THOSE WHO LEAVE

Those who leave their native lands are like a river — never stopping, always rushing, day and night.

Confucius

Ivar Rivenaes

THOSE WHO LEAVE

A NOVEL

VARDE BOOKS

British Library Cataloguing in Publication Data
A catalogue record for this book is available from the British Library

ISBN 0-9546583-0-2

Typeset by Amolibros, Milverton, Somerset
This book production has been managed by Amolibros
Printed and bound by T J International, Padstow, Cornwall, UK

Of previous novels by Ivar Rivenaes

"...A fantastic first novel. This is a big work, full of materiel—thoughts and experiences, and stamped with a lively ability to write..."

"...Ivar Rivenaes has at any rate imagination, a sharp eye for the essential feature of a character, and last, but not least, – he is in possession of a baroque humour that infects the reader..."

"...He knows like few others how to drive the action forward so that one simply has to read on..."

"...one can't remain indifferent, the book forces one to read on, to take a standpoint..."

"...This is well written! The 350 pages are entertaining, this writer shows an ability to express himself that is unusual in a first work. Passionate seriousness alternates with humour and irony to make exciting reading..."

"...I can find no parallels in my own time for such a sparkling talent in a first book...I would have to go—backwards—as far as Nordahl Grieg to find a partner of comparable quality..."

"...The language is excellent, with an effective, fast-moving idiom that is rich in variation. This book is clearly something beyond the ordinary among contemporary Norwegian books..."

"...Ivar Rivenaes is a master entertainer with an uncanny ability to switch from subtle irony to black humour..."

For Colleen

Acknowledgments

*To Jane Tatam for her invaluable support
and belief in my work.*

*To my wife Colleen for sound advice
and everything else.*

1

The late spring of 1958 had been promising, but the summer, like so many English summers, saw August fade into an early autumn.

A light mist touched the Hampshire hills like a gentle stroke from an artist's brush. From a distance came the faint whistle of a train. A kestrel hovered over the dirt-yellow field across the paddock and the row of chestnut trees stood as if carved in black against the leaden sky, heavy with rain. Then the wind ripped the clouds apart and the sun gilded the edge of the woods and the meadows.

Igor Parkhurst shuddered. He bit off the broken nail on his right thumb and wished that he'd bothered to put on a jacket. The smell of rotting leaves filled his nostrils as he sauntered through the remnants of his garden.

Parkhurst's mind moved in circles; he thought about life, life as it was, and life as it could have been.

He did not look up when he heard the rasping voices of the jackdaws approaching the big sycamore tree, its majestic trunk brown and moss green and glistening in the wet. Life had become a bad joke. His existence had been reduced to a vacuum between birth and death. He could not understand that he hadn't deserved better. Events had got on top of him, and, to crown it, he was no longer in the best of health.

Age, he thought, this merciless destroyer of good looks, hope and confidence; he was rapidly nearing three-quarters of a century and of late was convinced that his body would soon follow his reputation into decomposition, followed by terminal obscurity. It was as if, whatever he tried to do, the result was the equivalent of hoping for an orchid to grow by peeing on a weed.

His hands had begun to shake, on and off. He was arthritic. He carried two-hundred-and-twenty-four pounds on a five-foot-nine frame. His blood pressure could have blown apart a Sherman tank. It did not help that his daily consumption of cognac had increased from two fingers in a tumbler to a good half bottle, but the sense of succour was great and the feeling of loneliness became less unbearable as night closed in.

Parkhurst kicked a pine cone out of the way. He stopped in front of the greenhouse. Shards of broken glass ran like busted swastikas down the wall. He imitated a smile and recalled the scene of departure when Miriam, his third and final wife, had walked out two years earlier. Her words of farewell had not been nice. He shivered and rubbed the back of his neck with both hands.

"*You are not even worth the paper you don't write on,*" she had sneered. "*You can't afford to keep me and now you claim that you can't even afford to divorce me. What I wanted was a decent standard of living, but that was evidently too much. I tell you, Igor, when this divorce is over there won't be much left of you.*"

Parkhurst's grimace ended with a lopsided grin; he was clearly the kind of husband that only a widow with a failing memory could love. But Miriam had been right, in a way; he could no longer produce anything worthwhile, and he was nearly destitute. His creative mind, together with the rest of him, had long been hibernating.

How lucky women were, he mused; they never made mistakes, they had no faults and they were never wrong. Three attempts—and not once had he achieved the perfect balance; his imperfections and their virtues neatly synchronized in the conspiracy women effortlessly defined as love. It had been like doing a fandango with an eel.

The wind carried the smell of fertilizers across from the nearby fields. He plodded down the lawn towards the paddock. The ground was adorned with honey-coloured leaves from the beech trees.

He scratched the beard he'd grown to avoid looking at himself in the mirror every morning. His skin had gone the colour of sun-dried bones. His physique looked as if a eunuch had sired him. The hair on his head had the dull hue of pewter and the expression in his eyes was as lacklustre as melted lead.

The Web of the British Scorpion, he thought. He liked graphic analogies unconnected with realities.

He squeezed his left thumb with his right hand and saw the sun once more break through the clouds before it left the day. The pastures in the west became olive green and the pink softness of dusk turned mauve.

But the scorpion existed, all right, personified by Gregory Pritchard-White, Esquire, and he had been dangling in Pritchard-White's web for the past five years. Since the very first day, again and again, Parkhurst had asked himself: of what use could he possibly be to the Secret Service? Each time he came up with the same answer; hardly any, or probably none at all.

It had begun by sheer coincidence. With incredible naivety, or, rather, stupidity, he had conveyed to a then Member of Parliament a remark snapped up whilst visiting Washington in November 1953. In those days Parkhurst was a big name in literature; everybody flocked around him, including high-ranking politicians whose idea of a library was a storage room for discarded cheque books. He'd been invited to the White House, and there, on that occasion, he had forgotten to keep his nose clean. President Eisenhower had greeted him warmly, albeit, true to the best of American traditions, he'd been unable to get his name right. The President then turned around to continue his conversation with a silver-haired senator named Harold Wetherspoon. Baffled by the President's abrupt behaviour, Parkhurst stood where he was for a while, clinging to his glass, and just long enough to overhear the senator's description of the British as *totally unreliable homosexuals, too soft on the Russians and altogether unable to comprehend the peril of communism.* He is telling a joke, he'd reflected, but then he thought about God's generosity when it came to Americans and humour and decided to eavesdrop a bit more. *Apart from being a bunch of lily-livered eggheads hallucinating about an empire long lost,* the senator had continued, *no way were the British bright enough to understand Moscow's stealthy ways and neither were those isolated islanders sufficiently alert to the machinations of the KGB. In addition*—and at this point the senator had resolutely emptied his glass—*which had produced more spies, traitors and useless politicians per capita than the goddamn Brits? None. Which country had given birth to Neville Chamberlain and Oswald Mosley?* The senator shook his silvery locks vigorously before he strongly advised the President to *keep the Brits in the dark, which was where they belonged anyway, and not utter one single word about the latest Kremlin/White House overture.*

By then the grinning President had made himself busy by paying attention to a female admirer with a passion for golf. The senator's voice drifted, and from then on and forever after Igor Parkhurst had no idea what that particular overture was all about.

But the senator had been an important and influential man; he had once been to Europe for an entire week, and with this experience to his credit he quickly rose through the hierarchy and became the natural choice as USA's foremost specialist on all matters foreign and international.

Parkhurst thought about what he had overheard and did not give it too much weight. Obviously things were going on backstage, but that was politics. The subject had never been close to his heart.

What bugged him was the senator's remark about the British. Instead of writing it off as just another American inanity, he found himself increasingly annoyed, and, as he now saw it, a basically irrational sentiment became the catalyst leading to infinite misery.

Returning from Washington, he had called Wilbur Fletcher, an old acquaintance from Oxford and now a Member of Parliament; they had met for lunch in The House and Parkhurst had related what he'd overheard. *"Oh, never mind the Americans,"* Fletcher had said with an indifferent shrug. *"They're just a bunch of conceited, ignorant, shallow, arrogant, dishonest and humourless second-hand immigrants. Our inferior cousins across the pond cannot come to terms with the fact that we've got history, culture, traditions and class. It is nothing but envy, feeding from an enormous inferiority complex."* Fletcher had asked for another bottle of wine before he'd continued, *"What you heard was a piece of bungled politicking between two dilettantes, dear chap; annoying, yes, but of no significance. Suffice to say that we know substantially more about what is going on in this world than they do. Look at the way they deal with things they don't understand,"* he had added with a snicker. *"The Americans are so incredibly inept that one must almost admire their line of consistent mishaps from Wounded Knee to Panmunjon. I've met Senator Wetherspoon a few times in his capacity as Chairman of the Foreign Relation Committee, and, believe me, he's one of the biggest jerks they've ever produced. He's adopted this melancholy grin of an alligator pretending to be a friendly manic depressive, but nobody here takes him and his foolish mannerisms seriously."*

During the rest of the meal they talked about their days at Oxford, and that was it—or so he had thought at the time. What he did not know was that Fletcher had a high-ranking friend at the SIS, and that the friend had a young protégé who was as innovative as he was ambitious.

A week later Parkhurst received a telephone call. The man did not present himself other than as an acquaintance of Fletcher, but the caller would be grateful if he and Parkhurst could meet over a drink and discuss a matter of vital importance. Parkhurst had been both flattered and appreciative. His appreciation stemmed from the fact that a writer could never be in possession of too much raw material.

They met in a pub in Pimlico Road at opening hour. The place was quiet and they found a corner table. Pritchard-White said who he was and whom he worked for, stressed the confidentiality of the meeting, referred to Fletcher's version of the White House incident and praised Parkhurst for his unquestionable patriotism. People like Parkhurst were indeed rare, in Pritchard-White's estimate; a man who had the gift, or, possibly more precise, the transcendent ability to pick up pieces of intelligence from conversations and convey such priceless information to the country's designated collectors of the same. Such a person was no less than a national treasure.

Parkhurst grew a couple of inches as he listened. His stare was fastened on Pritchard-White's long and narrow face where a pair of brown-and-yellow-spotted eyes glistened with holy patriotism. Nothing wrong with that, he had thought; the man obviously believed in what he was doing, and, true enough, the world was a complex place. Everybody suspected everybody else of harbouring ulterior motives, acrimony was rife, there were mountains of nuclear weapons around, and—bottom line—*my country right or wrong*. Stalin's death earlier in the year had not made the Soviet Union less formidable, nor had the absurd Korean armistice made the world a safer place. The events in Iran, when Premier Mossadegh was ousted, demonstrated clearly that communism was a plague that could show up anywhere.

That about summed it up, and Parkhurst had smiled with controlled enthusiasm. Yes, if he could be of any help… a discrete nod and a conspiratorial line over his left eyebrow completed his new-found sense of flag-waving loyalty.

Pritchard-White had been delighted, in his self-effacing fashion. They'd agreed that Parkhurst would use his discretion and report whenever he picked up something that could be interpreted as being in the interest of the nation, however far-fetched it may sound at the time. And—by the way—nothing in writing, not a single note. Parkhurst had kept on nodding, but he did emphasize that incidents like the one in the White House were indeed few and far between; usually, he attended cocktail parties and other social events a bit further down the ladder. True, there were glittering get-togethers now and then where also politicians and ambassadors congregated—was it something like that Pritchard-White had in mind? Precisely. Big names from all walks of life, broadly speaking, preferably in the company of influential allies like women and alcohol—Pritchard-White had winked twice—that was when vanity took over and created the condition where an eagle like Parkhurst could pick up slices of raw meat involuntarily dropped.

They'd left an hour later; a partnership well and truly established and with the clear understanding that nobody was ever to know about this, and that Parkhurst did not liaise with anybody and that meant *anybody* but Pritchard-White.

He memorized the two code names and a couple of telephone numbers and went home, slightly bemused but all in all reasonably pleased with himself.

For the next two years not much happened. He reported back whenever he thought that something could be deciphered as being of national interest, and he remained in the dark as to the significance of his observations. During those years he'd been exceptionally prolific; his books and plays were well received and translated into a dozen languages. Money came in almost as fast as his succession of wives could get rid of it, and, thanks to his gift as a raconteur backed by his literary success, he'd become the darling of the intellectual masses from London to Paris and from San Francisco to Tokyo. His boundless energy and stamina allowed him to write for seven months of the year and to travel for four months. He gave himself one month during the summer to recharge his batteries, and for a long time he believed that this arrangement made everybody happy, family included.

Then one day Pritchard-White asked him to go to Israel; things were brewing in the Middle East. It was the first time a direct request had been made, and it didn't suit Parkhurst. He had other plans; one of his plays was to open in Berlin and he had promised to be at the premiere.

His objection had been met with stony silence. Pritchard-White sucked on his pipe for a long time, occasionally re-lighting it and permanently staring at a spot above Parkhurst's head. Half an eternity later their glances had crossed; Pritchard-White put his pipe in the ashtray, wiped the saliva from the corners of his mouth with the back of his hand and said, *"Really."*

Then he slowly shook his head as if he could not believe what he had heard, his molars grinding and the muscles in front of his earlobes moving like slugs under a strip of speckled canvas. *"Mr. Parkhurst,"* he said in a voice barely audible, *"presumably there is no need to remind you that we are talking about matters of national security. We—and I now speak on behalf of the British Government—we have reason to believe that the Americans are making a deal with the Israelis whilst telling us something entirely different. Furthermore, the Americans are also preparing some underhand scenario with Iraq and Turkey, trying to sneak in on the Baghdad Pact, consulting neither us nor the Israelis. That is utterly devious and totally unacceptable, my dear chap. We need to know what is going on. We can't ask the Arabs without their half-baked and perpetually paranoid political leaders immediately feeling betrayed by the Americans—most likely the final outcome, but anyway—and there we are. The Israelis not only distrust everybody out of sheer habit; for some arcane reason they also keep clinging to the misconception that we, the British, are primarily anti-Semitic and always have been. God knows where they got it from, but, regardless, how does one cure a permanent mental disturbance of such magnitude? Can't be done, old boy. It's pathological and beyond present means of treatment."* He again fired up his pipe, and for a while he sucked like a man offered his last smoke. He went on, *"You are popular in Israel, and Mossad can be quite leaky, when it suits them, particularly now with that old fox Ben-Gurion back in the saddle. Get down there and see what you can find out."*

Parkhurst repeated his desire to be in Berlin. He tried to reason, but Pritchard-White had cut him short. *"Just do it,"* he said in a tone of voice that Parkhurst found menacing, *"or you can read all about your father's interesting life in next week's newspapers. The sins of the fathers, and so on, my dear Mr. Parkhurst. It's amazing how colourful and nasty such a story can be made to appear—not to mention its repercussions. Think about it. If I hear nothing by tonight I shall presume that you are on your way."*

7

Parkhurst went home and locked the door to his study. He did not doubt that the threat was real, and it scared him. For the first time it dawned upon him that he was but a small pawn entirely at the mercy of a powerful and ruthless organisation and that his activities as a collector of intelligence, however insignificant, could one day seriously backfire and damage if not destroy him.

His father, Henry Parkhurst, had been an impresario, an eccentric character, vibrant and opinionated. He had been a friend of Bertrand Russell and shared his pacifism, although not to the extent of risking jail. As opposed to Russell, Henry Parkhurst could not accept that the Soviet Union wasn't likely to become the workers' paradise as outlined by Lenin and Trotsky. Henry could not be persuaded to read Lenin's *The State and Revolution*, characterised by Russell as a magnificent but perverse masterpiece of intellectual fraud—a description Henry Parkhurst found more amusing than instructive—and he flatly refused to rid himself of a residual sentimentality towards an -ism he'd never bothered to analyze. Even Russell's vivid description of his meeting with Lenin in the summer of 1920 could not make a dent in Henry Parkhurst's belief, and he continued to praise the revolution and the Soviet philosophy to anybody who cared to listen. He categorically discarded the theory that history repeated itself; in Henry Parkhurst's opinion it so happened that a vast number of events during the centuries had a tendency to reflect familiarity, and that was all there was to it. An explanation as to a possible distinction between the theory and the opinion was never produced—he just changed his facial expression from pitiful to resigned dismay.

Lenin's death and the arrival of Stalin made no difference. Russell's observation that Bolshevism was no better than Tsarism was wearily rejected, and it was only in 1933, following the Metro-Vickers case, that he began to question if there was indeed something rotten in the hitherto greatest of democracies. The assassination of Kirov a year later was not glossed over by Henry, but he was still reluctant to admit that he could have been so incredibly mistaken for almost twenty years.

Then came the Moscow show trials where Vyshinsky performed to Stalin's perfection; the blood purge swept away old-timers like Zinoviev, Kamenev and Bukharin among many others, and in 1938 only the ruins were left of Henry Parkhurst's illusions.

The relationship between father and son had been a harmonious one, mainly because young Igor from childhood displayed a will to understand and a desire to forgive. He knew that his father's rapport with reality was seldom intimate; on the contrary, most of the time it thrived on the far side of distant. Being a fantasist and a dreamer did not necessarily make a bad person, in Igor's view, and both as a child and in later years he found it impossible to judge his father as anything but a charming cross between Don Quixote and Walter Mitty; a quaint, capricious and ultimately kind and generous man who meant no harm. Yes, he did drive both Igor and his prim and proper mother Beryl up the wall more often than not, but always with such vivacity, exuberance and charm that it never seriously rocked the family boat.

Igor Parkhurst smiled as he recalled a story his mother had told time and again. It had been her wish that her one and only child should have a respectable English name, either Charles or, preferably, William, but her beloved husband had opted for Leon, after Trotsky. Mrs. Parkhurst refused to budge; no son of hers should walk through life with a distinctly un-British name like that, and to her astonishment Henry had just shrugged and seemingly accepted.

Three days before the Christening ceremony Beryl had by coincidence run into the local vicar who congratulated the Parkhursts with their choice of names for their little boy. No doubt he would use only one of them as he grew up. Beryl, baffled but composed, had said, *"Plural?"* and asked the vicar if he would be good enough to elaborate. The vicar had been quick to identify a Gordian Knot and knew that he had cornered himself. *"Your husband's list, Mrs. Parkhurst,"* he'd said, shifting his feet uneasily, *"Vladimir, Charles, Ilich, William, Leon. Am I to understand …?"* and he had stared towards heaven for further assistance. *"See you later,"* Beryl had said and hurried home. They had compromised the very same evening, landing on *Igor* and celebrating over a bottle of champagne. Henry had been extremely pleased with himself, and Beryl not seriously despondent.

Then, in 1939, Henry died. He did so before he had found the time or perhaps the nerve to denounce officially his past passion for communism. Having been a popular and successful impresario and a larger-than-life character, his essentially trivial political tenets were soon forgotten. Igor Parkhurst could not remember one single instance during his entire adult life when his father's once-held Soviet sympathies had been mentioned until Pritchard-White brought it up. Parkhurst knew that he was left with no choice. He believed that Henry's peripheral and innocent political past wouldn't make much of a splash in England, but America was a different matter. He feared that his immense popularity could evaporate overnight; the cold war was a fact and with Senator Joseph McCarthy permanently in the headlines, Parkhurst had no illusions about the Americans' horror of communism. This was more than a mere academic perception; during numerous visits the old ghost had been the topic of many a conversation, and his discernment, supported by solid experience, convinced him that Pritchard-White's threat, if carried out, would result in diminishing interest and ultimately the cancellation of lucrative contracts.

Parkhurst went to Israel and came back without the faintest idea about the value of his intelligence, as usual, but Pritchard-White had been pleased.

Since then he had made several trips to various places around the world; what had once been polite requests had been replaced by firm orders. He concealed neither his reluctance nor his displeasure, and their former amicable relationship soon became dominated by resentment and hostility.

In particular it annoyed him that Pritchard-White always managed to keep his cool. His attitude was contemptuous and patronizing, and he selected his words with the precision of a malicious schoolmaster. Career-wise he had done well for himself; he had rapidly risen through the hierarchy and operated a notch below top level. His contacts in Whitehall were many and influential.

Their relationship finally came to a point where Parkhurst decided that he'd had enough. He could no longer produce as he used to; his sources of income became fewer and the amounts smaller, and his family life was in a shambles. He spent a week in solitude evaluating his predicament, and he emerged with the conclusion that he'd rather lose America than his mind. The articles would surface—nobody squeezed Pritchard-White's nose without paying for it—but then Parkhurst himself would write a couple of articles, putting things in perspective. After a few weeks the whole shabby affair would blow over, and, who could tell, perhaps even the Americans would pay less attention than he'd originally feared. The year before, McCarthy's reign had finally come to an end when the Senate condemned him for "*conduct contrary to Senatorial traditions*" and perhaps common sense would continue its come-back now that phobia no longer was mistaken for patriotism.

The day of reckoning came in May 1956. They met in one of the pubs selected by Pritchard-White as appropriate for matters of national interest. Parkhurst showed up sporting a pair of baggy brown trousers and an old tweed jacket that he normally used when walking the lanes in rural Hampshire. Pritchard-White, tall and slim, was the epitome of elegance. His dark grey suit was tailor-made, with small lapels and four buttons. The tie was blue and narrow and with a small design embroidered in the centre.

Without overdoing formal politeness, he instructed Parkhurst to go to Moscow. The order was accompanied by the traditional comment about his mammoth popularity. Pritchard-White went on with details about pre-arrangements, events and the names of a good handful of interesting people with whom he should converse. That was it, really. Plain sailing, in other words. Nothing unfamiliar.

"Write your articles," Parkhurst said.

"Excuse me?"

"Write your articles about my father. I have had enough. My life has become a nightmare and I'd rather face the consequences than continue like this. I just can't go on. I think the time has come for you to accept that."

"What a shame."

"Is it? I am only a tiny little fish, merely a sardine, swimming aimlessly around in the seven seas of your world. I cannot see that I have been or ever will be of any real use whatsoever. The whole thing is just a farce. I am too ignorant about the world in which you operate, too naïve, too innocent and too amateurish."

"You are underestimating yourself. Grossly, I'd add."

"I don't think so. I am an incompetent and nonplussed dabbler, just as my father was an innocuous saloon philosopher of a left-wing quasi-intellectual kind. I ask you in earnest. Please let me go whilst there is still something left of my life."

"We never let go."

"I beg your pardon?"

11

"I am terribly sorry, old chap, but we don't operate that way. You are one of us. Apart from sympathizing with the frailness of your character there is nothing I can do about it."

"You know nothing about my character."

"Yes, I do. As you know, we exist to investigate, to counter, to advise and to assist. We are guided by our commitment to integrity, legality and objectivity. To serve our country is an honour and a duty. Once involved always involved. Betraying our mission is not acceptable. We've had enough of the likes of Burgess and Maclean."

"Are you comparing me with...?"

"Please, let's not get personal. However, the fact that those two gentlemen decided to emigrate five years ago does not eradicate another fact—namely that there are plenty of their ilk around. Funny, isn't it, how Cambridge was and is so fertile when it comes to treacherous perverts? Never mind. You're Oxford, I seem to recall, always a few steps behind, in all respects."

Parkhurst rose to leave. "Write your articles."

"Ah—the tip of the iceberg."

He sat down. "Am I supposed to follow?"

"Of course you are. Here—" he pulled a brown A-5 size envelope from his pocket and took out a photograph "—remember this gentleman?"

Parkhurst stared at the picture of two men passing in a park, one giving what looked like a small parcel to the other.

"I take it you recognize yourself. The other one, as you know, is your old friend Viktor Seleznyev from the Soviet Embassy. He's gone home to Moscow now, but I'm sure you've got no problems recalling name, place and, of course, data contained in your little parcel." He smiled. His visage made Parkhurst think of Count Dracula waiting for the twelve chimes of midnight.

"This is a fabrication," he said. "I have never seen that man in my life before."

"Is that so?" Pritchard-White pushed his glasses up from his nose and made them balance on top of his head. "What about this, then?" He took a piece of paper from the envelope and unfolded it on the table. "Look at this statement, one of many, as we both know. Haven't you amassed a small fortune in Switzerland, my dear fellow? I am impressed, to say the least." His eyes were glossy and with an expression usually associated with chemical assistance.

Parkhurst looked away. The smells of his own fear hit him like the stench in a public toilet. Then everything became blurred and Igor Parkhurst knew that he had lost. He could have fought his father's corner, but there was no way he could fight the evil machinery now facing him. For a brief moment he felt like a man whose mind was a satellite lost in space. He stared at the grin on Pritchard-White's face and thought that his teeth could have done with a monthly brush.

Pritchard-White's hands moved as if he was kneading dough.

Igor Parkhurst conceded defeat and knew that his life had become existence in decline.

He felt the rain on the wind and leaned against the solid trunk of the big chestnut tree. In the corner of the paddock his neighbour's horses stood as if chiselled in black marble.

He turned and began drifting back towards the house. Out of habit he tried to look slimmer by hunching his shoulders and keeping his arms straight with his knuckles pointing forward. His shoes made sucking noises on the damp and flattened grass. A peculiar ache penetrated his heart and spread across his chest. Laboriously he opened the French doors to his drawing room, reached for his last bottle of cognac and filled a tumbler. His hands were trembling. He let out a deep sigh and dumped himself heavily in the nearest chair.

His safety valves did not function any more. He missed them. Fits of rage, tears or any other appropriate emotional outburst had served him well in the past, but he had no tears left and anger and repugnance and the soothing sensation of feeling unscrupulously exploited were all of the past. He was burnt out, empty and seconds away from an all-consuming and irreversible indifference.

He looked out the window and up towards the sky where the clouds lingered like translucent greyhounds frozen in time. He quaffed his cognac and opened and closed his right hand as if squeezing water from a sponge. Life, he thought, what the hell was life but a graveyard with a forecourt. An echo of despair reverberated between his ears and he focused inward and reminisced.

Once, writing had been his life; purgatory extricated by catharsis. He'd seen it as both a duty and an intellectual challenge to emphasize the complexity of man without offering explanations or trying to influence the reader with unsustainable sentiments. He had agreed wholeheartedly with the Shakespearean technique of *presenting conflicts without giving answers*, and it had been fun. He smiled wryly. He had been good at it. Now he was dead from mental and emotional hypothermia, and whatever was left of his physical existence was as significant as an amoeba in orbit.

Two hours later his glass was empty and so was most of the bottle. He inhaled the stale smell of loneliness and got to his feet. He did not sway and he felt remarkably sober. I'll give it one more shot, he thought. I shall close the circle and if that does not work… he rubbed his cheeks with his knuckles as he walked across the floor, into the hallway and up the stairs to his bedroom.

Tucked under the sheets of his regal four-poster bed, Igor Parkhurst turned his pillow. It was brown from body grease and he heard his unshaven face rasp against the cover. He thought about his youth, so long ago, when his mind and his body were strong and virile and the notion of death was but a hypothesis, vague and elusive like the haze over a far-away mountain pass.

He listened for a while to the dialogue of the barn owls before he switched off the light. An hour later he was still awake.

Igor Parkhurst wished that he were the mortgage-free owner of a small cottage and not the occupant of a vast Victorian mansion belonging to a bank.

2

The early morning sun shone through and the wind lost its chill. The clouds drifted lazily towards the east, nebulous and auspicious like grey-white snippets of satin with edges dipped in mercury.

Parkhurst looked fondly at his shining black Rolls Royce and made himself comfortable in the driver's seat. For a few seconds he listened to the symphony from the engine. The car was his pride and joy, and, besides, he had kept it because it had no market value to speak of and he didn't have the money to buy anything else with four wheels, even with the Rolls as part exchange. The car was nearly half his own age, but he had maintained it well and it was in excellent condition. During the last five years he had not done more than a thousand miles annually on average, apart from Pritchard-White, who was there to go and see? Not many. His old contacts and his fair-weather friends had vanished together with the disappearance of his lucky star and his money. It was at this point that he had begun to suspect that the liquid seeping through most people's veins wasn't really blood but a chemical resulting from distillation of greed.

He put the Rolls into gear. No, he thought as the car moved silently down the driveway, there were only three left; Conor, Kathleen and Jennifer Moran. Conor had money and a heart bigger than the island he came from, but Igor Parkhurst had pride and integrity; his predicament was his own sorry affair and the word *alms* made his tongue swell and left a foul and repugnant taste.

Fletcher lived on Whetstone High Road, North London, and a few hundred yards before the junction between Ballards Lane and Woodhouse Road.

Wilbur Fletcher, he mumbled and put on his sunglasses; you got me into this mess in the first place. Now, let us see what you can do to get me out of it. A frail hope, I admit, but you are all I have got.

He was pleasantly surprised to find that the eastbound traffic was light. He noticed a black Mercedes coming up behind him, but it appeared to slow down and he paid it no further attention.

Parkhurst decided to enjoy the ride and let his mind flow. All his life he had tried to abide by the imperative of *constructive* self-awareness; he knew that he was gullible, bordering on uncritical trust in man's inherent kindliness. His other major shortcoming was his probity. From as far back as he could remember he had believed that honesty and rectitude were mankind's intangible capital; goodness and honour would always prevail and the values of morals and ethics could never become so diluted that man would destroy himself. He had always thought that man's conscience was a function of intelligence, however unevenly distributed, and he had kept alive his hope that one day the world would conclude that the *word* was more eligible than the *sword*.

All this had been in his *heart* for over seventy years. It was only during the last fifty years or so that his *brain* had begun to allude and at times insinuate otherwise. But even then it was too late, far too late; the mould had been cast and he had known since his teens that the discord would not go away and that his lot in life would forever be the perturbing conflict between his heart and his head.

It had paid off, though. Without this inner turmoil he wouldn't have been able to write in the first place. The raw material had seethed inside like the inextinguishable flames of hell. Observations, experiences and impressions had filled his pages as fast as his hand could move. His dreams had come true and for many years he had seen himself as less unlucky than most.

He had been enamoured of his own fame and he had loved his social life where men and women cultivated academic theories and gratifying philosophies. He had cherished his reputation and the adulation that followed wealth and recognition. Seldom did the notion that even gods could face misfortunes and pitfalls touch his consciousness.

How it all had changed. No longer was he sitting on life's fence with his vanity intact and his self-esteem reasonably unimpaired. Now, he merely existed under the heel of Her Majesty's most needed of rational outfits, the Secret Intelligence Service. It was surreal, beyond comprehension, why they had picked a man who couldn't qualify as a feeble caricature of an inept dilettante, but they had.

The responsibility rested solely with the regrettable existence of Wilbur Fletcher, previously Member of Parliament, Government Minister and now a destitute, broken and alcohol-sodden wreck.

Parkhurst had not been in touch with Fletcher since their fateful meeting five years ago, but he knew about Fletcher's fall from grace. Fletcher had been the favourite of the media during his entire career; skilled, eloquent, highly articulate and with the courage of his convictions. Not many weeks had passed without headlines. His constituency had adored him. Although nobody questioned his capabilities, there were those who opined that Fletcher had become a member of the Cabinet purely because Anthony Eden reckoned it was the only way to keep such a loose cannon under control. The reasoning was astute enough; for the first twelve months of Fletcher's ministerial calling, he had tried to be a team player and had caused no serious calamities.

The old Fletcher re-surfaced with the Suez crisis. He denounced the attack on Egypt as silly and irresponsible and all in all nothing but a cynical manoeuvre by a Prime Minister who was a prisoner of his own delusions. The outburst was glossed over by a unanimous Cabinet, minus Fletcher, and he escaped with a warning.

Then, simultaneously, came the uprising in Hungary and the West remaining passive. With his vituperative speeches and vitriolic comments Fletcher portrayed Britain and USA as enemies of mankind, void of dignity and unworthy of respect. Time and again he repeated J. F. Dulles, the American Secretary of State, who'd said: "*To all those suffering under communist slavery, let us say you can count on us.*"

Fletcher's popularity had earned him the nickname *The Untouchable* and used in particular by those who most despised the Government, but when the guns turned silent in Budapest nothing could save him.

The beginning of the end came for Wilbur Fletcher; a Cabinet reshuffle followed soon after, and he returned to the backbenches. Stories began to circulate about all his other political misjudgements during the years, about his colourful personal life that included a string of mistresses and a handful of illegitimate children, and finally there were rumours about his unstable mental condition caused by alcohol and possibly genes. His constituency were advised to deselect him and suddenly one day Wilbur Fletcher was gone, his career destroyed and his future as bleak as the fog embracing a frosty autumn's evening. His marriage copied his prospects and before long he was yesterday's man, condemned to obscurity and living alone in a small basement flat in North London, greeting each new day with a drink and a nod.

Parkhurst stopped along the way and bought two bottles of Chivas Regal. It was more than he could afford, but he anticipated reluctance if not downright hostility and figured that without a mental laxative Fletcher could well shut up altogether.

Parkhurst found an open space along the pavement and locked the car. He manoeuvred his bulk down the narrow and dirty staircase leading to the kitchen door. The small landing was packed with debris, empty bottles and a couple of torn plastic bags. The stench was nauseating. He knocked hard three times. He saw four cats scurrying across the floor. A minute later Fletcher appeared from a dark hallway. He showed no surprise as he unlocked the door, opened it and stepped aside.

"My dear Igor," he said softly. "I have been expecting you."

"What?"

"Come in, my friend. Come in."

Parkhurst went through. The smell of cats' urine hit him like a whiff of concentrated ammonia.

"This area is a haven for vagrants," Fletcher said and locked the door, "one simply cannot be careful enough." He smiled and put his hands in the pockets of his stained and ill-fitting brown trousers. "You took your time, dear chap."

"You've been expecting me," Parkhurst said, more a statement than a question.

"Does that surprise you? Your career is in the doldrums now. I am truly familiar with the feeling and who is there to blame but somebody else?"

"Heart-warming, Wilbur."

"Let us enter my spacious and elegant drawing room." Fletcher took the lead through the small dark hallway, swiped a cat from an easy-chair and sat down.

He said, "Did you know that Imre Nagy have been executed? They dumped him in an unmarked grave. Hail Kremlin and long live Hungary."

He shrugged and went on, "You are growing old and fat. You should have looked after yourself." He coughed violently. "The moral is that we soon enough reach the end of our biological destiny. Have a seat."

Parkhurst put the bag with the bottles on the floor in front of Fletcher, "I brought some Scottish aqua vitae," he said, remembering their Oxford days and Fletcher's passion for Latin phrases.

"That is kind of you," Fletcher said and picked up a bottle. "In my heydays I would have rejected the gift, needless to say, being as incorruptible as I was—*untouchable*." He made a snorting noise, opened the bottle and nodded towards the tawdry and faded cabinet. "You'll find my selection of crystal in there."

The odours of urine, excrements, sweat and tobacco had become almost unbearable. Parkhurst's intended sip of whisky became a mouthful.

"Please sit down," Fletcher urged. "You make the place look untidy."

Parkhurst eyed the threadbare carpet, the greyish-yellow walls where the paint was flaking off, the junkyard furniture and a crude painting of the Houses of Parliament hanging above the sofa.

Fletcher followed his gaze. "Happy days," he said and refilled his glass.

"Could we open a window?"

"I'm afraid not. My cats could disappear, and that would make my life meaningless."

Yes, I guess he's had enough of tragedies, Parkhurst thought and sat down in the corner of the sofa, the only place that was not occupied by one of Fletcher's feline beauties.

"You know all about me, of course," Fletcher said and brushed some ash from the sleeve of his shirt.

"I do." Parkhurst looked at the man who had once dominated their student days with his go-ahead spirit, his non-conformist ideas and his irresistible charm; six feet tall, athletic, fearless and agile as a lovesick squirrel.

The man opposite was round-shouldered, bloated and with a pallid complexion. The top of his head was decorated with unevenly formed blotches, like birds' droppings bleached by the sun. He was unshaven and unwashed, and his long, thin hair was greasy and tangled. His breath stank like a decaying animal. The collar of his shirt looked as if it had been chewed by an ill-tempered mastiff. Several dark brown spots indicated that Fletcher had run out of fresh razor blades.

"You've come a long way," he said. He could feel the dampness from the sofa on his thighs.

"Haven't we both?"

"You said you'd been expecting me."

"Yes, I have, for a long time. You ended up in the claws of Gregory Pritchard-White, I learned—" his nostrils moved as if he was going to sneeze "—thanks to my introduction, as we both know. Of course I have been expecting you." He lit a cigarette. They glared at each other through the thin blue smoke almost still in the air.

Parkhurst shuddered involuntarily and clasped his knees with both hands. There was no expression in Fletcher's eyes; no humour or remorse, just two little round balls the colour of wet granite. Parkhurst struggled to avoid clearing his throat. "Pritchard-White has ruined me."

"You mean that indirectly, I presume."

Parkhurst was taken aback. "Yes—yes, I assume one can say that. Indirectly. Let me rephrase …"

"That wouldn't be necessary," Fletcher interrupted. "I am familiar with his methods and their effect. He has paralyzed you. You can't write any more. You are on your knees. You've got no income. Three avaricious ex-wives and all your worthless friends have gone. I know." He took another sip. "Good stuff, this. You must come again." The corners of his mouth moved as if he was contemplating a sardonic smile. "This may surprise you, but I actually follow closely what is going on in this world. It keeps me alive, kind of. I would appreciate if you refrain from asking for which purpose—" he wet his lips "—I have yet to arrive at the answer. Or could it simply be that the more you know about life, the less you bother about the future?"

Parkhurst felt a pang of pity and averted his gaze. "How do I get out of this?" he said.

"You want your life back."

Parkhurst tried to chuckle. "What a brilliant observation."

"I am afraid you have wasted your Chivas Regal," Fletcher said. A touch of resignation vibrated in his voice. "Forget it."

It took a few seconds before Parkhurst fully understood that Fletcher's comment wasn't meant as a flippant joke. "*Forget it?*" he repeated.

The wrinkles around Fletcher's neck grew deeper as he lowered his head. "You haven't got a chance," he said and stumped out his cigarette with a tired movement. "There is no way they will ever let you go."

"You are really encouraging," Parkhurst muttered and could feel the perspiration on his forehead, "you've already made this trip worthwhile."

The stream of red-hot lava rippling across his belly made him close his eyes. He tried to stop his legs from trembling. Fletcher was indifferent; he had his own problems and, in all fairness, he was without influence, out of favour and too emotionally dehydrated to have any sense of empathy left.

Fletcher wiped his mouth with the sleeve of his shirt and helped himself to his third drink. "Allow me to tell you something," he said in a monotone voice. "Let me explain to you how Whitehall works. It is like a club, an enormous club in a world of its own and inhabited by people who basically dislike and distrust each other. It is a place where the truth, the whole truth and nothing but the truth does not exist and where rhetoric and not action is the key to survival. Ministers and the Civil Service alike are highly adept at blaming each other whenever needs be. Everybody's only concerns are short-term political gains and re-elections. Accountability is a worn-out joke and the good of the country and consideration for anybody outside the club are irrelevant quirks. You are supposed to know the unwritten rules and Rule Number One is loyalty—" Fletcher scratched his chest with his right hand and watched it move towards the glass "—loyalty, my dear Igor, however bizarre this may sound. That leaves you with two choices—" he drank greedily and let out a burp "—you conform and follow their code of conduct, or you are dead."

"But I was never part of the system," Parkhurst said.

"Oh yes, you were. You walked straight into it the moment you had your first tête-à-tête with Gregory Pritchard-White. That day the system swallowed you, and it is not its habit to throw up anything once devoured. Please do not ignore the nature and the character of the people you are dealing with. Whitehall is a place permeated with conceit, arrogance, cynicism and complacency. The overall incompetence is beyond belief. The absence of requisite erudition is staggering. The ignorance about real life is infinite and the passion for secrecy is pathological. Ministers and mandarins are intoxicated with their own feeling of power, and that, Igor, is a very contagious affliction. You hide your incompetence behind a contemptuous and patronizing attitude. Any outsider is a cross between a pariah and a commodity. You stay in your place and your place is where Whitehall have decided that your place should be."

"I see," Parkhurst said. His jaw was slack as if he'd made a regrettable slip of the tongue.

Fletcher looked at Parkhurst with unblinking eyes. "Do you? I am not so sure. Whitehall is a very sick place, corrupt, perverted and totally alien to your own little realm. In your kingdom you are an upright and dignified human being. To Whitehall you are just one of millions of other useful idiots. Unfortunately—for you, that is—your name is in the books of one of their departments, and, as I said, never to be erased. Hard luck, my friend, but that is the way it is and that is what you have to face. You must never forget that everything that springs from man's well of ethics is essentially no more than a sensory perception."

My legs have gone to sleep, Parkhurst thought; either that or paralysis is setting in. He moved his tongue from cheek to cheek and listened to the children playing in the street above. He said, "How many cats have you got?"

"Seven. I began to enjoy their company when I became allergic to human beings. I also used to have a talking parrot, but cirrhosis of the liver got the better of him."

"I am sorry to hear that."

Fletcher slumped in his chair like a boxer who wished the fight was over. "Life is a merciless surgeon. It's either the life-prolonging scalpel or the syringe of finality." He smiled. The tip of his tongue touched the small rust-coloured cracks on his lower lip. "It is amazing how much wisdom one can acquire in the company of King Alcohol."

"So it appears," Parkhurst said and shifted uncomfortably as the sofa's insufficient padding began to bother his buttocks. "Why didn't you try a comeback?"

A woeful smile spread across Fletcher's face. "I even stayed clinically sober for six months," he said, "but there was no hope. Nobody wanted to know. Finally I accepted my fate and here I am."

The white-and-ginger cat next to Parkhurst stretched idly and made a smell. "What keeps you alive?"

Fletcher smacked his lips and had another go at the bottle. "Oh, I just sit here and rue my stupidity and my weakness and my lack of fortitude. Cowardice prevents me from committing suicide whilst lassitude allows me to drink myself into oblivion. I must admit, though, I wish I could afford more than two bottles a day, but that's my lot, I'm afraid." He removed something stuck between his teeth with the nail of his little finger and shrugged as he flicked the brownish remnants of his breakfast across the room. "Not very many manage to rise like a dry-cleaned Phoenix from the sewer," he said as if struck by an afterthought. "However, it is a comforting thought that in the sewer you cast no shadow."

Parkhurst tried to smile. "A rational philosophy, but a bit short on genuine depth, I'd say."

"Of course it is. Unequivocal nonsense, would be more precise, but then we both went to Oxford."

The cats purred harmoniously and Parkhurst thought about his long drive back home.

"Igor."

"Yes?"

Fletcher's face seemed to have gone flat. There was a shine in his eyes as if the alcohol finally had taken effect. His voice was unsteady, "I am genuinely sorry that I can't be of any help."

"Thank you. I understand."

Fletcher massaged his scalp with his fingers. "You see, the Secret Service isn't staffed with gentlemen any more. In the old days it was a different matter altogether. People like Mansfield Cumming and Stewart Menzies were in many ways fantasists and in love with their cloak-and-dagger image, but they had honour and integrity. Those days are gone forever. Nobody can fight the Byzantine cabal that the Service has become. Once sucked in you have no hope of ever being released, and that is a fact you must now accept. By the way," he added and cocked his eyebrows, "Cumming had a very soft spot for writers. Did you know that?"

"I have never heard of either of them."

"No, why should you? Anyway, the old captain thought that writers were simply born for intelligence work, and maybe he had a point. You know, an inquisitive mind, the ability to form an overall picture and so on. Not entirely off the mark, I'd say."

Parkhurst breathed like a man who hadn't walked a flight of stairs for a while. "Pritchard-White knew this and adopted the concept? That makes sense. He doesn't strike me as an original thinker."

"No, he is not. People with philosophical leanings tend to be progressive. Spiritually they may be moral vegetarians, but they are not consciously destructive."

"Destruction and destitution," Parkhurst said and unbuttoned the collar of his shirt.

Fletcher pulled up his socks. His mouth became a horizontal line under his nose. "I take it that the name Kim Philby rings a bell."

"And—?"

"Three years ago Macmillan publicly denied that Philby was the "Third Man"".

"I remember."

"They've known all along what he's about. You too may have some years before you become a relic—if at all, that is."

"I don't follow."

"Your friend Pritchard-White can expose you at any one time, if it suits him, complete with photographs and statements, or he could decide to keep you under wraps. In my estimate you are too insignificant to be exposed, but that is only my personal opinion. Just play the game, Igor, and make the best out of it. As you may or may not know, the Official Secrets Act which was passed in 1911 contains two sections; one, that deals with espionage, and two, making it an offence to disclose any information on any subject. It was invented, in my modest estimate, to protect the high and mighty from embarrassment. Gregory can't lose, and you must cling to the hope that even a nasty philistine like him sees you as a toy he will one day tire of."

"Are you saying that his threat is an empty one?"

"No, not necessarily, and that's the problem. You can't count on it. What I am saying is that I advise you to go along with his whims. Do what he says and force yourself back to your typewriter. Keep your head up. Don't give up and find yourself in the gutter, like I did." Fletcher stared at the carpet. "You see, my mistake was that I could not make myself wallow in sycophancy *dressed up* as outspoken opinions, carefully selected. If I couldn't be genuine I had no right to be there. To me, principles were always more important than electoral realities. I genuinely believed that the moment a politician aimed for celebrity status *per se*, he'd shown that he was neither intellectually nor morally competent to represent the people. I still do. I joined Parliament with my innocence intact—my credulity was bottomless—but when they finally succeeded in forcing me out I was stripped of most of my little fantasies. I left behind my cherished illusions and espoused the dullness of a new day that has lasted forever since." He drank from the bottle. His laughter was hoarse and staccato. "And here we are, two people who refused to accept that mankind is perpetually rotten. Two thousand years ago gullibility was crucified once and for all, but somehow we misunderstood and the lesson escaped us. We —you and I—are the knights in shining white armour who stubbornly believe that the self can survive in the asylum for incurable perversity. We are the latter-day sons of the Great Satirist above, and now we are paying for our *ignis fatuus*." Fletcher blinked as if his eyes suddenly had been filled with hot ash. He rubbed them violently with the palms of his hands. The white turned crimson and a moist film gave him a look of despair. "Thank you for coming."

He found the car where he'd left it and checked for scratch marks. There were none. What a waste of a day, he thought, except for the charitable act of keeping Wilbur Fletcher company for a while.

The day had become brighter with only a slight chill in the wind. He was looking forward to getting home and thinking about an existence elevated from non-productive to prolific. He smiled with a bleak touch of mordant humour and cursed when the car wouldn't start.

He tried again. Nothing happened apart from the grovelling protest of an engine refusing to co-operate. Parkhurst wangled sideways out of the car.

He managed to get the bonnet up, bent over and stared at something that told him nothing.

His scalp started to itch. "Hilarious," he mumbled, "the car was perfectly all right this morning."

"Excuse me, sir," he heard a voice.

Parkhurst took a step back and saw a Japanese gentleman standing on the pavement. He was immaculately dressed in a dark grey pinstriped suit, white shirt, a green-and-orange tie and highly polished black shoes. He smiled genially and his one gold front tooth glittered in the sun.

"Yes?" Parkhurst snapped, "what can I do for you?" The chap probably wanted to know where the nearest camera shop was.

"It occurs to me that you are experiencing an acute mechanical problem, sir."

"Funny," Parkhurst said. "How did you guess?"

"No need to growl, sir," the Japanese said and smiled even wider. "It so happens that I have an intimate knowledge of automobile engines. With your kind permission," he added and bowed, "perhaps I can be of immediate assistance."

"I am sorry," Parkhurst said and regretted his own lack of manners. "Incidents like these do not bring out the best in me, I'm afraid. I do apologize."

The Japanese took off his jacket and placed it on the backseat of the car.

"Most graciously accepted," he said and rolled up his sleeves. "Now, if you would be good enough to place yourself in the driver's seat, sir? Switch on when I lift my hand but not before, if I may emphasize."

Parkhurst kept himself from smiling and got behind the wheel. A few minutes passed. Then he saw a hand waving and quickly turned the key. He listened for a few seconds to the purring of the engine and got out of the car.

"A big problem?" he asked.

"Not for an expert," the Japanese said and closed the bonnet. "May I explain the technicalities of the calamity, sir?"

"No thank you. It's probably beyond me, anyway"

"Very well, sir," the Japanese said and looked at the pub across the street, "I shall now go and wash my hands." He lifted his jacket carefully by the collar and placed it over his shoulder.

Parkhurst stood there, undecided, for a moment. Then he said, "You have been very kind, and I am grateful." He nodded towards The Virile Slug. "Would you care to join me for a drink?"

"Please, sir," the Japanese protested, "do not feel obliged. I was happy to be of assistance. On the other hand—" he smiled "—why not?"

Parkhurst looked into a pair of friendly brown eyes and said, "Good." They crossed the street and entered the semi-dark premises of the pub.

"If you would excuse me, sir," the Japanese said and headed for the men's room, "a quick clean-up."

"Certainly," Parkhurst said and greeted the barman. "I'll order as soon as my friend is back."

There was only one other person in the pub, a man dressed in black denims and a black leather jacket. There had been no reaction from him when they came in.

He kept staring into the mirror as if looking at something beyond his own image.

"Good afternoon," Parkhurst said.

The man did not answer. Neither did he turn his head. The expression in the eyes in the mirror was one of distant rumination.

Maybe he is deaf and half-blind, Parkhurst thought and quelled his annoyance. He didn't like to be ignored.

The Japanese came back.

"What would you like?" Parkhurst asked.

"A tiny Remy Martin, if I may," the Japanese said with a radiant smile.

"Two, please," Parkhurst nodded to the barman who was happy to have the monotony broken. "Same again, sir?" he asked the man in black who lifted his index finger but otherwise remained immobile. Parkhurst noticed a double measure of Irish whisky. He looked into the mirror and tried to meet the man's eyes.

Parkhurst was proud of his memory. One of his wives had compared it with a photo album; he could flick through the pages and instantly recognize anyone he'd seen before, however long ago.

The man continued to stare ahead. The face was unfamiliar, but Parkhurst did not relax. All his life he had trusted his instincts, and more often than not he'd been right. Now they told him that the man at the bar and the Japanese knew each other. Why was there no sign of recognition?

He turned to the Japanese. "My name is Igor Parkhurst," he said and offered his hand. The Japanese's grip was firm, and Parkhurst sensed a strength that did not surprise him. The man was five feet seven or eight inches tall and well built. His stomach was flat. He moved like a ballet dancer and carried an aura of self-confidence of the kind that could only come from exceptional fitness.

"Tadashi Ishihara," the Japanese said. He took out a visiting card from his breast pocket. Parkhurst studied it carefully. Once, almost six decades ago, Henry Parkhurst had given his son a piece of advice never to be forgotten: "*Before you start dabbling with the idiosyncrasies of any nationality,*" Henry had said, "*study their culture. Study their ethics, their habits and their code of behaviour and anything else that makes a person tick. This, my son, is so elementary that most don't do it. Instead, they complain about the awkwardness of the bloody foreigners. Never make the mistake of closing your mind to what is different.*" Parkhurst had taken the advice to heart, and it had served him well.

He studied the visiting card meticulously. He said out loud what he read and nodded appreciatively. He turned the card and looked at the Japanese calligraphy.

Just as Mr. Ishihara would expect; anything else would have been an insult.

"I am impressed. May I compliment you on a very tasteful design."

"Thank you."

"PhD—?"

"Indeed," Ishihara said. His brown eyes were twinkling. "I studied economics and politics at the University of Tokyo. Did you know that Japan established universities already in the eighth century?"

"I did, and I also know that your educational system is ahead of practically everybody else's. Do you work for one of the Japanese corporations over here?"

Ishihara frowned. "Good gracious me," he said sternly. "With all due respect, Mr. Parkhurst, I am a free spirit. I work for myself."

Parkhurst was beginning to enjoy himself. This fellow is quite a tonic, he thought, and a pretty unusual one, unless I am grossly mistaken.

"Your sense of humour is very refreshing," he said with a smile.

"Undisputedly so," Ishihara said. "I must add, though, being funny in England isn't particularly difficult. You are a most polite and well-mannered people, however ignorant."

Parkhurst pondered at that one, but he decided not to ask. Instead he said, "PhD and free-lance—?"

"I do simple things. Shares, commodities, currencies—I go in and out. It is rewarding, I am happy to underline, but also a tad boring, in the long run. Making money is much easier than losing it."

Parkhurst gulped. "Is that right?"

Ishihara nodded emphatically and sipped his cognac. He pulled out a short, thin cigar. "May I offer you one?"

"No thank you. I only smoke at night. So—making money is easier than losing it? I never knew that."

Ishihara smiled broadly. His gold front tooth gleamed in the reflection from his gold Cartier lighter. "Most people don't," he said. "The basic reason is that they never grasp the simple fact that money is merely a tool, neither more nor less. An emotional approach to lucre is the most common mistake. Anybody who realizes the simplicity of finance and economy can make a fortune."

"I find that fascinating," Parkhurst said. He inhaled. "Would you care to elaborate?"

28

The Japanese studied him charily. The friendliness was gone from his eyes. Parkhurst suddenly felt uncomfortable and wondered what had betrayed the excitement that surged through him. He turned to the barman and said, "Two of the same, please."

Ishihara ironed his tie with his forefinger. "An elegant little subterfuge," he mused.

"I beg your pardon?"

Ishihara laughed. He pushed his glass towards the edge of the table and folded his hands. The coldness was gone, but Parkhurst felt more confused than at ease.

"You beg my pardon," Ishihara said. "My oh my. Quite touching."

Parkhurst decided to keep quiet.

Ishihara continued, "I am a very sensitive man, which, added to my ability to observe, makes me a keen and exceptionally able student of the human element. A thrilling subject. Funny, too, most of the time."

Parkhurst waited.

"The voice," Ishihara said. "The voice is the problem. We can control almost everything, if we try; the body language, the expression in our eyes, our choice of words—the voice is what is letting us down. We know what we are saying—that is, some of us do—but we do not pay sufficient attention to *how* we are saying it. The instrument of betrayal, so to speak." He shrugged. "But I am sure you know all this. My apologies for lecturing."

Parkhurst's tension went. He looked straight at Ishihara. "You don't mean that, do you?"

"My apology? Not at all. We talk about money and you tell me—without a word—that you are getting all worked up. I say: why? Could it be greed or need?"

Parkhurst stared out the window and wondered how he had got himself into this conversation. The man opposite was a total stranger, an alien who gave the impression of being amused. The entire situation was ridiculous, humiliating and—no, it wasn't unnecessary, but forget that part of it. Cut it out, he thought, pay for the drinks and go home. There is nothing this man can do for me anyway. Or is there? Hope versus realism. *Making money is easier than losing it.* Shallow words, just an Oriental paradox dressed as irrefutable logic. Or was it?

"Being out of money can be as embarrassing as it is stressful," Ishihara said.

Parkhurst nearly lost his composure. "I—how do you know that?" he stuttered.

Ishihara leaned back and re-lit his cigar. "You are a very gifted man," he said evenly. "You are a brilliant writer, an excellent speaker, very knowledgeable, but an economist you are not."

"You seem to know a lot about me," Parkhurst said and wished he had phrased it differently.

Ishihara smiled. "Would you care to elaborate on your financial status?"

"I haven't done too well, lately."

Ishihara studied his fingernails. "The second of your predominant problems. Being a reluctant secret agent is worse, though, is it not?"

Parkhurst's hands gripped the edge of the table. What was going on? Who was this well-spoken and inscrutable Japanese? What did he know and why did they have this conversation? Had they really met by sheer coincidence? He sensed danger and something close to fear.

"I don't know what you are talking about," he said tersely.

Ishihara's eyes followed the smoke from his cigar as it coiled towards the ceiling. "Isn't that interesting? You are up to your eyeballs in alligators and you don't *know*? I am as soft and reverent as the kiss of a snowflake on a virgin's nipple, but please do not think that my gentle disposition gives you a right to insult me. Say that you do not want to talk about it, if you so wish, but do not try to outwit me. I have no desire to waste my precious time on unmitigated stupidity."

Parkhurst was baffled and knew that it showed. He said, "Good. Neither do I. Would it be too much to ask if you'd care to explain yourself, to tell me how you can help me? I take it that's what we are talking about, not to mention *why*."

At that moment Sammy the Skunk entered the pub, accompanied by his sidekick Mescaline Mike.

Mike and Sammy had been friends since Mike arrived from Kingston as a teenager. Sammy had spotted a potential ally. Mike needed someone who could teach him the law of an asphalt jungle bigger and more perplexing than that of Kingston's. Sammy had no illusions about the depths of his own feelings, whilst Mike genuinely believed that Sammy was the only person on this earth who was unreservedly trustworthy. The fact that Sammy was white was a naked truth that couldn't be denied, but Mike had no problems with his own reasoning; had he not seen, again and again, that *inside* no man was blacker than his reliable mate Sammy?

During his forty years on earth Sammy had spent more time inside than outside of prison; a petty crook that got his nickname because of a dark streak that ran through his long and unkempt hair the colour of a dusty daffodil. His face had the complexion of an under-baked meringue, and he had an ample collection of blackheads around his eyes, which were light brown with maroon specks. An ill-mannered police officer had once said, "*Sammy, who conceived you and how the hell did it happen? I bet that most of your sire's sperm ended up on the mattress greasing the fat rump of your mother-to-be. Christ, man, no wonder you look like sour milk in a condom.*"

Sammy was almost six feet tall, but his frail physique made him look smaller. His retirement scheme consisted of an antiquated Harley Davidson he'd never learned to ride, and his only passion in life apart from drugs and not working was the written word.

Whilst inside, Sammy did not waste time; there was practically no book available on psychology, economy and sociology he hadn't read twice. There's nothing wrong with knowledge, was Sammy's motto, as long as one didn't have to use it.

Mike supplied Sammy with his weekly requirements of drugs, preferably cocaine, and in return Sammy followed Mike wherever he went and even participated in a fight if there was no other way out. Most of the time there wasn't. Mike had matured into a consummate streetfighter with only one rule: no rules exist. One of Sammy's dearest possessions was a flick knife, and over time he had become good with it. Mike preferred a knuckle-duster followed by a razorblade when the enemy was down.

Mike's admiration for Sammy was limitless. It was good to be in the company of someone who was wise, educated and thoroughly reliable. Someone who had no scruples, who didn't have to go to work and to whom solving a problem was only a matter of time.

"Shit, mon," Mike said as they entered the pub, "we're skint."

Sammy nodded. "The situation needs analyzing. You've got nothing?"

"No. Maybe ten quid. You?"

Sammy hesitated. His funds were alarmingly low, and he was almost out of cocaine. Without Mike's generosity Sammy had no way of supporting his habit unless he sought additional income. The thought of strenuous and soul-destructive hard labour like progressing from muggings to assault on more affluent mortals filled him with horror.

"It is my considered opinion that something has to be done," he said.

"Like what?"

Sammy broke wind. "That's the question," he proclaimed. "That is really the question. We need to think. Preparation, then action. Not the other way round. I take it that you have no objection to this procedure?"

Sammy had never overestimated Mike's ability to think and didn't expect any input worth listening to. He was stunned when Mike said, "Blackmail."

Sammy pulled out a cigarette. He lit it and leaned closer. "Keep you voice down," he whispered. "What did you say?"

"I said blackmail. Simple. Piles of money. Why we never thought of that before?"

Sammy paused. "Because—because such an operation could easily jeopardize our treasured freedom to some considerable degree. I talk about years. Many years."

"I says it's a good idea," Mike persisted. He was offended and showed it by flaring his nostrils.

"Easy," Sammy said, "easy, man. I didn't say it wasn't a good idea." Jesus Christ, he thought, how do I get out of this one? Unless—he exhaled slowly as he began to realize that Mike might actually have dropped a seed that fell on the most fecund of ground.

"Mike my prince," he said with authority, "I think you've got something there."

Mike beamed. "Have I? What?"

I have no idea, Sammy thought, but maybe I will.

"We deserve a drink," he said. "This requires planning, preparations, strategy and overall understanding of the complexity of such monumental and intricate undertaking."

"Cool, mon," Mike consented. He was certain that his brilliant friend already had a plan in progress.

Too peaceful, Sammy mused as Mike ordered the drinks; one chap at the bar and two businessmen over in the corner. Within the hour the place would be packed and the noise would give his voice some much-needed cover. Sammy grinned. He had an excuse to defer strategy talk. He was sure that he would hit on something sufficiently convincing to appease Mike, but he was equally sure that even the most ingenious of ideas needed time to mature.

He had an hour to fill, though, since animals like Mike subconsciously assumed that instincts made brains superfluous.

They sipped their drinks in silence. Mike counted bottles. Sammy found himself staring at the two men in the corner. He wondered how it would feel to be a successful executive with plenty of money, pension, perks, secretaries and very little to do. Then he thought of their wives who had even less to do. They roamed places like Knightsbridge and Bond Street with their full wallets and had drivers to take them back to their palatial homes. Sammy's eyebrows moved like two caterpillars with itchy feet. If there were any justice in this life he would come back as a kept woman in the next. He looked again towards the corner and felt something stirring upstairs.

"Hey," he whispered, "see those two geezers? The fat one and the Jap?"

Mike nodded. There was nobody else over there. "Looks Chinese to me."

"No, he isn't. The eyes go the other way."

"Whatever. What about them?"

"Listen carefully," Sammy said and moved closer to Mike. "What I have to say now is part of the overall structure."

"You mean blackmail."

"I mean redistribution of wealth," Sammy corrected.

Mike waited. He didn't know what Sammy was talking about, but it sounded good.

Sammy continued, "You see, the Japanese won the war. The Japanese and the Germans won the war. That's a fact."

"You think that the fat fellow is German?" Mike asked and took one of Sammy's cigarettes.

"That could well be," Sammy nodded. "Look at him. A bucket of lard in a tweed suit. Personally, I find it very upsetting and offending the way foreigners exploit the weakness of our society. The Government is much to blame."

"Anyway."

Sammy knew that he'd seen the fat man before but couldn't place him. He was probably one of those publicity-seeking tycoons popping up on television and in the newspapers from time to time.

"Anyway," Mike repeated.

"Perfect," Sammy said. "Those two guys and a few like them are going to make us rich. Or at least wealthy."

"How come?"

Sammy rested his right elbow on the counter and scratched his lively groin. "Protection," he said. "You know, the proven Mafia system. Cosa Nostrum, as we call it. They pay us to prevent any harm coming their way."

"Who would harm them?"

"We would."

Mike spread his legs apart and adjusted the position of his balls. He had always known that there was no limit to Sammy's genius and wished there was a way of expressing it.

"What do you think?" Sammy said. He felt benevolent.

"Cool, mon," Mike enthused. "How we go about it?"

"I need to go for a pee," Sammy said and winked. The urge was creeping all over him.

"I thought you said you had no stuff left," Mike said.

"One. Just one."

"Okay."

Sammy's hands shook but he managed a snort without spilling anything. Easy now, he thought, this is going to be a piece of cake. It had to. He remembered to relieve himself and went back.

"One more," Mike said and beckoned to the barman.

Sammy preferred not to comment. Mike was still sober enough to put on an adequate performance and that was all that mattered. Sammy grabbed a paper napkin, spat on it and wiped his face. He yearned for a sneeze but nothing came. Time for action. The two moneybags in the corner might soon leave. Sammy's purple lips stopped an inch from Mike's ear. "Here's what we do."

Igor Parkhurst looked at the lanky, longhaired, bearded, scruffy, whey-faced and unwashed individual standing next to a menacing-looking and colourful hulk of a black man.

"We would appreciate if you could find another table," he said politely. "My guest and I are discussing some confidential matters."

"Business?" Sammy asked.

"In a manner of speaking, yes."

"Thought so. Big bucks?"

"I am afraid that is none of your concern."

"I think it is."

Parkhurst felt uncomfortable. He looked around for help. A few more people had drifted in, but they were busy talking some seven to eight yards away. The first guest was still not interested in his surroundings.

"What is it you want?"

Sammy pulled a roll of toiletpaper from his pocket. He tore off two sheets and blew his nose.

"We want to discuss finances," he said.

Parkhurst tried to keep calm and not show his fear. "I have—I have about forty pounds on me."

Sammy smiled benignly. "You're missing the point, fat boy. I'm not interested in your wallet. We operate long-term, me and my partner. Years, in fact. Just like the Japs."

Mike scowled. It was an expression that had petrified many a brave man. He was proud of his facial agility. "Years, mon," he sneered. "Got it?"

Ishihara rested his back against the wall and unbuttoned his double-breasted suit. "Get lost," he said.

Mike gaped. Slowly, he took out his knuckle-duster, caressed it and fitted it onto his right hand. Sammy made a swift movement. The thin blade of his flick-knife shot out and swished through the air. "Now, that's not very polite," he said ruefully. "I thought you Japs had manners."

"Yeah," Mike supported. "We don't take no shit from you yellow little slit-eyed monkeys who don't do this country no good. I says you better behave." He was pleased with that one. He leaned forward and extinguished his cigarette in Ishihara's drink.

"Listen, nigger," Ishihara said amiably, "why don't you and that slimy caricature of a reptile next to you go back to the latrine you came from? *Now.*"

Sammy sensed unease. This wasn't going entirely to plan. The Japanese was too unruffled, too confident. Unless he was bluffing. No losing face and all that crap. Got to be.

Mike, on the other hand, was far from hesitant. "You fucked-up shit," he sneered, "nobody but *nobody* but a nigger calls another nigger a *nigger.*"

Mike felt the weight of his knuckle-duster and experienced the deep, familiar and gratifying satisfaction of the red fog filling his eyes. He ignored Sammy's hand and took a step towards the Japanese.

"You're dead, mon," he snarled and threw a crushing punch towards an opponent who was no longer there.

He felt a devastating pain on his left shin. He hit the table with his chin and received a savage kick to his solar plexus as he fell and landed on his stomach. Unable to move, he did not see Ishihara leave the floor and deliver a flying round-kick to Sammy's jawbone but he heard him crash. As Mike tried to roll over, Ishihara's polished shoes generated a couple of broken ribs. Mike made up his mind to lie still. He heard Sammy scream when his hand, still clasping the knife, was shattered by the Japanese's heel.

Then everything became eerily quiet.

Igor Parkhurst looked around. Ishihara was standing a few feet away. He observed his victims as he methodically buttoned up his jacket. A dozen people stood motionless staring at the two on the floor. The barman had one hand on the telephone but did not proceed. The first guest had turned. His hands were folded in his lap. He appeared vaguely amused.

Ishihara gave Mike another kick. "Get to your feet. Pick up that other unsuccessful abortion and disappear before I get really annoyed."

Mike rolled into an upright position. He wondered what had hit him. "All right, mon," he whispered hoarsely. "Just leave us alone. We'll go."

Ishihara bared his teeth. Mike shuddered. He had once seen on television a dog with rabies. The Jap is mad, he thought and lent Sammy a helping hand. The pain in the side was excruciating, and Mike had lost all interest in an immediate redistribution of wealth. Sammy whimpered like an injured puppy and clutched his damaged hand. He did not fancy any further conversation.

Ishihara did not move until he saw the door close behind them. Then he picked up the knife and handed it to the barman who had not let go of the telephone.

"What do I do with it?" the barman asked.

Ishihara said, "Get it out of the way."

Someone began talking in a hushed voice. Another joined in. The barman shrugged. The ice was broken. Back to normal.

"Have one on the house," he said to Ishihara, "you and your friend. Same?"

"Deeply appreciated. Most generous. And one for the gentleman in front of you, please."

One too many, the barman thought, but he did not argue. Ishihara took the drinks and sat down.

"That black man looked vile," Parkhurst said. "I must admit that the situation with our ethnic groups here in UK is beginning to scare me."

Ishihara said, "Your successive governments have one thing in common with regard to immigration, and that is limitless stupidity. Blacks belong in Africa, nowhere else. Granted, I am a devout racist, like all Japanese, but at least we are being utilitarian about it. Blacks are born troublemakers. Their dysfunctional imitation of a brain contains one single idea, and that is that they are owed a living. My conclusion is, who the hell needs them."

"You evidently have scant regard for a liberal attitude," Parkhurst said.

Ishihara switched off the anger in his eyes and smiled jovially. "Tell me, Mr. Parkhurst, on what basis should I voluntarily and uncritically accept the sterile balderdash dripping from the septic skulls of intellectual mutants and self-absorbed pathological cocksuckers? With what *right* do these sub-human beings instruct me to employ a phraseology that is utterly absurd? I do hope you can provide me with an answer to each of my questions since both are entirely beyond my comprehension."

Parkhurst moved his lips but no sound came. He felt as if his tongue had lost contact with his larynx.

"Best of health," Ishihara said and raised his glass.

"Best of health. I— " Parkhurst fumbled with his glass "—I shouldn't really. I am driving."

"Drive slowly."

Parkhurst did not understand how the Japanese could be so relaxed, but then nothing else added up, either.

"Back to what we talked about," he began, "my— "

"—life," Ishihara assisted.

"Yes, if you so wish."

Ishihara pulled out his Cartier and lit a cigar. Parkhurst looked straight at him but could read nothing from the Japanese's expression. There isn't any, he thought. How do they manage to be so inscrutable? Some genes missing, perhaps.

"We have a lot to talk about," Ishihara finally said.

"That is interesting, but I still wouldn't mind an explanation. This entire meeting is no coincidence, is it?"

"Of course not."

"You fiddled with my car?"

"I did indeed."

"And those two thugs—?"

"That was a coincidence. I have no need for such a show. They were as welcome as a pair of porcupines copulating up my backside."

Parkhurst believed him. "You are obviously familiar with the martial arts."

"I came to The Old Master when I was twelve years of age. That is a very long time ago," he added with an absentminded nod.

Parkhurst was curious but he did not ask. The Japanese could be anything between thirty and forty. There were other relevant matters to consider.

"Where do we go from here?" he asked.

Ishihara looked at his Rolex. "Oh dear, how time has flown. My sincere regrets, but I do have to rush. We'll be in touch."

"*We—?*"

Ishihara nodded towards the first guest who had left his chair and stood waiting. "My partner. Have an enjoyable day, Mr. Parkhurst."

They left together.

Igor Parkhurst pushed his glass away. He placed his forearms on the table and tried to collect his thoughts. Who were those two? He had no idea. What did they want? Same answer. The Japanese had a remarkable command of the English language and hardly any accent. He was expensively dressed. The Rolex and the Cartier looked real. He was clearly not prone to silly mistakes.

Parkhurst scratched the tip of his nose. A man half an hour away from execution was not likely to get a visit from somebody trying to sell a life insurance policy.

Wishful thinking? Parkhurst trusted his instincts. There were times when all he got was an inner vibration, a voice telling him what was real and what was not.

Mr Ishihara was real, and so was his knowledge of Parkhurst's predicament.

We'll be in touch, he'd said. Parkhurst's telephone number was ex-directory and not printed on his card.

We.

Who was the black-clad white man and what part did he play? He certainly hadn't played any part during the fight.

On the other hand, Mr. Ishihara had not needed any help.

Wait and see, he thought. It does not stop here, whatever it is.

During the drive home, he thought about Fletcher. Wilbur had lost the ability to get excited. Passions had died out and he had become life's passive observer. Joy went by without leaving a mark. Each new day had become another drawn-out moment of blankness.

It could happen to anybody.

Parkhurst felt a bittersweet taste in his mouth.

He put on his sunglasses.

3

Days came and went. Days became weeks. Igor Parkhurst tried to work, but his concentration was wavering. Half an article here, a quarter of a story there, random notes—nothing came together. Most of the time he felt like a homeless orphan with a brandy bottle as his only companion.

He thought about defeatism, loneliness, bankruptcy and of losing the will to live. One early morning, unable to sleep, he shed a tear and knew that he had hit rock bottom. Igor Parkhurst abhorred self-pity; it was the road to destruction and it was paved with crystallized tears from the abyss of human instincts. He'd been there before, but he had never failed to drag himself out of the grey and turbulent ocean of despair.

Was it different, this time? Not really—only worse. Worse than the break-up of his three marriages, even more agonizing than having a kidney stone attack, once, when addressing the United Nations.

He was getting old; his willpower and steely determination were not what they used to be. He was indigent and—his crown of thorns—he was in the hands of evil and manipulative forces and he did not understand why.

Everything was patently more disagreeable than anything he could compare with, and he saw no way out. He was trapped; shackled and imprisoned in a cell without doors. There were no lights, and the silence was as total as it was oppressive.

It is all so unreal, he thought, so Kafka-ish. Could this be England; his beloved, liberal and *laissez-faire* England, the country he cherished and was proud of?

Igor Parkhurst got up and waddled over to the window. He pulled the curtains aside and greeted the rain that came down like slender grates of unpolished steel. It was England, all right; the other side of it. An England he had heard and read about, but not met. Until Pritchard-White.

How unforgivably naïve he had been, imagining that British politics were more decent that those of other countries. No, not imagining—*preferring* to believe.

Each man his illusions. Close the eyes and it does not exist. How utterly superficial could one allow oneself to get? Yes, he thought, we have many talents, and the ability to deceive ourselves is one of our more prominent ones.

Parkhurst felt a shade better. There could only be one way from here, and that was up. He was not ready to lie down and let life steamroll all over him; not yet and hopefully not ever.

He opened the window, sucked in a mouthful of fresh air and watched a pair of Canadian geese heading for the pond at the end of the garden. They honked as they passed. Parkhurst honked back. They were noisy buggers and pretty messy, but Parkhurst liked them as he liked and respected all wildlife. There was something arrogant about them, something composed and majestic. They were not as perfect as a kestrel or an osprey, but they were part of nature and with the same right to breathe. Parkhurst went downstairs and made himself a cup of coffee. For a brief moment he was tempted to add a drop of cognac, but he resisted.

For the next sixty minutes Parkhurst pondered, analyzed and contemplated. The state of the market wasn't the best it had ever been—it was unlikely that he'd get more for the property than he had paid for it. Paying off the mortgage plus the loans would leave him out of pocket—back to square one. He acknowledged with a calm that surprised him that the prospects of lucrative deals on writing were no longer realistic. There were several reasons. The most palpable was that his once fiery ability to feel indignation had been replaced by a despondency that had paralyzed his mind. He would never get back to his old self as long as the Secret Service had him in their grip; it was too demoralizing, too crippling.

The paradox was that even if he could live with being bankrupt and burnt-out and written off, how could he continue to exist in a mist of uncertainty, confusion and fear?

"They never let go," Fletcher had repeated between sips. *"Your usefulness is questionable, but one day you may be taken down from the shelf and there is a mission for you, a dirty task given to those who are more dispensable than others."*

Parkhurst had asked him to elaborate, but Fletcher had refused. *"Time will tell. Just do not have any illusions about having value as a human being. Humane consideration is a concept alien to Whitehall. The evidence is sitting in front of you."*

Parkhurst sighed. Who could help him? During the years he had learned the difference between an acquaintance and a friend, and he had tried to become selective. All those hundreds of people during the years, he mused, and there is only one single man I truly can call my friend; Conor Moran. He is the one person I trust implicitly.

Parkhurst walked the floor of his kitchen and knew that Conor could do no more than lend a sympathetic ear. Conor lived in a different world. He was independent and idealistic; he helped life's rejects, people with mental and emotional problems. Conor had no experience with the intricate cloak-and-dagger world of secrecy except that he had once studied to become a priest and that was a long time ago.

I'll call him, Parkhurst thought. At least Conor will listen and who knows …

Then Parkhurst remembered the Japanese who'd said he would be in touch. In between, Parkhurst had thought about Ishihara and their bizarre meeting—*it is easier to make money than to lose it.*

A charming, nonsensical Oriental absurdity. *We'll be in touch,* Parkhurst mumbled and rubbed his unshaven face; another don't-call-us-we'll-call-you situation remote from logic and common sense. He'd heard it a few times, now; it was horse-manure and nothing else.

It was hard to believe that Ishihara had arranged their meeting without a purpose in mind. I've nothing to lose by contacting him, Parkhurst reflected, I can invite him down here and tell him point-blank that I am interested in his financial services and take it from there. It can't do me any harm. If the worst comes to the worst I have wasted my time, but time isn't what I have the least of, these days.

Parkhurst thought about his knowledge of the Japanese culture; how they took their time, their passion for long-term planning and their reputation as skilled strategists.

An idea struck him. Why not try to find out something about the elusive Mr. Ishihara?

Parkhurst looked at the clock. It was seven p.m. in Tokyo.

Koji Nakamoto was one of Japan's most respected and influential reporters. His contacts within politics, police, science, the arts and crime were legendary. During the years he had developed a unique talent for being on the side of the winner without offending the loser. Every reader of his column knew that Nakamoto wrote the truth, albeit with due respect to all parties involved and always considering the subject's delicate feelings if so required. There was no piece of information he couldn't get hold of; he was honourable and he never revealed his source. The most powerful of the Yakuza families sometimes invited him to dinner when they entertained politicians.

Three years ago Nakamoto had attended when Parkhurst gave a lecture at Tokyo University about *Cultures and Humour*—courtesy of the SIS who wanted more information on what the Japanese were up to in their dealings with the Americans. Parkhurst had excelled and the applause had been more than just polite. Afterwards, when only a small handful of people had been invited to meet the esteemed guest, Nakamoto had approached Parkhurst.

His wit, tact and knowledge had impressed Nakamoto who had loved the understatements and admired Parkhurst's subtle irony. Parkhurst's jovial, friendly and well-mannered demeanour had won the evening, and with the added assistance of liquor everybody had got in a word or two. Parkhurst learned more about Japanese humour that evening than he had been able to accumulate during his entire research.

The following day Nakamoto had invited Parkhurst to dinner, and he'd found himself mesmerized by the charming and incredibly knowledgeable reporter. Parkhurst changed his plans and stayed for another week. Nakamoto had been keen to show his city and he had taken Parkhurst to the Hama Rikyu Garden, the Sensoji Temple, the Hara Museum, the Meiji Jingu Shrine and a few other places of outstanding beauty and tranquillity.

Parkhurst had fallen in love with Japan. During those few days he had absorbed as much as he could about the country's ancient history, the traditions, the structure of a complex and fascinating culture, the respect for the family, the strong sense of solidarity and the attitude to life's problems and challenges.

They had talked about the warlords, the samurais and the ninjas, about the gardens and the temples and the shrines, and on the last day they had talked about Nagasaki and Hiroshima.

That day they had also talked about the Americanization of the cities, and Parkhurst came home with a heavier mental cargo than he'd anticipated.

Nakamoto and Parkhurst had become intellectual allies, and although they had not seen each other since, they kept in touch from time to time.

Nakamoto answered the telephone at the first ring. "Ah, Igor-San! I am so pleased to hear from you. I trust that you are in the best of health and spirit?"

"Yes, thank you," Parkhurst said, "I am very well. How are you keeping, Koji-San?"

"On top of the world, thank you. Japan is buzzing with scandals, as you probably know. Perhaps I need a break. I may come over to England."

"I would be delighted to see you here. It's been a long time, and we have much to talk about."

"As always," Nakamoto said and waited.

"Koji-San," Parkhurst began, "I—something happened the other day which I do not quite understand. I was approached by a gentleman called Tadashi Ishihara."

"Not an unusual name."

"No, but that was the only thing that wasn't unusual about him. Can you spare a minute or two?"

"Of course, of course. Fill me in."

Parkhurst gave an abbreviated version of the event.

"Ah," Nakamoto said, "I don't like it. You have problems and Mr. Ishihara knows it."

"Spelling—?"

"Not over the telephone, Igor-San. Send me a detailed letter."

"I can telex—"

"No telex. A letter."

"A letter," Parkhurst consented and knew that Nakamoto had his reasons. "I'll send it today."

"Good." Nakamoto laughed. "I know it is difficult for an Englishman to describe a Japanese, but give it a try."

Parkhurst closed his eyes. "About five feet eight. Somewhere around thirty, I would assume. Very expensively dressed. A degree from the University of Tokyo, politics and economy. Referred to The Old Master after having exhibited his karate skills on a couple of local punks. That's about it, I believe."

"And his English?"

Parkhurst felt a bit sheepish. "Sorry. His English is not far from perfect. If he'd said he was born and raised here and had attended the most exclusive schools, I would have believed him."

"Obviously a gifted man, if all of it is true."

"That's the question, or one of them."

Nakamoto chuckled. "The truth always contains fewer complications than a web of lies. Mr. Ishihara could be as real as you and I. We shall know within a week or so. What about his partner?"

"He is white, blond going on grey. A bit younger than he looks, I think. Some two or three inches taller, strong looking and fond of Irish whisky. He never said one single word. Not a fancy dresser, by the way."

"My guess is that they have known each other for a long time. Just a hunch," Nakamoto added. "I shall start my investigations first thing tomorrow morning."

"I am very grateful," Parkhurst said.

"Nothing to it, Igor-San. A troubled mind is not a productive mind. I would like to see you back to your best. You have much to give."

"You are too kind," Parkhurst said. He felt strangely emotional.

"Part of my nature," Nakamoto giggled. "Cheer up, my friend. A problem is just another label for an inspiring confrontation."

"Thanks again, Koji."

"Take care. Speak to you soon."

The line went dead.

Parkhurst sensed relief. Something was happening. Not much, but it was better than nothing. Perhaps in a week or two he would know enough about Mr. Ishihara to approach him—or to forget him altogether. To drop him, though, would be a monumental disappointment since it was so much easier to make money than to lose it.

Money. Igor Parkhurst shook his head and smiled ruefully. What a mess. What have I come to, he thought. For years on end I had no financial worries to talk about, and now I am pinning my hopes on an enigmatic Japanese who I've met once and who could easily be a cheap con man.

Not much realism here, Mr. Parkhurst, he said out loud and decided to inspect his property. Do your best to keep the feeling of anguish at bay. Do contemplate, by all means, but don't analyze too much.

The courier rang the doorbell one afternoon eleven days later. Parkhurst poured a modest cognac and settled in his favourite chair in the library.

He began to read. The letter was typed. Parkhurst assiduously absorbed every word. He looked at the photo attached and started all over again.

Tadashi Ishihara was authentic enough. Everything he had told Parkhurst was correct. The fascinating part was what he hadn't told, which was quite a lot.

He was from a solid middle class background; his father was an industrialist and his mother an artist. The young Ishihara had turned out to be a brilliant but rebellious student with an independent mind and a wicked sense of humour. He had joined Ryutaro Kobayashi's karate dojo at an early age and twice won the Japanese Open Championship. He had become The Old Master's right-hand man and greatly assisted in making the school feared and renowned across the borders. What had once been a small outfit for idealistic karate-kas had become a powerhouse. There was clear evidence that Kobayashi had associated with the Yakuza.

Nakamoto went on to elaborate on the role and the prominence of the Yakuza in the Japanese society. He explained the function of the Sokaiya; gangsters who specialized in extortion by threatening to disrupt shareholders' meetings with questions that the Board of Directors had no desire to hear. Consequently, numerous scandals were being buried under mountains of money—a good estimate appeared to be some ten billion yen being paid to the Sokaiya annually.

It would probably amuse Igor-San to learn that this activity was perfectly legal. Age-old, healthy and respectable traditions had a tendency to survive, law or no law, in Japan as, presumably, in England. As far as young Ishihara was concerned there was no concrete evidence, but Nakamoto was reasonably certain that Ishihara had established and

46

developed his own private little business; it was unlikely that he had ever joined any of the syndicates. Presumably, he had operated solo, a profitable one-man Sokaiya, so to speak.

Then, at some time, tension had surfaced between Kobayashi and one of the Yakuza families, apparently culminating with an episode in Hong Kong.

Nakamoto did not know what had happened—given more time he probably could find out—but rumours had it that Kobayashi's other star had played a prominent role. His name was Angelo Vargas, and he was the first non-Oriental ever to be admitted to Kobayashi's dojo. Vargas never participated in the Sokaiya, but Nakamoto had little doubt that Vargas had been part of whatever Kobayashi and Ishihara had been up to. It was Vargas who had solved the problem in Hong Kong, and it was known that he had been included in Kobayashi's plans for the future of his organization. At that time Ishihara and Vargas had been allies for years, and they'd both been instrumental in dealing with the Yakuza after the Hong Kong affair.

Nakamoto admitted that he knew practically nothing about Vargas, except that he'd come to Japan on a Mexican passport. He had kept a very low profile during his years in Japan. Apart from causing a scandal in one of the tournaments by ignoring the rules, there was nothing on him. The odd myths and rumours, yes; hearsay had it that Vargas had little time for complicated solutions, in general, and that even the imperious and peremptory Kobayashi had treated Vargas with silk gloves. The opinion was that Vargas was a loner, exceptionally ruthless and even more vicious than Ishihara.

Then, suddenly, Ishihara and Vargas had left Japan. From then on, the trail went dead. Nakamoto could use his contacts and try to find out more, or Parkhurst could wait and see what happened. Nakamoto did not doubt that Ishihara was working on a long-term plan, and perhaps Parkhurst had little choice, gathering from his letter, than to play it by ear and evaluate whatever Ishihara came up with. Nakamoto could only advise extreme caution; any sign of altruism should be taken with a truckload of salt since neither Ishihara nor Vargas had left behind a reputation as Samaritans.

Parkhurst placed the letter on the side table. For a while he watched the bluetits attacking the peanut feeder hanging from the branch of an old oak tree that had once been hit by lightning. He rubbed his face with the palms of his hands. His lips parted and closed and he made little noises like a pup sucking milk.

Light clouds drifted towards the east like uneven slates of marble turning pink as the sun rose with regal idleness. The moss-green lawns were speckled with sherry-brown and glistening leaves from the chestnut trees. Igor Parkhurst stopped when he came to the end of his flagstone terrace.

He listened to a chiffchaff living up to its name. He watched a green woodpecker coming in for a rest in the Japanese maple tree that had been there before Miriam arrived. His lips silently formed the word *Japanese* a few times. He could feel the skin around his mouth getting tight when he saw a black Mercedes glide down the driveway and come to a halt.

No, he thought, I don't believe this; things just do not happen that way.

He walked towards the car and eyeballed Ishihara with a mixture of apprehension, surprise and anticipation.

"Good morning," Ishihara said. He closed the door behind him. "Why are you blinking like a bird pondering the plight of migration? Did I not say I'd be in touch?" He smiled. "By the way, it is indeed considerate of you to be at home. It is a long drive from London to here. Nice trip, though. It is very peaceful, this corner of our universe. Most pleasant." He stretched. "I'd better get the circulation going. I am as stiff as a cardinal in a whore's bed."

Parkhurst could not help smiling. The Japanese was dressed in dark grey trousers, fuchsia-coloured shirt with a sunflower-yellow tie and a midnight blue blazer. Parkhurst estimated that the cost of the shoes alone could have kept a taxidriver with fuel for a month.

It was quarter to ten in the morning. "Where else would I be?" he said and extended his hand.

"My exact conclusion," Ishihara said and walked past after the briefest of handshakes. "A lovely home. It would be a shame to lose it, particularly with no Mrs. Parkhurst around."

Parkhurst swallowed. "Is there anything about me that you do *not* know, Mr. Ishihara?"

"I can't think of anything. Would you be kind enough to show me your stately home, please? I am curious by nature and also a connoisseur of taste and beauty. Thereafter we can have tea in the kitchen." He bowed. "After you, Mr. Parkhurst."

They went through the entire house and ended up with the three drawing rooms. Ishihara was not in a hurry; he studied each object that caught his attention but he made no comments. From time to time he nodded.

"That is neo-Regency, correct? " He pointed towards the open doors to the hallway. "You do not see many sculptured galleries in Japan," he added and touched the heavy curtains. "I shall not bother with the cottages, the swimming pool and the tennis court today, Mr. Parkhurst. We have got things to talk about. Suffice to say that you have got a most exquisite home." He faced Parkhurst. "My compliments."

"Thank you," Parkhurst said uneasily. He wondered where all this would lead to.

"Heavens above!" Ishihara suddenly exclaimed. He was staring at a photograph of a woman. "How could you!"

Parkhurst looked at the portrait of Miriam. After the split-up he had been unable to drop the picture in the dustbin. He knew the reason; apart from being a silly old fool, he missed the company but not the person.

"Could what?" he asked.

"Marry her. She's got no lips."

Parkhurst looked again. It was true that darling Miriam had a rather thin mouth, probably as a result of firing from her impressive arsenal of sarcasms since the age of two. Parkhurst twittered. "We all make mistakes."

"Mistakes," Ishihara repeated. "She must be the most expensive erotic catastrophe your long and eventful life has hitherto experienced. The other wives cost you less, I seem to recall."

"They did."

Ishihara sat down on the side of an armchair. "But then they were just dumb creatures who could not cope with your lifestyle. This specimen of a lipless wonder is in a different aquarium altogether, the type of woman any man with only a feeble excuse for a brain would look at once and only once before he escaped faster than an obscenity in a cathedral. But not you. Good Lord! as you Brits are so fond of saying."

"Perhaps I am no exception, Mr. Ishihara," Parkhurst said and straightened his back. "I underrate women to the same extent as I overrate

49

men. You could call it the traditional, typical and unbalanced masculine mind, unable to fathom pure reasoning and incapable of absorbing any meritorious experience worth utilizing."

"An accurate annotation," Ishihara said, nodding approvingly. "The vast majority of men know next to nothing about women. She puts her dinky little pinkie finger on our hand, only a light touch, and we instantly imagine it as a feverish embrace by a vestal nun suddenly giving in to the less self-denying instincts ravaging her body and penetrating her immortal soul. Entirely assholistic, but there we are—or you, in this case."

Parkhurst began to feel annoyed. The last thing he needed was a lecture on matrimony. He cleared his throat. "Shall we consider the topic exhausted?" he said with polite irony. "I am sure you did not come all the way down here just to discuss the more personal aspects of my life."

Ishihara smiled. "Shall we have some tea?"

Parkhurst led the way to the kitchen. Ishihara insisted on making the tea, which he did without ceremony. He took off his blazer and hung it over the back of a chair. "With your kind permission," he said and sat down.

"Please feel at home."

"Most grateful. I do already." He lifted his cup. "Cheers," he smiled. "To a long, interesting and fruitful association."

Parkhurst was tempted not to move, but he could not make himself appear ill-mannered. "Cheers. To whatever."

Ishihara laughed and shook his head. "My friend, a mind cramped by suspicion is a barren mind. Seeds will fall on stones, as so eloquently expressed in the book of your quasi-constitutional religion. My friend Vargas told me that one. Mr. Vargas knows a bit about religions. He will be most impressed by your library. True bibliophiles are rare, these days."

"You must invite him down."

"That is inevitable. By the way, you do not mind being on first name? Skip the formalities? We know each other well enough, by now, I'd say."

"Don't we."

This is absurd, Parkhurst thought, crazy and unreal. This man just isn't true. The entire situation collided with every concept, every bit of knowledge he had about the Japanese; they simply did not behave in such a manner. Even if they had been abroad for some years, even if they purposely tried to break off their cultural roots, never did they conduct themselves with such supreme aplomb and seemingly natural ease as Mr. Ishihara. He's a freak, Parkhurst concluded. That leaves me with only two options; either get rid of him once and for all, or play along until the well has run dry and he seeks greener pastures.

Ishihara broke the silence. "You must wonder who I am, and you must wonder why I am here. It must also have occurred to you, as we briefly discussed during our first meeting, that coincidences are few and far between."

Parkhurst looked at him. The warmth and the humour had gone from Ishihara's dark brown eyes.

He continued, "It will all surface, sooner or later, but it is important that we take one step at a time."

Parkhurst said, "That makes sense. If I may be so bold, Mr. Ishihara, perhaps you would care to start somewhere? Anywhere. My mind is open, perceptive and eager to absorb."

A sharp noise came from outside. Before Parkhurst had turned his head, Ishihara was on his feet. "What's that!"

Parkhurst connected his molars and forestalled a smile. "Pheasants," he said.

Ishihara sat down and sipped his tea. The veins on his temples had become visible. "Tell me, Igor-San, why are English farmers so noisy?"

"Not peasant," Parkhurst said. "Pheasant—with a *ph*. It's a bird." He gave an easy smile. "Of Chinese origin, by the way. The Romans brought the pheasant to this country for decorative purposes. The English like to shoot them."

"Why this desire to annihilate?"

"Easy prey. The birds can hardly fly."

Parkhurst thought of Ishihara's quick reaction and added, "You are rather alert, I'd say."

"Old habits. Life in the country is not one of my experiences." He got up and walked over to the window. "Oh yes. A beautiful bird. Very pretty colours. Do they shut up at night?"

"That depends on the activities of the owls. The countryside is peaceful, but it is not necessarily quiet."

51

"Did it take you long to familiarize yourself?"

"Not really. It is much a matter of choice. You decide where you want to live, based on why, and you adapt accordingly."

"You have been discarded by practically everybody, and now you find that you are not cut out for a solitary existence. Not so, Igor?"

Parkhurst did not answer.

Ishihara went on, "Loneliness is a rat that eats his way from your testicles to your tonsils. It is not a pleasant ordeal, is it, Igor?"

I am not getting into this, Parkhurst thought. He said, "More tea?"

Ishihara returned to the table. He lit one of his thin cigars, leaned back and seemed lost in thoughts for a moment. After a minute or so he said, "Mr. Vargas and I have been operating on an international level for many years. We have now decided that our career is coming to an end. We have also made up our mind to settle in this country. We both like it here. It is not a bad place to live. The English are more liberal than they themselves realize, and we both have a passion for doing things our own way. We have been here for a while, now, so our decision is not a rash one. That would be out of character, anyway. However, we have been busy, we have travelled and not until now have we made any preparation for a new and quiet life." He flicked the ash from his cigar and gave himself a few seconds' respite. "In other words, Igor, *socially* we are non-entities. We don't exist. Step number two is to remedy said situation."

Ishihara paused again. His eyes did not leave Parkhurst's.

"Step number one is to get you out of the mess you are in, alleviate the situation, in more precise terms. You are virtually a wreck and therefore entirely useless. What you need is stability, harmony and the old famous percipience back in action."

I am not hearing this, Parkhurst thought; I am not sitting in my own kitchen listening to a complete stranger outlining my future. Why has the Almighty picked me as the victim of some cruel, nightmarish practical joke? I am sane, I believe, and I am not a bad person. I do have my problems; indeed, I have more problems than ever before in my life, but why should that concern a slick Japanese with a criminal background? What does he want from me; that is, what is the true reason behind all this?

"Igor my lad, you look utterly confused."

"Do I really? How odd."

Ishihara chuckled. "Almost an acerbic comment, and that's how I want to see you. That was an echo from the past, from the days when nobody could match your beautifully controlled but nonetheless vitriolic spirit." He tapped his gold front tooth, sparkling in the light from the late morning sun. "Pure gold, Igor, symbolizing days to come. Should not only the best be good enough? Should we not reach for the stars?" Ishihara stretched his fingers till they looked as rigid as the prongs of a pitchfork. "Most people mistake a problem for an obstacle, poor morons. You and I know that a problem is more precisely defined as an experiment, a personality test. You are with me?"

"Certainly, Mr. Ishihara, what else could a problem be."

"No-no," Ishihara protested. "Tadashi, please. Let us drop the formalities. I insist. This long chat has brought us closer than Siamese twins."

Parkhurst topped up his tea. "If you so wish, Tadashi."

"That's better. It is most heart-warming to notice that you are beginning to relax. Now, may I be so free as to continue my elaborate and well substantiated analysis of our present predicament, followed by a few essential suggestions and thereafter a temporary conclusion?"

Dear oh dear, Parkhurst thought. Maybe Nakamoto was wrong; Ishihara had studied law, not economy. Graduating, he had applied his formal training getting acquainted with the works of Dickens and Thackeray.

He said, "Not only do I agree, I could not have put it more eloquently myself."

"How extraordinarily kind," Ishihara said gravely. "Regrettably, though, I do not believe you, but in my world there is always room for the occasional dash of sarcasms of quality. Usually, irony is preferable because it is more subtle, a subject I myself study painstakingly and which you should revert to in your efforts to re-launch your flagging career. I can be of considerable assistance here, by the way, since I am intimately *au courant* with the secrets of moving with the rhythm of the heartbeat. Old Oriental wisdom. We can talk about that later."

Careful now, Parkhurst advised himself. Don't get careless with this chap. There is no point in offending him, even if I never see him again. And if I do—Parkhurst could easily imagine enemies less formidable than Tadashi Ishihara.

"I apologize. I should have shown more fastidiousness in my choice of words."

"Never mind. Buddha was the epitome of touchiness and impatience compared with me. A simple yet astonishingly accurate description of my good self would be a pure, forbearing and supreme mind in a divine body." Ishihara blew his cheeks like a trombone player. "There you have me."

Parkhurst laughed. A few more sessions like this, he thought, and I'll genuinely begin to enjoy my self-appointed friend.

"So," Ishihara mused, "we can now most categorically conclude that we need each other. You need me to become a full-fledged, contented and productive human being again, unrecognizable from the pathetic imitation sitting in front of me, and I need you in order to gain access to the upper echelon of the class-ridden and jingoistic British society."

Parkhurst said, "It may be all I want, but is it everything you want?"

Ishihara rose from his chair and went over to the windows facing east. He stood there for a while, a stocky, powerfully built figure seemingly admiring the birds and the bees and with nothing more to say.

"Is it?" Parkhurst pressed.

Ishihara turned. "You are far too intelligent to ask such a question," he said. "You clearly and quite correctly suspect that there is another dimension, or two. You also sense, I hope, that it has to do with your activities as an undercover agent, if you would pardon the bouquet. Indirectly, this is so."

"Indirectly—?"

"At some time in the future your esteemed masters will want to get in touch with Mr. Vargas and myself. You will be the medium."

"Why can't they—?" Parkhurst arrested himself. He had an uncomfortable feeling that he was treading water deeper than he appreciated.

"It does not work that way. I must beg of you not to ask any further questions. Please do trust that we know what we are talking about. We know what we are doing."

The sun had filled the room. Parkhurst could no longer see Ishihara's face.

It struck Parkhurst how happy he could have been here if only things were different, if only he was his old self again. He saw a wasp crawl across the windowpane and wondered if Ishihara had an allergy to stinging insects. Wasps were dangerous at this time of the year, seemingly lazy but nonetheless aggressive.

He tried to sound casual, "Why should I agree to all this?"

Ishihara opened the window, took in a mouthful of fresh air and hoisted himself up on the counter. He sat there, silent and relaxed with his feet dangling and his hands folded in his lap.

Parkhurst waited. Minutes passed. Ishihara appeared content to watch his latest chum.

"I asked you a question," Parkhurst finally gave in. "Would it be too much to expect an answer?" He wished he could see Ishihara's face.

"The tragedy is that you are so run down, so mentally disintegrated that you see fit to ask such a question at all," Ishihara said with chilling precision. "But you did, and the answer is; you have not got a choice."

He slid down from the counter and came back to the table. "Igor, I have presented you with a proposition. Give me a call when you are ready to take it a step further. I expect to hear from you within five days."

Parkhurst suddenly resented Ishihara's attitude. "I do have some imminent commitments," he said, " so perhaps…"

"That is entirely up to you," Ishihara interrupted. "If you want to devote yourself to a blank sheet of paper remaining blank in your typewriter and miss out on one hundred thousand pounds, then that is your chosen priority. Only you can determine the shape and direction of your future. No doubt your wisdom, experience and acumen will be your guiding lights."

Parkhurst felt dizzy. He cleared his throat but words would not come.

Ishihara's eyes clouded over. The colour went from dark brown to black. "Igor, I, too, have tasted the ups and downs in life, from divine sublimity to the inferno of hell. Appreciate, please, that I do sympathize with your situation, and please do accept that what I offer is a reciprocal arrangement."

Parkhurst hesitated. He struggled with the notion that somebody would come from nowhere and put forward a proposal that went against common human behaviour. "I am confused," he said. "I do not understand why you are prepared to do this. I heard your reason, but—but life isn't like that. If I'd still been a big shot—" his voice weakened "—I am a has-been, Mr. Ishihara. I am a burnt-out, wretched, decrepit fool facing oblivion and nothing else. You are simply too late."

Ishihara dropped the remainder of his cigar into the ashtray. "I disagree. Neither do I think that wallowing in self-pity does you any good."

He poured more tea and removed a couple of leaves with his spoon. "How many friends have you had during the years?"

"Oh—hundreds."

"Where are they now?"

Parkhurst's eyes drifted sideways.

"Let me tell you something about human behaviour," Ishihara said. "Most of us fail to recognize that loyalty is a function of requital. Not of blind devotion. We hail loyalty as perhaps the finest of qualities since we regularly fail to comprehend that it is just another of our intangible commodities. We buy it, Igor, with whatever currency is required in any one given situation. We buy it with whatever the recipient wishes to acquire—cash, help, security, sympathy, understanding—and the effect of this colourful little cocktail is unfailingly mistaken for fidelity. Then, when we no longer can or wish to provide yet another cocktail—or the recipient has found another supplier with a more intoxicating blend— the illusion of loyalty as a virtue has all but gone."

A vein under Parkhurst's left ear stood out like a piece of soft blue rope. "You find me rather easily taken in, don't you?"

"You are gullible because you are a decent and honourable man," Ishihara said. "Both are commendable qualities, as we know, but, unfortunately, man has a tendency to exploit the good and submit to the bad. You faded and became a pariah; I say, reach for my hand, leave the quagmire and let us enjoy the fruits of mutual efforts."

Parkhurst heard the horses whinnying over in the paddock and felt his eyes throbbing. "Re-cycled enthusiasm," he mumbled and rubbed his nose.

"Don't be such a jerk," Ishihara said. "Let us move forward, from now on. As of this moment, time is a singular line with no point of return, as Confucius would have said had he thought about it. Settled?"

"What about—about—"

"—your friend Gregory Pritchard-White, Esquire? Listen, Igor, the world is full of prats. Why shouldn't he be one of them? Don't overestimate the serpent."

"You know who and what he is?"

"Of course I do. Please, Igor. When it comes to intelligence work, I am one of life's few true professionals. Do not over-emphasize the importance of Pritchard-White. Basically, he is not much more than a fly in the arse."

"You mean a pain in the arse," Parkhurst said and tried a cheerful chortle.

"I wouldn't go that far. More of a buzz, really, soon ready to be blown away, hence fly."

Parkhurst shook his head and looked at the damp marks his hands had left on the wooden tabletop. "I admire your assertiveness."

The Japanese round face became a pond of tranquillity. "So do I. My superiority is more often than not mistaken for arrogance, for some reason. I am so pleased that you see me for what I am."

Ishihara got up, put on his jacket and went to the door. "May I presume that I shall soon have the pleasure of coming down here again? I have really taken to country life." He bowed. "Also, do try to remember the five-day limit for your little bonus. I wish you a pleasant day."

Parkhurst heard the engine start, but he did not move. There was a knock on the window. He looked up.

"I almost forgot," Ishihara beamed. "Please give Mr. Nakamoto my kindest regards next time you talk to him."

Then he was gone.

Parkhurst walked aimlessly from room to room for almost two hours. He saw without seeing and he heard without hearing. Finally he opened the French doors and went outside. He crossed the lawn and found a small grove where he sat down on a wooden bench.

He folded his hands behind his neck and watched two hares running figures of eight. In the distance he saw the gracious flight of a deer across the meadows. The blue of the Northeast sky was giving way to a red and grey shimmer where rain clouds were building up. With the wind came the smell of wet soil.

Igor Parkhurst closed his eyes and let memories and images float by like an old-fashioned newsreel in slow motion.

He had no idea what time it was. The sky was no longer ominous. A few white clouds tinged with magenta moved idly like amorphous cherubs playfully chasing each other.

He placed his feet apart, picked himself up from the bench and walked back to the house. He entered the study and poured a cognac before he sat down and telephoned Conor Moran.

4

It was a long way from Dublin to Chelsea where Conor Moran had lived for almost ten years. Too long, he sometimes thought when he recalled the tumultuous days of his youth and images of Ireland flashed through his mind.

Maybe one day, towards the evening of his life, he would go back and write his memoirs in between frequenting the pubs on Grafton Street and in Fleet Street where his fate had once been decided by a young and not yet famous Colm Begley.

Nobody had ever doubted that Conor would become a priest. A quiet, kind and mild-mannered boy, he was convinced that priests were good, perhaps saintly, and that the church was the one pillar of society that could forever be trusted.

From when he could talk, Conor longed to grow up and become a man of the collar. His most cherished dream, which he shared with nobody, was that one day the Pope would be Irish.

Conor's parents, Aenghus and Mairead, were gentle, sensitive and well read. They shared his enthusiasm for the church, but they never pushed him. Aenghus, a housepainter, was proud of his son's ambitions and achievements, and Mairead, who wrote poetry and had a beautiful singing voice, called him *my little angel* well into his teens. She only dropped it when she sensed that her six feet, one hundred and eighty pounds offspring with the constitution of a buffalo found her terms of endearment a shade embarrassing.

Conor was equally proud of his parents. Four of Mairead's poetry volumes had been published, and she sang at weddings, funerals and whenever there was a cause for celebration. Aenghus was an accomplished cartoonist but with no ambition to match; he sought the social company of artists, writers and other members of the Dublin intelligentsia and left it at that. Contrary to most, he drank and spoke with moderation, and he had no intention of changing either Dublin or the rest of the world. He was a good and popular listener, and many a confused soul asked for his advice on more serious matters.

Aenghus was a skilled and trusted craftsman, and he had few problems finding work. Occasionally he shared a job with a young man called Colm Begley who from time to time paid Union Hall a visit to see if anything worthwhile was available. Aenghus had difficulties swallowing Begley's extensive repertoire of blasphemies, but all in all Aenghus liked the young man and recognized early his other linguistic skills. *"I am a writer, first and foremost a writer. A born writer,"* Begley said repeatedly. Aenghus immobilized his brush and replied: *"If that is the case, why don't you put pen to paper as that is what I'm told that writers do. You most certainly should have enough experience to draw from by now."*

At this point Begley wiped his hands and rested his shoulder against the wall, wet or not. *"Jesus, Joseph and Mary, a truer word was never spoken. With the help of the Holy Mother of God I shall soon do exactly that."*

Then he started singing and they ended the day in the nearest pub where Aenghus enjoyed his pint and Begley drank everything except Protestant whisky.

Conor did not touch alcohol, but at the age of eighteen he joined his father in the pub for the first time. The year was 1932. Eamon de Valera and his *Fianna Fail* party had come to power, and Aenghus decided to celebrate the event with his son. Aenghus, like everybody else he knew, resented the demands for continuous land payments to the British Government, and although he realized that hardship would follow a trade war, there was no doubt in his soul that de Valera was right.

The lively atmosphere, tales and stories told with eloquence, the pathos, the humour, the songs and the verbal duels were to Conor like a breath of fresh air blowing through his mind. Most were considerate and moderated their language when he was around, but there were exceptions. Begley was one of them.

At first, Conor could not understand why he did not feel offended, why he did not resent the derogatory comments about the church and its disciples. There were men other than Begley who hated the church and all it stood for, either because of some personal experiences or because they found the entire concept of religion an intellectual abhorrence, or both. Conor listened intently without participating even when being bated beyond normal etiquette. Aenghus buried his face in the jug to hide his discomfort.

One day he said, "Son, maybe you should not come to the pub. It is not always—nice."

"Oh, I don't know," Conor said. "Perhaps the odd remonstration can do no harm. Where do I go if I cannot trust myself?"

Aenghus had no answer, and he knew it. What he didn't know was that his son had begun to harbour second thoughts about his vocation in life; there were nagging thorns tearing his soul and he no longer was sure which path to follow.

Conor recognized the void. One day the forces of guilt, doubt and naked shame would rip him apart unless he faced up to the turbulence inside and he found a balance that would make life bearable.

His self-control and willpower helped him to keep up the façade, but Mairead sensed that something was wrong. One day she asked with her usual candour, "What is bothering you, Conor?"

It was like all the windows had been opened in a room stuffed with the stale and musty odour from an unkempt, passive and starving human being. The sense of relief that swept through his mind brought tears to Conor's eyes.

Finally, Conor began to talk. He talked about Emperor Constantine and Bishop Hosius and their Nicene Creed conveniently inventing the Holy Spirit. He took Mairead through the vile and bloodstained history of the Church from 325 AC till modern time. He had little regard for most of the Pius XI encyclicals and, in particular, he could not accept the intolerance that dominated *Mortalium Animos*. He spoke about limbo and indulgence, about the rigid hierarchy and the Papacy seen as the brain and the heart of Christian faith. He made his comments about abortion, divorce, cover-ups, power struggles, corruption, intrigues, politicking, hypocrisy, cruelty, prejudice and infallibility. He touched the paradox that the crucifix as a symbol did not emerge until the Middle Ages, and he ended by quoting from Paul's Epistle to the Romans: "*The just shall live by faith.*"

Conor had laid his soul on the table, orderly and with precision. Mairead was touched and bewildered. Dear God, she thought, this son of mine has read more than theology for some while.

She saw a hitherto undetected defiance in his eyes and resigned herself to a future far removed from that of her dreams. What matters is his happiness, she thought, not my ambitions. She searched for words, but Conor had not finished.

"Added to all this," he said evenly, "I like women."

Mairead burst out laughing. "That seals it, doesn't it?"

"Just one of many factors," Conor shrugged. "We are all relieved, I presume."

She dried her eyes with her handkerchief. "So," she said, "I may have grandchildren, after all."

"That is not unthinkable," Conor mumbled and looked away.

Sweet Jesus, she thought, my boy is growing up. Why did it take me so long to realize? Mother's love, I guess, blinded by devotion, everlasting maternal instincts and wishful thinking. He is no longer my little boy; he is a man and a man soon ready to depart. "Where do you go from here, Conor?"

"I do not know, yet. First, I must talk to Father Michael. He will be in for a shock."

Indeed he will, Mairead thought. She liked and respected Father Michael, but she also had her reservations. He was a loud, blunt and opinionated bumblebee, and nobody had ever mistaken him for one of the Church's more flexible characters.

"He will try to persuade you," she predicted.

"I know. It doesn't matter. I cannot continue." Conor placed his hand on hers. "Thank you for listening. I know now that I needed this talk more than I was aware of. I feel—I feel at ease. It is like going through a wall and discover the wide open fields on the other side."

"Free at last?"

"Yes. I feel as if I do not have to pretend, any more. It is a strange sensation and not yet ready for words. The past twelve months or so have not been very pleasant."

There was silence for a while. Then Mairead said, "If you ever get married, or shall I say *when*, always communicate. It is the most important condition required in a marriage if it is to succeed and survive. Never bottle things up, Conor." She laughed. "And that is the only advice on marriage I shall ever give you."

61

Conor strolled down Fleet Street and into the Palace Bar. He saw Kathleen Keogh and did not avert his eyes. Her smile was sweet and confident, as if to say: "*I am not dangerous. You can talk to me.*"

I am imagining things, Conor thought. Before he could summon up sufficient courage to move a step closer, he had been spotted by Colm Begley who had recently been released from jail.

"God's teeth!" Begley shouted, "the Divine is amongst us. Come over here and let me buy you a drink, you sperm of the Holy Ghost."

He laughed rumbustiously. Several others joined in. Conor went across. Somebody made room.

"What is your preference, oh Father to be? A glass of milk?" Begley enquired.

Conor laughed with the others. He rested against the counter and looked squarely at the jovial face in front of him.

"May I first say how much I admire your command of the language, Colm? Your eloquence is admirable, and your vocabulary no less so."

"Jaysus!" Begley exclaimed, "I am a writer!"

"Yes," Conor nodded, "you are John Synge's worthy successor, or is it Frank Harris? I have read your entire production, and I am deeply impressed."

There was a stunned silence. Apart from the occasional pieces in *The Bell* and an on-off column in *Irish Press*, Begley had yet to produce anything of substance. Most of his cronies knew that this was a sore point with him. Sean O'Faolain, the editor of *The Bell*, had summed it up: "*You cannot talk, sing, drink and write at the same time. It's called priorities, Colm. Dreams alone do not produce volumes. Make up your mind and show the world your talent. Nobody will ever do it for you.*"

Begley had been careless enough to repeat this to whoever wanted to listen, and it spread quickly through the bars. After a while the bantering died down; Begley was good company, and, moreover, there were times when any excuse would do to start a fight.

Not this time. An expression of curiosity spread across Begley's face. "Is that so?" he said evenly and lit a cigarette. He smiled and met Conor's stare. "The blessings of Jaysus on you, my friend, or perhaps the other way round. What would be your choice of beverage in this hour of revelation?"

And change, Conor added in his mind and felt a strange sensation surge through him. He looked around. Kathleen Keogh stood less than five feet away. Her green eyes sparkled in the light. Begley glanced from one to the other, knowingly and amused.

"A single whisky would do me fine," Conor said.

Begley put down his own glass with a bang. "You heard the man!" he shouted to the barman. "Give him the fughing drink!"

Conor sipped, carefully enough to avoid tears coming to his eyes, but he wondered how this burning liquid could possibly be a pleasure.

"That's what I like to see," Begley barked, "a heavy drinker, like most priests. By the way, how is your revered bishop, these days? I hear he has appointed himself God's gift to choirboys."

"I am not a priest," Conor said. "Talking about rumours, I hear that you are an atheist."

"So I am," Begley said, "so I am." He slapped his knees and huffed. "At least a daytime atheist, which is a good start." The cigarette stuck to his lips, and he cursed as he burned his fingers. Then he looked at Kathleen Keogh, slid down from his chair, opened his arms and began to sing:

Do you remember, long ago
Kathleen?
When your lover whispered low
"Shall I stay or shall I go
Kathleen?"
And you answered proudly, "Go!
And join King James and strike a blow
For the Green!"

Begley climbed back onto his chair and asked for another drink. He nudged Conor gently. "You are drinking too fast, my friend," he said. "You must bear in mind that although the taste is sublime, it's the effect we are after. Slowly does it. Get the best of both worlds, like me." He chuckled genially. "So you are not a priest," he stated solemnly. "Please excuse my temerity, but why does a little voice tell me that you may never become one, either, praise heaven?"

Conor felt like he'd been hit in the stomach, but he quickly recovered. He had no intention of discussing his private and personal life with a half-drunk, would-be poet he hardly knew, least of all in public. "Your assumptions are your own," he said. He wasn't entirely pleased with the answer.

"Aye. Indeed they are," Begley agreed. "Would you like me to introduce you to the most beautiful maiden in the whole of Ireland?"

Conor reddened, but before he could get a word out, Begley shouted: "Kathleen! Come over and say hello to the finest blood this island of ours has ever produced. A virgin idealist, I suspect, but don't let that put you off."

Her handshake was as firm as her smile was warm.

When Conor came home two hours later, his parents were sitting in the kitchen. There was an awkward silence, as if he had interrupted or interfered with something deeply personal. His father looked tense and apprehensive. He had a glass of whisky in front of him. That was unusual.

Aenghus cleared his throat. "Care for something, son?"

"I'll make myself a cup of tea," Conor said.

Mairead smiled gently. "I have told your father about our talk," she said. She looked calm and serene. "Of course, only you can explain."

Explain. It had been so easy, when he had talked to Kathleen; words had flown freely, and she had said that no one should go against the grain of their own convictions. The more he had talked to Kathleen, the more certain he had become. He remembered with an inkling of embarrassment that only during the last half-hour of their long walk had they talked about her and her life.

"Have you lost your faith, Conor?" Aenghus asked. He pushed his glass around. His voice had a rough edge to it, but there were no signs that Aenghus had tried to drown his confusion.

He is lost, Conor thought, lost and bitterly disappointed. But do I become a priest for his sake? Conor knew the answer.

He said, "No, I have not lost my faith in God. What has happened is that I no longer believe that I can make a good priest. I have lost confidence in the Church. Its history, past and present, is not compatible with my ideals. I do not wish to become a politician with a collar. I have no desire to become entangled in a web of intrigues, hypocrisy, conspiracies and dishonesty shielded by the Bible and fended off with the Cross. I am not sacrificing my life on an altar of unhappiness and lost integrity."

Mairead focused her eyes on something at the far end of the kitchen.

He is older than his years, she thought and knew that her disappointment had given way to pride.

"It does not have to be that way," Aenghus said.

Conor folded his hands. "Yes, it does. Sooner or later, the system swallows you. We all give in under pressure if it persists for long enough—like a lifetime." His tone of voice changed. "Please understand, father. I am not leaving God behind. What I cannot do is to seek cover under the shell that man created in His name. The Church of today is too synthesized, a medieval relic. What it offers and what I need are mutually exclusive." He remembered Kathleen's word; "I cannot go against the grain of my conviction. I do not want to serve God in a compromised manner." He paused. "My reasons for wanting to join the Church were wrong. I was led astray by my ambitions, by a self-serving desire to *become* somebody." A tiny, subdued smile came and went. "That is not good enough, Father."

Aenghus puffed on his cigarette. His normally rubicund face had taken the colour of pearly white. He stared at the wooden tabletop and said, "I respect that, Conor. I really do."

Conor's eyes moved towards the window. He looked at the grey and misty veil embracing the closing of another day. "There is one more reason," he said. "I do not believe that I am meant for celibacy. I want to get married and have children." He put his hand on his father's shoulder. "I am sorry if I have disappointed you."

Aenghus grasped Conor's hand and squeezed it. "No, son, don't think like that. It was just—just a bit unexpected." He clinked the ice in his drink and gazed into the glass. "You must have gone through hell. Conor."

"Yes," Conor said and wanted to dry his eyes. "I think it is called catharsis."

The silence lasted for a few minutes. A sad little smile played around the corners of Mairead's mouth. Aenghus coughed and swallowed what was left of his drink.

"What are you going to do, Conor?" he asked.

"I don't know, but I believe that there is a solution, somewhere."

"There always is. Take your time and you will find it."

☞

Aenghus' only sister, Finola, had married Declan Hegarty from one of Kildare and Ireland's oldest and most prominent families of cattle barons.

The mutual admiration between Finola and Declan was without reservations, and the only blot on their life together was their inability to produce children.

Finola was an outspoken woman, shrewd and knowledgeable; she had an open mind, a well-honed tongue and a merciless memory. The families on both sides saw her as an eccentric, charming when it suited her but on the whole hard-headed and uncompromising in attitude and conduct.

Finola worshipped her nephew from when she first saw him at two days of age. She said to Aenghus, "Being your sister, he's half mine, you know. Don't worry if anything happens to you. I'll take care of him."

Aenghus had laughed, shaking his head. "You morbid cow. I shall hang on. I want him to grow up as a member of the human race. Go back to your foul-smelling dungeon and do something useful."

Finola had sniffed. "Promise me that he can spend his summer holidays with me. A few weeks in a civilized environment can only benefit him."

"When he gets of age and if that is what he wants," Aenghus had consented, "but I am not going to force him. Neither are you."

"Bullshit. He'll love it. I, Uncle Declan, all the animals, fresh air and acres and acres to explore. Bear in mind that my chicken coop is bigger than your entire property."

Young Conor had loved it. The holidays of his childhood became one unforgettable adventure after another, and he developed a profound affection and respect for all things living.

Nature and its treasures became Conor's temple, and during the years of his early adolescence he became convinced that his mission in life was to serve God and His creation.

His Uncle Declan was not the tallest of men; five-foot-ten, heavyset, immensely strong and with an untidy mane of dark blond hair. There were kindness and patience in his grey eyes, and he was as quiet and level-headed as his wife was extrovert and opinionated.

His inheritance had been formidable. He kept the cattle farm and with some of the money he bought a nearby stud where he moved in and made it his permanent residence.

Declan enjoyed teaching his young nephew about the land and the animals and nurtured a dream that Conor one day would take over. The boy's appetite for learning was limitless, and more than once did

Mairead and Aenghus feel a touch of jealousy when Conor came back and related his knowledge on farming and wildlife. He idolized his Aunt and Uncle, and before he was ten years of age he had unwittingly adopted for life Finola's critical attitude to anything confrontational. He could not always digest her acid comments or mordant descriptions, plentiful as they were, but there was never a dull moment in her company.

Somehow, young Conor did not mature and progress quite as Finola and Declan had expected, or, at least, had hoped for. Of all the animals on the farm he took a particular interest in the pigeon loft with its wide variety; tumblers, fantails, trumpeters, pouters, jacobiners and racers. Conor became the protégé of Garret O'Regan, the elderly gentleman who looked after the birds. Conor could spend days on end in Garret's company; listening, cleaning out, checking eggs for fertility and watching the birds fly. "Freedom," Garret used to say, "that's what they symbolize to me. Freedom. Like the spirit of St. Patrick."

Garret was deeply religious, averse to modern life, unmarried and suspicious of anything that did not have feathers. He was fond of reading history "*written by the victorious and therefore not to be trusted*" and his wry sense of humour appealed to Conor. Garret was a philosopher, in his own unassuming way, spicing each day with observations like: "*The Good Lord made the bird so that man could appreciate the flights of the angels.*" Not a bad analogy, Conor thought and watched Garret's large, gnarled and powerful hands caress a tumbler. He let go and his eyes followed the bird as it spiralled towards the sky.

"Chastity on wings," Garret said. "You don't find that with people. Except with newborn babies, that is. They soon learn, though."

One day Conor inadvertently cracked an egg from their only pair of pouters. He looked at the yellow mess in his hands with a feeling of horror and guilt.

"Garret," he called.

But Garret was outside, mixing fodder, and he did not hear.

Conor walked through the door. He stretched out his hands. "Garret, I don't know what happened. I am terribly sorry—" Garret looked up. Then he continued his work. Conor stood there.

Finally, Garret came over. He stared at what should have become one of his beloved birds. "Son," he said quietly, "you didn't try to cover up. You didn't try to lie yourself out of your predicament." He took off his glasses and rubbed the indentations on the bridge of his nose. "Let me tell you something, Conor, and must you never forget: it takes ten years for a man to build up a reputation for honesty, and it takes ten seconds to destroy it."

Garret went back to his work. Conor made a plea to himself never to forget what Garret had said.

☞

Declan was proud of his farms and all their inhabitants, but his real passion was his stallions. In his younger days Declan had been a fearless and successful gambler, and one day he had invested some of his profit in a brood mare. He had spotted *Tempest* as a promising two-year-old when she had won a handful of good races, but then she didn't train on and was a flop as a three-year-old.

Declan approached the owner when satisfied that the man was sufficiently fed up, offered a price too tempting to be turned down and brought *Tempest* home.

Declan decided to let her have a go as a four-year-old. She came back with a vengeance and won all of her six races, including two listed ones.

Declan knew that although *Tempest*'s bloodline was good, it was more interesting than outstanding, but, added to her remarkable turn of foot, she had a nice and balanced temperament.

He decided to breed from her.

"She'll pay us back," he said and looked fondly at his four-legged sweetheart. "You just wait and see."

Pay back she did. Her first offspring, a colt, went into training as a two-year-old and won both his races over five and six furlongs. As a three-year-old he won five out of five starts.

Declan suddenly had a fortune walking around on four hooves, and he was as pleased as he was proud of his achievement. "I can do it again," he said. "You wait and see."

Declan's pride and joy did not let him down. The stallion produced an impressive percentage of winners, and Finola took care of the gradual increase in nomination fees.

After the third foal, Declan retired his mare. "She deserves it," he said.

"What is the real reason?" she asked.

Declan hummed. "The real reason is that sooner or later this incredible luck will desert me. Something will go wrong. Let us quit whilst we're still way ahead."

Finola kissed him on the nose. Her eyes twinkled as she walked back to the house.

Although he enjoyed his uncle's equine success, Conor never managed to work up an all-conquering enthusiasm for horses and racing. They were beautiful and majestic animals, born to run and fascinating with their idiosyncrasies and personalities, but they never stirred his passions the same way, as did his birds.

Conor knew that he could never participate in the sport of kings in a way that would justify his uncle's desire for someone to share it with.

He would not become a cattle baron, or a breeder of racehorses. It was not in his blood. One day he would have to face Declan and Finola and come clean.

A few chosen words and he could defuse the entire scenario. It was simple, straightforward and honest, and his integrity and his ethics would remain intact.

But Conor held back. It upset him that his aunt and his uncle had adopted him as their heir, that they saw in him their dream of continuity come true. It also upset him that his parents were aware of this, although they knew that his preoccupation with the Church had never wavered.

Conor became worried. He lost weight and began to invent excuses. There was always an exam coming up and he was a bit behind. Or a new subject had been introduced and he had problems mastering it. He wasn't too impressed with himself, but, at least, he thought, he did operate within the vicinity of the truth.

He had a depressing feeling of getting closer to the first serious conflict of his young life.

Declan was sitting in his library doing the monthly accounts when Finola walked in.

"Give yourself a break," she said. "We need to talk."

"But this is important," he protested. "You know that."

"Of course it is, dear," she agreed, knowing from long experience that he probably had a few zeros wrong already, "but what is on my mind is even more important. Get me a drink on your way over here."

Declan obliged and sat down opposite her.

"You may need one yourself," she suggested.

"What is the matter?" he asked. He hardly ever touched alcohol, but something in her voice made him follow her advice.

"Cheers," she said and swallowed a good mouthful of the only good thing she admitted could be attributed to Russia. "It would not surprise me if you'll need another one before the day is over."

Declan smiled wearily; he heard in his wife's voice a determination that was blended with despair and unhappiness. A feeling of sadness and dependence came over him. He knew that whatever there was to come, he would need her more than ever before, but he also knew that she would not let him down.

"What is the cross you are carrying today, Finola?" Declan asked. He eyed his wife as she lit a cigarette. The coincidence that he did not smoke and hardly drank alcohol had never tempted him to impose his viewpoints on her. It wouldn't have worked, anyway.

"The lad will end up a bird-watching cardinal," she said. "He is not going to take over this place."

"Oh, come on," Declan protested. "Conor is young and he does not know what he wants. One day he will have had enough of theology and begin to see daylight."

"I don't think so."

Declan sat silent for a minute. "Why do I have this feeling of a dream disintegrating?"

Finola prayed that her compassion did not show and that her voice did not betray her emotions. "The sooner we accept it, the better," she said and patted the head of one of the wolfhounds next to her. "Young Conor will go through life like this fellow—with a collar." She touched the moisture on her glass and licked her finger. "He is avoiding us." She watched Declan's face as he sank further back in his chair. "He is avoiding us," she repeated. "That tells it all. You must have noticed."

Declan's eyes became unfocused. "I deluded myself."

Finola shifted her position to escape the light. She hoped that Declan did not see the tears in her eyes. "Never mind," she said. "Who the hell is perfect?"

Declan gulped down the first half of his drink. He looked dazed.

She said, "There is nothing we can do, except get on with our lives. I am as heartbroken as you are, but when did we ever have the right to expect anything?"

Declan shook his head as if coming out of a trance. "That is true."

She turned away. "A bloody priest with a pigeon on each shoulder. What a picture. That should please The Almighty."

"Now, now," he said consolingly, "no need to be blaspheme." He leaned forward and stroked her hand. "Life goes on. We'll make the best of it. We always do."

"I am not fughing blaspheme!" she hissed, "it's just that I hate to see you so—so…"

Finola clung to his hand and lowered her head.

Conor was not surprised at the urgency in his aunt's voice when she called and asked him to come over for the weekend. He had not been there for almost two months. Having run out of plausible excuses, he accepted with more guilt than gratitude.

The sombre atmosphere hit Conor instantly. He knew that whatever was coming, it was not going to be pleasant. They were friendly enough, as always, but Finola was visibly tense and Declan looked haggard and ill at ease. Conor braced himself and sat down.

"It is nice to be here again," he said. "It's been a long time."

"Yes, it has," Finola said and poured the tea. "You keep yourself busy?"

Not *have you been busy* or *your studies do keep you occupied*. Conor knew Finola well enough to recognize the importance of the distinction. Thank God, he thought, the moment of truth couldn't be far away; my aunt isn't noted for moving in circles.

He decided to test the water. "In a manner of speaking," he said tentatively.

Finola said, "Conor, your uncle and I love you as our own son. We had a dream. We wanted you to take over our farms before we got too old to run them properly. I believe you know that, too." She paused. Conor looked up. Past tense, he thought. That means that although they are disappointed, at least they are not in shock. I, too, am disappointed. I wish I had it in me to fulfil their dream, to repay, somehow, this incredible kindness over the years. The sad fact is that I do not have it in me. I would have had to decline even if the Church should cease to exist as my life's calling.

He said, "I have known for a while." He wanted to tell them about his anguish, but what good would it do? All three of them had acknowledged the factual situation. This was not the time for excuses or self-pity camouflaged as explanations.

"It cannot have been easy for you, and, I must admit, it was not easy for us, either," Finola said. "But, we made a mistake. For years we took it for granted that you would become part of the land, that the farms and all they stand for would begin to run through your veins and absorb you like it did with me. As I said many a time to Uncle Declan; I, too, came from the city, but Mother Earth grabbed me and gave me a richer life than I possibly could have had anywhere else. It will happen, I said; young Conor will become one of us." The expression in her eyes changed. She wiggled a finger but there was a bittersweet shade to her smile and voice. "The point is, though, we never asked what *you* wanted to do. We never queried if you were truly in love with the land, and more so than with the Church. You were not. We know now. That is the way it is, and we understand. We just happened to be infatuated by our own dream. We were so blinded that we ignored the individual that is you, Conor. It was a human error of immense proportions, mindless and unforgivable." She turned her face towards the window behind Declan's chair. "It was self-inflicted blindness, Conor, and now we are paying for it."

Conor felt more uncomfortable than he could ever remember. "I should have talked to you," he mumbled unsteadily.

"Don't be daft," Finola said sharply. "You are still in your teens and we are not. We blame ourselves, not you."

The lines on Declan's forehead became heavy. "She is right, Conor. Stick to your guns and you can't go wrong. Being true to yourself is life's most essential imperative."

"Even for a priest," Finola said.

Conor scratched his knees. "I am not a very good actor, am I?"

"Praise the Good Lord for that," Finola said. "It isn't in your nature being somebody who tries to be somebody else most of the time." Her lips curled. "Remember that when you become a Pope."

"But you already knew…"

Finola said, "That is not the point. Uncle Declan is telling you, in his own humble way, that you did not have to come here today. You must have had an inkling what it was all about, but you did not have to take us into your confidence. You could have stayed away. You could have kept quiet. You could have ducked and asked for time. You could have told us an outright fib. You didn't. That is what we are grateful for."

Conor could not look at them.

"Right," Finola declared abruptly, "why don't you go down to Garret and tell him to dust the feathers out of his hair? Uncle Declan has given him the green light to buy a pair of whatever it is and maybe you could go with him to pick them up. It's over in Naas, so better get going before it gets dark. We'll have supper when you come back."

Conor left the room with his eyes fixed to the floor.

Finola and Declan stood side by side and watched through the window as Conor walked across the yard towards Garret and his cherished birds.

"Poor boy," Declan said. "I feel sorry for him. It wasn't an easy day for a young man."

"No. And not exactly a piece of cake for you, either. Or for me."

"We'll get over it," he said and pondered for a while. "I think he is a bit confused."

"Of course he is. How can anybody consider becoming a priest without being confused?"

Declan laughed softly and put his arm around her. "You are incurable, my love. I thank the Good Lord above that you are too old to change."

She fought hard and the sob stayed away. "A priest," she said when she knew her voice was steady again. "What a fughing waste."

There was a bitter taste in her mouth. She hoped that a stiff vodka would wash it away.

☞

Kathleen Keogh knew within a week of having met Conor that the man she had earmarked as her future husband was not going to join the Church, and, fortunately, on his own volition. She knew that he had walked away from inheriting Ireland's most prestigious and successful farms. She also knew that he did not have the faintest idea where he was going; hence, she thought, why not hit the road to anywhere together? The prospect of facing no security whatsoever was a nice little challenge;

decidedly more exciting than being wrapped up in a marriage to a lawyer or an accountant where the entire masterplan was outlined for the next fifty years. Besides, Kathleen believed in love, and from the very first word between them she knew that she had found her man. He may be a no-hoper, materialistically, she thought, but respect, friendship, affection, togetherness, devotion and all the other aspects covered under the umbrella called love could not be bought for money, anyway.

Kathleen came from a family of six children; three brothers and two sisters. Her father, Patrick Keogh, was a prominent member of Fianna Eireann. Like so many tough and uncompromising men, he was soft as a silkworm when it came to his children; he seldom raised his voice, and he never hit them. They, in return, adored him, and as they grew older they began to understand more of the essence of his basic philosophies and his rules in bringing up children; fear must never be mistaken for respect. He ruled with a gentle smile, and when they overstepped he simply ignored them for a few hours, or even for a day or two.

He had his own scale of justice, and he placed his weights only after careful consideration. There was no worse punishment.

She had inherited her mother's temperament, and, particularly in Kathleen's younger years, it had a tendency to get the better of her. She became more balanced as she matured, influenced by her father's stability and deep-rooted habit of always thinking twice. All in all, as her parents noticed with pride, Kathleen developed into a young woman healthy of mind and body; strikingly attractive with her green eyes and amber hair, a slender figure with a levelled head, a temper under control most of the time and with a strong sense of fairness and justice and a considerable desire for independence.

One of her father's proteges was a youngster called Colm Begley. He had joined the Republican boy scouts at the tender age of eight, and Kathleen could vaguely remember him before he went to England and ended up in Borstal. She recalled his return almost three years later, but she could not take to his rowdy behaviour and colourful language. Shortly thereafter he again disappeared, following a shooting incident in a cemetery; this time, her father said, Begley had been sentenced to fourteen years.

Patrick Keogh could not hide his pleasure when Begley was released after only four years— "*a political amnesty, who would have believed that*"— Patrick Keogh mused again and again.

The two of them had some very long talks. Articles by Begley had been published in the *Irish Democrat* and *The Bell*, and Keogh urged the young man to become a writer, to fight with the pen and not with the gun.

"He is a romantic with a talent," Keogh told Kathleen. "He should use it where it can do Ireland and himself some good."

Kathleen by then knew enough about her country's history, the IRA and the individual named Colm Begley to understand what her father meant.

Begley did not immediately follow Keogh's advice. It was more fun and definitely easier to paint houses, to be an amateur smuggler, to sail the blue seas and to break deportation orders. Kathleen pleaded with him to change his reckless ways, and eventually Begley listened. Pieces from his pen again began to appear.

Kathleen was wildly enthusiastic and immensely proud of her friend; the only thing that worried her was his ever-growing desire for alcohol.

"You've got to stop," she begged, "or you'll end up dead before you are famous."

Conor's experience with women was non-existent. It did not enter his mind that the girl could be interested in him. The few times he had seen her, she had been surrounded by a dozen peacocks of all ages and descriptions, one wittier and more eloquent than the other, and Conor had written off as pure conceit the glances he thought she had thrown his way.

Why is everything different tonight? he thought. She is actually staring at me. She is smiling when she is staring at me. Perhaps she is just very polite and well mannered.

Why do I want to talk to her? Why should she want to talk to me? Oh Jesus Lord, she is so attractive. Maybe I should go home.

His mind was racing as he was half listening to Begley's unstoppable chatter, but Conor was still unprepared when he found himself face to face with a girl who in the space of a short evening had changed from a distant image to an intimate dream in a black dress.

"I see we have a mutual friend," Kathleen said and did not let go of his hand.

Conor felt as if he had a fishbone stuck in his throat. "I—I do not know Mr. Begley."

"Everybody knows me," Begley boomed.

"Of course," Kathleen said and released her grip, "I forgot. You are world famous in parts of Dublin."

Her eyes came back to Conor. He prayed that the signs of discomfort he felt were not visible.

"He is quite harmless, really," she went on and pinched Begley's cheek, "except to himself."

"Jaysus," Begley groaned, "don't start that again. Here I am, contemplating in solitude the start of a new and better life, and in you come after weeks of desertion only to shatter my honest but fragile rebirth. I am devastated. If ever I needed a drink, it's now. This is depressing." He lowered his chin but the belch escaped. "Find a table in a quiet corner, young man, and tell her all about yourself, however modest your tale may be." He grinned at Kathleen. "See you tomorrow, I hope."

"Tomorrow, Colm."

Conor spotted a couple leaving their table at the far end of the bar. Kathleen followed his gaze and smiled. They both nodded to Begley and left for the corner. Only when they sat down did Conor discover that he had forgotten to bring the drinks.

"My apologies," he blurted, "I'll go and get our glasses."

"Don't bother. I am fine."

Her smile was warm and tender. Conor had no idea how and where to start.

"I—I am…." he began and told himself to stop shaking his head.

Kathleen said, "Conor, I know who you are. You know who I am. You want to become a priest, I understand."

Conor sighed and wanted to wipe his forehead. The opening was there. Insecurity and shyness were in retreat and the drops of sweat trickling down his back no longer paralyzed him.

He said, "I did, but the vocation has left me, it seems."

"Dear me," Kathleen laughed and folded her hands. "That is one of the most candid statements I have heard for a long time."

He noticed that she did not wear a ring.

"Sorry," he mumbled and collected his thoughts. "What I mean is, I cannot join a Church in which I have no confidence. Similarly, I can't take over the Hegarty farms because I know that I'm not cut out for it."

Kathleen's eyes sparkled. "You have been offered to take over the Hegarty farms?"

"It's my family," he explained, "my aunt and my uncle. My Aunt Finola is my father's sister. She and Declan have no children."

"And you said thank you very much but I've got better things to do?" She leaned closer. "Let me get this right, Conor. First you break the Hegartys' heart, and shortly thereafter it's the Pope's turn. Sweet Jesus, Conor, am I curious! Your chosen challenge must be formidable."

"There isn't any," he said and wished that someone would switch off the lights. Never had he felt so utterly stupid and downright irresponsible. "I know it sounds strange," he continued with a helpless shrug, "it's just the way it is."

"Strange," she repeated. "Well, Conor, you certainly have a talent for understatements. Is there anything else I should know about you?"

Conor smiled wearily. She is leaving, he thought. She will walk away and never look at me again. Not since Pope Adrian IV's letter to Henry II in 1171 can there have been consequences on par with those of my fatuity. I must be Ireland's worst joke.

"I know," he said. "I have placed myself in the middle of nothing and I have no idea how to get out. A lost case, I think it's called."

She studied him with an expression of incredibility and puzzlement. "Conor, of all the nutcases in Ireland, you strike me as an interesting one. We may well have a lot to talk about. Would you like to come for a walk with me tomorrow?"

"Tomorrow is Saturday," he said and hoped to hide his joy and relief behind such a valuable observation.

"I wouldn't dispute that," Kathleen said. Her eyes were smiling. "Phoenix Park, twelve noon, at the Wellington Monument." She stood up. "You'll be there?"

Conor got to his feet. "Oh yes," he said firmly and extended his hand. "Thank you for listening to me."

"Sweet dreams, Conor."

Kathleen and Conor became inseparable. Before long they knew that life without the other was not a viable proposition. Kathleen continued her job in an accountant's office. Conor broke off his studies and accepted Declan's offer to work as a farmhand. He'll sort himself out, Declan told his wife, still praying for a small miracle.

Kathleen readily admitted that the love of her life was indeed the bleakest of prospects, but such a trifle was no serious obstacle to marriage. Conor despaired over his lack of direction, but Kathleen sympathized and told him to take one day at a time. They were young, only twenty, and who could tell what tomorrow would bring?

They got married in the Carmelite Church. The wedding was a quiet and dignified event. With the exception of Colm Begley, only the closest of relatives were present. Nobody, Begley included, got overly drunk. He gave a speech; touching, funny and affectionate, and Kathleen listened to her friend and wished that his restless soul would one day find the peace and harmony he so eloquently talked about.

Finola and Declan had offered to arrange the wedding at the farm; Finola promised the event of the year, but Conor turned her down.

"I can't accept," he told Kathleen. "I admit that I am a failure and I haven't got much pride left, but what little there is I cannot afford to sacrifice."

Finola and Declan showed no ill feelings. They said they understood. Their gift was a bank account with sufficient funds to furnish the small apartment Kathleen and Conor had decided to rent.

☞

Declan had become increasingly absentminded and no longer attended to detail the way he used to. He seemed to have lost his enthusiasm; the old sparkle was gone and from time to time he showed signs of depression. Finola's worries grew by the hour. One day she confided in Conor.

"Your uncle is not what he used to be. Something is troubling him but he does not talk to me. I wish I knew what to do."

Conor, who had noticed the trend months ago, tried to hide his discomfort and suggested that maybe a change of scenery could do some good. A holiday, perhaps a few weeks abroad; rest, recreation and everything at a distance.

Finola looked at him, pleadingly. "You know better, Conor."

He did. "All right," he said as they walked past the stables. "What about another *Tempest*?"

Finola stopped. "You mean, go back into breeding?"

Conor said, "Let us try to convince him that he can do it again. Now, there's a challenge, if there ever was one, so enormous that it might actually get Uncle Declan back on track again." He looked towards the paddocks. "I'd love to be part of it."

Finola turned away. "Thanks, Conor."

A week later, after many a heated argument and numerous objections, Declan announced that yes, he could most certainly do it all over, he and his young partner Conor. Knowledge, experience, youth and drive was an unbeatable combination; the spring was back in Declan' steps and the vibration in his voice matched the ardour in his eyes.

The oldest stallion grazed the heavenly pastures; illness had struck and he could not be saved. The second stallion enjoyed his retirement, but *Odin*, the youngest, still had a few drops left in him.

The only small problem was to find another *Tempest*.

Declan and Conor found the mare on a dilapidated farm near Cavan. The farmer claimed that he was *considering* breeding from her. It took a bottle of whisky and the better part of an afternoon to convince the not too knowledgeable farmer that a price equivalent to five top class foals was somewhat exorbitant. Near the point of exhaustion they settled on one third of the original demand, cash on the table.

The change in Declan was remarkable, and he could not wait for the mare to get in season. His only concern was that the stallion was getting closer to the end of his long and illustrious career; his last few crops had not all been successful, and there were signs that his interest in the other sex had followed the decline in his spermflow. Declan said to Conor, "Let's just hope and pray that we get a colt."

On the day of the big event, on his way to the stable, Declan suffered a heart attack and died an hour later.

For the next six months Finola continued to run the farms, but her heart was no longer in it. Kathleen and Conor visited her regularly. They did their best to distract her from talking about her husband and getting lost in memories. Their success was moderate. More often than not they were left with a sinking feeling of talking to the walls.

They were in the library. Finola sipped her vodka.

"What are you going to do?" he asked.

Finola smiled softly. "Not so fast, Conor. When are you going to stop blaming yourself for Uncle Declan's death?"

She adjusted the collar of her blouse. The skin on her hands had lost its smoothness. "You came to Declan with the only concept that could renew his zest and make him feel alive again. He was becoming mentally and, I'd say, emotionally stagnant. It had to be reversed, and you did exactly that. The last few months of his life he was the Declan of old. I know. I saw the transformation. There was a time when I believed it wasn't possible, any longer, but the miracle happened. He had a purpose, Conor, *a purpose,* and it changed his entire existence. He was happy." Finola's long fingers slid through her hair. "I am eternally grateful for what you did."

Conor fought his emotions. He wished that the room had been darker.

"I am leaving this place," Finola said after what he felt like being an hour later.

Conor remained silent. She came back to her chair. She lit a cigarette and stared into space with a look of bleakness in her eyes.

"It is not my home any more, not without Declan. I have tried, but it does not work. I have offered the farms to Declan's family for twenty percent under market value, and they have accepted. The staff is staying, if they so wish. I made a special provision for Garret to live here with his treasured birds until his weary little soul finally flaps out of sight. The one exception is you." She waved at the smoke. Her smile was tired. "You are out of a job. You don't belong here."

"No," Conor muttered, "I don't."

She went on, "I shall buy myself a house. I do not know where, yet, but it is not a problem."

At the other side of Dublin, Conor thought, far enough from here.

"I'll travel," she said. "I talked enough about it, so many times, but it never came to anything, as you know. It was as if we could not leave this place even for a day. Of course we could, but we didn't."

"Where to?" Conor asked.

"Oh, anywhere. Europe, America, The Far East—I want to see all those cultures I've read about. It shall be interesting." She stumped out her cigarette. "One day I shall be able to come back and settle down. What are your plans?"

Conor straightened his shoulders. The full force of having no plans hit him unprepared for an excuse and out of balance. "I ..." he began.

Conor decided to let go, to tell her his secret little dream, however far-fetched and with no roots in any reality beknown to him.

He said, "I would like to have a place of my own, a place where I could look after and help those who have fallen by the wayside; the downtrodden, the misfits, the lonely and the bewildered, those who for some reason or another can't cope with life, those who need somebody but cannot find one."

Finola nodded. "Quite a market." There was no smile on her face. "In other words, your private little church without the ominous cloud of religion hanging over it?"

"In a manner of speaking."

"Does Kathleen know?"

"I believe she has a vague notion."

"You never discussed it?"

"Not really. It's not very realistic."

"True." Finola rose and got herself another vodka. "I shall need some assistance when I move."

"I'll be here."

Finola stared into her glass. "Conor, I think you should go back to your wife."

He did, and he told her what had happened.

"Now we know," Kathleen said. "By the way, you'd better get yourself another job. I'm pregnant."

Jennifer was born on the last Saturday of December 1936.

The sense of despair had hit his aunt far worse than Conor had envisaged. Finola was slowly but surely committing suicide, intentionally or not.

"Let us bring her some travel brochures," he suggested.

So they did. Finola glanced through each glossy presentation of alluring and faraway places and said, yes, this was what she always had wanted to do. Perhaps next year.

"Not next year," Kathleen snapped, "now! This week. I seriously doubt that Declan would have approved of your sitting here wasting your life away. If you think that's to his honour you have misunderstood both past and present. Praise him by showing that you are able to cope.

Don't insult him by making this place into a catacomb for a contrite and pitiful widow."

The instant effect of Kathleen's words surprised even herself. She had barely stopped speaking before Finola burst into tears. For an eternity they watched her sob her heart out, Kathleen with relief and Conor with an expression of discomfort and confusion.

"Right," Finola eventually said and dried her cheeks. "Right. Where do I go?"

When she at long last made up her mind where to go, it was too late. The Second World War had begun.

The Moran, the Hagerty and the Keogh families had applauded de Valera's new constitution, declaring Ireland a sovereign and independent state in 1937. They agreed, two years later, when the government proclaimed that Ireland would remain neutral. Patrick Keogh spoke for all when he said, "It would amount to treason to become an ally of a country that occupies a part of our land."

Later in life, Conor concluded that the six years of privation had been an education he could benefit from forever more. The scarcity of supplies, the ration books, the censorship of newspapers, broadcasts and newsreels, the presence of the Glimmer Man upholding the gas laws, trains reduced in number as a result of being converted to run on turf and hardly any private cars around—it hadn't been easy for anybody, but only the mindless would fail to see that it had also been an invaluable lesson.

He never understood why so many young Irishmen had died for England during those years.

In 1948, a few days after the *Republic of Ireland Act* was passed, Finola finally decided to make her dream come through. She was away for eight weeks. They received postcards from Germany, then France, and thereafter Italy. She came back rejuvenated, more sure of herself and with the odd glimpse of the forcefulness and vivacity that had been her telltale sign.

She had also become restless. Within a fortnight she was off to the United States, travelled all over and returned three months later. After one week at home she declared her fascination in the Far East. It had become an obsession, she said, and the roundtrip she had in mind would take half a year, if not considerably more.

Conor persuaded her to give it a rest for a while, assisted by his twelve-year-old daughter Jennifer, Kathleen and his parents, and they spent some memorable evenings and weekends together. Finola postponed her intended departure a couple of times, but, as her restlessness grew, they conceded that further attempts to make her stay put could backfire and cause a relapse.

Finola booked a one-way ticket to Hong Kong. She explained that her experience so far had taught her not to pre-plan since her real desire was to go wherever she wanted to go whenever it suited her. They all agreed that this made sense.

One warm and sunny Sunday morning they took her to the airport and had drinks together before the flight was called.

A postcard from Hong Kong told Kathleen and Conor that Finola was going to Indonesia, and from there to Singapore.

Twenty days later they received a telegram from the British Embassy in Djakarta. The plane to Singapore had crashed shortly after take-off.

There were no survivors.

Conor inherited the lot, all in all to the tune of 1.2 million pounds.

"It's an awful lot of money," Kathleen said as they walked from the lawyer's office. "What do we do?"

She didn't expect an answer. She knew that Conor was too grief-stricken and too stunned to have an opinion about anything. I'd better guide him carefully here, she thought, or he'll once again go into himself to such an extent that he may never come out again.

She nudged him as they walked along. "Let us go and have a drink."

He stopped. "Now?"

Kathleen continued walking. "Why not?"

"I don't think that's a very good idea," he said.

Kathleen turned around. "Fine. What is a better idea?"

"It is—perhaps not very proper."

She took a step towards him. "May God in Heaven have mercy on your proper soul. I don't."

He saw her disappear down Harry Street.

It was quiet at McDaid's.

He—or we—have just inherited over one million pounds, Kathleen thought, and all he can think of is etiquette. Money was a tool, a commodity and a remedy; allow it to poison your mind and you'll forever pay the price. Conor was now in the position to appoint himself a saviour overnight. He could afford to get his little mission and do all the good he was capable of doing. Within reason, she thought; the money was going to last for a very long time. A lifetime, in short. She'd see to that. Her confidence in Conor's financial acumen was limited; so far, there had been no indication of its existence.

The picture of Sisyphus struggling with his stone crossed her mind. Kathleen shook her head and she wondered if her fate in life would be equally entertaining and rewarding. Don't be negative, she half mumbled. Defeat is a word excluded from my vocabulary. So is resignation. And pessimism.

Conor came through the door.

"Am I delighted to see you," she said. "There isn't one *proper* soul in here."

Conor went red. "I changed my mind."

"I've gathered that much already," Kathleen said and raised her glass. "Let us drink to the future. All we now have to do is to plan it. Carefully."

He saw the smile in her eyes and relaxed. "I am sorry, Kathleen," he said and circled the rim of the glass with his forefinger. "I am just very confused. It's an awful lot of money."

"But not unmanageable."

"It scares me."

"Why?"

Conor looked away. "Doesn't it scare you?"

"No."

He played with the ashtray before he pushed it towards her. "Why does it not scare you? I mean…" he cut himself off.

You do not know what you mean, she thought, and who can blame you. She said, "Conor, money is a commodity, and that is all there is to it. No more, and no less. That is, as long as you don't lose your head."

He looked shocked. "Dear God—no!"

"There we are, then. The key word is pragmatism. You and I are going to be very realistic about this. Remember your dream? You can fulfil it now. We'll do this together. I would like to quit my job and join you."

The blue of Conor's eyes went pale behind the mist. "I thank God for the day I met you."

Kathleen was touched but she tried not to show it.

He caressed her hand and seemed lost in thoughts. A wave of tenderness engulfed Kathleen's mind, and she thought how lucky she was to have the love and affection of this the kindest and most considerate of men. She thought about his strength and his principles, about his naivety and deep-rooted honesty and she hoped to God that life and maturity would not corrupt the essence of his being.

Colm Begley crashed through the entrance. He spotted them instantly and came over.

"My favourite couple," he boomed and sat down, "*Bec Fola and Diarmuid*. What a glorious day." He turned his massive head towards the barman. "The usual, young man."

"All of it?" the barman asked.

"That is *ree-ally* hilarious. Is there anything more challenging in life than the sparkling wit of a born comedian? Listen, you inchoate shadow of a primate," he sighed, "however much it hurts me to emphasize the obvious, you and I are planets apart. As a matter of fact, I seriously doubt that you are entitled to exist in the same universe. Cheers."

The barman remained stoical. He said amiably, "I'd say that the perpetual motion of glass-lifting doesn't require much brain, either. Cheers."

Begley huffed. "Touché. I didn't know you had a degree in logic."

Kathleen and Conor listened with mild amusement. Kathleen wished that somebody else would attract Begley's attention. "Please sit down," she said icily after he'd placed himself squarely at the end of the table.

"You are so kind," he nodded gravely. Then, still not touching his drink, he leaned forward and whispered almost inaudibly, "How does it feel to be millionaires?"

Kathleen and Conor stared at each other, stunned, then at Begley.

"How the hell did you know?" she whispered back.

Begley frowned and placed both elbows on the table. "My dear Kathleen," he said, keeping his voice down, "did you really imagine that a one million pound bombshell would go undetected? I know because somebody at the lawyer's office told me. Give it a couple of days and the whole of Dublin will know. Yes," he added and drummed his fingers on the coaster, "it is supposed to be confidential. *Supposed to be.* Just do not forget that confidentiality is a matter of honour, apart from an obligation, and honour has a tendency to evaporate when incomprehension takes over. As for obligations—" he snorted "—a *straight lawyer* is an oxymoron."

"I still can't believe it," Kathleen said. "It's preposterous."

Begley sipped for a while. "It is preposterously human to leak," he said flatly. "You ought to know that, by now. What I'd like to learn, how do the two of you intend to tackle problems to the tune of one million pounds?"

Kathleen sensed that Begley was in one of his more palatable moods. He was also more serious that she could recall for a long time. She looked at Conor who was watching Begley with an expression of curiosity mingled with a shade of amusement.

"What is funny, Conor?"

"Nothing, except that I've got a strange feeling that Colm is questioning the overall morality of our situation."

"Morality? Like what, like you don't deserve it?"

"He is right," Begley intervened, "although I am not so sure that we are talking about the same thing. It is not for me to query the mysterious ways of God, if that is what you mean, in particular since I am firmly convinced that a man's belief is a burden no one can carry for him. During my happy days at the convent school I was presented with the theory that the Almighty occasionally knows what He is doing, and that could well be the case here. No, *that* kind of morality is not what I have in mind."

Kathleen's lips parted. Her tongue flickered rapidly from corner to corner. "Could you get to the point?"

"Most certainly, but first, let me ask of you, what do you intend to do?"

"We intend to set up a place where lost and miserable souls can find comfort and consolation. You are welcome any time."

Conor sensed that his wife's temper was getting tested. He said, "We would like to do something good, something we believe in."

Begley scratched his thick mane. "That is indeed a most charitable concept. Admirable, I should add. I wish you luck, happiness and success, if such a yardstick is applicable."

Kathleen knew that she'd had enough. She stared at her friend and said, "Colm, you may think it's a stupid idea. It doesn't matter what you think. We know what we are doing."

Behan looked around. "No, you don't."

"We don't? Is this where your morality comes in?"

"Yes it is." He paused. "You still haven't got it, have you?"

"I am afraid not and neither do I care."

"You should. Conor has a dream, and you share it with him. That is nice, and you know I mean that. What I am trying to indicate to you, in my own polite and urbane way, is that the two of you will have a most uncomfortable future unless you take the first step in the right direction."

"And that is—?"

"Leave."

"Leave? You mean leave Dublin?"

"I mean leave Ireland."

The silence was long and awkward. Kathleen looked more puzzled than did Conor.

"Hear him out," Conor said.

Begley pulled his chair closer to the table. He searched his pockets for cigarettes. "A tiny ray of common sense is piercing its way through the darkness of ignorance," he said as the smoke rose towards the ceiling. "The ray touches lightly the vague hope of redemption still fluttering above the heads of the finest young man and woman joining the ranks of other fine youths forever lost to our beautiful and beleaguered island. That is, if your desire to survive is stronger than your faith in a fragile and basically flagitious mankind."

A minute vibration in Begley's voice made Kathleen listen with renewed interest. Conor squeezed his lower lip between the thumb and the index finger of his right hand. His left hand held the glass. There was resignation in his eyes when he looked at Kathleen. "I think I know," he said.

"Know what?"

Begley said, "What you should have been the first to realize, you vassal of King Mammon—" he glared at her "—as well as being your father's daughter."

"Double-M," she said. "*Money* and *Morality*."

"Precisely," Begley said. "Now we are getting somewhere. I must admit, though, it never ceases to amaze me what people are prepared to let money do to them." He moved closer to Conor. "I gather from your reaction that your vast and valuable knowledge of the history of the Church does include the sentiment that love of money is an evil. The reason I say *Church* and not *Christianity* is that the first is an institution and the latter is a dubious abstract. The Church, to the best of my humble understanding, knows everything there is to know about acquiring wealth and riches regardless of methods, means and consequences."

Conor nodded. One of the many factors when agonizing over his future had been the ruthless greed dominating so many of the Fathers, past and present. "I know," he said.

Begley continued, "Sad but true, and there is nothing we can do about it. Human nature is forever moulded."

Kathleen stared out the window. "How do we cope?" she said. There was weariness in her voice.

Begley said, "You can't, and here is another reason. In addition to relatives and friends, there are certain groups on this our peaceful little island that will show more than a passing interest in the sweetness of your pickle. You cannot fight them, Kathleen. Wherever you turn, you are doomed to lose. Your life will become hell on earth. Leave."

"Leave," Kathleen repeated tonelessly.

"Go to London. Take your dream with you and get lost in the big city. I am not saying that nobody can find you there, but the odds for survival and comparative harmony will improve considerably. Use your senses, act swiftly and leave no footprints in the sand. The low-profile strategy, Kathleen. I know what I am talking about." His hand moved along his jawbone. "You see, Kathleen, becoming a martyr requires one particular qualification, and that is leviathan selfishness. I don't think you are quite that accomplished, and Conor certainly isn't. Apart from all that, you have a young daughter to think of."

Kathleen tugged his sleeve. Her eyes did not leave the tabletop. "Thank you for your concern, Colm. We really appreciate it. I never knew you possessed such depths of wisdom. No," she added quickly and raised her gaze as he shifted uneasily on his chair; "I mean it. I know you are right. It's just so—so hard to swallow."

"Oh well," he said, still a shade embarrassed. "I am just being my adequate self."

The silence lasted for a good minute. Conor folded his hands. Kathleen rubbed her wedding ring against the lapel of her jacket. Begley stared into a glass he did not touch. He said, "It was just a suggestion," as if he regretted having interfered.

Kathleen looked at Conor. "Who do we know in London?"

"Nobody. We'll manage."

"You mean we are going?"

"Colm is right." Conor straightened himself up, placed his fists on the table and drew one sharp breath. "There is no choice, Kathleen. I do not want to live in fear, afraid twenty-four hours a day that something will happen to you, to our children or to myself. Other people have left, and managed. Why shouldn't we?"

Kathleen blinked. "No reason."

"God bless Ireland," Begley mumbled. "Perhaps one day we shall learn that peace and harmony are preferable to fear and terror."

"Maybe," Kathleen said. "Do you know anyone decent and English?"

"Jaysus, Kathleen, such a specimen does not exist. A contradiction of terms, if I ever heard one."

Kathleen put her hand over her mouth, but the sigh slipped through her fingers. "We need to buy a place," she said patiently. "We need a lawyer, an accountant and a bank manager. We need an investment advisor. You follow?"

Begley put his hand on Conor's shoulder. "Don't look so sheepish. The Good Lord was pretty selective when he handed out pragmatic minds."

Kathleen ignored him.

Begley continued, "By the way, I didn't say that I do not know *anybody* across the waters."

"Of course you have your contacts," she said, "a handful of wardens. Conor, we have to go."

Begley remained unruffled. "And somebody else."

"Is that so?"

"Yes. He is a writer, and an accomplished one. He also has his own radio show. He's a nice chap, actually. I've met him a couple of times. In his early sixties, I would think. He lives in London."

"Merciful Lord," Kathleen said and began to button her jacket. "Is that all you can come up with, Colm? Another bloody writer? No, thank you."

"Go and see him," Begley suggested. "What have you got to lose? I'll bet my last drink that you both will like him. He is a kind and generous man."

"You are serious, aren't you?"

"I am."

"Has he got a name?"

Begley looked perplexed. "Oh Christ," he muttered and rushed a hand through his unruly hair, "a name…"

Kathleen got up. "You bloody useless bag of shit!" She beckoned to Conor. "Let's go. Our friend has obviously been sober for too long."

"Sorry," Begley said hastily, seeing the tears in her eyes. "Sorry, Kathleen. It wasn't funny. His name is Parkhurst. Igor Parkhurst."

5

Igor Parkhurst was pleased with life. It had all gone well, lately; his second wife Emily had walked out on him, and his new agent Leo Dresbach had proved to be an efficient and prudent operator. No work sifted through Leo's manicured fingers unless it was being well paid for.

Parkhurst had discovered long ago that value for money was a relative concept. High-class work could be paid a pittance whilst some quasi-intellectual garbage would easily be paid handsomely. A funny world, Parkhurst mused as he prepared his morning coffee, but then, being seriously funny in an acerbic yet magnanimous way was his métier and the world should, for its own good, appreciate a philosophical entertainer.

It was Saturday. With the exception of an up-to-date chat with Dresbach, Parkhurst had the day to himself. The early autumn weather was unusually agreeable. The sun played with the clouds and the showers were few. For dinner he was seeing a couple of friends at his favourite restaurant.

The doorbell rang. Not again, he moaned and reached for another piece of toast. During the last ten days, Holland Park had been inundated with members of a religious sect—twice he had seen their fervour dampened when he informed them that he was a Catholic converted to Judaism. It did the trick.

The doorbell rang again, more firmly.

All right, Parkhurst muttered, it could be somebody else. He opened the front door and stared at the couple with a young girl facing him. The man and the woman looked at each other. Parkhurst felt uncomfortable.

"Is there anything I can do for you?" he asked tentatively.

The woman nodded. Parkhurst thought that the look in her green eyes was one of reservation and perhaps apprehension.

"We apologize for showing up like this," she said. "My name is Kathleen Moran, and this is my husband Conor and our daughter Jennifer. We came over from Ireland yesterday, and Colm—Mr. Begley said that you might be able to help us." She studied him for a few seconds. Suddenly, she smiled. "No," she said, "we do not need money. That is not why we are here."

"Ah," Parkhurst said, not entirely impressed with his own response. "Yes, I know Mr. Begley. How is he?"

"Himself."

"Still thirsty?"

"I am afraid so."

"It's such a shame. The young man has so clearly got a talent."

"He sends his regards," Kathleen said.

"Thank you," Parkhurst said. He stepped aside. "Please come in. To the left," he guided. "I hope you don't mind sitting in the kitchen. I enjoy the early hours of the morning in my kitchen."

It was just after ten o'clock.

"Early?" Conor said.

Parkhurst smiled. "I usually go to bed between midnight and two in the morning. It comes with the trade."

"I am sorry," Conor said.

He is ill at ease, Parkhurst thought. He recognized a shyness that had bothered him in his earlier years.

"Conor used to work on a farm," Kathleen explained with a melodious little laughter.

Careful now, Parkhurst thought. This woman can infatuate me before I even know it. If she's not a con, she is a gem.

"Coffee?" he offered.

They nodded.

He smiled at the girl. "Would you like a glass of milk, Jennifer?"

"Yes, please."

"We…" Conor began. He stopped and looked at his wife.

"Yes?" Parkhurst assisted with an amiable smile.

Kathleen took over; "It's a long story, Mr. Parkhurst. Perhaps I should start with the end. Conor inherited in excess of one million pounds."

"*We* inherited," Conor said.

"We inherited one million pounds," Kathleen continued. "Colm advised us to leave Ireland."

"I think I can understand why," Parkhurst said. He tried to comprehend what it would feel like to inherit a million pounds.

Kathleen said, "It is a lot of money, but we intend to use it, not spend it."

Parkhurst did not take his eyes off the woman. If this is a plot, he thought, at least the opening is magnificent.

"I appreciate if it is difficult for you to believe us," Kathleen said. "Would you mind if we tell you the entire story?"

Parkhurst shook his head. He saw no point in trying to hide his curiosity. "Please. This is most interesting, or should I say fascinating."

Kathleen's eyes rested against the ceiling for a moment. She searched for Conor's hand and moistened her lips.

Then she began. Parkhurst did not interrupt.

She finished, and Parkhurst's instincts told him that he did not need Colm Begley to verify their story.

Kathleen said, "All summed up, Mr. Parkhurst, you can see that we shall require some professional assistance."

Parkhurst buried himself in a pair of green eyes before he looked at Conor. "Thank you for telling me."

Kathleen picked up her teaspoon and gazed towards the reflection from the sun on the wall above Parkhurst's head. "Colm is a shrewd judge of character. He said that you are an honourable man."

Parkhurst smiled away his embarrassment. "It's like reaching for a star. You may never catch one, but life becomes meaningless if you stop trying."

Kathleen laughed. "That is a lovely picture. I shall definitely buy a radio and listen to you as often as I can."

Parkhurst chuckled. "Thank you for treasuring my sagacity. One day you may even get a television set and enjoy my presence in your drawing room."

"That brings us to the question of a property." Conor raised his head and looked at Parkhurst. "Our apology for having taken up so much of your time."

"Not at all. I am in no hurry. Please allow me to assist you in any one way I can."

"We need a lawyer and an accountant," Kathleen said.

"Right. I can introduce you to the people I am using. Neither firm are among the largest, here in London; that's never an attractive proposition for individual operators, if you don't mind my saying so, but they are as sensible and reliable as one can hope for in their respective professions."

Kathleen said, "Would you mind elucidating a bit?"

"There are a number of reasons," he said. "Large firms charge far more than their advice is worth. Clients have a tendency to overlook that there is fierce competition between the partners; that is, who can bring in the most revenue, and that you also pay for their rather luxurious offices, among other things. After the initial well-rehearsed spiel and friendly overtures you seldom get to see the actual partner himself—he is too busy checking timesheets—you become an account number and not a human being. Greed apart, they are mentally incapable of appreciating, let alone respecting that your resources may be limited. Their own income is far more important than your fate in life. More often than not, you will also find that whoever is dealing with your case gets busy with somebody else's case, and you have to start all over again. They seldom call you back; you are the one left chasing. Shall I go on?"

Kathleen laughed. "Point taken. Always listen to experience, my dad says. When do you think…?"

"First thing Monday morning. Where are you staying?"

Kathleen mentioned one of West End's less fashionable hotels, dug into her handbag and took out a small leaflet. "Room three-one-four."

Conor stood up. "Once again our apology for barging in on you like this, Mr Parkhurst. We are very thankful for your kindness, your time and your advice."

He extended his hand. The grip was firm and lasted only for a few seconds, but Parkhurst sensed a gentleness and a sincerity rarely encountered.

"You are more than welcome," he said and reached for Kathleen's hand. "It has been a pleasure, and I wish you the best of luck."

He followed them out.

Parkhurst was as good as his word. The following Wednesday Kathleen and Conor saw one of the senior partners in Parkhurst's recommended law firm. The day after they met with the accountants.

A week later Parkhurst could no longer contain his curiosity. He made two telephone calls. It did not surprise him that the young Irish couple were found to be genuine. Nothing that he learned contradicted what they had told him.

☞

One morning, on his way to the BBC, an idea struck him. It distracted him during rehearsal and became stronger in the course of the evening.

Morning came, and Parkhurst telephoned room three-one-four.

"Hello?" Kathleen said.

"Good morning. This is Igor Parkhurst. I just wanted to know that you are both well, and that everything is going fine."

"You must be clairvoyant."

"That has not bothered me in the past," Parkhurst laughed. "Why?"

"We were going to call you today. We would like to invite you to dinner as a small thank-you."

"Oh well, that is awfully nice of you, but please do not..."

"When are you free?"

Parkhurst grabbed his diary. "Friday," he said. "Friday night would be convenient."

"Could you suggest a restaurant, please, Mr. Parkhurst? I mean, Conor and I have been to a few, but we are not connoisseurs and we were not too impressed with the service, either. "She laughed. "It's probably the way we look, or our accent, or both."

Parkhurst already had his favourite place in mind. "Let me pick you up at about seven o'clock. I'll wait for you in the bar. See you then."

Parkhurst was sipping his cognac when Kathleen, Conor and Jennifer came around the corner spot on half past seven. Oh dear, he thought, they certainly do not spend their money on clothes. Kathleen's dress would not have caused a designer's attention; it was neat but very conservative. Conor's suit had all the hallmarks of an off-the-peg purchase. I'll guide them, he thought, conscious that he by now saw himself as their guardian and mentor.

Kathleen said, "We did not want to leave Jennifer on her own or with a stranger. We hope you don't mind."

Parkhurst laughed. "On the contrary." He looked at the young girl. She's going to be a beauty like her mother, he thought. Very quiet, though.

They were on first names before they left the hotel. Parkhurst, who was born garrulous, found a worthy competitor in Kathleen, and Conor loosened up and dropped the odd wry comment.

Kathleen was relaxed in Parkhurst's company. He was charming, attentive and amusing. The occasional side-glance reassured her that also Conor enjoyed himself. She could hardly believe it when she noticed that they were the only ones left in the restaurant; the maitre d' and the waiters hovered politely in the background, but Parkhurst seemed unaware of the time.

"It's almost eleven o'clock," she whispered. "I think they want to go home."

"Dear me! Where has the evening gone?" Parkhurst beckoned to the maitre d' and asked if they could possibly have their coffee in the lounge. He added, "Tonight I have the great and unusual privilege of being the guest."

The maitre d' smiled sympathetically. He returned seconds later with a folder on a plate and placed it next to Conor. "Thank you, sir. Give me a minute, and coffee will be served."

Conor opened the folder. Kathleen leaned over. "How much do we add?" she asked.

"Twenty percent," Parkhurst said.

Kathleen gasped. "That's a bit stiff, isn't it?"

Conor put his cash in the folder and got up.

Parkhurst shook hand with the maitre d' and thanked him for his excellent service.

Kathleen tapped Parkhurst on the shoulder. "Why do you get such good service? It can't be only because of your fame and your good looks."

Parkhurst laughed. "I adhere to a couple of simple rules. First and foremost, you treat those who serve you as your equal. Anything else is as preposterous as it is stupid. Secondly, do not expect something for nothing. The best tables do not come free. We all work for a living, and to ignore the human element is not very clever."

"You gave him something when you shook hands?"

"I did."

"Nifty," Kathleen said.

"Oh yes. Discretion is a craft."

They sat down in the lounge.

"Listen," Parkhurst said after the coffee had been served, "I have a proposition to make. It is just an idea, of course, but perhaps you would like to consider it." He adjusted his tie as he searched for words. "How do I phrase this...?"

"Straight," Kathleen said.

Parkhurst grimaced. "Yes. Of course. All right. You are spending a lot of money staying in a hotel. It could easily take months before you actually get a property and can move in. Things don't move fast, here in London. I am on my own in a large house with five extra bedrooms and four bathrooms." He covered his mouth with three fingers and cleared his throat. "Would it be an idea to move in until your property is a reality? It is just a thought, as I said—it may or may not appeal to you."

"It is a very kind and generous offer," Conor said. "Please do not take offence if we think about it."

"That goes without saying. I mean ..." Then Parkhurst experienced something strange, something he had not himself encountered during his married years. The young couple opposite him looked at each other for some ten seconds. The silence was almost surreal.

Suddenly, Kathleen turned towards him. "We have thought about it, and we accept gracefully."

Parkhurst shook his head as if waking up from a weird dream. "The three of you are something else," he said. "I am very pleased."

He glanced at Jennifer, who sat with her hands in her lap, wide awake. An unusual child, he thought; exceptionally well mannered and rather reticent—but she doesn't miss a thing.

Kathleen, Conor and Jennifer moved in two days later. They found the property they wanted towards the end of October; a big, rambling house in Chelsea. They reckoned that by March all necessary work should be completed.

The builders learned quickly that the new owners knew what they wanted, and that Mrs. Moran in particular was not easily taken for a ride. Shortly before Christmas, Kathleen and Conor locked up the building and went home for a quiet celebration with their families.

Parkhurst spent Christmas on his own. The emptiness depressed him. On Boxing Day his two daughters came over. Since nobody mentioned their mother, or the pending divorce, the day could have been more unpleasant. The girls each got their cheques in an envelope, duly decorated with a red ribbon.

Parkhurst wasn't excessively dejected when they kissed him goodbye.

Kathleen, Conor and Jennifer came back on the fourth day of January. By the middle of April their property was completed, including Conor's pigeon loft in the back garden.

Parkhurst asked, "Do we go out, or do we celebrate here?"

"Here," Kathleen said firmly, "at home. In a week's time we can have another celebration at home in Chelsea."

Parkhurst did not miss her point. He was moved and tried to hide it by polishing his glasses.

They sat in front of the fireplace in Parkhurst's vast drawing room when Kathleen said, "We would like to ask you something."

"Don't be shy," he smiled.

"My eldest brother was Jennifer's godfather. He was killed in an— an accident." She looked away for a brief moment. "As you know, we have no family here in England. Would you mind stepping in as Jennifer's godfather?"

Parkhurst abruptly checked himself and got busy with another log.

"G-Godfather," he stammered. "I don't know what to say. I…"

"You only say yes if you want to," Conor said. "Otherwise, you say no. We understand either way."

The tickle in his throat would not go away. Parkhurst bit his tongue, frowned and coughed discreetly. "You don't think I am too old?"

"No. Do you?"

"Well…"

"Is that all that bothers you?" Kathleen asked.

"Yes, it is."

"Hold on a minute," she went on. "If we can accept you, why can't you accept you?"

Parkhurst folded his hands and looked at each in turn. The smile was back on his face. "Against such logic I capitulate unconditionally."

6

Frost came during the night. There was still a smoky chill in the air when Conor got behind the wheel of his car. The streets were in shadows, but the turquoise sky curved like a porcelain cupola over buildings yet to buzz with life.

The westbound traffic was light, but Conor did not hurry. He had not asked and neither had Igor volunteered any information when he had called the night before. *"I need to talk to you,"* was all he'd said, *"please come."*

They were the words of a troubled man, but it was the tone of voice that had told Conor that his old friend and guru was more than worried; he was bewildered and depressed.

Conor switched on the radio. He never put undue pressure on himself, trying to accelerate the process; undirected guesswork was an exercise in futility and could more often than not lead the mind astray. He preferred to handle the unexpected with the serenity and patience required as details, shades and nuances bit by bit emerged. Impetuosity and lack of tact was a combination that produced an unattractive and counter-productive attitude; Conor had learned to listen. He never showed indifference, even when the seemingly most insignificant or irrelevant drops of intimacy splashed across the table from a soul in distress.

He thought of his ten years of experience with those unable to cope with life. He opened the window and wondered for how much longer he could continue. Kathleen and Jennifer pined for him to retire, and with some urgency, lately; they yearned for the day when he would get up in the morning and do what he *wanted to do* and not what he *had to do* before he got too old and the rocking chair became more alluring than walking the hills with the dogs he'd always wanted but never had. True, he could not go on forever and the world would never run out of misfits. Maybe the time really had come for a place in the middle of nowhere, for tranquillity and peace whilst the flames of the campfire were still bright enough to let him catch glimpses of a life faithful to the ideals of his youth.

But first there was Igor Parkhurst, a frightened old man who for the first time had asked for help. Conor knew; the tiredness and the resignation in Igor's voice pointed towards a situation too serious for him to deal with on his own. Something had gone wrong, and drastically so; Igor was not a moaner and he had always taken pride in sorting out whichever mishaps and calamities that came his way.

Conor pulled up in front of the farmgate. It was going to be a nice day; a few clouds, white with a tinge of pink and mauve and light grey edges where the sun had yet to reach. He saw Parkhurst standing in front of the house, a bulky figure dressed in green tweed and with a multicoloured hat on his head.

Conor got out of the car. "Good morning, Igor, and what a lovely morning it is. How long have you been standing there?"

Parkhurst tried a grin. "A couple of hours, I think. Not more."

"I thought so," Conor smiled.

"I feel better, now," Parkhurst said.

Conor lifted his hand towards the sky and exercised his fingers. During his career as minder of the downtrodden he had seen what loneliness could do to people. The mere presence of a sympathetic soul could lift a man's spirit from deep melancholy to the more comfortable spheres of tolerable dejection in a matter of hours.

"It is a perfect day for a stroll," Parkhurst said. He knew Conor's passion for leaving the streets of London whenever he could for a walk in the country.

"So it is, following a much needed and well deserved cup of coffee."

"Sorry," Parkhurst said. "I am just being my selfish and preoccupied self."

They walked up the stairs. "Kathleen and Jennifer send their love," Conor said.

"Thank you. They are both well, I hope?"

"Couldn't be better. Jennifer told me that she and James visited you a few weeks ago."

"Yes, that was a pleasant surprise. He seems a decent man, young James."

Conor looked at the curtains covering the windows. "Any reason for this total darkness?"

"I didn't notice. I was just sitting here, thinking."

Conor put the kettle on the Aga oven, which Miriam had imported from Sweden.

He placed two mugs on the table and sat down. "It's a long time since I last saw you."

Parkhurst avoided Conor's eyes. "I have been busy."

Conor studied his old friend. "Look at me, Igor."

Parkhurst lifted his head.

Conor said, "Listen, and listen carefully. Not once have you asked for a helping hand. Not ever have you asked a favour. You have coped on your own, which I admire, but somehow, somehow you are now facing a wall with no doors. I am your friend, Igor. I am here to do whatever I can do. You asked me to come. I am not leaving until I am part of your problem. Talk to me."

He clasped Parkhurst's hand and went on, "Begin somewhere. Don't bother with the chronology. We will put things in perspective as we go along."

Parkhurst began. Sometimes he was lucid, and sometimes he was almost incoherent. His voice revealed anger and frustration, bitterness and fear. He talked about his inability to understand the condemnation heaped upon him by each of his three wives. He talked about his sadness when he finally had to admit that they loved what he could give but not the giver. He bemoaned the greed and the obduracy of his children and how powerless he felt when he tried to tell them that no marriage was entirely cast in black and white. He mourned his incapability to write, and he lamented the lack of support from all those who had benefited from his creative talents and who now considered him history. He admitted his hefty financial problems, and he expressed his dread of old age, infirmity and loneliness.

One hour later Igor Parkhurst abruptly stopped, stared at the ceiling and said, "If you think I am drowning in self-pity, you are probably right. I have no strength any more."

"Why on earth did you not talk to me long ago?" Conor said. "Why did you wait till you are a hair's breadth from cracking up?"

101

Parkhurst said, "I am not asking for financial help." There was defiance in his voice.

Conor ignored the remark. "Let's go for a walk. You have not finished, yet."

"How did you know that?"

This is worse than I anticipated, Conor thought; the old Igor would never have asked such a question. "What do you think I have been doing for the past ten years? I have been listening to people describing the first half of their problems, the easy part. Then they invariably expect me to foresee, comprehend and finally explain the second half, which, as it happens, contains the roots of their anguish. Symptom and cause, Igor—ever heard that expression?"

"I don't follow."

"I believe you do."

Blood rushed to Parkhurst's face as he shook his head violently. "I never blamed anybody else!"

"Did I say that? Don't misunderstand me on purpose. I talked about the source itself. That source is you, Igor."

Parkhurst walked over to the table and sat down. "You are confusing me."

"Don't worry," Conor said. "Before this day is over you will see things more clearly. Tell me what else has happened to you lately, and we'll get back to square one and start structuring from there." His chin protruded. "Come on. Let us go for a walk."

They went outside.

"What a magnificent day," Conor said and inhaled deeply. "This is priceless. Kathleen keeps talking about buying a cottage down here somewhere, you know, a nice little weekend retreat. It is a good idea, I think, a hideaway with farmland all around. The ideal place to retire, eventually." He laughed softly, as if the notion of retirement was beyond the realms of reality.

"Why don't you and Kathleen come down for the weekend and you can start looking around?"

Conor thought for a second. "Thank you, Igor. We'll do that."

Parkhurst brightened. "Which way do we go?"

"I prefer the woods. There is something about trees that makes me feel relaxed, or less tense, whichever. Keep talking."

Parkhurst did. He revealed every detail about his involvement with the Secret Service, including Pritchard-White's threats of blackmail, the meeting with Wilbur Fletcher, and, finally the emergence of Ishihara and Vargas.

By early afternoon Conor had a good picture of what he saw as a ridiculous, pathetic yet nasty situation. What he failed to find was a convincing explanation for the appearance of Mr. Ishihara. Even more puzzling was the shadow of the enigmatic Mr. Vargas. Conor admitted that he was at a loss; logic was no longer applicable.

He stopped and watched a squirrel. "I hate to say this, Igor, but I am mystified. Mr. Ishihara offered to give you one hundred thousand pounds?"

"Yes."

"He did not say it's a loan?"

"No, he did not."

Conor sat down on a sawn-off tree trunk, picked up a cone and tossed it from hand to hand. "You are still famous, Igor. A name does not vanish overnight. You used to know a lot of important and influential people, the same people who now treat you as a pariah. Let us assume that you manage a comeback. The luminaries will once again flock around you, and money starts pouring in. All this requires some assistance, and that is what Mr. Ishihara is offering. In return, you open the doors for the two of them. They are foreigners, and the narrow path into our desirable society has fewer hurdles with you than without you. So far, so good." Conor looked at the pine trees swaying gingerly in the wind and ran his fingers through his hair. "You know, Igor, this could actually be less far-fetched than it sounds."

Parkhurst said, "I have got nothing to lose if you are right, and nothing to lose if you are wrong. Is that what you are saying? Can it really be that simple?"

"What are your instincts telling you?"

"My instincts tell me to be careful. Nothing is for free, Conor. We know that. Also, remember Mr. Nakamoto's warning. These two men are—I don't know; I have not come across people like that before. I feel there is something sinister about them, something methodical and ruthless. I feel that they know exactly what they are doing and that I do not. On the other hand—am I throwing away my last lifeline if I reject them?"

"I think there is only one way to find out."

"You mean, I haven't got much of a choice?"

"No, you have not."

"It scares me."

"More so than your present impasse?"

Parkhurst chewed on his tongue. "No."

"If Mr. Ishihara is the financier he says he is, you can be quite sure he has hedged his bet."

"I didn't think of that."

They walked for a while. The sun had lost some of its warmth, and the still naked trees stood like casual signatures in black against the pale blue afternoon sky.

Parkhurst said, "We could have lit a fire tonight, if you didn't have to go home."

"I don't."

Parkhurst looked to his left. He did not want Conor to see his face.

After a while he glanced at his friend and marvelled once again at the transformation that had taken place in the Irishman since they first met an eternity ago. Conor had been shy, reserved and taciturn, quiet, unassuming and modest. Funny, Parkhurst thought, in so many ways he is still the same Conor, but in other ways he is not. Maturity? Absolutely. Progress? Distinctly. Shaped and formed by experience; plodding about in the human cesspool trying to clear up the acts of muggers, thieves, robbers, prostitutes, drug addicts, alcoholics, dropouts, the homeless and any other misfit coming his way. Nobody was turned away, but—and this had become Conor's firm policy—anybody who did not attempt to improve their own situation was told to go somewhere else. Conor tolerated narcissism, but he did not accept self-pity. If there was even the tiniest sign of desire to rise from the gutter, Conor was there. People who weltered in self-pitying and shallow egotism were told never to come back, unless they began to understand and accept that nobody could help somebody who had no urge to participate.

Conor always made it clear that although the world was possibly *partly* to blame for their misfortunes, the same world wasn't getting any better and therefore they had no alternative but to look inwards and face their predicament in order to change it. "*True, and fair enough,*" Conor said to each newcomer, "*life can be miserable and unbearable, but since nobody can take over your existence, you either continue downhill, or you use whatever you have got to reverse the situation. The choice is yours. I am not here to carry you. I am here to assist."*

Some understood but most didn't. Some tried and most failed. Conor's rewards were meagre, but he never lost his conviction that a renewed life for one single human being could be measured, neither in quantity nor in efforts.

There were times when Parkhurst wondered how many disappointments Conor could take without cracking up, but the Irishman's instincts for mental and physical survival appeared to be beyond comparison with virtually any other man Parkhurst had ever encountered. Even Kathleen, after all these years, could not quite fathom her husband's incredible strength, his resilience and his ability to recover.

Once a year, though, she booked a holiday in the sun, and Conor had no say in the matter. She had found their haven in Barbados, and for two weeks in June Conor was out of touch with what his daughter called The Misfit Mission.

Coming back tanned and rejuvenated, Conor found his Mission intact. His staff of three men and one woman had coped adequately, as he knew they would. Apart from the odd broken window, a failed suicide or somebody falling off the wagon, nothing out of the ordinary had happened. The staff had been with him for a long time, and both they and Kathleen had convinced him ages ago that he wasn't entirely indispensable, at least not for a couple of weeks.

Jennifer was at the airport welcoming them home, listening with a smile to all that she had missed during a holiday more fantastic than last year's.

From time to time Parkhurst tried to draw a comparison between the Moran family life, and that or those of his own, but he'd had to admit that there wasn't any. Now it's too late, he thought as they swung up in front of the gate; I haven't got a woman, for a start, and I am too old to have any more children. Even if I exhausted my reservoir of experience, it is a fact that no donkey has ever won the Derby.

Conor lit the fire after the meal. He placed the cognac and the Irish whisky on the table and made himself comfortable. Parkhurst sat down in his favourite chair facing the windows. He stared at the soft and deep blue moment between darkness and starlight. Conor lit a cigar, sipped his whisky and seemed content with the silence.

Finally, Parkhurst folded his hands around his glass. "Where did I go wrong, Conor?"

"Part vanity, part kudos and part ambition. You also ignored the good use of your ability to read other people's mind. This ability you used for your writing and not for the improvement of your relationships. You are a good man, Igor, but the creative artist in you, who is considerable, has always taken precedence. Once upon a time your life became a function of your search for recognition. That became your goal, an everlasting dream from which you were not prepared to wake up. Now, in the autumn of your life, you have regrets. Yesterday is too late, but tomorrow is not. What is done cannot be undone, what is said cannot be unsaid. There is nothing uncomplicated or mysterious about either. You know that as well as I do. Tomorrow is yours, Igor; you are not dead, you are neither a mental wreck nor an emotional cripple—you have no valid excuse for not facing yourself and make your final years worth living. I shall refrain from elaborating on the distinction between life and existence."

"I am a good man—remember?" Parkhurst said. He instantly regretted the sarcasm.

Conor smiled and stretched his legs. "Don't play silly buggers with me, Igor. There is no winner."

He topped up his glass and blew a few smoke rings. "Let me tell you a story I once heard: An old man was lying on his deathbed. A younger relative came around to ask forgiveness for some nasty and untrue rumours he'd once spread. The old man said: "*Take this pillow and the knife on the table there, and go over to the window.*" The young man was confused, and he asked: "*Why?*" The old man said: "*Just do it.*" So, the young man did. "*Open the window,*" the old man said, "*cut the pillow and shake it till there is not one feather left.*" The young man said in despair: "*But it is a windy day. No way can I gather them all back again.*" The old man said: "*No, you can't.*" Only then did the young man understand what the old man was telling him."

Parkhurst was not sure how the story could highlight his own situation, but he nodded.

"You follow?" Conor asked. His smile was not overbearing.

"Well…"

"Getting out of the tunnel is your only imperative, Igor."

I know, Parkhurst thought, but *how*? He did not answer.

Conor threw another log on the fire. "Can we categorically state that you are in the hands of your creditors?"

"Yes."

"Is there no work coming your way?"

"Less and less."

"Kathleen and I have been wondering why we haven't seen your name around for some time. We thought you were having a prolonged sabbatical."

He continued, "We have a handful of alternatives. I could lend you enough money to fend off your creditors, that is, *today's* creditors. You could declare yourself bankrupt. You could go public with your cloak-and-dagger story." He looked over his shoulder and into the darkness. "Say you need fifty grand to calm the waters. Half a year later, or less, you need another fifty. Your expenditure is high, thanks to the running of this property, and your income is zero. How can you service a loan? You can't."

Parkhurst refilled his glass. It was only his second drink. He felt uncomfortably sober.

"What if I go public?" he asked.

"Don Quixote and his windmills. You will face an enormous series of battles you cannot win. You'll get entangled in a web of denials, lies, ridicule and, ultimately, a total and final defeat. Can you imagine any minister or mandarin actually verifying and supporting your story? It is a world where expediency is the only valid currency; a world where right and wrong, justice, truth, fair play and integrity are not even shadows on the wall. You'll be ostracized, annihilated and tossed aside; a wet rag of a human being begging for mercy where none exists. Unless, of course, they should be benevolent enough to kill you off, literally, at the early stage of your crusade."

Parkhurst rested his head against the back of the chair. "So much for getting closer to a solution," he said hoarsely.

"Oh, but we are. Have you not been listening?"

"Evidently not."

Conor re-lit his cigar. "We have already decided what you *can't* do. That is not bad in the course of two tiny drinks. We have also focused on what you *can* do."

"We have?"

"Your Japanese contact. Don't tell me you have forgotten. Did he not offer you a deal that would earn you a hundred thousand?"

"You take that seriously?"

"Yes, I do. Ask yourself why he approached you. I think there is more to your new-found friend Mr…"

"—Ishihara."

"—to Mr. Ishihara than meets the eye."

"Even if you are right, I am still short, long-term, that is."

Conor flicked the butt of his cigar into the yellow flames. "Mr. Ishihara wants a ticket to what he perceives as our cultural, refined and distinguished British society. This deal, or generous gift, whichever, is what he offers in return."

Parkhurst thought for a while. Then, on instinct, he decided to keep to himself Ishihara's second motive.

"So he said," he mumbled. "I just wonder what else is behind it."

"Pure guesswork is a waste of time, Igor. If there is an ulterior motive, it will come out in the wash. Let us concentrate on the money. Did you not say that Mr. Ishihara's got a friend?"

Parkhurst gawked. "You mean…?"

"Yes, that is exactly what I mean. One ticket per person."

"Good Lord, how do I get that across?"

"By telling him in plain words. You are fighting for survival, Igor. Reinforce your tender and sensitive soul and make a stand. Your Japanese benefactor may even appreciate your shrewd and businesslike approach. You've got nothing to lose."

"Except that he could get annoyed and walk away."

"That is a calculated risk you've got to take." Conor raised his head and listened to the war cries from the owls. "Predators," he said and smiled. "By the way, why doesn't Mr. Ishihara just give you the money and leave it at that? Why this charade?"

"That is not the Japanese way. Mr. Ishihara does seem thoroughly Westernized, but his roots are in his own culture. They simply do not operate that way."

"I see. You know more about the East than I do. Are you going to give it a try?"

Parkhurst said firmly, "Yes, assuming that Mr. Ishihara shows up again." He gave a thin smile. "I shall wait and see."

"He has made his opening move. He is not far away."

"What about my—my involvement," Parkhurst said. "How do I get out of this bizarre nightmare?"

"Creditors you can fight, governments you can't. There has to be another answer, something clever or, rather, sophisticated."

"You don't sound too optimistic."

"I am not. It is complicated because it is intangible, devious and ultimately evil." He chuckled into his glass. "This is one of the occasions when I wish that God had kept to Himself His passion for moving in mysterious ways."

"Amen."

Conor grinned. "Maybe I should have been a priest, after all."

"Heaven intervened."

"Yes, that is probably what happened." Conor screwed the cap back on the bottle. "Bedtime."

"Are you coming on Friday?"

"I mentioned it to Kathleen when I called her. Pure delight and no problems. She could do with a break. Jennifer is coming, too."

Parkhurst beamed. "Splendid." All of a sudden he felt less miserable than he'd done for months. "What about James?"

Conor got up and adjusted the screen in front of the fire. "He's in Germany. The great guns of our financial world are congregating in Stuttgart. I have no idea what they are going to solve. Perhaps we'll see poverty abolished next week."

Something in Conor's voice puzzled Parkhurst. "I thought you liked him."

Conor turned. "I have nothing against him. Yes, I even like him. He is nice, polite, respectful and considerate. I also believe that he is genuinely fond of Jennifer."

"There is a *but* in the air, Conor."

"I am not so sure whether Jennifer is yet aware of the depths of her own nature." There was a rare touch of aggression in his voice. "I fear that young James is a bit too uncomplicated for her."

He rose from his chair and said, "Let's lock up."

Friday came with a few early showers, but the weather cleared when Conor, Kathleen and Jennifer left London.

Conor had explained to Kathleen and Jennifer the nature and the dimensions of Parkhurst's problems.

They found him waiting at the gate. He wore his favourite green corduroy suit and his undersized multicoloured hat. He seemed preoccupied with the aerobatics of the swallows. Conor wondered how long his friend had been standing there. All right, he thought, you won't be lonely this weekend.

He rolled down the window. "Going for a walk?" he asked innocently.

"No —no," Parkhurst stuttered. "I am just coming back from one, as a matter of fact. I didn't expect you this early."

"Liar," Conor smiled. "See you up at the house."

"I can just as well come with you," Parkhurst said quickly and took off his hat.

Conor was stonefaced, "Sorry, but there is no way I can deprive you of this final bit of exercise. Complete your walk, Igor. It's only a few hundred yards. Besides, we haven't got room for you. Too much food and booze." He put the car into gear and drove off.

"That was not very kind," Jennifer said from the backseat.

Conor found her eyes in the mirror. "Don't you worry—Igor can move if he wants to. By now he smells food. Look—he is practically running."

Momentary peace and tranquillity. Good food and excellent wine. A glass or three of exquisite cognac. The presence of the Moran family.

Parkhurst counted his blessings and concluded that perhaps all was not lost. The night before he had sat in front of the fire in a mansion frighteningly quiet and disturbingly empty. He had tried hard to evaluate his past, his present and what was left of his future. He had recalled Conor's comments and advice. He had made an honest effort to be as objective, constructive and positive as possible.

He became aware of Conor's stare. "You have been watching me, haven't you?"

"Cheer up, Igor."

"I was just wondering what shape my life would have taken had I found a woman like Kathleen when I was twenty."

"And if your children had loved you as your goddaughter does. Why don't we all use the weekend to count our *ifs*?"

Parkhurst looked at his friend. "You are right. I shall pull myself together."

He woke up with a hangover, but otherwise well and at ease with himself. He put on his gown and slippers and wandered downstairs and into the kitchen.

Kathleen, Jennifer and Conor were enjoying their morning coffee.

"Top of the morning," Conor said. "I must declare, you look amazingly fit, almost supercharged."

"Like a gargantuan cherub," Kathleen said. "All rosy cheeks and pink eyes. You had a good night's sleep?"

Parkhurst pulled out a chair. "Better than, oh—I don't know—an eternity. What an evening. Where did the time go?"

"It's the company," Kathleen smiled. "Kindred spirits and, if I remember correctly, all kinds of spirits."

Parkhurst fumbled with the belt of his gown. "I love the three of you."

Jennifer came with a mug of coffee.

"Thank you, my dear," Parkhurst said and patted her hand. "I presume you picked that one accidentally on purpose." He looked at the picture of a polar bear with a bewildered look on his face. The text read: *LUCK FOOLS—TALENT RULES.*

"Pure coincidence," she said. "What a suspicious mind you have got, Uncle Igor." She stroked his hair and turned her attention to the driveway in front of the house. "Are you expecting somebody?"

They all got up and watched a black Mercedes come to a halt.

Parkhurst said, "No, but I think I know who it is."

"Who might the unexpected guest be?" Conor queried with a slight anticipation to his voice.

"Have a guess," Parkhurst said uneasily as both front doors of the car opened.

Conor smiled. "Your favourite Japanese and his friend."

When Conor had told Kathleen about Parkhurst's state of affairs, he had included the approach from the Japanese. Jennifer had yet to be informed.

"Who are they?" she asked. "Do you know them?"

"Kind of," Parkhurst said. "I'll explain later. Let me try to postpone the non-existent appointment."

He left the kitchen and went to the main entrance.

"Ah," they heard a voice, "Mr. Parkhurst. A very good morning to you. I do hope that we find you in the most ebullient of mind. May I have the pleasure to introduce my friend and associate Mr. Vargas? Please excuse this apparent intrusion, but may we come in for the briefest of moments?"

Parkhurst was taken aback, but he was too polite to consider an objection, or, as he suspected, temporarily too spineless to put up any resistance. Or was it the thought of a hundred grand multiplied by two that made him nod? "Please," he said and stepped aside.

Ishihara headed straight for the kitchen, followed by Vargas. Parkhurst closed the door, adjusted his gown and wondered if the two strangers' presence would turn out to be a calamity or a bounty.

"My oh my!" Ishihara exclaimed. "You have guests, Mr. Parkhurst. Why didn't you tell us? Now we feel like invaders. A most uncomfortable sensation." He smiled broadly and displayed his front gold tooth all around. "However, dare I presume that this is the esteemed Moran family? What a remarkable coincidence, not to forget the added bonus."

Parkhurst grounded his molars before he did the full round of presentations. The Japanese bowed formally, took a quick step forward and shook hands with each in turn. "A delight beyond words. It makes me indescribably happy that Mr. Parkhurst has some true friends to rely on, his pickle being what it is."

Vargas did not bow. Neither did he move as rapidly as the Japanese did. The movement of a cat, Conor thought, a beast of prey slowly approaching something of dubious interest. The handshake was firm but brief. Vargas' blue eyes showed neither friendliness nor hostility.

Parkhurst asked, "May I offer you something to drink?"

"That is frightfully thoughtful of you," Ishihara said. "Coffee, please. Milk and sugar for my good self. Mr. Vargas takes it black."

Jennifer turned to hide a smile. She had not been to the Far East, but she had encountered the odd Japanese during the years. This one was exceptional.

Ishihara was dressed in light grey trousers, shiny maroon shoes, mustard-coloured blazer, white shirt and a scarlet and indigo striped tie. He wore a gold Rolex and an expensive looking ring on his left pinkie finger. It struck Jennifer that there was no mismatch between his attire and his vocabulary. The gold tooth fascinated her, as did his entire demeanour and almost black and coruscating eyes.

Her gaze wandered from Ishihara to his less talkative companion who, in comparison, looked as elegant as a vagabond on the run. He was some three inches taller than the Japanese; black shoes with rubber soles, black denims, coal grey shirt with no tie and a black leather jacket. No jewellery, not even a watch. He was tanned, and, she surmised, had once been blond. His shortcut hair was greyish and looked bleached by the sun.

She tried to estimate the age group of the two guests; anything, she thought, between thirty and forty.

"Shall we move to the drawing room?" Parkhurst suggested. "It is a bit crowded here."

Jennifer found a tray and six coasters. They all put their cups down with the exception of Vargas, who decided to carry his. She looked at him, questioningly, but got no reaction. She smiled. Vargas remained impassive. Please yourself, she thought; a pity you haven't picked up some manners from your Oriental friend.

Comfortably seated, Ishihara raised his right hand. "Once again our most sincere apologies for this unannounced visit. The point is, however—" he stared at Parkhurst "—you and I have to reach a decision rather imminently. In fact, we must make our move not later than by ten o'clock Tuesday morning. These opportunities are comparatively few and far between, as you can appreciate." He smiled. "May I have your kind permission to smoke?"

"Of course," Parkhurst said, thankful for the respite.

Ishihara took a gold case from his inner pocket and opened it to reveal a dozen slender cigars. "Would anyone like to join me?"

Parkhurst and Conor accepted. Kathleen and Jennifer declined.

Ishihara lit the cigars with his gold lighter. "Ah," he sighed, " the unsurpassed pleasure of pure nicotine. Mr. Vargas smokes cigarettes, I'm afraid. Not quite the same, in my considered opinion. But then—" he shrugged "—we are all different." He looked fleetingly at Vargas who took no notice. His eyes rested on a painting.

"So," Ishihara went on and watched the smoke seeping from his nostrils, "shall we return to the all-important subject of Mr. Parkhurst's future since, I confidently presume, none of us here would like to see him disappear down the drain and into the big abyss from which there is no return. Let me be so bold as to presuppose that a second opinion does not exist." He fixed his stare on Conor. "Such a nice and talented man as Mr. Parkhurst should be allowed to blossom and find happiness in the autumn of his life."

Conor said, "On that point we certainly agree."

"Where might we disagree, Mr. Moran, if at all? I take it that you are fully familiar with the contents of my two previous meetings with

Mr. Parkhurst," he added and tapped his gold tooth with his forefinger. "Do not let my remarkable perception throw you off balance."

"It doesn't," Conor said. "My problem is that we do not know who you are and why you are doing what you are doing."

"That is indeed understandable. I do respect your being as cautious as a hooker counting an archbishop's money. Most commendable. I appreciate that you are a man whose experience with life's many facets and nuances is as wide as it is deep." He bowed, smiled benevolently and put his cigar in the ashtray.

There is not a trace of irony in his voice, Conor thought, and neither a hint of contempt in his eyes. This man is a very skilful player, and, I believe, equally dangerous. As for his sidekick—Conor looked at Vargas who had crossed his legs and did not seem to pay any attention to what was being said. Is it indifference, boredom or a mask? Conor thought; I can't place him, he's too laid-back. I can safely assume that he is here for a reason other than the lure of the countryside; the Japanese does the talking, but it could be parlous to write off this chap as merely a sleeping partner.

"Allow me to touch the subject of our background, an ungarnished outline, so to speak," Ishihara said, steadily watching Conor, "and I am sure that you will acknowledge that our motives for introducing ourselves to Mr. Parkhurst are as plausible as they are justifiable. You may heretofore have drawn the conclusion that we are both foreigners; I am Japanese, as you presumably have guessed already, and my brother Mr. Vargas is half Irish and half Apache. I take it for granted that you do not for a moment imagine that we are here seeking material gains. If that was the case—" he gave a quick smile "—Mr. Parkhurst would not head the queue. Nothing personal, Mr. Parkhurst, I am simply stating the obvious."

"Convincing, so far," Conor said.

"Indeed. You, Mr. Moran, know from personal experience what it is like to be a foreigner. This is purely an observation and not a judgement. Even the most resourceful and obstinate of people do find this an uphill struggle. Now, Mr. Vargas and I have been on the go for a good many years, and we have decided to honour this country with our permanent presence. The natives are less intolerant than most and it would not be far off the bulls-eye to say that England remains one of the few liberal countries on this planet. The reason for such attitude can of course be debated—personally, I am inclined to believe that the population here is mentally too lazy to bother about much at all—but, whatever, it is not a bad place to settle. We have been here for a few years, now, but commitments up to date have prevented us from exercising the delicate act of assimilation and integration. Withdrawing from past activities have given our existence another dimension, and we would now dearly like to become part of this most endearing and charming of stealthy xenophobic societies. However, realism ruling, not for one split microsecond do we envisage that we can achieve this target without the kind and most qualified assistance of an insider. Hence, Mr. Parkhurst. Would it be too immodest to assume that I make sense, so far?"

"It wouldn't," Conor said.

"Thank you kindly. Does it not also make sense that if you are prepared to take, you should be prepared to give? Not the most widespread of philosophies, I'm afraid, but one nevertheless distinctly expressed by a great soulmate of mine, and to which I rigorously adhere."

"Would that soulmate be Mr. Vargas?" Jennifer asked.

Ishihara did not blink. Then, suddenly, he turned and gave her a warm smile. "Not this time," he said and she noticed the humour in his eyes. "It was a Chinese gentleman by the name of Confucius, now deceased, sadly. Mr. Vargas' philosophies can be clearly expressed by himself, should he so desire."

Jennifer smiled back. She refrained from further comments. Vargas was sitting opposite her, less than three yards away. She wondered why his presence, his silence and everything else about him made her feel uncomfortable.

Ishihara continued, "Anyway. What we are offering Mr. Parkhurst is not a gift. What we all know, or should know, is that the act of giving is usually rewarded by the receiver with an unsavoury cocktail of emotions of which most are subconsciously negative simply because dignified gratitude is beyond ordinary mortals. Following this frivolous but excusable aside, what we are extending to Mr. Parkhurst is a helping hand, a short-term loan, in strict financial terms, enabling him to find his way out of his unfortunate wilderness."

Vargas moved. Jennifer saw a cigarette in his right hand and wondered where it came from. Ishihara lit another of his cigars and tossed the lighter to Vargas who caught it mid-air.

Ishihara added, "I have tried to be as explicit as the situation requires, but please do not hesitate to ask questions."

Parkhurst and Conor looked at each other.

"Let me see if I have got this right," Conor said. "You lend Mr. Parkhurst a certain amount to buy shares. The share goes up, Mr. Parkhurst makes a killing and you get your money back. In other words, you don't risk much."

"Only if it goes wrong," Ishihara said and placed his lighter edgeways on the table.

"My apology. For some reason I did not include that possibility."

"It is a calculated risk, Mr. Moran. Let me underline, for the sake of good order, that I am a businessman and not a charity."

"I would like to think about it," Parkhurst said, "digest it, so to speak. Can I call you tonight?"

"But of course," Ishihara said. His face beamed goodwill iced with attention. "I must emphasize, though, that we have to meet tomorrow if you decide to act. Let me also say that I sympathize with your most natural circumspection, but it is a fact of life, Mr. Parkhurst, that money usually dissolves any degree of apprehension. Never discount the human element, as Mr. Vargas is fond of saying."

"I believe I understand."

"Here," Ishihara said, "my card. You may recall that the one I gave you previously does not contain my telephone number."

Jennifer, who had enjoyed the Japanese's performance with a mixture of humour, awe and bewilderment, suddenly sensed that she was being watched. She moved her eyes from Ishihara and looked directly at Vargas. She told herself that there was no reason why she should feel ill at ease. Jennifer was not conceited; she did not allow herself to revel in the admiration most males so willingly displayed. She knew that men found her attractive; for years she had been aware of the signals of desire when men instinctively turned predators in the presence of a beautiful woman, and she tackled it by a display of formal courtesy fused with a touch of indifference.

Here, something didn't add up. Vargas continued to look at her; it was as if little electric sparks playfully criss-crossed his irises before disappearing behind a screen of reserved curiosity. Then the blue of his eyes turned deeper and made her think of a glacier reflecting in the cobalt of the Arctic Sea. The sudden coldness surprised her.

I'm not an object to this man, she thought, I am a *challenge*. He looks at me as if I am an unexpected archaeological discovery, either that, or those eyes of his are making a roundtrip inside my head. It is amazing how anybody can be so rude without saying a word or move a finger. He must be one of those lucky few whose facial muscles are never unduly exercised. Lots of practice, I suppose.

She settled for one of her deep-frozen stares. It didn't work. Vargas neither blinked nor looked away. She sensed that the palms of her hands were getting moist when she saw his lower lip half curl against his teeth. He's amused, she thought. The bastard is actually enjoying himself.

She heard Ishihara's laughter. It hit her like nails being shaken in a metal container. No, she thought, I am neither relieved nor disappointed if the Japanese breaks up now and take his mute crossbreed with him.

"We must be on our way. Thank you again for your kind hospitality and for giving us this opportunity to explain. I wish you a pleasant afternoon."

He got up, bowed and shook hands.

Vargas nodded to each in turn, Jennifer last. The expression on his face remained stoical, but for one transient moment Jennifer thought she saw the tiniest of smiles in his eyes.

Vargas went straight to the car, but Ishihara stopped on top of the staircase. "I do hope I shall hear from you tonight," he said.

"You will," Parkhurst promised. "By the way, is your friend always this talkative?"

Ishihara laughed. "I am afraid Mr. Vargas is rather reticent. Always has been. But don't worry, he will let you know should there be something he wants to get across." He turned and waved amicably. "See you tomorrow."

Parkhurst returned to the drawing room and found the other three deep in talk. None of them looked at him. He found his chair and eyed each in turn as if looking for guidance. The tiredness was coming back, and he felt a headache spreading from the top of his neck. He said, "I'd say our Japanese friend displayed the same unfathomable sincerity as a lawyer explaining his interim charges. You just do not know what to believe, and you've got no way of checking the facts."

"Seen isolated, I would say that Mr. Ishihara's rationale is fully plausible," Conor said to no one in particular. "It could even be entirely true."

117

He focused on Parkhurst and continued, "Why do I have this feeling that there is another truth, something we have yet to learn or discover? It is pure instinct, of course. What I am saying is that I am not entirely comfortable with this duo."

"Yes, it is quite a pair," Parkhurst said. "One is charming, eloquent, suave and logical, and the other is broody, sinister looking and less vocal than an oyster."

Kathleen laughed. "Maybe that's where the pearl is."

Conor beat Parkhurst to the question, "Meaning?"

Kathleen shrugged. "I don't know. I really have to dig into my well of intuition before I can answer that one." A thin line crossed her forehead. "Maybe he is just Mr. Ishihara's bodyguard, although…"

"—although?" Conor tapped her knee.

"Somehow, I don't think so. I am guessing. We are all guessing."

Parkhurst pressed his hands against his temples. "I do not think that Mr. Ishihara needs a bodyguard," he said. "From what little I have seen, he is fully capable of taking care of himself. Did I tell you that they have been together for a long time? They met in Japan."

Kathleen said, "They told you about themselves? That's nice, showing confidence, I mean."

Parkhurst stared past her. "Unfortunately not," he said and told them about Nakamoto's letter. "That's how I know."

There was a moment's silence. He poured himself a generous measure of cognac.

"Anyone else?" he asked.

They all declined.

"I've got a headache," he explained.

"You'll have another one tomorrow," Kathleen said.

Parkhurst sipped, closed his eyes and swallowed. "What the hell do I do?"

Nobody answered. He looked at Jennifer. "Tell me what you think. What would you have done? Sorry," he added quickly, "that was an unfair question."

"I think that Mum is right," Jennifer said. "Mr. Ishihara is telling the truth as far as his desire to assimilate is concerned. I do not doubt that. As for the other one," her voice became monotone, "it is impossible to tell. He gave me the impression of being indifferent and as sociable as a wounded buffalo."

"Something like that," Parkhurst said with a wry smile. He added, "Whatever else they could be up to, we have no way of knowing."

"I also think it's a waste of time sitting here surmising," Jennifer said. "They told us what they were prepared to tell us. We have to take it from there."

Parkhurst looked fondly at her. "You are certainly not one to misunderstand."

Jennifer leaned forward and stroked his cheek. "Thank you, Uncle Igor. Remember, though, this is only my personal opinion. Don't forget that nothing is easier than to advise somebody else. On top of that," she glanced at her parents; "I could be in minority."

"You are not," Conor said. He tried to hide the pride he felt for his daughter by adjusting the strap of his watch.

"Sanctioned," Kathleen said. "Another thing," she went on, "it is probably not important, but am I the only one here who think that Mr. Ishihara had one heck of a time regaling Mr. Ishihara? The more he talked, the more I got the impression that he sees himself as superior to us. His choice of words, his mannerisms, his entire *demeanour* radiated a certain lordliness, as if we were a bunch of bumpkins he'd degraded himself to take under his wings."

Parkhurst said, "That is the Japanese way. Anybody else is inferior. The distinction between this chap and any other Japanese I know about is that Mr. Ishihara has adopted those parts of our Western culture and attitudes that suits him, and this self-styled blend makes him unique. One thing is that he's picked up our language almost to perfection and uses it in a manner which is both superbly disdainful and loftily humorous, more interesting is it that he displays no trace of inhibitions whatsoever. Now, *that* is uncommon."

"Yes," Jennifer said, "that, too."

"The British have always believed that a true sense of humour cannot and does not exists anywhere else," Conor said. "Obviously a misconception, if I read you correctly."

"It is, Conor. I mean, how on earth can we tell? How can we possibly appreciate the humour of *any* nation without being familiar with their culture and in perfect command of their language? How do we grasp irony, self-deprecation, satire and subtleties without vernacular excellence? We can't. Instead, we dismiss the whole concept, which is the British way of coping with ignorance."

Conor laughed. "Harsh words, but dispute I shall not."

There was a hushed vibration in Parkhurst's voice when he said, "*Of all vulgar modes of escaping from the consideration of the effect of social and moral influence on the human mind, the most vulgar is that of attributing the diversities of conduct and character to inherent natural differences.*"

"That's profound," Kathleen said. "When did you write that?"

Parkhurst smiled. "I wish I had. John Stuart Mill wrote it."

"Lesson learned," Jennifer said. "Let us not make the same mistake as Mr. Ishihara and his identical twin."

At nine o'clock in the evening Parkhurst called Ishihara. They agreed to meet at The Connaught Hotel at noon the following day.

Jennifer did not say much during their drive back to London. She kept seeing the contours of a man behind snowflakes whirling through the night.

7

"A very good morning to you, sir," the doorman said as Parkhurst pulled up in front of the hotel. "I haven't seen you for a while, Mr. Parkhurst. How are you?"

"I couldn't be better." Parkhurst got out of the car and handed over the keys. "I am very well indeed. Life is rather hectic, though. How are you?"

"Splendid, sir. Top form. Having lunch today, Mr. Parkhurst?"

"Yes, I am."

"I think there is a gentleman waiting for you, sir—Mr. Ishihara."

"You know him?"

"He's been here a few times. Friendly chap. Very good English. Better than mine." He laughed. "See you later, Mr. Parkhurst."

Ishihara was waiting in the lobby. He was immaculately dressed in a dark grey suit—not much of a daring colour display on this occasion, Parkhurst thought; he looks as conservative and reserved as all Japanese businessmen want us to believe that they are.

Ishihara got up, smiled and extended his hand. "How nice of you to come, Mr. Parkhurst, and, if I may add, a most wise decision."

Parkhurst looked twice. Something was amiss. Then he suddenly realized. The gold tooth was gone, replaced by enamel. He smiled back.

They went into the lounge. Ishihara pointed towards a quiet corner. Parkhurst noticed the *Reserved* sign on the table. A waiter came over.

"The usual, gentlemen?"

Parkhurst nodded. Ishihara pressed the palms of his hands together and bowed.

"You have obviously been here before," Parkhurst said.

"Someone invited me to dinner here, a few years ago. I took to the place, and I have used it regularly ever since. It is quiet and discreet. Perfect for business talks, I'd say."

"The key words," Parkhurst said. He had been a patron for decades.

The waiter arrived with two glasses of cognac.

"Best of health," Ishihara said. "Today the gods are smiling behind the clouds. Soon there will be no clouds, and the heavenly powers will embrace you. Metaphorically speaking, I wish to emphasize."

"Poetic words," Parkhurst smiled.

"I do enjoy the odd poetical moment, and nothing makes me happier than to share my words of wisdom as they spring from my eleemosynary mind."

Ishihara was stonefaced, but Parkhurst was certain that he saw a glint of humorous irony in the Japanese's dark and staring eyes.

Ishihara lit a cigar. "Let us talk shop," he said and rested his elbows on his knees. "There is a small, listed company here in UK that has become interesting. During the past few years they have invested heavily in research and development and have come up with some unique geographical information systems. The technology has been thoroughly tested and will be on the market in the near future. Nobody in the City has paid any attention to them—yet, that is. The company is in the red and has been so for the last three years, but these guys know what they are doing. They are exceptionally skilled, inventive, prudent, pragmatic and ambitious, a rare phenomenon in this country, and they are heading for an enormous international success. I won't bore you with too many details; suffice to say that the company is grossly undervalued and is now on the verge of a dramatic recovery. The profit potential is mindboggling. The directors have steadily been buying shares, a point that should not be missed. You get the picture?"

"Yes—well, no, really" Parkhurst said. "I do not know much about business; rather, I know practically nothing, but why should the shares jump overnight, so to speak, just because a company is ready to launch a new technology? I mean, I thought that these things took time."

Ishihara lifted his glass. "Cheers," he said. "A shrewd observation." He leaned closer. "However," he continued, "and this is the secret: the company is up for grabs. The owners want to cash in. Very few know this, least of all that army of cretins in the City, but a handful of very large corporations are interested in acquiring this technology, among them Siemens and General Electric. Now, the moment *that* leaks out, the shares will go through the roof. It will become an auction; in other words, an incredible opportunity for those with a pocketful of shares. Need I say more?"

Parkhurst pondered for a short while. "Not really," he said. "I take it that you are absolutely confident."

Ishihara put a pillow behind his back and crossed his legs. The aura of comity was gone. "I beg your pardon?" he said icily.

Parkhurst knew his mistake and held up both hands in an attempt to display innocence and not suspicion. "Please, Mr. Ishihara," he said disarmingly, "it was not my intention to offend you. It is just that— well, we do talk about quite a lot of money."

"That is a matter of opinion, apart from the fact that we are talking about *my* money and not yours. Also, and I do apologize for repeating myself, don't ever mistake my supremacy for arrogance."

It was no joke. Parkhurst was tempted to shake his head but resisted. Never in his life had he come across a specimen like this Oriental nonpareil. He wondered briefly if Ishihara had even the faintest conception of the existence of self-doubt. Parkhurst dismissed the notion as too farfetched.

"You do not seem to have too much confidence in the City," he said.

Ishihara touched the knot of his tie. His eyebrows got closer to his hairline. "The pedigree isn't what it used to be. Today, a lot of people make money as effortlessly as a president of a Third World country; they collect for themselves a chunk of what other people have been stupid enough to invest unprotected. The methods are as cheap and effective as an abortion with a coathanger." Ishihara's smile faded. He touched the rim of his glass with the tips of his fingers and made a circular movement. "The old school is on the way out. Today's operators are basically vultures exercising their atavistic instincts and with no desire to contribute to a better world. Whatever overall cognitive abilities they once had have been switched off. They grab what they can today, and to hell with tomorrow. This affliction has befallen you British because you are infatuated with whatever comes across the Atlantic, however sick, mindless or quixotic. From the behaviour of today's braggadocios it is clear that the world is flat and that the sun circulates our planet. All that these manipulators can do with any degree of competence is to masturbate their egos with the hand of Mammon. Then, one day, they have had their final ejaculation; their talent could not match their vanity and they are back in their natural habitat, which is the gutter. The absence of common sense, pragmatism and insight gave free access to the stratosphere. Uninhibited greed became the god of their universe, and, as some of us know, there is no more fecund soil for mistakes than a mind dominated by avarice. Summary: termination of career, windup of lifestyle and goodbye oh rapidly vanishing rainbow."

The maitre d' emerged. "Ready to order, gentlemen?"

Ishihara said, "I leave the entire composition of our meal to your expertise, Mr. Comazzi."

"Very good, gentlemen. May I suggest a bottle of your favourite Chateau Haut-Brion, Mr. Ishihara?"

"You may indeed."

"Excellent. The table is ready when you are."

"Thank you," Ishihara said. "How is your shoulder?"

"Oh, far better, thank you," the maitre d' said. "The pain is practically gone. A few more treatments now, and I shall be as good as new."

"Splendid," Ishihara said, "I am pleased. Frozen shoulder," he explained as the maitre d' disappeared. "When a selection of mixtures from the pharmaceutical industry only made things worse, I introduced him to acupuncture."

"I find that interesting," Parkhurst said, careful not to tread on Ishihara's sensitive toes.

"Interesting? No, it is not. Acupuncture could have been introduced to the Western world ages ago had it not been for the fact that your medical profession is dominated by bigheaded, dogmatic, narrow-minded, overrated and covetous quacks who have allowed themselves to become serfs of the highly manipulative pharmaceutical industry." He balanced his cigar on the ashtray. "Let me know if you need some treatment. I know the best in the business. She can cure practically everything. Do you suffer from impotence?"

Parkhurst laughed. "I haven't had much of a chance to check, lately."

"Tell me, should the moment arrive. This lady can make you as virile as a rottweiler surrounded by a dozen bitches on heat."

"I shall bear that in mind."

The conversation during lunch was all business. Ishihara talked capitalization, yield, gearing, management strategies, finance, economy and marketing. Parkhurst found it fascinating and entertaining, but a fair portion of technicalities went over his head. Ishihara had little sympathy with the British obsession for short-term profits, which he considered fundamentally detrimental and therefore imbecile. Neither did he have much time for their management style. "Where the Oriental is assertive, the English is hubristic," he said and crossed his knife and fork on the plate. "I do find that quite astonishing, since the basic principles of all mercantile activities are as evident as they are uncomplicated. One is people," he continued and made a fist, "and the other is money. In that order—not the other way round. Dealing with people is an art. It requires a talent, but like all talents it can and should be cultivated. Those without this talent are not qualified to run companies, and this category includes accountants. Who are emerging as the running class of business here in England? Accountants." He shook his head. "It is insane. When did an accountant ever have a vision? Anyway. The ability to deal with money is less important. Don't look so surprised. You, the head of the company, can acquire a certain degree of knowledge and competence, but, since you are also a wise man, you employ somebody with the necessary know-how. Your function is to make people blossom in their jobs. That is a divine gift, and so is controlling them behind a smokescreen of subtle and congenial affectations. Feigning omnicompetence is as clever as opening a repair shop for hairdryers in the Sahara."

"You make it sound easy," Parkhurst said.

"It is. Everything is easy when you know what you are doing. It is the road to qualified adequacy that is difficult. Most people give up halfway; then they wonder, later in life, why they never succeeded. Human, and therefore pathetic."

"You do not rate businessmen highly, do you?"

"On average? No, I do not, although what I said applies to any category. People in general are not in favour of executing massive frontal attacks on anything that demands specific use of the brain. Life's tiny minority attends the school of reasoning and accomplishment. The rest drift through their pitiful existence mentally tighter than a gnat's asshole." He suddenly looked bored. "You should know."

"Yes, I believe I do."

They finished their main course, and the plates were taken away.

Parkhurst lifted his glass. "Your health." He whistled through his breath. "You know your wine, Mr. Ishihara."

"Yes, I do. Most people go for the price in order to impress, as you undoubtedly are aware of. I go exclusively for a taste that can fully satisfy my refined palate." The expression in his eyes was as impersonal as clingfilm over a pair of roasted chestnuts. He put his glass down and dabbed his mouth with his napkin.

Once again Parkhurst found himself admiring the Japanese's impeccable manners. "I must say…" he began but hesitated.

"Say what? Don't be shy."

Parkhurst chortled, delighted that an alternative compliment had crossed his mind. He said, "I find your command of the English language absolutely astounding. You must have a unique ear for languages."

"It is, and I have," Ishihara said. His dark eyes moved like a pair of erratic beetles. "I have to admit, though, perfect English isn't all that terribly complicated. Blunt the consonants, steer the vowels towards your nose and keep the *h* silent when first in a word. Constantly expand your vocabulary and do not sodomize your tongue like most Brits are in the habit of doing. By following these simple guidelines you'll be assessed as *cultured—*" he drummed all ten fingers on the table "*—no dight abight it, Mr. Paark-huurst.* My next career will be in *televussion,* and it is *frightfully* important that I instantly come across as the epicure that I am."

Parkhurst stared for a few seconds before he began to laugh. "I don't know what to make of you, Mr. Ishihara."

"Which, translated, means that how come this Japanese corsair has so eminently adapted to British etiquette."

Parkhurst searched for the right words but faced a blank.

Ishihara cupped his hands around his glass. "You've got the expression of somebody staring at an empty coffin with his own nameplate on it." He raised his glass with an enigmatic smile. "Don't feel uncomfortable, Igor. You'll get used to me."

"I'd better," Parkhurst mumbled.

Ishihara put his napkin on the table. "To finalize this most engaging part of our conversation, let me underline that there is not much point in gaining experience unless one has the will to understand and the aptitude to implement."

"Confucius?"

"Ishihara. Actually," he added and glanced at Parkhurst, "it was Mr. Vargas' idea."

"I am sorry?"

"Etiquette. Before we left Japan—it seems such an eternity ago—Mr. Vargas suggested that we should buy a book teaching us the habits and the traditions and the etiquette of each particular country. That's precisely what we did, and it worked. It facilitated greatly our assimilation; that is, to the extent that such is possible for aliens."

"There must have been places where books were not available."

"That is true, to the chagrin of Mr. Vargas, who is the most ardent bibliophile I've ever encountered. Instead, we observed and asked questions and made notes." Ishihara laughed quietly. "I wonder how many hundreds of pages Mr. Vargas is sitting on, now. He never throws anything away."

"You are very close, aren't you?" Parkhurst ventured carefully.

Ishihara focused on a painting across the room. For a while it was as if his mind had entered a different world. Finally, he said, "We are brothers. One day I may tell you." He watched as the waiter poured the coffee. "Back to business," he said abruptly. "We are seeing my broker in an hour's time. I shall place an order in your name for the agreed amount, and that is all there is to it, so far. This gentleman—his name is Alan Lynch—has proved himself to be reliable. He is young, talented and shrewd enough to stay clear of the usual tokens of prestige dominating the venerable City of London. He is, as the word goes, a man with a future."

Future. Parkhurst tried hard to remember the drill he had worked out in the early hours of the morning, but this was not his game. He was a complete amateur in Ishihara's world. Ruefully, Parkhurst admitted that he had neither the experience nor the acumen to phrase what weighted so heavily on his leaden heart confusing his shaky mind. Or, rather, he confessed and felt wretchedly deficient; he had lost whatever guts he once may have had.

Ishihara said genially, "Why do I sense that your otherwise creative and complex wits are virtually paralyzed by matters of a mundane nature? You look as if you are half a step away from a low-voltage electric chair."

Parkhurst felt as if he had swallowed a beehive. Hell, he thought, I've *got* to say it. My future, my life, my *everything* depends on it.

"The point is," he pressed and spoke slowly to keep control of his voice, "the point is that even if I make a hundred on this deal—" he swallowed and suppressed a gulp "—even then I am still roughly one hundred short, I figure. Long-term, I mean, since I can't rely on any future income from writing."

That was it. He had said it. Only the worst part remained. He ransacked his brain for the words that had come so eloquently during breakfast. "I mean—there are two of you." Good Lord, he thought, what a dilettante I am. I had it all worked out, and what do I do? I make the biggest splash in the history of high finance. No, I didn't splash; I blew myself straight out of the water.

Ishihara stroked the sides of his head with both hands, as if to array a hair-do that the wind had disturbed. He said with a faint smile, "Quite. There are two of us. That is an indisputable reality and an admirable end product of your clearly fatiguing mental exercise. You have expressed yourself with pellucid logic, Igor. You have stated beyond misinterpretation that you feel entitled to ask for one ticket for my good self, and one ticket for Mr. Vargas. There is no way I can object to this most lucid and patently intelligent conclusion, neither morally nor in any other way I can possibly think of."

Parkhurst stared at the Japanese. There was no mockery in Ishihara's voice, who went on, "As it happens, I have another company up my sleeve. The opportunity will surface in a couple of months' time. This is exceedingly fortunate, Igor, but then I am a lucky man—I would have found it shatteringly heartbreaking and eternally depressing if you had walked away."

Parkhurst shook his head as if to register that his ears were still in place. "You agree?"

Ishihara frowned. "Do I have a choice?"

I am dreaming, Parkhurst thought. "I appreciate—I am glad that we understand each other." he said.

"Don't we just," Ishihara nodded. There was still no apparent irony in his voice.

Parkhurst was elated with the outcome of his own clumsiness. He said, "Come to think of it, would it not be more correct and proper if the money went through my account and I purchased the shares in my own name?"

Ishihara nodded again. He said gravely, "There is no denying the sapience of such appropriate and ethically befitting strategy, except..." He paused and looked pensive.

"Except what?"

Ishihara shrugged. The deep line on his forehead did not correlate with the expression in his eyes. "That way, what will you tell your bank manager and what do you think his reaction would be?"

Parkhurst looked away. His glass was empty, and so was the bottle. He wet his lips behind his napkin. "Sorry," he said tersely. "Forget it."

"I already have. By the way, what do you think of my theory that the inherent pomposity of you Brits only mirrors immaturity that became hermetic after being raped by ignorance?"

Parkhurst wanted a cognac, and painfully so. He said, "I know we have our inadequacies, but are we really that bad?"

"Did I say *bad*? I did not. On the contrary; there is something endearing about your characteristic of benighted hypocrisy, distinctly preferable to repugnant bigotry. You are, in your own way, as unique as is a broadminded American. No wonder I prefer this country to anywhere else on this planet."

"Including Japan?"

"Japan is a strait jacket." Ishihara finished his drink. "We have to go." He signalled for the bill, signed and shook hands with the maitre d'. Parkhurst could not see the nomination of the folded note which the maitre d' put in his pocket; it was the movement of a magician, but he was certain it wasn't a fiver.

"We share the same philosophy," he said as they walked through the lobby. "Look after people and they look after you."

"Wisdom of Oriental proportions," Ishihara said.

Parkhurst smiled. "No less. Thank you for an excellent lunch. My pleasure, next time."

"Rewards await the trustworthy," Ishihara said.

The meeting with the broker was brief. Parkhurst took an instant liking to the young Alan Lynch. He was well mannered, respectful without being sycophantic, and obviously thoroughly schooled. Lynch reckoned that they had ten to fifteen days to buy Parkhurst's shares sensibly spread within that time limit. He gathered from the conversation that Ishihara was already sitting on a sizeable lot. Lynch mentioned that the share had gone up another two points during the morning; nothing alarming. Ishihara knew but didn't tell how.

Lynch clearly enjoyed talking to Ishihara; it was evident that he was a valued client. Most of the jargon was too technical for Parkhurst.

Wherever this will lead to I can't tell, Parkhurst summed up to himself, but it surely is an interesting world.

They stood on the pavement. "I'll take a cab back to the hotel," Parkhurst said. "Hopefully I can get out of London before the rush hour starts."

"I'll come with you," Ishihara said. "Somebody is waiting for me. I would like to introduce you."

Nothing was being said during the twenty-minute drive. Ishihara looked out the window, and Parkhurst let his mind wander into the brightness of his future. He would not have minded the odd comment about the events of the day, but he found Ishihara's silence forbidding and a touch eerie.

They arrived, and Ishihara paid. "After you, Igor."

Parkhurst went through the revolving doors and saw an Oriental woman of exquisite beauty. She sat in the same chair that Ishihara had occupied earlier in the day. Ishihara passed him, went over to the woman and kissed her on the cheek. "My empress!" he said, "I hope we haven't kept you waiting."

"Five minutes," she said and got up.

"This is Igor Parkhurst," Ishihara introduced. "Igor, meet my wife."

Parkhurst did his best to get the blatant stare out of his eyes. He had seen Oriental pulchritude before, but nothing in the class of Mrs. Ishihara. She was almost as tall as her husband, slender, with jet-black hair parted in the middle, surprisingly large almond eyes, and the most delicate chiselled features Parkhurst could recall having seen on any woman. Her skin had the soft off-white colour of moonbeams through a bubblebath, and her visage expressed curiosity dipped in alacrity. She wore her expensive clothes with a natural and casual elegance. Her few pieces of jewellery were a mugger's dream.

"Seen enough?" she said and displayed a perfect set of snow-white teeth.

"I—I am terribly sorry," Parkhurst stammered. "I did not mean to stare. Please call me Igor." He knew that his face had taken the colour of raw trout meat.

"Lucrezia Borgia of the Orient," she said and extended her hand.

"I beg your pardon?"

"Ignore her," Ishihara said. "My darling wife has got a twisted and decadent sense of humour. Her name is Yasmin. That is, it isn't, but it has been so for quite a few years."

"I see," Parkhurst said. He was still recovering from the first impact.

"Good Lord, isn't my husband explicit. By the way, Igor, please do not frown at my fondness for arch-English expressions should such occur during our conversation." She touched Parkhurst's arm with a light pat. "Your language is *so* hyperbolic, and I love it. The quaintness of your parlance is simply irresistible." She turned. "Come along, boys. I'm aching for a glass of champagne."

The lounge was half empty and the corner available. The maitre d' appeared from the restaurant and accelerated when he saw the company. "Madame," he beamed, "what a pleasure. May I organize a glass of champagne?"

"You read my mind with *awful* accuracy," Yasmin said. Her lips went oval. "I am not pleased with you. How come you missed your last appointment?"

The maitre d' shifted on his feet. "I had to take my dog to the vet. I did leave a…"

"I admire your sense of priority," Yasmin interrupted.

He said, "I'll be there on Friday."

"You'd better be."

"You do acupuncture?" Parkhurst asked.

"Yes, one of several enterprises."

Ishihara said, "The best there is, and the most expensive."

Yasmin's shoulders went up an inch. "Darling, you do not get a Bentley for the price of a bike. Do you know much about acupuncture, Igor?"

"I'm afraid not."

She gave him a radiant smile. "It is not complicated. My ancient and venerated forefathers formed the hypothesis that energy circulates in the body via meridians. Based on the idea of Yin and Yen is the amalgam of opposites. The balance between Yin and Yen is forever fluctuating, and if a body is out of balance, energetically, then acupuncture will re-establish this balance. The whole system is predicated on empirical laws from countless observations of ailments and their response to this treatment." She was sitting opposite him. Parkhurst was entranced. Her exotic beauty and the fragrance from her body made him oblivious to time, place and Ishihara's cryptic little smile. Yasmin continued, "The conclusion is that if you are not in balance, and the energy or life-force cannot circulate freely around the meridians, the result is an illness of some description or another. That's where I come in. What looks like pure magic is simply a method originating from knowledge and understanding of mind and body." She paused and sipped her champagne. "I take it that you have found my brief presentation sufficiently informative, Igor?"

"Yes, thank you. I'd say, that sounds very interesting." He looked at Ishihara and wondered about his inscrutable little smile. Pride? Yes, of course. Who wouldn't be proud of a woman like Yasmin? Parkhurst steered his glance towards Yasmin and said, "I have long been of the opinion that the Western world have quite a few things to learn from China."

Yasmin looked at the tip of her black Sobranie cigarette. She flicked it towards the ashtray. She stared at the ceiling. "Excuse me?"

How on earth can I have offended her, Parkhurst thought, alarm bells ringing. He looked to Ishihara for help. From the expression on his face Parkhurst knew that no assistance could be expected. He said, "I just commented…"

"I heard your comment," Yasmin cut in. "What baffles me is your monstrous ignorance. My dear husband led me to believe that you were an educated, well-informed and enlightened man. He evidently talked through a hole in his head."

Parkhurst had no idea where he had gone wrong. He wanted to apologize but did not know for what. His mouth was dry and his eyes were itching. I'll have to wait this one out, he thought; maybe she'll lower herself to offer an explanation.

"Mr. Parkhurst," she said with a drawl that made him quiver, "I am Korean. I am from the Land of the Morning Calm, a country that had a highly developed culture millenniums before the Chinese and the Japanese were up on their hindlegs."

"I do apologize," Parkhurst mumbled, "I…"

"Enough said," Yasmin chimed in. "I have come to acknowledge that my little Nipponese here was right when he warned me about the staggering extent of ignorance dominating the inhabitants of this island. Why is it that the educational system in your country does not allow room for even the tiniest piece of information about other civilizations and cultures? How come that you British can fumble your way through life without comprehending that Dover is neither the beginning nor the end of our universe? Nothing personal, Igor, since you can't help being a victim of your country's puny imitation of a culture."

Then the tightness around her mouth was gone and her eyes were no longer hard and black like two pieces of basalt left overnight in an icebucket.

Parkhurst laughed. He'd always had a soft spot for women whose personality and wits matched their looks and whose ability to play on their emotions stretched from stoicism to extremity. This one, he thought, has the added irresistible fascination of an orchid mirrored on frosted glass.

Yasmin's voice was soft and melodious. The expression in her eyes changed at will, and a will there was. As opposed to her husband, she had a distinct accent, which Parkhurst found utterly charming.

She's right, though, he mused; he did not possess a comprehensive knowledge about Oriental cultures. What he did know, however, was that Koreans were considered second-class citizens in Japan. He wondered why a sophisticated, proud and ultimately very Japanese man like Ishihara had chosen a Korean woman, even if she was, like this one, of an exceptional calibre. However independent and non-conformist Ishihara was, there had to be more to it than a sod-you-all attitude. Love, of course, was a possibility, but why had he not turned around when he discovered which way it was going? Could it be that Ishihara had managed to uproot himself to the extent of total emancipation, that he had gone through a process that had left him immune to pressure from traditions and dogmatism? If that was the case—Parkhurst looked at Ishihara with renewed respect—then the Japanese was indeed as rare as a mammoth alive and kicking.

Yasmin interrupted his line of thought, "You see, Igor, once upon a time the Chinese began to form their culture based on what they learned from us, and, in turn, the Japanese pinched whatever they fancied from the Chinese. That is thousands of years of history in a nutshell. The Chinese and the Japanese vehemently deny this, as is to be expected, but that does not alter the truth of the matter. Isn't this so, my Samurai?" She cast a sidelong glance at Ishihara and continued, "One day he may tell you why he no longer lives in Japan, and why he has no intention of going back. Not that I blame him, poor little bugger."

Ishihara emptied his drink and put the glass back on the table. "What did I do to deserve you?"

"Heavens know, but here we are. Which reminds me," she added, "we ought to be somewhere else, soon."

Parkhurst got the message. "Thank you for your hospitality and for an interesting and eventful day," he said and stood up. "I hope to see you both in the near future." He smiled at Yasmin Ishihara and wished that he had been up on his hindlegs a few thousand years ago. "It has been a great pleasure. Perhaps you would like to come down to my place in the country one day?"

She smiled. "That would be nice."

She stepped aside.

Ishihara said, "I'll be in touch."

A brief handshake, and they left.

Parkhurst gave it a few minutes before he joined the traffic.

Ishihara and his wife walked from The Connaught to their home in Belgrave Square.

Ishihara undressed, put on a black silk kimono and sat down in his favourite chair. He faced the skyline and closed his eyes. His hands rested on his thighs. He breathed rhythmically.

Yasmin came in. She sat in the Lotus position and looked up at her husband. She said, "You once promised that this is going to be your last assignment. Is that still true, Tadashi?"

"Yes."

"Is there no way you can get out of it?"

Ishihara opened and closed his fists and studied the muscles on his hairless forearms. "I can but I won't. I have been planning this one for years, Yasmin. I am not going to drop it. Nothing we have ever done in the past can compare with the magnitude of our final masterpiece." His eyes drifted towards his aquarium. "The achievement is one thing, perhaps not all that terribly important, seen isolated, but the reward will secure our future even if we live till we are one hundred and fifty years of age." He got up, found a bottle of beer in the fridge and did not bother with a glass. He went on, "It's only a few years away, Yasmin, and we can retire. Nothing in between, and nothing thereafter. I guarantee you."

"Do you? How do you know you won't be asked again?"

"Of course we'll be asked, but the answer is no."

Her eyes saddened. "Governments taking no for an answer? Wishful thinking, Tadashi."

He put the beer bottle on the table. "Anyone stupid enough to put pressure on us will learn the meaning of the word *backfire*. There isn't

134

one single clean politician anywhere in the world; they are all vulnerable, and they are all mortals." He shrugged. "They'll find someone else. Everybody retires, sooner or later, and there will always be young men keen on taking over from us." He picked up the bottle but did not drink. "The law of nature, Yasmin. Don't worry about it. We can be replaced. We'll soon be forgotten."

She did not look at him. "Men with your incomparable skills are neither easily replaced nor quickly forgotten."

Ishihara rested his elbows on his knees. His fingers supported his forehead like slanting miniature pillars. "We are moving in circles."

The late afternoon sun caught her hair. She got up and rocked on her heels. Ishihara could smell the heat on her skin and looked away.

"It seems that the Moran family have a certain influence on Mr. Parkhurst," she said.

"They are well-meaning, idealistic and harmless, what you'd call nice, sterling characters. Igor Parkhurst and Conor Moran have been friends for a decade, but they live in different worlds. My research told me that Parkhurst assisted Moran when he came over from Ireland with a lot of money and no experience."

"Why doesn't Moran pay off Parkhurst's debts?"

"Parkhurst wouldn't accept it. They both know that he would never be able to pay it back. Honour, and so forth. Apart from that, long-term it would not solve a thing."

"How did you find the daughter?"

"A piece of explosive wrapped in marzipan."

"That should appeal to Angelo."

"I don't think he even looked at her. He was bored, and when he is bored he is, as we know, so laid-back that he'd make a koala bear seem hyperactive."

"Can I come with you?"

He turned and looked at her. "Come with me where?"

"Down to Mr. Parkhurst's place. I'd love to see it."

"Of course you can. We'll go as soon as I have completed my initial business matters with him."

"He is a sweet old thing," Yasmin said, "a real gentleman. He's got class."

"Yes, he has. It pleases me that he has not once referred to himself as *honest*, followed by *deeply honest*, when we talk about money." He looked into her eyes. "Integrity, truthfulness, decency—people who have got it do not wear the labels on their sleeves. Parkhurst is an honourable man who knows that wherever you move, the shadows of your past move with you. He is also aware that the only way to eradicate shadows is to switch off the lights."

Yasmin's eyes took in Ishihara's entire physique. "Can we talk about something else, Tadashi?"

Ishihara did not seem to hear. He stared into space with a thoughtful expression on his face. "Parkhurst is one of the few I have met who understands the difference between what money can do for people, and what people allow the lure of money to do *to* them. We'll get him back on his feet, Yasmin. We shall have a Parkhurst who no longer crawls around in the suburbs of reality. He'll do us a lot of good."

"Only to be destroyed."

"That is beyond our control." He drained the rest of his beer. "Careful, now. Do not get too westernized."

"How do you mean?"

"Business and dewy-eyed sentiments do not go hand in hand in our world. Westerns are cheats, hypocrites and phoneys—we follow the invisible straight line. What our adversaries do not discover is their own problem."

"Why did you tell him that he may be contacted?"

"Because he is no fool. When it happens he will remember, and pay it little attention. He's got only a vague perception of how his masters operate; they have used him as an errand boy. He does not know what happens to *links* in major schemes. A blessing in disguise, as it is. Include that he will never learn what the plot is about."

Yasmin walked towards the bathroom. "I shall be glad when all this is over."

8

James Douglas Wilkinson had done well for himself since he left university and entered the real world. He was exceptionally well educated; accountancy and law. He had followed his father's maxim that it was better to stand on two legs instead of one. He got his reward when he was instantly snapped up by one of the City's most prominent finance houses.

James was capable of implementing what he had learned. He had a talent for saying the right things at the right time to the right people. His superiors took notice; James became a rising star, liked and respected. He ascended through the echelons faster than any of his contemporaries.

His flat off Wellington Road was spacious and within walking distance from St. John's Wood tube station. He had managed to secure a garage for his second-hand but emotionally invaluable Aston-Martin.

James was six feet tall and slim. He had short, dark hair and brown eyes. He was good-looking, and his smile was friendly or boyish, depending on whom he talked to. He was always immaculately groomed, and people in general took an instant liking to him. Notable exceptions were those of his colleagues who could not cope with his success, but James evaded them skilfully and with considerable tact, which, he believed, was always a strategy preferable to confrontation.

James had known Jennifer for three years. He had known for the same period of time that she was made for him. He was deeply in love with her, but he was shrewd enough not to allow his crush to overshadow respect and devotion.

He agreed with her that mutual respect was a vital ingredient in any relationship, be it friendship or marriage, and that sheer romance was no substitute for profound unity. James acknowledged that he had problems grasping the implications of Jennifer's stance in context with flat sharing, but, as his father had said so often, women were different. James had less of a problem concurring with his father's empirical observation.

James never doubted that Jennifer would marry him, although, when he had asked her earlier in the year, she had looked him in the eye and said that she would let him know when she was ready for such a commitment. He had known her long enough to learn that Jennifer was a strong-willed woman, and that there was a vibrant streak of independence in her that should not be underestimated. It was, he quietly confessed to himself, as if those green eyes were telling him: try to push me, and you push me out of your life.

Back from Germany the night before, he had called her. She laughed when he described the conference as tedious, pompous and probably completely unproductive. He listened when she mentioned her weekend together with her parents at Uncle Igor's place. It had been a good but uneventful break for all three of them. And for Uncle Igor, of course; he was a bit bored, these days. She thought he felt isolated, so maybe the two of them could visit him come next Bank Holiday. James went on to explain why he had been detained in Germany during the Monday, but he cut himself short when he sensed that the topic wasn't overly fascinating.

James loved to hear Jennifer laugh, but somewhere in the depths of his soul he knew that if he had any shortcomings, a well-developed sense of humour was one of them. He did not believe that he was completely void of this heavenly gift; he simply wasn't cut out to match the complexity of the wit and the humour of the Moran family. He thought it a rather tiny flaw, if a flaw at all; there were moments when he found Jennifer's weakness for black and cynical humour a shade disturbing—which was more of a flaw, quite frankly. But, weighing it all up, even if there were traits about her that he did not fully understand, who was to say that two people had to be identical to live happily together?

They agreed to go out to dinner the coming Thursday.

Every morning James followed the same route; the underground from

St. John's Wood to Liverpool Street, and then a brisk walk to the offices in Bishopsgate.

He liked the hustle and the bustle of the trains.

James' latest hobbyhorse was the government's passion for ever-increasing legislation, a vicious circle that would eventually make the entire population unwitting criminals. Getting rid of the spineless megalomaniac Anthony Eden last year was an unqualified blessing, but his successor Harold Macmillan was too left-wing and therefore a potential danger to democracy. It was a good sign for the nation, James concluded, that even persons of inferior intelligence and limited education agreed with him on this point.

One evening James worked till ten o'clock. A few of his colleagues were still there when he left; a lot of things had happened lately in the complex universe of sky-high finance.

He walked down Bishopsgate with his briefcase firmly clasped in his hand. The night was dark and few people were around. He had the pavement to himself. He stepped over a squashed sandwich and thought about life. One day Jennifer would come to her senses and they could get married and organize their lives in an orderly and proper fashion.

James left the pavement and stopped at the top of the stairs. He looked forward to getting home and relax with a gin and tonic. It would be too late to call Jennifer. He walked down to the almost empty platform.

The train was due in eight' minutes time. A man looking like a tramp leaned against the wall. He wore baggy trousers and army boots. The hood of his anorak shadowed his face. He held his head down and his hands were pressed against his stomach.

James walked towards him. "Is something wrong?" he asked.

The man mumbled a few words.

James got closer. "I didn't hear," he said.

The ground under his feet disappeared. His eyes disconnected with his brain. He was inside the archway with his face towards the wall and his right arm twisted behind his back.

James didn't move a muscle. He swallowed when his bladder refused to obey his brain.

He heard the crack a split second before he experienced the excruciating pain from his broken arm. Then something happened to his right ankle. James collapsed and fainted on the way down.

He woke up at Bart's Hospital. A figure in white appeared dimly, swaying from side to side at the foot of the bed. James heard a voice but could not understand the words. Gradually, he became aware of the plaster on his right arm. There was something wrong with his right leg. His head was swimming, but he registered no pain. His eyes were telling him that there were now several diffuse figures in white, at least he hoped so, since he saw different movements. Again he heard voices. The words *waking up* penetrated his mind. He laid still. Little by little he managed to focus on the person directly in front of him.

He groaned. "What happened?"

The figure, now more distinct, moved and came to the bedside. "I am Doctor McPherson. It appears that you were attacked last night."

James' mind began to clear. He stayed silent.

After a while he asked, "Am I badly injured?"

"It's all relative. You've got a broken ankle and a broken elbow. Anyway, with a bit of luck you'll be as good as new, eventually. That is, till rheumatism sets in, but don't let that worry you. It's years away."

James let out a grunt.

☞

Jennifer stopped for a moment when she came back into the lobby. She sensed an almost irresistible urge to light a cigarette. She felt exhausted, depressed and strangely confused. James had been such a pitiable sight, all wrapped up. His voice had been flat and there was hardly any life in his eyes.

She knew that she had left earlier than she should have. She regretted having sought refuge in clichés like *you-need-to-rest-now* and *I'll-be-back*. The hospital smells and people in wheelchairs and platoons of sad-looking relatives did nothing to enhance her frame of mind.

Whatever, she thought. Just get out of here, for a start.

She came into the yard and gazed at Bart's cold, dirt-grey stonewalls. A number of cars were parked. The trees looked as if they longed for a friendlier environment. The large fountain in the middle did not function. There were four identical resting-places with wooden benches. The design made her wonder if the architect had been influenced by pagodas whilst drawing a bus-shed.

Jennifer walked across the yard. She glanced at the sterile façade of the Paris Church to her right. She stopped for a moment and let her eyes wander over the names of those exterminated for king and country in the 1914-1918 war.

She walked through the gates. The wind played with her hair and carried the smell of exhaust and other intangibles marking progress on earth.

She heard a voice behind her, "Good morning."

Jennifer turned around. "Good morning, Mr. Vargas." Her lips did a four-seconds foxtrot. "Nothing wrong, I hope?"

"No."

"Annual check-up?"

"No."

"Just visiting, then?"

"Yes. And you?"

"Just visiting."

"I could do with a drink," he said. "Will you join me?"

Sweet Jesus, she thought, he can actually string together a whole sentence. The next surprise will be a change of expression in his eyes. She said, "Here?"

"Bad fluid. There is a nice little pub down the road."

Bad fluid. Jennifer wanted to smile, but she kept her composure. Some people were funny without being aware of it. "All right. Let's go for some good fluid down the road."

They walked down Giltspur Street a few feet apart, Vargas on the outside. Jennifer commented on the unpredictability of the London traffic. Vargas agreed. This is going to be fun, she thought; he is so soft-spoken that I miss half of what little he is saying.

He held her chair. "Just regular coffee, please," she said.

"Did you know that the first coffee house in England was opened in 1652?" Vargas asked. "They called them *penny universities* because the price was one penny per cup. Isn't that interesting?"

Jennifer nodded. "You really are a source of useless information."

Vargas went over to the bar.

Jennifer reached for her handbag and found that she had left her cigarettes behind.

"Have one of mine," Vargas said and put the cups on the table.

"How did you know I was looking for my cigarettes?"

"I am clairvoyant." He nodded in the direction of the hospital. "How did you know it was me before you turned around?"

"I did not."

"Is that true?"

Jennifer lowered her eyes. "I don't know."

Vargas said, "Compare your immortal soul with a deep and rugged canyon. Somewhere in the shadows a little voice struggled to be heard a few minutes ago. It succeeded. Some call it female intuition."

"You know a lot about women, Mr. Vargas?"

"I read a bit."

"Well read and suave. Did you go to a finishing school?"

The left-hand corner of Vargas' mouth moved an eight of an inch. Oh dear, Jennifer thought, he can smile, too. Even his eyes are smiling, kind of. Or maybe it is the light.

"The best," he said.

"I am pleased for you. Which one?"

"The well-known, world-wide University of Autodidacticism."

"But—oh, I see. You taught yourself. That is very admirable."

"Sheer necessity," he said. "Being a gringo in Mexico and a gaijin in Japan can be modestly entertaining. Being an ignorant alien when it comes to manners and etiquette makes it even less funny. So, I learned."

He stared at his cigarette. She noticed that he did not inhale. He took care blowing the smoke away from her.

He saw the puzzled look in her eyes. "Gaijin means foreigner. It also means inferior. The Japanese language is amazingly versatile, so vague in its structure that one can be extremely polite and equally insulting simultaneously. That can be useful, in between."

Jennifer smiled and stirred her coffee. His voice was husky and with a light rasp to it. He spoke slowly and with the clarity and deliberation of someone determined to master a foreign language, but with a tendency to cut his lines. It was different from Ishihara's; inflected, less flowery and with no attempt to camouflage or extirpate a natural accent. Some of the words he used amused her; he clearly consulted dictionaries and other sources of linguistic knowledge. At times he would pick an archaic phrase or expression.

"How did you go about tackling the English etiquette, Mr. Vargas?"

"I went into Hatchards and asked is there was a book available dealing with such a subject. The woman serving me said yes and it was a popular gift. I said it was a gift to myself. At first, she did not believe me. Then she began to laugh. When she finished she said I was the only person ever to admit buying it for myself. I thought it was a joke that I didn't understand. In retrospect, I have realized to what extent is was *not* a joke."

Jennifer extinguished her cigarette. "That's the English for you."

"So I discovered." He rested his hands on the table. They were neither too small nor too large. No manicurist had ever been near them. Jennifer eyed Vargas' hands with a mixture of curiosity and apprehension. There's a lot of strength in those hands, she thought. She suddenly felt a weird desire to touch them. The palms of her own hands went clammy. She said abruptly, "You spent some time in the Far East?"

"Yes."

"And before that?"

"Various places."

"And thereafter?"

"Same."

Jennifer gave him an easy smile. She was pleased with herself for keeping her annoyance under control. She said, "You are incredibly informative. Tell me, Mr. Vargas, are you half Irish and half Apache or are you a Japanese of Mexican origin, or, for that matter, a quarter of each?"

"I am not of an inquisitive disposition."

"That was not my question."

"It was the answer."

Jennifer looked at the elaborately cut mirrors across from the bar and from there to the maroon ceiling. "Are you trying to tell me, in your own tactful and delicate manner, to mind my own business?"

"Probing is impudent. It is a national disease and you should do something about it."

"I am not British, Mr. Vargas, but let that be as it is. I do, however, take your point. You are a secretive and exceptionally private person. That is of course your prerogative."

"Say again?"

"Excuse me?"

"Prerogative."

"Oh, it means an exclusive right, a privilege."

"Thank you." He took a pen and a small notebook from the breast pocket of his jacket and filled in the word. Jennifer saw that there wasn't much empty space. He said, "Coffee earned."

Jennifer turned and looked out the window to hide her smile. The rain hit the glass like pearls on marble. She said, "A question hopefully not too personal, Mr. Vargas, but what do you do for a living?"

"I am a fruiterer."

"A *what?*" She laughed more with relief than at his not-so-perfect pronunciation.

"I have fruit shops," Vargas explained patiently.

"Plural. A chain, in other words?"

He nodded solemnly. "I am getting close. Four, so far."

"That is not bad at all. Where are they?"

"Scattered around." He moved his index finger across his teeth. "The nearest is in Mayfair. It is not only fruit, by the way. I also sell olive oils, a few specialities like Polish sausages, and various goodies from the Middle East. Ahmed, the manager, calls the shop a delicatessen."

"Dear oh dear," Jennifer smiled. "You must be a very busy man."

"No, I am not. I have got managers; two Palestinians, one Portuguese and one Irishman. I visit them once a month, all in one day. Mr. Ishihara helps me with the books."

Jennifer thought of the money that Mr. Ishihara had offered to her godfather. "I understand. You and your friend Mr. Ishihara have made it in olive oil and potatoes."

Vargas folded his hands. There was a tiny pause between each word when he said, "To the best of my recollection, nobody has had a closer affinity with the potato than the Irish. I appreciate your respect and understanding, Miss Moran. Faithful to your history, you do not deride the value of the spud."

Jennifer covered her mouth with her hand. She had walked straight into that one. For a second she thought about James' attitude and demeanour—kind, gentle and eager to spoil her.

Vargas had leaned back. His eyes had the same inscrutable expression as when they first met. It irritated her that she could not read him

"You are evidently an avid student of history," she said tersely.

"I do scan through the odd volume."

Jennifer's exasperation grew. He is playing with me, she thought. He doesn't take me seriously. A voice in the back of her mind warned her that Vargas was challenging her—take it up and she'd play straight into his hand.

The voice died away.

"Is there anything particularly amusing about me, Mr. Vargas?"

"Anyone who isn't amusing is boring."

What a clever little twist. She hesitated. "Am I right in assuming that you are sitting there summing me up?"

"Yes."

Jennifer took a sharp breath. "Yes," she repeated, perplexed.

"It's a hobby of mine," Vargas explained with the patience of a cobra waiting for its prey to come closer. "I imagine myself as a lapidarist looking at a stone."

"A stone?"

"A diamond. The four Cs—carat, clarity, colour and cut. Interesting, and useful as a comparison."

"Indeed, captivating and intriguing," she said. She hoped that her dash of contempt did not escape his foreign ears.

"Please, Miss Moran, you must not be derogatory. As you know, or maybe you don't, but most people can be written off as a no-good piece of carbon."

How does he manage, Jennifer wondered; how can anyone make a misanthropic and depreciative remark like that and have innocence written all over his face?

"You are ostensibly not a lover of mankind," she said acidly.

Vargas' tongue showed between his teeth. "I have my reservations."

She said, "By the way, my name is Jennifer."

"I know."

She waited. Vargas remained silent. Christ, she thought, this stranger really is an outsider. "Would you happen to have a first name, Mr. Vargas?"

"Angelo."

Jennifer touched her lips with her fingertips, but the giggle slipped through. "Sorry," she said. "That was very rude of me. It's just that—" she laughed "—somehow I do not think there is much that is angelic about you."

"I find that shocking," Vargas said.

"Yes, I am sure you do—Angelo. It is a nice name, though. Apache, I presume, since it is definitely not Irish."

A blowfly caught his attention.

Ah, she thought, all in your own time, Angelo Vargas. Whenever it suits you, *if* it suits you. Oh dear, why am I sitting here thinking as if I shall ever see him again?

Vargas sipped his drink. "Been to Ireland, lately?" he asked and put the glass down.

"Yes. I went over a few months ago to see my grandparents. They used to come over here, once or twice a year, but they are getting old and fragile, now. So…" she drifted off.

"You are fond of them."

"Yes, I am. They are lovely people. It is a difficult situation for my parents, too. I know they would prefer to go back for good, but I do not think they will."

"I presume they have their reason."

"Oh, they do. It is such a strange country. So interesting, so beautiful—and then all this hatred, the violence, the clinging to the past. I do not understand it."

Vargas said, "Men are less rational, broadly speaking."

Jennifer sought his eyes. "Funny you should say that. It's like hearing my father, word for word."

"A wise man." There was no trace of disparagement in his voice, nor in his eyes.

Jennifer smiled. "Two wise men. How lucky can I get?" She instantly recognized the implications of her words and added quickly, "I admire your natural modesty, Mr. Vargas."

"What happened to Angelo?"

What was it about this man that made him so forbidding, so distant and yet so close? He is just reserved, she thought; he is a loner who takes time to open up.

He went on, "Pure self-assessment. Modesty is an artificial luxury, and, as such, utterly wasted on people with a sense of proportions and a distinct appreciation of unorthodox humour. Don't put your candle under a barrel, as the prophet shrewdly observed. He must have come to the conclusion that nobody could see it." Vargas opened another pack of cigarettes. "You remember Diogenes? The one who lived in a tub and walked the streets of Athens in full daylight with a lantern, looking for an honest man? No wonder his only close friend was a dog." He flicked his lighter. The smoke seeped from the corner of his mouth. "Do you like Toulouse-Lautrec's paintings?" Before Jennifer could answer, he continued, "I do. I find them enchanting, in a haunting kind of way. Irrelevant, in this context; the point is that this little self-styled bohemian had a very astute mind. He once wrote in a letter to a friend:

"This world is so full of answers. When shall we start looking for the questions?" Not a wholly original piece of philosophy, in itself; only praiseworthy if one tries to lead a life implementing it. Close your mouth."

Jennifer jerked her head back. Her neck had turned crimson and her green eyes gleamed with anger. "Do you take pride in being excessively rude?"

"It was merely a piece of advice. Ladies should not gape."

"Your lengthy speech took me by surprise, Mr. Vargas, and it showed momentarily on my face. Please do not overlook that when we first met, you very distinctly gave the impression of being a mute, illiterate, uncivil and ignorant savage from nowhere."

"You arrived at all that without my saying one single syllable? What a brain."

Jennifer pushed aside a lock from her forehead. *When we first met.* It was the second time the implications of those words had gone through her mind. She regretted what she had said, but she knew that Vargas would find an apology hollow. "I was flabbergasted," she said. "You baffled me. That is a compliment, if anything."

She saw the white of his teeth as a thin line between his lips. "Oh well, I guess I have my moments."

I am going to change the subject, she thought, let me find something neutral.

A grossly overweight woman sitting on a stool at the next table peered towards Vargas. She was dressed in a mauve outfit and wore a black woollen jacket of the style popular with dustmen. Suddenly she moved her bulk forward, glared at Vargas and said in a loud voice, "Blow your smoke away from me, please."

Vargas stared at the glow of his cigarette. He looked mindful. He turned towards the woman. "It bothers you?" he asked with a gentleness that made Jennifer moist her lips.

"Yes, it does."

"Something bothers me," Vargas said.

"Oh?" the woman said, "what's that?" Her tiny eyes nearly disappeared between layers of fat.

"The image of you undressed."

Her face went purple. She opened her mouth. Her tongue moved like a startled guppy, but she was too flustered to manage a riposte. Her male companion was half her size and looked as if he'd been splashed with iodine. The permanent grin on his wrinkled face made him look like a head-hunter's trophy. He put his hand on her shaking forearm and whispered a few words Jennifer could not hear. A minute later they got up, paid for their drinks and left.

Vargas' stare followed them until the door closed. Jennifer thought that the colour of his eyes had gone a deeper blue. No, she thought, that is impossible. It's just an expression revealing indifference.

"Maybe she's got an allergy," Jennifer said.

"She's a moralist and the moralist cannot survive emotionally without interfering and somebody is seen to suffer. The human element. Deplorable."

Jennifer said, "Does it entertain you to be provocative?"

"In between. By the way, I've got a handful of allergies myself," Vargas said. "People is one of them."

Jennifer's thumb slid up and down the stem of her glass. "Are you saying that you are socially inept?"

"Perfectly summed up."

She thought of his behaviour at Igor Parkhurst's place. "Why are we sitting here, Mr. Vargas?"

He removed a speck of ash that had fallen onto the rim of his glass. "I am at ease with you."

He said it offhandedly, but for an instant Jennifer's eyes flittered. "You are very direct."

"I am."

"We do not know each other."

He rested his back towards the curve of the chair. "Not yet."

I have to talk about something else, Jennifer thought. This is getting seriously personal.

"Are you going back to the hospital tonight?" she asked.

"No."

Jennifer told him about James and his horrible ordeal; strange, though, since the attacker had neither taken anything nor said a single word. James was a friend, she explained, casually, as if one of many.

She described her interior design business. She talked about her harmonious childhood, and she explained why she was still living in her parents' house. She had her own little apartment, and as much privacy as she wanted or could have had anywhere else. She described her father's work and his idealism, and she laughed when she touched upon her mother's wit and sharp sense of humour. Her father was a living saint, she was sure of that, but she was worried that he might wear himself out and not retire before he got too old and things got on top of him.

Vargas' eyes never left Jennifer's face; in between he nodded, once or twice he shook his head, but he stayed silent.

Lightning struck. "Jesus!" Jennifer gasped and looked at her watch. "Do you know what time it is? We have been sitting here for over two hours!"

"Imagine that."

"I have to go," she said.

"I understand," he said. "Even peripheral friends should be shown due attention."

Jennifer averted her gaze. Was that a shot in the dark, or what? she thought.

He followed her to the door and hailed a taxi.

She gave her address. The cabbie nodded, closed the window and drove off.

"Oh dear," she groaned silently, "what have I done? How could I sit there and tell the story of my life to a complete stranger? How stupid and silly—how could I let it happen?"

She thought for a while. It had happened because Angelo Vargas was a highly qualified listener. He had made her talk. In the most subtle and cunning manner had he tricked her into placing her soul on the table right in front of him. Very, very clever. Well, it would not happen again. She'd probably seen him for the last time, anyway.

Jennifer frowned. The ultimate question remained unanswered. Why, she thought, *why* did I wish to talk to this man? Because I did. I sat there *wanting* him to *know* me. I even wanted to touch him. A total stranger about whom I know nothing, except that he is neither Irish nor Apache. Oh yes, sorry, he's a success in potatoes, and he has got a Japanese friend to whom a hundred thousand pounds appear to be petty cash. What more does one need to know?

Need?

Jennifer tensed. This is crazy, she thought. I am behaving like a fifteen-year old school girl hooked on an entirely fictional obsession. What on earth is the matter with me? It is not very likely that Angelo Vargas and I have *anything* in common. He is probably one of those here-today-gone-tomorrow characters.

Well, Angelo Vargas, as of today you are history. No, you didn't happen.

The sun was trying to break through, but a strong wind from Northeast was gushing the heavy rain like arrows of lustrous silver past her window.

Angelo Vargas sat there, for a while, sipping his whisky.

His mind wandered back to the Sunday morning when he and Ishihara had shown up at Parkhurst's place and the old boy had feigned surprise. Vargas had read all of Parkhurst's books long before they had decided to appoint him their incognizant ally. Vargas had not let on that he was familiar with Parkhurst's works. There had not been much of a point, that day, nor appropriate, for that matter. Vargas smiled into his glass. With Ishihara around there was seldom a chance of getting in a word, anyway.

They had followed Parkhurst as he walked with the gait of a rheumatoid Shire horse into the kitchen to introduce them to the Moran family, who they knew were there. The daughter had been the surprise. Ishihara had not mentioned her existence. Irrelevant, he'd said, afterwards.

Vargas had looked into a pair of eyes sparkling like diamonds on green baize under overhead projectors. The image had not left him.

He paid his bill and went home. He lit two large black candles. The scent of cinnamon filled the air. He listened to the rhythmic sound of raindrops falling on the windowsills.

Vargas found a pillow, lay down on the floor and folded his hands under his head.

He did not move for a long time.

Jennifer did not go back to the hospital, that evening. She was not in the mood for a sickbed conference with James' parents. Neither was she in the mood for anything else.

She threw her head back and placed both hands over her face. What is wrong with me, she mumbled; I am a calm, collected, rational and sensible woman. Why is everything so hollow, all of a sudden?

I wonder where he lives.

She picked herself up and went downstairs and into her mother's kitchen.

Jennifer got a glass of water and sat down at the table. Kathleen eyed her discreetly. She said, "You are not going to the hospital tonight?"

"No. James' parents will be there, and—and I think he needs to rest."

"He possibly does," Kathleen agreed. "What a horrible thing to happen. Poor James."

Conor came in. "When do you think he'll be out?" he asked.

Jennifer shook her head. "I have no idea. I may know by tomorrow."

"Will you have dinner with us tonight?"

Jennifer rubbed her fingertips against her eyes. "No thank you. I am tired and not very hungry. I shall try to get some sleep."

She rinsed out her glass, smiled absentmindedly and went upstairs.

Conor sat down. His hands were flat on the table. "She is taking it badly."

Kathleen looked out the window. She watched a dozen of Conor's pigeons landing on the roof of the loft. "Yes," she said.

"Yes? Come on, my girl. I have known you for a few decades. There is something on your mind."

"It is just an instinct."

"Never mind what it is. Share with me."

Kathleen dried her hands. "Somehow I do not think that Jennifer will marry James."

"That's a relief."

"Sweet Jesus, Conor..." Kathleen shook her head and replaced the towel, "—do you realize what you just said?"

Conor got to his feet. He went over to the wine-rack and opened a bottle.

Kathleen looked at the label. "That's a damn expensive wine, Conor. What are we celebrating?"

Conor smiled. "We are raising a glass to your genius for seeing into the future. Cheers."

"Would you be so kind as to explain yourself?"

Conor had another sip. "Certainly. James is a fine young man. He is decent, hardworking and considerate. However—and you know this as well as I do—Jennifer needs someone with substance. Somebody who has seen more of life than she has. Somebody who has grown with his scars. Somebody who is a book she will never fully understand.

James is but a brief chapter she will soon tire of. Ideally, she should find a man about whom there are more questions than there are answers. Only to such a man will she ever give herself completely and without reservations. I pray he exists."

Kathleen blinked. "You said Jennifer takes it badly. That bit does not add up."

"It does. What troubles her is that she *knows*. What bothers her is how to tell him."

At nine o'clock the next morning Jennifer went to the hospital. Nobody else was present.

James was more focused, but he was clearly in pain. She kissed him lightly on his forehead. "Don't they give you anything?" she asked indignantly and sat down.

"Oh yes," he croaked, "every four hours. Two more to go. Whatever they give me isn't that effective, either. It lasts for twenty minutes, if that. The matron is without mercy."

How right she is, Jennifer thought. She had seen her share of addicts passing through The Mission, during the years. Some of them got their first introduction at a hospital. She wondered why her act of hypocrisy did not bother her.

"I missed you last night," he said.

Jennifer sensed a touch of accusation in his voice. "I am sorry, but with your parents coming and—who else was here?"

"I did not think of that. Of course. I still missed you."

And here I bloody well am, Jennifer thought.

James moved his upper body as if to find a more comfortable position. She could see him gritting his teeth.

"When are they letting you out?" she asked.

"They have not told me, yet. It won't be too long, I think."

Christ Almighty, she thought, why is this such heavy going? The last thing I need is an embarrassing silence. Please, God, give me something to say.

A rasping sound from James frightened her for an instant. Then she realized he was clearing his throat.

"Jennifer," he said and fluttered his eyelids like an ageing cabaret star, "I may need some time to recover." His gaze became steadier. "I'm thinking about the future. You know what I mean?"

Where the hell did that come from? she thought. Now what? I better steer this conversation in a different direction.

"I can get the Sloane job if I want it," she said. "It is tempting, don't you think?"

"Good news," James said.

"It will require some expansion. Dad said he would help me."

"Very good news," James said.

He does not mean it, Jennifer reflected. That did not come from the heart. James is not a liberal man. Actually, he is more conservative than most, but he is cunning enough not to reveal his true colours until he feels that he is in a stronger position. Until then he is all emancipated, positive and supportive. What he really wants is a wife who stays at home and looks after the house and the children, the garden, the dachshund and the budgie. His vanity will not allow him to have a wife who runs her own business. Mention pregnancy, and within half a glass of champagne those ugly words *your little business* will fill the room like a truckload of manure. Between sips he will ever so smoothly *suggest* that her creation should be on the market not later than the following day.

"Is something wrong?" James said.

Jennifer touched the tip of her nose with her little finger. The gap between her eyebrows got smaller. "I just feel tired. I did not sleep very well last night."

"That makes two of us."

"I am sorry," she said. "That was a feeble explanation, considering what you are going through."

"I wasn't complaining."

This is going nowhere, Jennifer thought. "Of course not," she said and got up. "See you tonight."

Halfway down the corridor Jennifer stopped. She blew a sigh towards the ceiling before she continued. The lobby was not particularly busy. She walked slowly. Three times she stopped to adjust the belt of her coat and the strap of her bag.

No Vargas.

Jennifer came through the gate. She looked to her left and remembered what her father once had said, "Soldiers die as a result of politicians' kudos and irresponsibility. So much for honour, glory and patriotism." Then he had quoted Leonardo da Vinci: "War—the utmost stupidity."

What in heaven's name had any of this to do with Angelo Vargas?

She began walking towards the pub. She stopped outside and pretended to look at her watch as she peered through the window. Not all of the tables were visible.

Jennifer turned, spotted a taxi in the distance and walked off.

She faithfully visited James twice a day until he was sent home. She participated in polite conversations with his parents. She endured witticisms from friends and colleagues and never dropped her chin. His mother had already moved in with a promise of staying for at least a month; a necessary evil, James privately told Jennifer, but Mum had little to do and saw this as a golden opportunity to be useful.

"Don't worry, dear," Mrs. Wilkinson said repeatedly to Jennifer. "I shall take ever so good care of him."

Praise the Lord, Jennifer thought.

Angelo Vargas never showed up.

9

Jennifer was dressed for the occasion; practical shoes, trousers, a white sweater and a blue windbreaker. The morning was sunny and bright, but a chilly wind whistled around the corners and tousled her hair. Mayfair, she thought; the extraneous fruiterer could have been a bit more specific. She could also have asked, in all fairness.

The evening before she had dug out her map and drawn a red line covering the area between Grosvenor Square, New Bond Street, Old Bond Street and Hertford Street.

She took a taxi and asked the driver to stop in front of the site of the new American Embassy. She looked at the photocopy of her map and at the red line of her rectangle. The wind had got stronger and she pulled up the collar of her windbreaker. This was going to be as easy as spotting a moth in a fog patch, she thought. She began walking towards South Audley Street.

Two hours and three cups of coffee later Jennifer was exhausted. Her feet were burning, she had a blister on her left heel and there was rain in the air. A couple of discarded chewing gums were sticking to the soles of her shoes.

Jennifer's mood darkened further. She had to be out of her mind, she thought, all this agony just to discover the whereabouts of some backstreet fruit pedlar. How to know your own city, she thought—just walk the streets for a few months.

Fruit. Had not Vargas dropped the word *delicatessen*? Was it indeed conceivable that this peripatetic, leather-jacketed immigrant of an undiscovered comedian had been serious, that he had given her a hint? Could it be that he had *anticipated* her excursion? His sangfroid made him difficult to read, but there could not be any other answer. He had planned it. He *knew* that she would go looking. Jennifer breathed through her mouth and sensed that colours swept her face like the Northern lights on a clear and glacial winter's evening.

There were two alternatives left; she had seen them both, but she had been too preoccupied with the concept of *fruit*.

If she failed she would go home and write in her diary *I am insane* and underneath she would add *Angelo Vargas get lost*.

The smallest shop was the nearest. She peeped through the windows and saw two men and a woman. One of the men looked of Mediterranean origin.

Jennifer walked in. "Excuse me," she said, "will Mr. Vargas be in today?"

The man stared at her, blankly. "Who?"

"Mr. Vargas. Mr. Angelo Vargas."

The man shook his head. "Never heard of him."

She wondered if she had a rash on her cheeks. She wanted to scratch but kept her hands still. "This is not Mr. Vargas' shop?"

"No," the man said, "this is my shop."

"Your name is not Ahmed?"

The expression on the man's face changed from bemusement to irritation. "It is not."

"I am sorry," Jennifer said and retreated, "wrong address."

The rain had become heavier. Continue, she told herself, go on and make sure. There is only one possibility left. Don't let your anger get the better of your goddamn mulishness. I'll bet my pair of wet shoes that those shops of his is just a smokescreen, for some imbecile reason; an outright lie produced for the sake of cheap temporary entertainment. What a perverted scum.

One more to go. Nobody would ever know that she had walked the entire Mayfair looking for the owner of a non-existing shop. Nobody. And—oh yes, when this waste of a day was over, the elusive Mr. Vargas would be written off, once and for all.

Her blister was getting worse. The rain continued non-stop.

Jennifer stopped and eyed the shop from the opposite pavement. It was brightly lit, well stocked and busy. She crossed the street and walked in. The blend of aromas appealed to her. She looked around. The place was spotlessly clean. Yes, she thought, it could justify the label *delicatessen*. An hour earlier she had ignored the shop because she did not associate the standard with an obscure bohemian like Vargas being the owner. The name on the stylish sign above the shop didn't sound too Vargas-*ish* either—*STORE OF DISTINCTION*—unless— Jennifer stared and smiled—unless she made an anagram out of the initial letters.

Last shot. Jennifer stared resolutely at one of the two young men nearest to her and said, "Who is the manager, please?"

The youngster smiled amicably. "My father." He nodded towards a portly, solid looking man sporting a white apron. She decided he looked like a Palestinian and walked over.

"Excuse me, but is your name Ahmed?"

The man smiled, but his eyes did not collaborate. "What can I do for you, miss?"

He is evading my question, she thought. Be open with him.

The man adjusted his apron and folded his hands. Suddenly, the smile seemed more gentle.

"Will Mr. Vargas be in today?" she asked.

"Not today. At least I don't think so."

Jennifer went numb. "Mr. Vargas," she repeated tonelessly, "Mr. Angelo Vargas."

"Yes, miss. My boss. The owner. Is there anything I can do for you?"

Jennifer wanted to sit down. Her stomach was in a knot. She felt dizzy.

"Are you all right?" the Palestinian asked with a worried look.

Jennifer tried to breathe normally. "Yes—yes, thank you. I am fine."

"I am Ahmed," the man said and extended his hand. "It is always a pleasure to meet a friend of Mr. Vargas'."

"How do you know I am a friend?" Jennifer queried with a smile.

The Palestinian measured her calmly. "I can tell."

Jennifer chose not to pursue the theme. "Would you mind if I sit down for a moment?" she asked.

"My apologies," Ahmed said. "Please, let me get you a chair from my office."

She looked into his warm, brown eyes. "My name is Jennifer Moran, and I am looking for Mr. Vargas." She sat down and crossed her hands without taking her eyes off Ahmed.

He laughed quietly. "Yes, Miss Moran, so I understand. You want me to leave a message?"

What is my next comment, Jennifer thought. Why did I not prepare myself for the most logical of all questions? She frowned. "Please forget it. I'll come back another time."

"No, Miss Moran," he said solemnly, "I cannot do that."

Jennifer did not know what to say. She could not believe, in retrospect, that she had not worked out a scenario for any possibility; Vargas being there, not being there—not even the wording of a simple message. She felt increasingly foolish. The Palestinian's kind and sympathetic attitude didn't help.

"You do not know Mr. Vargas very well, do you?" he said.

"No," she admitted.

He studied her carefully. "Mr. Vargas and I have known each other for a long time. I owe him much. There is no way I can hide from him that someone came looking for him. It does not matter what they tell me, and it does not matter who they are. I must respectfully ask you to understand."

Suddenly, Jennifer felt at ease. It was so simple, really. She had not planned her excursion in order to find out whether or not Angelo Vargas had told her the truth—instinctively she had believed him—the entire reason for her action had been an uncomplicated desire to meet him again. To see him, to talk to him and perhaps even to get to know him. This stranger from nowhere fascinated her, and she knew that only another meeting would prevent her wish from becoming even more of an obsession. She acknowledged that it was near impossible to comprehend; up till now but no longer had she deemed herself to be a sensible and rational human being and not prone to sudden whims and inexplicable behaviour.

But she also knew that there were voices in her that seldom could be heard. Only occasionally did she listen to the whispers from the depths of her soul; words and feelings that created a world different from the safe and uncomplicated existence she had hitherto known. She had no clear picture of who inhabited this world and how it functioned, but she knew that it contained elements of the unpredictable, the untamed and the non-conventional sides of the human nature. She admired her parents for the life they had created for themselves, but she knew that it was not for her. She had begun to envisage life with James as the suburban equivalent of an open prison.

Her godfather Igor Parkhurst had led an eventful life; things always happened to Uncle Igor, destitute or not, a surprise of some description or another was always waiting in the wings. She did not claim to understand him, entirely; however mild-mannered, considerate and kind, there were corners of his mind she sensed that she could not reach. Maybe this was what she was looking for; a tome where some of the pages seemed glued together and she could not separate them, a chapter or two she could not fully fathom or perhaps not even understand why they had been written.

"You are lost in thoughts, Miss Moran," she heard Ahmed's voice.

"I apologize," Jennifer said. The tension was gone. She straightened her neck. "I would appreciate if you could ask Mr. Vargas to telephone me."

Ahmed got up. What a lovely smile, he thought, but what does it tell me? I have seen people kill with a smile. "Certainly," he said. "I shall convey your message."

"I take it that you will not give me his telephone number."

"That is correct," Ahmed said.

Jennifer laughed. "I wonder what the two of you have been up to together."

The Palestinian looked past her. "You must come again, Miss Moran," he said and wiped his hands on the apron. "The quality of our produce is unsurpassed."

"I will," Jennifer promised and shook his hand. "Thank you for your patience."

"It has been my pleasure," Ahmed said.

Jennifer went home, showered and changed into a smart grey-and-green suit.

It was time to work. Time had come to throw herself into the deep end of her business whilst waiting for Angelo Vargas to call. She would take each day as it came and fill it to the best of her ability. The nights would be long enough for her to contemplate what to say to him when or if he eventually decided to pick up the telephone.

Maybe along these lines: *How nice of you to respond to my message, Mr. Vargas. Why don't you come over one evening for a meal? I am not the best of cooks, but I won't poison you, either. Been busy, lately? Just wondering. I mean, what the hell do you do with your time when you don't count green*

159

peppers and onions? Don't answer now. We must have something to talk about when you show up, that is, in case you do. You will? Splendid. And you actually mean this year. Next week? Marvellous. Yes, next Wednesday is fine. Eight o'clock. See you then. Good night.

Jennifer laughed helplessly and sat down in front of the mirror. Carefully, she put on a modicum of make-up.

"Jennifer Moran," she said slowly, "the only worthwhile knowledge you have about bio-chemistry is that it exists."

Kathleen knew that something worried her daughter, but, as always, Kathleen did not ask. From when she could talk, Jennifer had been taught the meaning of confidence and the virtue of trust; Kathleen and Conor never probed, and neither did they teach using meaningless platitudes and superficial moralism. Their method of upbringing was based on common sense, on mutual respect and on the volition to understand; the deep and never faltering feeling of implicit reliance and enduring harmony had been Jennifer's guiding light through her formative years and forever after.

Three days after her Mayfair raid, Jennifer came into her mother's kitchen.

Kathleen cast one look at her daughter's face and continued with her crossword puzzle. Something's coming, she thought, I wonder what. "Have you had your dinner?" she asked.

"Yes. Where is Dad?"

"With his pigeons. He should be here any minute."

"Could I have a glass of wine, please?"

Oh dear, Kathleen reflected, this must be serious. "Get the glasses," she said, "I'll open the bottle."

Conor came in. "Hello, my beauties." He watched as she poured the wine. "What are we celebrating?"

Jennifer pulled her glass closer. She looked up and into her father's eyes before she turned towards her mother. "I have broken off with James."

Kathleen sat down. Conor did not move.

Jennifer said, "He is not right for me. I have no wish to make his life miserable, let alone mine, but that would have been the result." She paused. "And yes," she added without apparent emotions, "I did give it some considerable thought, and no, I have not entered into another relationship."

Conor walked towards the table, pulled out a chair and sat down. "He took it badly, I assume."

Jennifer sipped her wine. "I don't know. I told him as gently as I could. He kept staring out the window. After ten minutes of silence I left."

That calmness comes from inner conviction, Kathleen thought. "You know what you are doing," she said quietly.

"Yes, I do. I cannot marry a man I do not love. "As for being friends—" Jennifer shrugged "—I do not think James is made that way. His pride is hurt and his vanity is shattered. I do not believe he wants to see me again."

Conor said, "And you?"

"I am indifferent. I have made my decision. I did what I knew was right."

Lord Almighty, Conor thought, there is more steel in this girl of mine than even I was aware of. Let there be a man out there who deserves her and let her find him.

Kathleen said, "Your father commented a long time ago that he didn't think James was the right choice."

Jennifer searched for her handkerchief. She dried her eyes. "How come, Dad?"

"Just an instinct. Nothing wrong with young James, except—"

"—except that there is nothing wrong with him," Kathleen completed.

"This is your father's polite way of saying that James is a bourgeois and parochial conformist. He would have bored you rigid." Kathleen giggled. "Come to think of it, he already has. Is that an adequate interpretation, Conor?"

"So it is," Conor nodded, "so it is."

Jennifer's eyelids moved rapidly. Then a warm and radiant smile broke out. "You two are something else."

Then she found her mother's eyes. "That was Dad's conclusion."

Kathleen did not avoid Jennifer's stare. "I knew that your father was right, but at the same time my maternal, egocentric instincts lingered on. I saw security with James, security and all the other trimmings like position, social respect, status and everything else that fills a mother's heart with pride." Her laughter was flat and brief. "Folly mixed with selfishness, Jennifer."

"Is that where you stand—no folly?"

"Yes, it is. Find your man, and your father and I will welcome him, whoever he is."

The image of Angelo Vargas flashed through Jennifer's mind. For a fleeting moment she wondered what her parents' reaction would be if she showed up with him by her side.

She smiled, but the sigh escaped and she lowered her head. "I am tired. Would you excuse me, please? I'll try to get a good night's sleep."

She kissed them both and turned in the doorway. "Thank you," she said and went upstairs.

The following night, at a quarter to ten, Jennifer's telephone rang. She felt a tingling in her hands and moved lazily towards the cabinet. She knew who it was before she heard his voice. "Hello," she said and imitated the end of a yawn.

"Good evening. This is Angelo Vargas."

"Already." The word slipped before she'd diagnosed its implications.

There was a slight pause. She wondered if he was laughing. *Could he laugh?* Hard to tell.

"I fancy a Japanese meal one of these days," he said. "Would you care to join me?"

"Why not? Go on."

"I have said what I wanted to say."

"No, you haven't. Does it not occur to you that I would need to know the name of the place, address, date and time? I am not a psychic apache squaw."

"Careful with that word," Vargas said.

"Which one—psychic, apache or squaw?"

"Squaw. I don't think you know what it means."

"Yes, I do. It means Indian woman, or wife, or both."

"Neither."

"Intriguing. Please educate me."

"The origin is Otiskwa, an Iroquois word. That was too complicated for the French, and we got squaw. It means *private.* Your breathless silence indicates that further elaboration is unnecessary."

Jennifer felt herself going hot. She rubbed her lips together. "You are evidently not burdened with any degree of inhibitions, Mr. Vargas," she said and was pleased with the chill in her voice.

"You asked."

Who is this creature? she thought. Am I really having this conversation, and why am I being so aggressive?

Vargas went on, "How about tomorrow, eight o'clock? The place is called Itoh, after the owner."

She wrote down the address. "That is fine with me," she said.

"Good. See you there. Good night." He hung up.

Jennifer stared at the receiver for several seconds before she put it down. She went back to her bed and laid down on her back with her eyes closed.

She had fallen into a pond. The water was amethyst blue. When she got out her clothes were dry. A million diamonds were attached to the fabric, sparkling in the rays from the sun. Angelo Vargas stood ten yards away. He reached for her hand. She ran towards him.

A tiny, esoteric smile was still there when she fell asleep.

Jennifer's rich, auburn hair was beautifully coiffured. She wore a simple, black dress, very little make-up, a gold necklace and a diamond ring given to her by Grandma Keogh.

"Are you sure this is the right address?" she asked the taxi driver.

She approached the staircase. She was apprehensive and had an unpleasant feeling of being ridiculously overdressed. It was all very well that the food was acceptable, but Mr. Vargas certainly hadn't gone out of his way to impress her. There had to be quite a few Oriental places more attractive than this dump.

Down the stairs an elderly Japanese was meeting her. His smile made his eyes disappear.

"Weh-come to my humbel establishment, Miss Molan," he beamed. "I am most honouled."

Jennifer tried to get eye contact. "How do you know who I am?"

"Ah. Easy. Valgas-San said an incledible beauty coming eight o'crock. Show the lady to my tabre. Easy. Vely easy."

Jennifer smiled back. Really. An incredible beauty. So, Mr. Vargas wasn't entirely impervious. Or was the friendly old Japanese making it up, being his polite self.

"Thank you, Mr.—"

"Preasure. Oh—a thousand apologies. I am Eisuke Itoh."

"I look forward to trying your food, Mr. Itoh."

"The best in Rondon. You see."

Vargas was sitting in a corner. His table was apart from the rest. He got up when he saw her. His eyes did not flicker.

Sweet Jesus, Jennifer thought, he doesn't even notice how I look. So much for the incredible beauty. God bless your Japanese manners, Mr. Itoh.

"Good evening," Vargas said and held her chair.

She sat down. "Good evening."

He wore black denims, and a royal blue shirt. The leather jacket hung on the back of his chair. It is probably safe to assume that he does not own a tie, she thought. I wonder if the rest of his wardrobe looks as if a one-eyed man suffering from amnesia has picked it.

She looked at the ceramic carafe and the two little cups on the table. "What is that?"

"Sake. Wine made from rice. Served hot. Would you like to try?"

"Please."

"Drink slowly and not too much of it, or you won't be able to get up."

"You are an authority on sake, I take it."

"That, too."

She took another sip. "It's good. I really like it."

He said, "Most Westerns don't. They just pretend they do. Funny how this side of Hong Kong is becoming full of Oriental fads."

Jennifer looked around. The place was small, some twenty tables, rather Spartan but very clean. The walls were covered with aquarelles; delicately performed motifs of mountains, bridges, gardens and tiny figures in kimonos.

The place was filling up. She noticed that she and Vargas were the only non-Orientals.

Mr. Itoh came over.

"What lovely paintings," Jennifer said. "Are they for sale?"

"Oh yes, every single one of them. I am deeply honoured that you like them."

"They are exquisite. Why do you want to sell them?"

"He painted them," Vargas said. "Being a modest man, he thinks he is on par with Utamoro but superior to Hiroshige."

Itoh's smile widened.

Vargas went on, "Regrettably, he paints better than he cooks. You've got something special for Miss Moran tonight, Itoh-San, have you not?"

"Most definitely so. Leave it to me. And one of my other specialities for you, great Shogun."

"Make a move, then."

"How do you know what I like," Jennifer whizzed. "Your arrogance is quite breathtaking. Perhaps you should go and buy yourself a book about How-To-Behave-and-Converse-Like-A-Civilized-Human-Being. I am sure there must be *something* on the market from which you could benefit, even if it is only a five-page volume for beginners."

The now familiar quizzical look was back in Vargas' eyes. "You are quite funny, you know."

"*Funny?*"

"Yes. That was a clever remark, that one. I like it. Very good English, too."

"It wasn't meant to be clever. It was—it was..."

"—an insult?" He nodded. "Not bad. I've heard worse, though."

"Now, isn't that an overwhelming surprise."

Then she saw the twinkle in his eyes and she smiled. "You don't really care what people think about you, do you?"

"It doesn't keep me awake. Why is it such a problem calling me Angelo? It is a nice name. Apt, too. We agreed on that, I seem to recall."

"We did not. So far, the only characteristic of angelic proportion I have discovered is your humility."

"So far."

Jennifer sensed that her face reddened. Careful now, she thought and swallowed some sake, this man does not miss much. What do I say now? I wish the damn food would arrive. She said, "Are we here because everywhere else was fully booked?"

She did not like the expression on Vargas' face. It wasn't mockery, but it wasn't humour, either. What a sordid remark, she thought, and snobbish, too. I did not mean in that way. What I said had more to do with my cryptic companion than with the place. Think twice, next time. I can hold my own with this man without resorting to cheap shots. What do I do if he suddenly has had enough of me and walks out?

Vargas continued to look at her. She glanced at the ceiling fan. The blades kept flapping like the wings of a condor taking off.

"You do not know much about Japanese food, do you?" he said. There was no aggression in his voice.

"No, and I apologize for my remark."

"There is no healthier way of eating. Japanese food is high in fibre, calcium, fatty acids and vitamins. Everything is very lightly cooked, which means that the nutrients have not been destroyed." Vargas rearranged his chopsticks without averting his stare. "You will also find that the Japanese take great pride in the presentation of their food. Contrary to most other cultures, they believe that appearance, texture and fragrance are essential parts of gastronomy; eating, to the Japanese, is a ritual, a ceremony that must not be treated with irreverence." He touched her diamond ring with one of his chopsticks. "I think that this evening will confirm what I have just said."

Jennifer's ears stung as if a pair of red-hot horseshoes had replaced them. She said, "Why did you not attack me for being snobbish and derogatory?"

"I am trying to understand you."

The softness of his voice made her look away. She studied her fingers. "I do not know how to use chopsticks."

Itoh and a kimono-clad Japanese girl stood next to them. "Noodles and rice," he said as the girl placed two bowls on the table, "and here, incredibly succulent lobster tail and some halibut steamed to perfection. All to your taste, I hope," he added with a worried expression.

"Perfect, Mr. Itoh," Jennifer assured him, "it looks fabulous. I am sure I'll have the meal of a lifetime."

Itoh and the girl went back to the kitchen. They returned a moment later; the girl with a pot of tea and Itoh with a large colourful plate which he put in front of Vargas.

"Show Miss Moran how to use chopsticks," Vargas said.

"Very simple. Here," Itoh said and demonstrated, then gently put the sticks in Jennifer's hand. "That's it," he went on as he helped her with the movements, "I think you are already in command. Let us try."

Why leave it to Mr. Itoh, Jennifer thought. Does not Angelo Vargas want to touch me?

"You are a very quick learner," Itoh said. "Please, enjoy the meal." He left.

"What happened to his accent?" Jennifer said.

"Just a show. Sometimes he likes to sound the way he believes he's supposed to sound. After a while he forgets. In between he does not care. Eusuke Itoh is a wise old warrior, and he's got a great sense of humour."

"Is he born in Japan?"

"Yes, but he came over some thirty years ago."

"You seem to know each other well."

"He is a family friend of Tadashi's."

"Tadashi?"

"Mr. Ishihara."

"I see. Your partner in crime."

Vargas played with his chopsticks; deftly and with rapid precision one overlapped the other and came back to its original position. She could not decide whether he looked thoughtful or amused.

She said, "Why are your chopsticks different from mine? They are beautiful. Can I see them?"

Vargas handed her one. Jennifer studied the intricate black-and-red pattern.

"Incredible," she said. "You must be a privileged patron."

"I am, but the chopsticks are mine. Mr. Itoh keeps them here for me."

Jennifer finished her second last piece of lobster. "Are you possessive by nature?"

"Only when it comes to books and chopsticks. I will lend you my car, but not one of my books."

Jennifer tilted her head. "Isn't that interesting. It sounds like an obsession, to me."

"It is. Each book is a universe of its own from where I can gather insight, wisdom and knowledge. Each book is a challenge; if I agree with the writer—which sometimes happen—I want to find out whether it is a conviction or a convenience. Each book has its own life, and I share it with its creator." The corners of his eyes went up. "A car is just a heap of metal."

Jennifer thought for a while. "Does that mean that you are not really reading, as such, it is more like an endless session of studying?"

Vargas de-tailed a shrimp. "Assiduously. I like to acquire knowledge from someone who knows something that I don't. If you've got a mind capable of covering a variety of territories, it would be a declaration of failure not to use it. I am not a disciple of the virtue of ignorance."

"You do not read novels?"

"Yes, I do. There can be a lot of lore in novels. During thousands of years there have been authors who knew as much about the human mind as is today presented as the so-called science of psychology." He leaned back and folded his hands. He said straightfaced, "In betwixt I also need to be entertained, to relax. Therapy, kind of."

"If you don't mind my saying, the word *betwixt* is not entirely up to date."

"Really?"

"Really."

"Thank you. I shall revise my vocabulary accordingly."

He's having me on again, she thought; his sense of humour is evidently as obscure as his background. She said, "The world of a grocer can be inhumanely demanding, then." She regretted the words before she had finished the sentence. That was neither funny nor satirical, she thought, just trite.

"I wouldn't go that far," Vargas said before she'd had time to form her defence in the shape of an excuse. " It has more to do with a respite from my demons."

Why are there no little alarm bells ringing? she thought. This situation can't possibly please me—or can it? James could not read me and that pleased me. I did not want him to. Am I finally coming around to admitting that I do not find a man attractive unless he's got *mystique* sprinkled all over him? Does it appeal to me that my poisoned arrows are ricocheting off the impenetrable mind of the man sitting here entertaining himself by summing me up? You may be on thin ice, here, Jennifer; it is quite possible that you are measuring his apparent indifference against your own infatuation.

She held her gaze and said, "Are there a handful of demons around, Angelo?"

For a moment she thought she saw a glimpse of sadness, like the shadow of a melancholy cloud swiftly crossing his face.

"Enough," he said.

There was an edge to his voice that did not invite to further elaboration. She wondered why Angelo Vargas was so reluctant to talk about himself.

Once again it struck her how softly he spoke, and she wished she could detect where his accent came from. She said, "As far as looks are concerned, you could pass for an Irishman, but your name is Spanish, isn't it? Were you a matador before the world of big finance and small bananas swallowed you up?"

Vargas lit a cigarette and gave no indication that he intended to answer.

"Please!" Jennifer said earnestly, "please do not reply. Kindly do not deprive me of the thrill of guessing. Let me see, now—" she stared towards the ceiling "—if not Spanish…of course! Why didn't I think? Mexican. Not Geronimo. Zapata."

"Yes."

"You are Mexican? Isn't it amazing what people can learn about each other just by keeping a dialogue alive, don't you think?"

Vargas blew a ring of smoke.

"Sorry for interrupting," Jennifer continued innocently. "I am *so* happy we managed to clear that one."

Vargas reached for his cup and turned it upside down. "You ask a lot of questions."

"Oh dear. Have you ever heard the word *conversation*? If it was up to you, we would be sitting here staring at each other."

"The capacity for talking and the ability to listen are not always commensurable."

"Is that a reference to me? Are you saying that I am not good at listening?"

"It's a reference to myself. Very few are given to differentiate between where the person begins and the shadow ends."

"What on earth does that mean?"

"It means that it is hard for someone aware of the distinction between probing and a genuine and profound sympathy to bare his ego."

"Ego?"

"You would call it soul," he said and undid the second top button of his shirt. "*Soul* is an abstraction not incorporated in the conglomerate of conceptions occupying my private world."

He picked up his lighter. She saw the veins disappear as he closed his hand. She rested her chin on the back of her hand as she looked at him; I am a Catholic and he is an infidel. The lure of his netherworld is becoming interesting.

"Have you no religion at all, Angelo?"

"No."

Dad will understand, Jennifer thought, Mum will not. She said, "The paragon of cynicism, is that it?" She touched her eyelashes with her index finger and smiled as if no theme could be more pertinent for a rewarding dinner conversation.

Vargas seemed to roll the words over his tongue before he said, "Cynicism or scepticism, Jennifer?"

She felt her neck getting hot. "Well—whatever."

"Not whatever. Cynicism is presumed based on contempt and scepticism is a consequence of solicitous reflections."

Jennifer turned the ring on her finger till the diamond no longer showed. She twisted it back to its original position. "You like playing with words, don't you?"

"I like to think that I have a clear idea of what I am talking about."

She saw Itoh come through the kitchen door and turned her burning face towards him. From the corner of her eyes she sighted Vargas staring at her. She pretended not to notice.

Itoh cast a quick glance at the empty plates. "You like my food, Miss Moran?"

She smiled warmly at him. "Absolutely fantastic, Mr. Itoh. I enjoyed every bite. Mr. Vargas never told me that you are a culinary master of exceptional distinction, but now I know."

"Mr. Vargas isn't famous for his compliments, Miss Moran," Itoh said.

He grinned and went on, "Always expect the unexpected, and you can't go wrong. However, I am most grateful for your appreciation of my cooking, very heart-warming. You are as kind as you are beautiful."

Jennifer looked into his mocha brown eyes and knew that it was not cheap flattery. "Thank you, Mr. Itoh."

"Do you know why she is so beautiful?" Vargas said and tapped Itoh's forearm.

"Tell me, wise man."

"It comes from within."

"I would not dare object to such a sagacious observation, oh warrior."

"No, you wouldn't, since it explains why you've got no looks at all."

Itoh sniffed and scanned the ceiling as if he expected a necessary

170

dash of additional patience from above. "A latter-day samurai with his tongue as his sword," he said and shrugged as he looked at Jennifer.

Jennifer fixed her gaze on Vargas' lighter. The badinage seemed good-natured enough, but she sensed an undercurrent that made her feel uncomfortable.

"Not to worry, Miss Moran," Itoh said and pressed his palms together. "If Vargas-San and I were enemies he would not have brought you here. It is just the way we are." He laughed and began picking up the bowls and the plates.

"I understand," she said without looking at either of them.

"No, you don't," Vargas said. "Itoh-San and I regard each other as ronins," he added and smiled at the girl who came with the warm towels, "an echo from a different culture."

Jennifer straightened in her chair. A drop of perspiration ran down her spine. What do I do, she thought; do I accept this dodo or do I walk away? My desire to be with him has not lessened during the evening, but from where do I get the understanding and the forbearance? Time. Give it time. I am hooked on an enigma of dubious origin. It is crazy, but that is an inseparable part of the attraction. Dear God, what am I walking into? And, by the way, dear God, don't make him lose interest.

Vargas got up. "Please excuse me for a moment," he said and walked across the room. She watched him when he went and she watched him when he came back with a glass in his hand. He looks supremely fit, she thought, the kind of fitness that does not come just from running. He's got the skin of a baby and hardly any lines on his face, yet his hair is thinning and has more silvery grey than blond. One day he will tell me his age. Not that it matters—just curiosity. Why do I think that it does not matter?

Vargas sat down.

"What are you drinking?" she asked.

"Irish whisky."

Jennifer sniffed. "Same as my father's. He says it relaxes him."

"It does."

Probably, Jennifer thought; the only difference is that Dad seems quite happy with half an inch in his glass at night. Vargas' glass was half full.

"I never took to it," Jennifer confessed. "It is an acquired taste, I assume. It burns."

"Part of the pleasure." Vargas stared into his glass. For a short while he looked remote, almost as if she was not there. Suddenly, he raised his eyes and said, "Whatever I tell you is true."

She got eye contact. "What do you mean?" she said.

The distant expression came back. "Think about it."

Jennifer listened to her instincts. "I do not think you are what you pretend to be."

"No?"

"No. You pretend to be stoic, but behind your phlegmatic demeanour and your attitude of indifference there is an intensity that goes to the core of your being."

"You are right."

His directness baffled her. "You admit it?"

"Wrong verb, Jennifer. I know about it, and I have done so for a very long time. The noun *admission* and its associated verb have connotations which are non-applicable to our relationship."

Jennifer pleated her lips. "Our *what?*"

"Is your problem with the vocabulary, or is it the grammar?"

She brushed a few imaginary crumbles from the table. "Is this your idea of having fun? If that's the case, I think you are confusing wit with lack of restraint."

"Do not mock modesty. *Intense* modesty, as you so shrewdly observed."

She wondered if her throat was turning crimson. "I also believe you are a nutcase."

"Borderline. Let me take you home."

Jennifer looked at her watch. It was twenty minutes to twelve.

They rose simultaneously. Mr. Itoh appeared like magic with her coat and a square parcel wrapped in brown paper. Jennifer thanked him for a lovely evening and a most delicious meal. She added that she hoped to see him again soon. Itoh bowed ceremoniously, smiled and handed her the parcel. "Please," he said, "for you."

Jennifer took it. "What is in here, Mr. Itoh?"

Vargas put the coat over her shoulders. "One of his paintings," he whispered.

"Oh, but I can't possibly—"

"Take it," Vargas said.

Something in his voice told her not to say any more.

"A great honour, Itoh-San," Vargas went on. "Miss Moran is deeply moved and eternally appreciative."

I should have put it that way, myself, Jennifer thought, but never mind.

"How can I thank you, Mr. Itoh?"

"May you derive much pleasure from it, and I have been blessed with a thousand thanks."

"It will hang prominently on her wall for the rest of her earthly life," Vargas promised. Then he said something in Japanese, and they both bowed. "Have a good night's sleep, Itoh-San," he concluded in English. "May your dreams be like a summer's breeze whispering to the flowers of the cherry tree."

Good Lord, Jennifer thought, isn't he poetic? "I share Mr. Vargas' wish," she smiled.

The pavement was deserted. Several cabs were looking for business.

"I'll see you home," Vargas said.

"That is not necessary."

"I know it is not necessary." He hailed a cab, opened the door and followed her in.

"What is a ronin, Angelo?"

"A samurai with no one to answer to."

The rest of the ride went in silence. It had been raining. Jennifer looked at the windows where spots of water hung like drops of crystal in the light from neon signs and passing cars. She saw her right foot moving as if tap-dancing in thin air and put it firmly down on the floor. Bewilderment and qualms ran like a stream of lava through her mind. She avoided glancing at Vargas. Lord in Heaven, she thought, where is this leading? What is happening to me?

The cab stopped. Vargas asked the driver to wait.

Jennifer said, "Thank you for an interesting evening."

Vargas stood with his back to the lights. She could not see his face properly.

He said, "I believe this was a good introduction."

Jennifer stood with her painting under her arm, more curious than expectant. Vargas did not extend his hand. He did not kiss her on the cheek. No, she thought, Angelo Vargas has no intention of touching me. I wonder why.

"Good night, Jennifer," he said.

"Good night." She turned around, went through the gate, along the driveway and up the stairs. Only when she was inside and the door was closed did she hear the car drive away.

10

The Sloane commission turned out to be more complex and demanding than Jennifer had anticipated. Mrs. Edith Mercante was a rich, loud, volatile and whimsical client, and she had become a nuisance. Jennifer reasoned that this was the kind of situation she had to learn to tackle with skill and diplomacy should she achieve a name for herself. Mrs. Mercante was friendly enough, but her constant change of mind made Jennifer wonder if the woman wasn't altogether unhinged.

Jennifer tested the water by asking for an interim payment. Mrs. Mercante wrote out a cheque on the spot. There was no hesitation and no query about the overall account.

Jennifer worked hard, harder than she'd ever worked in her life before. She gave it her everything; gradually, she began to believe that she could pull it off, and that her final reward would include a reference worth pages of advertisements.

In between, which meant numerous times a day and each night before she closed her eyes, she thought of Angelo Vargas.

Where was he? What was he up to? Why had he stayed clear of touching her? How come he had not called again? What did he mean when he said: *"Whatever I tell you is true."* The words kept echoing in her mind, time and time again.

One Sunday morning, whilst still in bed, Jennifer began to think that she had overcomplicated the significance of those six little words. Had she tried to interpret something that in reality was as clear-cut as it was straightforward, and had she invested hours looking for a profundity that did not exist?

She remembered him saying: *"You ask a lot of questions."* His words and his body language, to the extent she thought she could read it, conveyed in all likelihood one simple message: *Do not probe into my life. I will tell you what I want to tell you whenever it suits me, if it suits me. I am private and reserved, a recluse, but I do not tell lies.*

Could it be as patently evident as that? Yes, why not. There were no indications that Angelo Vargas was an extrovert. On the contrary; everything so far bore the marks of a loner who shared little if anything with somebody else.

But then, she wondered, why me? Do I behave and sound like a woman looking for an affair? Is that what he is after? He does not strike me as a man who thinks he is God's gift to women. And if, just *if* he is looking for an affair—Jennifer smiled—he is slower than a snail in a bucket of glue.

She stretched. Nothing adds up, she thought and peered at Itoh's painting. Ten days, and not a word. Bastard.

She looked at the clock on her chiffonier. The seconds ticked away like the heartbeat of a decrepit frog.

The telephone rang.

A battalion of butterflies broke lose from their cocoons and began exploring her intestines. After the seventh ring she lifted the receiver. She said, as casually as she could muster, "How nice of you to call."

"Clairvoyant," he said.

"A quiescent talent slowly unfolding. You are keeping well, I hope?"

"I am, thank you. How is the Sloane project coming along?"

"It is progressing. I think I will complete it with honours."

"You'll succeed." It was a statement, not a question. "I gather from your voice that you do find life acceptable."

"I do, thank you. How is your empire doing? Mushrooming?"

She thought she heard a low chuckle. "Nothing sensational happened during my absence."

"Absence?"

"I have been abroad."

"A successful trip, I presume?"

"I got distracted."

"What on earth can have disturbed your orderly mind? Sorry," she added quickly, "I just remembered that questions one asks do not."

"You," he said.

Jennifer's throat went dry. Her mind was racing. What do I say now? she thought. Keep it neutral. Sound sharp and composed. She said, "I am not too familiar with the Spanish language, Mr. Vargas, but I know the word *loco*. I take it that any true-blooded Mexican has incorporated the meaning as well as the implications in the lexicon of his mind."

There was a moment's silence. "I don't see the context, but, true enough, the word was once associated with my name."

"Why am I not astounded beyond the boundaries of human comprehension?"

Why do I say these things, she thought. Why do I hide behind nasty words? Why am I defensive and unfriendly?

Vargas said, "Are you free tonight? I know of a first-class Russian restaurant. Would you like to try? I'll wait whilst you consult your social diary."

Jennifer laughed with relief. This man is the most annoying person I have ever confronted, she thought, yet I can't wait to accept. "Where and when?" she said.

Vargas told her.

At the end of the following month they had been out together five times. He had lost some of his reserved attitude and had become less guarded and more relaxed. She found it easy to chat about anything that came to mind. She liked the way he never responded in a casual manner; everything seemed sombre, thoughtful and well considered. There were times she detected signs of a saturnine nature, but apart from the odd moment when there was a distant look in his eyes she did not find his silence heavy going.

Jennifer had seen little of the world, and she loved his tales from exotic places, his descriptions of people and their cultures, their customs and their history. His experience was vast, as was his knowledge, but somehow, once in a while, Jennifer had an uneasy feeling that it was all too innocent, too clinical, as if Angelo Vargas was one of life's spectators and not a participant.

That part of it did not hang together; a word here, the tone of his voice there—all her instincts told her that he had seen and been through far more than he hitherto was prepared to reveal.

It will come, she thought. One day Angelo Vargas will conclude that I have earned his confidence. Whatever is hidden in his past can't be undone, and broadminded Jennifer will clearly demonstrate her ability to accept and adapt.

One day, when he called, she said, "Angelo, tonight is on me."

"You invite?"

"I certainly do. It's a surprise, but you'll like it. Can we meet first at the Dorchester Hotel, in the lobby, at seven-thirty? By the way, you need to dress up a bit. No leather jacket." She laughed. "Would that be possible?"

"I think so."

When she arrived he was there, dressed in a pair of ill-fitting slacks, a dark blue blazer that had seen better days, a white shirt and no tie. At least he is wearing black shoes, she thought.

They went to the bar and found a table.

How do I phrase this without upsetting him, she pondered, it's delicate. The fact is that I do not know how sensitive he is. Well, I can always cancel, and we can go somewhere else.

Vargas said, "What's on your mind?"

She thought, If I look into those blue eyes I shall have to stick to my guns, delicate or not; there'll be other times when he can't show up as a candidate for the worst dressed man in London.

"You'll need to wear a tie where we are going," she said. "Have you got one?"

Vargas picked an olive. "I can go and get one. It won't take long."

She said, "Let us finish our drinks. We are not in a hurry. You live not far from here?"

"No."

"Walking distance?"

"Yes."

Slowly, and with distinct emphasis on each word, she said, "I would like to come with you."

She lit a cigarette. How does he manage to look so poised, she wondered? The expression in those eyes; not negative, not positive— just the way he did when we first met at Uncle Igor's house. Kind of searching, and without as much as a micro-flicker of anything resembling commitment. Have I gone too far? Is he ashamed of his place? Has he got an assortment of mistresses decorating his home or any other hidden agenda? He can always reject my suggestion. He'll probably do so in his customary, eloquent and flowery fashion—like *no*.

"That would be nice," Vargas said.

Jennifer lost control of her eyelids for a second. "Sorry," she mumbled and touched both with the nails of her thumbs. "Smoke in my eyes."

Vargas said, "A minor irritant, as long as it does not cloud your brain."

"Meaning what?" Jennifer snapped, surprised at her own pugnacity. "Why is it so damn funny?"

"You must stop looking for double meanings," Vargas shrugged. He was smiling.

Jennifer opened her mouth, thought better of it and had a sip of wine instead.

A few seconds passed.

Jennifer said, "Angelo, once in a while I find you the most irritating and ambiguous person I have ever met. God alone knows how your mind works. I certainly don't."

"Early days," he said.

"You must be one of the most laconic creatures ever to graze this earth."

And a few other things, she added to herself, like fascinating in a way that is beyond sheer attraction. I wonder what he'd be like to live with. A twenty-four-hour-a-day-seven-days-a-week ordeal, most likely, a situation no woman with her marbles intact should contemplate even hypothetically.

"I seem to have this repelling effect on people," Vargas said. He looked thoughtful. "Quite incomprehensible, come to think of it. Could the reason be that I am not a great advocate of recycled opinions? Or, and-or, that is, that I am not unduly communicative? An intriguing thesis." He emptied his glass. "Lucky is the woman who does not have to share such isolated existence."

She knew she had gone red in the face.

"Shall we go?" Vargas suggested.

"It is not far?"

He looked at her shoes. "We better take a cab."

"This is Belgravia," she said when the taxi stopped.

"You know your city."

Jennifer looked around. "I have always thought that this tacky little section of London was packed with small-time grocers. Now I know."

"You look as if you have been given the choice between the last rite and a one-way ticket to outer space. You can wait here, if you like."

"Thank you, but I read the latest crime statistics the other day. I'll come up."

"How do you know it is up?"

"Intuition."

He unlocked the front door. "After you."

"Your mortgage must be astronomical," she said.

"Haven't got one."

"I see. Apart from being in the right business, you must be an exceptionally parsimonious person."

"Parsimonious—?"

Jennifer was getting used to his tone of voice each time he repeated a word. It indicated that he was not acquainted with it and would like to know.

"It means frugal, prudent, economical, hardsaving—pick your choice."

"No need to. I am all of that."

He headed for the stairs.

She said, "Is the lift out of order?"

"No. I always use the stairs. Good exercise."

"You go. I'll take the lift. Which floor?"

Vargas came back and pressed the button. They went in.

"Togetherness," he said and stared ahead.

Jennifer lowered her head and hid her smile behind her collar. Since he talked so much less than she did, it had taken some time before she had acknowledged his low-key sense of humour; acute understatements, finely tuned one-liners and not so few acerbic observations. There were also moments she found disturbing; in between his humour could turn black, and his analytical remarks became mordacious. It was a side of him she found enthralling, yet, it was against everything that she had been brought up to reject. But persisted it did and the ambivalence was fascinating.

What she saw of his dark and cryptic nature had become a magnet; it was part of what she had fallen for. Jennifer knew that she had more in common with him than she at first had anticipated—depths she had not explored before she met him.

The lift stopped. Top floor, she noticed. It struck her that the entrance door to Vargas' apartment was unusually solid and equipped with a locking system she had not seen before.

"Please," Vargas said.

Jennifer walked in, and continued walking. The doors to each room were open. The space was overwhelming. She said, "You have got the *entire* floor?"

"Yes. Feel free to look around." He went into the drawing room and closed all the windows before he disappeared into what she assumed was his bedroom.

Jennifer was transfixed. The space, the décor and the colour scheme all blended in harmoniously. There is not much I can add to this, she thought.

Everything bore the stamp of a person with a penchant for neatness, except the books. There were books everywhere; on the shelves, on the tables and on the floors. No wonder I only see him once a week, she mused, I've got some serious competition here.

She counted seventeen cacti, some in flower. The paintings and the drawings were mainly Oriental. There were several sculptures carved in wood, some grotesque and some less so. She thought they were South American, but she wasn't sure. They could be African.

She flickered through a stack of LPs and came across names unfamiliar to her; Marian Anderson, Richard Tauber, Paul Robeson, Jan Kiepura, Tito Gobbi, and Beniamino Gigli. She recognized Jussi Bjoerling, Caruso and some contemporary names. There was a selection of Japanese and Chinese music. Brahms and Mozart were well represented.

Jennifer looked around. She wondered why he had closed all the windows. The place was warm, more so than she herself preferred.

She went into the kitchen. It was large, well equipped and very tidy. Towards the window facing the square was a rectangular, wooden table, heavy farmhouse style, but with unusual carvings. Jennifer slid her fingers across the top, touched the figures on the rim and on the legs and knew that this was a piece she would have liked to acquire for herself.

She opened a few cupboards. A small selection of glasses, cups and plates looked ridiculously lonely in the amount of space allocated. Jennifer shook her head. Vargas could hardly be known as one of London's greats for home entertainment.

She opened the doors of the fridge. Each compartment was surprisingly full; all healthy stuff, she noticed, and nothing that would require extensive preparations or, for that matter, outstanding skills. A bowl of fruit on the bench between the sink and the fridge completed the picture.

On the way out from the kitchen, a large room caught her attention. At first glance it was empty.

Jennifer stepped inside. She found the light switch, and stared. The room was at least forty by twenty feet, the wooden floor different from the rest of the apartment, but the eye-catching feature were the mirrors covering two of the walls from floor to ceiling. Then she saw some weight-lifting equipment and a heavy punchbag. A white pair of pyjamas with a black belt around hung in a corner.

"Take off your shoes," she heard Vargas' voice behind her.

"What?"

"Nobody walks into my dojo with shoes on."

Nobody. Jennifer went outside, kicked off her shoes and returned. She said, "Why did you close all the windows? It's pretty warm in here."

"I dislike being cold."

It was the tone of voice, not the words. Jennifer waited for a few seconds for an explanation. None came. "What's a dojo?" she asked.

"Japanese for gym."

She beckoned towards the mirrors. "Are you sure you see enough of yourself in here?"

"Sufficiently."

"Angelo," she said, annoyed, "explain to me. Try to string together an exposition containing more than three words. I do not know the background here; what it is, what it means to you or anything else."

Vargas took off his shoes and socks before he came in.

Maybe I should offer to take off my stockings, Jennifer thought. She decided against it.

Together they walked into the centre of the room.

"This is my Number One Temple," he said.

"You've got more than one?"

"I've got two. The other is also Number One."

"That is most original. Where is it?"

"All in due time."

"Right," Jennifer said patiently. "Let us deal with Number One first."

Vargas said, "In this Temple I try to reach perfection in the martial arts, a perfection which is unobtainable and therefore worth striving towards. In this Temple I meditate, my mind searching for the Way of the Budo. Here I clear my thoughts, and here I seek the inspiration to live my life in accordance with and in harmony with the principles I once decided should rule my existence."

Jennifer had no idea what he was talking about. "It is not religious, is it?"

She saw the briefest of smiles flash across Vargas' face. "No, there are no metaphysical concepts, no superstition, no heaven and no hell, no gods and no demons. That is—" he paused for a moment "—not outside or beyond the boundaries of my being. In time I shall elaborate, if you so wish; the caveat being, however, that you could find my tenets remote from the teaching of the Catholic Church."

Nice irony, Jennifer thought, quite subtle. She said, "Don't worry. Tolerance and flexibility of mind are part of my upbringing."

"I am pleased to hear that, although not entirely surprised. When I do my katas and my combinations," he went on, "it is easy to make mistakes. Not a problem when Tadashi and I train together—we watch each other—but very easy when training alone. Hence the mirrors."

Next to the door Jennifer saw a pair of sticks, joined together with a chain, hanging on the wall. She stepped closer.

"A nunchaku," Vargas explained, "originally used for trashing grain."

There were two long and sharp-looking pieces made of steel, with a half-moon crossbar towards one end, an old-fashioned bow with some arrows, a long stick and two bamboo swords.

Jennifer said, "A nice little collection, but wouldn't a gun suffice?"
She turned and faced him.

He smiled and said, "Hundreds of years ago, the peasants of Korea, China and Japan were not allowed to possess weapons. The rulers had no wish to experience revolts, and they figured that a bunch of unarmed farmers could not possibly pose a threat. Neutralize your vassals, was the motto of the day, and peace shall forever exist. Never underestimate a peasant, though. From ordinary household implements they developed an impressive arsenal of simple but effective weapons, some of which you see here on the wall."

"Clever," Jennifer confessed.

"The rulers eventually discovered that tyranny is a fragile policy. They forgot to remember that hunger and oppression only serve to feed the imagination of those suffering."

Jennifer walked across to the other end of the room. She eyed a small Oriental table in black lacquer. It was exquisitely decorated. The legs were short, about ten inches. A candle was centred on the top. "What is this for?" she asked.

"Here I meditate."

She stepped aside. "Can you show me?"

Vargas sat down on his heels. He rested his fists on his thighs and closed his eyes.

That does not look too comfortable, Jennifer thought. "For how long do you sit like that?"

"For as long as necessary. The measure of time does not come into it."

Then, suddenly, in one swift movement, he was on his feet.

"That was quick," Jennifer gasped.

"Speed is what you lose first and must therefore be maintained for as long as mentally and physically possible."

Close to the wall was a small cabinet. It had no ornaments or decorations. Jennifer looked at the roughly cut square stone, some six by five by two inches, placed on top of the glass lid. "What is this stone symbolizing, Angelo?"

"It's a relic."

"A relic is usually associated with something."

"My past."

Jennifer waited. I see, she thought, no further enlightenment today. Perhaps next year. She looked through the glass. "That is a samurai sword?"

"It is. You have clearly been hiding your vast knowledge behind an innocent mask of deceptive curiosity."

"Amusing."

Vargas removed the stone carefully and placed it on the floor. He opened the lid. She watched as he lifted the sword up from the cabinet, slowly and tenderly as if handling a piece of the most delicate and brittle porcelain. He held the sword by his side; his left hand on the scabbard and only the thumb and the index finger of his right hand on the handle. He took three steps back. The blade swished through the air.

Vargas held the sword still. "Do not touch it."

"I have no desire to touch it."

"This blade will cut your finger *however* lightly you touch it."

Jennifer took a closer look. "What do all those little inscriptions represent?"

"They tell the entire story of the sword; who made it for whom, when, where, shrine dedicated and so on. This one was forged in the Kamakura period." Vargas pointed without touching. "The name of the smith was Masamune, and it was made in the Sagami province in 1326."

"Beautiful and nasty-looking," Jennifer said. She put her hands behind her back.

"An accurate description, and the result of the most laborious and demanding workmanship you can imagine. They picked little granules of iron from the riverbanks, and finally they had enough to start forging. The result was a long, flat piece of steel of a quality that is practically unthinkable today. Under the most intense heat, this piece was hammered and folded, hammered and folded, over and over again, until the master was reasonably satisfied that his creation was even better than the previous one. It is difficult to fathom the pride and the skills that went into it."

He put the sword back into the cabinet as tenderly as he had taken it out. Then he replaced the stone and bent forward. "See you later."

Jennifer frowned. "Are you talking to me or to the sword?"

"The sword. It has been exposed. I must tend to it."

"Is that some kind of ritual?"

"Yes. And a necessity." He closed the lid. "It is also a token of respect."

She sensed his gaze taking in the lines she knew had appeared on her forehead.

He said, "Apart from Tadashi and Yasmin, you are the only one I have ever shown that blade."

The knot in her stomach squashed the compliment. "Yasmin?"

"Tadashi's wife."

The knot dissolved. No mistress, no knot. She wondered what part the stone played. She said, "Where is your other Number One Temple?"

"Where the sky is the ceiling. The mountains, the open fields, the woods and the hills, the sun and the rain and the wind."

"Rural anywhere, in other words."

"Yes."

"I like that. I take it that your gods and your demons wouldn't function properly if their owner was confined within the stonewalls of a man-made construction, like a church."

"I don't mind churches, as long as they are empty. I can sit there for hours, which I sometimes do, contemplating the skills and the abilities and the vanity and the folly of my fellow man. It is quite mesmerizing."

The edge in his voice did not escape Jennifer. I wonder what happened to him, she thought. That degree of resentment did not materialize overnight.

"You must be hungry," he said.

Jennifer looked at her watch. "Oh no!" she groaned. "I booked a table for nine o'clock. It is half past. Where did the time go…?"

"In here. Would you prefer to cancel? We can always go somewhere else," he added. "Or we cook something up here."

"I am fine. Really," she assured him. "What about you?"

"I go for days without food. It is good for my system. How do you like my tie?"

The pair of identical chairs was four yards apart, each at a forty-five degree angle facing the windows towards the Square. Jennifer sat down at the edge of the seat and said, "It is—unusual." How polite can I get, she thought as her mind absorbed the full extent of a handpainted fire-spitting red dragon on light grey silk.

"It was given to me by someone in Korea," Vargas said.

By a colour-blind little tart of a geisha girl, in all probability. Did they have geisha girls in Korea? Not the right moment to ask.

She did not notice that Vargas watched her.

"I have considered renewing my wardrobe." He smiled. "That's a nice euphemism for someone who does not own a suit."

"Replenishing," Jennifer said, grateful for his willingness to progress towards social acceptance.

"Replenishing," Vargas repeated. "I remember that word, now. Do you think you could help me?"

Stunned, Jennifer said, "I—I would be delighted to help you. Thank you for trusting me."

"You've got taste."

She looked into his eyes and smiled with a mixture of endearment and resignation. "Stop reading me, Angelo. It is spooky."

"I do not always read you."

Jennifer looked down, thankful for the dim lights and the distance between them.

She said, "You've got a lot of books here, Angelo."

He turned his head with the expression of someone eyeing a dear child. *"Read not to contradict and confute, nor to believe and take for granted, but to weigh and consider."*

The tone of his voice added to her feeling of devotion, an emotion she no longer denied. She said, "That was beautifully summed up, Angelo."

His vague smile made him look oddly melancholy. "I wish those words were mine, but they were written by Francis Bacon."

"Oh. So he can more than paint, then. Like Mr. Itoh."

The nuance of pensiveness went. "The other Bacon, a good three hundred years ago."

Jennifer listened to her own forced laughter.

"Angelo, do you not find me attractive?"

"I do."

"Then why do you keep away from me? Why do you not want to touch me?"

"I do." Vargas rose to his feet. "I did not want—I was wary of imposing myself on you."

"How many signals do you need?"

She woke up in the early hours of the morning. Through the open door she saw Vargas sitting in his chair in the drawing room. He was dressed in a black kimono. His hands rested in his lap. He stared towards the window at the break of dawn.

Jennifer wondered why his quiet tenderness had not surprised her.

11

Kathleen threw her newspaper across the kitchen table. The pencil followed. Conor caught it in time. "Easy, now, my dear," he said soothingly. "She'll come round."

Kathleen got up, pushed the chair away and sat down again. Her fingers began drumming on the tabletop. "I do not understand it," she said at the top of her voice. "This is so unlike Jennifer. Why does she not talk to us? She *always* talks to us."

The lines on Conor's forehead grew deeper. He eyed his wife. "We worry unduly," he said and knew that he did not sound too assertive.

"Unduly? If that is the case, why do you have *duly* written all over your face?"

Conor wished he were out among his pigeons. Being caught between two women was not his idea of peace on earth.

"Well?" Kathleen demanded.

Conor shrugged. "I think we must bear in mind that she is not a teenager. Jennifer knows what she is doing. She'll come round."

Kathleen jolted in her chair. "She has been seeing whoever it is for, what, four-five weeks now. We do not know who he is, not even his name. Nothing. Why hasn't she invited him to dinner and introduced him to us? Who is he? Why does she hide him?"

Conor fiddled with his wristwatch. "I don't know. Maybe she is just—just not sure, yet. I mean, she and James were together for over three years. Jennifer does not rush into things. You know that. Perhaps she has already dropped whoever it is."

"Jesus, Joseph and Mary! She came back on cloud nine this morning. I saw her through the window. All sunshine."

Conor stroked her hand. "I think that whoever she's met has made one hell of an impact on her, out of the blue, so to speak. She is confused because she's found herself in a situation unfamiliar to her. Jennifer has always been in control, and this time she might not be. She hesitates because she has not learned the answers to all of her own questions, and that, my love, is what keeps her back. She'll surface, one of these days. Don't worry."

Kathleen looked up and smiled wanly. "I wonder who he is."

"Intriguing," Conor said.

Jennifer had one precious day to herself; Mrs. Mercante had returned to her native shores for a week, three of the decorator's crew had reported in sick and the wallpaper for the dining room had been delayed.

When she'd left, Vargas had suggested meeting up again the following Saturday. A long time, she thought, but she ventured neither a challenge nor a question. She had things to do, and, possibly, so did he; regardless, she certainly wasn't going to push it.

Jennifer lay on her back, fully dressed, apart from her shoes.

She thought of her parents. A furrow showed between her eyes. It bothered her being secretive, it went against her nature, but the situation was an uncommon one. She had no illusions about her mother's ability to observe and conclude—Kathleen knew there was somebody in the background—but what in God's name was there to tell? So far, it could only go like this: "*May I present Angelo Vargas who you remember meeting at Uncle Igor's place. That's right, together with the Japanese gentleman. Mr. Vargas has got four little shops selling everything from cucumbers to figs. He lives in Belgravia—an entire top floor, no less—a very popular address with small-time grocers, as we all know. The whole Square is littered with them. Mr. Vargas has travelled a lot. He has been to many exotic places. As far as origin, background, age, experiences and what he really does for a living are concerned, I'm afraid this has yet to be revealed. I also know that he does own a tie but not a suit, and—no context—he is a misanthrope. Secretive? No, I wouldn't say that. Just abnormally introvert. No, not shy either. Reserved, is more appropriate; the distinct and unmistakable mind-your-own-business attitude. And that is it, really. Not bad, considering that I have only met him five times.*"

She let out a loud sigh and laughed helplessly. What in the name of the complete army of Irish saints do I do? At present stage there is no way I can introduce him.

Jennifer sat up. I've *got* to know more, she thought, I cannot play this cat and mouse game with my parents much longer. It is unfair, undignified and basically downright stupid.

Ask Vargas, a voice whispered. Yes, what a brilliant idea. "*Listen, Angelo. It is my intention to make you part of my life; actually, I am moving in with you. However, in order to do so, I must introduce you to my parents. That is how we do it, in our family. Traditions. Etiquette, if you like. Now, this requires that you give me at least a broad summary of your life till date. Start talking— I won't interrupt.*"

A touch of genius, that one. Jennifer could clearly envisage Vargas getting up, open the door and ask her to go back to the universe she came from.

Who, then? Who knew something worth knowing about Angelo Vargas? The Japanese. He and Vargas had known each other for a long, long time. How does one interrogate an inscrutable Oriental? Stillborn. It was a waste of time even thinking about it.

Jennifer knew that she was wary of Ishihara. He had struck her as a cold, shrewd and calculating character. Polite, yes, but not at all a person who readily accepted somebody else's terms. His wife? Why should she talk—they had not even met.

Jennifer crossed the floor and saw her father stepping into his pigeon loft. She knew that he was not too happy, these days; only the week before had he thrown out an addict whose self-obsession, lies, inability to accept responsibilities for his own actions and a pathological predilection for blaming everybody else had overextended even Conor's patience.

Why don't you retire now, Dad, she thought. Get away from all this. You have done your bit, and more. Why don't you and Mum find a place in the country where you can have your pigeons and any other creatures you want, away from this cesspool of misery and suffering and apathy? One day there will be little grandchildren running around in your garden, and you will have all the time in the world to enjoy them.

Ahmed.

The picture of the rotund and amicable Palestinian came to Jennifer's mind as clearly as if he'd stood in front of her. He had been nice to her; jovial, kind and so much more human than the smooth and businesslike Mr. Ishihara.

I owe him much, Ahmed had said.

That could only mean that there was a story, an episode or perhaps a section of time that could elucidate Angelo Vargas' past, or some of it.

Would Ahmed talk?

There was only one way to find out.

She took a taxi to Hertford Lane and walked from there.

Ahmed and his two sons were standing by the door, enjoying a quiet moment, and looking at people and cars passing by. He spotted her when she was thirty yards away. A smile spread across his face. He opened the door.

"I knew you would come back," he grinned. "This time, Miss Moran, you cannot leave empty-handed."

"I won't," Jennifer promised.

"Apples?" He picked one and held it up. "All the way from Australia. Delicious."

Jennifer said, "Ahmed, would it be possible to have a glass of tonic water? I have been walking for a while."

"I am so sorry, Miss Moran. Please accept my apologies. Where are my manners! Please come in."

He took a few steps back. Jennifer followed.

She saw him take a bottle from the shelf and said, "I insist on paying, Ahmed."

"Unthinkable," he answered and undid the screw top. "On the house."

Jennifer smiled. "What will Mr. Vargas say—customers drinking up his profit?"

"Nothing. I deduct it from my own profit. We have a profit-sharing system."

"Mr. Vargas exercises a rigid control?"

Ahmed shot her a quick glance, but the tone of his voice did not alter. "None at all. Mr. Vargas trusts me."

Cautious now, Jennifer thought, don't overstep. This man was not born yesterday. "I like to hear that," she said. "It's nice."

"Come into my office," Ahmed said. "Let us rest our weary legs for a few minutes."

The office was small, but neat and comfortable. Jennifer sat down. Ahmed left the door open. He went over to a corner and fumbled around with something she could not see.

"Do you like Arabic coffee?" she heard him ask.

"Are you making some?"

"Oh yes. All day long. Mind the shop!" he suddenly shouted to his sons. "I am busy. Do not disturb."

His mischievous grin was contagious. Jennifer said, "You are obviously a good organizer."

"The best," Ahmed nodded. "It takes a lot of competence to run this emporium."

"I think you like it."

His teeth were white and strong. "I love it. Mr. Vargas made me very happy when he asked me to run this shop. Can I tempt you with another cup?"

The coffee was sweet and strong. "Yes, please."

Now or never, she thought when Ahmed sat down. "Where did you meet?" she asked and hoped that she sounded and looked as casual and innocent as she had managed to do in front of her mirror two hours earlier.

Ahmed stretched his short legs. "In Lebanon," he said and stared into his cup. "An eternity ago, Miss Moran, and yet—and yet it seems like yesterday."

Jennifer kept quiet.

"Have you ever been to Lebanon, Miss Moran?"

"No, I have not. Please, call me Jennifer."

For a few moments he seemed far away. "It is a long story," he said at last, "and not a pretty one."

Her heart jumped a beat. "I am not in a hurry."

"Lebanon," Ahmed said as if he was talking to himself. "My beloved Lebanon. The days when Beirut was The Pearl of the Middle East. The days when we all lived side by side and there were no killings and no destruction. The days when all we wanted was to get on with our lives and live in peace. *Halas.*"

"Halas—?"

"Finished," he said, "it means finished." He offered her a cigarette. She declined. She watched as the smoke seeped through Ahmed's lips that had suddenly got thinner. "I was not born in Lebanon," he continued, "I was born in Palestine. Then, as you know, in 1948, thanks to the wisdom of the mighty powers, the country became Israel, the land of the Jews. Like millions of other Palestinians we moved out. Overnight we became a nation without a country. Not refugees. Exiles. My family found a new home in Beirut. My father and I opened a little shop there, similar to this one. I got my own family, and my wife and I were blessed with two sons and a daughter. We had a nice little apartment in the suburbs, and the shop was doing well. We did not became wealthy, but life was good, and we were happy." Ahmed topped up his coffee and stirred slowly. The ash fell from his cigarette onto the floor. He did not seem to notice. "Then my father suddenly died in 1950," he continued. His words were clear and distinct, but his voice was eerily apathetic. "He owed money, which I did not know about, and the creditor took over the shop."

Ahmed sipped his coffee. His eyes were focused on the wall behind Jennifer. Red dots had spread across his cheeks. He continued, "My mother stayed with her sister but there was no room for the rest of us, for me and my family. We had no money and nowhere to go, so we ended up in one of the refugee camps set up by the UN Relief and Works Agency, together with 950,000 other Palestinian."

He opened another bottle of water and filled her glass. He went on, "It was then that I fully understood to what extent we must credit the Israelis for being exceptionally factual and objective. They dutifully informed the world that all Palestinians are terrorists whilst the Jews fighting in Palestine in 1948 were freedom fighters. I also discovered, and have gracefully accepted, that God's chosen people have rights that nobody else have, and that their means, any means, always justifies the end. During the next few years, Jennifer, I learned a lot about weapons. Many a time did I witness three-and-four-year-old Palestinian terrorists screaming as their bodies were torn apart."

He covered his mouth with his handkerchief, cleared his throat and stared at her. "Did we try to fight the Israelis? Yes, we did. They had taken our land. We were barred from coming back to our homes. It was all so futile, though. All the great and powerful democracies supported Israel and the Arab countries kept quiet."

He wiped his hands on his apron.

"I could not see it getting any better, and I asked myself—is this a *life*?" He rubbed his forehead. He looked gaunt and tired. The sigh from his chest came like a gasp. He blinked, dipped one finger in his glass and wet his lips.

"Skirmishes with the Israelis went on and on. They always retaliated, which was to be expected, and then they avenged." he said and tossed his head from side to side. "They always *avenged*."

Jennifer found it hard to meet his eyes; never before had she encountered such grief and naked despair.

Ahmed lifted his head and stared at the ceiling. The age in his eyes shocked Jennifer. He straightened his fingers and looked as if a grim reality had been replaced by a horrific dream.

He had slumped in his chair. His left hand moved as if he was crushing an undesirable object. "A nephew of mine took it upon himself to try to contact the International Red Cross. We assumed that they would react when they heard that we were at the mercy of indiscriminate killers. I decided to go with him to the village and we sneaked through the deserted streets looking for a sign that could lead us to the Red Cross. After a kilometre or so a single shot was fired. My nephew was hit in the head and his young life was gone. Till this day I cannot remember how I got back to the camp, but I did, only to find that my little daughter had disappeared. I searched for her all over this dilapidated and grotesque parody of human existence, but nobody had seen her. In the meantime, the shooting had started all over again, but this time for only fifteen minutes. I came back to my wife and we could only conclude that our little girl had decided to follow me."

Ahmed reached for his glass. The expression in his eyes had changed from weariness to a cold stare. "So," he said through lips hardly moving, "I went out again. After some half a kilometre I saw a car parked outside a building which I had passed two hours earlier. The car had not been there the first time. Yes, I thought, that's where she must be. Someone got her in there when the shooting began. I went through one room, through another room, and then I saw him, an officer sitting at a table. He had a half-litre flask in front of him and a metal cup in his hand. I also saw my daughter. She was standing in a corner. Her eyes were wide open without seeing and blood was running down her legs. She was seven years old. The officer smiled at me and said, "You must be the father." I leaped forward, but he had already pulled his gun and he hit me so hard on the side of my head that I fell and lost consciousness. I woke up, lying on the floor, gagged with my own scarf, my belt around my legs and my hands tied behind my back. The officer was sitting at the table. My little girl was still standing in the corner. I tried to speak, but of course I could only make noises. I thought how unlikely it was that anybody could find us, and I knew that both my little girl and I would be dead before the officer left the house. Then I heard a few shots and suddenly someone came through the door. He wore a white coat and the emblem of the Red Cross. I could not believe my own eyes. Naturally, I knew that the doctor's life, too, was in danger, but at least there was a glimmer of hope, however small. The doctor will talk sense to the officer, I thought. The doctor will make him go away and allow me to take my daughter back to the camp. I tried to catch the doctor's eyes, but only to discover that I did not exist. How is this possible, I thought, that he has not noticed me? How is it possible that he has not seen my little girl standing in the corner? I heard the officer say: "Care for a drink, doctor?" The gun was back in the holster, but I saw what the doctor could not see; the officer's right hand resting on the handle. The doctor smiled. He leaned forward as if to take the flask. Then he hit the officer so hard between the eyes that he lifted from the chair, crashed against the wall and fell to the floor, unconscious. The doctor pulled out a white cloth from his pocket and used it as a glove whilst he removed the gun and took out the magazine which he put in an inside pocket. He tossed the gun under the table and bent down and untied me. Then he lifted up my little girl and put her in my arms, nodding towards the door. At that moment the officer came to. He started swearing and grabbed for the gun that wasn't there. The silence that followed was strange, no; it was surreal, mesmerizing in a way I have never experienced before or after. I stood there, with my daughter in my arms, enthralled, as the doctor unbuttoned his coat. All of a sudden and from nowhere there was a gun with a silencer in his hand. He lifted his arm till the barrel pointed towards the officer's groin. The officer began to cry. Whimpering, almost in a whisper he pleaded, begged and swore. He summoned his gods and promised the world and cursed his little mistake. Just go away, he whined, wars could do terrible things to people and he was only human. The doctor fired twice—plop! plop! and the screams, the screams from that officer will remain music to my ears for as long as I live."

Ahmed paused and drank some water. Jennifer's hands were damp. She felt a few drops of sweat running down her back. Her head was swimming. She searched in vain for something to say. She saw that a blood vessel had burst in Ahmed's left eye.

"Yes, Jennifer," Ahmed said softly, " those screams and the only three words the doctor said shall forever remain the most beautiful music to my ears."

"What did he say?" she whispered.

Ahmed swallowed like a man who wanted to extinguish a fire in his throat. "He said: "Enjoy your vasectomy.""

Jennifer's forehead was burning. She had cramp in her legs. Ahmed watched her carefully. His anger was gone, replaced by compassion.

He went over to a corner and came back with a dark brown liquid in a miniature glass. "Drink this," he said.

Jennifer grimaced as the elixir burned down her throat, but the effect was almost instant. Ahmed readjusted his chair. He sat down and folded his hands. He said, "I did not notice that the doctor had taken the keys from the officer's pocket. We went out to the car and the doctor drove us back to the camp. We got out, and as people came running towards us I turned only to see the car drive away." Ahmed twinned his thumbs and smiled. "That was the first time I saw Mr. Vargas. The moment the car disappeared, I remembered that I had not even said thank you."

"What was Mr. Vargas doing there?"

"I have no idea. He never told me and I never asked."

"And then you came over here?"

"Yes," Ahmed nodded, "for the sake of all of us, not least my daughter. It had become clear to me that we could no longer live with this fear. I had come to understand the eternal curse of politics infected by religion, and I knew that the Israelis would not go away, at least for a very long time. I knew about the suffering of the Jewish people during the centuries and I knew about the Holocaust, but perhaps one should not forget that the concept of being the chosen people was not forced upon them. They have now almost succeeded in replacing the entire history of the Second World War with one single epitaph: *The Holocaust*—supremely disregarding that another fifty million people also died." Ahmed ran a finger inside the collar of his shirt and loosened his tie. "Goebbels, with the rather apt first name *Joseph*, was a master teacher, and he left a legacy. It is ironic that the Jews have become his most brilliant students, a paradox they evidently and understandably prefer to ignore." Ahmed's eyelids moved slowly down, and then up again, as if he could not be bothered to nod. "So, Jennifer," he said, "I wrote to a cousin of mine who settled here in London many years ago. I knew he was running a successful import-export business, and I thought, maybe he is expanding and could do with some help. His business was indeed going very well, and he was kind enough to lend me some money, not only for us to come over, he also helped me with a loan so that I could buy furnitures and other essentials. A very kind and understanding man. We rented a small flat, still do, and we all did our best to adjust and adapt to become part of the English way of life. A foreigner can never succeed, of course—" Ahmed smiled wryly "—but at least there are no civil wars here. They don't kill you for having a different belief, and Golders Green is short on missiles and aeroplanes. Would you care for another glass?"

"Oh no, no thank you," Jennifer said, "that was quite sufficient."

Ahmed grinned. "Strong stuff. I make it myself."

"But I thought Muslims—" Jennifer stopped, sensing that she could be treading on delicate ground.

"—don't drink?" Ahmed commented lightly. "Oh well, we have our little indulgences, most of us. I am a religious man, but I am not a fundamentalist. A little bit of flexibility in life usually does more good than harm."

Jennifer nodded, thankful for Ahmed's understanding attitude.

"I think I'll have one myself," he said and steered his frame towards the corner, "and I shall re-live the day I met Mr. Vargas for the second time."

He came back, dumped heavily into his chair and emptied his glass. "I was walking down Regent Street, and I was not in a cheerful mood. My cousin's business had gone downhill, not entirely of his own making, and life had become difficult for us both. He had lost a few agencies, some of the markets were not what they used to be, and some debtors had let him down badly. It was a lot of money, quite a blow. My cousin was struggling, and eventually he lost his self-confidence and his entrepreneurial spirit. I did what I could to help, but it became obvious that the business could no longer support both our families. He deducted from my salary a certain amount per month as repayment for the loans, and one day he told me that the figure had to be increased. What was left in the first place gave us a living, but no more, and I could not see how I would manage with even less. So, with these cheerful thoughts running through my mind, I was one day on my way to see a customer in Haymarket who owed us money. I took the bus to Oxford Circus and I decided to walk from there." Ahmed lifted his eyes towards the ceiling and shook his head. "I could have been five minutes earlier, or five minutes later, or I could have walked on the other side—what luck! No, it was not luck. It was God's will. There, towards me, came the doctor from Beirut. He looked different. His hair was not dark any more, and he no longer had brown eyes." Ahmed smiled and rubbed his nose. "But I knew, I *knew*. Every instinct, every fibre in me told me who this was. I stopped. He looked through me and continued walking. I can't be wrong, I said to myself, he does not recognize me. I turned, and I followed, wondering how to approach him. Of course—well, it is easy to say now—he knew he was being followed. All of a sudden he was walking next to me. Not too close, but next to me. I said, "Thank you for what you did." He did not look at me. "Never seen you before," he said. Oh, did I feel foolish? Not because I was wrong, I knew I wasn't mistaken, but because he did not want to know, because he in effect told me not to bother him. "All I wanted was to thank you for what you did for me and my daughter," I said. "Please accept my apologies if I have inconvenienced you." Then, abruptly, he stopped and so did I. It was as if he had turned me around without touching me, and he looked me straight in the eye. "Ahmed," he said, "let's have a drink." I could not believe it, but that is what he said. "How do you know my name?" I asked. I saw this little smile on his face and he said, "You ask too many questions.""

Jennifer smiled. "That rings a bell."

"Well," Ahmed said, "that's Mr. Vargas for you."

Nothing in his voice indicated a double meaning. He continued, "For the first time in my life I found myself inside a pub. It was early in the day, and we sat down at a table in a quiet corner, facing each other. I had my coffee, and Mr. Vargas had his now so familiar Irish whisky." Ahmed laughed. "I keep a bottle over there," he gestured. "Mr. Vargas always has a glass when he drops in and listens to how the business is going. I think it bores him." Ahmed lit one of his sweet-smelling cigarettes. "Anyway, Mr. Vargas presented himself and asked how my daughter was doing and what had happened since. Just those two questions. One hour later I had told him practically everything and he had hardly said a word."

I am familiar with the pattern, Jennifer thought. Mr. Vargas certainly knows how to make people talk.

Ahmed went on, "Thereafter, he said, just out of the blue, that he was going to open a shop in Mayfair, and would I run it for him. I was terribly embarrassed, and I tried to convince him that I was fine, really. I thought he must have believed that the purpose of my story was to ask for help. It was an awful moment; I was so ashamed, and I did not know what to say or where to look.

"Ahmed," Mr. Vargas said, "Ahmed, you look like a man sitting on a camel's droppings. I need a manager. I need somebody who can run the shop for me. I'll pay you a manager's salary, and we split the profit down the middle. In return you do not bother me with details. You run the store as if it is your own. Once a month we go over the accounts, and that's it." I remember that I mumbled something about the offer being far too generous, but he just cut me off. "I shall answer the question you are too polite to ask," he said. "I am resident in this country, not domiciled. I need to own a business. That is all there is to it."

I said, "I do not know how to thank you, Mr. Vargas," and he said, "Don't. You are doing me a favour. Business is not one of my passions. Do we have a deal?"" Ahmed's face cracked into a web of fine lines. He clicked his teeth. "And here I am."

Jennifer sat still. Thoughts raced through her mind, and the chaos of her emotions made her feel unwell. Ahmed seemed relaxed and did not appear to expect a response.

"Why did you tell me all this?" she asked in a flat voice.

Ahmed looked over his shoulder. He touched his temples with his thumbs. The glow of his cigarette flared. He inhaled and used the palm of his left hand as an ashtray. "For your ears only, Jennifer. One day you will understand."

In other words, ask no more questions, she thought. One day I will understand. Or maybe not.

She got up. "Thank you, Ahmed. Thank you for talking to me, and thank you for your company."

There was no mistaking the warmth in Ahmed's eyes. She felt the calluses in his big, strong hand as he took hers. "Bless you," he said.

Bless me, Jennifer reflected, or do *you* include Angelo Vargas?

She took a taxi home and met her mother at the doorstep.

"Some come and some go," Kathleen smiled. "Been shopping?"

"Yes."

"Eating on your own?"

"That is not exactly unusual," Jennifer answered and regretted the edge to her voice.

"I didn't imply that," Kathleen said.

This can't go on for much longer, Jennifer thought as she went upstairs. The tension between us is becoming unbearable. I have alienated myself from my own parents who are my best friends and the nicest people on this earth. My mother is hurt; she does not understand why I am behaving this way. Neither do I, for that matter. But what is there to say? How can I explain this embryonic relationship with a man I know so little about, and what I do know is more disturbing than reassuring?

She sat down in an easy chair and loosened her belt. *Angelo Vargas,* she said out loud, *what have you done to me? How can I be in love with a man of violence; I, who abhor violence, and how can I find a future with a man whose life is shrouded in mystery and who does not seem to care about my need to know the human being behind the name before I can love him? Tell me, Angelo.*

She heard the sound of her own staccato laughter. Why this obsession, she thought, why am I so confused and lost and in doubt? How can I bring him here and introduce him to my parents? I can't. I am floating aimlessly around in a vacuum, and I have no idea how to get out of it.

Who can I talk to, she reflected, I *must* talk to somebody, someone who can listen and understand. There are not many—in fact, is there *anyone*?

For a short moment she thought of Delia, her best friend and confidante since their early school days. Many a little secret had been exchanged during the years; Delia confiding more in Jennifer than vice versa, Delia being the more talkative and gossipy and not minding that Jennifer was both by nature and by intentional design a good deal more reserved.

No, Jennifer concluded, not Delia. She would find it fascinating, thrilling and hugely entertaining, but basically she would not understand. Delia would not comprehend an involvement so intensely personal and deeply complex; she would find it exhilarating, like a minimal or superficial challenge with limited consequences.

Uncle Igor.

Of course. Kind, old Uncle Igor, her godfather and mentor.

The telephone rang.

No, Angelo, Jennifer thought and did not move, *I am not talking to you. I need to collect my thoughts and my feelings before we can meet again. I do not want to make an excuse. You will detect it, and that'll do no good. I am not here. I shall call you when I am ready. Please try to... how the hell can he understand when he does not know what is going through my mind?*

The ringing continued.

This is childish, she thought. Pick up the damn receiver and make it clear that—that next week will be more convenient. Something along those lines. Not unfriendly. Not negative. He would not push her. Not Angelo.

"Hello?" she said and wished she had cleared her throat.

"Hello," a female voice said, "my name is Yasmin Ishihara. I believe you have met my husband Tadashi. My husband and Angelo Vargas are close friends. Brothers, in a manner of speaking."

Her laughter made Jennifer think of a silver spoon rapidly tapping a crystal vase.

"Brothers," she repeated. "Yes, two of a kind, apart from the striking similarity."

Yasmin's infectious giggling continued. "I like that. Angelo said you are very funny."

Jennifer said, "I am flattered. What else did he reveal about me?"

"Not much, really. You know how talkative he is. Except—"

"—except what?"

"He said he'd never thought it possible to meet a woman whose class and humour matched her beauty."

Jennifer looked out the window. She pushed back a strand of hair that obscured her view. "Did he? Obviously an observation based on vast experience," she said. She wondered how Yasmin would interpret a comment coloured by infantile jealousy.

"Oh well," Yasmin said, "he's been around for a while. Anyway, the brothers said I would enjoy your company. Do you think we could meet up one day, say, for afternoon tea?"

There is a trace of an accent, Jennifer thought; added charm, if anything. Like Angelo, although his clipped and husky English differed from the smooth fluency of the Ishiharas'.

She said, "I'd love to. How do we recognize each other?"

The nightingale laughter came back. "I'd be surprised if the Harrods Tea Room is packed with Korean women."

Jennifer said, "Listen, the next few days are going to be rather busy, but I have got nothing on this afternoon. How are you fixed?"

"I do what I want to do," Yasmin said. "That is one of the advantages of being married to Tadashi. Shall we say one hour from now?"

Jennifer glanced at her watch. "I look forward."

"So do I."

The line went dead.

What an eventful life, Jennifer mused as she changed. I have recently acquired a lover of unknown origin and whose idea of getting a message across is basic, to put it mildly. I have collected one Palestinian and now one Korean friend, and, it seems, at least indirectly, one Japanese friend; that is, to the extent that Mr. Ishihara can lower his superior being through the strata and reach contact with the outskirts of humanity. Not bad for a girl who prefers to believe that she is reserved, selective, critical and the antithesis of a socialite.

Maybe I should revise if not overhaul the image I have of myself. Two introverts in one family is one too may.

Dad and Angelo will like each other. They are similar, in many ways, except that Dad does not shoot people in the groin. Should it so happen that Angelo likes pigeons, then eternal friendship is guaranteed.

I wonder what Yasmin can tell me about Angelo. She must have known him for a long time. Whatever it is, I hope it's not upsetting; I've had enough of that for one day. What do I do if she says that behind his thin veneer of good manners and his interest in books there is a ferocious tartar who lives by the sword; a latter-day samurai whose real market place is of a less docile nature than selling salad leaves to cost-conscious housewives?

Christ Almighty, what happened to my marbles?

The Tea Room was not full. Jennifer walked across towards the table where Yasmin was seated. She got up. Her handshake was firm and warm.

"I am pleased to meet you," she said. "I see that Angelo did not exaggerate."

They sat down. Jennifer eyed the Korean woman and did not try to conceal her admiration. "I can only return the compliment," she said. "Your husband is a very lucky man."

Yasmin's eyes did not leave Jennifer's face. "I know, but, in all honesty, the little rascal deserves me. He is an unusual man, my Nipponese eccentric. I was only a little girl when I first saw him, and he has bewitched me ever since. He is always fun to be with, always attentive and there is never a dull moment."

The waiter came over.

"Afternoon tea for two, please," Yasmin said.

"Thank you, Mrs. Ishihara. Scones?"

"The whole lot." She flashed a smile and turned to Jennifer. "You know," she continued, "boredom is a worse enemy to marriage than infidelity, but neither are as lethal as indifference. Tadashi taught me that. It is right, don't you think?"

Jennifer nodded. She was rarely impressed by other women's looks, but she admitted that she had to make an exception for the girl opposite. She had no way of telling Yasmin's age—she could be anything between twenty and thirty; her skin was milky white and looked incredibly soft, her long black hair parted in the middle was silky and rich, and the expression in her large almond eyes was warm and humorous. She was slender and gracious like a sylph, and her movements were finely measured and delicate. Jennifer knew that she had never seen a female as perfect as this Korean woman.

Yasmin said, "Are you in love with Angelo?"

Jennifer wondered if the rash she felt spreading across her face was visible. She managed a stiff smile. "I hardly know him."

"You can't let that worry you. Nobody knows Angelo."

"Not even you?"

Yasmin opened her handbag and took out a packet of Sobranie cigarettes. She offered one to Jennifer and lit them both. "Not even I," she said. "Angelo has been in my life for the last decade, but I do not profess to know him. Angelo is as solitary and closed as Tadashi is gregarious and extrovert."

"They must have *something* in common," Jennifer ventured.

The tea arrived. Yasmin paused until the waiter had left. "They do. They are both misanthropes; Tadashi by design—he loves it—and Angelo by nature or circumstances or probably a combination." Yasmin exhaled and smiled through the smoke. "One on purpose, and the other from experience."

"Not nature?"

"Nature formed by experience."

"That wasn't bad from someone who claims to know little or nothing."

"Just assuming and surmising, Jennifer. You don't mind being on first name? I think we should. My assumptions are based on observations. You will have to do the same. It is easier with Tadashi. He is not as recondite as Angelo, and Tadashi never lost his roots."

Jennifer put down her knife. "When did Angelo lose his roots?"

"Many, many years ago, but exactly when and why I do not know. It is what my intuition is telling me. It is also my intuition that somehow, somewhere along the way, Angelo got badly hurt. I do not mean *physically*."

Jennifer looked down and wondered how much else was hidden behind Vargas' impervious and laconic demeanour. She raised her eyes and saw that Yasmin was watching her with an expression of concern blended with percipience. "You are very fond of him, aren't you?"

Yasmin smiled with her eyes. "I am. And I trust him implicitly. Should it become your decision to love him—excuse the word *decision*—make sure that you never let him go. You'll never find another Angelo Vargas."

The waiter poured more tea. The picture of Ahmed flashed through Jennifer's mind. She heard the *plop* of a silenced gun. "On all accounts?"

Yasmin's eyes narrowed a fraction. "You either accept a man for what he is, or you don't. You cannot separate the bad from the good and the past from the present. You cannot recast the mould. You cannot disconnect facts and experiences and circumstances any more than you can replace realities with daydreaming."

"Is that how you evaluate Tadashi?"

Yasmin's smile was radiant. "That is how I see my Tadashi. There is a darker side to his nature which I am well aware of, but it is part of the person, part of the man I love."

"You are a wise woman, Yasmin."

"I have learned a thing or two. You know what Tadashi once said to me, many years ago? He said: *"One day, my girl, when you grow up and you are no longer emotionally and mentally short-sighted, I'll marry you."* It took some time, though, before he finally admitted that I wasn't a teenager any more and he consented."

"*He* consented?"

"Oh yes. Twice, I asked him. The third time he gave in. Tadashi did not become the ever so uxorious man I now know overnight. He is such a free spirit. He agreed because he knew that I would not be entirely happy without that extra little bit of security that marriage is supposed to provide. After all, he'd said all along that we belong together, which is true enough. He understood my point of view."

"Tadashi is a financier?"

"Yes. He plays the markets, and he is pretty good at it. He does not exactly love the City, but it does keep him entertained. He is gregarious, as I said, but his threshold of boredom is low. You have not heard him, yet, in full flow, but he's an expert at amusing himself."

Jennifer went for another scone. Unless she got rid of her insecurity and came to terms with a future with or without Angelo Vargas, she'd lose a stone in weight.

Yasmin continued, "I have never met anyone more capable of upsetting people than my darling husband, and the more he scores, the happier he is. His arsenal of invectives, cutting remarks and colourful descriptions are unsurpassed, which of course makes him admired, hated, adored and despised. He loves it."

Why is she telling me this? Jennifer thought. She said, "I have only met him once, and I must say I found him diplomatic, polite and eloquent. Even Uncle Igor sees your husband as both tactful and considerate, and my godfather is a very sensitive plant."

"Godfather?"

"I call him Uncle Igor, but we are not related. When my parents came over from Ireland, he was the one who helped them. They asked him if he would do them the honour of being my godfather. They have been close friends ever since."

"I think that is charming," Yasmin said. "What a lovely little story. So, he is more than just a family friend?" Her words met a sticky part in her throat. "You are close to your godfather, from the sound of it."

"He is the nicest man you could ever dream of meeting. We'll get together, one day." She placed the fingernails of her right hand on the tablecloth and made a circular movement. "When I first met your husband, at Uncle Igor's house, Angelo was there. He did not say one single word."

Yasmin smiled. "Tadashi and I have tried to make him socialize, but it's easier to pull a tiger through a keyhole. Angelo is happy with his books and his music, or less unhappy, whichever. I am not so sure that such a picture is complete, clinically speaking—I mean, not even Angelo is an island, however hard that is to believe."

Jennifer touched the corners of her mouth with her tongue. "You make me wonder what my contribution would be."

Yasmin held Jennifer's eyes. "You can give him a new lease of life."

Jennifer frowned. "What do you mean?"

Yasmin opened her packet of Sobranies. "One more, and I must rush."

"What do you mean by a new lease of life?" Jennifer pressed on.

They looked at each other. Seconds ticked away. Finally, Yasmin said, "That is for you to find out. You will."

Another cryptic message, like Ahmed's—*one day you will understand.* Christ, she thought, these foreigners do know how to veil their predictions.

Neither spoke for a while, but Jennifer did not find the silence uncomfortable. Instinctively, she liked Yasmin and felt that she was a warm and intelligent woman. There was a tinge of mystique about her that Jennifer credited to Yasmin's Oriental origin; it was hard to penetrate and probably impossible ever to understand fully for a Western mind, but that did not necessarily mean that a friendship could not be genuine, valuable and pleasant. Jennifer's instincts also told her that Yasmin knew Angelo Vargas far better than she was prepared to admit, and that the four of them could make company preferable to most people she knew about.

Yasmin signalled to the waiter. "On me," she said. "Your turn next time."

"It would be nice to see you again," Jennifer said.

"We shall have many a good time together," Yasmin said. Her smile was congenial.

Am I imagining things, Jennifer thought, or is her posture a shade restrained? She watched the elegant figure of Yasmin as she graciously strode through the main restaurant and was gone.

Yasmin went home and found Tadashi hidden behind the *Financial Times.* He got up when he heard her come in, embraced her and said, "It is terribly quiet without you. How did it go?"

To the point, Yasmin thought. That's my Tadashi. She sat down opposite him.

"As expected," she said evenly. "Angelo did not exaggerate. She is quite a woman."

Ishihara shrugged. "She isn't exactly the first in his life."

"True enough, but she could easily be the last."

"*That* serious? You must be joking."

"You talk against better knowledge, my Emperor. Angelo is getting on a bit, and he knows damn well that women like Jennifer Moran are few and far between. I am telling you—she moves in with him, and that's it. End of philandering for Brother Angelo."

"Sweet and touching," Ishihara said. His voice was heavy with irony. "Yes, I can see Angelo becoming an affable pillar of society, sanguine and equable, a minion and a conformist that any bourgeois little woman can be duly proud of. Sorry, my darling, but there are limits to miracles."

"He can change."

"Change? We are talking about a complete metamorphosis, Yasmin. It is a mental, emotional and physical impossibility. How the hell do you think that *anybody* can make a paragon out of someone who is fundamentally an untamed animal, a recluse and a dipsomaniac? Stop fantasizing, my orchid. It just does not happen."

He folded his hands on top of his head. Yasmin could hear his teeth working.

"Is that how you see him?" she said.

"I see him for what he is. What I said is an impartial and objective appraisal of a man who I trust and who is my friend."

"Is that right?"

"Yes, that is damn right. What do you think will happen when Jennifer finds out what he has been doing for a living since he left his native shores? How do you think she will react when she discovers the real Angelo? Mark my words, Yasmin, she'll disappear faster than she arrived."

"You and I have long ago admitted that we do not know the real Angelo."

"I know him well enough."

"Neither do we know Jennifer."

"What is there to know? She's just one of those millions of women who find the unobtainable attractive. *So* common, my dear."

Why is he getting upset? she thought. Why does it bother him that Angelo might wish for another life and settle down? For some reason, Tadashi sees Jennifer as a threat. Jealousy? Or is there something else— aspects that I have yet to learn about?

Ishihara lowered his head and watched his toes moving. "You wait and see," he said. "Adoration is a perishable commodity."

Yasmin gave it a few seconds. "If that is the case, how come we still love each other?"

Ishihara picked up the newspaper and tossed it onto the table. "Don't confuse love with adoration. Another thing is, we *know* each other. We have known each other since you came out of kindergarten. There was practically nothing we did not know *about* each other from the onset of our harmonious, caring and reciprocal relationship. Miss Moran is facing a drama of universal proportions. Tell me, wouldn't *you* have backed out, at this stage of your life, if you had discovered the naked truth about your new-found infatuation?"

"Not necessarily."

"*What?*" Ishihara's eyebrows closed ranks. "Don't give me that one. I agree that there are shocks and shocks, but in this case we are talking about a veritable and monumental earthquake."

He is not giving up, she thought. Is he not aware of the risk he is running if he alienates Angelo? She brushed her hair aside. The muscles in the back of her neck had become rigid, and she raised and lowered her shoulders. She said, "You and I have been partners for a long time. Your worldly image is that of an urbane, high-minded and benevolent person, but we both know what is behind this appealing façade. You are no more of an innocent from abroad than Angelo is. You are not less unyielding and no more of a Samaritan. Granted, there is a deep-rooted rancour in Angelo that you have not got, but you are both ruthless mercenaries. That's the man you are, Tadashi, the man I live with and the man I love. So," she said with a pensive smile, "I am not the victim of illusions, and I am not clinging to wishful thinking."

Ishihara's eyes jittered. The rays from the late afternoon sun hit the windows and he closed the blinds. "Angelo is wired differently," he said. "Apart from that, what are you getting at?"

"If I can, why can't Jennifer?"

Ishihara pulled his shirt up from his trousers and took off his cufflinks. "Try to understand what I am saying to you. Angelo is not I, and Jennifer is not you. Our situation is not their situation. She must be superhuman if she does not freak out."

"I think you are in for a surprise."

He placed the cufflinks side by side. "Am I?"

208

"There is steel in that woman."

"So what. In the unlikely event that nothing *else* scares her away, she'll come to her senses when it dawns upon her that Angelo isn't made for a domestic heaven on earth."

Yasmin stared at her husband with unblinking eyes. "Is there something you have not told me, Tadashi?"

He looked surprised. "Like what?"

"You once promised me that your next assignment is your last. Is that no longer the case?"

He began to unbutton his shirt. "I'll take a shower."

"Don't walk away from my question. Please answer me."

Irritation ran like a web of ugly scars across his face. "You know bloody well that I do not break my promises to you."

He left quickly. She could hear him slamming the door to their bedroom.

Wrong question, she thought. What is going on here? She knew that he saw his final assignment as the apex of his career; more complicated, more dangerous and infinitely more rewarding than anything he and Angelo had ever done before. She had no idea whom, when and where, as always. Tadashi had never subjected her to the burden of such knowledge, and this certainly wasn't going to be an exception. All he'd told her that it was a few years away, apart from intimating the magnitude of the task. She knew that she wasn't going to get any wiser.

Weariness descended like heavy chains around her neck and shoulders. She lay down on the sofa and closed her eyes.

I do not want to worry any longer, she thought. Why can't you retire now, Tadashi? Leave the rat race and take this terrible tension out of our lives. We have enough money to last us for another century. Can you not understand that I want to erase from my mind the thought of you in jail and Angelo in a grave?

Angelo.

Yasmin lay still for a while, barely breathing. She folded her hands over her stomach and stared at the ceiling. Her smile slowly spread. Of course, my precious Tadashi, she thought, what on earth are you going to do without Angelo? Jennifer moves in, Angelo mellows a shade or two and decides he's had enough. No more assignments. The living legend has become history. You are stuck, Tadashi. You are hopelessly cornered—you know Angelo's steely determination the moment his mind is made up. Much can happen within a few years, and, for once, time is on my side.

She massaged her cheekbones and stretched her legs. Thank heaven for little Jennifer, she thought, I am going to use you, my Irish rose, and I am going to use Angelo. Both are past the stage when biochemistry is mistaken for love, and you, Tadashi my darling, will be fighting windmills.

Yasmin sat up when she heard the door from the bathroom open. She lit a Sobranie and fixed her eyes on Ishihara as he came into the drawing room.

"I have a piece of news that may not be entirely welcome," she said.

He adjusted the obi on his kimono, sat down and put his feet on the newspaper on the table. "I am waiting."

"Igor Parkhurst is Jennifer's godfather."

Ishihara did not move for well over a minute. "Ironic," he finally said. "We found the perfect vehicle, and now this crops up. You say the girl is sharp?"

Yasmin's tongue showed between her teeth. "She is. If anything happens to Parkhurst, she'll add two and two together. You can also safely conclude that Angelo has figured out that one some while ago."

Ishihara was in no hurry selecting a cigar from his humidor. "Now, that is what I call interesting. Angelo is such a recluse. Women came and went during the years. All the time he claimed that he only bedded them for carnal pleasure and nothing else. No ties, no obligations and no future. I believed him. There were no reasons *not* to believe him, the way he behaved. I'll remind him of that, one day."

"Don't," Yasmin said.

He appeared not to hear. "A woman of steel, this Moran girl," he mused. "I bet she is as deceptively cold as a pair of knickers in a convent." He waved lazily at the smoke. "Anyway," he added behind a blue-grey mist, "life goes on."

Yasmin eyed him warily. His whole demeanour had changed; he seemed untroubled, almost indifferent. This is when he is dangerous, she thought; some plan is developing in that brain of his. Tadashi does not give up; there is no way he is going to drop his final and greatest project, godfathers or no godfathers.

"I'll have a bath," she said. "When do we have to leave?"

"Half past seven. It shall be great fun. A handful of Americans have been invited."

Yasmin smiled as she walked towards the bedroom. Ishihara loved diplomatic gatherings nearly as much as most embassies adored his presence. One of the worst kept secrets in London's social-political life was Ishihara's contempt for the Americans.

"You took to Igor Parkhurst, didn't you?" she heard his voice behind her.

"Yes," she said and turned around.

He filled his mouth with smoke and said, "Mourn him, if you like, but not in my presence."

12

Ishihara joined Elvis Presley in a "Don't I beg of You" duet as the Mercedes hummed its way down towards Igor Parkhurst's country estate. The day was bright with a promise of late sunshine and nearly compatible with Ishihara's state of mind. His concentration drifted from Elvis to the image of Parkhurst standing with a cheque for £101,450 in his hand. The amount was not sufficient to get him out of the doldrums, but it was a decent kick-start to a new and better existence.

Ishihara was reasonably pleased with himself. He had sold a fraction before the share peaked, as any investor knowing his métier should do, and the only problem now was to find another little goose with a golden egg in her belly.

Ishihara admired geese. Once, in Malaysia, one had chased him. The tenacity and the single-mindedness of the bird had impressed him forever since.

He lit a cigar and left Elvis to struggle on his own.

Yasmin's analysis of the situation of the Parkhurst-Moran-Vargas triangle bothered him. The constellation was not conducive to his final operation; without Vargas there was no instrument and therefore no operation. A dark and acrid cloud of resentment blinded Ishihara for a few moments. He swore silently and asked himself how he could have missed such a simple piece of elementary intelligence.

At the first meeting at Parkhurst's house, the Moran family had been an unwitting ally, exactly as he had planned, but that aside, he had seen all three of them as minor players. When he learned about their close friendship it had not occurred to him to delve into the minutest of obscure details, like the godfather bit; that information had not come forth, and it would still have been of no significance whatever had Vargas managed to keep his hormones under control.

Ishihara shook his head. He had not foreseen that his hypercritical partner could get interested in a prudish, conventional, pious and self-righteous female whose entire background inevitably would clash with Vargas' world; those two would be like a pair of vicious rhinos on collision course in a cage.

Ishihara removed a tobacco leaf from his lower lip. This Irish nymph of steel was as welcome as a sneeze during orgasm. How could *anyone* have predicted such a carnal cock-up? He had known since they first met that Vargas was unpredictable. His troubled mind was never at ease. In his heart he was constantly yearning for redemption and salvation and whatever else the Western part of the universe could supply as relief for a spiritual nomad prone to existentialism. All this was well and good—every man had a right to nurture his own delusions—but how could Vargas possibly believe that this saintly little local ingenue would provide him with the key to eternal harmony? The entire predicament was as pathetic as it was ridiculous. Regrettably, it was also a massive headache. Ishihara had an uncomfortable suspicion that it would not disintegrate all by itself and vanish without a trace overnight.

Ishihara slowed down and rested his eyes on a field surprisingly green for the time of the year. He saw two dominant problems. One was that Parkhurst was ideal for the purpose and it would be a formidable task to replace him—his credentials were impeccable. The other was that although it was long overdue that Vargas found someone who could introduce life into his existence, the timing could not have been worse.

Ishihara changed gear. A problem was merely another wager in disguise, and no barrier was insurmountable. He would have time to prepare and to make his arrangements. All complexities seen in context, time was but an open-ended resource for the ingenious that knew what made the world function.

The morning was still and misty; a mild breeze came with the sun and the sky cleared like steam evaporating from a blue mirror. A sparrow hawk circled over the pine forest across from the farmer's barley field.

Parkhurst knew that as a gardener he could not grow weeds in a greenhouse, but it upset him to see his once lovely grounds deteriorate. He was attending to his roses when he heard a car coming down the drive. Puzzled, he looked up; he didn't expect anybody. He straightened his back when he recognized the car. The man who makes appointments, he thought. Well, somebody is better than nobody.

He shuffled heavily towards his guest and said from twenty feet away, "What a pleasant surprise, Mr. Ishihara. Welcome to the wilderness. Would you like a rose for your button hole?"

Ishihara stepped out and locked the car.

Parkhurst said, "There is no need to lock the car, not in this neighbourhood."

"I always lock my car. My cautious mind does not allow me to take liberties with the criminal fraternity even here among hedgehogs, yokels and other creatures of limited ability and feeble imagination."

"I would not dream of opposing your sensible and presumably hard-earned philosophy," Parkhurst smiled and stared at the expensive-looking leather case in Ishihara's hand. "Are you staying overnight?"

"That's the idea, provided that such arrangement does not inconvenience you."

I was only joking, Parkhurst thought, and he obviously isn't. "Of course not," he said, "I'll be delighted."

Ishihara smiled genially. "You are the kindest of men, Igor. Your hospitality is most appreciated. I have never before spent a night in such a magnificent edifice as your country estate certainly is. In fact, I have never before stayed overnight outside of London. Quite a hole in my cultural education; one should indeed get to know the rural beauty and esoteric attraction of the country in which one has decided to invest one's future."

Dear me, Parkhurst thought, isn't he flowery today, more so than usual. Something positive must have happened. I hope it is associated with investments.

They went through the kitchen and up the stairs. Parkhurst opened the door and Ishihara walked in. It was a large room; light green walls with a magnolia ceiling, a four-poster bed, bookshelves with a hundred or so volumes neatly placed with attention to size and colour, television, telephone, built-in wardrobes, windows facing the garden and a spacious adjacent bathroom.

"Splendid," Ishihara said and rubbed his hands, "absolutely magnificent. You have made my day, Igor my lad. This is a haven for someone with a lifestyle as hectic as mine is. I shall return to the asylum of London in a rested and relaxed condition, in health as well as in spirit."

"I am glad you like it."

"Your kindness and generosity overwhelm me."

An apt remark from someone who invited himself, Parkhurst thought and headed for the door.

"By the way," Ishihara added, as if he suddenly remembered, "take this with you." He took an envelope from his inner pocket and handed it to Parkhurst.

He felt out of breath. "What is it?"

Ishihara said, "Go down into your kitchen. Place yourself on a chair. Then open the envelope. In that order, if I may be so free as to suggest."

Parkhurst was holding the cheque with both hands. His eyes were still glazed when Ishihara came in. He had changed into denims, a cardigan and thick-soled boots. There was a smile on his face. "You look like a colt being promoted from racehorse to stallion," he said.

"I can't believe this," Parkhurst mumbled, "I do not know what to say..." he looked at Ishihara and shrugged helplessly.

"Your attempt to thank me in the most profound manner is duly observed, but I fail to notice my reward in the form of a cup of tea. I do not easily permit the dark cloud of depression to obscure my mind, but at this very moment I am getting close. I make this downhearted statement because you once made it clear that you expect a second payment, and all you can say is that you do not know what to say. You are a wordsmith, and I must therefore interpret your lack of enthusiasm, or should I say indifference, as sheer and unadulterated ingratitude. However, since you so clearly have proved yourself to be a cold-hearted person, I shall no longer look for signs indicating that you appreciate the extent of my dejection, or even its existence. I think I'd better go home now, Mr. Parkhurst."

Parkhurst half rose from the table. "I am so sorry," he said, his neck and cheeks turning scarlet, "it was not my intention to... I am..."

"—stunned," Ishihara suggested.

"Yes," Parkhurst jumped in, "stunned and confused. Please try to understand."

Then he saw the humour in Ishihara's eyes and sank down onto his chair. "Please, Mr. Ishihara, don't give me a heart attack."

Ishihara said, "Calm down, my son. Everything is forgiven. May I add that there is no reason to be confused."

Parkhurst looked out the window. The melancholy smile lingered on when he said, "I fell through the roof and crashed through the floor and not one single associate from the past was willing to assist. Nobody wanted to know. I became a leper, a name best forgotten. I left messages and no one returned my calls. I sent out my manuscripts and they came back with a compliment slip. People quickened their pace when they saw me coming down the street. Why do I no longer exist? I asked myself. I even thought of getting out of this world, but my nerve failed me."

"Where was your friend Mr. Moran?"

"He didn't know about it. Conor knew nothing until recently. He would have lent me the money, but I could not have taken it. How could I have paid him back without any prospects of future income?" Parkhurst wiped his eyes with the back of his tie. "Then, in comes a stranger. He offers to help me, and he delivers. Not in my wildest dreams did I think that such a miracle could happen." He sniffed and pressed his thumbs against the bridge of his nose. "A stranger who is also a foreigner—pretty ironic, isn't it?"

"Let us weed out a misconception. I am not a foreigner, I am an alien. Critters like blacks and Asians and such-like are reluctantly tolerated foreigners; I, a Japanese, am an accepted alien. The difference is that aliens have class and culture. Foreigners do not, or, to be exceedingly broadminded, in the least worst of cases they may possess a tarnished and defect replica. Please do not let an issue of such magnitude muddle your mind. You Brits know that I am right. What I find regrettable is that most of you have neither the wit nor the guts to phrase your real attitude in exact terms. Instead, you label it racism, which is not at all what you mean, but it is the easy way out. You do what Pontius Pilate made fashionable in public when a precisely formulated analysis hits you in the face."

He is serious, Parkhurst thought, not certain of the relevance of Ishihara's digression. "I follow," he said, keen to change the subject. Parkhurst was familiar with the Japanese' contempt for hairy barbarians, but it had never occurred to him that even the most vehement atavism from feudal Japan would resort to such merciless and inflammatory rhetoric. Ishihara was not the archetype of modern Japan, that had become clear from day one, but it still surprised Parkhurst that this well-spoken, successful albeit eccentric man was so entirely void of inhibitions.

"Now we must think of repayment," he said. "Part of the deal," he added with a grimace that he hoped would pass for a smile.

"We must indeed, and that is one of several good reasons why I am here. However, let us first deal with the financial picture. You require another cheque to get you out of your crocodile-infested pond. I shall attend to the matter as soon as the first opportunity presents itself on one of my many City inroads. The ticket for my friend Mr. Vargas, you may recall."

Parkhurst nodded.

"Turning now to the subject of repayment, I have a problem," Ishihara said. "It does bother me that Mr. Vargas is as sociable as a mongoose in a snake pit. I shall need considerable help and expertise here, something I am sure that a man of your competence can provide. Over time, that is," he added. "I fully accept that thaumaturgy can be an arduous and lengthy affair."

Is he pulling my leg, Parkhurst thought, or is this a message? He said, "I am sure we can work something out."

"Your self-confidence is reassuring. It may not surprise you to learn that I did not pick your name out of a hat, though."

Oh, I believe that, Parkhurst thought. You do not exactly give the impression of orchestrating *anything* in a casual manner.

Ishihara was staring out the window. He tilted his head as if he was listening intently. "The silence," he said. "What a place to rejuvenate oneself and recharge the battery. I understand why you are fond of your home."

"I am," Parkhurst said. He wondered what Ishihara was leading up to. Suddenly, he got to his feet. Once again Parkhurst noticed the speed and the agility of the stocky Japanese.

"We shall now get your career back on course," Ishihara said. "I have got a few ideas, but we can talk about that later. First, I have a suggestion to make." He smiled as he watched Parkhurst's attempt to organize tea for two. "Or shall I call it a small favour," Ishihara went on, "if I may be so audacious?"

"Please," Parkhurst said and poured water into the teapot.

Ishihara said, "Your ex-mother-in-law was going to occupy the west wing, and, as far as I recall, it is fully furnished and in excellent condition. Does my memory prove me correct?"

"It does," Parkhurst confirmed. Yes, the lady was indeed going to take over that part of the house, and the barn, and the stables. He shuddered. She'd never been short on ideas, Miriam's mother, as long as somebody else paid for their implementation. Parkhurst looked at Ishihara with a growing anticipation of what was to come.

"Yasmin and I will eventually buy a property in the country," Ishihara explained, "but not yet. Could it possibly be an idea that we rent your west wing for a year or two? Primarily, it will be for weekends only, although we may use it the odd day in between. We need a place where we can relax and unfold, and this is ideal. Also, it would be the perfect base from where we can search for a house of our own, in due time." He raised his hand. "Please, I have no wish to impose on you. If it is not convenient or desirable, I shall fully understand. Let me add, though, that I would offer you a rent fifty percent over market rate, such being the premium for the privilege of access to your magnificent estate, and, of course, the pleasure of your company whenever so wished by both parties. I sincerely hope that you do not find my proposal inappropriate."

Parkhurst was delighted, but he decided to play it cool. The place had been a very lonely abode for longer than he cared to remember, and he knew that for even a penny a month he would have welcomed the Japanese and his delightful wife.

"I am honoured," he said and put on an air of quiet dignity, "but are you sure it won't be too tranquil for you? Not much is happening here, you know."

"That is precisely what I am looking for."

"Would London not be too far away?"

"Just far enough."

Parkhurst looked at the pokerfaced Japanese with a sinking feeling of having overplayed his hand. "Excellent," he beamed with the width of his smile properly measured, "I could not have asked for a more pleasant surprise."

"Except for the cheque."

"In addition to the cheque."

"I am happy we have an understanding," Ishihara said. "I would not commercialize our arrangement and thereby cheapen it by saying that we have a *deal*. That is an odious word. Yasmin will be delighted."

They sat down facing each other. Parkhurst said, "I feel uncomfortable with anything above market rate."

Ishihara lifted his cup as if to take in the aroma of the tea. "My dear Igor, during my walk through life I have made the odd observation. My memories, so far, could be compared with a bouquet of flowers, each clearly imprinted on my sentient mind. Some are beautiful, some less so, some are smelly, some have thorns and some are poisonous. Altogether they constitute what people with an alert consciousness call *experience*." He tasted his tea, nodded approvingly and put his cup down. "People who learn and who diligently utilize their attainments are indeed rare; the brutal fact is that the vast majority of what we so charitably call mankind do nothing but crawl from cradle to grave without any worthwhile experience at all. Does this sound cynical? Instantly, the answer would be *yes*, but, alas, how does one define cynicism? Let me quote my friend Vargas, who once remarked that cynicism is conceived by mortification, born by realism and brought up by experience."

Ishihara smiled. Parkhurst could not decide whether the Japanese' eyes expressed derision or amusement.

"I presume you can see the context," Ishihara went on. "Let me now reveal that one of my little flowers is called: *Do not expect something for nothing*. Why this name, you may ask. Because doing anyone a favour appeals to the recipient's worst instincts. It is not the most attractive of flowers, but it does justify its place in my collection."

Parkhurst said, "There have been moments when I have seen that flower, and one or two others equally unattractive."

"The human element, as my friend Vargas so aptly describes it when man rears his ugly face from the slime he is feeding on."

Quite a pair, Parkhurst thought, no wonder they found each other.

Ishihara said, "I made you an offer which I think is fair, and which I believe you should accept. Let us keep everything on an even keel; you owe me nothing, and I owe you nothing. That way neither is beholden to the other, and we have neutralized the worst of our instincts."

"I can't argue," Parkhurst said. "Do you always adhere to your principles?"

"Yes, I do. This is not because it makes life easier—it doesn't—but because being true to myself gives me a feeling of fulfilment. When I failed, which I did once in a while in the past, I sensed that I was betraying myself, that I compromised my convictions to ease the burden of self-discipline enabling me to pretend that life was more agreeable that way, whilst all I did was to adjust my self-respect. Such an attitude is not very rewarding, in the long run, so I decided to face the consequences of no longer prostituting my character. It was worth it. The ultimate accolade is of course that ordinary minds find you unacceptable, objectionable and unpalatable."

Parkhurst had not come across too many self-contained units of Ishihara's stature, and secretly he admired those who possessed such a scrupulous tunnel vision. People like that always succeeded. The minus was that they did not seem to care about the effect they had on other people. Was that necessarily a bad thing? Not absolutely, he thought, pleased with his new-found conclusion, but how long would it take to achieve such a level of rock-solid assertiveness? Was it too late for himself? Perhaps Ishihara would prove to be an ally also in life's moral playground.

"You are quiet, Igor."

"I was thinking about what you said. It adds up."

Ishihara held out his hands, bent one finger at the time and made a cracking noise with his fists. "Let us go for a walk," he said.

It had turned partly overcast, but with no rain and the ground was dry. They walked across the fields and into the forest and over the hills, and Parkhurst pointed and described.

They admired the beauty of a Speckled Wood and a High Brown Fritillary butterflies. They saw a rare red kite circle above the hedges. Parkhurst gave a running commentary on Redstarts, Pied Wagtails, Hoopoes, Blackbirds, Goldfinches, Collared Doves and other birds he recognized as they sauntered along and listened to the chorus of the avian world. He gestured and explained where wheat and barley were growing, the fields looking as if millions of coffee beans had been scattered among small and oddly shaped white-and-grey flints. He enthused about the majestic dignity of the oaks and the elms, the sycamores and the chestnut trees, and about the beauty of the whitebeams and the maples. They both stopped and stood still when a pair of deer crossed a glen fifty yards away, and Parkhurst's neck turned crimson as he was holding his breath. When he recovered, he continued his narration; he talked about harvesting and long established rituals, about shooting and hunting, and about the people and their attitude towards the land.

All the time Ishihara listened intently, but apart from the odd question he barely spoke. Parkhurst related how he came to this part of the world with no knowledge at all; he was a city-dweller, ignorant of rural England and how it functioned. In the beginning he saw it as tactically wise to pick up a piece of knowledge here and there; the local church became his first target. Then he began to talk to farmers, gardeners, foresters and other well-established locals who clearly loved and respected the countryside. Gradually, a genuine interest replaced his initial expediency, and in the relatively short space of time since Parkhurst replanted his roots he had amassed a knowledge and an understanding which impressed even those most sceptical to newcomers. It was accepted, but not necessarily respected, when he politely but firmly declined to participate in shooting and hunting. To those who queried, he made it clear as tactfully as the subject allowed that it gave him no pleasure to kill animals. He took great care in expounding that he neither criticized nor condemned these activities of century-long traditions; he nodded sympathetically when they emphasized the need for culling, and he uttered agreeable little noises when staunch supporters vividly described the essence of the balance of nature. He did not make the point that they *bred* pheasants and partridges for shooting, and neither did he question why they imported foxes from other counties on occasions when the little red terror was in short supply. He did not say that he found it ridiculous when the fearless gunmen all dressed up in their traditional uniform gathered to face the challenge of the season, and he contained himself when he heard congratulations exchanged after a viciously dangerous partridge had been blasted out of the sky.

All in all he behaved in a thoughtful and urbane manner, and it was now his impression that he was being tolerated, just about, as a country squire. His good humour, his natural friendliness and his easygoing ways all helped, and it had done no harm that he had befriended the local vicar, The Reverend Arthur Thornton.

The vicar was a liberal, knowledgeable and respected man who seldom said no thanks to a good cigar and never to a drink or two, and he could tell a bawdy joke as well as anybody. He had come from another county twelve years earlier, and he and Parkhurst quickly discovered the invisible bond between *immigrants,* as they called themselves when nobody else was around.

Be warned, though, Thornton had said during his third whisky one evening, down here you will learn what is meant by a *closed* society. Don't be fooled by feigned acquiescence. To most, you will remain an outsider with his roots elsewhere, never the true article. It was an incestuous little community, and they were hell-bent on keeping their bigoted cliques intact. There was no clear dividing line between what was being perceived as community spirit versus religious rituals; they all went to church and took part in and supported arrangements benefiting the church, but few were genuine believers. Petty idiosyncrasies were sacrosanct and vigorously defended, and snobbery and pretence were mistaken for virtuous characteristics. The same went for self-righteousness frequently confused with bluff sincerity, as did hypocrisy and a generous allowance of pomposity. Gossiping was like an ever-present wind singing through the treetops, and the less they knew, the more they made up. It went without saying that the locals had no perception of their own folly. But, never mind, Thornton had concluded as his eyes requested one for the road; God's children were mainly fatuous and only in part malicious, and there was nothing Parkhurst could do about it, except keep smiling. And—by the way—the whole picture had to be understood as a neutral and clinically accurate description, like a disease being illustrated by its symptoms.

Parkhurst's agnosticism did not faze Thornton; on the contrary, many a time they had enjoyed a good debate on life and death, heaven and hell, sin and salvation, miracles and illusions, faith and indifference, and, not least, would this world be a better place if man put more efforts into developing and engineering his intellectual potential towards human progress instead of clinging to pillars built from dogmas and uncritical reverence for irrational myths?

The vicar argued that although man was equipped with a mind, sort of, evolution had run out of steam aeons ago—admittedly with the odd specimen confirming the rule by exception—and therefore the ordinary Homo Sapiens—a frightfully flattering label—had no choice but to succumb to obeisance and diktats, supernatural or otherwise, from first to last breath.

Parkhurst had a lot of time for Arthur Thornton.

The clouds parted, and the warm rays from the sun cast alluring shadows across the hills and the meadows. Ishihara was walking with short steps, forward-leaning and in a way that indicated that he could go on forever. Parkhurst sensed that his own stamina was getting close to an end and suggested that they should walk back. Ishihara nodded, but he kept his silence. Parkhurst wondered what went through the Japanese' mind, but he did not ask. Ishihara would talk if he so wished.

They passed a small valley, went over a brook and into a pine forest. Suddenly, Ishihara began to speak. He talked about Tokyo; the pulsating life and the vitality of the city, the bright lights at night, the crowds and the smells, the discipline and the uniformity of its citizens, the long established corruption at all levels, the might of the underworld, the oppressive educational system, art, architecture and the monotony and the inflexibility which ultimately had made him decide to leave.

But, before that, whilst they were still very much part of Tokyo's kaleidoscopic scenery, Vargas one day said that he was travelling to the mountains of Shirakawa-Go where he had heard that an old ninja lived. Vargas was determined to find this man. He ignored Ishihara's advice that the ninjas ceased to operate several hundred years ago, and that chasing rainbows was not a worthwhile exercise. Instead, Ishihara suggested, if Vargas was so eager to get acquainted with the remnants of the past, why not join the Togakure School of Ninjitsu, which was reasonably qualified and probably adequate. The original ninja, Ishihara explained, was a true craftsman of Japan's glorious feudal era from the thirteenth to the seventeenth century; their specialities being assassinations, but they were also adept at anything from espionage and abduction to extortion and sabotage. Black-clad, ruthless, deadly and incredibly fit and agile, they sold their services to whoever paid the most, and their reputation became the raw material for countless legends.

Ishihara did his best to convince Vargas that the ninjas didn't exist any more; copies, perhaps, but the direct line of thoroughbred ninjas became extinct when the Tokugawa Shogun made them outlaws. Vargas was unmoved. He had made up his mind to go, and Ishihara knew that nothing or nobody would change his friend's decision. Not even Ryutaro Kobayashi, The Old Master, as he was known, the founder of the school and a teacher of cult hero status, not even Sensei's most scathing and sarcastic remarks had the slightest effect on Vargas.

This, in itself, did not surprise Ishihara, since Vargas was the only student who openly rejected Sensei's legendary methods of controlling the mind and the body of his subjects. What amazed Ishihara was Vargas' fixation with a non-existing ninja and with the echoes of the past, unless, of course, the whole idea was simply a desire to get out of Tokyo and into the fresh air of the Shirakawa-Go Mountains. The more Ishihara thought about it, the less derogatory he became about Vargas' obsession, and one week before Vargas' departure, Ishihara decided that he, too, was going.

The Old Master showed his fury and disappointment by instantly ignoring them completely; the loss of his two star students hurt him deeply. Only when both Ishihara and Vargas promised to return, did Sensei mellow; not enough to wish them goodbye and the best of luck, but he afforded himself the briefest of nods and a terse comment about his door being open irrespective of the stupidity of whoever came through it.

They arrived at Shirakawa-Go in Ishihara's car. A farmer at the foot of the mountain range allowed them to park after lengthy negotiations over the weekly fee, and they began their search for Vargas' elusive ninja.

Whoever they asked shook their head; no, never heard of a ninja. Some displayed ignorance and others averred that no such being was alive any more. Some were prepared to relate legends and tales from a bygone era, and that was as far as they got.

One day, increasingly annoyed but still with his manners under control, Vargas stopped an old man on his way home from the paddy fields and asked him if he had ever heard the name Yoshiri Sakaigawa. The skin on the old man's face was wrinkled like crumpled papyrus and as dark as chew tobacco. He remained impassive and continued his walk with no apparent intention of dignifying them with as much as a shake of his head.

For some mysterious reason, that was enough for Vargas. He concluded that the evidence was indisputable. All they had to do, was to criss-cross the mountains for a week or two; Yoshiri Sakaigawa was up there, somewhere. He was a ninja, and he was going to share his secrets with them.

Vargas flatly refused to tell from where the name had emerged. For the rest of the day Ishihara battled with his temptation to go back to Tokyo. His curiosity got the better of him, and he consented to another seven days.

After three weeks, only interrupted by excursions down to the valley for supplies, they came across a small wooden cottage with its solid beams kept together by ropes. A man who looked like being in his sixties sat in the Lotus position outside, staring at the embers of his fire and ignoring their presence. Vargas stopped ten yards away and asked the man if his name was Yoshiri Sakaigawa. There was no reaction. This did not seem to surprise Vargas, and he suggested to Ishihara that from then on they should show up every morning. Sooner or later the old man would make up his mind to communicate. Vargas was convinced about the man's identity, but how and why Ishihara could not tell.

Every morning they left their camp a mile away, went over to the old man's cottage and sat there till the sun went down. Sometimes the man was there, and at other times he was not. Every so often he plodded about with various chores, and then there were hours when he just sat there, meditating with his eyes closed.

Ishihara's irritation grew steadily by the day. This was an utter waste of time, he thought, and even if the man really was a ninja, it was patently clear that he was not going to share so much as a cup of tea with them.

Go back, Vargas suggested, knowing full well that Ishihara dreaded the ridicule that would meet him if he returned without even some cherished ninja weaponry, like a *tetsu-bishi* or a *shuriken*, as evidence of their rigorous training in the secrecy of the Shirakawa-Go mountains. Moreover, he needed a bit of time to make his story at least remotely plausible, since, according to legend, it took more than a couple of weeks to become a full-fledged ninja.

Ishihara wondered what he had let himself in for. Each night he prayed to every single one of his Shinto gods brought along, pleading with them to persuade the old man to open his mouth and deliver a carefully selected collection of profundities from which Ishihara could spin his story.

On the morning of the thirtieth day, when the first rays from the sun tinted the mountaintops, the old man spoke. He said that his name was Yoshiri Sakaigawa, and that he was deeply honoured to be visited by two of Sensei Kobayashi's students. They had come to learn the Way of the Ninja, and they had demonstrated to him the humility and the patience without which nothing could be achieved. One thing, though; they were not to ask questions; listen and learn, learn and listen.

The two of them spent the next six months with Sakaigawa. Within two days Ishihara was convinced that the old man was determined to break them. Ishihara reckoned that Sakaigawa was somewhere between

225

sixty and seventy years of age; it was impossible to be more exact, but the man's strength, stamina and agility were beyond belief.

They sat under ice-cold waterfalls. They ran for hours with a massive boulder under each arm. They repeated endlessly minute techniques that proved to have incredible effect. They meditated and lost track of time. They stretched till they thought that their limbs were going to fall off.

Sakaigawa taught them about nutrition. He revealed how to read an opponent's mind. He showed them which plants could be useful in case they needed to paralyze or kill an enemy without leaving a clue behind. He explained how to train the eyes to see better in the dark, how to move in total silence, how to destroy any evidence of ever having been present, how to climb effortlessly using toes and fingers, and how to control tenseness. Each day he ended the lesson with the caveat that *The Way Of The Ninja Was Without Remorse.*

The more Ishihara listened and learned, the more he believed that Vargas had been right all along; Sakaigawa's knowledge, experience, wisdom and insight were all part of Sensei Kobayashi's repertoire. The deeper secrets of this erudition were something that Kobayashi was not going to pass on to anybody, including his carefully chosen protégés.

It made sense, Ishihara thought. It kept alive The Old Master's need for superiority and the aura of mysticism. Ishihara had known for years that Sensei Kobayashi was a wily and devious fox, but would not he, Tadashi Ishihara, have done exactly the same? The answer was *yes*, and up there, in the wide open temple of the Shirakawa-Go mountains, he and Vargas made a pact: they would never share with anybody what Sakaigawa had taught them.

On the way back to Tokyo, Ishihara could no longer contain himself. Once again he asked Vargas how he had come about the existence of Yoshiri Sakaigawa, and this time Vargas complied. Ishihara was more shocked than surprised when Vargas told that he had locked himself into Sensei's office one night, gone through his drawers and found an old, faded picture of Sakaigawa together with a letter. Vargas had not taken in the entire contents of the letter, but he had picked up enough to grasp Sakaigawa's true identity and whereabouts, and that he was Kobayashi's teacher.

The advantage of being Vargas, Ishihara had contemplated; no Japanese would have considered breaking into his sensei's office.

During the years, before they finally left Japan for good, Vargas had returned to Shirakawa-Go, staying away for months at a time. Ishihara never went back. He felt that continued contact with Sakaigawa amounted to disloyalty to Kobayashi, a sentiment that did not bother Vargas.

Kobayashi treated them as if they had never been away at all; no comments, no questions and not once did the name Sakaigawa pass his lips. Ishihara admired Kobayashi's stoicism and self-control. Vargas discounted the attitude as an attempt not to lose face. A bit of each was probably closer to the truth, Ishihara reflected.

Vargas' often indifferent and callous attitude used to annoy Ishihara until one day, much later, it struck him that his friend's conduct was a shield against a world that more than once had treated him badly during a time when immaturity, vulnerability and inexperience ruled his existence. Ishihara did not know much about Vargas, a man not prone to confide in others, but he sensed that his partner had encountered his share of lonely and turbulent days. Vargas was restless; his mind was in constant turmoil, and his emotions were like antennae searching for signals. It was a Vargas that nobody but Ishihara saw. To anybody else, Vargas was cold, methodical and ruthless; a fighting machine dominated by an iron will and with a self-control that even the most calculating or apathetic Japanese could not help admiring.

The last time Vargas went to Shirakawa-Go was the year when the two of them decided to seek their future and fortune elsewhere. Vargas came back with a samurai sword. He showed it to Ishihara, but nobody else, before depositing it in a bank. Ishihara knew that the sword was more than a gift; it was an honour only bestowed on someone Sakaigawa had become fond of, a fondness added to admiration and respect.

Ishihara's openness surprised Parkhurst as he listened to the tales from a life he knew nothing about. It was this little walk of theirs, Ishihara continued, that had reminded him of the Shirakawa-Go mountains; the serenity, the harmony of nature, its beauty and the melancholy yet pleasant state of mind that it had created.

Yes, Yasmin and he were certainly going to buy a property in the country, hopefully in the not too distant future, and, who could tell, one day a few little Ishiharas would be running around. There could be no better place to grow up than in the civilized wilderness of rural England; if cliquey, so be it.

As they got closer to Parkhurst's home, they passed a farm. Without further explanation, Ishihara stopped and said that he wanted to buy eggs. The farmer and his wife were in the courtyard. The wife was feeding her assortment of Bantams and Italians. She and her husband hailed Parkhurst with the natural amicability of good neighbours. Parkhurst introduced Ishihara as a friend from London, and they greeted him politely and tried to avoid showing any sign of finding a visitor from Japan a bit of a local oddity. If Ishihara sensed their curiosity, he hid it well. For a few minutes he entertained them with his opinions on poultry and its relevance and importance to society. He concluded with a few compliments on the invaluable benefits of free-range philosophy. The farmers could clearly not decide whether Mr. Parkhurst's friend was an expert on the subject, or simply a big-city know-all asshole, but since the guest was unfortunate enough to be a foreigner, one should courteously give him the benefit of the doubt.

Parkhurst, on his part, suspected that the entire performance was a piece of self-entertainment. Ishihara paid for the eggs, wished them *sayonara* and hoped to learn more from them when next in the area.

Fifteen minutes later they were in Parkhurst's kitchen. Ishihara said, "I am on a diet. I need to shed a few pounds."

"That makes two of us," Parkhurst said.

Ishihara kicked off his shoes. "Correct. I am four pounds overweight, and you are obese. Even your eyelids are fat. My advice is that you get rid of at least three stones. Wobbling around with all that excess fat does you no good at all. Do not forget that also your mind is affected by being out of form, shape and condition. I take it that you are not so vain, or dumb, rather, that you get offended by number one friendly advice. Bear in mind that what you need the most, is somebody who has your overall interest at heart—apart from money, that is."

"Thank you," Parkhurst said, bemused.

"You are welcome. As soon as we have settled your debts and secured a few extra pennies to live on, you need to resume your career. It needs a kick-start, and, luckily, you've now got a friend who knows how to do it. I shall nurse your talent till it once again blossoms like an orchid among thistles. Your fame and fortune will rise like a cyclone from nowhere, and the world will be at your feet. Doesn't that sound tempting?"

Parkhurst did not know what to believe. "It sounds impossible," he said.

"Balls and apeshit," Ishihara sneered and held an egg up against the light. "By the way, did you know that penicillin can be retrieved from the dung of Japanese monkeys? Even our apes are ahead of you Westerns." His eyes were all over Parkhurst's face. "Anyway, Igor, following this succinct and useful but admittedly impertinent aside, may I continue from where you interrupted me?" Ishihara got his eyebrows closer to his hairline and gave one of his bullfrog stares. "From this very moment, the word *defeatism* is erased from your vocabulary and eradicated from your mind. Does one understand what I recommend, or is one's faculties so blunted that this simple imperative is beyond one's comprehension?"

Parkhurst's smile was gloomy. "Do you really believe that I can come back to what I used to be?"

"I do not *believe*," Ishihara answered, "I *know*. The only one who can stop you is yourself, and that is not going to happen. I have a plan and I have the resources. You have the talent, and what more do we need?" Ishihara snapped his fingers. "You are not a parasite, Igor, you are a creator. Those who create nothing in life are those with the biggest words and the most vacuous minds. They are the scavengers, they are the leeches who feed on somebody else's efforts without which the scavengers and the leeches have no existence. Look back, Igor, and think of all those people who during the years borrowed your light. They were strutting around in the shine from your sun and your moon, and they disappeared when the clouds came and darkened your life. Think back—your fair-weather friends were obsessed with the *process* far more than with the final product; they were mesmerized by the *source* of your material because this gave them access to the evolution and its progress and thereby to your inner life. They sensed involvement by infringing the privacy of creation. That is how human scavengers survive, and when the aorta runs dry they find another victim. Don't look so dazed, Igor. You know it is true. Those very same people, those with the big words and the shallow minds, the non-productive and the non-creative, what do you think will happen to them? They will approach their final day remembering whom they used to know, and their appropriate epitaph should read: *Here rots an unfulfilled wretch.* Not so for you, son. You have achieved, and you will achieve again. Where is your wok?"

Parkhurst's tongue changed from pink to purple as it whizzed across his lips. For years he had tried to rationalize away the emptiness of his life; the lonely hours and the harrowing feeling of being deserted. Ishihara had mercilessly ripped away the shroud of consoling deception, and Parkhurst knew that the Japanese had spoken the truth.

"Where is your wok? Wake up."

"Excuse me?"

"Good grief! Your frying pan, man. I am going to make us my delicious, succulent and low-calorie omelette. Secret recipe. One day I may write a sensational cookbook and become world famous. Who knows?"

"What else can you make?" Parkhurst asked. The thought of food stimulated his mental energy. He sat down, sensing that he was in the way.

"Not much."

"Thin books do not appeal to most publishers," Parkhurst said.

"Ah, but you are leaping to the most cursory of illations. One day, when I live in harmony far from the city lights, I shall throw myself into the deep end of my huge and exceptionally well-equipped kitchen. With my fertile imagination at large, an endless stream of culinary masterpieces will flow like stir-fried butterflies from my pots and pans. That is indeed a mouth-watering metaphor, if you will forgive my acute and highly unusual attack of immodesty."

"Indeed," Parkhurst applauded, "Ishihara, the master chef. I can see the headlines. When are you retiring, then?"

Ishihara said, "I do not retire, I change universe." He searched through the cupboards till he found an apron. "Kindly excuse me for a moment." He left and came back with a bottle of cognac.

Ten minutes later, a large and exotic-looking omelette exuding the most titillating aroma was placed in front of Parkhurst. "This is fantastic," he said after the first bite. "Don't wait too long, or you're wasting a formidable talent."

"I know, but a man's *gotta do* what a man's *gotta do*. Not to worry. My time will come."

Parkhurst decided to push it. "Retirement—sorry, your change of universe is not imminent?"

Ishihara straightened up, put his knife and fork on the plate and rested his chin on his folded hands. "Retirement, like defeatism, is to some people a concept of purely academic nature. They exist as words only, not as realities. We, the exceptions, never give in; we continue our battles regardless of odds because otherwise life would lose all meaning. Neither do we *retire*. The mere thought is overloaded with negative connotations. We change professions, we struggle on, one way or the other, and there's always a challenge, another alp to climb. Only life's little squirts allow themselves to be swept aside, at one time or another, the spineless and the degenerated creatures whose only function is to make up the numbers. I apologize for my choice of nouns and any other insensitive grammatical aid enabling me to express clearly my passionate viewpoints. My excuse is that the effect of harsh words in a foreign language is somehow mollified and diluted in one's own mind." He smiled. "You'll get used to me. My enthusiasm for verbal firecrackers is here to stay. After all, each of us is entitled to entertainment of his own choice; too bad if it offends delicate souls." Some of the humour went from his eyes. "I almost said *the intellect of delicate souls*, but there are limits to compassion. However much I admire my kindred spirit Confucius, in that respect he went too far. He was pursuing true benevolence in man to such an extent that he finally convinced himself that the non-existent is well and alive. I quote from The Master: "*Benevolence is more vital to the common people than even fire and water. In the case of fire and water, I have seen men die by stepping on them, but I have never seen any man die by stepping on benevolence.*" It is possible that he tried to be cannily ambiguous, he was Chinese, after all, but I think we can classify this precious fragment of wisdom as a touching illusion." Ishihara's face was a mask of serenity. "Added to that," he went on, "neither you nor I are common people, so it's irrelevant, anyway. The moral is, never overdo what is essentially an artificial attribute."

He is entitled to regale himself, Parkhurst thought, I'll let that one pass.

They finished, and Parkhurst rinsed off the plates and the cutlery and put them in the sink. Ishihara took care of the wok.

"It is very important to clean utensils properly," he explained. "It has struck me, though, were there a Nobel Prize for cleanliness, no Brit would be a contender."

Parkhurst glanced at Ishihara's cognac and suggested that they withdrew to the comfort of the drawing room.

Ishihara seemed contented as he sank into one of the deep, eiderdown-cushioned chairs, relaxing with his cigar and a liberal measure of cognac.

Parkhurst was facing the French doors. Dark and heavy clouds were amassing; dusk came early, and he wondered if it was a coincidence that Ishihara had placed himself with his back to the greying light. No, he thought, there is nothing coincidental about him. I am still not comfortable in his company. I feel a kind of disquietude the way anything unknown disturbs me, an element of wariness, but not fear. At least I do not think so.

"Light a candle," Ishihara suggested.

Parkhurst obliged. Once more, silence befell the room. Parkhurst kept thinking of what Ishihara had told about Tokyo and the Shirakawa-Go Mountains. Halfway down the glass Parkhurst found the courage to ask, "How did you and Mr. Vargas meet, Tadashi?"

The silence that followed was like a still day in a desert. After a while Parkhurst began to listen to the distant tolling of bells from a church. The ringing grew louder. Another few minutes of this, he thought, and my head is going to explode. He tried to fight off the feeling of unease that had seized him, but it was as if his aorta had been icecapped and his intestines injected with mercury. He looked out. Dusk had come. The trees were black silhouettes against a gunmetal sky. A soft mauve haze rose from the lawns. The splashing of the fountain took over from the church bells.

"What did you pick up from the lane?" Ishihara said.

"Pick up? Oh, snails."

"Snails?"

"Yes. I always do that when I walk the lanes. I hate to see those pretty little things squashed by car tyres. It is so unnecessary." The words came slowly. Parkhurst could hear his own voice as if coming from the strings of a cello touched by a rasp.

"You pick up a snail by its shell and place it on the verge?" Ishihara said.

"Is that strange?"

"Snails," Ishihara repeated as if the image of snail saving was beyond comprehension. "I see." He placed his lighter upside-down on the table and stared at it for a while. "When we walked the fields, you sometimes moved like a tipsy ballet dancer. How come?"

"I do not like stepping on flowers."

Ishihara seemed spellbound by his lighter.

Parkhurst wanted to explain, but all that came were snorting little noises, like a potbellied pig begging for attention. He felt a strong urge to wipe his forehead, but he kept still. In the flickering light from the candle he saw that the Japanese had closed his eyes. His face was as peaceful as if he had fallen asleep with a sweet dream.

"How did I meet Angelo Vargas?" Ishihara said. His voice was soft and low, almost like a chant. He shook his head. "Amazing," he mumbled as if addressing himself. "What a day that was."

Ishihara refilled their glasses. His face was in shadows. "What a day," he repeated with a laughter that was barely audible, "not to forget all those years thereafter. Quite a life, come to think of it. Do you really want to hear?"

Parkhurst made a double gesture with his hands. "I did find it interesting, what you told me earlier today."

"Fascinating, perhaps?"

"That would sum it up."

Ishihara stretched his legs and rested his elbows on the sides of the chair.

"Make yourself comfy, Igor."

13

Ishihara and half a dozen other *karatekas* stood outside Ryutaro Kobayashi's dojo when they spotted the stranger carrying an old suitcase coming towards them. That he was a stranger was one thing, nothing unusual about that in a city like Tokyo, but the fact that he was a *white* stranger was a different matter altogether. A blond, blue-eyed gaijin in Ikebukuro was nearly as rare as an elephant in an ice cube. Even Ishihara, more worldly and sophisticated than any of his contemporaries, had problems concealing his astonishment.

They instantly forgot the coffee bar and their well-deserved rest before the afternoon session. Nobody moved when the gaijin put his suitcase down on the pavement and politely asked in English if they knew where he could find Mr. Kobayashi.

One of the boys giggled. He did not understand what the gaijin was saying, apart from the name of their sensei, but somehow it was funny. Ishihara put a stop to the snickering with a stern look.

"Behave yourself," he said. "This man has the most courteous manners, and you behave as if our entire teaching on etiquette has been a waste of time. You are a blackbelt, not a whitebelt who does not know his nuts from his earlobes. Do you read me?"

The boy lowered his eyes and wished he had kept quiet. He knew that his stupid little gaffe would cost him an assorted number of bruises later on. Ishihara's adherence to discipline coupled with his ferocity was widely feared.

"Please excuse this digression," Ishihara said in English and looked at the gaijin. "You wish to meet Sensei Kobayashi?"

"I do."

Ishihara studied the stranger through narrowed eyes and liked what he saw. This gaijin could be genuine, he thought; crazy, perhaps, but genuine.

Ishihara already knew how Kobayashi would react. His animosity towards anybody non-Oriental was as legendary as was the man himself. In particular, he hated the Americans; a sentiment that did not make him stand out among any generation of the Japanese population.

The fact that Ryutaro Kobayashi was born in Korea and had taken a Japanese name had, in his own opinion, nothing to do with his many and diversified Japanese philosophies on race, origin, culture, politics and history; he was Ryutaro Kobayashi, and patriotism was a valuable quality and should not be taken lightly, whether original or adopted. Nobody dared mention that he had more reasons to hate the Japanese than the Americans, and nobody said to his face what he and everybody else knew all too well; a Korean in Japan was a second-class citizen.

Ryutaro Kobayashi hungered for recognition as much as he hungered for fame and riches, and most of the time he played his cards deftly and with considerable understanding of the human psyche.

"Are you American?" Ishihara asked.

"No."

"Have you been to America?"

"Yes."

"For how long?"

"Some years."

Ishihara's mind changed gears. He sensed the first little blob fermenting somewhere in the back of his brain.

"*Doko kara kitano?*" he said.

"Pardon?"

Good, Ishihara thought, satisfied that the gaijin could not speak Japanese.

"Where do you come from?" he translated.

"Mexico."

"Ah. The land of the Aztec people. A very rich culture. Most interesting."

"It is."

Unflappable devil, Ishihara mused. All I have to do now is to convince Sensei that we have stumbled over something that might be worth keeping.

It was long established that Ishihara was The Old Master's crown prince, the one who would take over and run the organization when Kobayashi decided to call it a day. Ishihara's influence was strong, but he had no illusions about who made the final decisions. Ishihara could suggest and advise and recommend, but, added to all his other qualities, Kobayashi was a stubborn man and not easily moved. It would take substantial skills to persuade Kobayashi to accept the gaijin. All in all, Ishihara thought, it would boil down to one, simple argument. Hopefully, it would work.

"My name is Tadashi Ishihara," he said and extended his hand.

The grip of the stranger was firm, but not demonstratively so. "Angelo Vargas."

Ishihara said, "No offence, but you do not look like a Mexican. Like Pancho Villa," he added in an attempt to neutralize what could be perceived as scepticism.

"My ancestors came from the North of Spain," Vargas said. "They were all blond with blue eyes."

"Ah," Ishihara nodded, not sure he was being told the truth, "that explains it. Kindly wait here whilst I go upstairs to speak to Sensei Kobayashi."

He knocked on Kobayashi's door, heard a noise, entered and bowed ceremonially. Kobayashi was sitting behind his huge desk, lost in the intricacies of accounts and correspondence. At long last, he looked up.

"Yes, Tadashi-San?" The voice was surprisingly mellow for such a powerfully built man, like a soft whisper gliding gently through the air.

"Sensei," Ishihara began respectfully, "I am afraid that we are facing a most intolerable situation."

Kobayashi was sitting in a captain's chair. It rated as one of his more precious possessions, a gift from a wealthy student who later became a successful politician, and thus even more wealthy. The chair was in green leather with the wooden parts made from walnut tree; it could lean backward and forward, the seat could be adjusted to the desired height from the floor, and it could swivel 360 degrees. Kobayashi regularly took advantages of these artifices; which one depended on who he talked to and the subject in question, or both, in most cases. It was a chair with built-in psychological perspectives, and Kobayashi was not a man who lightly ignored whatever upper hand life or furniture makers provided him with.

He put his huge hand on the knob at the right-hand side of the chair, leaned backward till he reached an angle of 45 degrees, and said, "Speak."

Ishihara folded his hands in front and bowed for the second time.

"There is a gaijin downstairs," he began. "He wants to talk to you."

Kobayashi had, during the years, developed a sophisticated way of using his eyes to maximum effect; he could close them to a fraction of a millimetre and still see anything that happened around him without the drawback of eye contact, and he could open them so wide that they virtually became circular, which he thought was no mean feat for an Oriental, plus anything in between these two extremes. This time he closed one eye whilst the other scrutinized Ishihara.

"Talk about what," he said with all the indifference of a seasoned operator.

"That I do not know," Ishihara replied. "Naturally, I did not find it appropriate to query what might be for your ears only. However, I would not be surprised if it is the gaijin's intention to train here. Nothing but an assumption, I must add. I am bearing in mind your enormous reputation."

Kobayashi's eyes were wide open. "That is out of question," he said. "No gaijin will ever set foot in my dojo. You know my policy."

"I do indeed," Ishihara reassured him.

Kobayashi shook his head. "What makes a hairy barbarian believe that I, Ryutaro Kobayashi, will teach him the martial arts? It is insane. How dumb can a white man get?"

"Very dumb," Ishihara confirmed.

Kobayashi adjusted his chair and placed his enormous hands on the desk with a crashing sound. "So, Tadashi-San, since you so generously agree that all white men are imbeciles and no white man will ever train in my dojo, what are you doing here?"

Ishihara bowed. "I consider it my duty to inform you of everything that is going on in connection with our great school, however disagreeable and unwelcome the issue may be."

Kobayashi battled with his curiosity. "Where is he from, this gaijin?" he asked casually.

"He says he is from Mexico."

That seemed to amuse Kobayashi. His voice suddenly changed, and his laughter thundered like the echo from a sizeable avalanche. "Mexico," he choked, "a tiny little insect from Mexico. Even worse."

"He is quite tall and well built," Ishihara said matter-of-fact, "and he is blond and has got blue eyes."

Suspicion clouded Kobayashi's eyes. "Are you sure he is not American?"

"I can only quote what the gaijin told me, Sensei. He has been to America, though."

Ishihara knew that Kobayashi itched to have a look at the blond Mexican insect. He also knew that The Old Master—cunning, complex and devious as he was—had a healthy respect for Ishihara's sharp and pragmatic intelligence, his outstanding abilities on the floor, and his organizational talents coupled with his business acumen. Kobayashi was secretly proud of the fact that Ishihara was university educated, a glory Kobayashi borrowed whenever he found it convenient, appropriate or necessary.

Ishihara said quietly, "Sensei, would it be an idea to say hello to this gaijin?"

Kobayashi opened a drawer and took out a piece of sugar cane. He had ulcers, and a *shaman* with an impressive medical reputation added to his mystic powers had once strongly recommended nature's sweet ways. Any professional medical advice replacing whatever Kobayashi preferred to believe in had yet to be invented. He chewed for a while.

"Why should I?" he said at last.

"I am merely thinking of your great and worthwhile ambition, Sensei, your long-term plan to make our school into an international organization. As you have stated on several occasions," Ishihara continued, pleased with his knack for turning wishful thinking into facts, "we will need to send our own instructors out to the various parts of the world. Now, and I dare say this because it is logical that the notion has crossed your own brilliant mind, some countries could prove more difficult than others, particularly in the West, and we might deem it advantageous to lower ourselves to the level of training the odd gaijin and place him wherever so required. It all depends on how fast you want to move and the potential of the markets. Like America, for instance."

Kobayashi went for the closed-eyes technique. "That is precisely what I have in mind," he said. "I am pleased that you follow my thinking."

Oh, sure, Ishihara thought. He said, "Thank you, Sensei. You are most kind."

Kobayashi, wondering how to do a U-turn without losing face, added, "But don't you think it's a bit early?"

A line appeared on Ishihara's forehead. "Say we accept this gaijin today, it will be another five years before he gets to the black belt and is a *shodan*. At *least* five years," he emphasized and nodded as he surveyed the future, "and, come to think of it, perhaps we should not send out anyone below *nidan* or even *sandan* status."

"That very perspective has given me food for thoughts for a long time," Kobayashi declared. "In spite of your reservations, I think it wouldn't do any harm to have a look at this Mexican."

Half the battle won, Ishihara thought. The other half is up to the gaijin.

They went downstairs. Vargas was sitting on his suitcase, observing life as it passed by. He got up when he saw them.

"What do you want?" Kobayashi said in guttural English.

"I want to train here."

"Why? What do you know about my school?"

Vargas reached for his inner pocket and took out a newspaper clipping protected by a plastic folder. He carefully unfolded the paper and gave it to Kobayashi.

Kobayashi's English was better than he wanted most people to know about; feigning ignorance could from time to time be a useful strategy, but he was not in Ishihara's class. Kobayashi pretended to read every word before he handed the paper to Ishihara, who quickly scanned through it.

"Seattle," he drawled, "you got it from a newspaper in Seattle? Interesting. A very good piece, actually. Sensei is obviously extremely famous in America," he added with a glance at Kobayashi.

"Looks like," Vargas said.

He's talkative, this fellow, Ishihara reflected, rather unlike other Westerns he'd met. He asked, "You came from America to here?"

"No. I spent some time in Hong Kong."

"A fascinating place," Ishihara said. "Full of Triads, I believe."

"They exist."

Kobayashi was quietly pondering over the newspaper article and the fame he did not know he had. There and then he decided to make a move towards his long-term plans. "This is not the place for you," he said, fixing his stare at Vargas. "You are too old. This is not *Sankukai* or *Shotokan*. This is real karate. I am Ryutaro Kobayashi."

"I know who you are," Vargas said, staring back. "That is why I am here."

"Go away," Kobayashi growled with a sudden vehemence. "Find yourself another dojo. Look at them all. One of them will suit you."

Vargas picked up his suitcase and glared at Kobayashi for a few seconds. Then he turned around and walked away.

"I do not follow, Sensei," Ishihara said, bewildered.

Ryutaro Kobayashi smiled benignly. "It is called experience, Tadashi-San. If this gaijin is made of the right stuff, he will come back."

Crafty, Ishihara thought. The Old Master is still on top of the game.

When Ishihara went home that night, he admitted to himself that he could not fully explain why he wished it wasn't the last time he had seen this gaijin called Vargas.

Two weeks later Vargas was back, same outfit, same suitcase.

Ishihara ran upstairs with the news. He waited patiently for half an hour before it pleased Kobayashi to come down.

"Well?" Kobayashi said and looked at Vargas with eyes nine-tenth closed.

Vargas said, "I followed your advice. I saw ten different dojos."

"Very good. Which one shall have the honour of your presence?"

"This one."

Ishihara did not move. He had no desire to interfere with the peculiar tension he sensed was building up between Kobayashi and Vargas. They stared at each other for what seemed like minutes. Neither gave in. Ishihara knew that whoever made the first move would make or break the future of Vargas in the world of the martial arts.

Ishihara had to exercise substantial self-discipline when he saw Kobayashi reach for Vargas' hand and say, "Come in."

That night there was an eerie silence in the dojo. Sensei Kobayashi stood in front of the class of elite blackbelts. His hands were crossed and his eyes were closed. He was lost in meditation.

Everybody was aware of the presence of the gaijin, sitting on a chair next to the door, but no one, save Ishihara, knew who the white man was. Neither did they know why he was allowed to sit there. Curiosity and bewilderment hung like a tarnished halo over the class. Nobody considered asking; they all knew Sensei's passion for secrecy when it pleased him, which was most of the time.

Kobayashi had long adopted the policy of keeping his motives under wraps; it was his philosophy that all true masters were mystics. He was also convinced that nobody could match the complexity of his sublime mind, so why bother anyway.

"Keep them guessing," he once confided in Ishihara, who did not disagree with this particular viewpoint.

The beating of the drum reverberated through the dojo, and the training began. During the katas and the combinations, Ishihara noticed that Vargas watched impassively; there was no visible trace of awe or admiration on the gaijin's face.

An hour later, Sensei cleared the floor, picked out two blackbelts, and the fighting commenced. Kobayashi's school was widely known in the world of karate for being by far the most ferocious and brutal; knockdown was the rule and not the exception. There were also far fewer restrictions to which techniques were allowed and which were not. The result was that Kobayashi's students either quit or developed into highly efficient fighting machines, a fact that delighted Kobayashi no end. His tournaments were famous for their spectacular display of the martial arts, and the relatively few students from other schools who had the guts to show up were usually disposed of in the first round. Any protest about prohibited techniques was dismissed with ease and contempt. It was Kobayashi's tournament, and the thousands of spectators were always on the side of the aggressive fighter; the more savage, the better.

Perhaps, Ishihara thought, perhaps it was the inexplicable presence of the gaijin that spurred the students to new heights; the fights that night were of supreme quality. Each time someone was knocked out, two of the blackbelts ran across the floor, grabbed one ankle each and dragged the victim close to the wall where he was left to recover on his own initiative. Nobody paid the slightest attention to injuries; there would be time later. Clemency was a concept nowhere to be found in the syllabus.

Finally, Kobayashi nodded to Ishihara. Even those badly damaged sat up—they knew what was to come. Ishihara entered the floor, his glance sweeping the entire class before he picked the one who had giggled when Vargas first arrived.

The boy was visibly scared, but he tried to hide it by walking quickly to the line. He bowed and instantly took his fighting position. Ishihara played with him for a full three minutes and inflicted enough bruises to last for a month. A supremely executed round-kick to the head sent the boy down for good.

Another three fights followed. Ishihara did not waste too much time. The dim smile on Kobayashi's face told everybody that he was reasonably satisfied with the performance of his crown prince.

Ishihara bowed to his Sensei and the class. Then, as if a second thought had entered his head, he turned and went back to the line.

This time there was no sweeping glance. He looked at a man called Sadayuki Watanabe, a blackbelt of massive proportions; at least a head taller than Ishihara and with a weight advantage of three stones.

Ishihara bowed, and Watanabe stepped forward. The tension in the dojo was almost tangible. Even Kobayashi straightened up and watched through open eyes. His smile was gone.

Ishihara had never seriously fought Watanabe, a member of the Yamaguchi yakuza family, but Kobayashi had spotted Watanabe's potential at an early stage and paid him special attention. He had arrived as a clumsy teenager, but Kobayashi gradually shaped him into one of the best and most feared fighters the school had ever produced.

For a minute or so, the two men appeared wary of each other; then, slowly, Ishihara started to dominate. His incredible speed began to tell, and again and again he outwitted the bigger man with skills, precision and sheer talent. Despair and confusion etched their lines on Watanabe's face; although he got in a few kicks and punches, Ishihara seemed to flow away without being hurt. Watanabe realized that he had to use his weight advantage, get Ishihara into a corner and let knees and elbows do the rest. As Watanabe lounged forward, Ishihara whipped around. He planted his heel with considerable force into Watanabe's family jewels, pivoted again and sent his right knee into Watanabe's solar plexus, followed by a sweep that lifted the big man up in the air and saw him crashing to the floor. Ishihara leapt, fell heavily on his opponent and completed the performance with a vicious elbow strike to Watanabe's temple.

Ishihara did not bother to look as Watanabe was being dragged off the floor. Instead, he eyed Vargas, who, very slightly, nodded once.

Fine, Ishihara thought, it'd be interesting to see what this gaijin is made of. If he didn't have an idea about true karate before, he's got it now.

The class assembled and went through the rituals. As Kobayashi approached the door, Vargas rose. "When can I start?" he asked.

"When I tell you," Kobayashi said without stopping.

A week passed. Vargas showed up in the afternoon, placed himself in the chair and left when everybody else did. He watched every single class, from whitebelts and up. He saw groups disappearing for runs through the streets of Tokyo, coming back exhausted, feet bleeding and dripping with sweat. He asked no questions and made no comments. He showed Kobayashi polite respect, but not a word was exchanged between them.

Vargas appeared to have limitless patience, but Ishihara began to wonder for how long it could last. Neither did he know what Kobayashi was up to; Ishihara could only surmise that this was Kobayashi's idea of a character test.

One day, halfway into the second week, Ishihara invited Vargas for a drink after training. Vargas accepted with a nod. They went to one of the numerous, seedy little coffee bars frequented by small-time yakuzas, prostitutes in the lower price range, fixers, lay-abouts and others whose reality was stacked with cherished but faded dreams.

Ishihara ordered two cups of coffee. They headed for a table occupied by four of his students, loudly enjoying their evening. The conversation died away the moment they spotted Ishihara. Quietly, they got up and left.

"Efficient," Vargas said.

Ishihara shrugged. "What is the point of having authority and not use it when needs be?"

They sat down. Vargas took a packet of cigarettes and a cheap plastic lighter from his pocket.

"You *smoke*?" Ishihara asked, horrified. "It is not good for you."

Vargas lit his cigarette. "Neither is sitting on a chair for weeks."

Ah, Ishihara mused, now we are getting somewhere. He still did not understand his fascination with the gaijin, except—a notion Ishihara was determined to keep to himself—except that Vargas came from the white man's world, a world that was multifarious, unregimented, vibrating and as diversified as Japan was homogeneous, a world that Ishihara yearned to learn about and perhaps one day would enter.

243

"You are a very patient man, Vargas-San," he said.

"Stoical," Vargas said and blew a smoke ring away from Ishihara, who wondered if he'd seen on Vargas' face the shadow of a smile flicker by.

"How long do you think you can last on that chair?"

"For as long as it takes."

Ishihara continued, "You know, Sensei is a very wise and complex man. Nobody can read his mind or understand the way he thinks. He knows the human nature, he is the most astute and..." Ishihara stopped.

"—cunning?" Vargas suggested.

Ishihara looked away. "That could be the word." He smiled as he again focused on the gaijin. "He's testing you, you know."

"Is he? Thank you. That had not occurred to me."

Ishihara laughed.

Vargas folded his hands in front of him. They are strong, Ishihara thought, I wonder to what extent he can already use them. This man may come from nowhere, but he hasn't arrived without an experience or two behind him. My guess is that he is a streetfighter, keen on furthering his education. On average, though, streetfighters don't last long. Five years of hard training before reaching *shodan* is an eternity to most people, far more than they are prepared to invest. He had seen them come, and he had seen them go. Of the vast number of students registering each year, only a tiny handful made it to blackbelts.

This man also had the great disadvantage of being a gaijin. When it came to contempt for barbarians, Ishihara wasn't much different from any other Oriental. The dissimilarity was that Ishihara was open-minded enough to concede that the odd barbarian could actually turn out to be likeable, but, more important, it was not entirely inconceivable that a white man could teach him a thing or two about their basically degenerate but enticing world.

"And the other way round," Vargas said.

"What?"

"Are you having your line of thought interrupted? I am trying to get across to you that *I* am testing your complex and revered Sensei. Sooner or later he'll have to show his hand, or do you think that this possibility has not occurred to Japan's greatest living philosopher?"

Ishihara smiled. The sarcasm appealed to him.

He concentrated on the remains of his coffee, eager to hide that he found the gaijin's laconic sense of humour appallingly attractive.

"I'll give it another two and a half weeks," Vargas said.

"Till he lets you train, you mean?"

"That is what we are talking about."

Ishihara looked doubtful. He said, "I am not pessimistic by nature, but I do not want you to get disappointed. Believe me, nobody can foretell the outcome of Sensei's mental exercises. I read him occasionally, sheer luck, I suppose, but I fail more often than not."

"Try harder."

Ishihara chuckled. "All right," he said, "my all too dominating modesty sometimes gets in the way. Let me predict: I say, three months in that chair."

"Two and a half weeks," Vargas repeated. "I bet you one thousand American dollars."

Ishihara did not lose his composure. He examined Vargas' face for almost a minute. "Are you serious?" he finally asked. "That is a fair amount of money."

"Can you not count that far?"

I think he means it, Ishihara thought, now what? The one thousand dollars was not beyond him, far from it; Ishihara had done very well for himself since leaving Tokyo University with degrees in economics and politics, apart from being an only child of a wealthy family.

So, he contemplated, do I take the gaijin's money, or what? Say he can't afford it. Well, that part is simple; then he should not have bet and he'll lose his money as well as his face. Let me call it part of his education; that is, teaching him not to rush into things he knows nothing about. I'll do him the favour.

"You're on," he said, "one thousand it is." He sipped his coffee and tried to ignore that Vargas lit another cigarette. "May I ask, Vargas-San, where do you live?"

Vargas mentioned a cheap little inn less than a mile away. Ishihara had seen the place; it was opposite a love-hotel he frequented from time to time.

He said, "If you do not mind my advice, it would be far more economical in the long run to get yourself an apartment. They are not too expensive, around here."

"I have tried," Vargas said. "Nobody wants to know."

Ishihara nodded sympathetically. "You know why?"

"No."

"They think you are American."

"Explain, please."

"Hiroshima and Nagasaki."

They drank their coffee in silence. Eventually, Ishihara said, "Could I be so free as to offer my assistance? I believe I can open the door for you."

"Thank you," Vargas said.

"Good. Meet me here at eleven o'clock tomorrow morning. Bring your passport." He thought for a second. "As a matter of fact, just check out from that place."

"Confidence?"

Ishihara laughed. "Not another bet."

Vargas lit his third cigarette. "Sensible," he said through the smoke. "You've lost enough for one day."

Ishihara grimaced. "I'll tell you what—if I lose this bet, I'll never bet with you again."

Vargas rested the thumb of his right hand against his chin and stared at the glow of his cigarette a few inches away. "There are other suckers."

Ishihara leaned against the wall. He crossed his legs. His eyes flittered all over Vargas' face. "So that's what you are doing for a living. You are a—a…"

"—hustler," Vargas suggested.

"Yes, hustler. You operate with cards and coins and that sort of things?"

"From catching flies with chopsticks to predicting the ins and outs of great minds, and everything in between."

Ishihara could have done without the reminder, but he grinned. "Just a word of caution, there are some less than savoury characters around here."

Vargas said politely, "Thank you. I have never looked after myself before."

Ishihara sighed. "I am sorry. It was not my intention to offend you. I was also going to advise you on something else, but evidently no assistance is required."

"Don't sulk," Vargas said. "Give it a shot, and I'll tell you if your advice is useful or not." There was mild humour in his eyes.

He is easy to forgive, this fellow, Ishihara thought. I wonder why. He said, "I notice that you smoke American cigarettes. Buy Japanese."

Vargas put his hand over his half-full packet and crushed it.

"You do have a way of expressing yourself," Ishihara said.

"What are we doing here?" Vargas said.

"I beg your pardon?"

"Your reason for inviting me. I know that all Japanese are polite and have the greatest respect for decorum, but I also know a few things about motives and the human nature."

"I see," Ishihara said, trying to win time. "As you said …"

"Please," Vargas cut in, "no clichés. I want to learn from you. You are curious about the world I come from. Exchange of platitudes is pointless."

Ishihara flinched inwardly. He was on unfamiliar ground. It did not take him long to recover. "You are most direct. You clearly know why we are here, but, granted, I should have been open with you from the onset of my invitation. Kindly forgive."

"Being direct is a simple way of avoiding misunderstanding, circumstances permitting. In most cases it pays off."

Ishihara said, "That is an interesting observation, but you must know that directness is not the most common of Japanese virtues. Personally, I agree with you, but believe me, you will find that I am an exception."

"Duly noted."

Ishihara went on, "One of the benefits with the Japanese language is that we can actually say something and nothing at the same time. We have made it into an artform. Furthermore, if I may continue, do not place too much reliance on our refined and elaborate etiquette. Any decent and self-respecting Japanese will apologize when stabbing you from behind."

Vargas' blue eyes showed a trace of amusement. "You are not going to stay here forever, are you?"

It was a statement, not a question, and the preciseness of Vargas' intuition rattled Ishihara. "I think you would like to travel," Vargas continued. "I think it is your dream to seek your future, fame and fortune away from these overpopulated islands. Not a bad idea, if I may be so bold as to advise. Japan is interesting, but it isn't exactly the birthplace of individualism."

Ishihara tried to laugh away his confusion. "I do not know what made you arrive at that conclusion, leaving Japan, I mean." He looked past Vargas. The reply could have been a notch or two more subtle.

"Just surmising," Vargas said evenly.

Ishihara glanced at his watch. "Time for your chair."

Vargas put the crushed packet of cigarettes in the ashtray. "Another two and a half weeks to go."

They met the following morning. Within two hours Vargas had found what was to become his home for years ahead. Mama-San Yokota had no problems renting out her number one apartment to a man who, although a gaijin, was a friend of Ishihara's and a student of the great Kobayashi, both well known and deeply respected in the neighbourhood. She learned to her immense delight that the Mexicans hated the Americans as intensely as the Japanese did, and, for good measure, this particular Mexican had the grace to show her his passport. He also gave her an abbreviated history of his homeland and promised to buy her a map of the Americas south of the US border. Mama-San Yokota nodded politely, too civil to tell her new tenant that nothing interested her less.

The rent, however, was a different matter, and she became visibly agitated when Vargas offered to pay six months in advance. From that moment on there was nothing she would not do for him, a promise Ishihara recommended Vargas to take with a bucket of salt.

Mama-San went downstairs, and Vargas and Ishihara sat down on the floor.

Ishihara said, "A bit Spartan, even to Japanese standards."

"It'll do."

"You will need to buy a few things, like a futon, tatami mats and a kettle. Please let me assist. I know where you can get value for money. Let us go over to your hotel and pick up the rest of your belongings."

"That's it," Vargas said and beckoned towards his suitcase.

He got up and his eyes swept the room. "I shall need also need an oil heater. I dislike being cold."

Five days later Vargas' one-room apartment looked reasonably fit for human inhabitancy, and twelve days thereafter Ishihara lost his bet. Sensei Kobayashi came through the door of the dojo clutching a *gi* in his hand—a white cotton jacket and pair of trousers. He nodded to Ishihara whilst dumping the *gi* with a white belt wrapped around it into Vargas' lap.

Ishihara ran across the floor, and the whole class turned to find out what was going on.

Kobayashi made no attempt to whisper. "Tadashi-San," he boomed, "as of today, the gaijin is all yours. You insisted on him, you'll have him. Start by teaching him how to do the *obi*. Five hundred repetitions should suffice, I hope."

Kobayashi grinned as if he'd dropped the apothegm of the century, turned on his heels and was gone.

Ishihara had never before experienced a more spooky silence. Nobody could hear anybody breathe. Never *ever* before has Sensei *given* a *gi* to a student; a gi was something purchased at an inflated price—Sensei's gesture was beyond comprehension. Generosity was not the most prominent of his quirks, and besides, the beginner was a gaijin. What was going on?

Ishihara could not be bothered to search for an explanation, partly because Sensei's behaviour was unfathomable, but mostly because he was both hurt and offended. First and foremost, he thought, Kobayashi had his ulterior motives for taking on Vargas. Then Sensei played his little game for a month, and now, when it came to the crunch, he implied in front of a full class of elite blackbelts that the presence and the future of the gaijin had been Ishihara's idea, and, therefore, so were the responsibility and the obligations.

Brilliant thinking, Ishihara conceded; if Vargas failed and dropped out after a few months, it was all down to Ishihara, and if the gaijin did not fail, Kobayashi would step in and claim the credit. No problem with the logic, so far, but the gi was the mystery. Also, why insist on Vargas doing the belt five hundred times? Anyone, gaijins included, who could not do the knot after the second attempt had to be a write-off.

Ishihara seethed. Not having Kobayashi's full confidence was one thing—nobody had Kobayashi's confidence—but to be used as a pawn and reduced to teaching a whitebelt was something else. He, crown prince and sixth dan, dealing with a beginner—Ishihara shuddered. That was history, a situation gone years and years ago. It contravened his rank, his status and every other aspect of the school's structure. It was unheard of, and, to add injury to insult, he'd lost one thousand dollars.

Ishihara crossed his hands and feigned meditation. He could not let his self-control desert him. Slowly, the cramp in his jaw muscles abated. He opened his eyes and glared at Vargas' stolid face. The damn gaijin was just sitting there, showing absolutely nothing; no triumph, no surprise—indifference, if anything.

Another one with a labyrinth of a mind, Ishihara thought. Then, as if touched by the gods, Ishihara smiled. Yes, he thought, the gaijin is all mine—*my* way.

An hour later he dismissed the class. Vargas stood up when the last student left.

Ishihara pointed at the *gi* and said, "Time to begin. Go and change."

Vargas attended the regular classes instructed by a variety of *shodans* and *nidans*, but in the early hours of the morning and late at night, Ishihara spent never less than one hour with his new-found friend. Vargas' physical strength was way above average, and his reflexes were so lightning fast that Ishihara began to compare his student with himself— no greater compliment existed. It also impressed him that Vargas never tired, his stamina seemed limitless. He never made excuses, and he never complained. Injuries were treated as minor inconveniences, quickly attended to and thereafter ignored.

It's all in the mind, Ishihara thought, and we shall see; this may become interesting. The second year of endless, fatiguing and tedious repetitions was empirically a breaking point. Few were chosen; only a minute percentage showed the same steely determination as did the gaijin Vargas.

Ishihara soon acknowledged that Vargas wasn't unfamiliar with fighting, albeit of a different and more primitive kind; certain movements, instinctive reactions and the expression in his eyes told their own story.

One day, sitting in a sushi bar in Akihaba, Ishihara asked, "You are a streetfighter, aren't you, and you have been so for a long time. Am I right?"

Vargas picked a slice of tuna with elaborate care. "So what."

Ishihara ignored the comment. "How come?" he said. "Tell me."

"Circumstantial necessity."

Ishihara played with his chopsticks. The expression on his face showed only mild curiosity. "I haven't seen any scars."

"Losers get scarred."

Ishihara laughed. He helped himself to more sake. The toe of his shoe touched Vargas' right ankle. "I have never seen you without that knife strapped to your leg. A true and faithful friend, I take it?"

"Faithful and efficient."

Ishihara pondered for a while. They had known each other for a year, and it irked him that Vargas was still the stranger he'd been since he first arrived. The man was too closed, too reticent and too private; a recluse determined to share nothing with anybody. Fair enough, he had talked about places he'd been to; he shared his knowledge of history, culture and ways of life. He described and informed like an interested and observant reporter, objectively and impassionately. But he never talked about his own involvements and experiences and never about his personal life. Vargas related with clinical precision and verbiage. There was a barrier there, like a wall of ice around him, and Ishihara saw no way of getting through it.

Still, he spent as much time as he could in Vargas' company. Ishihara believed that the sympathy was mutual, but another reason, far more important than the degree of reciprocal rapport Vargas had allowed them to develop, was Ishihara's conviction that Vargas' appearance was no coincidence. Fate had decided that he should come into Ishihara's life, and fate had staked out their future together.

How and where Ishihara did not know; the ways of the gods could not be questioned. No, Ishihara told himself, I shall not query. I shall accept at face value, as I accept that the man opposite is not, thank heavens, one of life's privileged individuals. He comes from the streets, but there were signs that he once had been introduced to some kind of education, an echo of which manifested itself in Vargas' insatiable passion for literature and learning. His tiny room looked like a miniature library, and he was immune to any derogatory remark about his hobby— a grossly inadequate euphemism for an all-conquering zeal. Somewhere behind Vargas' shield there were qualities that complemented Ishihara's own—whatever they did, they would make a perfect team.

Ishihara trusted Vargas on instinct, and he had no problems in dismissing logic in favour of fatalism. The gods had linked them together, and the gods were never wrong. Gods and humans, faith and fate; what was life but a carefully engineered balance between heaven and earth?

Ishihara glanced at Vargas who was staring ahead, lost in thoughts of his own. He had swapped the sake for Japanese whisky. Ishihara had noticed that expression from time to time; Vargas looking distant and sphinxlike, as if he had entered a world no one else had access to. A mind in turmoil, Ishihara thought; a mind tormented by conflicts and where the demons outnumbered the gods.

During one of their first talks, Vargas had said that he did not appreciate personal questions. It was up to Ishihara to show the discretion required.

251

Ishihara had said that he understood. He wasn't convinced that he did, but he had trod carefully each time he sensed that Vargas reacted in a negative manner. Ishihara quickly devised a technique of casually commenting instead of asking, and by now he was satisfied with his ability to master equilibrium on a tight rope. He still got frustrated when his curiosity was being met by a cold stare, but with a blend of fatalism and dignified resignation he concluded that time and patience were his allies.

The warm sake had made him sombre. He wanted to talk, but not to himself.

"You are making good progress," he began. "You are well ahead of the rest of the class."

"I know."

"Don't get bigheaded," Ishihara advised with a forced laugher. "You are not exactly at my level."

"Not yet."

Suddenly, Vargas changed. The aloofness disappeared; it was as if he had snapped himself out of a trance, and he smiled. "You are so damn nosy that it is absurd, Tadashi. You must learn to control yourself. It's a virtue, I've been told, and you have not got many to lose." Vargas shook his head as if mildly disturbed. "Your lack of inhibitions is worrying, amigo. Where is your sense of propriety? Being sanguine and garrulous is one thing—outright probing does not fit the profile of a Japanese gentleman."

"For heaven's sake!" Ishihara hissed. "What are you talking about! I have hardly said a word all evening. Did I ever interrupt your endless and interesting monologue?" He knew that he had walked into one of the little traps that Vargas enjoyed setting up in order to irritate people, but it was too late.

"Body language, Tadashi," Vargas said with a patronizing gesture. "You know, tiny movements; eyes, tone of voice, tics—you get the picture?"

Ishihara's voice was heavy with irony, "Most certainly. From now on we shall restrict ourselves to staring at each other. Who needs words?"

"You do."

"I do not. I am perfectly at ease with profound serenity and total silence."

"Nicely put, but misleading. Would you like to know why I came to Honbu?"

Ishihara clasped his knees with both hands, steadied the dragon in his stomach and emptied his sake. He's having me on again, he thought—the sphinx talking?

Vargas pushed his empty glass away and asked for another.

"Do you know what a stowaway is?" he asked.

"Yes, I do."

Vargas sipped his drink. Ishihara stared in disbelief as the colour of Vargas' eyes changed from sapphire to midnight blue.

"I entered a cargo ship in Amsterdam," he said. "I had no idea that she was destined for Mexico. I thought that I was going to the United States. Misinformation. After a few days I decided to surface. The night before I hid the parcel containing my money, my knife and my stone under the port side anchor and almost fell overboard in doing so. Anyway. I needed water, I needed food and I needed to clean myself. The captain was Dutch, as were the rest of the officers. He wanted to know if I could pay for the fare. I told him that I had fifty American dollars. The amount was deemed insufficient, and I would have to make up the difference by working my way over. He did not say to where. I was left in the care of the cook, a Belgian.

One day, the cook and two of the officers hit on the assumption that my affluence could possibly exceed fifty dollars. They decided to find out. They didn't, but it was one of life's little miracles that I survived.

That night, the odd moment when I was conscious, I made up my mind to learn to fight. I vowed to acquire the strength, the skills and the ability to destroy whoever came in my way. Sooner or later I would find someone who could teach me to perfection. Not boxing or wrestling; somebody who knew about sheer annihilation of an opponent or three."

Vargas paused. He lit a cigarette and frequented his glass, all the time without losing eye contact. Ishihara felt as if the room temperature had gone below zero. We all have a desire to be able to defend ourselves, he thought, but this was different. Deeply embedded in Vargas' psyche was an immensely strong and primitive desire to become indestructible, to seek invincibility. It required a degree of ruthlessness that was inhuman. It demanded an attitude that saw savagery as a mere necessity. Not quite the average student, Ishihara concluded without letting go of Vargas' stare, but then, that was the impression from day one. Could this have been the vibration that had made a blip on Kobayashi's built-in radar screen? Had he instantly recognized that Vargas had not come all the way from Seattle in order to pick up a dan-grade and a diploma, but to become a skilled and unmerciful warrior? Such a mentality would appeal to The Old Master, more than anything else. *That* was his real reason for accepting Vargas, and it explained the *gi*.

Vargas continued. "Halfway across the Atlantic I dreamed of blowing up the ship, but explosives weren't part of the cargo. Come to think of it, the suicidal instinct was missing, as well. Explosives and arms is a very lucrative trade, by the way, should you ever plan to get rich."

Ishihara did not comment.

Vargas smiled. "Anyway, a chap at the Amsterdam Port Authority informed me that the ship was destined for the Americas, which was true enough, but he did not specify and I did not distinguish between USA and the rest of the continent."

"You wanted to get lost in the United States," Ishihara said.

"The land of freedom and opportunities, of milk and honey; yes, that was the idea. The captain's idea was to keep me on board, hidden away during the stay, and to exploit further the fruits of free labour back to Amsterdam where I would be handed over to the appropriate section of the Dutch law enforcement brigade. This I learned one day prior to arrival. I also learned that the port in waiting was Veracruz in Mexico. From other conversations overheard I got the impression that the local authorities could be surprisingly quick with formalities if properly rewarded."

Vargas rubbed the palms of his hands against his ribcage and looked amused. "From my reading about Mexico, I knew that my chances of survival and prosperity did not match the odds available in the United States, but there wasn't much I could do about it. No way was I going back to Europe, and I had twenty-four hours to devise a plan. Mexico was to become my adopted country, at least for a while, and I knew I had to disembark on the first night when everybody was too intoxicated by drink or elation to pay any attention to an inexperienced kid locked up and filled with horror stories about Mexican brutality. The lock on the cabin door wasn't the most complicated on this earth. Shortly before midnight, accompanied only by the clinking of bottles and the shanty songs of unseen performers on the mess deck, I walked unnoticed down the gangway and into the shadows."

Ishihara undid three buttons on his shirt to let fresh air circulate.

The tip of his fingers touched his skin. It was as damp as his mouth was dry. He said, "What about your money?"

Vargas licked the inside of his empty glass. "I could not risk getting caught carrying my entire capital. My money was safely carried ashore by the cook. He discovered that a few hours later. This fine gentleman was fond of tequila. Before we arrived at Veracruz, he told me something that turned out to be the second favour he ever did me. The first I've already mentioned. Cookie was going to get enough of tequila to last him for the stay, plus another roundtrip. For this purpose he had a large leather bag. I hid the money in a side pocket of his bag and hoped for the best, being short on options. My knife and my stone I carried on me. When he finally emerged from the cantina, that night, bottles merrily saluting each other as he walked, I followed him. He wasn't drunk, but he wasn't sober, either, and at one point he vanished behind a shed to relieve himself. Time to collect, in other words. He still had no idea he was my appointed courier. I took him by surprise. The area was not well lit, but I had my one and only scarf over my face and a black cap almost down to my eyebrows. I knew that he carried a long and sharp butcher's knife; he never went ashore without it, he once told me. As expected, for a split second he could not decide whether to go for the knife or for the bag standing on the ground next to him. Then something connected in his little brain, and he went for both. The knife came out, and he bent forward to grab his bag. I had my stone in my hand, and I hit him across the neck. He tried to get up, so I repeated the exercise. This time he stayed where I intended him to stay. I took my money and bade him farewell with a sweet little gesture of my own design, conceived and cherished under the stars as I crossed the ocean towards an unknown destiny."

Ishihara badly wanted his whisky to take effect.

"You killed him," he said when he came back with the drinks.

"No," Vargas said evenly. "He wasn't worth the risk." He ran his thumb across his lips and sniffed the drink before he tasted it. The expression of mild amusement had come back. "You see, Tadashi, apart from what he did to me, he was a lousy cook. I ensured that he'd never cook again."

"How?"

"I cut off his thumb and his index-finger on both hands."

Ishihara cleared his throat and asked, "Why did you let him go?"

Then he realized that Vargas had already answered the question. "I mean, it must have been hard, considering what you went through."

Vargas said, "It was, but I was young and immature. My ability to evaluate human life was not what it is today, and neither was my talent for analyzing the permutations of consequences. I did the right thing, circumstances considered." He paused. "In retrospect, I now know that my destructive instincts were only germinal at the time."

Ishihara fiddled with his glass. He had yet to develop a taste for the more potent of life's liquid godsends. He wanted to ask about Vargas' life in Mexico. No, he thought, let him tell me in his own time. He said, "Then you saw the article about Sensei in a Seattle newspaper."

"I did, some years later, and here I am."

"Just like that," Ishihara said and hunched his shoulders to avoid shaking his head. The dark shimmer had gone from Vargas' eyes; he looked his normal self and Ishihara wondered if he'd been the victim of his own imagination. How the hell can anybody change the colour of his eyes? he thought. It's impossible.

Vargas' smile was open and genuine. "Just like that," he said. "You never give up, do you? No, I am not Mexican, and I think you have known that all along." He focused on a point above Ishihara's head. "In between Mexico and here, I lived in the United States and thereafter in Hong Kong. The story of my life. Satisfied?"

Ishihara knew that he'd been told more than he could possibly have hoped for, but he still could not resist: "No, since you are kind enough to ask."

Vargas shifted his cigarette from left to right between his teeth. "Those were the years in the wilderness," he said with a softness that contradicted the look in his eyes. "I was young, impressionable and vulnerable, so young and inexperienced that I either adapted instantly and I mean *instantly* to the concrete jungle called Mexico City, or I perished. I transformed; against the grim drabness and quiescence of my background in an occupied country I became a savage whose primary instincts were directed towards survival. Only the library kept me sane. Once again, books became my salvation, my rescue from an unconditional primeval existence."

"What made you seek the library? You just decided to read, all of a sudden? I can see that it made sense, though, seeking a balance, so to speak."

Vargas crushed out his cigarette. All right, Ishihara thought, I've gone too far. Call it a day.

"My grandfather," Vargas said. "Legacy from my grandfather. He loved books. It was through him that I discovered the captivating world of literature. He taught me to read, among other things."

"Do you keep in touch with your grandfather?"

"I left the day I learned about his death, but yes, we do keep in touch."

There was a haunted look on Vargas' face. Ishihara bit his tongue and cursed his frivolous mind. "I am sorry," he said in a low voice.

Vargas looked away.

Fate, as Ishihara knew it, could never be explained. At that moment, two American sailors came into the sushi bar. They were both laughing and evidently in need of something to sustain their high spirit. Their white navy uniforms were stained and they had taken off their caps.

"Sake," one of them suggested. "It is better than that bloody awful imitation of whisky they produce here."

Ishihara could see that malice was lurking under the surface of joviality.

"Sake!" the other concurred. He banged his fist on the counter.

They drank heavily. In between greedy slurps they began to make loud, derogatory remarks about Japan, the people and the culture. One of them remembered that etiquette was just goddamn humbug, a load of horseshit that shouldn't fool anybody.

Both were in their mid-to-late twenties, six feet tall and around 180 pounds. The most talkative had a broken nose, the other a scar that ran from over his left eye and across towards the flip of his right ear.

"Pearl Harbour!" Broken Nose suddenly yelled and slammed both fists on the table.

Bar room brawlers, Ishihara thought, the pride of the US Navy showing their true colours in the most unmistakable way. He nudged Vargas. "Let's get out of here. They are looking for a fight."

Vargas did not move.

"Please," Ishihara whispered. "Remember *The Way*."

The teaching of The Old Master was simple. The Way of the Warrior was to avoid a fight whenever possible, and not to seek it. Only when no other options were available should the Warrior engage in battle, and only then should he use his skills in order to maximize the effect and minimize the extent of the confrontation.

But Ishihara knew it was too late. From the moment the two sailors came into the bar, some sixth sense told him that Vargas had no desire to follow the Way of the Warrior.

Scarface turned to Broken Nose and said with elaborate slowness, "You know, Chuck, there's a white man sitting over there. You hear me? A *white* man in the midst of a bunch of slit-eyed yellow little baboons. I think he deserves better company, don't you?"

Broken Nose nodded enthusiastically. "Surely. Hey!" he bellowed, glaring at Vargas, "come over here!"

"Thank you, but I am fine where I am," Vargas replied so amiably that Ishihara barely recognized the voice.

"Oh you are, are you. That Jap there your fiancée?"

"He is my friend," Vargas said and looked at Ishihara, who noticed that the dark shimmer was back in Vargas' eyes.

"Goddammit!" Scarface exclaimed. "This guy ain't normal. I think he's an insult to white mankind."

"That's precisely what he is," Broken Nose clarified.

"Tell you what," Scarface said. "I think we gotta do something here. Tell me," he shouted across to Vargas, "how would you fancy your fiancée if he ain't got no ears no more?"

Vargas dropped his hands onto his lap. "I would not advise that," he said softly.

"Now is that right?" Scarface snarled contemptuously. "Well, I ain't in the mood to listen to no lily-livered renegade." His right hand went inside his jacket and came out firmly holding a gun. The American put the barrel of his nine millimetre Browning to his lips and kissed it gently. Ishihara stared in disbelief. For a moment he was too amazed to be scared. Guns in the streets of Tokyo were practically unheard of; not even mindless barbarians were stupid enough to walk around waving firearms.

Scarface placed his left hand on the wrist of his right arm. "I ain't got much patience left. His ears, and your kneecaps, you sonofabitch."

"You are a long way from home," Vargas said. "Perhaps this is not a bad place to end your career."

"It ain't over yet," Scarface snarled and showed his teeth. He stretched his arms above his head and lowered the barrel.

Ishihara was halfway up when Vargas exploded into action. The light caught the steel as his knife whistled through the air and sank deep into the American's shoulder, one inch below the right-hand collarbone.

He screamed, dropped his gun and fell to his knees. He stared in horror at the knife and the blood quickly spreading. Vargas moved, landed in front of the American and pulled out the knife with a violent jerk. Before the other American could react, Vargas had slashed him twice from shoulder to navel, proceeding so fast that he escaped a single drop of blood.

"Let's get out of here!" Ishihara shouted. "Now!"

Vargas wiped his knife on Scarface's trousers. Ishihara raised his hands, palms outwards. He looked at the twenty odd customers frozen to their seats. He said, "There were three Americans here, those two and a black fellow. They had a fight between them. The black fellow used a knife and ran off. Do you understand?" They all stayed silent, but Ishihara knew that his version would become the unanimous version. He thought quickly. Under no circumstances could he allow Vargas to get caught—his visa had expired. Within minutes the police would be there; Ishihara was familiar with their efficiency, as he was aware of their mentality. They would not be too bothered about a fracas between three Americans; they would do no more than what they had to do, which was to ensure medical care and thereafter leave the rest in the hands of American justice. The search for the third culprit would officially enter the records and unofficially fade away overnight. The visa was another matter.

"We are out of here," he said.

They found Ishihara's car and drove to Vargas' place.

Vargas had bought a rosewood table, two bamboo chairs and a fusuma to give the room another dimension. Ishihara could see Vargas' movements through the thin rice paper of the partition.

"I have to clean and polish the knife," Vargas said. "Make yourself at home."

Ishihara sat down in one of the bamboo chairs. The wooden floor was creaking, and some of the boards were loose. Stacks of books were neatly organized against the wall. The place was spotlessly clean.

"I know you've got contacts," he heard Vargas' voice behind the fusuma. "Can you get me a case of Irish whisky?"

"Can do."

"No offence, but your local stuff can't compete."

"No problem."

Vargas appeared and sat down on the floor. There were a couple of yards between them. He faced Ishihara. Neither spoke for a while.

Ishihara broke the silence. "There's a nice scent here, like the burning wood of the apple tree."

"My candles. You can buy them in Shinjuku. Sometimes I lay on the floor and the scent brings back memories of my nights with my pigeons. The loft was my shrine."

Ishihara lit one of the candles. He wanted to ask about the memories, but it was not the right moment. Instead, he said, "You've got quite a temper, haven't you."

"I have."

"Funny. I have never seen any sign of it, until today, that is."

Vargas cracked his neck and placed his hands on the floor behind him. "I used to be my own worst enemy until experience told me to impose some discipline and control. It took a long time. Fighting your own nature is a gigantic challenge. I am better off, though, being in command, as you so shrewdly observed."

Ishihara was not convinced that Vargas was being entirely serious. "What happened today, then—you just let go?"

Vargas shrugged. "Once in a while I feel this urge to exercise my atavistic instincts. It keeps the balance. Call it a safety valve."

Ishihara thought for a while. "Do you think that gun was loaded?"

"Yes, I do. They're Americans. I didn't see much mileage in trying to get it confirmed. Also, they were stoned out of their minds."

"You mean on drugs?"

"On drugs. Mixing it with sake didn't make them any more rational."

"How can you tell?"

Vargas smiled. "Believe me, Tadashi, if you live in Mexico and the United States for a while, you can't miss picking up a few things about drugs."

Ishihara gripped the sides of his chair. "That bullet could have hit me in the face. I could have been killed."

"If he was a lousy shot, yes. Any nagging doubt can be erased from your mind if we go looking for them."

"I like your mild sense of humour."

"None better."

Ishihara stretched. The tension in his body was gone. His mind began to relax. He promised himself to pray to a carefully selected choice of his revered Shinto gods when he came home.

The neon lights from a nearby massage parlour flashed through the room. Vargas closed his eyes. "Time to meditate."

"Just a thought," Ishihara said. "Do you have any regrets about your life?"

He saw a glimpse of what he read as resignation when Vargas opened his eyes and stared at the candle. "Why is the usual precision of your mind absent, all of a sudden? Do I regret what I have done, or do I have any regrets about what happened to me? Which one is it, Tadashi?"

"Both, I guess."

"Neither."

Ishihara believed him, but he did not know why. His own life had been sheltered; regulated and protected, and with no serious upheavals. He had used his education and his wits and ambitions to get him to where he was, and, so far, he had been spared an imperilled existence. The odd hiccup, yes, but nothing compared with what he knew and sensed that Vargas had been through.

"Scars on the mind stay," he said, seeking clarification. "There is no surgery for emotions."

"You are implying that I have rationalized away my wounds? A logical conclusion, but not quite what happened. I nursed them carefully, over time, and gradually they healed—" he ran a finger across his lips and squinted at the lights coruscating through the window "—although not all equally well. The mould can't be re-cast and the past can't be undone. You are stuck with who you are, and all there is room for is minor corrections. Over the years, I found my balance, broadly speaking. I concluded that bitterness has only one victim, and that is oneself. Having regrets is a negative and destructive preoccupation leading nowhere. Am I rationalizing? Some will say so, particularly those of academic disposition and with a tendency to confuse scratches with wounds, those who never had to hide in the sewer and never stared death in the eye. Their major contribution to mankind is to exercise unrestrained judgmentalism. This they do to such an extent and with such talent that reason disintegrates in the toxic vapours from their stomachs where, as is invariably the case, their brain is located. They preach, recommend, dictate and condemn; the pillars of society who will never discover that life is cheap, that it has no value beyond its own existence. Regrets? I have trained my mind to eradicate any sentiment that resembles self-pity, and that is how I live with myself."

Ishihara's right hand moved as if playing chess with invisible pieces. Had Vargas' reference to *those of academic disposition* been aimed at him?

Ishihara did not like the thought; it collided with his image of himself and it certainly did not fit in with his notion of the future.

Vargas rested on one elbow and turned lazily. He said, "Does the way I lead my life make me a nefarious person, amigo, a paragon of culpability? It does, by most standards. The point is—*my* point is—I could not care less. My life is my own responsibility and I have no desire to feign transmutation from wolf to turtle."

"No," Ishihara said, still dazed, "one should not mess with nature." Vargas' monologue had stunned him; never ever had his friend revealed that many thoughts in any one go at any one day.

Silence fell. Vargas had again closed his eyes, seemingly unaware of the impact his words had made on Ishihara.

Slowly, almost imperceptibly, Ishihara moved his chair to his left, away from the flickering lights. Vargas' presentation of himself as an insensitive and one-dimensional being did not make sense. Clearly, Ishihara thought, behind the carapace was a man whose world once had been shattered, leaving behind nothing but devastation. On the ruins of this cataclysm Vargas had re-invented himself; taken stock and with single-minded tenacity set his goals in order to emerge as the god of his own universe. Nothing and nobody was to get in his way, never again was he to submit to another mortal. Ishihara could sympathize with the ambition, but he had problems believing it humanly possible to convert such a rigid philosophy into prevailing praxis. Life was not that simple. Only a man carrying no emotional baggage could achieve that kind of fulfilment, and such a person was either dead or incurably insane. Vargas was very much alive; he certainly had his crazy moments and could behave in the most bizarre manner, but insane he was not. Also, Ishihara recalled, there had been instances when Vargas momentarily dropped his shield, and those rare glimpses had convinced Ishihara that there were other sides to Vargas' callous and uncompromising nature.

Ishihara did not see Vargas as capable of becoming a harmonious person, that Vargas himself could possibly envisage a life where his mind was at peace, even if he wanted to. Did he want to? Ishihara dismissed the question. Ten years ago, perhaps, but not any more. The margins were gone.

Interesting, he thought; Vargas had always looked so composed. The real Vargas had come out a couple of hours earlier, like a grizzly bear stepping on a bed of nails. What fascinated Ishihara was not so much the evidence of his friend's temper as the vehemence behind it. The flare-up had been genuine, but, looking back, everything pointed to a cold fury; Vargas' entire act had been performed in a calculating, methodical and professional way. The expression on his face when he'd slashed the second American had been a strange mixture of intensity and indifference, an action reflecting his words *life is cheap—it has no value beyond its own existence.*

The words echoed through Ishihara's mind and he smiled when he thought of the jigsaw puzzle that eventually would give him a clear and concerted picture of times to come.

From far away Ishihara heard Vargas' voice, "Would you like to know what it feels like to be perpetually disturbed?"

Ishihara smiled. "I would, amigo."

"Like climbing Mount Everest barefoot and without a rope."

From that moment on, any lingering doubt had gone. Ishihara knew that he and Vargas complemented each other to perfection.

Neither Ishihara nor Vargas told anybody about the episode in the sushi bar, and, as Ishihara anticipated, every single customer had seen three Americans break into a fight. The police soon lost interest, but Ishihara nevertheless decided to stay clear of the area for a while. Vargas agreed.

It worried Ishihara that Vargas' visa had run out; he was, in effect, an illegal immigrant. Ishihara was uncomfortable with the situation; although the control was slack, there was always a chance of discovery by accident. He urged Vargas to stay put in Ikebukuro and to keep a low profile.

Vargas did not object, but Ishihara knew that his friend from time to time wandered up to the Ginza or Shinjuku districts where there was no shortage of beautiful women. His other reason was monetary transactions; Vargas preferred to use the major banks in central Tokyo when exchanging his dollars. Ishihara offered to assist; he could use his own contacts and discreetly arrange whatever Vargas needed. Ishihara, who had a substantial income, tactfully suggested a loan, if needs be. Vargas thanked him, but said that he had enough money to last him for another decade, possibly longer, depending on the bets he could pull of. He added that central Tokyo was full of foreign businessmen and diplomats; one more white face made no difference, and the likelihood of being questioned by the police was negligible. Ishihara repeated his warning; discovery by coincidence did happen, and how would Vargas feel if he found himself in a police van heading for the airport?

Vargas became invisible for a few months.

The incident in the sushi bar kept haunting Ishihara; he could not forget the sequence of the episode, and how close to death he had been. Neither could he clear his mind of what had happened to Vargas on board the ship to Mexico; the attempt to rob him, how he had got his money ashore and how he had dealt with the cook. Ishihara no longer believed that the warrior in Vargas had been born during the voyage across the Atlantic. His disposition was innate and not acquired; nascent instincts had *surfaced* the moment he came to believe that the world was his enemy, all he had needed to release his primitive violence was a catalyst. On board that ship, Vargas had become conscious of his compulsion, of the forces in him that had forever opened the door to an existence where ferocity and brutality ruled, and where callousness was the key to survival.

The other side of the coin added to Ishihara's bafflement. Vargas' sense of humour wasn't always black and cynical. His craving for books and learning were not traits usually associated with troublemakers. He had shown signs of consideration and generosity.

Ishihara's observations made him deduce that Vargas had his own code of honour, and that he could be trusted. Ishihara had never sought the friendship of other men before; he was a loner who, he now knew, had happened to find empathy and rapport with another loner. Ishihara did not see himself as one of life's pure and innocent bystanders, nor as alien to coercion, but he knew that he lacked the ultimate killer instinct. He had other qualities. *Jointly,* he and Vargas would become a considerable operational force.

Ishihara's experience with non-Japanese was limited, but, people being people and thus human beings even if they were gaijins, Vargas was not an exclusively unique specimen. Ishihara had seen such men before. When they matured, they usually ended up as heads of big and powerful yakuza syndicates. They grew into urbane and charming men, they were knowledgeable and ingenious in their methods, but their killer instinct bubbled happily behind a carefully presented mask of dignity. Ishihara respected their acumen, their traditional role and the part they played in the Japanese society, but he'd never had any ambition to join them. A vibrant individualistic streak in him rejected the notion of becoming part of an organization, criminal or otherwise. He wanted to act on his own, to be his own master and to enjoy the fruits of independence.

Was such freedom to be found in Japan? No, it was not. The structure of the entire Japanese society was like a gigantic anthill—misfits strayed at their peril. Japan was a strait jacket; influence from abroad could little by little loosen the ropes, but it would take many decades before liberalism became a concept in the Japanese mind.

Ishihara acknowledged that his plan for the future was still in its embryonic stage, but he identified the contours. He would need time to develop the project—years of analysis, intelligence work and case studies. Its most attractive advantages—apart from the rewards—were that he could operate from anywhere, and that only a limited initial capital was required.

Other than that, all he needed was a qualified accomplice. Ishihara's cool and calculating brain supported his instincts telling him that he had found such an ally in Vargas.

The snag, spadework aside, was that, since he had yet to confide in Vargas, it was impossible to tell how his friend would react. Another potential drawback was that Vargas clearly enjoyed living in Japan. He could decide to stay on for longer than it suited Ishihara.

Ishihara made up his mind to ignore the time factor. Pragmatism, a fatalistic streak and infinite patience were his partners. He resolved to develop and complete his plan and otherwise take one year at a time.

Ishihara made his living as a *sokaiya*, an activity nobody knew about except his victims, and they kept quiet. His parents, as well as Kobayashi— a man with an almost pathological curiosity and an insatiable appetite for hearsay camouflaged as need for inside information—had accepted Ishihara's explanation that he was a financial consultant to small and medium-sized businesses with cashflow problems.

In one way, this was perfectly true; the difference from the common conception of consultancy was that the companies' cashflow headaches worsened as a result of Ishihara's advisory services. This was only temporarily, as he was quick to point out; it was not his long-term strategy to acquire the golden egg *and* kill the goose.

His clients were also delighted to learn instantly that Ishihara had nothing to do with the yakuza, a bunch of scruffy, tattooed and loud brawlers making a company's annual meeting into a nightmare for the management unless the yakuza's demands were met in advance. Since most businesses had something to hide, primarily of a nature that would not go down well with the shareholders, the companies paid up and everybody was happy, relatively speaking.

One thing was that such crude methods did not appeal to Ishihara. More important, competing openly with the yakuza and thereby challenging them in their own backyard would have been sheer folly. Joining them would have been equally stupid.

Simplicity, discretion and intelligence became the hallmarks of Ishihara's operation. His preys were medium-sized listed companies. During his search, he left no stone unturned. If a company had something to hide, Ishihara would find it.

His opening tactic was to make an appointment with the chairman over the telephone; he was a shareholder who had become worried—and a shareholder Ishihara invariably was, however minor—and could he possibly see the honourable chairman for half an hour, preferably the following day? Should the chairman not get the message, Ishihara became more explicit; not enough to compromise either the company or himself, but sufficiently clear for the chairman to understand that Ishihara was indeed welcome, ideally the same afternoon, if possible.

Ishihara showed up, and the two of them—nobody else was ever present—went over the problems in the most courteous, businesslike and analytical fashion. Ishihara then presented his conditions for dropping the matter; it being embezzlement, corruption, bribery, use of illegal labour, dubious funds abroad or any other common practice accepted by everybody except the authorities.

Ishihara took care never to come across as outright greedy, and in most cases an agreement was reached there and then.

Ishihara worked on two levels; an upfront payment in proportion to the size of the problem and the profitability of the company, and a twelve months' retainer, correspondingly calculated. In return for these monthly fees, he would keep the chairman oriented about any internal irregularities prohibited by inconvenient laws and deplorable ethics borne by far-fetched theories, in addition to those problems created by disloyalty, avarice and stupidity.

It was not uncommon that Ishihara and the chairman parted as best of friends; Ishihara satisfied with the latest improvement of his financial status, and the chairman forever grateful that he had been caught by a solitary gentleman of a buccaneer and not by the brutal and unrefined yakuza.

It even happened that Ishihara was sent invitations to expensive parties thrown by his quarries, a gesture he without exception declined. There was always the risk that one or two of his previous contacts could show up at the same party; mixing business with pleasure was unwise, and particularly so when virtual anonymity was one of the essential ingredients to his success.

But, however lucrative and easy his business was, somewhere in the shadows of Ishihara's mind stirred an inchoate desire to see the world, to experience something else, to face a more formidable and parlous challenge. There was much about Japan that he loved and admired; he was immensely proud of his ancestry in straight paternal line to the Shogun Tokugawa, and he knew that he would forever be part of a culture alien to that of any country to which destiny would take him.

He also knew that he had placed himself in the most ambiguous of positions; in his heart, no other country could take the place of Japan— in his mind, several could. There was something alluring about the Western world; more individual freedom, less of a rigid lifestyle, a happy-go-lucky mentality, and a frivolous depravity that from a distance seemed irresistible.

The seed of an all-conquering plan had been sown, and Ishihara began to engineer its development and growth.

His first move was simple; a complete search of all foreign embassies in Tokyo.

☞

The child who called herself Yasmin came and went as she pleased. She was Kobayashi's pet and known as The Mascot, a term of endearment instigated by The Old Master himself. Already at the age of twelve it was clear that she would grow into an exceptional beauty, a probability Yasmin fully agreed with.

She lived with her Korean mother three-quarters of a mile away. Everybody in the dojo spoiled her rotten, and she manipulated everyone with consummate skills and boundless charm. Nobody dared to put her in her place; in Sensei's eyes she was pure divinity and could do no wrong.

Her given name was Kimimo, but no sensible cousin from the Korean peninsula would consider living in Japan with an indigenous name. At the age of seven she stumbled over the name Yasmin which she instantly fell for and adopted. Sensei was not too pleased, and neither was her mother, but, as usual, Yasmin won the war. Within days one and all adored her new identity.

Yasmin was not overly keen on karate. It was too much work, but she was eager to learn self-defence techniques. Kobayashi gave her private lessons most of the time, and he appointed Ishihara to accommodate her should Sensei be otherwise occupied with extremely pressing engagements.

It would forever remain an unanswered question if Ishihara were the only person in the entire school who did not take to Yasmin, but he was the only one who had the guts to make it patently clear. In Ishihara's eyes, Yasmin was a spoiled brat and a devious bitch, all of which he told her to her face, although never in the presence of anyone else. Yasmin responded with icy disdain and referred to him as *the fat little Nipponese with the brain of a dead monkey and the attraction of a plucked duck.*

To Ishihara's surprise, Yasmin kept the animosity between them to herself. She did not complain to Kobayashi or, for that matter, seek his support or comfort in any other way. Ishihara reluctantly admired her spirit and her very visible streak of independence, but in their daily life his rudimentary veneration was overshadowed by a seemingly unadulterated antagonism and a non-stop competition in trading insults.

Ishihara allowed none of this to influence his teaching. Yasmin became proficient in the most cruelly effective art of self-defence; there was a touch of ferocity in the young girl, and she showed him enough to convince him that being merciless wasn't beyond her.

Then came the surprise. The more Ishihara saw of Yasmin, the more he realized that he was developing a soft spot for her. For several years he kept his feeling well hidden behind a shield of tutorial discipline and, to support his emotional balance, a patronizing attitude.

This is crazy, he thought one day; she is just a teenager well ahead of her years, but still a child. Perhaps in five or six years' time, but until then close your mind and the whole thing may fizzle out by itself. Squash any fantasy in its infancy and treat her like the intolerable pest that she is.

What Ishihara did not know at the time, was that Yasmin adored him. She played her game to perfection, but in her mind she had decided that Ishihara was the man in her life. Never suspecting such a degree of maturity, Ishihara continued as before, ignorant of the reciprocal aspects of their situation.

Yasmin, fully in control, persevered in treating him as a necessary evil with little under his harsh hairdo. It did not help Ishihara that Yasmin singled out Vargas as her friend, confidant and soul mate. At first, she had been wary of Vargas' aloofness and asperity, but after a while she began to talk to him. She was delighted when Vargas accepted her invitation to have a drink together, and over their first pot of tea she concluded that he was an individual from whom she could learn a lot about a world she barely knew existed.

Vargas treated her with kindness and consideration; he never made fun of her, and he was always ready to answer questions however infantile or naïve. The exception, which Yasmin quickly picked up, was any reference to his personal life, and she accepted that her new friend was by any yardstick a very private person. In the beginning she had used her feminine finesse and touched ever so lightly on his childhood and his deeper feelings, but each time Vargas had steered her away from the subject. Yasmin understood and resigned herself to the fact that Vargas was not going to confide in her—at least not yet.

Ishihara was aware that he resented the bond he saw evolving between Yasmin and Vargas, but he knew that any indication would do more harm than good. Each time Yasmin and Vargas talked or went out together, Ishihara put on his most inscrutable face, his body language making it obvious that he was relieved to get rid of her, and that he failed to grasp Vargas' patience with the little rattlesnake.

Sensei Kobayashi's reaction was less subdued when one day a lower grade student, Atsushi Matsuda, deemed it his duty to inform about Yasmin and the gaijin. Matsuda disliked Vargas intensely and saw this as his great opportunity to make life unbearable for the barbarian; the sense of duty appropriately supported by a verbal display of care, consideration and concern for Yasmin's vulnerability.

Kobayashi summoned Yasmin to his office and asked what on earth she thought she was doing. Was she not aware of her own age and, for that matter, of the advanced years of Vargas? Could it possibly have escaped her that this man was nothing but an abominable gaijin, vitiating her entire existence and leading her straight into an underworld of turpitude and insidious behaviour, mannerisms and attitudes? Had she any idea what this looked like in the eyes of the school, the society, the gods and whoever else were involved?

When Kobayashi stopped for a gasp of air, Yasmin softly told him to mind his own business. She liked the gaijin, he was funny and pleasant and polite, and he had been to places that Kobayashi probably hadn't even heard about. She could learn a good deal from Vargas, and, that aside, nobody told her who to see and who not to see. Was this really all that difficult to comprehend, and could she be shown a bit of respect, please?

Kobayashi adhered to traditions and gave in, but only after having promised himself to cure Vargas' misconceptions once and for all.

The fun began the next day. Kobayashi came into the dojo, stepped up in front of the class and took over. The most gruelling two hours followed. The same technique was being repeated over and over again, and Kobayashi made it clear that nobody did it to perfection, least of all Vargas. Then, suddenly Kobayashi stopped, cleared the floor and asked Vargas to perform *Pinan Ichi*, the most basic of katas.

"You've got the floor all to yourself," Kobayashi smiled with his eyes half closed. "Go ahead."

Not once during the next hour did Vargas falter, and, to make things worse, not once did he even look at his Sensei. Sweat streamed from Vargas, his gi became wet and soggy and clinging, but on he went.

Finally, Kobayashi discovered that he had other things to do. "Useless!" he shouted, bowed without overdoing it and vanished.

Two days later Kobayashi showed up again, and the same pattern followed. To add to his own amusement, he dropped his gi on the floor as he walked out at the end of the session and ordered Vargas to have it cleaned and ironed the next day.

This was something Kobayashi did to beginners, when in the right frame of mind; Vargas was in his second year and the insult was as blatant as it was unheard of. Vargas picked up the gi and returned it the following morning in pristine condition.

Kobayashi's behaviour neither amused nor impressed Ishihara. He had guessed what was behind it but he knew that any interference would only make the vendetta last longer. After a week he intuited that Yasmin was unaware of what was going on, and he casually gave her a hint. Yasmin instantly grasped the picture, and he saw her eyes go black with anger. Admirably in control of herself, she finished her lesson, showered, dressed and went upstairs.

She walked into Kobayashi's office without knocking and sat down in front of him.

"What are you doing?" she asked quietly.

Kobayashi mistook her composure for dejection and asked innocently, "What are we talking about?"

Yasmin smiled sweetly. "We are talking about Vargas and your stupid and loathsome attempt to break him. We are talking about your pitiable desire for revenge, which means, in case you have problems figuring it out, that we are talking about me."

"You?"

"Me. You detest the fact that I like the gaijin, and you resent the fact that Vargas and I are socializing." She threw her head back and glared at him. The smile was gone.

"Not at all," Kobayashi replied hastily, avoiding the eyes of the little madam who had crossed her legs and folded her arms. "I just thought that the class was lagging behind in techniques and vigour."

"Is that a fact," she said, barely moving her lips, "and Vargas in particular?"

Kobayashi shrugged before he nodded. "Quite."

Yasmin said, "If that is true, then please explain this to me: a couple of weeks ago the gaijin was one of the most promising students you've ever had."

"He is slipping," Kobayashi said meekly.

Yasmin sighed. She moved a strand of hair from her forehead. She pursed her lips and her second sigh echoed between the walls. She said, "Listen, if you want to behave like a psychopath, do so. Be yourself. I am not telling you what to do, but I am telling you what *I* am going to do. I quit. Problem solved."

Kobayashi swivelled back to front position and grabbed the sides of his chair. "You *what?*"

"I quit. I walk out. I am not coming back. How much clearer do you want it?"

Kobayashi closed his eyes, opened them wide and exploded. "You can't quit!"

Yasmin did not blink. "Try me." Her smile did not reach beyond her nose.

Kobayashi knew that she had him by the balls. His only problem now was to get out of her grip with his dignity intact. "You shouldn't talk to me like that," he mumbled affectionately. "Nobody else does."

"I am not nobody else."

Kobayashi resisted a comment on grammar and logic. Any further provocation would not come out in his favour. He said, "You know, a little chat between you and the gaijin now and then is probably a good idea. He's been to places, and I think you have the talent to extract a few things from him. A part of your education, so to speak." A thoughtful expression flooded his face. "I am convinced that I am right, and if anybody makes some inane or offending remark—promise to let me know. There are limits to discrimination, I'd say, and narrow-mindedness is something I cannot and will not tolerate."

Yasmin got up.

"You are not quitting?" he asked earnestly.

"Don't play your own mindless version of shogi with me ever again," she said with a stern expression. "You should know by now that you can't win." She tossed her head with such force that her hair swirled across her face, and left.

Kobayashi stared at the empty chair for a long time. There was a smile on his face. "What a girl," he muttered, "what a girl."

In the early part of the fifth year, Ishihara recommended that Vargas went for his black belt. There were only eleven names on Ishihara's list. Kobayashi studied it carefully, as was his habit. He took a pen and a piece of paper and wrote something that Ishihara could not see. Kobayashi folded the paper and placed it under the picture of a famous film star that had once visited the dojo for an hour in his search for authenticity and perfection. Kobayashi's admiration for celebrities was common knowledge, and he had been overjoyed when the actor in a television interview had described his gruelling training under the great Old Master himself.

Kobayashi put a massive finger on the piece of paper. "This is something we shall have a look at after the grading."

Ishihara was puzzled. Sensei had never before made any comment prior to a grading.

Eight names came up on the board the day after the grading. Three had failed, Vargas among them. Ishihara was bewildered. Vargas had been outstanding; there had to be something else behind Kobayashi's decision. Ishihara tried to be objective. Nobody could question Vargas' technical competence and neither his fortitude nor his perseverance. Ishihara found Kobayashi's decision incomprehensible.

Kobayashi and Ishihara were alone in the office. "You wonder why I failed Vargas," Kobayashi said and looked out the window.

"I do, Sensei," Ishihara answered and hoped that he sounded neutral.

"Vargas is brilliant," Kobayashi said evenly. "He's got the potential to become great, like me and you."

There was another lengthy silence. Ishihara tensed his abdomen and breathed with his mouth open.

Kobayashi's upper lip moved vertically like the pink arm of a squid caressing a row of white pebbles. He placed his elbows on the sides of his chair and his fingertips came together. "Vargas does not have much regard for our ethics and our principles," he said. "He came here to learn to fight, which is fair enough, but he has no humility. He has made up his own tenets, and he does not care about our spiritual teaching. Except when it suits him, that is."

"How are you going to change that?" Ishihara asked.

"I can't," Kobayashi confessed. "I failed him because I want to put him through one, final test. As far as our beliefs are concerned he is a lost cause, that I admit, but there is something else that will tell me if I judged him correctly from the very beginning." He pulled the piece of paper from under the picture. "I knew that Horiuchi and Yamada were going to fail. You did the right thing by recommending them, but I think we both knew that an improvement in spirit was required." He pushed the paper towards Ishihara. "Open it."

Ishihara read: "Nagai never to return. Yamada back in two weeks. Vargas back same afternoon." He put the paper on the desk. "Great thinking, Sensei. I would not have gone against your predictions."

"Of course not."

Ishihara looked at his watch. "Vargas should be downstairs, by now." He inspected his fingernails. "What if he isn't?"

Kobayashi frowned. "Let us first assume that he is. That means that

273

he has swallowed his pride and shown the first ever sign of humility. Failing to get the belt is a tremendous blow to one's ego. Very few can tackle it in a dignified manner." He raised and turned his right fist. "It further proves that he does possess a microscopic element of propriety. My masterstroke is that I have brought it out in the open. Characteristics like respect, consideration and flexibility of mind can follow, and then we have a truly great warrior." Kobayashi's eyes opened wide. "Like yourself. I have great plans for the two of you." He put his hands behind his neck and made a noise like someone blowing into a bottle. "It is my aim to make this school the most powerful in the world. Do you follow, Tadashi-San?" A warm gloss veiled his eyes. "More about that later."

Not much more, Ishihara thought. Your plan and my plan are as far from being congruent as our gaijin brownbelt is from ever falling into line. More about that later. He said, "That sounds very interesting, Sensei. I can't help thinking, though—what if Vargas-San has called it a day?"

The papers in front of Kobayashi fluttered when he exhaled. "A great loss," he grunted, "but I did not have a choice. A calculated risk, in other words. I cannot cooperate with a man who does not understand that life is two-way traffic."

A befitting observation coming from a steamroller like yourself, Ishihara thought. He knew he was getting closer to Kobayashi's vision of the future. "Cooperate?" he asked.

Kobayashi got up. "America," he said and fixed Ishihara with a hypnotic stare. "I am going to split America in half. You will be in charge of the East, and Vargas will run the West. I have looked at the map."

"How are you going to finance it?" Ishihara could not resist, painfully aware of the day to come when Kobayashi would have to admit that his plan was a delusion.

"I am working on something," Kobayashi said airily, "big money." He stretched his neck. The skin around his mouth tightened. "Should we not go downstairs and say hello to our brownbelt?"

Vargas was there. He ignored their arrival and finished his kata with spotless precision. Then he stripped to the waist and began working on the punchbag, methodically and with intense concentration. Kobayashi and Ishihara did not exist.

"What did I tell you?" Kobayashi whispered, brimming with satisfaction.

You do not understand the man, Ishihara thought; you do not read him at all, and neither do you read me. For a moment he felt sorry for Kobayashi and his grandiose plan. Kobayashi would never understand that he lacked the necessary competence and the qualifications to become the organizer and administrator of an international school.

They went outside.

"The next grading is in six months' time," Kobayashi said. "Put him up. He'll pass."

"Very good, Sensei."

"Let me know when he asks you why I failed him."

Well into the second week after the grading Vargas still had not asked, and Ishihara's curiosity got the better of him. He invited Vargas to dinner in one of the top restaurants in Ginza. Ishihara was in a particularly good mood. Everything had gone according to forecast; his bank account was swelling, and his plan for the future was now more than a vague idea.

They enjoyed their first aperitif in silence. Ishihara ordered another round and lit a small cigar, one of life's other little graces recently discovered.

"I am intrigued," he said out of the blue.

"I know."

"I do not mean in general terms," Ishihara explained. "I mean specifically, one particular question, or issue."

"You do."

"Yes, I do. Every single individual failing his belt wants to know *why*, but not you. How come?"

Vargas said, "Why should I?"

Ishihara stared at him, baffled. "Because—because there are lessons to be learned."

"Drivel."

I see, Ishihara thought; he is not in his most communicative mood. "Sensei had his reasons for failing you," he said firmly.

Vargas pushed his glass to the side. He straightened his back. "Listen carefully. The colour of the belt does not make me a fighter. I can't stop Sensei playing his half-witted little games. You and Sensei have taught me as much as you probably can during these years. I appreciate that, as far as appreciation goes. I have paid my dues and I owe nothing to anybody. Soon, I shall be ready to move on, with or without recognition from Sensei. It does not matter. My life is my own, and time has come to think ahead." The smile was brief but friendly. "Am I getting through to you?"

"You are," Ishihara said. He fought to control the feeling of unease that Vargas' words had stirred in him. "Where are you going?" he asked passively.

Vargas gazed into his empty glass. "To the mountains," he said. "All this talking makes me incredibly thirsty."

"Which mountains?" Ishihara asked. He was not sure if Vargas was to be taken seriously.

"Where the ninja is."

The heaviest sigh of the evening dropped into Ishihara's glass. "Now *that* is drivel," he said gently. "Ninjas don't exist."

"This one does."

"Balls and bananas. Who told you this?"

"Nobody. I found out. Come with me and I'll prove it. This gentleman can teach us what nobody else can—or will," he added and smiled wryly as he reached for his lighter.

"What's funny?" Ishihara said, unable to interpret Vargas' private show of amusement.

"Life is funny. So is revenge in its most refined form. Come with me, and you'll see."

Supposing I let him out of my sight and he disappears for good, Ishihara thought, I can't afford that. There will be nothing left of my plan. I would have to start all over again, and that is not a very attractive option. Where am I to find another Vargas? Perhaps a bit of ghost hunting up in some mountain is worth the price, however inane. "I shall think about it," he said and was pleased with the degree of certitude in his voice.

"Do that."

Ishihara said, "By the way, you know that Sensei's big tournament is on, next spring."

"Who can have missed it."

"Are you going to participate?"

"I don't see myself as a tournament fighter."

"I think you should."

"I think not."

Ishihara did not like the situation, but there was no way out. "You owe it to him," he said quietly.

"I owe him nothing."

Ishihara slurped his cognac. "He fixed your visa."

Kobayashi had used his political contacts and a considerable amount of money to provide Vargas with the necessary documents; enabling Vargas to stay in Japan for as long as he wished. He could also leave the country and return on the same permission. The implications of the action were manifold; the papers gave Vargas an identity without which he would have faced problems wherever he went—no country welcomed a man with a hole in his existence; sooner or later it would emerge, equally unpopular, that he had been an illegal immigrant.

"I'll think about it," he said with an indifference that didn't fool Ishihara.

"Do that."

Vargas returned the smile of an American redhead who sat two tables away. She had large, brown eyes, a freckled nose and generous lips.

"She's interested," Ishihara said. "Her boobs are swaying like a pair of anemones in a backwash."

"Not tonight," Vargas said.

"Got things on your mind?" Ishihara deadpanned.

Vargas did not answer.

The tournament, Ishihara thought; he is actually thinking about what I said. He's facing a personal conflict. Nothing else would explain the silence; it was unheard of that Vargas declined an invitation to exercise his testosterone.

Six months later Vargas again went for his black belt. His name came up on top of the board.

Kobayashi's forthcoming tournament was to be the most spectacular and impressive martial arts event ever staged in Japan, and he used every means available to him to guarantee its success. Securing the Dome was his first significant triumph. The hall was immensely popular with anybody arranging anything, and the rivalry was fierce and uncompromising. Kobayashi's growing influence with prominent politicians tipped the scale in his favour, but Ishihara knew that nobody got the Dome *gratis,* and he wondered where that kind of money came from.

To Kobayashi's immense pleasure, over eighty fighters from abroad had been entered. The moment the lists of participants were completed, he smoothly manipulated the draws in a way that would virtually guarantee the first ten places being awarded his own fighters.

Through his contacts in the business world he launched an advertising campaign, the design and format only matched by its immodesty. The results came quickly; all tickets were sold four weeks prior to the event.

Kobayashi's intention behind his fiddle with the draws was glaringly obvious; Ishihara and Vargas were to meet in the final, and the other eight top places generously distributed among his other favourite warriors.

Ishihara's first fight caused him little concern, but he did not like that Kobayashi had matched Vargas with Watanabe. The plan was simple enough; Vargas would beat Watanabe, but the big Japanese was no slouch and he had a proven ability to inflict damage on his opponents. With Watanabe out of the way, Vargas would be steered through the rest of the tournament, and the final between the crown prince and the gaijin would be the great climax everybody had come to see.

Should Vargas be ahead come third and last round, in spite of injuries caused by Watanabe, Kobayashi would arrange a disqualification; Ishihara would be the winner and the gaijin technically and morally an undisputed second. Elementary, Ishihara thought; straightforward, clear-cut and pragmatic. The entire tournament was designed to enhance the reputation of the grand Old Master and his school, a vehicle to carry his influence to hitherto unscaled heights and for the world to recognize him as the greatest ever. The tournament and its participants were the stars, but in Ryutaro Kobayashi's solar system there was room for only one sun, and that was himself.

The whole scheme left a sour taste with Ishihara, but he knew that he was powerless to interfere. This was Kobayashi's grand and illustrious event, and any objection would have been brutally and contemptuously brushed aside.

The first twenty fights had been between foreign competitors, an uncomplicated method of getting rid of half of them. The combats were reasonably entertaining; the packed audience applauded politely but waited with strained patience for the first big one, the clash between Watanabe and the gaijin Vargas.

Kobayashi's talent for drama and suspense was in full bloom; he decided to let the audience wait a bit longer. He arranged for the first of several breathtaking displays of the martial arts, culminating with his own *tameshiwari* where he knocked a piece of glass out of a full beer bottle.

The spectators went wild. Then, suddenly, lights flickering for a moment, Watanabe emerged on the mat and the temperature rose another ten degrees.

Ishihara did not like the look of Watanabe; he showed aggression and an arrogance surpassing even his usual attitude, and the adulation from the audience had no subduing effect.

Vargas appeared, and the hall fell silent. He ignored Watanabe, adjusted the belt and sat down in the *seiza* position with his eyes closed. Something is wrong, Ishihara thought, nobody could be *that* relaxed in a competition like this. The judges were in place, as was the referee, and Watanabe stepped forward and took his position on the line.

The commentaries from the loudspeakers reverberated through the hall. Still, Vargas did not move. Ishihara glanced briefly at Kobayashi who looked as if he was frozen to the floor, his fists clenched and with an expression of fury mixed with confusion. The referee went over to Vargas and said something Ishihara could not hear. Vargas looked up and nodded. Then he yawned. It took a full ten seconds before he blinked several times and slowly got to his feet. He walked to the line where he stood with his hands down.

This is unreal, Ishihara thought, he looks as if he is bored out of his mind. What the hell is he thinking of?

Ishihara could see that Watanabe was not amused; Vargas' indifference infuriated him to the point of losing control. His eyes narrowed and he opened and clenched his fists, swayed rhythmically, gritted his teeth and signalled to the audience that he could not wait to annihilate the ill-mannered and disrespectful gaijin.

Ishihara knew that Watanabe nurtured a deep-felt hatred for Vargas. Ever since Ishihara had humiliated Watanabe on Vargas' first day in the dojo, Watanabe had in no subtle terms broadcasted to one and all that Ishihara did what he did to impress the barbarian—in other words, it was Vargas' fault. Ishihara knew that Watanabe did not possess too many qualities associated with cerebral activities, but a knack for putting square logic in a circular vacuum was within his repertoire.

Ishihara had kept Vargas and Watanabe clear of each other during the years. This was the day of reckoning, a moment Ishihara had been waiting for, ever since he realized that Vargas was probably of the same class as he, the magnificent Tadashi Ishihara.

The moment had come, and what happened? His friend Vargas looked disinterested. His entire behaviour indicated that he'd rather lie down and go to sleep. Ishihara moistened his lips and tried to dry his sweaty palms on his white and spotless gi. He heard himself scream *"Mushin!"* to Vargas and then the referee yelled *Yamate* and Watanabe leapt forward in a frenzied attack, fists and feet flying.

Vargas sidestepped, ducked, pirouetted and danced away with his hands open and barely above his hips. Whatever Watanabe tried, Vargas was out of reach. His ability to read his opponent, combined with incredible reflexes, made Watanabe miss again and again.

Mushin, Ishihara thought. Maybe he did not hear me. *No thought—focus on nothing but winning. Mushin, Angelo!*

With one minute left of the first round, neither had scored. Ishihara sensed the uneasiness of the crowd; they had come to see some appealing brutality and heart-warming bloodshed, and not to watch the redoubtable gaijin perform his own version of the Swan Lake.

Watanabe attacked again, this time so violently that he momentarily lost his balance. He was quick to find his stance, but not quick enough. Vargas hit him with considerable force just above solar plexus. He followed up with a savage kick to Watanabe's right kidney and another two kicks to the upper arms. Vargas completed the attack with a sweep that sent Watanabe crashing to the floor.

He was halfway up when the bell rang. The audience was pleased with the action, although they would rather have seen the situation reversed. Anyway, it was value for money, and the acrid scent of anticipation filled the hall as the second round began.

It became a repetition of the first. Vargas danced away and Watanabe got increasingly frustrated, snarling insults at his evasive opponent. Then, with less than a minute to go, Vargas attacked, hitting both Watanabe's shoulders almost simultaneously and ending the round with a devastating kick to Watanabe's right thigh, a few inches above the knee. Watanabe tried not to limp as he walked towards his line, but Ishihara knew the paralyzing effect of Vargas' kick, as he knew the damage Vargas had inflicted on Watanabe's shoulders and arms.

Every single spectator now knew that Watanabe could only win by knocking out Vargas. Only Kobayashi and his students knew that neither Vargas nor Watanabe had much regard for the rulebook.

Ishihara shook his head and wished that he could stop the fight there and then. One of those two was going to get seriously hurt, and probably with lasting consequences. This was not tournament fighting, this was—Ishihara stopped his flow of thought and stared towards the ceiling. The bright lights hit his mind like a nuclear explosion—why on earth had he not seen it earlier? The message had been there the moment Vargas yawned, or even before, long before—from the day Vargas had told him about the days on board the ship across the Atlantic Ocean and the fate of the unfortunate cook.

During the past six minutes, Watanabe had been lured into a trap from which there was no escape. He could only win by trying to demolish Vargas, and he would do so with the greatest of pleasure and with all of his accumulated hatred.

What he forgot was that blind fury more often than not resulted in making mistakes, giving Vargas the opportunity to capitalize on every error made by Watanabe's lack of rational thinking.

Ishihara felt as if invisible powers had lifted him several feet up in the air. There would be no final between himself and Vargas. His friend had engineered it all in such a way that this was going to be Vargas' first and last fight in his first and last tournament.

Ishihara did not like the emerging excitement he felt stirring in his belly. The yakuza versus the gaijin was undeniably a thrilling piece of entertainment; one had begun his education in the streets of Tokyo, and the other in the streets of Mexico City. Both had been trained by the great Kobayashi, both had the streetfighter's skills and instincts and both readily employed whatever means necessary whenever accepted techniques proved insufficient.

As Ishihara had anticipated, Watanabe was the first to show that he'd left the rules behind. Having missed with a tremendous *mawashi-geri* which would have knocked Vargas' head off had it connected, Watanabe lifted his left leg and sent his heel with all the force he could muster towards the toes of Vargas' right foot, missing by an inch. A knee to the groin was similarly unsuccessful, whilst a kick to the ankle was enough to bring Vargas out of balance. The referee stopped the fight and issued a warning to Watanabe who stared through him and did not even bother to bow. Vargas looked at Ishihara and smiled. Ishihara recognized the shimmer he'd seen in Vargas' eyes on other occasions and knew that only a miracle would make the third round last for the full three minutes.

Ishihara had to admire Watanabe's spirit. He limped and was clearly in pain each time he lifted his arms, but the adrenaline was flowing and he was impervious to anything but the detested gaijin who had the audacity to make him look outwitted and second-rate.

Suddenly, Watanabe changed tactics. He began circling Vargas whilst feigning kicks and punches without actually throwing any. He got closer and closer. He hunched but held his guard high. Then he jumped but was hit by an almighty kick to solar plexus. Watanabe went down, but before the judges had finished waving their flags he was up again, his enormous strength and willpower coming to his rescue. He inhaled deeply and made a rasping sound as he got his wind back. He turned sideways, kicked and missed to the inside of Vargas' left thigh, and then, with all the strength of his 190 pounds muscular body, he lunged his right fist towards Vargas' face.

This time he connected. Blood spurted from Vargas' right eyebrow, and the hall erupted. This was the business, and there were still one and a half minutes to go. Vargas took a step back, seemingly unshaken, and wiped the blood from his eyes. Watanabe, encouraged by his success and stimulated by the change of colour on his opponent, attacked again.

Vargas' next two moves were executed so fast that very few actually saw what happened. Watanabe was on his way down with a shattered shin when his jaw collided with Vargas' knee, but the third move was clear for all to see. As Watanabe swayed on one leg, Vargas grabbed with both hands Watanabe's left arm, swung around and broke the elbow. Vargas let go of the arm, clutched Watanabe's gi and headbutted with such force that nobody missed the sound of the crack when Watanabe's nose spread across his face.

The referee and the judges stared at the unconscious Watanabe, bloodied and on his back in an unnatural position. Ishihara could have sworn that the silence lasted for at least half a minute. Then Kobayashi took a step forward and the paramedics rushed in and got Watanabe on to a stretcher.

Ishihara could hear a low humming from the crowd. The noise grew in intensity until Kobayashi raised his hands, turned three hundred and sixty degrees in slow motion and reached for a microphone. He announced that he, the referee and the judges would hold a conference and shortly convey the outcome of this exciting bout.

No, Ishihara thought, not even Kobayashi could get away with that one. Ishihara knew what Kobayashi's argument would be; the incident was *accidental and unintentional* and therefore Vargas was the undisputed winner. Every single spectator could well have missed Vargas' first moves when Watanabe went down, but nobody had missed the headbutt. The referee and the judges were in awe of Kobayashi and feared him, but they could not possibly disregard the crowd, the media and a large number of Japanese luminaries and a good handful of foreign dignitaries.

Ishihara saw Kobayashi shake his head as he glared at Vargas who sat in the *seiza* position, relaxed and seemingly at ease with himself.

The decision came. Vargas had been disqualified, and the audience applauded enthusiastically. Nobody should be rewarded for using dirty tricks, least of all a gaijin.

Vargas' plan had worked to perfection. Ishihara knew that Watanabe's fighting days were over. Moreover, he knew that only Kobayashi's influence with the Yamaguchi family could prevent Vargas leaving Japan in a coffin.

Ishihara went on to win the tournament.

☞

One day Ishihara picked up a well-worn book from Vargas' table and said, "*Thesaurus*—what is this, Angelo?"

"Open it," Vargas suggested

Ishihara did and kept quiet for the next twenty minutes. "Fantastic," he finally said, "what a gold mine. Can I borrow it?"

"No."

Ishihara was hurt. "Why not? You know I take good care of things."

"I don't lend my books. Not even to you. They are part of me."

"That is a very possessive attitude."

"It is also the way it is."

A month later Vargas gave Ishihara a brown parcel. "From London? Not a bomb, I presume."

"It is, symbolically."

Ishihara opened the parcel and stared at the brand new Thesaurus.

Vargas said, "It is a necessity, complementing your dictionary. You need to improve on your vocabulary if you are going to conquer foreign soil. I don't know where your obscure plan will take you, but English is the language understood practically anywhere in the world."

Ishihara opened the book and flicked through the pages. "Is that why you never bothered to pick up much Spanish, or Japanese, for that matter?"

"I never saw much point in wasting time and effort on something that was only going to be a transitory part of my life. English is the language, amigo."

Ishihara caressed his gift. "I agree. In a few weeks' time you won't understand half of what I am saying."

"Don't bet on it."

"Five thousand American dollars. I'll pick one hundred words at random two weeks from now. If you miss one word, you have lost."

"Let's put some excitement into it. Fifty thousand dollars."

"That's crazy. Far too much. Nobody should bet that kind of money."

"I do," Vargas said.

Within days of the knife-throwing sushi bar episode Kobayashi knew all about it, and he began to treat Vargas almost as an equal. Vargas' flagrant audacity and uncurbed brutality at the tournament added to the glory, and one day Kobayashi invited his gaijin protégéé to a party at one of Shinjuku's most distinguished *ryoteis*.

Ishihara urged Vargas to accept; to come along with Kobayashi to such a prominent entertainment house, frequented by big shots only, was a great honour. Ishihara was certain that Vargas would find it amusing, and possibly also rewarding.

That evening, Kobayashi was to meet with some wealthy industrialists and a small selection of frontline politicians—all of whom had been present at the tournament. A few of the guests had reputations as habitual gamblers.

Vargas acquiesced, and Kobayashi opened the evening by apologizing for the strict but necessary rules that had forced him to disqualify Vargas. The applause died down, and Kobayashi followed up with a graphic description of what had happened in the sushi bar. Five American navy officers had been dissected by this gaijin and his knife, something that of course would have been extremely difficult if not impossible without Kobayashi's personal tuition during the years—just for the record.

All the guests nodded silently; the gaijin was obviously a warrior of great distinction and worthy of Kobayashi's patronage. He went on, for a few more minutes, his fertile mind working overtime, and he concluded to universal acclaim that Vargas was as close to being a Japanese as any gaijin could ever be.

Having exhausted the theme, they went on to discuss a forthcoming basketball game. The sake and the whisky flowed freely, the hostesses moved in and out with bottles and food as fast as their attire allowed and gradually the atmosphere changed from urbane and suave to loud and aggressive.

One of the nabobs, Yasutoshi Arimoto, became particularly agitated, and his voice cut through the din like a drill in a crematorium. He wanted to make a bet, and it annoyed him that nobody had the guts, or was drunk enough, to take him on. They all knew that he was as fearless as he was rich, and for several months in a row his luck had been running high.

Vargas, who had been quiet all evening, suddenly flipped the butt of his cigarette into an ashtray across the table and raised his hands. "Arimoto-San," he said politely, "you should not bet on this game."

Arimoto did not take much pleasure in being contradicted. "And why not?" he sneered, forgetting that officially he did not speak or understand English.

Vargas said, "Because I know the outcome of this game before it's been played."

Sweat trickled like drops of cod-liver oil down Arimoto's cheeks. A geisha handed him a towel. He wiped his face and dropped the towel on the floor. There was an expression of intensity in his eyes as he snatched his full glass and swallowed the lot. He said, "Who fixed the game, Vargas-San?"

"Nobody, to the best of my knowledge."

Arimoto belched and shook his head. "Then you are talking rubbish. If it is not fixed, nobody knows."

Vargas said, "I do. I am a *shaman*."

Arimoto's laughter could have shamed a cockatoo into embarrassed silence. "You are a bloody gaijin," he snarled. "You can fight, but there is nothing mystic about you."

Vargas put his hand inside his oversized jacket and began placing stacks of money on the table. "I bet you fifty thousand American dollars, Arimoto-San."

Nobody moved. Kobayashi lowered his eyelids and stared at his feet. The geishas stood like colourful statues, beautiful and expressionless. Arimoto's tongue was hanging out. He inhaled rapidly through his nose. "Fifty thousand American dollars," he repeated hoarsely. "Now, that is what I call a bet. You're on, gaijin."

Vargas said, "Where is your money?"

"Don't worry about the money. You win, I pay."

"Give me an IOU," Vargas said, "date, amount and signature. Either that, or there is no bet."

Arimoto sat still, but the hatred in his eyes matched the venom in his voice when he said, "Do you doubt my word, gaijin?"

Vargas said, "This is business, not a moral contest."

Arimoto's pride battled with his greed. He grabbed his bowl of noodles and slurped loudly for a while. During the last mouthful he said, "Nobody doubts my word."

"Suit yourself."

Arimoto put the bowl on the table. "I shall take into account that you are not Japanese," he said, visibly satisfied with his face-saving phrase. "I shall therefore give you an IOU." He wrote quickly and dumped the piece of paper on top of Vargas' money. "Now tell me the result," he said and glared triumphantly at the blank faces of the other guests. "What is it?"

"Nil-nil."

"What?"

"Nil-nil. Before the game's been played, the result is nil-nil."

With the exception of Kobayashi, everybody roared with laughter; how hilarious, how utterly ridiculous of Arimoto to walk straight into the gaijin's age-old little trap. Fifty thousand American dollars down a wide, open drain; it was simply too stupid to be true, the great Arimoto conned by a small-time hustler. They'd all seen it coming, but it was none of their business to interfere—perhaps Arimoto could get his money back by betting on the gaijin turning into a dragon before the night was over?

Finally, the laughter subsided amidst the clinking of glasses. Kobayashi continued to observe his feet. Arimoto took an empty whisky bottle from the table and studied it as if it was a valuable artefact. Vargas stretched his right leg and put his hand on his knee.

"Someone will bring you the money tomorrow," Arimoto said without losing sight of the bottle.

Shortly thereafter the party broke up. Kobayashi and Vargas walked in silence for a while; Kobayashi apparently lost in thoughts and Vargas taking in the hectic rhythm of life emanating from the *pachinko* parlours and the tea saloons, the stand bars and the Shinto shrines, the coffee houses and the noodle shops; the smoke and the smells and the constant humming of restless human activity. The neon lights shimmered like dissected rainbows in the late night drizzle, and the wet surface made squeaky little noises under their shoes.

"You just destroyed my chances of a new dojo," Kobayashi said and stared into space with a look of fury mixed with deep concern.

"Did I?"

"Yes, you did. Arimoto-San and some wealthy associates were going to back me. That is now history, thanks to you and your dishonourable behaviour."

Vargas pointed towards a *nomiya* across the street and said, "Have a drink with me. I've got something to tell you."

"There is nothing more to say."

Vargas stood at the corner of the wooden counter with a Japanese whisky in his hand when Kobayashi arrived. Kobayashi, who did not touch alcohol, asked for a soft drink. "Speak," he said.

"You have got very little money of your own, Sensei. You go to bed with Arimoto and his buddies, and they'll own the dojo. One day they will manufacture a disagreement, and then what."

"Everything is worthless without me. I am Ryutaro Kobayashi."

"I know who you are. I also know who Sadamasa Nagai is."

The bottle broke in Kobayashi's hand. He licked the blood from his fingers. "Nagai is a filthy little insect who knows nothing about karate," he snapped. "Nagai is a clown and a piece of shit."

Vargas asked for a wet towel and another two drinks. He said, "True, Sensei, but Nagai and Arimoto are close and have been so for years. There is no denying that Nagai is a bad joke in the world of martial arts, but it remains a fact that he does control three different organizations, each of them bigger than yours. You are not in their division, Sensei, and you know it. Don't let your ambitions blind you—one day you'll pay for it if you do, and that price will be too high."

Kobayashi wrapped the towel around his hand and made a fist. "Nagai is a nobody."

"Untrue. He's an extremely wealthy and influential man who loves the glory and the mystique of the martial arts, and he buys what he otherwise can't get. To everybody else, you are a legend, Sensei—to Nagai you are just another Korean who can be disposed of whenever convenient."

Kobayashi stood with his feet apart as if he was afraid the earth was going to move. "I have known Arimoti-San for several years," he said. "He is a good man."

"Arimoto is a manipulating, ruthless bastard. If you refuse to see him for what hc is, so be it. It's your life."

Kobayashi looked at the faded poster clinging to the ceiling. His eyes were lifeless, his thoughts had been pushed back into his subconscience.

Vargas' fingers scratched the white rings left by countless glasses. "Look, Sensei, their plan is simple. Good and innocent Arimoto moves in with his money. You get your magnificent dojo, for a few years. Then Nagai takes over. Arimoto gets his ample reward from Nagai and you are left with yesterday's dream. No more legend. Why the hell can't you see it?"

☞

Ishihara said, "I am not Arimoto, Angelo-San. I believe I can win, but I am not going to bet with you, not for that kind of money; no, not at all. Forget it."

Vargas said, "Wise. You only bet that kind of money when you know you are going to win."

"Such a situation requires an instinct I haven't got. It is probably congenital. Do you know that word?"

Vargas smiled. "You are confusing the issues. You are an ardent exhibitionist and I am not. You are a compulsive talker, and I am not." He patted the Thesaurus. "The message is, you should not judge a book by its cover. Do you fathom the analogy, or am I getting too labyrinthine for you?"

Ishihara laughed. He loved their little duels. "I admit that you are far more devious and complex than my simple self could possibly aspire to. Perhaps that is why we get on so famously."

"Your modesty is earth-shattering, Tadashi. Let me see if I can help you. What about two unscrupulous creatures, each are possessing useful but different characteristics, which met by coincidence and discovered

288

that they complemented each other to near perfection? Condensed— a symbiotic alliance destined to experience prosperity together. Use the book," he added with a nod towards the Thesaurus. "I wouldn't want you to miss the essence of my interpretation of your hitherto convoluted ambitions."

"You said *near* perfection?"

"Nothing is perfect."

Ishihara sensed a sweet smell. It came from himself. It was the scent of relief. He looked out the window. There was lightning behind the clouds. He could feel Vargas' eyes in the back of his head. "But you do not know my plan," he said and was pleased that the shrillness of surprise was wanting.

Vargas said, "Not the core of it, but I think I know its form and shape."

It all came a bit too sudden for Ishihara. He was not thrown off balance, but he knew that he needed time to prepare his presentation. He picked up the brown wrapping paper. "Who is Hatchards?"

"It's a bookshop in London. Very old and respectable. You can get almost anything there—any subject. Which reminds me," he added and searched for another parcel behind a pillow, "these two came a few weeks ago, but since I do not like ceremonies I decided to let you have all three in one go."

Ishihara ripped the paper open and placed the books in front of him. They were Ayn Rand's *The Fountainhead* and Machiavelli's *The Prince*.

"I have never heard of either of them," he said, pleased but not embarrassed.

"Excellent literature," Vargas said. "Study them assiduously, and thereafter your horizon will be altogether different."

"Thank you," Ishihara mumbled. "I don't know what more to say."

"Good. I would hate sitting here listening to a speech you are not qualified to make."

Ishihara laughed softly. "No bet."

Vargas got up. "Study them," he repeated. "Together with Sun-Tzu's *The Art of War* you'll be as prepared in theory as you will ever get. The rest is practice; from practice you get experience, and from experience capitalization."

Ishihara lowered his head and pretended to examine the books. It was evident that Vargas knew, or, at least, knew *enough*. Had he bought the books because he had decided to go his own way, or had he acknowledged and accepted his part in the plan?

He looked up. "Angelo-San, I have got something to talk to you about. Can you come to my place tomorrow night?"

He saw a smile on Vargas' face.

Ishihara lived near Kitanomaru Park; prestigious, reasonably quiet and hugely expensive. His apartment was spacious and luxuriously furnished, but apart from his bonsai trees and a small collection of personal items there were no attachments; nothing that he would have problems leaving behind. The few belongings he treasured could be stored away and forwarded whenever convenient.

Ishihara cast a final glance on the drinks-tray and the Cartier clock and thought of Vargas and his books when the doorbell rang.

Ishihara was ready. He had prepared himself with acute precision. Anything but a plain, honest and simple presentation could easily prove counterproductive. He had no wish to underestimate Vargas' perception; an attempt to shroud the issue would be likely to fail, and Vargas would change the subject, finish his drink and walk out. The plan rested entirely on mutual trust. There was no room for even the shadow of a hidden string.

He handed Vargas a glass of his relished Irish whisky and poured a cognac for himself. They sat down opposite each other.

Ishihara began. He explained his plan soberly and in prosaic terms. All the time he watched Vargas who listened with intense concentration. Once in a while he sipped his whisky with uncommon frugality. He did not interrupt.

"That is the blueprint," Ishihara concluded. "It will make us rich, and we shall enjoy freedom and excitement. There will be no boundaries and no commitments apart from the implications of each undertaking. We can do what we want whenever it suits us."

"You have done your homework," Vargas said.

Ishihara chewed on his cigar and put a forefinger on each temple. "Thank you. I anticipated that the embassies would be sources of information, but I did not expect them to be veritable gold mines. We could virtually start tomorrow and keep ourselves busy for the next decade—without overdoing it," he added with a disarming gesture.

"Tomorrow," Vargas repeated.

"Not literally," Ishihara said quickly, sensing Vargas' hesitation. "I mean, I have to sell this place and make a few other arrangements. I was thinking more like, say, two or three months from now."

"Too early."

"What?"

"I am not ready. I need more time."

"I don't follow."

"I am going to see the ninja. I am also going to Korea for a few months."

"Is this your nice way of saying that you want no part of my plan, that you are not coming with me?" He instantly regretted the sharpness of his voice. It had not been called for. Vargas owed him nothing.

"Am I not in the habit of making myself clear?" Vargas said quietly.

"I did not mean it that way. It's just that this talk about the ninja…"

"He exists. I guarantee you that he exists. That is, unless he has died recently, but I don't think so. Join me. Let us find him together."

"And then—?"

"Give me another drink."

"And then?" he reiterated.

Vargas focused on his whisky. He rose and went over to the window. He stood there for a few minutes. Ishihara waited patiently, determined not to break the silence. After all, he thought, the plan must have given Vargas a lot to think about; it wasn't exactly a parochial, anaemic and tenuous little mirage of a desiccated fantasy that could be converted into remunerative realities overnight.

Vargas said, "I will come with you when I am ready. I'll let you know."

He came back to his chair and sat down. The wave of relief that engulfed Ishihara was so all-embracing that for once he was lost for words.

Vargas said, "Louder. I can't hear you."

Ishihara nodded. "Let us find the ninja together."

The lightning had stopped. Moonlight spangled the leaves on the bonsai trees.

Vargas said, "I take it that you have prepared your farewell speech to Sensei."

"More or less. I will tell him the truth."

"Which part of it?"

Ishihara chuckled. "Which part—I like that. The part that concerns *him*, his school and myself. I shall tell him, as tactfully as I can, that I am not destined to spend the rest of my life in a dojo. I will sympathize with his disappointment, and I will ask him to try to understand that I must use my education and devote myself to my ambition, which is to become wealthy. Fair enough?"

"He'll understand *that* part of it, but not much else."

"I am afraid you are right. Sensei has changed. He is no longer the man I used to know. All his ideals have gone down the drain; now, he just *preaches* them, he no longer *lives* by them. He has become obsessed with money and power, and he is using his concern for the future of his school as a blatant excuse for his aspirations. The idealist has become an unscrupulous opportunist. I always found him a bit devious, but it is only during the last few years that I have grasped how formidable this talent actually is. He has even become inexorably cocky about his involvement with the Yamaguchi family since he dropped Arimoto, but Yamaguchi is just another recipe for disaster. Sensei's entanglement with some politicians I know of is equally hazardous. I wish he knew his limitations, but he doesn't. He thinks that because he is the most impressive karate master the world has ever seen he is also a genius at everything else. He has become his own false god and it will only get worse."

"I agree," Vargas said. "Sensei is a major martial arts character and a minor Machiavellian prototype."

"Is that what he is? I have not fully digested the book, yet."

"Try concentration."

Ishihara put his sock-less feet on the table and stared at the ceiling. "Tell me one thing," he said after a while. "You got disqualified on purpose, didn't you?"

"Don't tell me you've already figured out that much."

"Otherwise we would have met in the final."

"We would."

"Would you have tried to break my arms and legs? Would you have headbutted me?"

"No."

"There we are," Ishihara grinned triumphantly. "I knew it, all along. Sensei was wrong. He failed your first try at blackbelt because you'd never shown any respect for ethics, whilst I argued that you had your own ethics and that he should have respected that. He never listened. I *knew* I was right."

"Nice feeling, being right."

"After the tournament, Sensei bragged about his psychological insight—never mind that he tried to influence the decision—whilst I emphasized that a dirty thug like Watanabe wasn't worthy of ethical considerations. That went over Sensei's head. He does not understand that there are *ethics* and *ethics*." Ishihara's forehead glistened, and he smiled so broadly that his upper lip touched his nose. "Thank you for confirming it."

"Confirming what?"

The beads on Ishihara's forehead fused with four horizontal lines. "About your ethics. You just said that you would not have headbutted me."

"You are mistaking ethics for *aesthetics*. Funny how the real reason has escaped you."

Ishihara scratched his chin. He was not entirely at ease. "What might the *real* reason be, Angelo?"

"You are ugly enough as it is."

"Heavens above," Ishihara sighed. "Why did I open my mouth?"

"An incurable habit. Let's go for a meal."

During the evening Ishihara got inebriated, but not enough to become careless. The next morning he remembered a remark Vargas had made about Mammon being the only god never to fail his disciples, and a seemingly casual aside about England being a good place to settle when their safari days were over.

Ishihara spent the early part of the day trying to analyze Vargas' final comment on life having its own justifications, and how boring it all would have been without the ever-thriving presence of the seven deadly sins.

Two months later, on Ishihara's birthday, Yasmin vanished. He discovered her absence by coincidence; Vargas had arranged for a surprise party and immediately told Ishihara when it became clear that Yasmin was nowhere to be found. Vargas had asked all over the dojo; nobody knew, and even Kobayashi was blank.

Vargas went to see Yasmin's mother, but Mrs. Obuchi had no idea where her daughter was. She was gone when Mrs. Obuchi came home from shopping early that morning. Vargas was halfway down the street when Mrs. Obuchi came running after him. Some of Yasmin's clothes were missing, together with a small suitcase. He went back. Over a cup of tea he reassured Mrs. Obuchi that he would find Yasmin and bring her home safely. Did she have any relatives somewhere in Japan? No. Was it plausible that Yasmin had got into her head to visit Korea? Most unlikely. Had she ever disappeared before? Never. Had she been secretive, lately? No, they had always enjoyed an open and trusting relationship. Had Yasmin been depressed or elated or shown any other emotion the last few days? Pause. Emotions? No—well, yes, perhaps anxious. Somewhat tense, maybe, or preoccupied. Mrs. Obuchi had not paid too much attention; Yasmin could be up and down, but, given time, she always came around and confided in her mother.

Then Vargas said something that surprised Mrs. Obuchi. He asked her not to talk to anybody about his own concern for Yasmin's absence, and that included Mr. Kobayashi.

Mrs. Obuchi looked at Vargas for a long time before she quietly consented. She asked no questions.

Vargas went straight to Ishihara and related the entire story. He omitted nothing and said as he finished, "Go upstairs and ask Sensei if he knows where Yasmin is. When he has finished denying any knowledge of her whereabouts, you ask him where Astuo Tanaka is."

"Is he too gone?" Ishihara asked, visibly alarmed. "What the hell is going on?"

Vargas sat down on the staircase. "I'll wait here. Move."

Astuo Tanaka was Kobayashi's secretary and accountant, a quiet, unassuming and highly efficient man in his thirties. He was uncommunicative, reserved and burdened with Kobayashi's trust and confidence, or as close to it as anyone could get. Vargas knew that Tanaka was involved with Sensei's dream about the majestic monument that he was going to build, a palace of a dojo surpassing what most mortals could possibly imagine as the ultimate school for the martial arts. It was therefore probable that Tanaka had a fair idea where the money was coming from. He would also know, to some extent, about Kobayashi's other dealings with the yakuza and the politicians.

Vargas did not put it beyond Kobayashi to involve an eighteen-year-old girl if it could help him to reach his ambitions. Whatever Kobayashi was up to, it stank from one end of Japan to the other. Yasmin was sharp, clever, street-smart, well educated and incredibly charming, but to use her, as an innocent pawn in a sinister game of criminal activities was so cynical and outright asinine that even Kobayashi should have thought better of it, however megalomaniac he had managed to become.

"Sensei doesn't know," Ishihara said, coming down the stairs. "And Tanaka is off sick, he said."

"We shall bring him some aspirins," Vargas said.

They drove to Tanaka's apartment twenty minutes away. There was no sign of life. A neighbour had seen Tanaka leave in the early hours of the morning, carrying an overnight bag and a briefcase.

"Now what?" Ishihara said. There was despair in his voice.

The corners of Vargas' mouth downgraded. "Now we shall earn the confidence of our great mentor, whether he likes it or not."

On the way back they ran into traffic problems, and they reached the dojo forty-five agonizing minutes later.

Kobayashi had disappeared.

Ishihara would forever remember the next two days as a grotesque nightmare whose impact made him feel paralyzed with fear and worry. He had long understood what Yasmin meant to him; her strong personality, her wit and her integrity played constantly on his mind, and he believed that no other woman could replace her. The precocious child was gone. Yasmin was now a radiant belle whose magnetism had encompassed him beyond limits and reservations. During the past year she had treated him with less disdain, she had become more coquettish and her previous acerbic demeanour had given way to amiable teasing. He was still painfully aware of the difference in age, something Vargas discounted as antediluvian thinking, but Ishihara had yet to accumulate sufficient nerve to invite her out.

He also knew that time was no longer on his side; soon, he and Vargas would leave.

Many a night had Ishihara composed the words that would reveal his love for Yasmin; he would come back and together they would go away and live happily forever after. But all those divine and alluring lines were still imprisoned inside him, and now Yasmin was gone.

Late afternoon of the second day there was still no sign of Kobayashi. Ishihara and Vargas were sitting in a nearby coffee bar. Ishihara had moved in with Vargas and they had spent every single hour trying to find clues to Yasmin and Kobayashi's hiding places.

"This is driving me insane." Ishihara groaned. He did not touch his coffee. "Isn't there something else we can do?"

Vargas looked in the direction of the dojo. His tongue flickered from side to side. "Sensei is bound to come back to his office. Any message will come to the office and go from the office. My guess is that he will show up late at night when nobody is around."

"Then what do we do?"

"We wait and see. He can't work without a light on, even if it's only the lamp on his desk. We'll be able to see it."

Ishihara nodded. Kobayashi had never bothered with blinds or curtains. Yes, the light would be visible. Then he got an idea. "Why don't we wait outside," he suggested. "He'll walk straight into us."

"No, he won't. He'll sneak around corners and spot us before we can see him. Then he will evaporate. Don't forget that he knows this area inside out."

"Why would he not want to see us?"

"Why did he leave? When did he confide in either of us about his dealings with the yakuza and the rest of the mob that he is busy cultivating? Add Yasmin, and you have the answer."

"Add Yasmin? I am not with you."

"You are not," Vargas said sharply. "Let me explain, then. He knows, as I do, that you and Yasmin have a soft spot for each other. Is it getting any clearer?"

"Nobody knows that!" Ishihara protested.

"Don't be infantile. It does not help to underestimate the old gorilla."

The connotation began to dawn on Ishihara. He felt physically unwell and wanted to lock himself away. He said, "I am the last person he wants to see."

"The second last. I wouldn't be surprised if Yamaguchi-San is the very last."

Ishihara put his hand on his friend's arm. "Is there something you have not told me?"

Vargas did not move. "I am surmising, adding two and two. My theory is that Sensei has got himself involved in a get-rich-quick situation and has come unstuck. Somewhere in the background is the esteemed Mr. Yamaguchi, enjoying himself by pulling the strings. Your local Japanese don is a crafty, accomplished and experienced miscreant whilst Sensei has got neither the brains nor the make-up to become an accomplished villain. Our precious Sensei may be many things, but an abstract thinker he is not." Vargas stroked his nose with his little finger and smiled. "As you said, the other night—life is like a game of Shogi; if you can't see a few moves ahead, don't play."

Ishihara took his hand away. He suddenly remembered that Vargas detested being touched by anybody, except women.

Ishihara stirred the sugar in his coffee and pointed the spoon at Vargas. "This is not the time to make an indirect inference to my plan," he said, tight-lipped.

"Oh yes," Vargas said, still caressing his nose, "it certainly is. Assuming that Sensei shows up, which he will do, sooner or later, what do you intend to do? What is your strategy? How are you going to implement whatever tactics required bringing Yasmin back? Do you have a contingency plan? Are you willing to sacrifice Sensei for Yasmin?" Vargas lowered his hand and covered a yawn. "A few minor details like those, amigo."

Ishihara's teeth began to ache. "I—I presume that he will tell me," he said. "If he's got serious problems, why should he not talk to me?"

"Loss of face, the omnipotent Mr. Yamaguchi and your infinite infatuation with Yasmin."

Ishihara' shoulders hunched. "Can you make him talk?"

"He'll either talk, or he can prepare himself for another existence altogether."

Ishihara jolted into upright position. "No! Do not kill him. Please, Angelo."

Vargas lit a cigarette and stared at the flame from the lighter. "How irrational can you get? I have no intention of killing him. The motive is there, but not the reason."

Ishihara had run out of cigars. He eyed the blue smoke drifting across the table and inhaled what came his way. He looked relieved. "Surely, motive and reason is the one and same thing," he said. There were still aspects of Vargas' logic that weren't immediately decipherable.

Vargas said, "Not if you define motive as impulse and reason as faculty of thinking. If those two concepts do not coincide, you are making a mistake. Never forget that, Tadashi, or your career will be short-lived."

Ishihara felt as if a flame-thrower had been aimed at his back. At that moment he knew that this was the last time he would ever walk into a situation without strategies, tactics, contingency plans and a crystal-clear picture of how to implement whatever measures he had arrived at.

He said, "How are you going to make him talk?"

"Wait and see. It won't be difficult."

Ishihara took one of Vargas' cigarettes. "I wonder about you, Angelo. Do you know what is the biggest question on my mind?"

"I shall consult my tea leaves."

Ishihara grimaced and picked up the lighter. "Sometimes I see you as a serious and deep person, and at other times I am convinced that there is nothing on this earth that you take seriously. Which is it?"

"You really are in a screwed-up state of mind today."

"There is nothing abnormal about my question. Why don't you answer it?"

"If you insist."

"I do not insist. I politely query the intricacies of your mercurial interior."

"Is that what you do?"

"Yes. I most courteously and with considerable diplomatic finesse put forward an observation about the nomadic ways of your petulant psyche. That is all. I apologize if you find my innocent parenthesis provocative."

"Learn to distinguish between what is the carapace and what is the human quintessence behind the carapace. Do not assume that one excludes the other. Without panoply you do not survive."

"Some armours have more chinks than others?"

"Yes. You mend your own and exploit those of anybody else's, when needs be. The human element, amigo. Not the most attractive of philosophies, as we have been told with coruscating sophistry by blameless purists during the centuries; just a basic necessity, like it or not."

"I believe I trace a sense of bitterness."

"You are mistaken if you do. There was a time when I was so inclined, but then I discovered the price for harbouring such sentiment, and that nobody else was going to pay it." Vargas nodded thoughtfully. "It is amazing what a few grams of self-assessment can do for the nomadic ways of one's petulant psyche."

Ishihara laughed. Silently, he thanked Vargas for his help and moral support during their long hours of agony and frustration. He said, "It is a quarter to ten."

"Sit here," Vargas suggested. "I'll go and have a look."

He came back a few minutes later. There was no expression on his face. He walked like a cat moving towards the milktray.

"Well—?"

Vargas did not sit down. "The light is on."

Ishihara tried to shake off the tension that had penetrated every fibre of his body. He rose unsteadily and stared towards the door. "What are we waiting for?"

Vargas took a step closer. "First we pay for our coffee, and then we walk over." He lowered his voice. "Leave the talking to me. Have you got the key?"

Ishihara fumbled in his pockets and nodded.

Vargas paid, smiled at the girl and slithered across the floor. Ishihara followed.

"Give me the keys," Vargas said. He opened the door quietly and closed it behind them. They climbed the stairs without making a noise, Vargas first, and entered Kobayashi's office without knocking.

Kobayashi sat slumped in his chair. His eyes were fixed on a small white box resting on a sheet of brown wrapping paper. An opened envelope and a letter lay next to the box.

"Good evening," Vargas said and sat down. "I do hope that we find you in the best of health and spirit, Sensei." He beckoned to Ishihara and then towards the other chair in front of the desk.

"I did not invite you," Kobayashi said. His voice croaked like a radio during a thunderstorm. He did not look up.

"I'll be damned," Vargas said. "How could I possibly have overlooked a non-existent invitation? Anyway. Here we are."

"I don't need you," Kobayashi snarled. He still did not look up.

"I am afraid your personal needs are irrelevant," Vargas said genially. "On the other hand—talking about needs—kindly tell us where Yasmin is."

Kobayashi raised his head. His eyes were bulging. "I don't know where she is."

"I think you do. As a matter of fact, I *know* that you do."

Kobayashi leaned back and covered his face with both hands. A groan came from deep inside, and his massive body began to shake. "Look!" he screamed through his hands. "*Look!*"

Vargas pulled the brown wrapping paper with the box closer and took off the lid. The box contained a finger, a toe and an ear. Vargas put the lid back on. He crossed his legs.

Numb from shock, Ishihara found himself staring at the sheath strapped to Vargas' leg.

Vargas folded his hands. "Something wrong, Sensei?"

"*Wrong? Look!*" Kobayashi screamed once more. The sound vibrated through the room like the anguished cry from a tortured prisoner.

"I have looked," Vargas said. "In fact, we have both looked. May I respectfully ask you to enlighten us, Sensei?"

Vargas' ice-cool attitude began to unnerve Ishihara. Sweat was streaming from him, down his back, down his forehead and into his eyes. He was burning to interrupt, but he kept his promise.

Vargas continued, "I take it that the digits and the organ used to be integral parts of your most faithful Mr. Tanaka's anatomy. I further assume that the rest of him has gone to where his forefathers reside."

He waited. Finally, Kobayashi seemed to get a grip on himself. The hands came down, and he jerked the chair closer to the desk.

Ishihara could not take his eyes away. Never before had he seen his old mentor in such a state of despair, dejection and outright bewilderment. He is completely squashed, he thought, he's got no idea what to do.

"Kindly excuse me whilst I acquaint myself with this piece of communication," Vargas said and took the letter. He began to read. Then he frowned. "What horrible English," he said and looked at Kobayashi. "How can you possibly associate yourself with such a bunch of illiterate morons?"

"Please, Angelo," Ishihara whispered.

"All in capital letters," Vargas said, "and it goes, as follows:

DEAR MR. KOBAYASHI WE UNNERSTAN THAT YOU ARE INTRESTED IN DOING BIZNESS. SO IS WE. TWO REPRESENATIFS FROM YOUR OFFICE NAMELY MISS YASMIN AND MR. TANAKA IS NOW OUR GUESTS THAT IS NOT MR. TANAKA WHO IS DEAD. PLEASE FIND ENCLOSED GREETINGS TO THIS EFFECT. MISS YASMIN IS SO FAR ALL FINE AND WELL. YOU CAN

HAVE HER BACK IN ONE PEACE FOR ONE HUNNER TOUSAN AMERICAN DOLLARS. WE WILL TELEPONE INSTRUCTIONS. BEST REGARDS.

Vargas lowered the paper and added, "This is incredibly rude."

Ishihara leaned across. "There is a mark," he said, feverishly, "a sign."

"14 K," Vargas said. "Triads. She is in Hong Kong."

"You know them?"

"We have met."

Ishihara clutched his trouser legs. "Can we find her?"

"We'll find her."

"You believe them?"

"I do. She is fine and in one piece." He glared at Kobayashi. "She is their bargaining object. They'll only get funny if they realize there is no money to collect. To go there without the money would be the end of her. Limpy-Ho isn't noted for benevolence and a subtle sense of humour."

"Limpy-Ho?"

"Ng Sik-Ho. He is the most powerful of them all. To give you an idea, he is honorary member of both 14 K and the Wo Shing Wo. Limpy-Ho does drugs for a living. Isn't that interesting, Sensei?" he added and eyed the dishevelled figure across the desk. Kobayashi lowered his head. There was no other reaction.

Vargas went on, "Well, that one we can sort out later." There was a faint smile. "Limpy-Ho really must have enjoyed himself, instructing one of his more literate sidekicks to compose this letter. I take it that your associates have not called yet?"

Kobayashi shook his head.

Vargas sucked in air. "Give me the hundred thousand, Sensei."

A gargling sound came from Kobayashi's throat. "I haven't got it."

Ishihara said, "I can..." but stopped when Vargas kicked him on the shin and went on, "I need the money *now*."

"I told you. I have not got that kind of money."

Vargas leaned back, folded his hands behind his neck and stared at the ceiling. "Tell me exactly what is going on, Sensei," he said icily.

Kobayashi shifted uneasily in his chair. He wet his lips and fumbled with the sleeves of his jacket. Vargas continued to stare at the ceiling. "I am losing my patience, Sensei, something there's not much of in the first place. You either tell me what is going on, or you will never see Yasmin again."

The sigh that came from Kobayashi's throat could have shattered the egg of an ostrich. Slowly, searching for words, he admitted that it had all to do with his dream, his Honbu. The land had been purchased, the plans were approved, and every single yen of his capital was salted in the project. The rest was going to be financed by Yamaguchi-San; a long-term, low-interest loan, no interference and a built-in option for Kobayashi to repay the loan at any one time and with no premium added. What clsc? Well, in return for these generous terms, Yamaguchi had asked for a small favour. He wanted to set up a *sokaiya* outfit in Hong Kong; there were plenty of Japanese companies in Hong Kong, and he saw no reason why his business should not employ the same successful operations there as in Japan. The research, however, could not be performed by his own people; too conspicuous. A far better idea would be to send two charming, educated and professional representatives unconnected with the *Oyabun* and his syndicate, under an umbrella of disguise; observing, learning and reporting back in a business-like manner.

That had struck Kobayashi as a rational notion, and, eager to please and even more eager to impress, he had told Yamaguchi-San that none were better suited than Yasmin and Astuo Tanaka. Yamaguch-San had accepted most gracefully, and that was it. If it had occurred to Kobayashi that something like this could have happened, he would have declined Yamaguchi's offer out of hand. But, who could have guessed—?

"Shogi," Vargas said.

"What?"

"Forget it. Yamaguchi is into drugs. He is a minor player whose ambition it is to become a major player. The *boryokudan* have only scratched the surface, so far. The potential of the Japanese drugs market is enormous."

"I wouldn't know," Kobayashi said.

"Of course not. Putting one and one together isn't easy."

"I swear to you," Kobayashi said and raised his voice, "Yamaguchi-San never spoke to Yasmin and Astuo."

"No, he didn't," Vargas agreed. "Yasmin would have spotted a scumbag like Yamaguchi a mile away. Do you also know if Yamaguchi did or did not communicate with the Triads?"

Kobayashi's chin fell. He looked old and haggard.

"All this for a bloody mausoleum," Vargas said. He got up, crossed the floor and stood by the window, admiring the skyline. "Déjà vu, except that Ramirez did not hallucinate," he mumbled.

"What's that?" Ishihara queried.

"Something that took place in Mexico and shouldn't have happened to nice people like me. Let's go and raise the money."

"*Now?*" Kobayashi said. "Where?"

"Your buddy Yamaguchi."

"I can't!" The utterance came like a scratch of nails on glass.

"Why not?"

"It is out of question!"

Vargas turned. He came back to the desk and fixed Kobayashi with eyes showing nothing but mild surprise. "Is that a fact, Sensei? Could you possibly lower yourself to explain why?"

Kobayashi crossed his arms. "Not Yamaguchi."

It did not stick together, Ishihara thought; Vargas was too calm, too composed. He had put himself in the line of fire, but why did he behave as if the entire matter was nothing but cheap entertainment? He was fond of Yasmin, and Ishihara was his only friend—and yet, Vargas seemed strangely indifferent.

Ishihara did not believe that he could control himself much longer. Something drastic had to be done, and soon. Hong Kong was far away, and Ishihara knew that the Triads' reputation for ruthlessness was well earned. Why hadn't Vargas accepted that Ishihara should raise the money, which he could have done the moment the banks opened? Why this apparently pointless game involving Yamaguchi? He looked at the telephone that had yet to ring and gulped when he saw Vargas light a cigarette. Smoking was strictly forbidden in the dojo. In Kobayashi's office it was pure sacrilege.

Kobayashi's eyes disappeared and he tightened his arms across his chest. "No cigarettes!" he sneered.

Vargas inhaled, leaned forward and blew the smoke into Kobayashi's face.

"Listen, you screwed-up sonofabitch," he said and planted his hands on the top of the desk, his cigarette pointing vertically between two fingers, "I refuse to believe that you are willing to sacrifice Yasmin for your mausoleum. I refuse to believe that the risk of losing face is more important than the risk of losing your daughter. I refuse to believe that you are scared of a slimy turd like Yamaguchi. I even refuse to believe you are so incredibly bloody stupid that you fail to comprehend that if I do not bring down Yamaguchi, which will take less than a week, then you are the one who will vanish on a one-way ticket.

Now, try to add all this up, and what does it mean? It means that Yamaguchi is financing Yasmin's safe return. It means that you are undeservedly saved from ruin and destruction." He straightened his back. "Take your time, Sensei. I want you to appreciate fully what I am trying to implant into that stinking, septic lump of mucus passing for your brain."

Ishihara understood what Vargas was doing, and sat motionless. Never before had he heard him using foul language and nobody had ever dared throwing in Kobayashi's face that Yasmin was his daughter.

Vargas was changing tactics, and his aim was to derail Kobayashi. Ishihara did not doubt that worse was to come unless Kobayashi saw daylight within the next few minutes. Ishihara almost smiled when he recalled what Vargas had once said: "*You only use the rulebook if nothing else works, not the other way round.*"

Behind his mask of control was a white-hot fury kept in check by an iron-willed discipline developed from experiences Ishihara was glad he'd never suffered.

Kobayashi coughed. "You said *financing*—you mean temporarily?"

Vargas dropped his cigarette in Kobayashi's teacup. "Temporarily," he confirmed, "guaranteed by Tadashi-San."

Kobayashi looked at Ishihara, who nodded. He wondered what Vargas was up to.

"Short-term financing?" Kobayashi said. "That's different."

"Isn't it," Vargas said.

Ishihara wiped his eyebrows with the back of his hands. "Tell me, would it not be an idea to inform the Hong Kong police?"

Vargas nodded. "It would, if you want to upset Limpy-Ho. The Hong Kong police are notoriously corrupt and infiltrated by the Triads. Limpy would know within five minutes, cut his losses, order the disposal of Yasmin and wash his hands. Nothing if not pragmatic, our Chinese adversary."

Kobayashi stirred in his chair. "They didn't have to kill Astuo-San," he said angrily.

"Yes," Ishihara concurred, "what on earth was the purpose of killing Astuo?"

Vargas took off his jacket, hung it on the back of the chair and sat down. "Excuse me," he said acidly, "but are the two of you telling me that I still haven't got through to you? Have you completely lost whatever faculties you once had?"

Ishihara said, "Sorry. What did we miss?"

"You missed the entire point, which is that the whole scenario is a set-up. Yasmin and Astuo's trip has got nothing to do with the blackmail market. It has all to do with drugs. Yamaguchi wanted two guinea pigs, two complete innocents as *couriers*. He wanted to find out how easy it was or wasn't to get a kilo or two through customs. If he succeeded, he'd have a few spare yen to invest in Honbu.

You've got to give him credit, Sensei, using your own daughter to bring in the money with which he planned to take over your school, in due time. Now, if they'd got caught, Yasmin and Astuo were not *his* people, nothing to do with him and everything to do with you. Then Astuo figured out what was going on and refused to cooperate. By killing him, the Triads sent a message to Yamaguchi: be a bit more professional, or forget it." Vargas lit another cigarette and put his feet on the desk. "Left is Yasmin, now too frightened to be a worthwhile risk as a courier, but far from useless as a bargaining piece. Limpy gets his hundred thousand in addition to the upfront payment from Yamaguchi, keeps the drugs and forces Yamaguchi to get his act together if he wants to do business. Simple, and efficient."

Ishihara said, "In other words, Yamaguchi indirectly killed Astuo."

"Assisted by Sensei." Vargas took a pad and a pen from the desk and began to write. "Here," he said and handed the paper to Kobayashi. "These are the cue words when they call. Under no circumstances must you mention that *two* of us are coming. Only me. Agree to anything they say. If you are in doubt about something, write it down so that I can see it."

Kobayashi took the paper. He looked drained. "Now what?" he said in a broken voice.

"Nothing," Vargas said. "It may well take hours before they call. Let it ring four times before you answer."

"I'll make some tea," Ishihara said.

Vargas went over to the couch and lay down under the enormous painting of Kobayashi in his heyday. When Ishihara came with the tea, he found his friend asleep.

The telephone rang at half past five in the morning.

Vargas was instantly on his feet. "Let it ring," he said sharply to Kobayashi who had been slumbering and for a moment was trying to find out where he was.

Ishihara stood next to Vargas who pushed the pad in front of Kobayashi. "Remember, say *yes* or *no* whenever appropriate. They can't see you nod or shake your head. Here," he lifted the receiver. "Enjoy yourself."

Kobayashi said *yes* twice and *no* once during the first two minutes. Then he gave a description of Vargas and said, like he was repeating: *yes, a white man.* They heard a click. Vargas took the receiver from Kobayashi and put it back on.

Kobayashi pulled out his handkerchief and wiped his head. "They want you to wear a red-and-white striped tie."

"Ingenious. Now, we have got a few things to do. Sensei, ensure that Tadashi and I get through the airport without any formalities, and I mean *any*. No passports, no customs and no security. Tadashi, book one single economy with return first class, one first class return and one single first class from Hong Kong in the name of Mrs. Ishihara. Return is tomorrow, first available flight. Arrange for a car to take us to Haneda and for a car to be ready when we call from Kai Tek. Sensei, the same when we return—*no* formalities. Ensure that we walk straight through. Use your contacts." He stared from one to the other. "I take it that no explanation is necessary."

"What about Yasmin," Ishihara said, "her passport and the name on her ticket...?"

"Just do it," Vargas interrupted. "I don't need any questions."

"All right. When do we leave?"

"We can't be at the airport much before ten this morning. Any time thereafter. Use your combined influence if the plane is full." Vargas turned to Kobayashi. "I take it that our friends did not leave a telephone number, and that you confirmed I am coming today."

"Yes," Kobayashi said. "Yes, today."

Vargas pulled a small notebook from his inner pocket. "I need to make a few calls."

Neither Kobayashi nor Ishihara moved.

Vargas said, "It's private, which is my polite way of asking you to get the hell out of here. The less you know the better. Close the door after you."

He let them back in again ten minutes later.

"It is time to pay our respects to the honourable Mr. Yamaguchi," he said.

The traffic moved in a steady flow. Fifty minutes later Ishihara stopped the car.

The two guards in front of the gates of Yamaguchi's luxurious mansion instantly recognized Kobayashi and bowed respectfully.

Vargas turned his back to the guards, faced Ishihara and said, "Tell them to inform their master that Kobayashi-San is here with two of his financial advisors. The business is very urgent. Add our sincere apology for showing up at this ungodly hour. That's all."

Ishihara translated. One of the guards went over to the telephone. He nodded a few times, hung up and pushed the button to open the gate.

Yamaguchi stood by a small palm tree in his exquisite drawing room. He was clad in a black kimono and was watching an exceptionally beautiful girl preparing the tea. He was of Ishihara's height, but skinny and with a wrinkled and dark face. He looked seventy, but was in his late fifties. His hair was steely grey, combed back in a way that made him look ascetic, like a latter-day shogun ruling his fiefdom with the abacus in general and the sword only when more refined methods of modern times proved insufficient.

The two bodyguards were both dressed in rat-coloured suits. They stood three yards away on either side of their chieftain. They stiffened when they discovered the identity of Kobayashi's financial advisors but they did not move. Like the guests, they wore slippers provided for indoor use.

Yamaguchi showed no emotions. He bowed gracefully and wished them welcome to his humble abode. He hoped they would join him for tea.

"Get the niceties out of the way," Vargas said to Kobayashi. "Thereafter, I take over."

Kobayashi apologized profusely for this early intrusion; he sincerely hoped that Yamaguchi would appreciate the urgency and rounded off with a few well-chosen words about Yamaguchi's status, importance and most contributory role in the entire Japanese society.

They both bowed twice. Yamaguchi's permanent smile added to the impression of the benevolent samurai.

"My honourable friends," he began and ignored Vargas, "whatever I can do..." he let the essence of what he could do float in the air.

"Translate accurately what I am saying and every word that he is saying," Vargas told Ishihara. "No liberties, no camouflage and no cosmetics regardless of your own opinion of the verbal exchange between him and myself."

"Shall we sit down," Yamaguchi suggested and pointed towards the dark red, oblong leather cushions around the low and ornate table where the tea was ready. Vargas remained standing.

"Please," Yamaguchi said with a sweeping gesture and looked at Vargas for the first time.

Vargas said, "Order your two anthropoids to sit down."

Yamaguchi barked an order without waiting for a translation and without turning his head. The two bodyguards sat down on the floor.

"Tell them to keep their hands on their knees," Vargas said.

Yamaguchi barked again. Vargas sat down. He positioned himself in such a way that neither Yamaguchi nor the bodyguards could see the knife.

"You are of a suspicious disposition, Mr. Vargas," Yamaguchi said smoothly.

"Paranoid, considering the anodyne nature of the company."

Yamaguchi did not lose his deadpan expression. "A white man with a sense of humour. What an asset you must be to your race." He smiled benignly. "Thank heavens for little miracles."

"Thank heavens," Vargas reiterated. "Who knows, we may soon experience another supernatural phenomenon."

The girl poured the tea. Vargas eyed her with undisguised admiration. "Your sense of beauty is unequalled, Yamaguchi-San. I wish I could say the same about your common sense."

For a split second, Yamaguchi hesitated. Then he bowed slightly and said, "Thank you. Beauty does appeal to me. Anything common does not."

Vargas returned the bow. "Which brings me to our mission here."

Yamaguchi slurped his tea and looked at Kobayashi. "Is Mr. Vargas your appointed spokesman, Kobayashi-San?"

Vargas said, "I am, unanimously elected. Now, I am going to take something from my inner pocket and give to you. Please inform your two guardian angels that it is only a piece of paper."

Yamaguchi raised his hand. Vargas reached for his pocket, took out the letter from Hong Kong and gave it to him.

Yamaguchi minimized the distance between his thick eyebrows. "I am sure it is interesting, but what does it say?"

"Cut the bullshit," Vargas said. "Your English isn't that bad."

Yamaguchi's eyelids became heavy. "I do not speak English," he said. There was a touch of malice in his voice.

"Have it your way, for the time being. Tadashi, please translate to our linguistically illiterate host the contents of the letter."

Yamaguchi appeared to concentrate as he listened. It had not taken him long to regain his self-control. A few seconds of silence passed before he shook his head. "This is most depressing," he said. "It makes me sad to hear about such misfortune. However, I do not understand how I can be of any assistance. I would if I could, of course, but my influence in Hong Kong is non-existent."

Vargas said, "We are not interested in your influence in Hong Kong. We are interested in the one hundred thousand dollars here and now."

Yamaguchi pressed the tips of his fingers together and tilted his head. "Another joke, I presume? You are a very gifted man, Vargas-San."

Vargas looked down. Then, slowly, he raised his head. "Listen carefully, you filthy little insect," he said almost tenderly. "We are here to collect. You have not got a choice. Kindly do not test my forbearance any further."

The insult was so gross that Ishihara felt his legs go rigid, as if seized by cramp. This is not going to work, he thought, this time Vargas had overplayed his hand by a very wide margin.

Yamaguchi did not change his position. "Are you threatening me, Vargas-San?" he asked as if only vaguely surprised.

Vargas smiled. "No, Yamaguchi-San, I am not threatening you. I am not even warning you. I am making a statement. Would you like to learn the implications involved?"

Yamaguchi did not answer. Ishihara could see his eyes as two little pieces of shiny coal, focusing on Vargas.

Vargas said, "To start with, every single one of our fighters will hunt down your pathetic army of tattooed apes and have them comfortably placed in wheelchairs for the rest of their unworthy lives. Those who survive, that is. Secondly, your shady little operation will be exposed. Shall I mention the names of a few reporters who are rather keen on the yakuza? Thirdly, your suppliers of drugs will deliver but not get paid, something I believe would upset them. Not only will your incipient career as a drug baron come to an abrupt end—where will you hide, Yamaguchi-San? Lastly, but not least—consider it a bonus—this mansion and every one of your neat and tidy drug depots will burn down." Vargas sipped his tea without taking his eyes off Yamaguchi. "Now, that is what I call a statement, Yamaguchi-San. Please feel free to ask questions should I not have expressed myself clearly."

A web of red veins had appeared on the whites of Yamaguchi's eyes, but his physical impassiveness remained obdurate. A true warlord, Ishihara thought, no wonder he is a success. It shall be interesting to see how he is going to deal with the gaijin's *statement*, and how quickly.

"We are talking about a loan," Yamaguchi said evenly.

Vargas looked surprised. "But of course. What else? Five days, maximum. One hundred percent interest on the entire amount, guaranteed by Ishihara-San here."

Yamaguchi shook the sleeves of his kimono and put his flat right hand over his left. "What stops Ishihara-San coming up with the cash?"

"All in bonds and shares. It will take a few days to convert, and I am going to Hong Kong today. Do not forget the one hundred percent, now, Yamaguchi-San. Easy money, wouldn't you say?"

The corners of Yamaguchi's eyes extended to a line towards his temples. He said, "Tell me, Vargas-San, just as a matter of curiosity, what makes you think that I have got that kind of cash within reach, that is, here and now?"

Vargas' frame was silhouetted against the window. His elbows rested on his knees. His gaze took in the entire room. "Where else would you keep black money?"

Yamaguchi got up. He came back ten minutes later with a pilot case. "Would you like to count it, Vargas-San?"

"No. I think we understand each other."

They all rose. Vargas took the case that Yamaguchi had placed on the table.

"A pleasure doing business with you, Yamaguchi-San."

"The pleasure is mine. I hope you will have a rewarding trip."

"You are too kind."

This would have been a perfectly normal exchange of civilities had it taken place between two Japanese, Ishihara thought. He could see that Yamaguchi was aware of Vargas' veiled irony and he knew that the *Oyabun* was already well into his plan for revenge. First, though, he had to get his money back, but thereafter—the more Ishihara pondered, the less he liked Vargas' initiative. Obviously, his friend had not gone into this without evaluating the consequences; Ishihara's problem was that he could not see how Vargas was going to conclude successfully such a sordid and dangerous game with a seasoned and unscrupulous opponent like Yamaguchi.

"Allow me the honour of following you out," Yamaguchi said.

As the heavy wooden doors swung open, Vargas demonstratively inhaled a few lung-fulls of air. "A nice change," he said, adding a dash of elation to his voice. "And what a lovely cherry tree, Yamaguchi-San. Do you think I could have a sapling when I finally leave the birthplace of the rising sun?"

The Japanese bowed. "With my good wishes." His voice sounded like tractor wheels on gravel.

Vargas turned and faced Yamaguchi. "One final detail, Shogun. Do not lose yourself in feverish fantasies about an elaborate and bloodstained vendetta. Consider this as my last and most friendly advice. Kobayashi-San here would be most deeply upset should he find you helpless and forsaken in the sewer you came from."

Ishihara spread his feet and searched his mind for words that could defuse the tension. Kobayashi stared towards the sky where the sun had begun to whiten the blue.

Yamaguchi's skills as a poker player did not betray him. Not a single extra wrinkle appeared on his teak-coloured face.

Vargas walked down the drive and through the gates, opened the backdoor of the car and tossed the case onto the seat.

Kobayashi and Ishihara bade farewell in the traditional, urbane manner. Neither apologized for Vargas's insults.

Halfway to Ikebukuro, Kobayashi opened his mouth. "I do not understand what you are doing, Angelo-San." He sounded strangely subdued.

"You will, eventually. Thank you for keeping up the façade. It cannot have been easy, considering that Yamaguchi is responsible for Atsuo's death and for Yasmin's life hanging in a thread."

"It was not easy."

"Add that Yamaguchi duped you. May I now take it for granted that your heart is filled with hatred?"

"It is, Angelo-San. No forgiveness. We have got ourselves an enemy for life."

Vargas said, "Not that long."

On the way to the airport they stopped at a shopping centre. Vargas left the car and came back with a large briefcase and a plastic bag containing three soft parcels. He opened two of the parcels. Ishihara looked at the red-and-white tie and a pair of dark blue trousers of a material he had not seen before.

"Strange stuff," he said and felt the texture between his thumb and index finger.

"Waterproof," Vargas said.

Twenty minutes later he asked the driver to pull over at first available site. The driver obliged and went for a ten minutes walk, as instructed. Vargas looked around to ensure that nobody was close before he opened the pilot case and the new briefcase. He split the money into two equal portions and put one half in each case. He pulled a three-by-fifteen inch box from his inside pocket and put it on top of the money in the briefcase, together with the third and unopened parcel. Ishihara noticed that the oblong box was wrapped in plastic on paper loosely folded without tape or rubber bands.

He said with a thin smile, "You've got a plan, and a contingency plan."

"I do. I wish we had more options, but we didn't exactly create this situation."

Ishihara gazed out the window. "What if neither plan works?"

Vargas closed the two cases, but left the combinations locks untouched. "I shall have to improvise."

Ishihara had followed Vargas' instructions to the letter. He was dressed in a dark suit, with a white shirt and a discreet tie. He carried an elegant briefcase that contained stockmarket reports and a financial newspaper.

With his gold cufflinks and expensive watch he looked like any other Japanese executive on his way to an important meeting.

"What is my function?" he asked quietly.

"You haven't got any."

"Please, no jokes. Do not torment me. It is bad enough as it is."

Vargas put his feet on the pilot case. "Here is what we do," he began, ignoring Ishihara's plea. "From the moment we get out of this car, we do not know each other. Under no circumstances do we make any contact; not at Haneda, not during the flight and not when we arrive at Kai Tek. I shall be among the first leaving the aircraft. You will be among the last. Take a taxi to The Peninsula Hotel. When you get into the lobby, turn right and find a table at the far end. Order some tea or coffee, read your reports and ensure that nobody shares your table. If Yasmin and I are not there within one hour, take a taxi back to Kai Tek and ask for John Mullenberg, security. You, John and a few other chaps will then wait in the entrance hall. When you see Yasmin and I coming accompanied by three or four Chinese, leave it to John. He knows what to do."

"Is that all?" Ishihara said, perplexed.

"That's all."

"Why am I coming with you?"

Vargas faced him. "Would you rather sit at home, twiddling your thumbs, each minute feeling like an eternity?"

Ishihara understood. "I do appreciate your thoughts, but isn't there *something* I can do?"

Vargas adjusted Ishihara's tie, a highly unusual act of affection, he thought.

"Remember Sensei's message," Vargas said. "One white man is coming. How do you think they will react if we both show up? I sympathize with your frustration, but we haven't got a choice. Limpy-Ho is well informed and equally well prepared. One minute after we left Yamaguchi, he was on the phone to his Chinese counterpart. Yamaguchi wants his money back. The only thing I don't know, is what he promised in return."

"Are you saying that you know where Yasmin is?"

"Roughly. I'd say that she is within five minutes from The Peninsula. The reason why she is not in the Walled City or at some obscure address in the New Territories is that Limpy does not believe in giving his competitors any natural advantages. Limpy is no amateur."

"How can you be so sure?"

"You ask too many questions, Tadashi. I know where she is."

The driver took his seat. They rode in silence. Five hundred yards from Departures, in the midst of heavy traffic, Vargas asked the driver to stop the car.

"Get out," he said to Ishihara.

"Here?"

"Here. Walk the last bit. See you at The Peninsula."

Ishihara began walking. Vargas closed the door. He bent down, unwrapped the two parcels and placed the contents at the bottom of the pilot case, the smaller object on top of the larger one. He folded the paper and the plastic sheet and put them in the outer sidepocket before he readjusted the stacks of dollars and did the combination locks.

Vargas left the plane with a case in each hand. He entered Arrivals carrying only the pilot case. Two Chinese approached him as they spotted his tie. They bowed politely and asked if they could have the honour of driving him to his destination in their most comfortable limousine. No expression on the faces of the two Chinese indicated playing with words.

Vargas said, "Excuse me, but would you by any chance have a name?"

"Charlie," said the one who had spoken.

"Right, Charlie. Have you got a message for me?"

The Chinese dug into his pocket and produced a small piece of paper. Vargas unfolded it and read *Amsterdam*. He nodded. "Take me for a ride."

A black Mercedes was waiting outside, with a third Chinese behind the wheel.

In less than fifteen minutes they swung into Nathan Road and stopped after a few hundred yards. Charlie got out. Vargas and the other Chinese followed. The driver remained in his seat.

"That's the entrance," Charlie beckoned.

Vargas eyed the dilapidated and timeworn edifice, strangely out of style with the modern architecture of the area. Outside the windows of the fifth floor a faded sign read ....*Factory*, the first word or words unintelligible. "How high up?" he asked.

"Just a bit of exercise," Charlie said.

Vargas nodded towards The Peninsula. "A pity we can't have a drink whilst we exchange merchandise."

Charlie showed his goldspecked dental work. "A pleasure to be cherished afterwards."

They fell in with the rhythm of thousands of other pedestrians. Inside the door, Charlie stopped. "Just for the sake of good order," he said. "Johnnie would like to make sure that you are clean. Only a routine precaution," he added, grinning as if he enjoyed an obscene joke.

Vargas put down the case and spread-eagled whilst Johnnie frisked him. Charlie had his right hand in his pocket but looked relaxed. Johnnie shook his head.

"No," Charlie said, "I didn't think so."

"Who comes armed to a business meeting?" Vargas said.

"You tell me."

"Johnnie does not speak English?"

"He is very shy."

Charlie turned towards the staircase. "After you."

On the fifth landing, Charlie passed Vargas, with Johnnie still behind, and approached a door with vertical remnants of green paint in an uneven pattern. He knocked four times and said something in Cantonese. Vargas heard the clicking of the locks. The door opened.

Vargas entered.

The room was large, some thirty by fifteen yards. Whatever had once been produced there, nothing was left except a long, wooden table on cast iron supporters, and half a dozen primitive chairs.

One Chinese was seated at the table. Another moved as if he contemplated sitting down. The one seated was dressed in an ash-grey suit and looked as complaisant and assertive as a senior partner in an accountancy firm. The one on the move wore blue jeans and a black T-shirt. Suddenly, he sat down. They both had a cleaver in front of them.

Yasmin was sitting on a chair with her back to the wall. Her feet were tied to the legs of the chair and her hands tied behind her back. A dirty bandanna covered her mouth.

Vargas took in the details. Then he ignored her. The one in the suit got up.

"I am Herbert," he said. "I am pleased to make your acquaintance, Mr. Vargas."

"Likewise. Is your friend there as bashful as Johnnie?"

"He is very reticent," Herbert smiled. He looked at the cleaver. "More of an action man, really. He is amazingly adept with his little potato peeler. Practically an artist, I would not hesitate to emphasize."

"Aren't all Triads?"

"Some are more gifted than others, like in all walks of life. Take it as a *cumshaw*. He has not yet been elevated to the dizzy heights of negotiations and diplomacy. You can call him Teddy, like in bear." Herbert laughed, satisfied with his verbal dexterity.

Vargas saw that Charlie and Johnnie had taken their positions inside the door. They had locked it. He continued to ignore Yasmin.

"Would you mind if I take off my jacket?" he said to Herbert.

"Please." He made a sweeping gesture. "Feel at home."

"It must have taken you some while to compose that exceptionally amusing letter to Mr. Kobayashi."

Herbert laughed again. The odour from his lunch whiffed across the table. "Thank you. I appreciate the compliment. You see, I used to work for a British law firm for some years, hence my intimate knowledge of their language and its infinite wealth of nuances and room for any conceivable permutation of inanities. Yes, it did give me a great pleasure to produce a piece of garbage so bad that any Japanese would take it as being authentic, familiar as the turnip heads are with the subnormal standard of their own dim-witted yakuza." Herbert took a bright blue fountain pen from his breast pocket and scratched his right ear. "If you wonder about the little parcel attached to my greetings, the reason was to make my message genuinely sincere."

"You didn't fail," Vargas said. "For a moment I thought that Ng himself had written the letter, but then I realized there weren't enough spelling mistakes. How is his lordship, these days?"

Herbert did not answer. His smile had gone.

Vargas went on, "He still lives in Kent Road, I take it? A most impressive property, I'd say. I was once his guest, there. Limpy-Ho knows how to throw a party."

"You are well informed," Herbert said. The smile was back.

"I used to hang around here."

Herbert said, "I am pleased that Mr. Kobayashi fully comprehended my message. It was a pity with poor Mr. Tanaka, though. The honourable gentleman flatly refused to cooperate."

"Some people do not know what is best for them."

"Sadly not. However, it is as nice as it is encouraging to meet a *gweilo* with a measure of intelligence and an ounce of common sense." He moved the chair with his foot and sat down. "You work for the great Mr. Kobayashi?"

"No, I do not. We are not business associates. I make my living as an independent courier. Mr. Kobayashi's penchant for violence does not appeal to me. Call me Angelo, please. Amiable informality does make the world a better place, don't you think?"

Herbert patted the hair above his ears with his fingers. "Angelo," he mused, "that does not sound English. Neither does Vargas, for that matter."

"Far from it. Mexican, as fate would have it." He placed his left foot on the seat of the nearest chair. "Tell me, Herbert, of all the *gweilos* on this earth, I understand that you find the English the most contemptible. How come you all adopted English names?"

"Ah," Herbert said and caressed his cleaver absentmindedly, "sheer convenience, I am ashamed to say. We operate in an international milieu, here in Hong Kong, as you undoubtedly are aware of, and the question of names is one of expediency, really." His laughter ripped through the air like a dentist's drill. "You hit the nail on the head, Angelo—there are no bigger swines than the pompous, deceitful, eggheaded excretions known as Brits."

"One learns something new every day," Vargas said. "Now, convenience and expediency being the key words, shall we get down to business? I do not want to appear rude, but I have a plane to catch."

Herbert nodded gravely. "A most timely observation. I sincerely hope you won't be offended if we count the money?"

"Not at all," Vargas said and placed the case in front of him. "Anything else would be highly unprofessional. It is locked," he explained as he adjusted the wheels of the combination locks with his thumbs. "Safety reasons, as one would expect. There are so many dishonourable characters around."

Herbert stared as Vargas piled up the money. "And here we have the entire lot?" he asked when Vargas patted the top of the heap, indicating completion.

"No, we have not. Here we have half of it."

Herbert placed his right elbow on the back of his chair. "But surely, Angelo, I seem to recollect that my little note, to which you so kindly referred, clearly stated all and not half of it. How could we possibly have misunderstood each other?"

"We didn't," Vargas said and straightened his back. "The other fifty are in a briefcase at the airport, together with my passport and my ticket."

A thin blue vein on Herbert's forehead began to pulsate. "Ah," he said in a silken voice, "I think I understand. You want us all to go to the airport, the lady included, pick up the rest of the money and there we bid you adieu. Am I grossly mistaken?"

"You read me."

"An ingenious and commendable scenario," Herbert said and glanced fleetingly at Charlie across the room. "As a matter of fact, I believe I would have devised something similar, bearing in mind the viable options available. I do sympathize, or should I say *commiserate*."

"I value your understanding."

A tic between Herbert's eyebrows did not seem to bother him. He smiled. "Your plan is as good as any, my friend, but, however regrettable, not good enough." He scanned the grey and flaking ceiling. "How can I put this without hurting your feelings—well, suffice to say that I dare assume my own thinking to be superior. May I respectfully request that you, Charlie and Johnnie go back to Kai Tek, pick up the other briefcase and return at your very earliest convenience? Should you decide not to return—and it does cause me pain to say this—you leave behind fifty grand and a dead lady." He picked his nose and eyed Vargas for a few seconds. "Come to think of it, there is actually a fair chance that you will miss your plane altogether, added to the misfortune as just described. You see, Charlie and Johnnie are well trained, and it so happens that they understand the concept of *loyalty* infinitely better than they comprehend the illusion of *conscience*." He smiled without parting his lips. "Not much of a bargain, is it," he sneered, showing the first sign of annoyance. "No, do not sit down. You are on your way to Kai Tek."

The next sequence of events happened too fast for Yasmin to follow. Vargas' hand disappeared into the pilot case and came up with the knife. The blade turned red as he slit Herbert's throat from ear to ear. Vargas pivoted and the knife whizzed through the air. Teddy was on his feet with the cleaver in his right hand and his arm raised when the knife hit his neck under the left-hand side of his jaw. Charlie and Johnnie were closing in when Vargas grabbed Herbert's cleaver, moved forward, sidestepped and embedded the cleaver between Charlie's eyes. Johnnie began to circle with a stiletto in his right hand and his left hand held flat at waist height. Vargas pirouetted, jumped and shattered Johnnie's larynx with a sidekick.

Vargas breathed heavily for a moment before he looked at Yasmin. He pulled his knife from Teddy's neck and went over to the sink. He rinsed his hands and the knife before he walked across and cut her free. He took care not to get his bloodied clothes too close. He undid the bandanna. Yasmin gasped and tears came to her eyes.

"Don't get up," Vargas said sharply, "You'll fall over. Move your arms and legs. Try to get some circulation going."

He went over to his jacket, took something from a pocket and gave it to her. "Swallow this."

Yasmin looked at the white pill. "What is it?"

"A mild tranquilizer. You should feel the effect within twenty minutes."

Yasmin gulped down the pill. She watched Vargas pick up a cleaver from the floor. She looked away when she realized what he had in mind.

Only when she heard the water running did she raise her head. Vargas had stripped to the waist. His bloodstained T-shirt covered Charlie's face. Meticulously, Vargas washed off any trace of blood before he undid his trousers and left them in the sink for a few minutes with the water running. He gave the trousers a good shake before he wiped off remaining drops. He folded them neatly, went over to the pilot case and took out the white T-shirt he had bought on the way to the airport. The sheath came up. He strapped it to his leg and inserted the knife before he put on his jacket. He put the parcel wrapped in plastic over paper at the bottom of the case. The trousers followed. Finally, he threw in the money and secured the locks.

Yasmin tried to get up, but her legs refused. She felt giddy and numb and her arms were paralyzed. She began to cry.

"Come," Vargas said and took her hand. "I'll support you down the stairs."

Yasmin managed to get to her feet. She swayed and clung to Vargas' arm.

Vargas said, "I have to unlock the door. Don't faint."

They walked down slowly, step by step. Between the second and the first floor an elderly Chinese woman scurried past on her way up. She did not look at them.

Before he opened the entrance door, Vargas said, "Can you walk fifty yards up and down the pavement?"

Yasmin moistened her sore lips and nodded.

They walked, pretending to window-shop.

"Tadashi is waiting at The Peninsula," Vargas said.

Yasmin sobbed and clung harder to Vargas' arm. He said, "We'll go in there, now. Be as natural as you possibly can. We shall have a cup of well-earned coffee and a chat about nothing for a while before we move on."

They turned.

"You are safe now," Vargas said. "Everything is under control. Is the pill working?"

Yasmin pressed her tongue against her teeth. She tried not to weep. Her throat was burning, but the acute sense of pain and fear was waning. "I think so," she whispered.

"Do you reckon you can walk on your own when we enter the hotel?"

"I will try. Yes, I can."

Ishihara was facing the side entrance. He got up when he saw them. "I am *so* pleased to see you," he smiled. He had rehearsed the line for the last twenty minutes. He held out a chair for Yasmin. She avoided looking at him. "Cheer up," he said in a low, even voice. "Let us try to behave like anybody else in here."

Yasmin's grimace resembled a bleak smile. She wished she could giggle at Ishihara's non-committal grin, but she had no laughter to spare. He said, "My display of self-control supersedes normal human endeavour. The last half hour has been like a year."

The waiter came over. Vargas ordered coffee and water. He touched Yasmin's hand. "Drink slowly."

Yasmin sipped, and sipped once more. Her hands were still trembling. Vargas picked up one of Ishihara's stockmarket reports. He read for a minute. His face showed deep concentration.

He said, "It is most peculiar. How can anyone propose a merger without accepting that there has to be a deadline?"

Ishihara tried to avoid the smoke from his cigar getting into his eyes. "You mean, they would not or could not see the sense in our proposal?"

Vargas said, "Overconfident people have a tendency to neglect due diligence. It is a classic mistake, usually associated with gross incompetence."

Ishihara threw a glance towards the Nathan Road entrance door. "I take it that re-negotiation is out of question?"

"They have accepted their position."

Ishihara heard his own laughter as if coming from outside himself.

"Reduce the volume," Vargas said. "You sound like a hyena with a throat infection." He tossed the report back to Ishihara who said, "What about Mr. Mullenberg?"

"We have an arrangement. He'll be our host tonight. His house is safe."

Ishihara studied the badly chewed end of his cigar. Any lingering doubt had gone from his mind. He killed them, he thought, and his only concern is that I keep my laughter under control. He tried to get eye contact with Yasmin, but she stared into her glass that she held with both hands. There was an expression of melancholy mixed with apprehension on her face. He saw that Vargas, too, was looking at her.

Vargas got up. "Yasmin," he said and took her hand, "I would like to show you something."

"What?" she said and rose, robot-like.

"Just come with me."

Ishihara watched as they crossed the lobby and entered an antique shop at the opposite end.

"Don't surround us," Vargas said to the three attendants who appeared from nowhere. "We'll let you know if we find something we like."

They looked for a few minutes. "How about that one?" Vargas said and nodded towards an exquisitely carved jade orchid. "You caught on to that one the moment you came in, didn't you?" he smiled.

"Please, Angelo, I can't accept—"

Vargas turned to the nearest attendant. "How much?"

The attendant unlocked the glass door and glanced at the tag with a proficient expression of disbelief. Yasmin gasped audibly.

For the next few minutes Vargas and the attendant duelled with the good-humoured and pigheaded dignity of experienced hagglers. They finally shook hands when each reckoned he had won.

"Wrap it well," Vargas said. "I'll be back in half an hour's time."

"Why?" Yasmin said on their way through the lobby.

"Because you have given me the yardstick with which I can measure the woman I hope will come into my life."

Yasmin did not turn her head. "You'll find your orchid, Angelo."

They sat for another half-hour whilst Vargas entertained them with his knowledge of Hong Kong, the islands and the New Territories.

Then he went over to the shop and came back with an elegantly presented parcel, which he placed in Yasmin's lap. "To happy days ahead, darling."

Ishihara's cup stopped an inch from the saucer. "What is it?" he said.

"A present," Vargas said. "We just got engaged."

My world is falling apart, Ishihara thought, but it is not going to show on my face. My future is in ruins, and my big plan is but a speck of ash disintegrating into the night. Yasmin is spellbound, infatuated and drawn to the gaijin like a ladybird to a carnivorous plant. Why have I not seen it before? So much for loyalty and friendship. Can I blame him? No, Yasmin is a unique woman, but her deficit is that she is too young to understand the implications of her desire. The gaijin saved her life, and her inexperience has led her into a predicament where she can no longer synchronize her feelings with her thinking. Once again I shall conclude that Confucius was right: "*The five worst infirmities that afflict the female are indolence, discontent, slander, jealousy and silliness.*" Add *gullibility*, and the picture is complete. Does it matter? Not any more. The millions of molecules constituting my humble being have dispersed into and all over the mighty universe. As of today, I only exist as an empty shell.

"Congratulations," he said.

Vargas lit a cigarette. "With what?"

"The engagement."

"Whose engagement?"

Ishihara's shirt was clinging to his damp skin. He used his thumb and little finger to allow some air between the cotton and his body. Stoneface him, he thought, let nothing indicate that you are either dejected or over the moon. "You and Yasmin," he said.

"*Me* and Yasmin? How incredibly thick can you get, Tadashi?"

He could hear his own heartbeat. "Excuse me?"

Vargas' sigh could have toppled a church candle. "The *we* refers to *you* and Yasmin as the happy couple, and to my good self as the devoted and delighted friend. Had I remembered that your ability to deduce is practically non-existent, I would of course have phrased it differently. Not to worry. Can I be your best man?"

Yasmin giggled.

Ishihara's hands opened and closed and made dents in his kneecaps. "Your sense of humour contains a good measure of cruelty, Angelo."

"My apologies. It should have come to mind that cruelty is a concept unbeknown to the Japanese. Nanking was but a mild joke, I now recall."

Ishihara's mood vacillated between sunshine and thunder, but he decided to let go. "All right," he said and picked up his briefcase. "It is time to leave this place."

Yasmin rested her hand on his shoulder. She said softly, "Tadashi, you were not there, across the street. Please understand what Angelo is trying to do." Her tone of voice did not match her smile. Ishihara averted his eyes. "I am sorry. I should have thought."

"Forget it. Think of tomorrow and how you are going to cheer up our revered and loveable Sensei."

They were on their way to Kai Tek early the following morning. Yasmin sat in the backseat, tenderly squeezed between Ishihara and Vargas. The driver tried to keep up a conversation half in English and half in Cantonese. He gave up when the gweilo said he looked forward to Hong Kong becoming another Tibet.

Mullenberg had left twenty minutes earlier. He met them when they arrived. They headed for the gates. Nobody approached them.

The passage through Haneda went as smoothly as it did on the way out. The car was waiting.

Ishihara sat in front, Yasmin and Vargas with his two cases in the back.

When they came closer to the City Centre, Vargas told the driver to stop in front of the Nippon Credit Bank, circle around and not lose sight of the main doors. Neither Ishihara nor Yasmin made any comment when Vargas took the two cases and vanished inside the building.

When he came out, he was still carrying the cases. "Ikebukuro," he said to the driver, leaned back in the seat and closed his eyes.

Ryutaro Kobayashi was in his office. For the briefest of moments, an expression of immense relief swept his face. He regained his composure and did not move in his chair. Yasmin sat down opposite him.

"Hello," she said tonelessly. "Astuo asked me to convey his regards."

Kobayashi coughed. The bags under his eyes were dark and heavy. A red vein ran like a scar down the side of his nose. "I did not know, Yasmin. I had no idea what Yamaguchi was up to. You must believe me." He stared at her, pleadingly. "I should have thought, but I didn't. The Honbu..." His voice faded away.

Ishihara leaned against the doorframe. "Sensei is telling the truth. Yamaguchi duped him. It was a human error."

Yasmin turned. "Astuo is dead!" she screamed. "I saw him die! I saw what they did to him!"

Kobayashi sat motionless. Drops of perspiration ran down his forehead and into his eyes. He did not blink. "Please forgive me, Yasmin."

"*Forgive* you? How could you be so incredibly stupid as to mix with the likes of Yamaguchi? Don't you know what he is? I hope that Astuo's death and what I have been through shall forever haunt your damn Honbu!"

"I am finished with Yamaguchi and the yakuza," Kobayashi rasped.

Until the next time, Ishihara thought. He said, "We can't bring Astuo back, Yasmin. Sensei would never have allowed that either of you went to Hong Kong had he known about the drugs and the Triads. You must believe that."

Tears dripped onto Yasmin's lap.

Ishihara continued, "We must look to the future. I think we have all learned from this." He walked across and stroked her hair. "It is behind us, now. Let us look ahead, Yasmin."

Kobayashi focused his vision on the briefcases. "I shall tell Yamaguchi-San to collect his money."

"Proposed with admirable timing," Vargas said and sat down on the couch. "We must not forget that Yamaguchi is the rightful owner of an expensive pilot case. I could not bear the thought of not returning it."

Ishihara smiled. A flash of life showed in Yasmin's eyes.

"What's funny?" Kobayashi said.

Yasmin ran her fingers through her long black hair. "It is empty."

"Almost," Vargas said.

Kobayashi raised his shoulders. He got closer to his desk. "What is going on?"

"Not much," Vargas said. "Just call Yamaguchi and ask him to collect his leather. Under no circumstances will any of us go over there."

"Where is the money?"

"Where it ought to be."

"You took the money?"

"*Took* it?" Vargas looked crestfallen. "Sensei, Sensei—what's got into you. Can you not remember what I said to your former sleeping partner? One hundred percent interest, I promised. Not much room for a misunderstanding, I'd say. Not with Yamaguchi."

"Misunderstanding what?"

"My intentions. Clearly, nobody in his right mind could possibly have expected me to get involved without taking an interest; a one hundred percent interest, as it were, and well deserved, in retrospect. This is pure logic, Sensei. Do not forget that Yamaguchi is accessory to murder, for which he will not be indicted, and that his personal little realm is still functioning without repercussions. What is a touch of distress caused by having to pay a finder's fee in comparison? Actually," he went on, "everything considered, a hundred percent is ridiculously cheap, but that's me."

"You will be dead within two days," Kobayashi said with a mixture of disbelief and awe.

"I don't think so. By the way, the case is not entirely empty." Vargas rose, picked up the case and went across to the desk. He opened the lid and turned the case upside-down. A parcel fell with a thump a few inches from Kobayashi's fingers.

"What is it?"

"A gift."

Kobayashi had always taken a childlike delight in gifts, but his hands did not move. "A gift?"

"That's right. From me to you, Sensei. Open it."

Kobayashi hesitated. Then he began to unwrap the paper. He stopped when he saw the brown spots on the non-transparent sheet of plastic. "What is it?" he repeated.

"Greetings from Hong Kong. Don't be overmodest, Sensei."

Kobayashi pinched a corner flip and pulled. Yasmin looked away. Ishihara stared at the strangely twisted hand on the desk.

"It used to belong to a gentleman called Herbert," Vargas explained softly. "His real name was Wu Tak Hoi. He won't need it any more. As of yesterday, the Chinese heaven has been greatly enriched by the arrival of Herbert and three of his soulmates."

Kobayashi dropped the sheet faster than he'd grabbed it. His lips moved, but no words came out.

Vargas continued, "Herbert was one of Limpy-Ho's trusted lieutenants, an urbane and sophisticated young man known for taking great pleasure in the slow demise of other people. He wasn't as charismatic as Limpy, but definitely a devoted and conscientious disciple. A bit too impressed with himself, as luck has it, but then, few are perfect."

Kobayashi squinted and puffed out his cheeks. "What am I supposed to do with it?"

"Put it in a jar of formaldehyde and look at it with love and affection each time the thought of your new Honbu crosses your mind."

Kobayashi put his chair in recline and folded his arms. "There is a vicious streak in you, Angelo-San."

Vargas smiled. "That observation is the prerogative of the Japanese. You are only a Korean." He looked at Ishihara who was busy cleaning his fingernails. "Anyway, before you go to bed tonight, Sensei, remember to thank your entire army of gods for whatever your hunch is telling you I consist of. Also, if you are really lucky, your daughter may be willing to substantiate the depths and the validity of your remarkable intuition. Thereafter, thank her, as well."

Yasmin jolted in her chair. She looked wide-eyed at Vargas. He touched her shoulder. "Do not worry. My discretion supersedes my cruelty and even Sensei's indisputable knowledge of the human interior. I would have liked to say *soul*, but that is an esoteric conception and therefore beyond our catatonic Sensei."

Ishihara looked up. There was no mistaking the acrimony in Vargas' voice. Kobayashi seemed perplexed and fixed his stare on the contorted hand in front of him. Yasmin fought the shine in her eyes and shook her head as if to stop the tears from getting any further.

Ishihara said, "Angelo, leave Tokyo. Yamaguchi will find you if you don't. There is no safe place anywhere in the city."

Vargas stretched his arms horizontally. For a few seconds he did not move. Then he said, "I'll call you tomorrow."

He left.

Four weeks later, on a Wednesday, Vargas was back. The following Friday, around midnight, Yamaguchi was rushed from his favourite restaurant to the nearest hospital where he died in agony within a few hours. It appeared he had eaten something that disagreed with him.

On the Saturday, before sunrise, an early bird of a salaryman found Sadayuki Watanabe lying in a narrow side street. There were no signs of violence. The police informed his family that the expression on the deceased's face, a mixture of fear and surprise, was quite common when people suffered a sudden coronary attack.

Yasmin showed no emotions when Ishihara told her that he and Vargas were leaving. Her countenance revealed only half-hearted interest when he added that he would come back for her.

"Why?" she said. "What for?"

But Ishihara had prepared himself, and he stuck to his script. "For you," he said. "I would like you to come with me even if by then I have yet to settle."

"Could you be a bit more categorical?" she said with an appropriate blend of weariness and detachment.

Ishihara wanted to gnash his teeth. "I think we belong together."

"You *think?*"

"I feel. I know."

"That's better. See you, sometime in the future."

She walked away.

My wife to be, Ishihara thought; confident as a tigress, gracious as a gazelle and benign as a tarantula. It will be quite a marriage.

They had given themselves plenty of time. Ishihara was elated; he had problems keeping still and investigated even the most trivial little shop as he raided the terminal from one end to the other.

Vargas followed. There was no visible enthusiasm.

"Don't you ever get excited?" Ishihara challenged.

"No."

"But the whole place is buzzing. All these people travelling to whichever destination. I find it exhilarating."

"I can see that. Let's find the lounge. I am getting thirsty." He looked out the window. "All those years…" he mumbled as if talking to himself.

"What about them?"

"Nothing."

Ishihara lifted his glass. "Cheers. To a long, happy and fruitful life. Our apprenticeship is over. At long last are we ready to become the masters of our trade."

"The best," Vargas saluted, deadpanned.

Ishihara never narrowed his eyes except when he tried to avoid looking irate or embarrassed. "We leave a lot of memories behind," he said and attempted to look absentminded.

"No, we don't. We take them with us."

"You know what I mean."

"I know that you feel bad about walking out on Sensei and his prodigious plans. That is the way you see it, however misconstrued. I also know how you feel about leaving Yasmin behind."

Ishihara stared at his glass as if it contained a fourth dimension. "I did talk to her. I said that I would come back for her. It won't change anything as far as you and I are concerned," he added quickly.

"You just want a cosy little family life. Someone to look after you."

"Most people think that's normal."

"No doubt she'll wait faithfully for the return of her knight in shining armour."

Ishihara's eyes clouded over. "You know Yasmin. She didn't exactly make a farewell scene."

"I am stunned. You intend to keep your vow?"

"Of course I do. You know what she means to me."

Vargas measured his almost empty glass. "A sensible decision. Not in a million years will you find another Yasmin."

Ishihara's gaze drifted. The ringing in his ears reached his temples. "Would you like another drink?"

He came back, put the glasses down and said, "Still a mite melancholy?"

"Pensive."

A bit more than that, Ishihara thought. "You never found the one in a million, did you?"

The expression on Vargas' face was neither sullen nor humorous. "She would have to be the equivalent of Yasmin. Long odds, I'd say."

"Why shouldn't there be another Yasmin, somewhere? It is not like you to be pessimistic."

"Pessimistic? Only a hardhearted tart or a snow-white saint would consider living with me. The first I don't want, and the latter is in short supply."

328

"Yasmin is neither."

"No, but I was around when she grew up. No mature woman would allow herself that span of time trying to establish the potential existence of compatibility. The moment she learned about my past she would find herself in a permanent state of emotional paralysis, and the only way she could recover would be to wave the relationship goodbye. I admire your spawning imagination, but no woman of exceptional quality can accept what I am. Infatuation is a short-lived phenomenon and without substance."

"Supposing you find your goddess, why tell her more than she needs to know?"

Vargas showed his teeth. There was no sign of glee elsewhere on his face. He said, "Because I am naïve, however prosaic this observation may echo in your semi-idealistic mind. You cannot have a fulfilling relationship based on deceit and stealth. That is a contradiction, an absurdity and a recipe for disaster." He picked some peanuts, but kept them in his hand. "So, you see, Tadashi, I have well and truly cornered myself. I have yet to relinquish my little dream of finding my shrine, but you must agree I am walking on pretty thin ice. Exciting, yes, but not particularly soothing."

Ishihara knew there was little he could add that did not sound hollow or insincere. He said, "Life goes on. Let us take it as it comes."

"Amen."

"I wonder how many terminals we'll pass through during the next few years."

"One is one too many."

"Oh, come on, Angelo. Cheer up. One day we will retire and then we can sit in peace and harmony and cherish the memories of a wandering life."

"The terminal terminus."

"What was that?"

"Nothing of profound significance. Just a thought playing with itself."

"Do you associate a terminal with something in particular?"

"Void," Vargas said. "The state of being nowhere. You know what you are leaving behind, but not what awaits. Void."

Ishihara looked at his watch. Vargas was clearly in one of his more abstruse moods. There was no point in getting contaminated.

A gong chimed. Ishihara listened intently. "That's our plane."

They approached their seats. Ishihara said, "Would you like the window?"

"I prefer the aisle."

The smile did not escape Ishihara. He stared at the lights from the boats and the ships on Tokyo Bay, the sea smoky grey and the wing of the aircraft glinting like moonbeams on polished steel. The thin, flaming horizon over the city met the clouds, and the contours of Mount Fuji closed behind the mist on his eyes.

☞

The big candle had almost burned down. It flickered, now and then, but the flame stayed alive and cast eerie shadows on the walls. Somewhere a clock tolled three times. The only other sound was the occasional uneasy squeaking of the woodwork.

Parkhurst was wide awake, barely aware of the cramp in his legs and the stiffness in his neck.

Only when he sensed that Ishihara had finished his story did Parkhurst notice that he had hardly touched his cognac. He wanted a sip, but he had no wish to break the spell still lingering. Maybe there was more to come, even if the body language from Ishihara indicated that such was not the case.

Ishihara yawned and covered his face with both hands. "There you have it," he said, stretching his arms and legs. "Now you know how Mr. Vargas and I met, how we became brothers."

Plus a bit more, Parkhurst thought. He raised his glass. "Thank you for your confidence in me. I find your story incredibly interesting. Most unusual, I should add, really captivating." And what *raw material*, he contemplated, momentarily forgetting that the writer in him was slumbering like The Sleeping Beauty with the prince even faster asleep.

"I am glad," Ishihara said. He did not specify what pleased him. He covered another yawn. "Now I shall need my beauty sleep." He got to his feet with no sign of fatigue and blew out the candle.

Parkhurst heaved himself up from his chair. "One thing," he said tentatively, "maybe I missed it, but this idea of yours, you know—the embassies, Mr. Vargas' participation, the plan you conceived and developed…"

"Oh, that," Ishihara said indifferently. "It's just a lucrative way of making an interesting living. Certain transactions on the international stage can be potentially sensitive, as you know, delicate, even. There are cases when governments choose to distance themselves from the inevitable implications following a given decision and thereby requiring the assistance of a neutral hand. A niche market, one can say, necessitating discretion and certain advanced skills in the handling of such transactions."

"It all sound fairly clandestine to me."

"It is. When did any one country ever enjoy open government? A contradiction of terms, I dare say." Ishihara smiled amicably. "Are you forgetting your own predicament, Igor? Even a banal little concoction like the one you are caught up in bears witness of how these chaps work. Cloak-and-dagger isn't part of their life, it *is* their life. A universal phenomenon, I am afraid. In that respect, there is no distinction between democracies and tyrannies."

"That is true," Parkhurst said. "Yes, even in my case, however trite and cockamamie." He shrugged. "I suffer, and you benefit. Vive la difference."

Ishihara laughed. "Conclusion—life is a bitch. Don't wake me up. See you whenever."

Ishihara came down half past ten in the morning. He made a cup of coffee and declined breakfast. Parkhurst had been up for an hour; he had not slept too well, and it showed under his eyes. The rest of his face looked as if two armies of angry ants had made it their battleground during the night.

Ishihara opened a couple of windows and did his breathing exercises.

Parkhurst said, "It is nice to greet a cheerful man. You obviously had no problems sleeping through the night."

"I never have. A peaceful rest comes natural to an undefiled and innocent heart. No inducement needed."

"That is good to hear."

Ishihara rolled a sugar cube between his cheeks. He sucked for a while. "I find the smell of muck invigorating. Do you think there's a psychological clue, somewhere? I must give it some thought."

What is he up to, Parkhurst mused.

Ishihara said, "Start preparing, Igor—*today*. I shall be back in a week's time."

Parkhurst steadied his mug with his left hand. "Preparing for what?"

"For the re-launch of your career."

"I have explained to you that I have got nothing more to give. It wasn't a joke, Tadashi. I wish it was, but it isn't."

"I disagree. You can if you want to."

"Excuse my intransigence, but I'm afraid that my opinion is the only one that counts." He pressed his back harder against the wall. The ceiling had begun to move.

"Sit down," Ishihara said. "You don't look too well." He watched as Parkhurst made his way across to the table and said, "Defeatism is the dubious privilege of the semi-illiterate section of our society, which, in round figures, constitutes roughly ninety-eight percent of the population. You are a member of the *elite*. You have a moral obligation to hoist your brain up from your ass and use your creativity. The only valid excuses for not doing so are death and senility. Am I reasonably clear, Igor?"

"I appreciate what you are trying to do," Parkhurst said. He made an effort to smile away his deep-rooted feeling of tiredness and dejection. "Let us not fool ourselves. I have not got it any more."

"Burnt out?"

"Yes, however much I detest the thought."

Ishihara said, "We have established that you abhor your status as a has-been; self-appointed, but nevertheless. Is it your intention to die a bitter and reprobate old man? Is it your ambition to spend the autumn of your life in a vegetative state? Do you prefer to live your remaining years as someone that nobody wants to see because no one enjoys the company of a wasted talent wallowing in self-pity?" The look in Ishihara's eyes was distant, as if he was reluctantly confronting a long-forgotten dream. His voice was flat when he said, "There is a difference between a set-back and being burnt out."

Parkhurst took off his glasses and began to polish them with the wet paper towel.

"That is theoretically correct, but…"

"Forget your *buts*." Ishihara's eyes were bright, but not from humour. "I have made up my mind. I know *what* you are going to do, *where* to do it and *when* to do it. You have got three weeks to prepare yourself."

"Would it be too much to tell me what you are talking about?"

"Oxford Union."

"Now, that is *really* amusing."

"There we are, again. Instant enthusiasm."

Parkhurst tried to catch Ishihara's eyes, but the Japanese was busy watching a lone and timorous fly.

"You cannot be serious. That is—that is insane!"

"Is it?"

"Assuming I have a theme, which I have not, those youngsters will tear me apart. It is out of question. Five years ago, perhaps, but not today."

Ishihara bounced his fists on the table. "I don't believe this! Am I being asked to accept that your mind has lost its teeth when I *know* that such is not the case? Am I supposed to swallow that the richly fragmented mushroom thriving in the darkness of your skull has withered into total lethe overnight? I am doing my best to be kind, but it does upset me to be subjected to the stench of bile condensed in a gormless jerk who seemingly loves rolling around in a filthy dungeon of moronic smugness." He picked up a biro and snapped it in two. There were yellow sparks in his eyes. "A few more minutes of this, Igor, and I am inclined to concede that your intellectual cornucopia followed the vortex of your financial collapse."

The web of lines on Parkhurst's face exuded shock and horror. He raised his hands as if to defend himself. His voice sank to a hoarse whisper. "There is no need to be virulent. I plead with you to understand that the well has run dry. You know this—I mean, what you said is the truth. I am in all respects an indigent old man; financially, physically, mentally and probably also morally."

Ishihara rolled his eyes. "Back to square one," he muttered. "What am I doing here? Why am I wasting my precious time in the company of an insipid, spineless, degenerate and stinking old turd who hasn't even got the guts to wipe his own ass? I had everything arranged. Three weeks from today, and your comeback would have been a fact. What do I get in return? I get whimpering sobs from a shrunken, ignominious and repugnant imitation of an impervious prick. Good Lord! What have I done to deserve stumbling over this crawling piece of carrion? Why am I cursed with the acquaintance of a goofball whose quotient of moral fibre cannot be detected under a microscope?" He sighed and looked gloomily at his host. "What a pitiful little wanker you are. However much it hurts me, I shall accept that you mentally have committed *hara-kiri*. Why don't you go upstairs and swallow a bottle of cyanide? I'll pay for the funeral."

Ishihara kicked his chair back and left the table. "Kindly excuse me, but I have got better things to do. This is too harrowing. I shall now leave this birthplace of equivocation and iniquity."

Parkhurst pushed out his tongue and left it between his lips for a moment. He looked up. "That was not very nice," he said. "That was awful and ugly."

"Truth is, on occasions. As a matter of fact, there is nothing *like* the naked truth, provided that you know what it is and how to handle it."

Parkhurst pushed his cup to the side and rested his forehead on the table. His fingers were buried in his grey and unruly mane. "What do I talk about?" he whispered.

Ishihara sat down. "You talk about the sweet taste of life," he said. "I shall be back within a week." He grinned. "Don't worry, Igor. We will give those little prats something that'll make their testicles pop out from their ears."

"There'll be women there, as well," Parkhurst mumbled. He hoped that such a revelation would somehow prolong Ishihara's stay.

"You'll make them float on their pussies."

Ishihara left his cigar in the ashtray and went upstairs.

Parkhurst walked outside and stood under the big oak tree at the end of the lawn. He could see his farm-gate from there.

It had rained during the early hours of the morning, but the sun had broken through the putty-coloured clouds speckled with a tinge of charcoal and magnolia. The raindrops hung like miniature Easter eggs from the leaves.

He saw the Mercedes wait for a tractor to pass, and then it was gone.

Ishihara's words about moral fibres had hit Parkhurst's brain like blows from an ice pick. No, he thought, I am not a crawling piece of carrion; I am a man who has proved himself in the past and who once again is going to walk tall and with his head held high. I shall accept Ishihara's helping hand and dig deep and give this opportunity everything I have got. I shall forever more believe in myself and in my forthcoming era of *rank fecundity*.

The undoing of Igor Parkhurst is a sophism but his re-birth is not.

He watched a squirrel running along the rails of the paddock. It stopped with its tail held high and a pair of little brown eyes twinkled in the morning light.

Parkhurst nodded respectfully and strode up to the house with his hands on his back and his gaze towards the peacock blue sky.

14

Parkhurst was pleased and relieved when the telephone rang.
Since Ishihara's departure, the feeling of fear and timidity had augmented and become almost unbearable. Once again Parkhurst faced problems by admitting that Ishihara was right; without a bold and eye-catching resurgence, life would slowly disintegrate. On the other hand, was a busted comeback better than none?

It was easy for Ishihara to say that unconditional surrender was tantamount to intellectual suicide; it was *he*, Igor Parkhurst, who had to meet the audience eye to eye, and it was *he* who had to live with the consequences of defeat, of his second and ultimate downfall.

He still had no idea of what to talk about; not a single topic had emerged, and he could not shake off a feeling of anguish closing in on panic. Ishihara had promised to help; surely the imaginative Japanese would produce a string of cue words enough to spin a reasonably attractive yarn, handsomely decorated with borders of catching embroidery, but it wasn't Ishihara who had to glue it all together, and it wasn't he who had to *deliver*.

With a degree of self-control that surprised him, Parkhurst managed to stay off the cognac until late afternoon. For the second time, he read John Osborne's *Look Back in Anger*, Colin Wilson's *The Outsider* and Kingsley Amis' *Lucky Jim*.

I was better than these chaps, he thought; my books showed a deeper understanding of the human psyche and my talent for satire were unsurpassed.

Was. Showed. Was. Past tense.

He read Boris Pasternak's *Doctor Zhivago* and found it shallow and melodramatic. He plodded through Jack Kerouac's *On the Road* and

336

wondered if Kerouac's writing was an omen for things to come in literature.

In between, one or two formless ideas surfaced, like the fin of a shark searching for its prey and then quickly disappearing long before he could get an image of what was lurking beneath.

Or maybe it was only a mirage; there wasn't really anything moving around—it was just a minor flash of wishful thinking.

His nights were short, intercepted with bouts of heavy perspiration and nightmares he could not remember the next morning. The first cup of coffee was a boon, but the second activated the chemicals consumed the night before.

A week, Ishihara had said, and still three days to go.

On the fifth day, the telephone rang.

Parkhurst got up faster than his constitution allowed. He heaved for breath for a while before he walked towards the most ingenious, useful and philanthropic of all inventions. It *had* to be Ishihara. He'd probably changed his mind and would like to come earlier.

Parkhurst cleared his croaky voice and lifted up the receiver. "Hello," he said, acutely aware of the tension gripping his jaw muscles.

"Hello, Uncle Igor. It is Jennifer. How are you?"

Not Ishihara. Still, it was a human voice.

"Eh—fine, my dear. I am very well indeed. How are you?"

He thought the line had gone dead. "Jennifer?"

"I am here." Again, there was a moment of silence. "I could have been better."

"What is wrong, Jennifer?"

"I need someone to talk to."

Don't we all, Parkhurst thought. He said, "Any time, Jennifer. You know that."

"Yes, I do. Can I come now?"

"But of course you can."

"I'll see you in a couple of hours," she said. The strain in her voice was unmistakable. She hung up.

Parkhurst stood for a while with the receiver in his hand. No clues, he thought, not as much as a vague hint. The voice didn't even sound like Jennifer's; she was always so calm, composed and in control.

Conor had said that Jennifer was like a quiet stream; no one could really tell the secrets and the mysteries held in the depths of its waters.

There was no point in trying to guess the nature of her problem. Soon he'd know and he would help if he could.

Jennifer wore jeans, a black sweater and a pair of thick-soled boots. There was no trace of make-up on her face. Her hair had lost some of its gloss. Her movements were not as agile and light as usual. The twinkle in here eyes was forced.

She stared at Parkhurst. "You look awful, Uncle Igor."

"I know," he confessed with a grin. "Believe me, I avoid mirrors whenever I can."

"When did you last shave?"

Parkhurst touched his jaws and missed her eyes. "Three or four days ago. Maybe five."

She gave him a hug. "Don't let yourself go, Uncle Igor."

Shame swept through Parkhurst. He had not had a bath, either, for five days. He knew he was reeking from body odour blended with garlic and cognac. "Listen," he said, "I'll go and have a shave and a shower. You make some coffee, and I'll be down in fifteen minutes."

Her lips moved. No, he thought, that is not a Jennifer smile. She said, "Positive thinking."

He smiled. "Why wasn't I blessed with a woman like you?" He saw the strain on her face. What did I touch, he thought—who, rather than what, is the core of your problem?

Parkhurst came down twenty minutes later, all refreshed; doused with after-shave and his thick, grey curls still moist and shining.

Jennifer sat at the kitchen table. She was smoking a cigarette. She looked apprehensive and stared through the smoke out the window.

Such a beautiful face, Parkhurst thought, but not a happy one. What on earth was wrong? He had never seen Jennifer depressed or morose. Quiet, yes, but not dejected.

It was ironic. Here he was, in desperate need for someone to communicate with, to confide in and to seek comfort from. He was at his lowest, and the future, immediate and long-term, frightened him.

And there was Jennifer, in exactly the same predicament, or so it appeared.

"I've got a problem," she said. She did not move.

"Do you recognize the nature of your problem?"

"I do."

"Recognizing a problem is halfway to solution. Pardon the cliché, but it is true."

She turned and faced him. "I need advice, Uncle Igor," she said quietly. "I do not need clichés and I do not need hollow bits of superficial consolation."

"I am sorry," he mumbled. "I meant to be constructive."

The aggression went from her eyes. "I know you did. It's just that— that I have never felt so helpless and confused in all my life."

Oh dear, he thought, this must be serious. Jennifer was his beloved goddaughter. She needed him. He was going to be there for her.

He put the flat of his hands on the table and straightened his shoulders. "Talk to me."

Her head sagged to the side. She tried to smile, but her lips quivered. "It is a man," she said, and stopped.

Parkhurst put on his glasses. "What happened?"

A sigh vibrated across the table. "Nothing."

"Nothing? I do not understand. Oh, I see," he added, "I think I follow."

Jennifer looked down.

"You are in love," he said.

She fiddled with the ashtray. "It is worse than that," she said in a husky voice. "I think I love him."

Good grief, Parkhurst thought, which way is this going?

"Is it not being reciprocated?" he asked gently.

"I don't know. I can't tell. The problem is…"

"—yes?"

"Who he is."

The more I hear, the less I like it, Parkhurst thought. "Do I know who this gentleman is?"

Jennifer's laughter was brief and nervous. "Angelo Vargas."

Oh Christ, Parkhurst thought. The blood in his veins had gone from cold to frozen. "You mean, Mr. Ishihara's friend?"

"How many Angelo Vargas' are there?"

One too many, Parkhurst reflected. He said, "You have kept this to yourself, haven't you?"

"Nobody knows. That includes my parents. It probably also includes Mr. Vargas." She looked away. "I do not know what he knows. I do not know what he thinks, and I do not know who he is."

Some relationship, Parkhurst mused. He put his hand over hers. "You are attracted to him." Yes, that was pretty obvious, but he couldn't think of anything else to say.

"I can't get him out of my mind. I see him and I hear his voice when he is not around. At present, that is twenty-four hours a day."

"He is away?"

"I don't know. I am avoiding him, and he does not call me."

This sounds like trench warfare, Parkhurst concluded. "Why are you avoiding him?"

She focused on the window. A dove shattered the silence. Parkhurst squeezed her hand. She said, "Somebody told me something about him."

Here we go, Parkhurst thought. This can only get worse. "You want to talk about it?"

For a long while, Jennifer neither moved nor spoke. The expression on her face changed from worried to resigned. Parkhurst knew better than to push her. He waited patiently.

Finally, Jennifer began. Initially, she searched for words and corrected herself a few times on the chronological sequence of events, but, gradually, Parkhurst got the story from the day when she first cast her eyes on Angelo Vargas and up to what Ahmed had told her. She omitted any mentioning of their physical relationship. This, Parkhurst understood and respected. Anything else would have been out of character for Jennifer.

Parkhurst took his hand away. He could feel the tightness of his skin around his nose and eyes. *Now* what do I say, he thought. I can't gloss it over, but neither am I prepared to condemn it out of hand. That would be inappropriate, counterproductive, moralistic and, in the final analysis, utterly unhelpful. It does not matter what I personally think of Mr. Vargas. He looked at Jennifer's pale face and touched her chin with the back of his hand.

She said, "How can I condone what he did?"

"Jennifer," he began and kept his voice close to a whisper, "we all have a tendency to sit in our ivory towers dishing out assorted fragments of moralism, securely disconnected from what we are viewing, and with no personal experience of the predicament in question."

She stared at him with an expression of innocence, as if she had just woken up from a peaceful dream. "You really mean that, don't you?"

"Yes, I do. I cannot discard from my mind how *I* would have felt were I Ahmed and it was *my* daughter standing in the corner."

She closed her eyes.

"Succour is a rare quality," Parkhurst continued quietly. "Most people turn their heads and walk away."

She said in a low voice, "And yet, he does not come across as a savage." The look behind the glimmer was distant.

"On the contrary," Parkhurst said. "I seem to recall him as a polite, quiet and rather soft-spoken gentleman." Please, God, he prayed silently, do not ever let her know about Tokyo and Hong Kong.

"Nothing adds up," she said and rested her forehead against the palm of her hands. "I wonder if I am in denial. I am confused." She looked up. "What do you know about him?"

Oh no, Parkhurst thought, I did not hear that. He hid his feeling of alarm by walking across the kitchen. He opened a window at the far end. The wind whispered sweetly through the foliage of the Japanese maple tree and the sun caught a fatigued leaf in the slow dance towards its final resting-place.

"It is such a nice day," he said. "Shall we go for a stroll?"

He turned. Jennifer had not changed her position. She said, "You must know *something*."

"Honestly, I have met Mr. Vargas—what is it—twice? No—once. We didn't say a word to each other. Believe me," he added and made his voice stronger, "he has never volunteered one single detail about himself." And that is the truth, he thought, if only indirectly.

"What about Mr. Ishihara?"

"What about him?"

"You have seen a bit of him, haven't you? Or doesn't he talk, either?" She raised her head. There was a different look in her eyes; defiant, then demanding. "That is not exactly the way I remember him."

Catastrophe looming, Parkhurst thought. How in God's name do I get out of this one? He felt flushed and the rate of his heartbeat had gone up.

She said, "My intuition is telling me that you know something. I am equally confident that you would not hide anything from me. I also know that you would never lie to me." There was no softness in her voice when she went on, "I need all the help I can get. You are the only one who can provide it."

Parkhurst did not bother to nod. He could no longer escape relating Ishihara's story, and relate it accurately. The Japanese had not been reluctant to talk about Vargas and himself. He had not requested confidentiality. Ishihara knew what he was doing and, Parkhurst suspected, so did Vargas.

A jolt of elation came from nowhere and hit him like an ample measure of cognac on an empty stomach. I am facing a blessing in disguise here, he thought; if Jennifer still harbours a shade of hope about a future with Angelo Vargas, surely Ishihara's story would effectively extinguish any lingering flame and naïve illusions about the man's character and true nature? What a divine little twist. She would get over it, in time. Not for a while, but the facts would speak for themselves and time would heal. Eventually.

"Shall we go for a walk, Jennifer?"

The air was crisp and carried the scent of autumn. The leaves of the chestnut trees blushed as the sun rose higher and the breeze became a faint whisper through the branches.

Jennifer did not seem to notice. She walked with her hands in her pockets and her eyes to the ground. Once in a while she brushed her hair from her face.

Parkhurst's exceptional memory made him repeat Ishihara's narrative almost verbatim, nothing added, and nothing deducted. He kept his voice neutral, but he could feel his tension building up and he spoke more slowly when he came to what had taken place in Hong Kong. He paused following the get-together at The Peninsula hotel; a sense of weariness and exhaustion came over him, and Jennifer's silence added to his anguish. He glanced at her from the corner of his eyes. Suddenly, she stopped.

"Can we sit down?" she said and nodded towards the trunk of a fallen tree.

"I could do with a rest," he answered with a strained smile. The worst was over as far as his knowledge of Angelo Vargas was concerned. Now it remained to be seen how Jennifer would stand up to what she had learned about the love of her life. Parkhurst could not imagine a more devastating way of squashing her infatuation. He had seen too much in life to find it strange that women got themselves attracted to a feral, half-polished atavism like Vargas, but Jennifer would see daylight. She would, ultimately, acknowledge that her world was a universe away from his. Being in love with love was one thing. Pursuing happiness in the midst of a primitive and pitiless jungle was something entirely different. She would come around.

"You have not finished," she said.

Parkhurst undid the buttons on his jacket. He was getting warm. He picked a flower and twirled it between his fingers. He kept looking at the white and purple colours when he took up the story from where he'd left it. When he came to the very end—the aeroplane leaving Japan—he removed his cap and wiped his face.

Jennifer sat with her shoulders hunched.

He said, "I am so sorry, Jennifer. I wish there had been another story to tell."

He saw no reaction, and he could not hear her breathe. He stifled a sigh. He wanted to stroke her head and say something that would alleviate her pain, but all he could feel was emptiness mingled with compassion and sadness. He wished he had brought along his little silver flask with cognac.

"He wanted me to know," she said.

Yes, Parkhurst thought, I'll credit him that much. Ishihara had his permission to tell—or, more likely, had been *asked* to tell, like the Palestinian. I may have underestimated Mr. Vargas' subtlety—or perhaps his wisdom blended with a dash of integrity. Who can tell? There's nothing stranger than the human mind.

"I agree. He wanted you to know."

"He is still looking for his shrine."

Aren't we all, Parkhurst pondered wearily, but that does not make him a person worthy of you.

"A woman of Yasmin's calibre," Jennifer said. She straightened her back and stared at the blue and cloudless sky. "Tell me about marriage, Uncle Igor."

Parkhurst gaped. "Marriage?"

"Yes. You know more about the subject than most, don't you?"

He laughed. "My girl, I was a complete and utter failure, a total disaster. I have got three ex-wives to verify it."

"You were the only one to blame in all three cases?"

"Well—no, but I know I wasn't easy to live with."

Parkhurst turned his mind inside out trying to find an explanation—how come she was all of a sudden so relaxed and rational? Where did this serenity come from, and why? Had she not fully comprehended what he had told her? No, that was unthinkable. Shock, perhaps. And, if so, when and how would the reaction manifest itself—Parkhurst's throat dried up.

She said, "That's why I want to know. Not everybody can expect to be as lucky as my parents."

"To the extent that luck comes into it." Then he caught on. "Oh, I see," he smiled, "you want to learn about compatibility. A good question. I have wondered, myself, many a time; is compatibility something that is either present, or, if not, on the outset, can it be achieved? I wish I knew."

She returned his smile. She no longer looked ashen and gaunt. The vibration was back in her voice, and there was life in her green eyes. Parkhurst was relieved, and he was apprehensive. The change in her was inexplicable.

He said, "Few marriages should last longer than ten years, since thereafter the two cell-mates have little or nothing to say to each other. Beyond that span, our holy wedlock requires more effort than most people are prepared to invest. The physical attraction is on the wane and there is no longer much to explore. Excitement has been replaced by ennui. Communication has degenerated from interesting to trivial and become essentially meaningless. Body, mind and emotions; nothing is perpetual, everything wears out and becomes stagnant before it all fades into oblivion."

"An alluring picture. I'll frame it."

Parkhurst rubbed the corners of his mouth with his thumbs and continued, "It begins with a bio-chemical reaction and ends with isolation. Apart from children, where such dubious godsends exist, the only two common factors preventing total detachment are television and supermarkets. Nothing can rekindle the flame of earlier days, and still there are those who do not see the sanity in getting divorced."

"Bar insanity, what keeps them together?"

"Badly digested delusions, like fear of loneliness passing for loyalty. Dread of financial upheaval and economic insecurity purposely camouflaged behind a fog referred to as common sense. Misconstrued concern for children. The path of least resistance neatly covered with little golden petals described with tumid magnanimity as a potpourri of affection, devotion and—most apt—sweet nothing. Mechanical adaptations consciously confused with tokens of endearment. It is pathetic, simply lamentable and absurd. Love makes blind, as generations have observed before us, and when sight is restored, deafness takes over. Shall I go on?"

"You should re-marry. With all that insight, how can you go wrong?"

"An alchemist knows more about gold than I know about marital felicity."

"How does one avoid all those pitfalls?"

"Ask your parents."

"Don't be so negative."

"Even my children hate me."

"Your children live in a selfish little world, grossly obsessed with themselves."

"Why do you ask all these questions?"

"I am picking your brain and milking your experience."

"There is not much point in having experience if you do not know how to change and take advantage of it."

"You wouldn't be feeling sorry for yourself, now?"

"Possibly. You know, if—no, forget it." Parkhurst patted his stomach and watched a kestrel hovering over a row of hawthorns.

"Tell me."

Parkhurst's laughter came as a short series of grunts. "My brain is telling me that age is but an irrelevant concept of time, and that nothing is more natural than seeing the roaring flames of the mind and the soul taper off, slowly diminishing and turning to ember and ash as midnight gets closer. Still, you can't help thinking back on what *could* have been. All you are left with is a myriad of memories, most of them tinged with discontent, and a future more insecure and shorter than the past ever was."

Jennifer got up. "You sound like a dried-up old misanthrope. Is that the way you want me to remember you?"

He put his hands on the tree trunk as if to push himself up. "I am sorry for this mental cul-de-sac. I did not mean it that way. And I am not dead, yet," he added with a vigour that made him feel comfortable.

"Good, and that is what you should tell yourself every morning when you wake up."

She walked over to a small brook nearby and stopped at the edge of the water. She bent down, splashed her face and dried her hands on the grass. "You don't approve of Angelo Vargas, do you?" she said.

Parkhurst did not hesitate. "You can't overlook that he is a killer, Jennifer, a killer and an anachronism. He may be well read and have interesting opinions and be worth listening to—I grant you all that—but my question is, how can you—*you*—expect to find harmony, devotion and everlasting affection with and from such a man?"

Gently, she put a leaf on the rippling water and watched as it danced gracefully away. "You were less condemning a while ago."

"All right—so there were mitigating circumstances in between, but, basically, that does not make much of a difference. You called me a misanthrope, but compared with him I am naivety personified. His opinion of mankind does not exactly cling to the clouds."

"He told Yasmin that I've got class. What does he mean?"

"How do I know what he means? Why don't you ask him?"

"It is not that simple."

Evidently not, Parkhurst thought.

"Think," she said.

"Class comes from the heart. Nobody without kindness, consideration and generosity of heart can lay claim to having class—that's the way I see it. I also believe that anybody who feels a need to make such a claim for themselves hasn't got it and does not know what it is."

"Thank you. That sums it up?"

Igor Parkhurst raised his gaze towards a few white clouds drifting by, the rays from the sun shining through like lucid sheets of white satin. "No, not entirely," he said. "To me, class and grace make femininity complete. Many of today's women consider grace undesirable because they for some reason believe that it is not compatible with what they perceive as equality and emancipation. How wrong they are, sacrificing this noble blend of qualities for *appearance*. Who are they trying to impress? Remove the esoteric aura and you are left with a female who is void of enigma. She has deprived herself of the glamour and the magnetism that makes her a genuine *class act*. No level of intelligence, education, position or status can replace the sublime and radiant effect of true refinement." He eyed a rabbit jumping a ditch and smiled. "Those who can but do not try to reach this level are committing a crime against their own gender."

"Do you believe that Angelo Vargas shares your viewpoint?"

How the hell can *I* tell? Parkhurst thought. He said, "That is of course possible."

"Thank you."

Good grace, Parkhurst thought, she is besotted with this chap, helplessly intoxicated. He thought of what Conor had said about his daughter and the depths of her character, but not even *he* could have envisaged that somewhere inside Jennifer there was a hunger for the incomprehensible; a relationship with a man of Angelo Vargas' disposition.

"I hope you know what you are doing, Jennifer."

"Only I can answer that question."

"Can you?"

"Not yet," she said and looked away. She felt as if rime was covering her irises and her tongue severely bitten by frost. Uncle Igor had been helpful, in his own clumsy way, but it was the old story; nobody could make somebody else's decision. It had not been a waste of time, listening, but she should have known.

They walked back. Parkhurst told her about Ishihara's recent visit. She nodded and patted Parkhurst on the back when he slipped the word *comeback* into his monologue and gleefully described Ishihara's merciless insistence.

She returned to London late in the evening.

Two sleepless nights, and Jennifer knew that she had to make a move. Jesus, she thought, I need this like Cromwell needed advice on cruelty.

She had been presented with a picture of Angelo Vargas' life—parts of it—an incomplete sketch that revealed unsettling complexities of his nature and traits of a character that she associated with primitivity and barbarism. He had been judicious enough to let somebody else present what he *so far* wanted her to learn. Jennifer genuinely respected this; she knew intuitively that Vargas himself would have given an abbreviated version, and that a number of vital details would have been omitted. He would have given her a rough and wanting draft, whilst Ahmed and Ishihara both were in position to apply colours and nuances that Vargas would not have included. Ahmed and Ishihara were partial and subjective—personal involvement could not possibly make it otherwise—but at least they had *watched*. Had Vargas told those stories himself, she would not have doubted the authenticity, but the truth would have been given to her in its barest and most clinical form. The human side would have been missing and therefore most or all aspects of the afflictions which were the true heart of the matter.

Vargas knew this. He had wanted her to know what had happened and why it had happened. He had done so after they'd become intimate; a clever, calculated and understandable measure, like saying: do not judge me on what you have heard—judge me on what you have *seen* and heard. He had wanted to give himself a chance, and his timing had been good. It was human, and she could not blame him; after all, he did not *have* to tell her, in the first place.

Didn't he? Jennifer stared at Itoh's painting in search for an answer. Yes, he did. Their liaison was still rudimentary; they were circling each other and the depths of a true relationship had yet to develop. If, by some accident, she had learned what she now knew in two or three years' time, her faith in him and what they had together would have collapsed. The impact of the shock would have blown them apart, irreparably, and this, too, must have crossed Angelo's mind.

She knew that she had a long way to go before she could begin to sort out the turmoil that raged inside her. She concluded that although her life was in chaos, her ability to rational thinking was not entirely eradicated. She knew that her rationality was *influenced*, contaminated by dread, horror, bewilderment and distress, but that was an issue of her own making. She had chosen to allow a premature birth of illusions, and she had ignored the potential negative repercussions of their debacle.

Why didn't she just walk away?

As hours went by, Jennifer began to ask herself the questions she hoped would lead to a final conclusion. She knew that she could not back out of her relationship with Vargas without facing him—what she did not know, was the true depths of her feelings for him.

After two long and distressing days of soul-searching, Jennifer believed that she loved Angelo Vargas. What she questioned was her ability to cope if she joined his world.

Her father would have said, *Cut your losses whilst you still can. There are instances in life when the mind must overrule the heart.*

Her mother would have asked: *Do you want to carry the responsibility of having this man as the father of your children?*

They were both right; any sensible person had to agree. But was she the sensible person everybody seemed to think she was? Being sensible meant being rational, stable, pragmatic, down-to-earth and emotionally prudent. It meant being logical and willing to listen to healthy advice, and that was most commendable since the reward was stability guaranteed.

She smiled, stripped and looked at herself in the mirror. She had lost weight, and there were dark shadows under her eyes. *Here stands a victim of her own making,* she whispered to the mirror, *a grieving martyr, suffering not because of her beliefs but because of her scruples and misgivings. None of this is your fault, Angelo. I am the one to bear the consequences of what I do or do not do. Life would have been so much simpler had I not met you—the question is: what price simplicity? Your bloodstained hands have caressed this body, and your soft-spoken words continue to vibrate like a knife just thrown. Are you still wearing your knife, Angelo, ready to slice up whoever crosses your path in a manner you find disagreeable?*

His face appeared behind her own in the mirror. She saw the clarity of his eyes, his expression of serenity, and behind the calmness a shade of melancholy.

Yes, Angelo, I do not have a problem believing that you are what life has made you. The issue is the question of compatibility. Is it hypothetically conceivable that two cultures, as opposite as ours, can merge and assimilate, that balance can ever be achieved? Mere speculation, Angelo, a theory floating somewhere between heaven and hell.

She put on her thick white bathrobe and a pair of sandals and walked up the narrow staircase to the roof. The night was clear with a nip in the air. She looked at the violet sky and wondered why the colour of the full moon was dark amber and not bright yellow.

She thought of Igor Parkhurst and his characterization of marriage; the voice of experience interpreting the prototype. He had meant it well. He did not want to see her hurt. Then she thought of Yasmin—*a woman of the highest calibre*—who saw Vargas as a trustworthy, loyal and endearing friend.

But Angelo had saved her life—Yasmin's feelings did not represent a balanced appraisal. That said—Jennifer pulled the robe tighter across her chest—Yasmin had known Angelo since she was a young girl. He had become her friend and confidant many years before they experienced Hong Kong together.

Am I looking for an explanation, she thought, or am I looking for excuses? There was only one way to find out, and that was to live with him. Was she prepared for such a leap into the unknown? Her body and her instincts said yes, but her mind said no.

The night became eerily still. Jennifer shivered and stared into the darkness that had squashed the earth, like a garden shed hit by a missile.

She went to bed and switched off the light. She would contact Angelo Vargas the next day. They would meet, and she was going to expound, as honestly as possible, what she thought of the ambiguity of her predicament.

15

Vargas was waiting on the pavement outside Itoh's restaurant. He greeted her with a friendly smile and asked how she'd been. She'd half expected him to be reserved, but there was no trace of tension.

His affability angered her for an instant, but her annoyance subsided when she reminded herself that it was she who had asked for this rendezvous, and that he had all the rights to behave as he saw fit. She was not his alter ego, nor the other way round, and it wasn't improbable that he would listen with sympathy when she explained her doubts about a future together.

What if he said that such future had not entered his mind? Jennifer was pleased with her precautions; she would ask him to forgive her conceit and kindly ignore her unfounded bout of vanity. Perhaps they could have the odd meal, in between, and still remain friends. Something like that.

Itoh was delighted to see her, but with customary tactfulness he soon left them alone. She asked Vargas to order and added that she was not particularly hungry.

Could they start with some sake, please?

The dry run earlier in the day had gone well. She had been satisfied with her reasoning and with her choice of words. The only unknown factor was her feelings. She looked at Vargas, unable to understand that this quiet and soft-spoken man was the same person who had caused such carnage in Hong Kong.

Jennifer wanted to speak, but her mouth was dry and the sake had yet to take effect.

Vargas said, "The point is that we do not know."

Jennifer went for a refill. "Know what?"

"How life would be living together. Let us find out. We do not need anybody's advice."

She finally looked at him. "I have never been so hopelessly torn apart, Angelo."

He said softly, "I think I understand. Our backgrounds are very different. I am not a natural product of your section of society." He raised his hand. "No, Jennifer, these are facts. All I can promise you with any degree of certainty is a bumpy ride. I never saw fit to become a conformist, and it would surprise me if I am easy to live with."

"At least there is nothing wrong with your perception of honesty."

He took his hand away and had the first sip of his whisky. "I live by the Ten Commandments," he said solemnly, "circumstances permitting."

Jennifer laughed. "You are pretty irreverent, Mr. Vargas. Honestly, I don't think you care one bit about any written or unwritten rule that makes society function."

"A harsh judgement," he said and opened a packet of cigarettes. "Truth is, I have been chiselling away on my imperfections ever since I left the mould."

She began to relax. Her well-rehearsed speech had disintegrated, but she no longer thought she would need it. Things would work out. The two of them could find an agenda that took away the pressure and gave her time to reflect.

"Could I have some more sake, please?"

Vargas obliged. Itoh was hovering in the background but was obviously instructed to keep his distance until further notice.

"Can I ask you a few questions?"

"As long as they are relevant."

"Of course they are relevant. What do you take me for?"

"You'd be surprised."

"What does that mean?"

"Ask your questions."

She undid the top button of her blouse and brushed a lock of hair from her face. "How did you know I'd been to see Mr. Parkhurst?"

"I watched you. I saw you leave, that morning, heading west. I followed till I was certain where you were going. The way you looked confirmed it, as well."

His frankness baffled her, but an unexpected question popping up in her mind helped her to recover. "How did I look?"

"Shabby, hollow-eyed and grim."

"You really know how to flatter a woman, don't you? So," she added, " you spied on me."

"That is a pointless statement and not a relevant question."

She took his packet of cigarettes and placed it edgeways. Her shoulders were erect. "Did you have anything to do with James Wilkinson's accident?"

"Yes."

"Why?"

"He was in the way."

"*He was in the way? You could have made him a cripple or even killed him!*"

Vargas' left hand was resting in his lap. His right hand held his glass. "You have the Irish' matchless talent for humorous narrative."

She covered her lips with her fingers. There was a red smear on her cup. She wanted to wipe it off. "You are not normal, are you?"

"Your past lover is young. He'll heal. In a year's time he'll be as good as new."

"But —"

Vargas' smile did not match the tone of his voice when he said, "If I had wanted to kill Wilkinson, where do you think he would have been today?"

Oh God, she thought, my head feels like a jellybean in a deep freezer. "That is awful," she said, "that is—that is wicked and primitive!"

"We are getting to know each other."

She fumbled with the ring her grandmother had given her. "You couldn't think of any other solution?"

"I could, but this was the simplest one." He sipped his drink. "As we both know, it worked to perfection. Any other question to which your profound intuition has not already provided you with the correct answer?"

"You almost crippled a man in order to chat me up. You could not employ a more civilized way?" She looked into his eyes and saw that he did not think an answer was necessary. He's got frostbite on his soul, she thought. I wonder which animal appears somewhere on his line of descendants. *Whatever I say, it will be the truth.* Yes, Angelo Vargas was being honest with her, brutally honest. Strange, she thought, but there is something attractively reassuring about his unrefined integrity.

She said, "You have a unique way of introducing yourself. I can't think of anyone else doing what you did." And, she thought, no way would I ever let you know that your barbarism appeals to me. Worse— or better—I actually feel good about it.

"I wanted to meet you and talk to you. Labyrinths don't excite me." He beckoned to Itoh whose speed and agility belied his age. Within minutes the starters were on the table.

She looked around. "He has forgotten my chopsticks."

Vargas reached for his inner pocket. "He hasn't," he said and handed to her a long and thin parcel.

She opened it and stared at the pair of chopstick almost identical to Vargas', only the paintwork more elaborate. Well, she thought, some girls get diamonds, and I get a pair of chopsticks.

"Memories are made of these," Vargas said. "Consider them a treasured relic from something that could have been—should you so decide."

You bastard, she thought, you are not exactly making it easy for me. Or are you?

Vargas dug into the vegetables. "I've got a question for you," he said.

I am sure you have, she reflected, and I am equally sure you already know the answer. She felt a knot in her stomach. *Anything* could be expected from her suave dinner companion. "Yes?" she mumbled and concentrated on the rice.

"Why did you dump Wilkinson?"

She had not dumped him. They had calmly discussed the matter, as befits two adults. They had concluded that they were not suited. It had been a mutual decision, going their separate ways, the dignified outcome of common sense and discerning cogitation. A most plausible explanation, she thought, sophisticated and civilized—except that it wasn't true.

Why not be as outspoken and primitive as Vargas? She giggled and said, "He bored the pants off me."

Vargas said, "Mmm—a logical ground for dismissal. As of this moment the ways of the female mind are no longer mysterious. No moral hangover, either?"

I'd better change the subject, she thought. "Why are you drinking whisky with your food?"

"Because I like it."

"I thought one is supposed to drink tea or sake with Japanese food."

"Is one?"

She could feel her cheeks changing colour. "All right, that was very conventional of me."

"You are still young."

She placed her chopsticks on the *hashi-oki*. "Are you patronizing me?"

"Just guiding you through life's maze which ends where the wide open field of independent thinking begins."

"That is the most arrogant statement I've heard in my entire life."

The smile on Vargas' face was still visible. He said, "I am trying to get something across to you, which is: if it is your target in life to be put on a pedestal, you should stick to the Wilkinsons of this world."

He really is an irresistible pervert, she thought. There is no *sound* reason why I should find this man alluring, and yet I do. I have no wish to be put on a pedestal, and a stable and uneventful life has no temptations. Angelo Vargas appeals to me because I am yearning for the excitement of the unknown. The darker side of his nature is stirring up something I find seductive. His mind and his body are like two magnets, and I am the piece of metal that has voluntarily placed itself in the middle. All this I can tell nobody, not a living soul. Not even Angelo—and that is the indelible sweetness of it.

Jennifer scissored her chopsticks and picked up a piece of sushi. "Tasty," she said and kept a straight face.

"Tell Itoh," Vargas suggested. He eyed her in a way she preferred to interpret as admiration. "He'll be delighted."

Itoh heard his name and came over. "Everything fine?" he queried, "you are happy?"

"Marvellous," Jennifer smiled. "You are a true master."

"The light of my life has had her first bit of sushi," Vargas explained.

"Fantastic," Itoh beamed, "you like it?"

"Delicious," Jennifer said. "By the way, Mr. Itoh, I cannot thank you enough for the painting you gave me. It is lovely. It hangs in my bedroom, and I look at it every night before I go to sleep."

"Strong calming effect, then," Itoh assumed.

"Very much so," Jennifer nodded.

"Like Mr. Vargas." Itoh's sparkling brown eyes had almost disappeared. He bowed and focused his attention on some newly arrived customers.

Jennifer composed herself. "Angelo," she said, taking time wiping her hands with the hot towel Itoh had brought, "please do not call me the light of your life."

"Why not?"

"Because it is—it sounds pretentious."

"Does it? Mistress, then."

"From pretentious to vulgar does not take you long," she said acidly.

"I was being neither. Exact, I would think."

She repeated the words in her mind and listened to his tone of voice. She swallowed so fast that her tongue made a click. "You really mean that, don't you?"

"I do."

A woman of the highest calibre. Angelo Vargas looking for his shrine.

She was moved and did not try to hide it. She touched his cheek with the tip of her fingers. "Thank you, Angelo."

He put on his jacket and held out his hand.

"One final question," she said.

"Yes?"

"Have you always been a loner?"

"There are times when I am more at ease on my own."

"*Times?*" Jennifer choked back a hollow laughter. "What else is new?"

"Make your point, if any."

"I am trying to get to know you. You're not exactly the most loquacious person I have ever come across."

Vargas said, "Let's get some fresh air."

They went upstairs.

"Would you mind walking for a few minutes?" Vargas asked.

"Not at all." She put her arm under his as they strolled along. She saw a couple in their thirties and a boy of five or six who had glued himself to the window of a toyshop. The man asked the boy to come. There was an immediate reaction; the boy responded in the most obliging manner. He apologized for having caused a delay, he certainly did not mean to.

"What a delightful child, so polite and well-mannered," she said.

"Poor kid," Vargas said. "Not a happy child."

"Why is he not a happy child?"

"Too eager to please. He's been kept in a strait jacket and won't have much of a mind of his own when he grows up. Unless he somehow manages to break off. That's always a possibility, however remote."

One day, she thought, one day I'll know more about you, Angelo Vargas. That observation wasn't taken out of thin air.

"Jennifer!" she heard a voice behind her. "Jennifer, it has been ages!"

She felt a hand on her upper arm and turned around. It was Delia, her close friend from their early schooldays.

"What a thrill to see you again," Delia went on. "What are you doing with yourself, these days? This is my betrothed, Frederick Sandrich. Don't call him Freddy, he hates it."

Jennifer shook hands with Frederick and introduced Vargas. She tried not to compare his leather jacket and denims with Frederick's sharp suit and camelhair coat. Insecurity tightened the skin over her cheekbones when she saw Delia's eyes scrutinize Vargas.

"I am very pleased to meet you," Frederick said, shaking hands with each in turn. "Delia has said more than once that the two of you must meet up again. I understand you are very close."

"Oh, we are," Delia said. "Distance in time means nothing. Why don't the four of us go out to dinner one evening? We have *so* much catching-up to do."

"That would be nice," Jennifer said, acutely aware of Vargas' silence. She could not be the only one sensing that he exuded a mixture of indifference and animosity. "We would love to, wouldn't we, Angelo?"

Delia showed her perfect, white teeth. Her smile would have been nice had she not made excessive use of her lipstick. "Frederick and I are looking for a weekend retreat, and I think we have found one," she said. "What an *ordeal*, Jennifer. Frederick is a stockbroker. We'll keep the flat in Chelsea, but come weekends we shall definitely unwind in the wilderness. You can't imagine how busy I have been."

Jennifer smiled at Frederick and wondered which number he was in Delia's collection of grooms-to-be. Delia was a sweet and likeable girl, but already when in her early teens had she made it clear that she was not going to settle for a one-room flat in Bethnal Green. There was nothing wrong with ambitions, but Jennifer had pondered more than once if Delia's idea of priorities and happiness one day would lead her astray. Men found her hugely attractive, and her ability to get what she wanted was legendary.

Delia eyed Vargas. "What do you do for a living?" she smiled.

"I am a monk."

"A *monk?*"

"Retired. I ran a monastery, which I owned. It stood in two hundred acres. One day a developer gave me an offer I couldn't refuse."

Delia laughed. "That's a good one. Excuse me, Mr. Vargas—this is terribly rude of me—but somehow I don't believe you. You wouldn't be an undercover agent or anything like that?"

"I only dress like one."

She tittered. "How delightful."

Jennifer said, "Why don't I call you next week, and we'll arrange something?" She smiled at Frederick who gave her a sympathetic nod. Delia opened her bag and handed Jennifer a card. "My new telephone number. Promise to call, will you?" She took a step closer to Vargas, but continued to face Jennifer. "How long have the two of you been together? I mustn't allow myself to get so hopelessly out of touch any more."

Vargas said, "All evening, and preferably what's left of it."

Delia caught him by the arm. The tip of her tongue moved between her lips. "What a sweetheart," she said. "No wonder you want to keep him for yourself."

Vargas looked amused. Delia's laughter did not match the look in her grey eyes. "Next week, Jennifer. I can't wait."

"Next week," she said and put the card away. She avoided looking at Vargas and fought to keep her cool. "It's really a pleasure seeing you again. Nice meeting you, Frederick."

They bade goodnight for half a minute. Jennifer resumed walking. Her heels clicked angrily against the pavement.

"Was it necessary to be so incredibly rude?" she said and looked at him. The anger in her eyes rose like vapour from acid on green marble.

"I am not good at small talk."

"So you resort to insults instead."

"Your friend Delia isn't easily insulted."

"You do not like her?"

"I found her well-drilled smile and the acquired shyness in her misty eyes very siren."

"Delia may be a bit of a character, but she is a nice and kind girl. I have known her since for a long time. We have got a lot of good memories together."

"Why did you lose touch?"

"I—I don't know. I got busy with my work, and—I don't know what she has been doing. It is just one of those things."

"I'll get you a taxi," Vargas said.

He gave her a hand as she climbed in. "Jennifer," he said and leaned closer, "take as long as you need. I have read that it's easier getting into a relationship that it is getting out of it."

He closed the door and walked off.

Yesterday it was yes and no, Jennifer thought as the taxi snaked its way through the traffic. Today, it is yes-yes and no. Why is he so acrimonious, so downright asocial? How can I cope with an existence where one is comparatively congenial and civilized and the other an ill-natured recluse? Is there any hope of influencing him, of achieving an improvement, or is he too set in his ways? I wish I knew. I wish I knew a lot of things.

She saw the driver switch on the wipers and heard the downpour clattering against the roof. The car moved slowly over films of oil on a wet surface that looked like the colourful bubbles of soapwater she used to blow as a child. The water ran like threads of silver down the window. The rhythmic swishing of the blades made her sleepy and she saw Angelo Vargas' face when he said *let us find out*.

16

I do not expect Mr. Ishihara to surprise me any more, Parkhurst thought, or, rather, I expect anything from him, however bizarre.

He therefore took it in his stride when Ishihara called and said that it had all been arranged for the following day; a suite waited at The Connaught, and would Parkhurst respectfully transfer his gargantuan frame enveloping his titanic talents and be there by ten o'clock in the morning. All he needed to bring, apart from necessities, were a thick pad of his favourite design and colour, half a dozen pencils and an open mind.

Parkhurst duly obliged however much he hated driving during the rush hour. He arrived fifteen minutes early. It had taken him almost two and a half hours, and he was exhausted. The doorman took care of the car and the luggage. Parkhurst went straight to the lounge and asked for a cup of very strong coffee.

I need a few moments of peace and quiet before I face the loony Japanese, he mused. It's going to be a long day.

Ishihara smiled broadly as he opened the door. "Igor my lad, welcome. You look as fresh, ready and sharp as the biting gusts from the North Pole, all set to sweep away the cobwebs from the minds of the next generation of lawyers, accountants, bureaucrats and all the other meritorious members of our genteel society. I trust that you feel as deliriously anticipatory as a sparrow behind a horse suffering from frequent bowel movements. Enter, oh Samson of the intellectual elite."

He stepped aside. Parkhurst saw Vargas sitting in a chair with his back to the balcony.

"Good morning, Mr. Parkhurst."

He is plainly in a friendly and talkative mood, Parkhurst thought. What in God's name is he doing here? "Good morning, Mr. Vargas."

Ishihara had taken off his jacket and tie. He placed his thumbs behind his braces and stretched the elastics. "Nice, aren't they? I had them specially made."

"The first thing I noticed," Parkhurst said. He tried to count the white elephants on fuchsia background as they climbed up Ishihara's chest and continued over his shoulders. "Nothing symbolic, I presume."

Ishihara said, "They are indeed. Shall I get you a pair?"

"No thank you. What is the symbolism?"

Ishihara rolled up his sleeves. "When does an elephant become a white elephant?"

Parkhurst put his briefcase on the floor next to the coffee table. He liked mind games. He said, "When something has become entirely unrealistic; it being a load too heavy to carry, a burden to stay clear of, or a dilemma one should have avoided."

"Or no longer of value to one person but desired by another person," Ishihara supplemented. "Not bad, Igor. Your mind is already in second gear. I do find it tremendously impressive that you didn't go for the normally accepted interpretation."

I'd better be careful now, Parkhurst thought; Mr. Ishihara has spent the morning honing his razorblade of a tongue. He sat down in the sofa with Vargas at a forty-five degree angle to his right.

"Don't bother to thank me for the compliment," Ishihara said.

Parkhurst undid his shoelaces. "I am sorry, but you are ahead of me. I did not catch the bottomless depth and infinite wisdom of your allegory."

"It is not at all complicated. You claim that you have lost your talent and what is lost cannot be of value to anybody. I claim that it is impossible to lose a talent as long as one is alive and compos mentis. What you *really* have lost, is your self-confidence. Figuratively speaking, you see the rest of your career as the vague and one-dimensional relief of a white elephant, like a primitive drawing on the wall of a cave. That is why we are here, my son. We are here to eradicate this most horrible of misconceptions. Together we shall prove to the world that Igor Parkhurst is still a formidable force. You get it?"

"The world, no less," Parkhurst muttered.

"Yes. After Oxford, Harvard is waiting in the wings."

Before Parkhurst could react, Ishihara pointed to a sideboard. "Tea,

361

coffee and mineral water. No booze. Throw your jacket and roll up your sleeves." He poured three cups of coffee and placed them on the table. "You wonder why my friend Mr. Vargas is here?"

"To contribute, I suppose."

"That is correct. I commented because I noticed an expression of surprise on your face when you spotted his presence."

"You did not mention that Mr. Vargas would be here."

"I didn't have to, but, granted, an explanation is not uncalled for." Ishihara lit a cigar. He got up and opened the balcony door ajar. "The reason is that Mr. Vargas has got opinions that are not commonplace. He has got viewpoints that a lot of people have problems digesting, I am pleased to add. He has a penchant for throwing Molotov cocktails when least expected. He also has an insatiable hunger for the mysteries of the past, for some obscure reason." Ishihara came back to his chair. "I cannot guarantee that we shall benefit from any or all of this. You never know with Angelo. He may prefer to keep quiet, or he may not. He wanted to show up, and here he is." Ishihara pressed the palms of his hands together, his fingers pointing upwards. "I sincerely hope that you have no objections."

Parkhurst said, "Not at all. On the contrary." He glanced quizzically at Vargas who looked indifferent. The neck of his black shirt was open, and he appeared more at ease than his imperious friend.

"Good," Ishihara said. "With the assistance of Angelo's virulent and nefarious mind, as opposed to my own humble and debonair disposition, the combined efforts of our exceptionally sagacious triumvirate cannot fail. All set?"

Parkhurst opened his briefcase and took out a pad and a pencil. "Ready to soar," he said. He still had no idea how, with what and to where.

Ishihara said, "We need a caption, an inspiring heading." He looked at the other two.

"Distorted experiences in free fall," Vargas said.

"Meaning?" Parkhurst queried politely.

"Nothing, but nobody knows that. Bear in mind to whom you'll be talking."

"Excellent," Ishihara said. "Intriguing, meaningless and thus a challenge to clever-clogs."

"What if somebody takes up that challenge?" Parkhurst asked.

Vargas crossed his legs. "Then you shake your head and tell that person that he or she is probably better off permanently unemployed."

Parkhurst scrutinized his pencil. Vargas had clearly decided to be helpful.

"We are progressing fast," Ishihara said. "Igor, write down the caption."

Parkhurst wrote. "Are you advocating an offensive style?"

"Absolutely. Does that bother you?"

"Well—yes. I was thinking of a more humorous approach, along the line of mild satire, perhaps. That is what I used to be good at."

"Brilliant," Ishihara smiled. "Saying what?"

Parkhurst cursed silently. "I haven't got anything."

Ishihara folded his hands behind his neck. "There is something you must understand. Your misfortune is that you are a gentleman. You are a dying breed. People are no longer sufficiently educated to comprehend what you stand for. It simply isn't part of their curriculum. You can only succeed if you are able and willing to *adapt*. Am I getting through to you?"

Parkhurst pencil fell on the floor. He picked it up. The muscles in his face displayed unease. He said, "I feel as well prepared for the challenge as a chicken breaking the shell of his egg." He drank from his glass of water. "I know you are right."

"Of course I am right. As Angelo said, bear in mind who you'll be talking to. You must not forget that students quickly get bored. The reason for this sad state of affairs is not that they are particularly literate, experienced, above-average intelligent, intellectual, rational or cognizant— all of which sums up the totally misconstrued image they have of themselves—the indubitable reason is that they are too vacuous to grasp that mentally they are practically decomposed and will remain so for years to come. If the three stallions *Conceit, Vanity* and *Arrogance* penetrate the virgin *Ignorance*, out comes a student. Now, *there* is an opening for you."

"Are you suggesting that I write down what you just said?"

"Yes, I am. They will only find you interesting if you are being controversial, and they will continue to listen *only* if you can maintain being bold, contentious and belligerent. Be unreservedly hostile in your appraisal of accepted maxims. Let each word be a poisonous arrow. Be inflammatory. Cause confusion."

He thought for a while. The other two watched in silence. He wished he could go downstairs for a quick cognac. Ishihara crossed his arms and demonstrated his endless patience by inhaling loudly through his nose.

Finally, he clasped his thighs. "Pay attention, Igor. Acknowledge that you have to perform a veritable blitzkrieg. Only by being aggressive can your scholarly address be sufficiently spiced to make your audience gung ho, advertent and appreciative."

Parkhurst's chin came up. He tapped his pencil against the paper. "Right. To get their attention, I seriously affront them for a minute. Where do we go from there?"

"Close to home," Vargas said. "Education. It is a lamentable fact that children are not being taught to *think*. Almost all education systems are designed in such a way that children are being forced to *remember*. Stress that this wilful misapprehension is as universal as it is age-old. Only an exceptional tutor knows the difference between stimulating guidance and mental dressage."

Ishihara said, "That is depressingly true. The most important word in our vocabulary—*why*—has less status than *because*. The answer is more important than the question. Result? An uncritical mind." He smiled when Parkhurst's pencil slithered across the paper. "Try something like this: if most of you leave this university with the belief that you are well educated, then most of you will end up as pompous, bourgeois, shop-worn and snotty little stereotypes. Your goal in life will be to replace the Vauxhall with a Ford and to move from a flat in Clapham to a cramped but *executive-style* detached house on one eighth of an acre nicely located on an estate in the suburbs. Your friends will all be haughty little replicas of yourself, *smart* but disgruntled, and at the age of sixty you will wonder what happened since those glorious days at Oxford. Your retirement will be ruled by hardship since your pension did not turn out to be what you supposed it would be, and each morning you will stare out the window and wonder what to do with yourself. A bleak picture? Yes, and only avoidable if you enter the real world with humility, drive and an unrelenting desire to keep your integrity intact."

"They'll love me," Parkhurst mumbled.

Vargas said, "They'll respect you."

Ishihara crowed. "Do not lose sight of the objective, which is: I am Igor Parkhurst, and I am here to create a stir."

They circled around the theme of education for another half-hour. Parkhurst grew in confidence.

"This is not bad," he said. "How do you suggest I round it off?"

Vargas said, "Moderately. I once read that the essence of education is that you learn to find what you do not know. Tell our paragons of the future that they have a hell of a lot to find. Tell them that the burden of indoctrination has its roots in an inflated vocabulary where aroma and mode are more important than exactitude and probity. Then you jump straight onto the next subject."

Parkhurst eyed his assistants. "Any preferences?"

The room was getting smokefilled. Vargas got up and opened wide the balcony doors.

"Listen," Ishihara said. "Your mind is a jungle, a fertile soil for diatribes, caprices, ideas and denunciations, a Garden of Eden where the orchid feeds on sulphuric acid and from where your words sweep the audience like a Siberian blizzard interrupted by the odd whiff from a tropical heat wave. That is how you must see yourself."

"Science," Vargas said. "No student worth his grant would forgive you if you dodged this most distinguished of disciplines. Paint a picture of the unselfish humanitarian; the person, to whom the microscope is God, genetics is the Holy Ghost and any conclusion—outlandish, unsubstantiated or purchased for a purpose—is the word of Christ. Do not forget to emphasize that the mind of the scientist is so pure in its logic and so refined and rational in its altruism that weeds like moral and ethics are permanently deprived of nutrition."

The lines under Parkhurst's temples looked like scratch marks. His complexion had turned from ruddy to the colour of a tropical sunset. He wrote vigorously.

Ishihara said, "Calm down. You are heading for a university, not a hospital. Go and get some fresh air."

Parkhurst straightened his neck. He rose and walked out on the balcony. He looked down and counted the cars parked.

He came back. "That helped."

"A brief dissection of politics will be expected," Ishihara said. "Just make it sufficiently repugnant, which shouldn't be difficult."

"I'll advocate a revolution, emotionally violent but physically bloodless. How's that?"

"Splendid. Don't forget to include that those who contemplate this abject profession are intellectual mastubators who could find psychiatry financially more rewarding."

"Could it be an idea first to give a brief presentation of the British as I see them, see *us*, I mean?"

"Fabulous. Go ahead."

"I beg your pardon?"

"Talk. Describe. Outline."

Parkhurst opened and closed his right hand and massaged the wrist. "Allow me to make a few notes." He wrote fast. "How does this sound," he said and adjusted his glasses. "We British are a liberal lot, not by design but as a result of mental idleness. We love to talk, but save us from having to implement much. Work, efforts and initiative are abstracts, and may we forever remain liberal."

"Is that it?"

Parkhurst looked stunned. "So far."

"Improvise. You can edit afterwards. Is there not anything you find particularly surprising or alarming?"

Parkhurst pressed his thumb against his lower lip. His nose twitched. "I do find it surprising that all post-war governments have shown disdain towards the teaching of history. This attitude has been steadily growing. The lamentable result is a diminished sense of national identity. Now, *that* is alarming. Also, why is it that initiative, motivation and the urge to seek adventure and take risks are no longer socially agreeable? Why is it that individuality, non-conformism and any degree of distinction are being frowned upon? Too many people opt for *security*, which, if achieved, leads to an uneventful, parochial and insular existence where the worst reality is the payment of the mortgage. They end up having lived a life deprived of experiences worth looking back on, and the only risky return-trips to hell are those watched on television. We talk incessantly about fair play—I think we invented the phrase—but we are unwilling or unable to identify the undignified truth that fair play benefits the loser. We possess the provincial, narrow-minded mentality of the islander, incapable of comprehending that other countries have cultures, traditions, etiquette, history and an educational system possibly superior to ours. We mistake arrogance for pride, and we do not recognize that our attitude is a case of inane ignorance masquerading as justified contempt. In short, my beloved England has become the land of passivity, greed, laxity, carelessness and road works."

Ishihara smiled. "Who said he was burnt out?"

Parkhurst felt good, better than he had for a very long time.

"A few more observations along those lines, and they'll give you a standing ovation," Vargas said from the window. "You think what *they* should have thought, and you state what your generation is not supposed to express, that is, those few who know the truth you so eloquently formulated."

"You think I'll get away with it? It is pretty harsh stuff, however true."

Vargas rolled his shoulders and glanced out the window. "Crucifixion is the fate of the meek."

Ishihara rubbed his hands. "Religion is one of Angelo's pet subjects."

"I shall have to tread carefully on that one," Parkhurst said. "The line between constructive criticism and blasphemy is a rather thin one."

Vargas said, "Religion—any religion—is an impenetrable roadblock to progress. No true intellectual evolution and therefore no human progress can take place as long as dogma, creed or any other droppings from this monster of superstition swaddle the mind. The moment man invented religion, his ability to reason came to a standstill, confirmed by the absurd existence of the concept of blasphemy."

"Can you spin a bit further on that one?" Ishihara asked.

Parkhurst said, "I think so, but I do not really want to present myself as someone who objects to religion *per se*. Critical, yes, but not with disparagement. I can't express hate or scorn for man's need for something beyond himself to believe in."

Vargas said, "You can't hate an abstract. You can only abominate man for allowing himself to cultivate the bacteria that will eventually destroy him."

Parkhurst looked at Vargas for a few seconds. "I'd like to use the quintessence of that, if I may."

"Be my guest."

Parkhurst continued to stare. Somewhere in the back of his mind he began to sense why Jennifer found Vargas' company stimulating. He's an unorthodox specimen, Parkhurst thought, a Daedalian character. I wonder what made him what he is. He smiled inwardly as the concept of *raw material* flashed by.

Vargas stared back. Parkhurst coughed and said, "Another subject that might arouse the audience is science versus religion. That is always a popular show of transcendent juggling in academic circles."

Ishihara said, "What do you think, Angelo?"

Vargas smiled. His eyes had not let go of Parkhurst who started to feel uncomfortable. Vargas said, "A quasi-intellectual game for the narrow-minded, a game with no beginning and no end and with a black hole in the middle."

Parkhurst averted his gaze. "How do you validate your verdict?"

"Try assumed evidence against arrogated sentiment. Such a game is a farce, and it is illustrating our inability to break the cycle of the establishmentarian's stranglehold on evolution and progress as seen in context with religion. Conclusion: even if we by some coincidence *could* advance one step further, the will is absent. The earth is flat, and seeds fall on stones. It is better and less complicated, that way. Consult Galileo."

Parkhurst made notes.

When he finished, Ishihara said, "Any thoughts about your venerable monarchy?"

"Oh, I think we better leave the royal family alone."

"I said *monarchy*, which is not the same as royal family. On the other hand, you may be right. The vast majority of Brits are neither sufficiently mature nor pragmatic enough to appreciate the blessings of a republic, and the illiterate dwarf who at present decorates the throne is too bland to be worth a shot."

Two hours later, Parkhurst believed that he could make it. He scanned through the pages, nodded to himself and felt reasonably sure that he had sufficient material in hand to produce what was required. He sensed an incipient anticipation and a feeling of elation he had not experienced for half an eternity.

"A good day's work," Ishihara said. "What remains now is for you to have the script ready within a week. Then you and I go through it and edit together. How is that?"

"That is perfect," Parkhurst said. "I am actually beginning to look forward to this. I never thought..."

"There we are," Ishihara smiled.

Vargas asked, "What is the time?"

Parkhurst looked at his watch. "I don't believe this! It's six o'clock. Where has the time gone? I am not even tired."

Vargas stepped into his shoes. "Evidently a rejuvenating process."

Ishihara tapped Parkhurst on the shoulder with his pen. "I'd like to use your shower. In return, I'll pay for dinner."

Parkhurst wondered why it had not occurred to him that the hotel bill would end up in his lap.

Ishihara said, "I suggest we honour the restaurant here." He turned to Vargas. "Coming—?"

"No thank you. I am playing poker."

Ishihara shrugged. "Yakuza," he said.

Vargas put on his jacket. "Enjoy your dinner," he said and left.

"That was quick," Parkhurst said. "I wanted to thank him."

Ishihara shook his head. "Some other time."

"Is something wrong?"

"He'll be wasting his money tonight."

"Is he not a good player?"

"He can be when he sets his mind to it. The problem comes when he goes there to relax, to divert his thoughts from whatever he's preoccupied with, but, regrettably, only half-heartedly so. He concentrates on neither, with the result that he's gambling instead of playing, calling when he should have folded and folds when he should have raised. That sort of things. Bad economy and questionable therapy."

"Maybe he does relax, to some extent. By the way, I thought yakuza was the Japanese word for Mafia."

"My native tongue is complex. In this context, *ya* means eight, *ku* means nine, and *za* means three; in other words, the worst possible hand you can be dealt in poker. It was a hint to Angelo that he should play and not gamble. Believe me, Igor, the difference is monumental."

"His choice," Parkhurst said diplomatically. He stretched his arms and legs, called room service and asked for two large cognacs. He thought of his newfound belief in himself and smiled. A decent meal, a good night's sleep, and Igor Parkhurst would wake up assertive and more at ease than he'd ever been. He crossed the floor and looked out. It had become overcast, and daylight was fading like a glow turning to ash and carried into oblivion by the evening breeze.

He pulled the curtains. "Your friend is an unusual man," he said. "I pride myself of being able to read people, but Mr. Vargas escapes me."

All signs of joviality had gone from Ishihara' face.

"Do not ever try to probe," he said. The menace in his voice was unmistakable. "I will tell you what I want to tell you, but there it stops. Have I made myself clear?"

Parkhurst nodded, dumbfounded. Why were those two so protective of each other? Loyalty was a fine quality, but why this apparent need for a Chinese wall? Was this the way true friendship manifested itself? Parkhurst had experienced the gamut from obsequious hangers-on, acceptable acquaintances and to the odd reliable ones, but he had never come close to sampling anything resembling the bond that he perceived existed between Ishihara and Vargas, not even with Conor.

He looked up when he heard Ishihara close the door behind him.

☞

Parkhurst had hoped for thirty to forty students to show up, with a bit of luck; he had not expected a packed hall and people still queuing outside. Nobody had warned him about the presence of reporters from both tabloids and broadsheets. The sight of a BBC television crew was another shock.

Ishihara apologized profusely; had he really forgotten to mention that some coverage was part of the strategy? An abysmal oversight, quite unforgivable and equally incomprehensible.

"You did it on purpose," Parkhurst barked.

Ishihara laughed. "Of course I did. Otherwise you would have been so petrified for days that you'd probably gone into hiding. It is all for your benefit, Igor. Tomorrow you are once again headlines. Here," he added and gave Parkhurst a paper cup, "one swallow of your favourite cognac, just enough to let the butterflies settle down."

Parkhurst emptied the cup and began to feel better. He knew that Ishihara was right; a nation-wide coverage was essential to the re-launch—assuming that everything went according to plan. And if it didn't? Parkhurst longed for another sip but knew it would be unwise. The dice had been thrown; whatever happened, he had no choice but to take it in his stride.

Two minutes to go.

He spotted Jennifer and Yasmin standing in the front row. Well, he thought, at least I am guaranteed *some* applause.

He nudged Ishihara. "Is not Mr. Vargas here?"

"He is having a drink. Don't worry, the four of us are not going to miss one single word. We'll all be in your corner tonight."

"I feel as if someone has injected me with a gallon of curare."

"You are not having another drink."

Ishihara glanced at his watch. He said quietly, "When you enter that little podium, stand there and look at them until the last trace of commotion has died down. Employ an expression of patience blended with mild amusement. Do not panic—just wait. Let your entire demeanour demonstrate that you are in command."

"These kids are good at heckling—even before somebody starts."

"Should that be the case, smile benignly and say: "I'd love to wait till you've grown up, but I may not live that long." Pause for a few seconds, and add if necessary: "It is as indisputable as it is heartbreaking that our world is overpopulated with morons, but I can honestly say that I did not expect this wretched fact to be demonstrated and confirmed here tonight." That should do it. The vast majority will suppress any residue of cheap witticisms from a handful of self-appointed wags. It is safe to assume that without a certain puerile inquisitiveness they wouldn't be students, most of them, but I think you will find that they are here to listen to what you have to say *provided* it's interesting, which it is, and *provided* you don't lose your composure. Here," Ishihara added and handed him a piece of paper. "It's all there." He paused for a few seconds. "Time to go," he added. "I am not going to wish you the best of luck since you won't need it. You have scripted your act—now go and act your script. You cannot fail."

Parkhurst listened to the well-phrased, courteous and flowery introduction. He took a couple of maximum breaths and began his walk towards a podium that seemed a mile away and yet all too close.

The first of Ishihara's punchlines came in useful, and the audience laughed. From that moment on, Igor Parkhurst was in control. He had the audience under his spell, and he gave them a performance that surprised even Ishihara. It was vintage Parkhurst, the old magic was back and his acerbic *obiter dicta* in the shape of good-humoured and seemingly off-the-cuff observations were several times interrupted by thunderous applause.

It culminated with a standing ovation.

Parkhurst stood there, for a moment, too stunned to move. He folded his script and adjusted his glasses and hoped that no one could see his eyes. Then he looked at his goddaughter and her friends and he wondered what he had done to deserve his Second Coming.

☞

Parkhurst woke up with a hangover. He could vaguely remember up to and including his performance, but thereafter the white mist of alcoholic daze blurred the rest of the evening.

Slowly, pieces from a shattered memory came drifting back. He recalled diffusely that everybody had been shaking hands with him and that nearly as many had bought him a drink. The odd faces of celebrities, reporters and other luminaries reappeared and they'd all wanted to know where and why he had been hiding for so long. Ishihara and Vargas had not left his side, and Jennifer and Yasmin—what did they do?—oh yes, several times they'd taken the drink from his hand and given him a glass of water instead.

Parkhurst looked around. He was in his own bed, little doubts about that, but how on earth had he got there? Also, the house wasn't quiet; voices came from downstairs.

Parkhurst got up, staggered into the shower and stood under a cascade of cold water until he'd decided that his faculties were staging an initial recovery.

Jennifer, Yasmin, Ishihara and Vargas were sitting around the kitchen table. It was covered with newspapers.

"Good morning, everybody," Parkhurst said, He wondered what had happened to his voice. He sat down. "What do they say?" he asked.

"Total fiasco," Ishihara said.

Parkhurst wanted to hide his face, but his hands did not obey. "What?" he whispered.

The two girls looked away.

"Stop interrupting," Ishihara went on. "You make me repeat myself."

Parkhurst's voice cracked. "I heard you."

"No, you didn't. I had not finished. Before you so rudely cut me off I was going to say: total fiasco for those who thought that Igor Parkhurst was burnt out."

Parkhurst managed a cackle.

Yasmin came over and stroked his head. "Ignore him," she said. "His mother's milk was spiced with venom and razor blades. He can't help it."

Jennifer and Ishihara laughed. Vargas smiled.

Yasmin continued, "Fantastic, Igor. Success is a mild word. You did it, as we all expected."

"You'll be on television tonight," Ishihara said.

"How did you get them up there?" Parkhurst asked. He did not know what else to say.

"I have contacts. However, I did promise them exceptional value for money."

Parkhurst folded the newspapers. "I'll read these later."

"Next stop is Harvard," Ishihara said. "I have made some tentative enquiries—I told you that. In view of yesterday's performance, an invitation is now in the box. That will be followed by an interview with one of the top American television presenters. Which one, I haven't decided yet. Thereafter, with the accolade in the States behind you, we shall arrange for an interview here. What is important now is the sequence of things, and not least that you pace yourself with proper care and consideration. None of these pays well, not bad, but not astronomical; which means that you better start writing as soon as you are back from the colonies. A good little program, Igor—you are going to prove the old adage that nothing succeeds like success. In a few months' time you won't need us any more."

Parkhurst looked at each in turn. "Are you going away?"

"No, no," Ishihara smiled. "When did *need* and *want* become synonyms?"

"But first of all we have to arrange your party," Jennifer said.

"My party? What party?"

"The one we talked about last night. Luckily, I made a note of all those you invited."

Parkhurst had no recollection of having suggested a party. "This is the second joke of the morning, I take it."

"No," Jennifer said. "It is true, Uncle Igor. We are not having you on."

"Dear me," Parkhurst groaned, "how do I get out of this one?"

Ishihara said, "You don't. Giving a party is actually a very good idea. You cannot operate without contacts, without people. Whatever reason anybody has for supporting or cultivating you, it is there for you to use and exploit. This time *you* are in the driving seat, and never again do you let go. We shall compose a proper list of guests—a drink's party—and we will establish the network required for keeping you in the limelight. You produced last night, Igor, and you'll produce again."

"I could not have done what I did without your help."

Vargas said, "We were only the catalyst."

"Incentives do not make talent," Ishihara said. "You must not confuse stimuli with creativity."

"I'll add a feminine touch," Yasmin said, "stop being such a prissy whimp. You are Igor Parkhurst, the gifted and prolific writer."

"Resurrected, if that helps," Vargas said.

Parkhurst did not dare look up. He was still feeling vulnerable and emotional. "I—how do I go about it, the party, I mean?"

"Don't worry, Uncle Igor. Yasmin and I will take care of it."

A forlorn smile showed on Parkhurst's face. "When do I give this party?"

Ishihara clicked his tongue. "Timing is essential. We have gone for Saturday two weeks from now." He looked thoughtful. "Let us make it a really interesting get-together, say, a few from the American Embassy, and not to forget that particular friend of yours employed by Her Majesty."

Parkhurst's rubicund complexion had gone. He moved his head as if hit by a spasm. "You can't be serious, Tadashi. That is not even a preposterous joke."

"No joke. I think it is time they learn that you are no longer helpless and unprotected."

Ishihara's lips had parted and moved sideways, but Parkhurst could not read the expression. It could be a mistake to object, he thought; he is serious, and he does have a habit of knowing what he is doing.

Vargas opened a window. They could hear the neighbour's rooster in the distance. Dogs were baying up on the hill.

Parkhurst scratched his jawbone with his index finger. He looked at Ishihara. "There is one thing I do not understand, Tadashi. All those people, yesterday, you know, from television and the newspapers…"

"What about them?"

"You once said that you needed me as your ticket to a social life, but clearly you already know a lot of people."

"It doesn't figure?"

"No, it does not, unless you have made your contacts since we first spoke."

"You think we have misled you."

Parkhurst kicked off his slippers and put his feet on the cold terracotta floor. "I did not say that."

"I believe Uncle Igor is entitled to ask," Jennifer said and looked at Vargas.

"He is," Vargas said.

Parkhurst raised his hands. "Listen, I am very grateful for what you have done, but was it because you felt *sorry* for me? All this talk about social life was a shenanigan, however nice, to make me feel better, was it not?"

Jennifer said, "There is nothing wrong with compassion."

Parkhurst lowered his hands and closed his eyes for a moment. "There is quite a difference between compassion and pity."

"You achieved something yesterday," Yasmin said. "Does it matter *how* you arrived?"

Parkhurst said, "Yes, and that is the entire point. I cannot do anything in return. We had a deal, and there is nothing to repay. Do you not understand how small this makes me feel?"

Ishihara banged his fists on the table and left his chair. He said sharply, "Igor, sometimes you are too damn bloody stupid for words. I am getting fed up with this." He clapped his hands, raised his arms and made a wailing sound as if to underscore that the strain had become unbearable. "How did I do what I did yesterday? I used my contacts in the dull and dreary world of the media business by exploiting their need for headlines; by sheer commercial manipulations, by selling them a piece of sensationalism and nothing else. It was a transaction. I promised them a stunning and controversial performance—they bought it and you delivered. Why the shivering hell is this so difficult to understand?" Ishihara began to circle the table. "Angelo and I did and still do need you as our vehicle. We want to advance into the dizzying heights of the most exciting social life where the quality is measured on the intellectual Richter scale. Did you not use to mix with writers, historians, scientists, painters, film producers and philosophers, people who are creative and not merely reproductive? The eagles, Igor—we are seeking the eagles and not the jackals of the society. Yesterday, you re-emerged. The doors shall once again be opened wide. You will walk in, and we'll follow. *That* is when you have paid us back. Whatever happens thereafter is up to us to accomplish. Have I ever spoken a truer word, Angelo?"

"Not to my recollection."

Parkhurst's shoulders sagged. The expression of bewilderment and compunction waned. Ishihara's words made sense. Parkhurst looked fondly at Jennifer who smiled. He saw Yasmin staring at her husband and thought she had good reasons to be proud of him.

17

Hardly inside the front door, Yasmin dropped her coat on a chair. She strode into the drawing room and stopped in front of the aquarium, Ishihara's pride and joy, and glared at its inhabitants.

Ishihara came in. He undid the knot of his tie. "What is the matter?"

"Nothing," she said. "Everything is just perfect."

He sat down. "If that is the case, why do you behave like a witch who has lost her broomstick?"

"Because I can't stand imbecilic questions."

"Get me a drink," he sighed.

"Why should I? Are your fat and short little legs no longer obeying your twisted brain?"

"My legs are not fat, and they are long enough to reach the ground."

"Good. Go get it yourself, then."

Ishihara found a glass and feigned hesitation eyeing his selection of cognacs before he made his decision. "One for you, my cherry tart?" he asked.

"No thank you. I don't need a tranquilizer at the moment."

He went back to his chair. "Is there a remote chance of having a civilized and rational exchange of words?"

Yasmin glided across the floor and descended gracefully into the large chair opposite him. She curled up and rested her chin against her right-hand forefinger.

What an incredible woman, he thought. I must remember to thank my gods tonight for having awarded me this most beautiful of jewels, as rare as a cross between a scorpion and a cobra. He said, "Speak, my recherché."

"You overdo it with Parkhurst."

Is that all? he thought. I doubt it. He said, "In what way?"

"Why do you have to be so overwhelmingly charismatic, so friendly and considerate? You gave quite a performance, this morning. Poor Parkhurst is completely taken in by you."

"What is wrong with that?"

"He is a nice old chap, kind and gullible, and his perception of what is going on makes me feel uncomfortable."

"Jennifer has got to you, hasn't she? The positive influence of an upright and decent woman, stuffed with the ethical values of the Western world."

Yasmin studied her slender and perfectly shaped fingers. One minute later she raised her gaze. "Do not ever again speak to me in a derogatory manner, Tadashi."

Ishihara drank. "Sorry," he said. "It came out the wrong way. I know who and what you are."

"Yes, you do."

This is a prelude, he thought. There is something else on her mind. He said, "It does not matter which way we treat Parkhurst. Ultimately, he is a British problem, and why not make the best out of it for as long as it lasts."

"That's a point."

No, he thought, this is too easy. There is an overgrown, firespitting dragon in my stomach, and he is getting restless.

"Tadashi," Yasmin said so slowly that he knew the subject to be as unwelcome as he'd anticipated, "when are we going to start a family?"

He could hear his own molars working. "We are not a in hurry, are we?"

"*In a hurry!*" she repeated icily. "Dear oh dear. Don't you realize that soon we'll be middle-aged?"

"Let there be limits to exaggerations."

"Limits? A few more years and you could have been a grandfather. I am sick and tired of this—this existence. I want a life, a life that fulfils me as a woman. We have been through all this before, and each time you shy away and tell me that we are not in a hurry. *I* am in a hurry, Tadashi. I have no desire to try to enjoy my children as a geriatric. Look at me."

He did not like the coldness of her stare. She went on, "I think you are hiding something from me. I never thought the day would come when I should find myself forced to say those words, but I believe them to be true."

Ishihara moved uneasily in his chair. A fine web of lines appeared around his eyes. For an instant he looked distant. He pressed the back of his hands against his temples as if to prevent his attention from escaping. His voice was low but clear when he said, "You know that you are only indirectly part of my operation. We made a pact once—it cannot ever be broken. You know a lot, but who, why, where and when you never should know and you never will."

"Which of those have got anything to do with what we are talking about—the pronouns or the adverbs? You can answer in your own superficial way, and I shall do my best to grasp the essence." She lit a cigarette. The smoke hid her eyes. "Is it the *who*?"

He said, "It's *when*."

"Can you elucidate?"

His usually cherubic face looked gaunt and tired. "Correction," he said, " it's the *who and* the *when*. The timetable is not up to us."

"I see. How many years are we talking about?"

"Two and a bit. "

Yasmin nodded and stared out the window.

"I always thought it right that I should retire before we settled down and started a family," he continued. "You know that. It's a risky business, what I am doing, and I would like to close the book and enjoy my children without having to travel any more."

"You have got nothing more to prove. Why can't you retire *now*? We have the money and we like it here in England. What is there to stop you?"

"I do not feel financially secure. Raising a family is a pretty costly venture. We talk about some twenty years of expenses. Also, should something happen to me, I do not want you to have to worry about your economy."

"Do not talk like that. I don't like it."

"I am being factual, like it or not. I have been through the figures, and I am not entirely comfortable with what we've got."

She saw past him. There was a vacant look in her eyes. "How long is this going to last? How many more years? How many more assignments?"

"One assignment. Only one. It is bigger than anything we have done. *One*, and that's it. I guarantee you it will be the last."

"Does Angelo know?"

"Yes, of course he knows."

The vacant look in Yasmin's eyes had not gone away. Ishihara watched his fishes. The dragon in his belly had calmed down. The silence bothered him, but it had yet to become oppressive.

She said, "Why are you being so nice to Igor Parkhurst?"

"I need him. You know that. Why do you bring it up again?"

"Give me the other real reason."

Ishihara took his time cutting the tip of his cigar. When in the right mood, Yasmin was as gentle as a nutcracker on a sore thumb. "You know I picked him because he is ideally suited for my purpose. In due time he'll be contacted, and he'll pass me the message. That's the way it works." He tossed the matchbox between his hands. "The other reason is merely a by-product."

"Of what?"

"Of his delight in experiencing his Indian summer."

"That's it?"

"I have taken a liking to the old dog. I guess it is my way of paying him back, albeit, I admit, in a perverted manner. So what. It's part of the game. I do not mind that he is happier now than he was when I first met him."

"Don't insult my intelligence, Tadashi."

Ishihara sighed. "To see him make a comeback developed into a challenge I could not resist. I wanted to find out if I could do it, if I could really handle this and convert the challenge into an achievement. I began to cherish the thought of venturing into something entirely new, face the confrontation and carry the matter through to fruition. Parkhurst became secondary, in a way."

"Now you make sense. A pity he's a nice person."

Ishihara folded his hands around his knees and rocked back and forth. "I don't disagree."

"I have asked you before, and I ask you again—is there not some way you can bend the rules?"

"I do not make the rules. The British do. Please remember, he is their man."

Yasmin slid out of her chair. "I think I'll have a tiny one." She selected her drink and said with her back towards him, "You'll have to find a solution with Parkhurst. You will lose if you don't."

Ishihara raised his chin and turned his head. He had an inveterate respect for Yasmin's ability to analyze a situation. He watched as she came towards him. She sat down on the floor in front of him.

"How come?" he said.

"Angelo."

The dragon turned and twisted. He said in a flat voice, "Kindly explain."

"Angelo cannot allow the elimination of Parkhurst. There is no way he's going to risk losing Jennifer. He does not want the hazard of her godfather's disappearance hanging like the sword of Damocles over their relationship."

"When did Angelo develop a conscience?"

"It is not a question of conscience. It is pragmatism, sheer common sense. Jennifer may never learn the truth, but *if* she does, one way or another, he knows that he's lost something he'll not ever find again. That is a risk he is not prepared to take."

"I can have a chat with him."

"A *chat?*"

"Of course, the chance is that you are right; he'll double-lock the door to his arcane mind."

"In this context it is not a door, it's a miniature cat-flap in a concrete wall. You won't get through."

"In other words, I have cornered myself?"

"You have always said that nothing can be planned to perfection, that there's forever going to be an unknown factor somewhere. In this case, that unknown factor happens to be an elderly gentleman who you are helping to re-visit the glory of former days. What a beautiful little snip of irony. It could have been funny, had the circumstances been different. Now, it's just utterly unfortunate."

"I learned about Jennifer's existence when I did my homework on Parkhurst, but only to the extent that she's the daughter of his closest friends. I did not pick up the godfather bit. Also, who the hell could have anticipated that she'd get to Angelo the way she has? Talk about negative miracles. No woman has ever before bewitched him, and it had to be this one, and it had to happen now."

"Hard luck, Tadashi."

His back was damp and his nose was itching. He said, "There must be a way out."

"Tread carefully, my love."

He looked past her. "You are right. Without Angelo I am like a sculptor without his chisel."

"You have a talent for delicate analogies."

"Supposing I tell him I have made a deal with the Brits not to touch Parkhurst?"

"Splendid. What do you tell him when he reads Parkhurst's obituary?"

He shrugged. "They broke their word, an accident—whatever."

"Why has your brain come to a standstill? What is the matter with you?"

Ishihara gulped down the rest of his drink. "I *have* to find a solution. I am not going to lose my pension fund."

"You could lose a bit more than that if you don't start thinking along straight lines."

He got up, went over to the credenza and opened his humidor. He picked a cigar. "What do we do?" he said.

"We avoid Angelo turning on you."

He stood still, like an actor transfixed in a burlesque position. "*Turn on me?* That is unthinkable."

"Nothing is unthinkable. It is a potential reality, and a reality that *I* have to live with. You can close your eyes, if you so wish, but I can't."

He lit the cigar. He put half an inch of cognac in his glass and walked back, dragging his feet. He sat down, leaned forward and scratched his head.

"Keep your dandruff away from my glass," Yasmin said.

"I need to think."

"No, you don't. Who is number one in your life?"

"You know that."

"I want to hear it."

"I am. If I cease to exist, so does my reality of you and us."

"Correct. You, then I, and us. *We* are number one only for as long as we are together. There is no other reality. It comes before anything else."

"But of course it does."

"What makes you think that Angelo has a different philosophy?"

"He hasn't."

"Then why do you say it's unthinkable that he could turn on you?"

Ishihara heard the pigeons on the windowsill. He closed his eyes. He had no answer. He tried to look as stoic as his jade Buddha.

She turned her face towards the light from the sinking sun. "Without you, I am not even a number any more. If Angelo eliminates you, I am nobody. I am without a reality and with nowhere to go."

"The joker in the pack."

"Say again?"

"Igor Parkhurst—the joker in the pack."

She tilted her head.

Ishihara waited. He squinted as he eyed her face. Like a porcelain doll, he thought; fragile and entirely innocuous—but that's on the *outside*. He believed that a solution was not far away.

She said. "Forget about making a deal with the Brits. It is universally known that they are untrustworthy." She kept staring ahead. "Angelo is toying with the idea of calling it a day. *That's* your real problem."

He gave the briefest of nods. "Identified and accepted. Now what?"

"We must convince him that the money from your *final* assignment is vital to us. We must persuade him to assure the Brits, in a way that renders logic and reason superfluous, that it is in the best interest of all parties involved to leave Parkhurst unharmed."

Ishihara rolled his tongue inside his glass before he sipped. "Angelo's got a way with people."

"Has he? I wouldn't know."

Ishihara ignored the irony. He pondered for a while. "No," he said, "I can't see him do it. He intends to live here. It would be foolish of me even to suggest it."

"There is a way," she said. "No, let me correct that: there is *possibly* a way, and I underline *possibly* because it would be witless to take him for granted." She smiled. "Almost as witless as making the mistake of going behind his back."

Ishihara stared at his wife as if he wanted to hypnotize her. "Which way?"

She raised a hand and waved airily. Her eyes darted past him.

"Which?" he repeated.

"I have heard that the end justifies the means," she said.

"I am not in the mood for riddles."

"The solution comes with a price. I want something in return."

Surprise, surprise, Ishihara thought. He kept his face a stony mask.

She said, "I do not want to put any pressure on you. It's just a simple request—not blackmail."

"Making excuses does not suit you. Tell me the solution."

"Let us first deal with the price."

Not blackmail, he thought, no, of course. Do I need a map to find out in which direction we are heading? I don't think so. "I am listening," he said.

Her smile was no longer cryptic. Her eyes were like embers in the dark. "I want a family," she said. Her voice was as clear as a bell in the night. "I want a family and a house in the country. I want it *now*, Tadashi—not in two or three years' time. We have enough money to buy a decent property and live comfortably for years ahead. You do your assignment, whenever it comes. When that book of yours is finally closed, I and a child or two will be there to help you on your road to a different life. Your mind will be at ease, and we will be there waiting for you."

He chewed on his fingernails. "Give me the solution."

"*I'll* persuade Angelo."

"How?"

"Leave that to me."

"Go find your house."

He could feel cramp coming on in his legs. He wiggled his toes. "Imagine that," he mumbled, "Angelo helplessly consumed by this Irish ingenue. I never thought I'd see the day *any* woman would make him lay down his sword."

"Get out of the fog, please."

"I momentarily forgot what an excellent shogi player you are."

"She is part of the game. How I play, is my business."

"That is perfectly true."

"Angelo deserves a bit of happiness," she said. "He has his wicked ways, but he is not all bad. Jennifer knows this, and I'm beginning to think she's got the guts to admit how well suited they are."

Ishihara removed his socks. "We can't but assume that she is an exceptional woman looking for an abstruse eccentric"

"On the other hand, Angelo isn't exactly everybody's cup of tea, as the English so eloquently phrase it, and I believe that subconsciously she is fearing disapproval."

"From her parents, you mean? I understand that she is close to them."

"Not only from her parents, but from society as a whole. Angelo is an outsider, a stranger in any and all respects of the word. Jennifer harbours a feeling of uncertainty, a scepticism of which form and shape a life with him will take."

"Brilliant. It will solve our dilemma if she drops him."

"Yes, it would, but, to be on the safe side, we'd have to presume she doesn't."

She fiddled with her lighter. "Perhaps my most astute move would be to make her well and truly believe that not in a million years will she find another Angelo."

Ishihara laughed. "Funny. That is what he said to me about you."

"Did he? When?"

"Honestly. He said it when we left Japan, sitting at the airport."

Her lips parted. Suddenly, she smiled. "We shall overcome, young Tadashi. Invite me out tonight. I want to celebrate a dream come true."

"A pleasure and an honour, my fallen angel, but first I'm having a bath. I need to soak away my aches and pains."

He could hear the water running. He leaned back and rested his head. The line between his eyes came back. Why would Yasmin persuade Jennifer that Angelo was one in a million? A piece of logic was missing. It'd be tactically unwise to ask for a few more details, though; usually, his beloved wife knew what she was doing.

He opened his mouth and breathed rhythmically. One day it would be over. All of a sudden that day seemed an eternity away, and there was nothing he could do about it.

Yasmin would be safe. Yasmin and the child or the children would be safe.

And he?

Safer.

Ishihara wondered how it would feel to live a life in peace and quiet; a life without tension, doing all the small things that altogether had to substitute the lure of the sword.

☞

As Ishihara had predicted, or knew, the invitation from Harvard came two weeks after Parkhurst's memorable Oxford performance.

His telephone had not stopped ringing. People who alleged to be old friends could not emphasize strongly enough how happy they were for him, and people who wanted to become new friends were equally delighted. Parkhurst followed Ishihara's advice and leaked the Harvard news to the press. He declined any speaking engagements and told his once co-operative publishers that options were being kept open. Yes, a lunch would have been nice, but at present moment he simply could not find the time. Next month? It was hard to say—why not give him a call?

His one-time enthusiastic agent rose from the dead and offered his renewed and improved services. Again, Parkhurst listened to Ishihara and told the agent that no such services were required, for the time being. Stay in touch? By all means.

Parkhurst and Ishihara went through a list of sixty names for the party, half of the names suggested by Ishihara. Within a week, most of the invitations had been accepted. Parkhurst tried to shake off a feeling of horror when it twigged that his run-down property would be invaded by altogether some one hundred and twenty people.

Jennifer understood that he was still in a state of convalescence, and she assured him that there was nothing to worry about. She and Yasmin would take care of whatever it took to guarantee a success, and he watched in awe as they proceeded with merciless efficiency.

☞

Parkhurst had been nervous and tense since he woke up. He was relieved when Jennifer, Yasmin, Ishihara and Vargas showed up a good three hours before official party time.

The weather was nice, not too mild, but dry and with no wind. Night would come early, and a variety of lamps had been placed between shrubs and bushes, assisted by four large spotlights mounted on the roof of the house, ensuring an easier life for those in need of fresh air.

Jennifer had got the local electrician to check that everything also functioned inside; most of the rooms had not been used since Miriam ruled. The window cleaners and the gardeners had come and gone. The carpets had been shampooed. The glasses were done and the flower arrangements were in place.

"There is nothing to be nervous about, Uncle Igor," Jennifer said and took his hands. "Everything is under control. The caterers will be here by five o'clock, at the latest."

Yasmin came over. "A worried look on such a handsome face is out of place," she smiled. "Cheer up. It will be an evening to remember with fondness and pride." She took a step back. "Never before have I seen a Greek god in a tuxedo. You look very dignified."

Ishihara strolled in with a glass of wine in his hand. "This is your evening, oh famous bard. Bask in the glory. Use your natural charm and wit." He paused. "Remember this—any snide remark from *anybody* you squash instantly. Do it with a smile, but do it. Some will try, in view of circumstances. That is inevitable, but you are not going to be pushed around any more."

Parkhurst wished that he, too, had a drink in his hand. "You are probably right. I have allowed myself to be knocked about a bit. No more."

Ishihara beamed. "That's my boy. The good thing about experience is that it makes you realize how many shits you have wasted your time and money on, during the years."

Jennifer said, "It is true what Tadashi inferred—the reborn Igor Parkhurst is a rock, not a punching bag."

"Least of all a drivelling clown," Ishihara said. "As of today, the Parkhurst they all know is a man of stature, a towering giant re-emerging from the mist of voluntary obscurity. Yasmin, my orchid, why don't you go and give those caterers a final call. Tell them they've got fifteen minutes to get here."

Parkhurst and Ishihara watched the two women walking across the lawn. Both wore long dresses, Jennifer's dark green and Yasmin all in black. Both were discreetly made up; Yasmin displayed an exquisite but limited selection of her most precious jewellery, and Jennifer none apart from her diamond ring.

"Quite a sight," Ishihara said.

"They are breathtaking. Why couldn't they be forty years older? By the way, where is Angelo? I have not seen him since he arrived."

"He's around, somewhere. He likes trees. This is not his scene. I do not think he's feeling too comfortable." Ishihara chuckled. "His presence demonstrates the grip Jennifer has got on him. My oh my—the age of miracles."

Jennifer and Yasmin came back.

"It is all under control," Yasmin said. "The caterers will be here any minute."

"Has anyone seen Angelo?" Jennifer asked.

Ishihara pointed. "Try where the big oak trees are. Ten to one he is there."

She found him leaning against one of the massive oaks. A glass was placed on a nearby stone. He stood staring up through the branches and looked at ease.

"Hello," she said.

"Hello. Incredible, these trees. So old and majestic and awe-inspiring. I could walk the forests for days."

Jennifer could smell the whisky. "You know that my parents are coming."

"I do. You and I are strangers."

"Yes," she said, gratefully. "I would like to introduce you properly. I mean, not here, not tonight. When it's only the four of us."

"Fine with me."

"It is important to me," Jennifer pressed. "I love and respect them, and I know that they would appreciate a—a..."

"—formal introduction."

Jennifer smiled. "Yes, a formal introduction. You do not mind, do you?"

"Anything you say. Your parents are very lucky, and so are you."

Yes, we are, she thought. For how many years had Angelo roamed through life without anybody? Once, there must have been somebody.

The caterers were as good as their word. Nothing was missing, and everything looked up to standard. Under the guidance of Jennifer and Yasmin, the chef organized smoothly and with great efficiency. Jennifer's feeling of anxiety began to subside.

By seven-thirty the first guests arrived. Parkhurst greeted each with a few chosen words and an amiable smile. His unhurried assertiveness surprised Ishihara who did not leave Parkhurst's side until the last couple had arrived. Jennifer and Yasmin took on their roles as hostesses with a quiet and natural elegance.

Parkhurst had made up his mind to stick to white wine for at least three hours, and in modest quantities. Any compliment or flattering remark was received with grace and decorum. A small orchestra—piano, flute and guitar—played softly in the background. Soon the atmosphere superseded Parkhurst's dreams of a thoroughly successful evening.

He saw his long-time publisher Peter Howard making a move and smiled genially.

"Igor, my old friend," Howard enthused, "this is marvellous! As I have always said, you can't keep a good man down." He turned to his wife. "Have I not always said that, Daphne? Have I not always said a talent is a talent is a talent? I should know, having got a pretty unique one myself." He laughed rumbustiously when he saw Parkhurst smile and moved a step closer. "Now, what is my greatest talent, Igor!" he boomed and nudged Parkhurst.

Parkhurst looked at the bloated face of a man he had never really liked, a man who readily swapped integrity for opportunism whenever convenient, a man whose god was safely deposited in a compartment of his wallet.

"As you know, Peter, my ability to observe has its limitations. I am afraid I shall have to ask you to illuminate."

Howard's skin was as thick as the doors of his Rolls Royce. "I have always said, give a man a break, and he'll prove that his gift is imperishable. I never fail to read a writer—no pun intended. His mind is an open book to me. I read him like I read his works. Have I not always said that, Daphne? *Insight*, Igor. *That's* my greatest talent."

Daphne said, "It is nice to see you back, Igor."

"Thank you for those kind words, Daphne," Parkhurst said and smiled. He wondered why she had stayed married to someone as morally inferior as Peter Howard for all those years.

Ishihara bowed. "I'm afraid we have to circulate, Igor. Please excuse us. That was perfect," he added when they were out of earshot from the publisher. "Keep it up, now. No slips. Let us say hello to your loyal and industrious agent."

"Igor!" Leo Dresbach blurted, "I wish I could express in words how happy I am for you. When will your next script be ready? Let us have lunch next week. We *must* discuss your future. I've got some options you wouldn't believe."

"I appreciate your kindness," Parkhurst said. "However, for the time being I am rather busy counting my onions."

"Divine!" Dresbach giggled, "same, good old Igor, mellifluous and urbane as ever. Do not spend too much time with your onions, though. They make your eyes water, you know, preventing you from seeing properly." He glared at Ishihara the way a vicious mongrel eyed a rival. "Just like sewage."

"You know a lot about sewage, Mr. Dresbach?" Ishihara asked.

Dresbach had the hairdo of a Shetland pony. He fumbled with his mane before he made a dramatic gesticulation. "It's part of life, I'm afraid."

"So is puking, but that does not make viewing compulsory."

The fissure under Dresbach's nose widened. "That was incredibly amusing and well coined. You must be born in this country." He licked his nicotine-stained teeth.

"Thankfully not," Ishihara said with a hint of exaggerated patience. "Where I come from, agents do not talk in capital letters and produce in invisible ink. Kindly excuse us. The host wishes to say hello to some of his more unsullied guests."

They moved towards the French doors.

"You are still holding back," Ishihara said. "You left it to me to tackle this excretion. Why?"

Parkhurst nodded and smiled to his guests as he and Ishihara strolled into the garden. Ishihara's eyes did not leave Parkhurst's face. They stopped in the centre of the lawn. Both smiled as if they enjoyed a most amicable conversation.

"Well?"

Parkhurst looked at his watch. His second glass of cognac was still hours away. "I do not mind the odd ironic or satirical comment," he said, "that does not cause me any problem. Sarcasm, on the other hand, is not what I do best. You are a natural, and I am not."

"There is room for improvement in all of us."

"Arguably."

"Let us assume that there is. What is not debatable is that no progress can be made unless the will to move forward is present."

"There certainly have been moments when I wished I could be more acerbic, but it seems to go against the grain. Perhaps I am just not made that way."

"Made? Nobody is entirely made this or that way. To some extent we *make* ourselves. Anything else would be like claiming that everything is genetic and we are therefore unable to shape and form and discipline ourselves towards the image of what we *want* to be."

"Where does this lead us?"

The Japanese raised his head and gazed at the sapphire sky where the first stars had become visible. A hue of yellow in the west indicated an early moon.

"You are a fine man, Igor," he said gently. "You are polite, well-mannered and considerate. You do not want to hurt other people's feelings. You have a strong tendency to give them the benefit of the doubt, even where none exists. All commendable qualities, in any human being, seen isolated, but dangerous in a world less than ideal. Such qualities leave you vulnerable, simply because most people mistake overall decency for leniency. They think you are weak, somebody who can easily be pushed about and laughed at behind his back. Are you weak? No, you are not. You do have a *weakness*, though, and that is that you render yourself susceptible to lesser beings' exploiting your chivalry. You allow them to retain their conviction that you are a human jellyfish, a gifted but spineless gentleman."

Parkhurst moved to get out from the glare of the spotlight. "Perhaps," he said.

"No perhaps. You have to put your foot down whenever so required. You see, it also goes against the grain to be a pushover. During the short time we have known each other, you have indeed demonstrated that you have the wit and the will to instigate measures when necessity so demands."

Parkhurst suddenly felt weary and dispirited. He suspected that the anxiety of preparing for the party had taken its toll; it had been more of a strain than he had hitherto acknowledged.

Yasmin came towards them. Her radiant smile made Parkhurst feel better.

She said, "What a party. Everybody is enjoying the evening. This is what I call a stunning success. Be proud, Igor."

Parkhurst looked at the moon rising over yellow fields. There was a squawk to his voice when he said, "Thanks to you and Jennifer and my protective shadow here."

Yasmin laughed. "Why do you always underestimate yourself?" she said. The words reverberated through Parkhurst's mind. She put her arm around Ishihara. "Have you seen Jennifer?"

"Keeping an eye on Angelo, I guess."

"Don't be nasty. Let us go and cheer him up."

They went inside and ran into Jennifer. She was talking to her old friend Delia who was accompanied by a high-ranking member of the American Embassy.

Jennifer made her excuse and joined them in their search for Vargas. "Strange," she said to no one in particular.

"What?" Yasmin said.

"Delia. The man she is going to marry is in Singapore, and here she is with this American fellow."

"Why is that strange? They are probably old friends. He got an invitation, didn't want to come on his own and Delia was available. What's the mystery?"

"They seem kind of intimate."

"So what? It is not your problem. She likes men and wants to have a last fling before being incarcerated."

"You are right," Jennifer said. "I am being prudish."

They found Vargas sitting on his own in the corner of a sofa. He had a glass in one hand and a cigar in the other.

"Is everything all right?" Jennifer asked.

"Fine," Vargas smiled and got up. "I am enjoying myself. Lots of funny people about."

She nodded. "That is one way to look at it."

"I hope you are having a good time, Mr. Vargas," Parkhurst said.

"I am, thank you. It has been entertaining, so far."

Jennifer sat down. The other three nodded and withdrew.

"Are you sure everything is all right?"

"Yes," he said and sat next to her. "Why do you keep asking?"

"Well, you are sitting here on your own. It's like you are a bit…"

"—lost? Not so."

She looked at his glass.

"Do you see that woman over there?" he asked.

"Which one?"

"The one who looks like Lucifer's idea of the Virgin Mary, next to the fat chap with glasses."

"What about her?"

"She came over and talked to me. First she gave a summary of her own life and that of her husband's; very successful people, I was made to understand. Then she began asking me questions."

"And—?"

"I dislike it. My life is none of her or anybody else's business. She got the message, to her credit, and went off to pester someone else. Empty chatter. Is this what-do-you-do-for-a-living and where-do-you-come-from and related palaver all people can hit on? Have they not got anything of substance on their minds?"

"It is known as conversation and generally perceived as a way of getting to know each other."

"I have no wish to know her. She came across as a vacuous bore. Besides, I have no talent for idle chit-chat."

"Put you next to an oyster and you'll both be happy?" Jennifer glanced at the raven-haired beauty that was staring back. "Maybe she fancies you."

Vargas waited till she looked at him. He smiled. "Oh well, it takes more than physical appearance to be interesting. Bear in mind that I discovered the person Jennifer before I enjoyed the woman Jennifer. Not the other way round."

She felt her cheeks getting hot and tingly. "There is no limit to what you are prepared to say, is there?"

"No, my blushing cactus—not in your company, that is."

"Did you see my parents?"

"We exchanged a few words when they arrived. My first impression was positive. I would not go so far as to say I like them since I don't know them, yet, but the initial signals were positive. Does this cheer you up?"

"Good Lord! Are you actually telling me that there might be the odd human being you do not instantly dislike?"

Vargas did not answer. He did not let go of her eyes.

"I am sorry. Of course it matters that the signals were positive." She wanted to squeeze his hand, but didn't. "I am supposed to be the hostess," she said and got up. "See you later."

Vargas' eyes followed her until she was out of sight.

Gregory Pritchard-White had come on his own. He invariably did, Parkhurst knew; Pritchard-White never took his wife anywhere. He always used the same excuse; one of his four children wasn't too well or, more often, some virus had hit his wife. Parkhurst also knew the real reason; Pritchard-White kept his private life strictly apart from anything he suspected could have even a hypothetical association with his work. It was an official secret that he was obsessed with his organization, and that he was a rock solid believer in the old maxim that prevention was better than cure, that was, when expediency so demanded. Some of his colleagues wondered if his family was of less importance to him than what he deemed to be his mission in life, and then there were the odd cynics who did not wonder at all.

Ishihara said, "Don't put it off any longer, Igor. Show the maggot who is in command here."

Parkhurst feigned surprise. "What do you mean?"

"You know bloody well what I mean. It is time to have a few words with Her Majesty's representative, even if you find him less mesmerizing than a decaying corpse."

"The curse of my life," Parkhurst muttered.

But Ishihara had heard him. "And the cause of your re-birth. Be positive. Come, let us have a look at him," he added with a smile that Parkhurst found disturbing. He could feel the muscles in his lower back stiffen as he cast a sideways glance at his old foe.

Pritchard-White was tall, but since they first had met his posture had changed; he stooped and he had developed a tendency to keep his chin close to his chest. Deep lines ran from the jawbone and up to his brownish-yellow eyes. The gauntness of his face gave him a look of attenuation, enhancing the prominence of his nose and accentuating the protrusion of his cheekbones. His slick, dark hair was combed back with no sign of greying; a mite too dark, Parkhurst thought, but where was the evidence that vanity was stillborn in civil servants.

Pritchard-White was deep in conversation and visibly amused by Lady Margaret Hunter, a striking woman in her late twenties. Parkhurst had met her, on a few occasions. She was known as a *scream* and a *riot* by some and as a pain-in-the-arse by most. Nature had provided her with stunning looks whilst her parents had instilled in her from an early age the imperative that anything goes in the name of happiness. This euphemism for success had been defined as the combined blessings of prosperity, fame and social prestige.

Three years ago she had been the blushing bride of Lord Hunter. He was forty years her senior, a wealthy landowner who was also the chairman of a large publishing group. He was her third husband. According to the gossip columnists, her previous ones had both paid dearly for the privilege of her fleeting intimacy.

Parkhurst had seen but not met the honourable lord before. The invitation had been Ishihara's idea. He had gone through a list of the most powerful publishers in town, and Parkhurst had seen no reason to object. He only hoped that Lady Margaret for once would behave and not seek out some artless soul to be the victim of her caustic tongue and impressive knowledge of foul language.

"Mr. Parkhurst," Pritchard-White said, "what a fabulous evening. I must compliment you on absolutely everything." He glanced at Lady Margaret. "That does include the most delightful of guests. You clearly know a lot of interesting people."

"Doesn't he," Lady Margaret concurred. Parkhurst thought that she sounded like her own image of the commoner's idea of true aristocracy. "A really splendid get-together," she concluded.

Parkhurst said, "Thank you both. You are as kind as you are observant."

Lord Hunter took it upon him to participate. "Indeed," he said in a voice that reminded Parkhurst of a kettle running dry on a hot plate. "A jolly good party, Mr. Parkhurst." His pale, grey eyes under rustcoloured eyebrows pored over his host. "When can one expect your next literary crusade, Mr. Parkhurst? I would certainly be interested to have a look."

His eyes left Parkhurst and fixed Ishihara without waiting for a reply. "Are you in the car business, Mr.—?"

"Ishihara"

"Japanese, I take it?"

"So do I. And you?"

The sneer of bafflement coupled with indignation was etched on Lord Hunter's face. "I beg your pardon?"

Ishihara's face showed infinite patience. "Do not rush it, Mr. Hunter. It can't be an easy task to decide whether you are a Brit, a Great Brit, an Englishman or a UK-anian."

Lord Hunter twisted his neck as if following a tennis rally. "Frightfully sorry, old chap. That one was lost on me."

"Like the empire. I see. Never mind." Ishihara made his expression as blank as his voice was bland. "To answer your question, I am not in the car business."

"Ah. What, then? You chaps seem to be taking over what there is to take over, these days. Can't say I approve. The reward for winning the war, you and the Germans, I suppose." He sniggered as if it impressed him that his knowledge of history blended with his corrosive wit.

Ishihara said, "This may surprise you, but there is actually more to Japan than cars."

"Ah, yes, of course. We saw that during the war, didn't we? One does not approve of such behaviour, quite frankly." Lord Hunter opened his mouth wide and revealed that he did not believe in dentists' right to exist. "Nothing personal, if that needs to be added."

Ishihara 's face showed mild amazement. "As far as cars and everything else go, we only do with skills and efficiency what you Brits have lost the ability to do, namely to produce and market profitably quality products," he said as if talking to someone showing signs of senility.

"As for your other scholarly articulation, there are numerous occasions in our day-to-day life when a comment can only be perceived as an offence if one assumes that the originator of such comment possesses sufficient intelligence to comprehend what he is actually saying. Hence, Mr. Hunter, your obiter dictum cannot possibly be classified as an offence. Nothing personal, if that needs to be added, my dear chap."

Lady Margaret's lips curled like a pair of snails set on fire. "It is *Lord* Hunter."

Ishihara looked at her for a few seconds. "Madam, may I compliment you on your jewellery. A Christmas tree pales in comparison."

Her eyes went glossy. She flicked a lock from her eyes and turned to Parkhurst. "We shall be ever so delighted to evaluate your next manuscript, Igor. It is an old truth that the best writers are those who are the most besmeared by lowlife experiences, baseness and the odour of foreign, quasi-intellectual squalor." Her full and red lips parted. "We won't hold that against you, dear, personally, I mean."

Ishihara said, "No, that's not cricket."

Parkhurst was too baffled to react. Lady Margaret took her husband by the elbow. "Shall we go and get some fresh air, darling?"

But Lord Hunter was not quite ready. "Do get in touch," he said with the grin of a hammerhead and patted Parkhurst on the shoulder. "I would love to have you in our stable."

Lady Margaret pushed him. "We *really* should move around, dear."

Parkhurst shuddered. Her voice resembled a chainsaw running low on fuel. As they turned, she added loud enough for the other three to hear, "Don't worry, darling. I'll get the fucking Jap."

Parkhurst shook his head as if waking up from a bad dream. Pritchard-White smiled and blinked feverishly. "I could not help enjoying that," he said. "Well done, Mr. Ishihara. Lord Hunter is not famous for being tactful, and as for his wife..." He shrugged as if partly responsible.

Ishihara crossed his hands. "Two true three-dimensional characters," he said, "arrogant, pompous and ignorant."

Pritchard-White laughed. Parkhurst smiled feebly.

"Do not think that you have been discarded," Ishihara said. "The honourable lord and in particular his vile and vulgar little vanity-supporter will walk on nails to get you on their lists." He smiled. "Yesterday shunned, today worshipped."

Parkhurst said, "I am not so sure."

"Human nature, Igor. Failing to catch you now would be tantamount to a declaration of failure. They are all here to cash in on you. The lady is a leech. No way have you seen the last of her."

"A leech," Parkhurst repeated and wondered how far away cognac-time was.

Ishihara looked at Pritchard-White. "Not the rarest of specimens, regardless of profession, I'd say."

Pritchard-White had stopped blinking. The light from the candelabra played with the yellow specks in his eyes. "You wouldn't be a psychologist, would you, Mr. Ishihara?"

"Only by vocation and lifelong training." He paused for a while. "And, I would say, by fascination. My métier is one of Japan's most traditional, noble, revered, thriving and natural crafts. I am a diplomat."

"A diplomat," Pritchard-White said and eyeballed the straightfaced Japanese. "That is interesting. You have recently joined the Embassy, I take it?"

Ishihara looked towards the sofa where Vargas was sitting on his own. "My work is not directly associated with the Embassy. The political implications of my occupation are somewhat more Byzantine. I am sure you appreciate the nuance."

Pritchard-White blinked. "The world of politics is indeed an arena of intricate contests and often of the most clandestine nature."

"That is a most exact comment," Ishihara said. "It is regrettable, though, that some of life's callings originate from man's remarkable gift for keeping the seven deadly sins alive and healthy." He raised his glass towards Vargas who nodded in return.

"This is really intriguing," Pritchard-White said. "My own thinking follows parallel lines. May I supplement your reflection with the notion that one should never accept anything that defies clinical interpretation? A shockingly high percentage do not possess the insight necessary to understand that solipsism and altruism are mutually exclusive." He peered in Vargas' direction.

Ishihara said, "A subtle theory, and not easily discredited."

Parkhurst was lost. He had no idea what the other two were on about. He sensed an undercurrent of esoteric parlance, but he was unable to decode the significance. Neither did he understand why Ishihara had suddenly jumped from finance to diplomacy.

Parkhurst's feeling of unease grew. The three of them know each other, he thought; there is something in their body language telling me that they have met before.

Pritchard-White said, "It is a great pity, but I am afraid I'll have to leave now." He looked at his watch and smiled ruefully. "My wife isn't very well."

He turned and faced Parkhurst. "Thank you so much for a most enjoyable evening."

Parkhurst said, "You are welcome." He hoped that his smile looked unaffected.

He suddenly noticed that Vargas stood between himself and Ishihara.

"I take it that the two of you were introduced earlier this evening," Ishihara said and looked from Pritchard-White to Vargas. "Mr. Pritchard-White and I have concluded that the world is a dreadful place."

Vargas dumped the butt of his cigar in the nearest ashtray. "You must know something I don't," he said.

"You are old friends?" Pritchard-White asked casually.

"Friends and colleagues," Ishihara confirmed. "We complement each other, in a manner of speaking. Yes, we do indeed go back a very long time. Anyway, don't let us keep you, Mr. Pritchard-White. You've got a fair way to go."

Pritchard-White showed no surprise. He nodded his farewell with a polite smile.

"Drive carefully, now," Ishihara added suavely. "Deadly sinners prefer the protection of darkness."

Pritchard-White's chin moved an inch further from his chest. Any trace of facetiousness had been wiped off his face. He tugged the sleeve of his jacket and said, "I appreciate your concern, Mr. Ishihara."

"Nothing to it," Ishihara said. "It was just a skittish aside of mere microscopic importance—" he looked at Vargas for a few seconds "—although it is anybody's guess what the future may bring."

They *do* know each other, Parkhurst thought, all three of them. There is an almost tangible crosscurrent here. He waited till he saw Pritchard-White putting on his coat in the hallway. "What was that all about?" he said.

Ishihara's round face radiated innocence. "What are you talking about?"

"Never mind," Parkhurst said. He had a feeling he wouldn't get a straight answer.

Ishihara said, "A very dangerous man and a true professional."

Parkhurst sensed discomfort. He shifted on his feet. "Meaning?" he asked.

"Meaning no integrity and total indifference to other people's fate in life. Meaning ruthless, blatant, cynical and highly efficient. He is somebody who considers the concept of morals to be a perverted joke and not an encumbrance. I can understand your inability to cope with a person of such distinction and the effect he's had on your state of mind. An interesting challenge."

"Challenge? In what way?"

"In making him release the grip he's got on you. He enjoys it immensely."

"What is on your mind?"

"Oh, just thinking aloud. I do believe, however, that anyone of such hubristic disposition is bound to have a serious weakness. We'll find it. It could take some time—his advantage is that he is made for the sewer in which he operates."

Yasmin and Jennifer came in from the study.

"Aren't you guys supposed to enjoy yourselves?" Yasmin said. "You look like an assembly of unsuccessful undertakers."

"Just a brief intermezzo," Ishihara said and smiled at his wife. "We were trying to solve a purely rhetorical question."

"Who was that gentleman just leaving?" Jennifer asked.

"Igor's Nemesis," Vargas said.

Yasmin stepped closer to Ishihara. She put a hand on his shoulder. "I see," she said. "Why is it that Nemesis has a face like an oversized cucumber carved by an irate child?"

"That's exactly the conundrum troubling us," Ishihara said. "How did you arrive at that observation?"

Yasmin brushed some invisible dust from the front of her dress. "A shot in the dark."

"How do you feel, Uncle Igor?" Jennifer said.

Parkhurst squinted. "I feel eternally grateful for having you around me," he said and hoped that nobody heard the tremble in his voice.

Yasmin adjusted her necklace and looked towards the garden. Vargas sipped his whisky and looked towards Conor Moran who was deep in conversation with the vicar Arthur Thornton.

Kathleen came in from the kitchen and stood next to her daughter. "What a pleasant evening," she said and stared at Vargas.

Jennifer felt numb. She wished that she could interpret the flicker of a smile that had crossed Vargas' face.

"Not least thanks to Yasmin and your daughter, Mrs. Moran," he said at his most soft-spoken. "Perfection exemplified."

Jennifer did not know where to look.

"Both Mr. Vargas and Mr. Ishihara have been of tremendous help," Parkhurst said and put his arm around Kathleen. "Without them I would still have been in the doldrums. You have no idea how much better I feel. Night and day, my dear."

Kathleen folded her hands. "I am sure that Mr. Vargas has earned his Christian name. What do you think, Jennifer?"

The smile had not left Vargas' eyes. "That is perhaps a premature assumption, Mrs. Moran. I could not resist the temptation to introduce myself to your daughter, but the pleasure was all too brief."

Clever, Jennifer thought; he did not say *when*, and can he be fluent when it suits him.

"That is nice to hear," Kathleen said. "The *too brief* bit, I mean."

Vargas said, "Thank you. I am beginning to understand why Jennifer's apparent lack of ambiguity is no coincidence."

Jennifer wanted to interrupt but could not find an appropriate comment.

But Kathleen would not let go. "What is your favourite drink, Mr. Vargas?"

"Irish whisky."

"Heavens above! Now, *that* is what I call a coincidence. You must meet my husband, Mr. Vargas. He fancies the stuff and he loves a bit of competition."

"I am looking forward to the event."

"You shouldn't happen to fancy pigeons, as well?"

"I do."

"Jesus! This is weird." Kathleen paused for effect. She ignored Jennifer's stare. "What else would you have in common with my husband, I wonder?"

"With luck on my side I shall find out," Vargas said. He lifted his glass with a slight nod towards Kathleen. "However, with the vain hope of answering your question, Mrs. Moran, your husband and I could have in common that we agree on the fundamental difference between reciprocation and retaliation."

Kathleen balked, but she quickly recovered. "You know," she said with less aggression in her voice, "my husband once contemplated joining the church. I wonder why that suddenly came to mind."

"Hear a suggestion," Ishihara said. "Could it be that neither your husband nor Mr. Vargas are particularly adept at imitating feelings?" He smiled disarmingly. "You see, Mrs. Moran, my friend Mr. Vargas is utterly hopeless when it comes to disguising explanations as excuses."

What triggered off this conversation? Jennifer thought. Has my mother taken an instant dislike to Angelo? Does she sense something and resent not being told?

Her mother could turn quarrelsome when she'd had too much to drink, aggressive and argumentative for the sake of it.

Her instincts told her that somehow her mother was struggling. She did not wish to be provocative; on the other hand, something was bothering her. She knew that she would have told the truth and introduced Vargas on the spot had the three of them been alone. She said, "Can I get anybody a drink?"

"A glass of white wine, please," Kathleen said. She avoided Jennifer's eyes.

"I'll give you a hand," Yasmin said.

They came back the moment Parkhurst rejoined the group. Conor and Arthur Thornton came over. Lord and Lady Hunter emerged from the library.

Conor smiled proudly at his daughter and nodded to Parkhurst. "I am happy for you, Igor. This is truly an evening to remember."

"It isn't over, yet," Lady Margaret said and glared at Ishihara. "Now is the time for party games."

Ishihara bowed. "I notice that you have rearranged your war paint. Your eyebrows look like Siamese twins of the Nematode family and your pupils radiate the tenderness of a lovesick chameleon."

Oh no, Parkhurst thought, here we go. I don't deserve this. He looked pleadingly at her husband, but Lord Hunter was busy studying the ceiling.

"What do you have in mind, Lady Margaret?" Parkhurst grimaced.

"Nothing too complicated," she said innocently. "Just a bit of intellectual table-tennis, perhaps. The balls could be customs, habits, traditions—you name it. After all, we are such an international crowd tonight, aren't we? We have English and Irish and Japanese balls—" she gawked at Vargas "—and whatever you are, and, who knows, there could be more contaminated blood within these four walls." She looked around, satisfied. The twenty or so remaining guests had fallen silent; Lady Margaret's reputation had not been created overnight. She took a step back, measured Ishihara from top to toe, and said, "Let us begin with you—what's-your-name." The line between her eyes went as quickly as it came. "Just a theory," she continued, "but had I not been a happily married woman, don't you think that you and I could have been the most ideal of imperfect partners?"

"Theory? Oh, I don't know," Ishihara said and scratched his chin. "Dubious compatibility is one thing, possessing a genuine and comprehensive common experience is a different and more complex aspect. I fear that you are confusing the two, Mrs. Hunter."

Lady Margaret's smile could have extinguished a bonfire. "You are implying that I am short on experience, my dear?"

"Not at all," Ishihara protested amiably. "Implying *anything* would not be worth the effort of activating one single brain-cell—my dear."

"I am afraid you are getting a tad too sophisticated for your own good, now, Mr. Ishihara," she said, suddenly remembering his name.

Ishihara puffed on his cigar. "We do have to get to the bottom of this—your fascination with the concept of experience, that is."

The silence was absolute.

Ishihara, smile in place and gold tooth glistening, raised his hand. "I have heard that you are fond of horseriding, Mrs. Hunter. Whilst we are still within the fascinating perimeter of somatic experiences, would it be too daring to suggest that the saddle gives you what your husband does not? Now, *there* is a ball for you to excogitate, my dear."

Lady Margaret threw her head back and moved her lips as if there was a cyanide pill under her tongue. "This could have been an interesting and informative conversation had you not been such a vermin," she scoffed. "You evidently do not know what *class* is."

"Funny you should say that," Ishihara said. "I was just thinking how regrettable it is that your mother did not bank on a better-class sperm producer."

Lord Hunter snapped out of his trance-like fixation with the chandelier. "That's a bit heavy coming from a Japanese," he said. "Your bloody banks are all over the place now. Being wealthy isn't everything, you know. Don't think that we have forgotten your Second World War atrocities. You chaps have a lot to apologize for, I'd say, but you never did." His gap-toothed grin was as endearing as the beak of a vulture ready for the feast.

Ishihara tugged his left earlobe and looked sorrowful. "We are waiting for someone to take the lead," he said.

Lord Hunter stretched his neck. "Oh? Who, and for what?" he said with the expression of somebody forced to chew on a chilli.

"The British, when their greed and indecency destroyed other cultures in a mindless and ultimately otiose attempt to establish an empire. Or the Americans for the Indians. Let me supplement with Spain for the Inquisition, Germany for Martin Luther, France for Napoleon and Russia for Lenin, to mention but a few. Let me throw in England for Cromwell, for the sake of balance and good order. You see, Mr. Hunter, any renouncement of past generations' activities will forever remain rhetorical, a fact that has escaped only the mentally flatfooted. Your own understanding of human nature and your perception of history can safely be written off as lukewarm academic goulash, I'm afraid." He made a circular movement with his cigar. "One thing does please me, though, my dear chap. The two of you have demonstrated that the merger between an emasculated patrician and an authentic philistine shows that there is still hope for the British aristocracy."

That did it, Parkhurst thought as Lady Margaret turned to her husband. "It is time for us to go home, darling. It is getting late."

One or two smiled. Some studied the carpet. Others paid attention to the glass in their hands.

"Allow me to see you out," Parkhurst said. His face was a mask of concern. "Thank you so much for coming."

"Good night, everybody," Lord Hunter said. "Jolly nice."

"Good night," came the chorus back.

Yasmin moistened her lips and took Ishihara's glass. "Poor plebeian cow."

"She met her match," Delia said. "That was hilarious."

Not the word I would have used, Jennifer thought.

Vargas had looked unruffled except for the blue of his eyes getting darker during the parley; an expression Jennifer had begun to interpret as a sign of amusement.

"What a pity she left," Ishihara said. "It is not often one comes across a female with the body of a shrunken Venus, the heart of a centipede and the mind of an unwashed slut."

Yasmin touched Jennifer's arm. "I know. Strong language and how could the paragon of gentlemanly behaviour conduct himself in such a manner. Those are your thoughts, aren't they?"

Jennifer stared back.

Yasmin continued, "Tadashi takes no nonsense from anybody. He simply cannot understand why he should. He leaves to his opponent to choose his or her weapon, and then he uses the very same weapon against them. You and I would not have employed such language, but that is irrelevant. I am not Tadashi, and neither are you. Tadashi and Angelo are winners; they are extremely competitive by nature, and the thought of defeat does not cross their minds, irrespective of the nature of the battle. They have scant regard for rules in general, and none whatsoever if the opponent plays dirty." She paused, took her gold cigarette case from her bag and lit one of her Sobranies. "I do not feel that I have a right to criticize them. Do you?"

Jennifer, unprepared for what she thought to be an attack rather than a vigorous speech of defence, shook her head. "I presume you are right," she said. "Most of the time I find aggression unnecessary, but none of us have a right to apply our principles to anybody else."

Yasmin's eyes were neither friendly nor hostile. "Good," she said. "I have lived with Tadashi for many years, and I love him for what he is. I know that a few things could have been different, which means that I do not approve of everything he does and says and stands for. *However*, my dear Jennifer, should I be stupid enough to try and alter some of him into an image of unreality, I can just as well say goodbye instead."

Jennifer tilted her head. "Message received."

"Fine," Yasmin said with a clear trace of irony, "but before you secretly criticize my opinionated self with too much disdain, please bear in mind that there is one fundamental difference between us; I speak from experience, and you do not."

"It was not my—"

"Of course not. We both know, to our tremendous personal benefit, why most relationships are in shambles; lack of respect, want of tolerance, inattention to felicitous and legitimate idiosyncrasies and the demonic consequences of self-righteousness. Are you still in agreement, my dear Irish fairy?"

Jennifer smiled. "Food for thought. You maketh sense. I don't think I could argue even if I wanted to."

"Which you don't."

"No. As a matter of fact—" she stopped short, censored by her own ingrained instincts for privacy. She had never met a woman so easy to talk to as Yasmin, but being familiar was a far cry from being open-hearted.

"What?"

Jennifer quickly made up her mind. "It so happens that my mother has the same philosophy."

"A sensible woman. She does what she preaches. I must get to know her." She flashed a smile.

Jennifer felt tired. It had been a long day. The tension of having Vargas and her parents under the same roof did not help. Nor did she find it conducive to her peace of mind that her mother seemed to have her suspicions about her daughter and Angelo Vargas.

On her way to the kitchen she saw Vargas heading for the sofa. He returned her smile.

She sat down at the kitchen table and exchanged some well-meant niceties with the chef. She checked the invoice and signed on behalf of Parkhurst.

A few minutes later Jennifer was alone. She looked out the window at the fir trees, black against the moon and the velvet sky.

The fatigue began to lose some of its grip, but she decided to ask Parkhurst if she could stay overnight. It would not be wise to go back with Vargas, and she had no desire to fend off seemingly innocent but in reality intricate questions or comments from her mother.

Tomorrow would come soon enough, and she would take care of what did not take care of itself. What poetic resonance, she thought and laughed softly at her own wishful thinking. Tomorrow was another slog. Nothing came without efforts or sacrifices, or both.

She got up with her mind focused on her future with Angelo Vargas and their life together. Why not tell him now that she would introduce him to her parents in the course of the week and she could bring her things over the day thereafter?

Yes, why not; the moment was as good as any.

Jennifer came through the door from the hallway into the drawing room the moment Delia got up from the sofa. She was white-faced, visibly trembling and unable to hold back her tears. She said something to Vargas that Jennifer could not hear. Then Delia turned and marched straight past towards the cloakroom and began a frantic search for her coat.

Jennifer followed. "What is it, Delia? What happened?"

Delia turned around. Her makeup was in a mess and her voice quivered. "I—I cannot tell. It is too..." she lowered her head with a sob and buried her face in her coat. "Find Daniel for me," she wept. "I want to go home."

"Please tell me, Delia."

There was no response. Jennifer waited, but Delia remained silent.

Jennifer felt helpless. She raised her hands, dropped them and said, "I'll find Daniel."

She knew that Vargas looked at her as she crossed the floor.

She said calmly, "I am sorry, Daniel, but I believe Delia is not feeling very well. She wants to go home."

Daniel quickly excused himself.

Jennifer waited till she heard the entrance door close before she went over to Vargas. He stood up.

"What happened, Angelo?"

"She got upset."

She swallowed. "I realize that. What did you say to her?"

Vargas kept his stare. Seconds ticked away. "Not much."

His indifference annoyed Jennifer to an extent that made her almost blind with fury. Easy now, she thought, you are tired, you are tense and you can very readily turn irrational.

"Did you insult her?" she asked, surprised at the harshness of her own voice. "Delia is one of my oldest friends, but what do you care?"

Vargas showed no emotions.

"Can't you even be bothered to defend yourself?" she said, her eyes all over his impassive face.

"There is nothing to defend."

Something snapped inside her. "I see," she said and tried to fight uptightness, fatigue and tears. "I understand. You and Ishihara are two of a kind, vile and cruel and primitive behind your feeble little facades of civility and skin-deep manners. You are just a carnivorous animal in spite of your books and your archaic lore and your quasi-erudite observations. You have a deep hatred for everything and everybody, Angelo. Your intransigence and your asocial attitude is beyond normal comprehension." She paused, unable to understand why the expression in his eyes did not change. She inhaled sharply. "I do not think that you and I have much in common, Angelo. I do not wish to see you again."

Vargas put down his glass and left.

Jennifer walked slowly towards the French doors and out into the garden. She looked up towards the stars when she heard an engine start. The closing chapter of my dream, she thought. She could not feel the chill of the night, only exhaustion and emptiness. The breeze made the leaves on the ground dance with a mournful rustle around her feet. She thought of how badly she had wanted him and of how little it took to shatter a life and leave it in ruins. Dear God, she whispered, please save me from my own thoughts and please let me rest and help me to wake up with the strength to face another future.

"Come inside," Yasmin said. "It's freezing, out here."

They went back in. Parkhurst came over. There was a worried expression on his face. "You look absolutely drained, Jennifer. Is anything wrong?"

"I am just very tired."

"Of course you are. It has been such a long day. I can't thank you enough. Could you do with a night-cap?"

"I want to go to bed. Do you mind if I stay overnight?"

"I would vigorously object to anything else."

Jennifer walked over to her parents who stood on their own. "Uncle Igor persuaded me to stay overnight," she said. "I am exhausted."

"Sensible," Conor said.

Kathleen embraced her. "Some rest will do you good," she said. Her voice was as neutral as the expression in her eyes.

She knows, Jennifer thought, but she can't figure out why Angelo suddenly left. She won't ask, and she has yet to learn that there is nothing to tell.

Parkhurst faced the few remaining guests. "Listen, everybody. Jennifer wishes to retire, and I would like to thank her and Yasmin for their marvellous efforts. Without their assistance I could not possibly have arranged this evening." He raised his glass. "To Jennifer and Yasmin. Good night, my dear."

Jennifer laid on her back and waited for sleep that did not come. She toyed with the idea of sneaking back for a glass of red wine.

She listened to the wind softly caressing the branches of the trees. She tried to think of the moon as a barren piece of rock and dust and the stars as masses of gas and fire. She wished that the curtains had been heavier so that the light could not come through.

The universe exploded and she thought of Angelo Vargas as a kind and gentle human being. The flame flickered and died out and she saw only the cold blue eyes of a man who had nothing to say.

Something stirred her memory. As from a distance she saw her mother's face and then Yasmin's. Had they not stared at her when Angelo left?

They had; Kathleen with an expression of disbelief mixed with worry, and Yasmin's face, usually so insusceptible, had shown a trace of amusement and—yes, there was something else, a look that resembled mild despair.

She never looked at the clock and she did not know when sleep came.

18

Kathleen and Conor praised the evening on several occasions. To Jennifer's relief, her mother made no comment about Vargas. Nor did she indirectly hint that she harboured her own thoughts about a presumed relationship. Both she and Conor had fallen for Yasmin's charm and beauty. Kathleen did not find it easy to swallow what she described as Ishihara's offensive treatment of Lady Hunter; not that the crude bitch didn't deserve any better, *but nevertheless*. Conor excused Ishihara and said that he had done nothing but pick up the glove and thrown it back. Admittedly, the language could have been more refined, but the Lady was infamous for her vulgarity and sorely needed to be taught a lesson.

Kathleen said that Yasmin would be welcome any time. Conor argued that Ishihara would behave himself if treated with respect and dignity and should therefore be made to feel equally welcome. Kathleen had her doubts, but she did not put down a veto.

Jennifer listened politely and said, yes, it would be nice to invite them to dinner one evening. She would do it as soon as pressure from work eased. She smiled warmly at her father and avoided her mother's eyes and knew that sooner or later an explanation was required so that the tension would go away and the reassuring feeling of normality could come back. Life would go on as before—the way it was prior to the day she first set her eyes on Angelo Vargas.

He never called.

Jennifer buried herself in work. She dodged social life, lost weight and made money. With the job in Sloane Street long completed and rewarded with a glowing reference, she discovered that she could choose her clients practically at will. She had never doubted her own skills, but her ability to negotiate and drive a hard bargain surprised her.

Once in a while she wondered how much her business would be worth on the open market, but she knew that she was its main asset. She had to build up a wider clientele basis, a larger staff with more overall experience, and a more solid reputation before she could sell out and do something else.

What, she did not know; what she did know was that she wasn't destined to be a designer for the rest of her life.

Destiny.

Vargas never called. Why should he?

Once, she called Delia and asked what had happened. Delia refused to speak; she had never been so offended, so hurt, so trampled on *ever* in her life, and that was all she was going to say. She sounded genuinely pleased when Jennifer told her that Vargas was history. Very sensible, Delia said; the man was obviously nothing but a latter-day Attila, if not *more* primitive. Jennifer certainly deserved better than to be chained to a pernicious Neanderthal like Vargas.

Delia's outburst irritated Jennifer almost to the point of defending him, but she kept a neutral tone and suggested half-heartedly that they had lunch together in the foreseeable future. Delia promised to call. Jennifer had not heard from her since.

She admitted that she missed him. He was very much alive in her mind, but she kept telling the mirror that little or no compatibility existed. There was an abyss between them that no bridge could span.

In order to maintain a degree of mental equilibrium, she tried to convince herself that time would heal. In a few months' time Angelo Vargas would be forgotten, or at least reduced to a faded memory.

She also missed Yasmin but wasn't all too surprised not to hear from her. Yasmin's loyalty was with Vargas; the three of them were old friends and, however disappointing and hurtful, she was but a passing ship vanishing over the horizon and into the night.

Jennifer tried to quench the feeling of being written off, discarded and forgotten, but with little success. She could ignore that Ishihara stuck to his friend, but it puzzled her that Yasmin could walk away so effortlessly. Jennifer had come to like and respect Yasmin, but, evidently, it wasn't mutual. The thought of being tossed aside like a broken toy nagged Jennifer, but she couldn't make herself call Yasmin and ask if they could meet up.

The telephone rang one Sunday morning. Jennifer had not had a good night's sleep, and she answered with a grumpy "Hello."

"Praise heaven," a female voice said. "You are there. I admit that this is awfully early—ten o'clock, oh dear—but I simply *have* to know if the rumours are true."

Jennifer did not recognize the posh voice. "Who is this," she said sharply, "what rumours?"

"That Miss Moran is hibernating. Could it be nothing but cheap and illfounded gossip? The Irish rose is out and about in full bloom?"

"Yasmin!"

"Ah! Wasn't I good! All I need now is for Tadashi to get his knighthood. Slim chance, admittedly, a Lady Yasmin joining the aristocracy where she so clearly belongs. How does that grab you? Try to ignore my features before you answer."

Jennifer was so relieved that she did not dare to laugh. "Yasmin," she repeated, "how are you?"

"Very well, thank you. Tadashi and I are looking for a house—what an ordeal. My apologies for not having called you before, but I have been terribly busy. Why is it that all estate agents have whipped cream for brains? Anyway. I have picked out two possibles, so far. Do you think that you could come with me one day and have a look?"

"Of course. That would be so nice, Yasmin. I feel like I have not seen you for ages."

"I miss you, too. Why don't we tear ourselves loose one day next week and have lunch together?"

"Super," Jennifer said. She was still trying to recover.

"Wednesday, high noon, at Harrods? It's convenient, and I like it there. The tables are not too close."

"That would be fine."

"Splendid." She hung up.

Jennifer sat on the edge of her bed for a long time. She felt at ease. The moment of calm, of magic peace, was like watching the first fall of snow.

Yasmin was already there, immaculate and radiant as ever. She got up and embraced Jennifer, took a step back with her hands on Jennifer's shoulders and said, "Are you on some stupid diet?"

"Not intentionally."

"You are not, and that is all you can say—*not intentionally?*"

They sat down. Less than a third of the tables were occupied. Jennifer blessed the quiet atmosphere.

Yasmin ordered and put a Sobranie in her cigarette holder. "So," she said and turned the holder between her fingers as she watched the smoke drift away, "how is life treating you?"

"Very well. I have got more work than I can cope with at the moment. I think I must learn to pace myself. How is the house-hunting going?"

"What a mess. I tell you, it is a nightmare. Those estate agents are like politicians; you can't believe a word of what they are saying. Misleading? The understatement of the century. But, not to worry. I shall find what I want, eventually."

"Where are you looking?"

"Berkshire, Hampshire, Oxfordshire—it does not really matter. Tadashi and I agree that there are four deciding factors; namely the layout and the quality the property itself, the condition of it, location and value for money. There is a place on the Berkshire-Hampshire border that very much appeal to me. Tadashi hasn't seen it yet. It is a picturesque house, with lovely grounds and several outbuildings, one of them perfect for a dojo. I feel that the asking price is too steep—the whole property requires a bit of work to get it up to standard. Would you like to come along and give me your opinion one day?"

Jennifer said, "I would be delighted. Tadashi wouldn't mind?"

"Not at all. The more he can leave to me, the happier he is. Quite a shrewd little Nipponese, that husband of mine. He knows that I won't rest until I have found something that suits us both."

Shrewd he most certainly is, Jennifer thought. She said, "Are you keeping the flat in London?"

"Tadashi wants to keep it, at least for the time being. I don't care one way or the other as long as we can afford it." Yasmin stumped out her cigarette. "Let us go and get tempted."

They stood next to each other at the salad bar. Yasmin said, "How is Uncle Igor?"

"He is fine. I have called him a couple of times, but I have not seen him since—since the party." Jennifer put salad on her plate. "He is disappointed that Harvard got delayed, but he is writing again and he expects the manuscript to be completed in six months' time."

"I understand that Harvard is only a few weeks away," Yasmin said. "Tadashi can't wait."

"Is he going over?"

"He certainly is. He wouldn't miss it for the world. He and Parkhurst have created a gem of a speech. The Americans won't know what hit them."

"That sounds ominous. I thought he had a soft spot for the Americans."

"He may well have, but Tadashi hasn't. Pure hatred is a mild description."

Jennifer smiled. "That's a bit dramatic, isn't it?"

"Not if you had almost your entire family wiped out by an atomic bomb."

She stopped. "Is that what happened?"

"Yes. His grandparents on both sides and most of their offsprings lived in Nagasaki."

"I am terribly sorry, Yasmin. I did not know."

"How could you? Tadashi does not talk about it."

She asked for two glasses of white wine. They ate in silence for a few minutes. Yasmin dabbed the corners of her mouth with her napkin, sipped her wine and smiled sweetly. "How is your friend Delia?"

I am not getting into this, Jennifer thought. I am not going to mention his name or ask if they have seen each other or anything else. On the contrary. I shall make it quite clear that there are other and more interesting things to talk about.

"Delia is fine," she said with an aura of indifference. "We shall have lunch one of these days."

"Now, isn't that nice. Did she say when?"

"No, she did not actually specify. Is it important?"

"Perhaps not. I would have thought that she needed some time to nurture her tender emotions."

"It is all in the past. Delia wants to forget."

Yasmin nibbled at her bread. "Am I to understand that she wants to forget so badly that she hasn't confided in you?"

"Delia wants to forget," Jennifer reiterated stubbornly. "She does not want to talk about it. Neither do I."

"Mmm," Yasmin purred and reached for the butter. "That's understandable."

It took a few moments before the words sank in. Jennifer said, "What do you mean—*understandable?*"

Yasmin brushed some crumbs from the table. "Neither would I, were I Delia."

I am missing something here, Jennifer thought. "Would what?"

"Talk about it." Yasmin shook her head. "Horrible, is the word." Her gaze wandered all over the restaurant as if in search of divine clemency. "Heaven forbid it ever came out, would have been my reaction."

Jennifer put down her knife and fork. She crossed them with great care over the plate and folded her hands in her lap. "Are you actually saying that you *know* what Angelo said to Delia?"

"Of course, my dear. How else could I have had an opinion?"

"Good," Jennifer said. "Let us have Angelo's version of events."

"It is not Angelo's version. Angelo has not mentioned Delia—or you, for that matter—since the party."

Jennifer looked away. "How do you know, then?"

"I was standing less than four feet away during their intimate tête-à-tête."

"Would you mind telling me?"

"Oh, I could not possibly do that. It was just *too* horrible, as your close friend Delia so vigorously expressed. Let us talk about something else." She asked the waiter for another piece of bread. "Tadashi wants a ten by four foot aquarium incorporated in the wall between two drawing rooms. What do you think about that?"

"Please do not torment me, Yasmin."

"Torment you? Less than five minutes ago you made it patently clear that neither you nor dear Delia have any desire to recapitulate an episode about which Delia knows everything and you know nothing. Please, do show some consistency."

Jennifer took one of Yasmin's cigarettes and lit it. Her hands were shaking.

"Can you remember your very last words to Angelo before he left?" Yasmin went on.

"He confided in you?"

"Angelo *confided?* No, he has not. Tadashi and I have seen him a few times since the party, but he has not mentioned you with one single word. I told you."

The pain in Jennifer's stomach increased. A sense of dejection encapsulated her mind like a thick, acrid fog. She did not know what to say.

Yasmin said casually, "I was there, Jennifer. I heard it all. Some chap, whoever it was, tried to entertain me with the story of his life. I was bored rigid and was just going to excuse myself when darling Delia made herself comfortable next to Angelo. Praise the businessman—he gave me the perfect cover for eavesdropping. Terribly naughty, of course, but what can you do—it was *so* entertaining. Would you like another glass of wine? Now, where was I...?"

"I am glad you are enjoying yourself."

"Oh, it was hilarious, and contagiously so. Poor Delia." Yasmin laughed with a shake of her head. "I fully understand if the two of you shall never again forgive your God for allowing Adam to escape from Eden."

Jennifer quaffed down the rest of her wine as the second glass arrived. She knows that I do not know, she thought, that is why we are here— or one of the reasons. I believe that Angelo has not said anything. She is telling the truth. The fact that I did not notice her, or can't remember, is perhaps not too surprising. I was shell-shocked and I have been so, more or less, ever since.

"I recall what I said to him."

"So do I, and that leads me to ask: why should I tell you, and why would you like to know? Am I to assume that you did not *mean* what you said? *I* certainly believed you. The look on your face told it all. Has Angelo called you?"

"No."

"There we are. He, too, believed you. He presumes, quite correctly, that you are not the type who plays with other people's feelings. You mean what you say."

Jennifer saw that she was halfway down her second glass. Careful now, she thought, this is not going very well. Keep your head clear. She said, "It would give me some peace of mind if I learned what happened." She heard the whiz of her own breathing and looked across the room. "I am asking you to help me."

A touch of compassion showed on Yasmin's face. She leaned forward and said, "Delia came over to Angelo. He got up and she dumped herself

414

in the middle of the sofa with the result that they were sitting close together. The expression of expectancy made her face shine like a lighthouse on a clear night. She said, 'How nice to see you again, Mr. Vargas. Not that a tuxedo doesn't suit you, but you *do* look better, more genuine, kind of, in a leather jacket.' She chatted about the party, made comments about some of the guests, and then, out of the blue, she said, 'I am meeting Frederick in Paris on Monday next, but I am going over on Friday. He has booked a very nice suite at the George V. Why don't you come over and we'll have some fun together?' She laughed and purred like a cheetah when she added: 'No need to book a room. What do you say?' At that moment I changed position so that I could see Angelo's face as he turned towards her. He had that expression in his eyes, you know, as if studying some strange animal, and he said, very quietly, 'What makes you think you can compare with Jennifer?' Delia practically jolted, where she sat, but then she must have thought is was a joke, and she said, 'Please, *Angelo*, don't tell me that you are just another conventional, bourgeois stereotype. I refuse to believe that. We could have such a great time, the two of us, turn the city upside-down, lots of fun and no commitments.' Angelo kept looking at her. She went on, 'No offence to dear innocent Jennifer, of course. She's a sweet little thing, but a bit of a homebaked pie, wouldn't you say? Perfectly all right for day-to-day consumption, granted, but not what I would call *exciting*. Trust me, I'll give you the weekend of a lifetime.' At that point Angelo smiled—a smile I shall never forget—and he said in that inimitable soft-spoken way of his, '*Delia, you do not reach Jennifer to her ankles*.' " Yasmin sighed. "And that's when darling Delia got up and you came in."

Jennifer had her eyes fixed on her napkin. Her face was burning.

"Your lip is bleeding. Here," Yasmin said and gave Jennifer a paper tissue. "Dear Lord," she whispered, "what have I done?"

"I am sure Angelo is eternally grateful for having been given the benefit of the doubt," Yasmin said.

"But I *asked* him."

"Dear oh dear. Did you really expect him to tell you? I thought you knew him better than that."

"I wonder if I know him at all."

"I am inclined to agree, in view of circumstances. Heavens above, Jennifer! You are an intelligent and sensitive woman—how come it escapes you that Angelo is a very complex man? I was twelve years of age when I first met him, and I believe I know him better than anybody else does, Tadashi included, but *far* from entirely. Perhaps nobody ever will, but that should not stop you from *trying.*"

Jennifer finally looked up. "Why should he want to see me again?"

Yasmin rubbed the tip of her fingers against her cheekbones. "Why indeed," she said emphatically, but the smile was back in her almond eyes. "If you need to ask that question, you do not deserve to know the answer. I could do with another glass of wine." She placed her hands on the table and leaned closer. "Listen, Jennifer. Go and see him. Say what is on your mind. Angelo is made for you and vice versa."

Jennifer's eyelids moved rapidly. She tried to smile. "You are a true friend, Yasmin."

A shadow of embarrassment crossed Yasmin's face. Then she threw her head back and laughed softly. "We Orientals are taught never to talk about our feelings, never mind show them. It is part of our culture and so unlike you Westerns. Tadashi schooled me to disagree with this and many other uncritically adopted concepts of our heritage and our philosophies, when appropriate, but it still causes me problems, now and then." Her fingers played with her long, dark hair. "Thank you for your kind words."

"It is I who should be thankful, and I—I admire your loyalty to Angelo."

A strange little smile played at the corners of Yasmin's mouth. "You may think it is because he saved my life and risked his own in doing so," she said quietly. "There is more to it than that, much more. Angelo became my friend the day he walked into the dojo for the first time. Believe me, I was quite horrible in those days, a right little madam, as we say, but he was always kind to me and incredibly patient. I knew that I could trust him. Intuition, I guess. He told me about a world that I hardly knew existed. He guided me and he always understood. I could not make him out. He was such an enigma, such a free spirit and a tearaway, and yet he had all the time in the world for a snotty kid who was much too big for her knickers. Thinking back—"Yasmin shook her head and laughed "—no wonder blond turned to white before time. He and Tadashi did exactly what pleased them. I can still remember the look of despair on my—on Sensei's face each time he talked about them. He knew that one day they would be gone. It was a terrible blow to him, but he never let on—except to me, that is."

"You were twelve when you met Tadashi?"

"No, I was younger than that. Tadashi had been around for a long time before Angelo appeared. God, did I hate that little creep, Tadashi, that is. He was such an arrogant shit. It wasn't love at first sight, believe me!"

She got up, left and came back with two plates, a cheesecake on each. "Here, eat this. You are too skinny. Another few pounds off, my girl, and you'll look like an ascetic on hunger-strike."

She went on, "Actually, Tadashi and I developed a love-hate relationship. I think such a beginning is fortunate—it seems to form the basis for something more long-lasting. I began to see Tadashi in a different light when he made this gaijin from nowhere his protégée, and Angelo always spoke of Tadashi with respect and sympathy. Another thing with Tadashi was that although he could be arrogant and indifferent and even seem to lose heart when I was at my worst, he never patronized me. I don't know about you, but I believe that any man who patronizes a woman is revealing his insecurity and his limitations. He is the victim of a culture he never had the wit and the courage to challenge. Tadashi did not fall into that category. Slowly but surely my feelings for him changed from a teenager's infatuation and into mature love and affection. I really worship my little Buddha. He is such a sweetie."

Yasmin ordered coffee. Neither spoke for a while.

She continued, "Tadashi and Angelo are the most magnetic and entrancing men I have ever come across. Nobody can ever classify them as handsome, poor devils, but they have got *quality*. By that I mean that I have unlimited faith in them. If you can place your full confidence in a man, if he has got a sense of humour, if he knows what he wants and is prepared to go for it, if he is unorthodox and as kind as he can be unforgiving—what more can a woman ask for? You tell me."

"Unforgiving?"

"Aversion to compromise, broadly speaking. When you have lived with Angelo for a few years, you will understand better."

"But—unforgiving? It is such a harsh word. I do not follow."

"Let me illustrate. Once, in Japan, I asked Angelo a question: *'Tell me about your background, please.'* He looked at me in such a way that I quickly changed the subject and never again asked that question. Are you with me?"

"Not entirely."

"As you know, Angelo is a private person, exceptionally so. My intuition, triggered off by his reaction, told me that there were memories from his past that he was not prepared to share with anybody. I was left with a feeling of having tried to uncover deep and ugly wounds. It scared me, literally. This was not the Angelo I knew. His reaction lasted only for a split second, but it was enough. Those memories are well and truly alive, and whatever happened is, to a nature like Angelo's, unforgivable."

"You consider that a quality?"

"Yes, I do. You can sweep your misfortunes in life under the carpet, or you can immerse yourself in self-pity. You can also use your experiences to strengthen your character by exploiting the fact that the reward of vengeance is comparative peace of mind. This is not my own inference— Tadashi once told me—and in this connection it means that you can cripple your own mind if you capitulate to forgiveness not due."

"I always thought that forgiveness was a sign of strength."

"It is a noble sentiment, on the face of it. The entire Christian ideology reverberates through it, and it is a perfect guideline for those who do not admit to the darker side of their nature. That is a problem Angelo hasn't got."

Jennifer thought for a while. "Are you trying to tell me, in the nicest possible way, that he is not going to forgive me?"

Yasmin laughed. "You'll find out. No, seriously, what you did was a mistake caused by confusion. You made an error of judgement, followed by an act of stupidity. It was *not* betrayal, and it was *not* malicious."

I wonder if she knows more than she is willing to tell, Jennifer thought. She said, "How do I break the cycle of damage?"

Yasmin glanced at her watch and signalled for the bill. "I think you have yet to discover to what extent he longs for someone close to talk to," she said. "Try affection, Jennifer—also known as love. Go and see him. Now."

"*Now?*"

"I can't see what you have got to gain by delaying it."

Jennifer smiled against her will as the ambiguity of the irony flashed through her mind. What a situation, she thought, with James Wilkinson I feared what I *did* know, and with Angelo Vargas I fear what I *do not* know.

She rang the doorbell without giving herself time to pause and reflect.

"Yes?"

"It is Jennifer. Can I come up for a moment?"

The entrance door to Vargas' apartment was ajar. She went through the hall and found him standing in the drawing room. He was facing the large windows, barefoot and dressed in a black kimono. An open book and a thick pad lay on his carved, hardwood Indonesian coffee table. She saw a pen and some loose sheets with his characteristic writing. A lit candle stood on the table. It gave off a scent that reminded her of primula on a late spring's morning. He did not look at her.

"I have come to apologize," she said. She could hear her own voice like a shrill cry from a distressed animal. "I now know what Delia said to you and what you said to her." Oh Christ, what do I sound like and why are my words so flat? "I am very sorry for my reaction and for the way I misjudged you and for the accusations I threw at you. It wasn't you I judged. Unwittingly, at that moment, I condemned myself for not having the guts to admit that I love you for what you are. I am sorry it took so long."

Vargas stood with his hands crossed in front. He did not move.

"I do not expect you to forgive me, Angelo. All I want is for you to know that I am not very proud of myself."

There was no reaction. He seemed lost in his own thoughts.

His lack of attention is beginning to annoy me, she thought. *Say something,* a voice within her screamed. Throw a fit, sneer, blame, accuse, ask me to get lost—*demonstrate,* please, that you are at least marginally human.

The statue eight yards away remained immobile.

"Very well," Jennifer said, her voice trembling with sadness and chagrin, "I am leaving now. I shall not pester you again."

She saw his head move up and down in slow motion. She tasted the blood on her lips and said, "Goodbye, Angelo. I am out of your life."

"Too late."

"What?"

Vargas turned ninety degrees. His hands were still crossed. He said, "When are you moving in?"

The black-clad figure faded as mist filled the room. Oh no, Angelo, she cried silently, please do not do this to me. I know I made a horrible mistake, but do not torture me. Do not seek your revenge by annihilating what little is left of my dignity.

Vargas said, "I'll meet your parents whenever convenient."

The mist lifted. She saw him coming towards her.

Early next morning she woke up from the sound of the shower. She stretched, put her hands behind her head and felt rested and content.

When Vargas finally came out, she said, "It is beyond me how anyone can spend twenty minutes in the shower." She eyed his naked body. The way he moved pleased her.

"One of my hang-ups," Vargas said. "There was a time when soap and water were luxuries."

Echoes from the past; when, she wondered, where and why? She asked, "What are your plans for today?"

"Quite a hectic schedule. I am going for a run in the park, followed by an hour in the dojo."

"You are not overdoing it? I mean, there can't be much energy left for anything else."

Vargas dressed with methodical care. "I have got this book that annoys the daylight out of me," he said. "On every single page I find something that I instinctively disagree with. Can't leave it like that. I have to find out why."

"I saw all those notes on the table," she said. "So, that is what you are doing—analyzing your thoughts."

"I am analyzing my instincts. I try to transform them into logical thoughts. It's an interesting challenge, if a bit arduous at times."

"You've got a yearning for knowledge, haven't you, all kinds of knowledge."

He smiled. "Possibly a consequence of being unable to believe that life has a meaning."

"It has not?"

"No. Purposes only. Plural."

She pushed the cover aside. "Dizzying heights, and too early for me to get into. My father would love a discussion like that. I can see the two of you sitting in the pigeon loft dissecting anything from God's will to the mystery of the homing instinct."

Vargas put on a black shirt. "One being a euphemism for the other."

"Why are you always dressed in black?"

"I am attracted to the colour of innocence."

"That is nonsense. *White* is the colour of innocence."

He did his buttons. "Only if you are a mortal heavily under the influence of the most lethal of drugs, widely taken and yet generally unknown."

"What are you talking about?"

"Self-deception."

"I am having a shower. Are you making breakfast?"

"As you wish."

Vargas was sitting at the table when she came into the kitchen. She had a towel around her head and was dressed in a gown that swept the floor. She stared at the two bowls of chopped-up fruit. "Is that all? Is that what you call breakfast?"

"Fruit is healthy and nutritious. There are lots of vitamins and minerals in that bowl. Sit down and be grateful."

She focused on a third bowl, filled with a white substance. "And that is—?"

"Natural yoghurt. Mix it with the fruit."

"What is that jar of Mexican honey doing here?"

"Nature's nectar, straight from the world's most soberminded and cleanliving bees. Pour it over the top and stir gently. A good start of the day is important."

"Not bad, coming from someone addicted to cigarettes and whisky."

"Isn't my Irish hedgehog eloquent today? Answer: contrariety is one of my characteristics."

"It certainly is."

Vargas took the honey jar and unscrewed the lid. "Here," he said, "but don't overdo it. We do not want your tongue much sweeter than it already is

She said, "When can you come to dinner?"

"Whenever."

"I have been struggling with what to say to my parents. First and foremost, there is little to tell since I hardly know you, and, secondly, there is no way I can relate what happened in the Middle East and in Hong Kong." She faced him. " That means that I have to boil it down to your business activities here and the fact that you have been travelling a lot and have been living in various countries." She chewed her upper lip. "I feel like a cheat, Angelo. Please do whatever you can to help me when you meet them. Use your discretion, is all I ask. They are such nice and gentle people, and the last thing I want is to upset them. Can you understand?"

"I believe so."

She picked up a handful of almonds and munched absentmindedly. "I better head for home, now. I'll go and get dressed."

She decided to walk up to Knightsbridge and get a cab from there. The forthcoming encounter with her parents was heavy on her mind. She knew that she had to talk to them, but she had no idea how to explain her relationship with Angelo Vargas. She knew so little about him, and yet there was so much she could not tell. Her father would listen sympathetically and keep his questions to himself, but her mother— Jennifer did not relish the thought of her mother's scrutinizing eyes and astute interjections, her surmises and her knack for intuitive conclusions and explicit judgements.

Well, so what. I'll just have to economize with the truth and improvise where necessary. Nothing is going to stop me sharing my life with Angelo. I must do what I believe is right for me, and, so far, I have no options but to let the future take care of itself. It is simple, really; not moving in would be a far bigger mistake than moving out later should things not work out. Admitting a mistake is nothing compared to living with the nightmare of what *could have been* had I not been timid and afraid of taking a risk when it mattered the most.

She spotted a pub. She went in and asked for a cup of coffee. Something else bothered her, and it irked her that she could not put her finger on it. She tried to be constructive; she sensed that whatever it was that bugged her, it had to do with something that was missing. The feeling came over her each time she left Vargas' place.

There was nothing wrong with his choice of colours. The furnitures were comfortable and of top quality. The wooden floors were attractive. His oriental rugs were superb in colours and design. His cacti and his variety of candles were acceptable. The absence of any other floral or additional decorative arrangements was not remarkable. Some of his paintings and drawings could be deemed bizarre by conventional standard, but they were not outrageous.

Paintings, drawings, conventional—absence.

Suddenly, Jennifer knew.

422

There were no photographs in Vargas' apartment.

The house was empty when she came home. She opted for her parents' drawing room as the strategically most suitable venue before she went downstairs.

She sat down in one of the large armchairs facing the open door. I am emotionally ready, she thought with a wry smile, but mentally I am unprepared. Or is it the other way round?

One and a half hours later she heard the car and the front door being unlocked. Jennifer took a sip from her fourth glass of juice and put on a mask of geniality bolstered by an easy smile. Not necessarily adequate, she thought—I can't but try and here we go.

"Good morning," Kathleen said, nonplussed. "Are you having the day off?"

"Yes. I need to talk to you."

"To both of us?"

"Yes."

Conor looked at his daughter with a worried expression. "Is everything all right?"

"I am fine, Dad."

Conor did not look convinced. He said, "We'll be with you in a minute."

Jennifer felt a calm that momentarily surprised her. No, she thought, there is nothing strange about it. I have made up my mind. No more games, no more secrecy and, most important of all, confidence restored. Just one thing, God, please ensure that they do not reject Angelo out of hand. I deserve better, even if he does not.

Kathleen and Conor came in. They each carried a cup of coffee. Conor's hand could have been steadier. Kathleen sat down and looked at Jennifer. Conor placed himself next to Kathleen.

"I would like to invite someone to dinner," Jennifer said and folded her hands.

Conor's jaw fell. "Is that all?"

Kathleen said with exaggerated patience, "My dear, this is not some fish and chips joint. I very much doubt that we are talking about a casual guest."

"Of course," Conor said. "I know that." He paused before he looked up. "When do you have in mind, Jennifer?"

Kathleen said, "Excuse me, but would it not be appropriate to ask *who* before *when?*"

"Somehow, I think Jennifer is going to tell us," he said and stared at Kathleen.

She mellowed. "Darling, I do not dispute…"

"His name is Angelo Vargas," Jennifer said.

Silence fell like the aftershock of an earthquake. Jennifer was determined to go no further until a reaction loomed one way or the other.

Conor said, "I think we have met him."

"You have, twice, at Uncle Igor's place."

"A rather quiet man," Conor recalled. "I do not think he said a single word, the first time."

"Did you know him before that?" Kathleen asked.

"No, I did not."

"You met him and split up with James the following day, so to speak."

Conor said quietly, "This is not an inquisition. Let Jennifer talk."

Kathleen touched her neck where some red spots had become visible. "I am sorry, Jennifer. I did not mean to upset you."

Jennifer shook her head. "I am not upset. James and I had nothing in common. The relationship had no future. I knew I was going to end it well before this stranger from nowhere appeared on the horizon." She smiled at her mother. "If a daughter of mine came riding into the yard with an Angelo Vargas, I, too, would probably have had some misgivings."

Conor touched his nose, a sure sign of bewilderment. "What makes you say that?"

Here it comes, Jennifer thought—the moment of truth, and my lips are dry. She said, "I do not know when or where he was born. I do not know his real name. I do not know much about what he does for a living, that is, what I do know, does not measure up. There is not one single photograph in his apartment, and the only people he seems to have some contact with, are Yasmin and Tadashi Ishihara."

"Mr. Vargas does not talk to you," Conor said.

She laughed. "Oh, he talks, all right, but on his own terms."

Kathleen brushed her hair from her forehead. "What *do* you know about him?"

"I know that he has travelled widely. I know that he is above average erudite. I suspect that he left home at an early age. I assume that some of his education would not fall into the category of *formal*."

Kathleen said, "How much more informed and intimate can one expect to get?"

"That was uncalled for," Conor said with more volume to his voice. His expression of bewilderment had given way to indignation.

Jennifer kept her calm. "Mum, you are not all that surprised, are you? Do you remember Uncle Igor's party? You kept looking at us. You knew then, didn't you?"

"I had my thoughts," Kathleen admitted. She knew that *thoughts* sounded better than *suspicions*. "Yes, I did. It's just that…"

"What?"

"I don't know. I can't place him."

Conor said, "You don't know him. Come on, Kathleen, he is not from another planet. Let us have him to dinner. Meet him, and judge thereafter. Not before."

Kathleen looked at her husband. She faced Jennifer. "Is there anything else we should know?"

"Yes. I am moving in with him."

Kathleen bit her tongue, but too late. The sigh escaped between her teeth and drifted like the pungent smoke from a gun just fired towards her daughter.

Conor's eyes wandered from Kathleen to Jennifer. He said, "God bless you, my girl. We both hope you will make each other happy. Don't we, Kathleen?"

"Yes, we do."

He went on, "We appreciate that you want us to meet him before you leave. We very much respect that."

"You are not all that amazed, are you, Dad?"

Conor looked warmly at his daughter. "No, I am not."

Kathleen got up. She said, "I suggest Saturday, if that is convenient for Mr. Vargas. I'll go and think about a menu." She walked out and left behind the scent of her perfume and a silence that was welcome.

Eventually, Conor said, "Did Mr. Vargas object when you made it clear that he should meet us?"

"He suggested it."

He sat still for several minutes. The lines around his eyes looked as if delineated with a sharp pencil. His expression of aloofness made Jennifer think of Angelo Vargas.

19

Jennifer heard the monotonous gargling from the diesel engine. She pressed her hands against her stomach and got up when the taxi drove off. She walked slowly towards the entrance door, readjusted her dress, undid the lock and took a step back.

"Welc…." Jennifer's tongue froze and she stared unblinkingly at the stranger in front of her.

Angelo Vargas was wearing his tailor-made dark suit, a light blue shirt, a grey tie and black Italian shoes—altogether the result of Jennifer's taste and assistance. The transformation from the denim-and-leather clad Vargas to the prototype of a fashion conscious gentleman was so startling that Jennifer unwittingly shook her head in disbelief.

"Good evening," he said. "Am I too early?"

She pulled herself together. "No—no," she said, "not at all." She saw that he was carrying a parcel; a square box wrapped in glossy white paper. "Please come in."

He kept looking at her as he walked up the stairs.

Strange, she thought; he knows I was startled to the bone when I saw him all smartened up, and still no comment. Well, that's Angelo—the man I am gradually beginning to know. Very gradually, she mused and stepped aside.

He leaned forward and kissed her. "You look your true self."

Jennifer was pleased with her black, simple, elegant and highly overpriced designer dress, her dark green suede shoes and her latest hairdo. She wore a single-stranded pearl necklace, pearl earrings with a small diamond and her one and only ring. Her makeup was as discreet as the scent of her perfume. "Thank you," she laughed. "What is my true self?"

"Radiant—the reward for no longer being in denial."

She could feel her cheeks glowing. She turned quickly and headed towards the drawing room. "This way, please. I'll get you a drink."

Vargas followed. Carefully, he put the parcel on the coffee table, took the glass and looked around.

"I'll tell my parents that you are here."

She was reaching for the doorknob when she heard Vargas' voice, "Jennifer."

She turned.

"Try to be less formal and you won't be so tense," he said.

She moistened her lips. "I have been walking a tightrope all day. I just can't help it. It is so important to me that…" she broke off.

He came closer. "Jennifer, I shall do my best, but I can't *make* your parents like me. They either do, or they don't. I understand that you find the situation difficult. There is an abyss between you and your parents on one side, and me on the other. All we can do is to try to bridge it. I cannot undo my past, but I can try to create a different future." He smiled. "After all, I am human, you know—given the benefit of the doubt." He put his arm around her and squeezed gently. "I know that I can never live up to your mother's image of the perfect partner for her daughter," he whispered into her ear. "Our target is to prove that the way we lead our life is more important than anybody else's interpretation of it. Let us take one minute at a time."

She touched the back of his neck. "Mum is all right. It is just that she compares everybody with Dad, and he is too perfect and clean-cut even for his own good." She smiled. "We shall overcome."

He placed his hands on her shoulders. "That's the attitude. Have faith."

Jennifer felt relieved; the talk had helped, but she gave herself plenty of time on her way from the drawing room to the kitchen. Once inside, she smiled brightly and said, "He is here."

Conor followed her into the drawing room and said, "Good evening, Mr. Vargas, and welcome." He extended his hand. "It is nice to see you again."

"Thank you, Mr. Moran. Your gentle words are most appreciated. May I reciprocate your kind greeting."

Jennifer flinched. Neither Vargas nor her father seemed to notice.

Conor nodded towards Vargas' glass. "I see that Jennifer has looked after you. Irish?"

"Yes."

"Have you tried it before?"

Vargas smiled. "Occasionally."

"No ice, I observe. Would you like some water?"

"I prefer it straight from the distillery. Whisky, like integrity, should not be diluted."

Conor laughed, but his eyebrows went up. "An interesting analogy, and not entirely a shot in the dark, I presume."

"It is difficult to aim in the dark."

The lines on Conor's forehead became more distinct. "So it is," he said, "so it is. Please, have a seat."

The two men sat down. Jennifer opened a bottle of sherry. She had no idea where Vargas was heading. His remarks seemed out of context with anything she could think of. Maybe her father understood, or, if he didn't, it would not take long. She joined them.

"Do you like living in London?" Conor asked.

Vargas put his glass down and leaned back. "So-so, I must say. It is very convenient, in many respects, but there are times when I could wish for more tranquillity."

"Same here," Conor said. "My wife and daughter have unanimously decided that I am going to retire in a few years' time, and that we shall disappear into the wilderness of the English countryside whilst it is still there."

Jennifer held back. Under almost any other circumstances her father would have said *Kathleen and Jennifer*—not *my wife and daughter*.

"I sympathize," Vargas said. "Sooner or later we shall probably follow suit."

Jennifer sipped her sherry. *We*. She avoided looking at either of the two men.

"It is the sensible thing to do," Conor said. "I'd really love to have all the space in the world for my pigeons and my dogs and whatever else I want to surround myself with. Do you like dogs, Mr. Vargas?"

"I do, but I would not want one here in London. I still travel, and the thought of a kennel does not appeal to me." The smile on his face was barely detectable. "I would probably suffer more than the dog."

Sweet Jesus, Jennifer thought, feelings. Angelo is baring his soul here. What is wrong?

"Exactly my sentiment, too," Conor said. "What kind of dog would you be looking for?"

"A malamute, for a start."

Father and daughter looked at each other.

"No," Jennifer said, "not with one word. Never. Honestly."

Conor grinned. "What a coincidence. A malamute. That's the dog I am going to have. My knowledge is limited, I must admit, but there is something about their appearance that appeals to me. I know that the malamute is a very ancient breed, and I have heard that they are loyal and affectionate. Is it also true that they are unusually clean and not at all noisy?"

"That is true, and it is a fact that they are as bright as they are docile. Powerful animals and excellent guard dogs. One minus, though; a malamute is not very good with other male dogs. He likes to rule his territory. Have one of each, if you want two of them."

The door opened and Kathleen sailed in. Conor adjusted his facial composition. Jennifer's eyes widened. To her, Kathleen had always been an ageless beauty, but never more breathtakingly so than when she smiled at Angelo Vargas and said, "At long last, Mr. Vargas. Jennifer has told me so little about you."

Vargas was on his feet within a split second of Kathleen's appearance. He bowed formally as they shook hands. "Thank you for inviting me to your home, Mrs. Moran. I am deeply honoured."

Dear God, Jennifer pleaded silently, please see that Mum does not find Angelo's attempts at social graces too hilarious. Please put a clamp on her wicked sense of humour. I do not know what I will do or say if she begins to ridicule him.

But Kathleen was sweetness herself. "Don't mention it. The pleasure is mine. It is a very nice suit you are wearing, I must say."

"Thank you, but all credit to Jennifer. My sartorial talent has its limitations, as you may have observed previously."

"I did, hence the salute to progress." Kathleen looked straight into Vargas' eyes and wondered if the flicker of amusement had its roots in profundity or mischief. Walk lightly, she told herself; Jennifer has not chosen this man because of his looks. He reminds me of a panther in a cage. It may be a good idea to keep the door closed.

Kathleen had changed into an ankle-length dress the colour of holly but without the gloss. It enhanced her figure to perfection. Her amber hair, a shade more red than Jennifer's, fell softly around her neck, and her green eyes sparkled in the light from the candles. She had put on a selection of her most eye-catching jewellery, all gifts from Conor who had developed a knack for gems during the years. Jennifer asked herself if also Vargas, whose social experience was so evidently limited, found Kathleen a wee bit overdressed for the occasion. He showed no expression, not even the admiration most men had problems hiding when facing a beautiful and attractive woman.

"Please sit down," Kathleen said. "Conor, could you get me a glass of sherry, please?"

Vargas picked up the parcel from the table. "I should be most grateful if you would accept this small token of appreciation," he said.

Jesus, Joseph and Mary, Kathleen thought; where the hell did he get his social phraseology? I better keep a straight face—Jennifer is watching like an adder ready to strike. "How sweet of you. Can I open it now?"

"Most gratifying if you would."

Jennifer sensed her tension growing. She had no idea what was in the box; she could only hope that Vargas' concept of an appropriate gift was more advanced than his ability to exchange adequate pleasantries in proper English.

"Oh dear God!" Kathleen exclaimed, "how exquisite!" She held up one of the two rice bowls. "I have never seen anything so delicate." She turned it upside-down. "Japanese. How on earth do they paint those minute little figures?"

"Chinese," he said. "They used the tiniest of bamboo sticks."

"Are they old?"

"A few hundred years."

Conor cleared his throat. "Which dynasty?"

"Ch'ing. The Shun Chih period."

Kathleen began to realize what she was holding in her hands. Carefully, she put the bowls on the table, unwrapped the two carved wooden bases and placed the bowls side by side. She did not take her eyes off the bowls and continued to touch them with the tip of her fingers. "I can't get over it," she said dreamily. "They are too beautiful for words."

"Most apt," Vargas said.

That must be the compliment of the century, Jennifer thought; he means it well, but I have to get him out of this quagmire of solecisms before somebody starts giggling.

Kathleen looked up. "I do not know how to thank you."

Vargas' eyes wandered from Kathleen to Jennifer and back again. "You already have."

Two red spots appeared on Kathleen's cheeks. She said quickly, "Listen, I am afraid that dinner is being delayed by some thirty minutes. Why don't you chaps enjoy yourselves whilst Jennifer and I get things ready?"

Vargas stood up as the two women left the room.

Conor said, "Would you like to see my pigeons?"

"I would."

"I mean, only if you want to. Not everybody…"

"I would."

"Let us go through the backdoor from the kitchen," Conor said. "That way the girls will know where we are."

"Just passing through," he said to Kathleen. "Mr. Vargas wants to see my pigeons."

"Thank heaven you are both dressed for the event," she mumbled.

Conor said, "Ignore her. She thinks that God made pigeons by mistake."

"A sentiment Noah would have disputed," Vargas said.

They walked through the garden. The cooing from the birds grew louder. There were two padlocks on the door. Cautiously, Conor opened the door and went in. Vargas followed. The loft was large; some fifteen by twelve feet, and eight feet to the lowest point of the slanting roof.

Vargas said, "Tumblers, Racers and Orientals. A nice selection."

Conor cast a quick glance. He said, "Yes, about forty, all in all." He opened the door to the storeroom at the back and took out two small, circular wooden stools. "They are not overly comfortable," he said with a grin, "but it is only for half an hour, at the most."

Vargas sat down. "You keep it spotlessly clean."

"I have to. I do not want any diseases if I can possibly avoid it. Besides, I do not feel entirely at ease unless the place is in mint condition." He opened a small window with re-inforced, non-transparent glass above the entrance door and went back to the storeroom. He returned with a bottle of whisky and two thick glasses. "I always keep a reserve here. Would you care for a drop?"

He poured a good inch in each glass before he sat down. They were facing each other at an angle, seven feet or so between them.

"Cheers," he said. "To life and whatever it contains and to whatever it may bring."

"Can't be more specific than that. Cheers."

Conor looked around as if counting his pigeons. He tried to avoid studying too openly his daughter's choice.

Vargas made a circle in the layer of shellsand on the floor and put his glass down. He reached out, and in one fluent movement he took one of the racers from its perch. He carefully placed its feet between his fingers. "Quite a beauty," he said as he studied the bird's head and felt its breastbone. "Should be an eminent flyer, this fellow."

Conor said, "He is, but I do not race them. I keep them for company and because I think they are divinely beautiful. As a creation they can't quite match the falcon for perfection, but it is not far from. If I ever get a place in the country, I shall have a couple of falcons, too." The corners of his mouth twitched. "I'll just have to ensure that nobody can let them out at the same time."

Vargas smiled without his eyes leaving the pigeon. "You'll get there if you want to."

"I guess so," Conor said and looked into his glass. "I can see that you are familiar with birds."

Vargas put the racer back on the perch. "It is a long time ago."

Something in Vargas' voice that made Conor hesitate; a shade of indifference, a dismissal of a past not worth the memory—or was it bitterness? No, it was not bitterness. It was camouflaged animosity, repugnance blended with contempt; a rage buried but not forgotten and seldom allowed to leave its dungeon. Conor had seen it before; he knew the corrosive effect of emotions not understood or admitted and he knew the damage that inner turmoil could do to the mind. The difference in this case was that Vargas was aware of his turbulence; otherwise, he would not have made a reference to his past. Conor said, "What happened?" and hoped that he sounded casual.

"Someone killed them."

Not the nicest of memories, Conor thought; this goes deeper than the mere slaughter of a handful of birds. Will he tell me? I do not think so. Maybe another time, when we know each other better. Change the subject.

He said, "As a young man I studied theology. I had this alluring dream of one day becoming an archbishop or perhaps even a cardinal."

He picked a feather from his sleeve and smiled. "So long ago, and look where I ended up."

"No longer hell-bent on going to heaven?"

Conor smiled. "One day I realized that I was deceiving myself. I came to understand that my big dream was not to serve God, it was to make a career out of a church for which I had a dwindling respect. I began to think that humanity was in danger of disintegrating if we allowed orchestrated religiosity to dominate the mind. I concluded— and it was at that point I broke off—that I either surrendered and gave up any hope of communicating with a wall of clichés, dogmas, quotes and maxims, or I collected the ruins of my integrity and got out. So, there I was, having left a world overburdened with shallow pity and short on genuine compassion, a culture wealthy in hypocrisy, cunning, cruelty and unlimited self-righteousness, and with nowhere to go."

Vargas drank. His put his empty glass on the floor. "The road to Damascus, or *from*, rather—in your case."

Conor chuckled. "You know your Bible."

"There was a time when it was the only literature available."

Conor did not ask. He had an idea what kind of place Vargas referred to, but he also remembered Jennifer's summary: *Angelo Vargas talks on his own terms.*

"What saved you?" Vargas asked.

Conor laughed. He appreciated the double entendre. "Kathleen, primarily. She came into my life at that very crucial time. She, and a friend of hers, a chap called Colm Begley. He was…"

"I have read him."

Conor nodded. "He was a good man. It was just so sad and unfortunate that his lifestyle got more attention than his works. Anyway, he put me on the track that led to this, to The Mission." He waved his hands as if embracing his kingdom.

"Any regrets?" Vargas said.

Conor laughed quietly. "In all societies, and at any one time in history, there are people who have no conception of their own absurdity. They are commonly known as priests. No, I have no regrets." He touched the beak of a tumbler standing next to his shoe. "Would you care for another drop?"

"I could be persuaded, thank you."

Conor refilled the glasses and put the bottle on the shelf in the storeroom. He still had his back to Vargas when he said, "You don't think much of what I am doing here; The Mission, I mean."

"I cannot recall having voiced an opinion."

Why am I defending myself, Conor thought? Is it because this man represents an independence I wish I had for myself? He said, "It is not within everybody's power to come to grips with life. There are many a lost soul who gets hurt too early, and then too many times."

Vargas said, "That is true. Whatever a journeyman tries to do, he ends up against the ropes. The world versus a broken man will always be a mismatch. You believe that it should not be allowed, but that's the way we are. That is man, and man's behaviour is the reason why Conor Moran keeps asking why his God is turning a blind eye."

"Without my doubts I would have been an even more imperfect servant."

"Genuine believers ask questions and true non-believers do not?"

Conor picked up a handful of sand and sifted it through his fingers. "With the odd exception," he said.

"You are a compassionate man, Conor."

The use of his first name startled Conor. "There are still moments when I wonder whether compassion is a blessing or a curse."

"Back to doubts. You do what you believe you should do, and that is all that matters."

"Rightly or wrongly, but I have a feeling you do not care much for religious beliefs."

"Rightly. Faith is the ability to convince oneself that an illusion is a reality."

Conor stared at him, nonplussed. "You do not accept *any* religion?"

"I accept it as a man-made phenomenon with its origin in ignorance blended with fear and supported by an irrational tendency to sycophancy. The ability to oral communication made man assume that he was the creation of a divine power. It is hard to imagine a more limitless conceit. It reflects nothing but a perpetual state of hallucinations, a state of mind that man is too ill equipped to fathom. Religion, any religion, is the manifestation of man's limitations. The side-effects are devastating, as we have seen during the centuries."

Conor swallowed a mouthful and tilted his head as if he'd got water in his ears. "Side-effects," he said. "Like what?"

"Intellectual paralysis and emotional cancer."

Conor cupped the glass in his hands. "You do make yourself clear."

Vargas stared at him for several seconds before he answered, "That's intentional."

Yes, Conor thought, and I am grateful because I believe you do it for Jennifer. You want me to know where you stand. He said, "Once, there must have been a God in your life."

"There was, forcibly introduced by Lutheranism at its worst—if one should be generous enough to grade it in the first place. My whole being turned into one of belligerence and hate and only so many years later did I manage to transform my attitude to one of indifference. Today, I am past entertaining labels like atheist, agnostic, non-believer or any other description which by its mere nature is meaningless."

"Not even solipsist?"

"A world without labels is inconceivable?"

The irony in Vargas' voice did not escape Conor. "I did not mean it that way."

Vargas nodded but did not comment.

Conor said, "One of my experiences in life is that most people do not live by their wits. We live on the fringe of our emotions. I cannot fathom an existence without God. God is life itself, and therefore life has a meaning. Forgive me for sounding like a preacher, but that is the way I have brought up Jennifer."

"I hear your message and I apprize it," Vargas said. He gently stroked a pigeon that had jumped up on his left shoe. "Two things, though; one is that I do not confuse meaning with purpose—which is my prerogative—and, secondly, the last person a man should look for is a woman whose mind is a replica of his own."

Apprize, Conor repeated silently and gulped down most of what was left in his glass. He said, "I think we understand each other."

"I believe we do." Vargas picked up the bird and continued to caress it.

Conor did not find the silence uncomfortable. He studied the man three yards away and wondered how much Jennifer actually knew about him.

"What a stunner," Vargas said. He eyed the pigeon as it balanced on his index finger. He smiled when a dropping missed his hand by a short inch.

Conor said, "Jennifer tells me that you are spending a lot of time on your own."

"I do. Demons should be exercised in solitude."

"How can there be demons without gods?"

Vargas put the bird back on the floor. "Rhetorical substitutes for conflicts and benedictions."

This man is born four hundred years too late, Conor thought. What a career the Inquisition could have given him, assuming that the right Jesuit monastery had managed to mould him the way Lutheranism didn't.

"Would you mind if I go outside for a quick smoke?" Vargas asked.

"Have one here. I'll have one with you. These birds are not susceptible to chronic respiratory problems."

Conor's eyes followed the grey-blue smoke drifting towards the open window over the door. "You have seen a bit of the world, I understand."

"Most of it."

"I never travelled much. Once a year we go to the same spot in Barbados, and that is all, really, apart from the odd trip back to Ireland." Conor inhaled and rubbed the lighter as if hoping a genie would pop out with a round-trip ticket. "There are moments when I wish I had experienced more, seen different cultures, faced the unexpected under another sky, listened to people whose lifestyle is alien and heard the wind rustle through the ruins of long-forgotten temples." He shrugged with an expression of woeful regrets. "I am not complaining. One can't have it all, I guess." He stared at the few remaining drops in his glass. "What would you say is the essence of your experiences from what you have seen of the world?"

"That we all come from the same cesspool."

Conor moved on his stool. "That is a rather negative conclusion."

"It's a factual conclusion."

Conor balanced the glass on his knee. "Is there not something of value wherever you go? Is there not something nice and good and beautiful and worthwhile?"

"Everything is of value, one way or the other, but that does not necessarily make it worthwhile. And, yes, to specify, my memory does contain remnants of the good and the beautiful, but I seem to recall that you asked about the *essence*."

Conor opened his mouth but Vargas continued, "Please allow me to elaborate. I admit that my answer was not entirely adequate. What I have learned, so far, is never to underestimate to what degree the human being is ruled by irrationality. The human element is accurately identified and summed up by the Seven Deadly Sins." His eyes met Conor's who could not interpret the expression on Vargas' face.

Conor cleared his voice. "God did give us a free will."

Vargas smiled. "The eternal pretext. Man's most indispensable and precious intellectual hybrid. I would have thought it more honest by the followers of any persuasion to advocate that their Great Handicapper never manages to catch up with his runners when it comes to depravity."

Conor did not try to conceal a smile. "There is a voice in me agreeing with you."

"It must have been there for a long time. Otherwise, you would have been a cardinal, by now."

Conor laughed and looked at his watch.

Vargas said, "Your wife said thirty minutes."

"So she did," Conor muttered and looked longingly towards the storeroom, "so she did." He got up. "We need not worry. The message will come through loud and clear. A final wee drop?"

Vargas held out his glass. Conor poured but with restraint. "I'd better show moderation," he smiled. "A bloodhound would give his right paw for my wife's nose." He added quickly, "Not that she is judgmental, but she does favour sobriety when meeting someone for the first time." He straightened up. "However, we are still entirely coherent, suave and utterly articulate. What more can a woman ask for?"

"What indeed."

Conor found his stool. "Whatever your experiences, Angelo, I wish I had seen more of this world."

"By choice."

"What?"

"By choice," Vargas repeated. "By seeking out your destination, go looking for whatever you want to see, and then return to your safe and private little harbour. That is a bit different from finding yourself in the middle of nowhere without any idea of what to do and where to go from there. Add youth and inexperience, and you start your journey on another level altogether."

"Is that what happened to you?"

"Yes."

Conor hesitated for a few moments. "I see," he said warily. "Yes, that is a different story. I presume, no, I don't really—it is just a conjecture…"

"Please go on."

"It did occur to me, from the way you described it, that there must have been some experiences you probably could have done without."

Vargas waited for a while before he said, "When the ghosts from bygone days pay their visit, there is no choice but to let them stay for as long as it lasts. Eventually, they go for a respite."

"Are your travelling days over?"

"Almost."

"I take it you are looking forward to another way of life."

"I am."

"Jennifer mentioned that you once expressed a wish never again to see an airport."

"True, but not an entirely realistic sentiment."

"It's funny, in a way," Conor said. "I like airports." His eyes darted from bird to bird. "They kind of remind me of our existence, drawing a comparison, so to speak, with our life here on earth."

"How come?"

"Well—you arrive, you sit there or you maunder about; people passing by, you see your destiny on the board, and then, the final call. Sort of sums it up, doesn't it?"

"Yes. We come, stay and vanish."

"Do we vanish? We are only lost if we do not know where we are going."

"A bewitching parable, but exclusively for the redeemed."

Conor stumped out his cigarette. "I have another one," he said. "Imagine that the airport is the world, our world. We move about, the prey of our demons and our gods—your conflicts and benedictions—and cleverly they guide us towards our final destination, and all along they play their little games with us. You know, all those seemingly inconspicuous and at times inexplicable one-acts which we interpret as coincidences or fate."

"That is a bit closer to earth," Vargas said. There was a glint of satire in his eyes.

"I thought you'd say that," Conor quipped. "Who knows, we could both be right. Truths can at times be obscure creations." There was a look of compliance in his stare. "On the other hand, when the sun goes down, I know that I shall close my eyes in the firm belief that all roads lead to God's Terminal."

"Destination, if any, unknown."

"That is where we differ," Conor said.

The silence was broken by a knock on the door. They heard Jennifer's voice, "Dinner is ready."

"Coming," Conor said and exercised his ankles and massaged his knees. "I have enjoyed our talk, Angelo. May we have many more in time to come?"

Vargas said, "That would be a privilege."

Conor closed the window and put the glasses away. No, he thought, I am not going to ask this man to look after my daughter. Any admonition, however well presented, would be a stupid mistake. He must have feelings for Jennifer, or he would not have shown up. Jennifer may not know what she is walking into, but then, who does, at the beginning of a relationship? I hope that they will find harmony. I also hope that he is as kind as his past is opaque. *That* kind? Conor smiled and secured the door to the storeroom. Kathleen and I can only wait and see. At least they'll live nearby and not in some faraway country.

Vargas was gone and Kathleen and Conor assembled around the kitchen table. Following what he wrote off as a minor indulgence in the pigeon loft, Conor had been careful all evening, but now he poured a generous night-cap. Kathleen's fingers touched the slender stem of her champagne glass. She stared dreamily at the bubbles as if they contained the secrets of questions not asked. Conor opened a window, found an ashtray and lit a cigar. Kathleen did not like the smell of tobacco in her kitchen, but she had long ago decided not to make an issue of it since neither Conor nor Jennifer was habitual smokers.

Conor sat down and adjusted the collar of his pyjama top. "What do you make of him?" He looked into his wife's eyes and saw naked and vulnerable honesty.

She said, "I don't know. He…" she stopped when the door opened and Jennifer came in. She had not changed. It was a sign that she did not intend to stay for long. She looked at them in turn. "Thank you for what you did tonight, and thank you for making Angelo feel welcome."

"Same thing," Conor said jovially.

"No, Dad, it isn't."

"Oh?" Conor looked embarrassed. "No, I suppose you are right."

Kathleen said, "It was a pleasure, dear. Your Mr. Vargas made everything so easy. He is very polite and well mannered."

Your Mr. Vargas. Jennifer did not comment.

"He's got a sense of humour, too," Conor said. "I liked his one-liners. There's a certain—well, not exactly cynicism, but—what's the word I am looking for—scepticism, I think."

"Less considerate people call it a *black* sense of humour," Jennifer said, smiling with her eyes only. "Sometimes he cuts through with the sharpness of a samurai sword, and at other times he prefers arrows dipped in acid. That is what you mean, Dad, is it not?"

Conor shrugged. "You said it."

"Yes, I did, for the benefit of us all. I love his humour, even when it is patently obvious that his regard for humans is not detectable. It appeals to someone with a stable, secure and conventional background."

Why is she defensive? Kathleen thought; neither Conor nor I have said one single negative word about Mr. Vargas. She said, "Yours, as opposed to his."

Jennifer stared stubbornly at her mother. "Yes."

Conor sensed the tension and said, "He and I had a very interesting chat before dinner. I bet he can tell some captivating stories, when you get to know him."

Hedge your bet, Jennifer thought. You may hear some nice and moderately colourful tales about pyramids and pagodas and historical events and cultural differences, but you won't hear much about asperity, cataclysmic incidents and his prowess when it comes to gory solutions. There will be nothing that indicates the nefarious side of his nature, not a hint about anything you could find disconcerting. Behind all this are his memories. One day he will share those memories with me, and that shall be as far as they ever go.

Kathleen watched from the corner of her eyes. She is in the grip of this man, she thought. Not only is she defensive about him to a degree that has yet to be warranted, she is, God forbid, one short step away from becoming utterly obsessed. Perhaps I do not know my own daughter as well as I thought I did.

I need time to think. She said, "What happened at Uncle Igor's party?"

Jennifer told them.

Kathleen's eyes got smaller. "I have always thought that Delia's a bitch," she said bitingly.

Conor chuckled. "You don't reach Jennifer to her ankles," he repeated. "That's a good one."

Then Jennifer told them how it all came about; her meeting with Yasmin and the quintessence of the visit to Vargas' apartment.

Conor nodded. "The chap loves you, Jennifer."

"Yes, I believe the chap does."

Kathleen looked away. She waved at the smoke. Her mouth had lost some of its fullness.

Jennifer said, "I do not know him, either. Bits and pieces, yes, but he is almost as much of an enigma to me as he is to you. What I *do* know is that I want to be with him. It will either work, or it won't. I have no guarantees, and I can't tell. The way I feel, I have no option but to give it a try." She gave a wan smile. "Who knows, Angelo and I may be ideally suited."

"I do hope so," Kathleen said with a sincerity that did not escape Jennifer.

Conor took her hand. "You have got as much of a chance as anybody else, Jennifer. As you know, it's amazing what goodwill, mutual respect and unqualified devotion can do. Add broadmindedness and a dash of humour, and you've got the recipe." He gave her hand a squeeze. "The voice of experience."

"I know," Jennifer smiled. "I have seen it close up since the day I was born." She got up and pretended to stifle a yawn. "Bedtime," she said. "Have a good night's sleep, and I'll see you in the morning." She gave each a hug and left.

Conor heard the clock on the wall tick the seconds away. A door closed upstairs. A single drop of water from the tap over the sink splashed onto a plate.

"What is wrong, Kathleen?"

She stared ahead. Then she suddenly shook her head as if waking up from a trance. She sighed, widened her eyes and said, "I cannot place him. There is something about him that makes me feel ill at ease."

"We do not know the man."

"No, Conor, and we never will."

"What do you mean?"

She did not answer.

He said, "Listen, he and I had a good talk. I mean, credit me with some insight. He certainly did not strike me as a low-class and shoddy philanderer. If that was the case, he would have gone to Paris with Delia and not cultivated a class act like Jennifer. I think he is serious." His voice went up a notch. "They could well be lovers already, but it does not make sense that mere carnal exploitation is the core of their relationship. Not Jennifer."

"That is not what I mean."

"What *do* you mean?"

Kathleen refilled her glass. She sipped slowly. "He is carrying a lot of luggage. He has been around for a long time, all over the place. I have some problems perceiving him as a saint reincarnated."

Conor knew better than to challenge her intuition. "Jennifer does not need a saint. She does not *want* a saint. She has clearly demonstrated that she's had enough of the James Wilkinsons of this world. Look at her past acquaintances. They were all nice, well educated, conventional and basically glib little chaps. A marriage with any of those would have ended in disaster. She has become aware of the depths of her own soul. She is looking for a match. I think she has found him."

"To some extent I agree with you," Kathleen said wearily. "She has certainly leapt from one extreme to another. What baffles me is, why did she pick one from the jungle?"

"The jungle?"

"That man is primitive. Mark my words."

"Oh, come on," Conor protested. "We could not possibly fault his manners or his behaviour or anything else about him tonight, could we?"

"Ignoring his bizarre ideas of compliments he knows how to conduct himself, I'll give him that. What I am saying is, behind that façade there is a different person."

Conor looked at his empty glass and poured a modest shot. "Are we not being a bit selfish, now? We can't choose for Jennifer, and, another thing, I do not think that we have even a remote reason to underestimate her. Let us write him off if she does, but not before." A tiny smile appeared and he continued, "Perhaps she has discovered that they are compatible."

Kathleen kept quiet for a while. Then she said, "I so want her to be happy."

"But she *is* happy. She is *radiating* happiness."

Her voice sank to a whisper. "Yes, I suppose she is."

"He likes pigeons."

"Need I know more."

"He doesn't live on the skin of a rasher."

Kathleen hesitated. "That is true. At least he can look after her—should he so decide."

"He—they, I mean—want a place in the country. Perhaps we can arrange it so that we do not live too far apart."

Kathleen dabbed her eyes with her handkerchief. "Or too close." She tried to smile. "I am just being sensible. I do wish you mean it."

"Mean what?"

"Retiring."

"I do. We have done our stint. I honestly feel that we owe the rest of our lives to ourselves."

Kathleen saw the sincerity in Conor's blue eyes and smiled warmly. He stroked her chin. "Go to bed, my Irish rose. You look very tired."

She stood up. "Just one question."

"Yes?"

"How come the two of you are on first names?"

Conor put his half-smoked cigar in the ashtray. "He started it. Out there," he gestured. "We talked about this place and beliefs and he said *you are a compassionate man, Conor*. It surprised me, but then, in this day and age…" he shrugged as if to indicate that the world wasn't what it used to be.

Kathleen said, "In spite of his Oriental manners and old-fashioned behaviour he tried to be up-to-date?"

"I presume so."

"How can you be so naïve?"

"I don't follow."

"I do not believe that Mr. Vargas cares one bit about what is in and what is out in today's society. Use your head, Conor."

She went on, "Rapport, my love. He found rapport with you, and vice versa, from what I can gather."

"Is there anything wrong with that?"

"No. I just wonder what the two of you can have in common—apart from Jennifer."

"He is easy to talk to. We exchanged quite a few viewpoints. I have to take him at face value. What else can I do?"

"He never used *my* first name."

Conor grinned. "You are more forbidding."

"That man has crossed the tropic of Cancer a few times," she said in a terse voice. "He knows what he is doing. Bear that in mind."

They heard the click when Jennifer switched off her light.

20

A week after Jennifer had moved in, Ishihara called Vargas. The conversation lasted for fifteen minutes. Ishihara did most of the talking.

Jennifer always felt uncomfortable when other people were on the telephone; it was as if she was eavesdropping, and she preferred to keep her distance.

On her way to the kitchen she heard Vargas say *presidential election*, but she missed the context. She made a cup of herbal tea and came in when he put the receiver down.

He said, "I invited Yasmin and Tadashi to dinner tonight. Itoh's place eight o'clock. I hope you don't mind."

"Of course I don't mind. It will be nice to meet up again."

"I'll go and attend to my stubbles," Vargas said. He usually shaved once a week, but he made exceptions for social events.

She sat down in the chair that had become hers. She felt strangely annoyed. What is the matter with me, she thought? We have been on our own for an entire week, and Yasmin and Tadashi are friends. Did I not promise myself to help Angelo become less of a recluse? Careful now, or we shall both end up as hermits.

She rose to her feet, pulled the curtains wide apart and gazed towards the sky. Twilight had given way to darkness. The heavy grey clouds over the city looked as if sprayed with a thin, misty layer of orange.

No, she thought, her frame of mind had nothing to do with fear of becoming a recluse. He should have *asked*, not just made an arrangement over her head as if she had no say in the matter. Such behaviour was unacceptable; it would not work, in the long run, and she had to arrest it before it grew into a habit.

Habits. He had so many of them, having lived on his own for such a long time. He was not used to sharing. He was not familiar with small talk, intimate conversations, reading out loud and all the other little routines of successfully living together. His companion had been silence, he came and went as he pleased; partaking was alien to him.

Jennifer began to relax. Thank heaven she had not moved in without *some* concepts of the imperatives of adapting. She, too, had lived on her own, basically, although not to the extent of isolation, as Vargas had. I can see the need for flexibility on both sides, she thought, the necessity of patience and the will to understand. The most dominant obstacle was Angelo's reticence, his seemingly intransigent tendency not to allow anybody to enter his personal and private world; a clandestine realm where the ghosts and the shadows and the memories of the past were never allowed the privilege of daybreak.

But little signs now and then told her that he was aware of this predilection, and that he struggled to overcome it. She had no illusions about the forbearance and dexterity required on her part to make Vargas leave the monastic existence of his twilight universe, but, equally, she had no doubt that her love for him, assisted by his own conscious efforts, would eventually be rewarded.

She felt better. I knew I would be in for a bumpy ride, she thought—he told me so—but there is nothing that love and affection can't overcome. He can be quite sensible, when it suits him, and all I have to do is to ensure that his adoration for me remains undiminished. She laughed softly. What a modest requirement, she thought; an everlasting effect dipped in profundities and sprinkled with the glittering gemstones of ardour and expectations.

"What was that?" Vargas said. He stood in the doorway, drying his face with an oversized towel.

"Sorry?"

"I thought I heard something."

"I was humming a song I heard the other day."

"Humming." He came in and faced her.

"Correction," she said. "I wasn't humming. I was talking to myself."

"Anything I should know?"

"There is nothing you do not know already. I was thinking of how much I want us to succeed."

"We have not done badly, so far."

She suppressed a smile. "I hope that you do not consider this one week of relative concord a major achievement."

"Not at all." He moved closer and put his hand on her shoulder. "I am as easy to live with as I am placid, tolerant, predictable and exposed. Since you are not too bad, either, why should we not succeed?"

She touched his hand. "It scares me sometimes."

"What does?"

"Your uncanny knack of seeing through me. You knew all along what I was thinking, didn't you?"

"Would the opposite be better?"

"No." She smiled at him. "I suppose my apprehension is caused by not being used to it."

"That applies to quite a few things for both of us. The question is, are we willing to learn?"

"I am."

He sat down. "So am I, but you've got to give me time. Since I lost my roots I have been living in the shadows of futility all around. They don't disappear overnight."

Vargas' shoulders dropped. He said, "The snakes in my brain keep licking the back of my eyes. Sometimes I feel that my irises are a pair of forked tongues flickering all over my face."

A shiver went through her. She saw a vein pulsate under his ear. He said, "It's the demons. Most of the time I control them, but sometimes at night…" He shook his head.

She kissed his temple. He looked at her. There was a strange intensity in his eyes. She said, "Don't worry. If I want something badly enough, I can be incredibly patient."

"You'll need to be."

The tension lost its hold. Jennifer looked past the Angelo Vargas she had not seen before; a man with his shoulders hunched and who had allowed her a glimpse of his torments and a share of his loneliness. She sensed a soothing feeling of serenity. The image of a majestic and snow-covered mountain against a porcelain sky went by. She said, "Thank you for telling me."

He looked up. "I am at ease with you."

Outside Itoh's restaurant, Vargas stopped.

"You are right," he said.

"Good. In what respect?"

"I should not have invited Yasmin and Tadashi without consulting you beforehand."

"No, you shouldn't."

"Two-way traffic. I thought about it. Bad mistake. Kindly ignore."

She squeezed his arm. "Hereby ignored, kindly." Funny, she thought as they walked down the stairs, the word *forgive* does not seem to exist in his vocabulary. Neither does *sorry* or any variant of forthright apologies. Does it matter? No, not as long as regrets are recognized and expressed in an identifiable form.

Itoh demonstrated his delight at seeing them again in no uncertain manner.

Jennifer opened her handbag and took out a gift-wrapped parcel. "Please, Mr. Itoh," she said. "You have been so good to me. I want to give you something in return."

Itoh's eyes widened.

"Don't look at me," Vargas said. "I had no idea she'd bought you a present, otherwise I would have done my best to prevent it."

"Oh no," Itoh said and focused on Jennifer, "I am not worthy of this gift."

"How can you tell?" Vargas said.

"Can I open it now?"

They watched in silence as Itoh's liver-specked hands caressed the parcel before he undid the paper. "Oh dear oh dear," he said and stared at the eagle carved in crystal, its wings outstretched and with a savage look of defiance. "How incredibly gorgeous," he exclaimed. "I shall not know how to thank you, Miss Jennifer."

"It's Miss Moran to you," Vargas said.

"Angelo!"

Itoh held up the eagle. The lights played with the crystal. "I am so honoured," he said. "*Domo arigato*, Miss Jennifer. Very many and most sincere thanks."

"I am glad you like it," she said warmly.

"Take good care of it," Vargas advised. "It is the most symbolic gift you are ever likely to get."

"Symbolic, Vargas-San? In what way, dare I ask?"

Vargas pretended to study the eagle from different angles. "It will never take off—just like your cooking."

"Angelo, don't be so cruel!"

Itoh laughed. "I am used to him, Miss Jennifer." He was still smiling when he said, "As you will be, in due time. There are remnants of kindness in there, somewhere deep down inside. Liberties in the light of true friendship are easy to accept." He spoke with apparent indifference, as if making a casual statement, but Jennifer understood.

"You are a wise man, Mr. Itoh," she said softly.

Itoh bowed. "May I show you to your table, please."

Yasmin embraced Jennifer and Vargas. Ishihara smiled at Jennifer but did not go beyond a handshake.

He said, "How does it feel, experiencing the illegitimate imitation of marriage?"

Jennifer frowned but covered up with a smile. She wondered if there was a trace of animosity in Ishihara's voice.

"Fine," she said. "Actually, neither Angelo nor I are too concerned about conventional formalities."

Yasmin said, "That is good. The whole point is that you enjoy being together."

"Oh yes, we do."

Ishihara took off his jacket. "Itoh-San, could we have some more sake, please. The usual for you, Angelo?"

"Yes. What's up, Tadashi?"

"The States. Parkhurst and I are going over next week." He stroked his forehead. "There are times when I fear he is cracking up. What a slog it has been."

"In what way?"

"He is too timid, our friend Parkhurst. Either that, or he does not understand that you cannot impress the Americans without insulting them." He looked thoughtful. "Probably a bit of each, I'm afraid. I have supplied him with dozens of superbly offensive comments and observations, top quality slights all the way, but I have my suspicions that the final product will be pretty diluted." He banged the flat of his hand on the table and sighed. "The poor bugger is in awe of the Americans. When he talks about Harvard, he refers to *the chapel-like lecture hall of the Ivy League campus*—can you believe it? It is as if he thinks that Harvard is the birthplace of sacrosanct progress. It's unreal. Igor, of all, should understand that the more you suck up to the Americans, the sooner you'll lose your dignity."

"Why should he choose to be offensive?" Jennifer said.

Ishihara studied her. She tried to read his expression but failed to conclude. He said, "I just told you. No one can have much of an impact on the Americans by being subtle, refined or ironic. They are incapable of comprehending fine-spun oratory. Mentally and emotionally they are brawlers, intellectual philistines with a baboon's sensitivity. At *best* they understand a gentle kick—allowing time for their brains to register— but only impetuosity guarantees their full and instant attention. Do not forget that we are dealing with a nation whose protagonist is a cattle attendant and whose heroes are addressed as either *Mr. President* or *Don*—the difference between these two categories of legendary villains being that the Mafioso has a code of honour."

Itoh came with the drinks. "Show patience, Miss Jennifer," he said. "Tadashi-San has got this problem of not being adept at expressing himself clearly."

Jennifer and Yasmin laughed. Vargas smiled. Ishihara said, "Why don't you do what flatters you the most?"

"And what might that be, oh warlord?"

"Keep quiet."

"Ah, but my friend, are you not forgetting the teaching of the great Confucius?"

"Am I?"

"So it appears. Did he not say:

> 'Not to learn
> not to be able to talk about what one has learned
> not to be the better through having learned
> not to be able to change things towards the good —
> all this would seem terribly sad to me.' "

Ishihara said, "That is more romantic poetry than self-assessment and therefore engaging only to a quasi-idealistic and uncritical mind. You must not overlook that Confucius was only a Chinese." He looked towards the ceiling. "The Chinese, like the Koreans, have their limitations, a lamentable fact that should not be ignored when borrowing crappy aphorisms passing for wisdom. Quote from Miamoto Musashi next time you want to make an impact, unless, of course, substance with origin in experience no longer matters to you."

"I cherish your advice, but may I remind you that Musashi was a *ronin* and not a philosopher."

"Who later became an artist and who, in his writing, displayed the deepest insight into the human psyche."

"Who are we talking about?" Jennifer asked.

Vargas said, "Miamoto Musashi was a free spirit and a believer in self-applied didactics."

Ishihara raised his cup as if saluting Vargas. "Praiseworthy, and an attitude we both applaud." He turned to Itoh. "Musashi took great interest in himself and always did what he deemed proper. Why don't you do the same?"

"Like what, oh heir of Tokugawa?"

"Cut your throat."

"What reason would I have for such an act, my kind-hearted friend?"

"I can think of two: one is that if the concept *restaurant* was protected by intellectual rights you would be back in the fishing village you came from, and the other is that you evidently believe that dinner should be served at breakfast time."

Itoh straightened up. "Ah. The kitchen." He bowed. "My sincere apology. I must not forget that an empty stomach sucks oxygen from the dehydrated blob that some people call their brain. I shall hurry in order to prevent a total blackout."

Ishihara nodded. "Fine. You had the last word. *Sayonara.*"

Jennifer was getting used to the constant bantering between the three of them, but this time there was something else in the air. Ishihara was clearly not in the best of moods. She sensed that Yasmin was watching.

"Don't worry," Yasmin said. "Tadashi is just going through his emotional period. He gets depressed once a month. Don't ask me if there is any plausible reason, psychological or otherwise, since I have yet to discover."

Vargas smiled. Ishihara played with his chopsticks and said, "It's Parkhurst. He needs a steroid injection up his nose. I am afraid the Americans will find him so wet that, should he die over there, they won't have to cremate him. He'll evaporate."

Jennifer was beginning to resent Ishihara's negative attitude towards her godfather. She said, "Why don't you leave him alone? Why bother?"

Ishihara leaned back and hooked his thumbs behind his braces. "I want Parkhurst to succeed," he said, his dark brown eyes glazed with vehemence. "I thought that I had expounded beyond the shadow of a doubt how to achieve this, how to leave sufficient impact to be remembered, or, in simpler terms, how to become the recipient of numerous invitations. If Parkhurst plays his cards right, he can indeed make a substantial amount of money merely by telling the Americans a few home truths. Look at the fortunes they are paying on the circuit for the indigestible porridge served by faded politicians."

"Yes, I know that, but I believe it is possible to be entertaining without being sordid or libellous."

"Libellous? It is true that America has proudly developed into the world's largest litigious dungeon, but they have yet to grasp the fine legal art of making fortunes on even the most earthy piece of vilification, in stark contrast to this country, as we all know." He concentrated on his sake for a moment. "Apart from that, one should not forget that libel necessitates an unequivocal statement. After all, it is not quite that easy to claim defamation simply because somebody is expressing an opinion. I have tried to get this point across to your beloved godfather, and, to his credit, he is at least considering it."

Jennifer began to feel more rattled than she knew it was worth. "Would there be anything personal in your eagerness to assist and support?"

"Absolutely. My contempt for the plebeian natives of your former colonies is boundless, and I am shamelessly exploiting this opportunity to express myself through Parkhurst, thereby rewarding both of us."

He knows how to disarm his opponents, she thought, using naked honesty as his sword. Very clever. She said, "I like your candour, Tadashi. It adds to your charm. I had my suspicions, I have to admit, that there's quite a nice and decent little fellow hidden behind the armour of the *ronin*."

"Thank you," Ishihara said. The touch of humour had gone from his eyes. "I shall treasure this compliment for the rest of my days."

"You are welcome." Jennifer glanced at Vargas who looked as if he wasn't paying much attention.

"I suggest we change the subject," Yasmin said and put her hand over Ishihara's. "Let us drop the Americans."

"You mean *forget*, don't you," Ishihara said. "I can do much, my cherry blossom, but *forget* is something I cannot, shall not and will not do. I can *regret*—which I do—that when Roosevelt needed a miracle to save the American economy, we, my forefathers, were unwise enough to give it to him in the form of Pearl Harbour. Four years later they gave us Little and Big Brother, and we, the Japanese, needed a miracle to make Phoenix rise from the ashes. We succeeded, but their act—which was politically and not militarily motivated—was one of pure evil, a tour de force of such infinite immorality that everything from the Crusades, the Inquisition and the Conquistadors pales in comparison. Nowhere in history has man witnessed such limitless degeneracy, such an act of debauchery and cowardice. My only consolation is that the United States is decaying from within. Before the end of the next century it will have destroyed itself through corruption, ethnic heterogeneity, wholesale ignorance and moral atrophy."

Jennifer said, "Why do you want to visit if you have such a seductive image of the place?"

Yasmin tapped her chopsticks against her bowl. "Tadashi aspires to The Grand Cordon of the Supreme order of the Chrysanthemum." She smiled at Jennifer. "It's Japan's highest order."

Ishihara did not look at her. "Sheer compassion, Jennifer. Parkhurst needs me. After Harvard, I have arranged for a television interview with one of their brightest stars; a female whose main asset is the shrill, nasal, penetrating and high-pitched voice unrivalled by any woman born outside of the United States. Like most of her contemporaries, she knows little and understands less, but the show should be good publicity provided Parkhurst does not play his cat-and-mouse game in such a manner that it becomes either too obvious or too subtle for his audience."

Itoh arrived with the starters. He placed a dish in front of Jennifer. "This, Miss Jennifer, especially for you. The most succulent prawns ever to leave the ocean." He smiled genially. "And this, Miss Yasmin, especially for you, the best-best tuna with crab ever composed and prepared."

Ishihara said, "What about Mr. Angelo and Mr. Tadashi?"

"What about you?"

"Have you not prepared anything special for us?"

Itoh's visage changed from joviality to jaded weariness. He shook his head. "I could not be bothered." He put a large plate of sushi on the table. "Somebody ordered this three days ago but changed his mind. Hopefully it hasn't gone off. I have kept it in the fridge." His brows went up. "Not to worry. I have a stomach pump on the premises. Regulations, as I understand them. Please do not panic. Eat well, my friends."

Ishihara said, "Keep the sake flowing, and another glass for Angelo-San."

453

Vargas took a slender etui from his pocket, opened it and gave Jennifer her chopsticks. "Anything else whilst visiting your favourite nation?" he asked Ishihara.

"Yes," Ishihara said between mouthfuls. "I have lined up a televised debate between Parkhurst and the honourable senator Rufus Thurlow. Said Rufus, as we know, has declared that he is ready and willing to serve the great American people as their next great president. He will run out of steam long before he runs out of money, but at least he is one of the few declared runners of any value, publicity-wise, at this stage." Ishihara clicked his chopsticks. "Rufus—what the hell is the matter with parents who name their offspring *Rufus*?"

"Probably an unwanted child," Vargas said.

"That shouldn't surprise me. He is of Catholic stock."

"Is he entertaining?" Yasmin asked.

Ishihara picked another piece of sushi and gave himself time. "Incredibly so. Rufus has absolutely no sense of history and therefore no understanding of or respect for traditions. His mind has got only one gear, and it never moves without seatbelts securely fastened. He firmly believes that American foreign policy is without equal and fails completely to see the irony in this statement. He also believes that the Christian God Almighty first saw daylight somewhere between Maine and San Francisco. Rufus' favourite expression is *Wow!*—a cherished and widely popular outburst easily understood by those of his countrymen who want to leave an impression of being intellectually astute."

"You opted for the right opponent," Jennifer said. She hoped that she did not sound overly sarcastic.

Ishihara imitated a blithe grin. "I know it sounds contradictory in view of my description, but Rufus is actually ideal for our purpose. He has even managed to produce some form of program. Rufus has concluded that he is an ardent admirer and supporter of arts, he wants nobody to pay more than twenty percent income tax, and—his most repeated declaration—America should withdraw from all commitments abroad. No more policing; America has done her stint, and foreign aid should only be granted where return is guaranteed. Not exactly original, that one—that is what they have been doing all along, one way or another—but he knows that no American can resist investing a dollar when promised five in return. Rufus comes from a wealthy family and has all his life been disconnected from the real world. His greatest asset, though, as far as we are concerned, is his uncanny ability to confuse objectivity with pomposity and pragmatism with expediency. Parkhurst should annihilate him."

"You'll be in the studio?" Vargas said.

"Most certainly. Rufus will provide the experience of a lifetime. I have never before had the chance to witness the process when somebody's two single brain-cells meet, have an orgasm and produce the simulacrum of a prematurely born thought."

"Don't spill your coffee when it happens."

"Coffee!" Ishihara barked. Then he saw Vargas' smile and turned to Jennifer. "The Americans' formula for coffee is one bean per cup. Funny," he added and lost some of his aggression, "they import but two products from Colombia, and they know how to utilize only one of them."

Jennifer wished that he would let go of his pet enemy. She said, "Look at the bright side, Tadashi. At least you won't have too much of a problem trying to understand what they are saying, if nothing else."

"That is not entirely applicable to my good self," Ishihara said and half closed his eyes. "I can, however, see the linguistic advantage for one who is unable to distinguish between niggerish rock 'n' roll and a Beethoven symphony." He waved dismissively with his right hand. "It is a deplorable situation," he went on, "but what can one expect from a nation that consider Hemingway a great writer, Tennessee Williams a playwright of distinction, the mumbling morons Brando and Dean superb thespians, and—to crown it—hailing Jerry Lewis, Dick van Dyke and Bill Cosby as comedians?" His chin came forward, and he picked his teeth with the nail of his little finger. "My viewpoint is not unique," he continued and looked at his nail. "I am merely expressing observations shared by *civilized* nations, which, in this context, does not include Ireland. There is nothing wrong with the Irish culture, of course—let us not confuse the issue—but, clinically speaking, one must not overlook the link between the Irish and the Americans since 1840 and till today's support of the IRA." He lifted his cup. "Nothing personal, Jennifer. Lack of judgement is a birthright."

Yasmin said sharply, "Tadashi, I think you have sucked every milligram of marrow out of your little bone by now."

Jennifer's palms were clammy. She failed to see a reason, but she had no doubt that Ishihara had been waiting to drop a deliberate insult. He studied his chopsticks as if he'd never seen them before, seemingly unaware of Yasmin's comment. Suddenly, with an aggressive movement of his head, he said, "Another thing, come to think of…"

"Tadashi," Vargas said quietly, "I believe that the four of us would benefit from a conversation free from personal references. Would you not agree that an amicable and courteous atmosphere is preferable?"

For a split second Ishihara lost his composure. He shifted uneasily on his chair, grabbed his sake and stared across the room. Then he said, "I am sorry if what I said was being misinterpreted in any one way. It was not my intention to cause offence. I just summed up some of my sentiments."

Vargas said, "You would not want anyone here to take umbrage." He kept staring at Ishihara who finally looked back. "Would you, Tadashi?"

"No. Of course not."

"*Shazai*," Yasmin said.

A chill went down Jennifer's spine. The look that Ishihara had thrown his wife contained very little affection. He got up. "Excuse me. I'll be back in a minute," he said and headed for the men's room.

Vargas said, "Don't push him, Yasmin. I'll go and see if he is all right."

"No need to," she snapped. "He does not deserve sympathy."

Vargas left without answering.

Jennifer asked, "What does *Shazai* mean?"

Yasmin sighed. "It means that I have committed a sin for which I humbly apologize. Please forgive him. I know what is troubling him." She raised her hand. "Not now. I will tell you later, and you will understand. Tadashi is a good man, but there are times when his ego overshadows his common sense. He is not *entirely* perfect," she added with a forced laughter.

Jennifer decided to let the matter rest. She preferred to assume that Yasmin one day would explain Tadashi's weird and uncharacteristic behaviour.

"Strange men, those two," Yasmin said with a wry smile. "What have we got ourselves into? Tadashi will listen to Angelo. He always does."

"There is a good deal of understanding between them, isn't there? Has it been like that all the time?"

"Yes, it has. Once, whilst still in Japan, Tadashi said to me: 'This gaijin is a peculiar man. He has got a very cold brain and a menacing heart. He is my brother.'" Yasmin smiled. "That was long before Hong Kong. Tadashi still sees it that way."

The scenes from the Middle East and Hong Kong flashed through Jennifer's mind. She scraped the rest of the steamed rice from the dish into her bowl and said, "We all change as we get older."

"Don't count on it."

Jennifer rearranged her napkin with deliberate slowness. "Do I detect a warning?"

"Angelo has been searching for his shrine for as long as I have known him, which means *longer*. He is restless and mercurial and I think he would reject peace of mind even if he knew how to achieve it. My advice is that you accept him for what he is. He may mellow a bit, thanks to your presence, but he won't *change*. I told myself exactly the same when I decided to marry Tadashi, and I was not mistaken." She touched Jennifer's arm. "Accept realities, my friend, and you can't go wrong. If any one woman on this earth is compatible with Angelo, it is you."

Jennifer asked herself if she should feel flattered or patronized. She said, "Tell me, on what do you…" she stopped when Yasmin turned her head and said, "Here they come."

"Hello, girls," Ishihara grinned. "How did you manage without us?"

Yasmin said, "We suffered in silence."

Ishihara pushed out Vargas' chair with his foot. "I thought so. Well, here we are, the shining knights ready for the rescue."

They sat down. Jennifer looked at Vargas. She saw a friendly smile and nothing more.

Ishihara was at his most charming the rest of the evening.

During the taxi ride home, Yasmin refused to utter a single word. Ishihara finally gave up.

She went to the bedroom where she changed into a white and yellow kimono. She splashed a good measure of tequila into a glass, lit a Sobranie and blew the smoke towards the aquarium.

Ishihara loosened the knot of his expensive silk tie. "I wouldn't mind a drink."

Yasmin made no comment. She walked across to the sofa, sat down and closed her eyes.

Ishihara unbuttoned his collar and took off his jacket, "Do you mind if I change before we continue this rewarding conversation?"

"Do what the hell you like."

457

He went into the bedroom and began to undress. Yasmin's attitude was ominous. It was not often she brushed him aside and refused a discussion. He put on his favourite cotton pyjamas, black with white lapels and a white tiger on the back. He did ten *ibukis* before he concluded that no breathing exercises would make him feel any more relaxed. He wandered into the drawing room and stopped in front of the drinks tray. He filled up his glass and picked a chair in relative darkness some ten feet away from Yasmin who still sat with her eyes closed.

He said, "Are you going to talk or not?"

Yasmin lifted her glass to her lips as if performing a pantomime act. She opened her eyes and said, "You bloody prat."

Ishihara rested his right ankle on his left knee. "Informative."

Yasmin patted her chin with the tip of her fingers. "How could you be so incredibly moronic?"

"I am afraid you have lost me. What are we talking about?"

Yasmin's smile could have paralyzed an alligator. "Condescension will get you nowhere."

Mistake number two, he thought, whatever the first one was. He said, "It was not meant that way."

"Please do not insult my intelligence."

Ishihara eyed his wife. She studied her toes. He decided to drop all pretences. He knew from long experience that nothing constructive would be achieved unless he put the entire deck of cards on the table. "You did not like the way I spoke to your Irish friend."

"The issue is not whether you are entitled to your periodical displays of pathological nastiness. What I find incredible is your timing, your inability to grasp when it is better to shut up. You made a very serious mistake tonight. I hope there is still time to put it right."

Ishihara began to feel annoyed. "That was no mistake, my dear," he said sharply. "That woman is bad news."

There was a long silence. Then, Yasmin said, "Oh, really."

"Yes, *really*. For the life of me I cannot see why I should be under any obligation to feign an enthusiasm that isn't there."

Her eyebrows moved. She smiled. "That wasn't your mistake. You just don't get it, do you? Obligation is irrelevant."

Who is condescending, he thought? She evidently thinks she's got a point invisible to anybody else. I shall remain calm and listen to whatever short-circuited conclusion she has arrived at. "Please tell me," he said and kept his voice neutral.

She got up, walked towards him and sat down on her heels. She kept her glass in both hand and stared into his eyes for a moment before she said, " Your mistake was that you let *Angelo* know how you feel about Jennifer. Think about it. Is not Angelo the last person in this universe that you can afford to offend? Forget how close the two of you have been during all these years. Forget the sentimental notion that he is your proclaimed brother. Forget the humane observation that Angelo deserves to find a shade of happiness at long last. Remember only this one single question: what are you going to do if he drops out; how are you going to carry through that final and in all respects ultimate coup of yours without him? We have discussed this before, and it is beyond me that you fail to get the message."

Ishihara stared back as the consequences of her words began to dawn upon him. "With that woman out of the way we won't have a situation like that," he said and sensed that he was not at his most convincing.

Yasmin said with deliberate slowness, "Let me get this right—*out of the way*—does this mean that you are contemplating getting rid of her?"

He looked past her. The skin under his nose was moist.

She continued, "Because if you do, remember to kill Angelo first."

"You misunderstand," he said. "I do not think like that at all. My point is that Jennifer is bad news in as much as Angelo wishes to retire for *her* sake. Same result, I mean. I really fear that he will."

"You are not supremely logical tonight. He can be persuaded, but only—*only*—if we both clearly demonstrate in the most positive manner that we accept Jennifer as part of his life. Believe me, she is not going to walk away. I have told you before, and I am telling you again."

Ishihara sniggered. "There have been a few other women in his life."

"Yes. They came and went. We know that, and we also know that none of them were of Jennifer's class. She is an unusual woman, Tadashi, with or without your approval. My prediction is that she and Angelo will become as inseparable as you and I are." She sat down, put her glass on the floor and threw her head back. "Angelo's only problem is that he subliminally suspects that he does not deserve her, a misconception he has to get rid of all by himself."

"Maybe he won't," Ishihara said and wished that his wife would go back to the sofa.

She said, "Sadly, he is not the only one with a personal problem."

He didn't like the look in her eyes. "Go on," he said with a strained smile.

"For a start, you are jealous."

"I beg your pardon?"

"You heard me. Ever since Angelo showed up in Tokyo, you've had him to yourself. Neither of you ever allowed anybody or anything to come between you. Now, suddenly, here is Jennifer. He realizes what has come into his life, and you fail to cope."

"That is not perfectly correct. What about you?"

"Oh no, I never came between you. I was there from the beginning, something you both accepted from the onset. Don't confuse yourself."

Ishihara kept quiet. He knew that his wife was not far off the mark.

Yasmin said, "Your other problem is the contradiction that colours your existence. How come that a man with your intelligence appears unable to create a balance between *where* he is and *what* he is?"

He bit his tongue and suppressed a noise that could have been taken for a sigh. "What contradiction and what balance?"

"You despise practically everything the West stands for, yet you prefer to live here. It is time you scrutinize your instincts and revise your priorities, my darling, or your immortal spirit will continue to limp through an earthbound wilderness instead of flying free and happy high above."

"Has this got anything to do with Angelo and Jennifer?"

"Very much so. He was never a problem; he's a godless nomad who follows his own selfish rules whenever it suits him, whilst *she* is exactly the opposite. In your book she epitomizes Westerns traditions at its most despicable level, and what better grounds are there for disliking her. Fear of Angelo refusing to participate in your assignment is not your only motive. Get your scale adjusted, or I shall seriously begin to suspect that there is a third reason."

"Like what?"

"Like that you have no intention of quitting. Like there is no such thing as the *last* assignment. Why? Because you fear the emptiness when the *thrill of the danger* is no longer there."

"I have given you my word."

Yasmin did not answer. The skin under her eyes was tight and she looked weary.

Ishihara moved to the edge of his chair. An expression of despondency crossed his face. "What do I do?" he said tonelessly.

"Accept her. Idolize and worship her the way I idolize and worship Angelo."

"That is impossible."

"I know. *Pretend* that you do. Open your mind. Sooner or later you will like her. She is a nice and kind human being. She is honest, and she is genuine. Few are."

He tapped her on the nose. "You do idolize him, don't you."

"I always have. You know that."

He shrugged. "I'll do my best."

Yasmin laughed. "Do not underestimate your acting talents. Make Angelo believe that you are happy for him."

"I will."

Her silence did not reassure him. "What is it?"

She went back to the sofa and curled up in a corner. "Forgive me for being slow, but how badly do we need this last assignment?"

He looked down. Not again, he thought. He said, "Added security. I told you."

"Is there something you have *not* told me?"

He got up for a refill. "I don't think so."

"Why is it, then, that Angelo can afford to retire and you cannot? Don't say he is less money-conscious than you are, because he isn't."

Ishihara felt that his head was spinning the way it did when he was short of sleep. "He has got more money than we have."

"Why is that? You always shared down to the last penny."

"His capital has grown considerably during the years. He picked his brokers with great care, and they've done a good job. He is watching his portfolio, and he doesn't do anything wild. He is pretty well off, by now."

"And we?"

"You know that I speculate. I gamble. I take chances. Sometimes it pays off, but not always."

"Excuse me, but are you trying to tell me that Angelo does not gamble?"

Ishihara put his glass on the side table. He sat down. "No, I am not. We both know that he is an inveterate gambler. The difference is that he does not touch his capital. He's using the money from his shops."

"I see. That is why the ice on Angelo's pond is thicker than on ours?"

"That is exactly the way it is."

"Are we in trouble?"

"No, we are not."

"You promised to show me the figures."

"It skipped my mind. We'll go through everything tomorrow. You will see for yourself why we cannot afford to discard one or two unwelcome permutations."

"Unwelcome?"

"I have to face that you could be left on your own with a child or three. That is why the prospects of extra security are so heavy on my mind."

"And the last assignment will take care of everything?"

"Yes, it will. I talk about a few millions." He nodded. "Each."

"Who is worth that much?"

An exceptionally prominent corpse, Ishihara thought. He said, "I didn't hear that question."

"Just hypothesizing. It wasn't a question."

He moved his head from side to side until he heard the crack from his neck. "One more detail," he said. "The money will go into a trust. Your trust, and in your name only."

Yasmin sat still. Her hands rested in her lap. She lifted her face towards the ceiling and closed her eyes. She did not wish to break the silence. What he said had been on his mind all along. She thought how meaningless life without him would be and the burning sensation in her head became acute. She saw the mighty Mount Fuji, the cherry blossoms, their favourite shrine and the quiet river nearby, and then the image of the rustic English home where they were going to live in peace and quiet and watch their children grow up.

21

Vargas was more quiet than usual when they got home, but Jennifer was in no mood to leave him to ponder on his own. We share, she thought, and he damn well is going to let me know what is on his mind.

They sat down.

He stared ahead. The thumb and index finger of his right hand touched his lower lip. He still had his jacket on and he had yet to get himself a drink.

Lord Jesus, she thought, this must be serious. She said, "Why doesn't Tadashi like me?"

He did not move.

"Excuse me, I am talking to you."

"I am trying to figure it out," he said after a while.

She brushed a newspaper off a chair. That is one of the things I like about you, she thought, you do not try to feed me a meaningless cliché. "What happened in the loo?"

"He urinated."

"Was he capable of talking at the same time?"

"He didn't try."

"That was it, then. You watched him pee, and, being your considerate self, you guided him back to the table, having helped him with his zipper. Forgive me for complicating your process of thought, but why did you follow him?" I've gone too far, now, she thought. Angelo may be stoical, but he does not eat barbed wire.

He took off his jacket whilst still sitting down. "I think he sees you as an intruder."

"Who told who?"

"Nobody." He got up and slid past her towards the hallway. She heard him hang up his jacket. She heard the sound of a glass being filled. This is spooky, she thought. How did he manage to move from the hallway to the cabinet without my noticing? She said, "Have a drink."

He made no comment.

She studied his profile and said, "There are times when I find your verbosity overwhelming."

The corners of his mouth remained static.

She said wearily, "Kindly let me know what you said to Tadashi. I believe I have a right to know, and I believe you have that obligation to the two of us."

He turned and faced her. She saw something in his eyes that she had not noticed before; not anger or disapproval, but like a smouldering glow reflecting on glass. He said, "It's you, Jennifer and I, or it is Jennifer and I."

She put her fingers to her mouth. Vargas kept staring at her. She said, "Jesus Christ, is that what you told him? I did not mean..." She did not know what she meant and she saw that her hands shook. He was still eyeing her but the glow was gone.

"You don't compromise, do you?" she said.

"There are times when I don't."

Yes, she thought, like most of the time. Even Tadashi, your long-time and only friend. I do not understand. I, a woman you hardly know and who could walk out on you tomorrow—not that I will, not that I *ever* will—but you do not know that. What made you so relentless, so unyielding, so absolute in your dealings with what comes your way in life?

He said, "You watch your end of the bridge, and Yasmin will watch the other."

"And Tadashi?"

"To his credit, Tadashi has the ability to change course mid-air. The odd pearly-white spots of a carefully trimmed conscience, also known as opportunism stain his egomaniacal soul. Hence his mental and emotional dexterity."

She remembered Yasmin's reaction when Ishihara had dropped his acid comments. She was not too sure what Vargas actually meant. All she could do was to heed his advice. She said, "Does Yasmin know something about you that nobody else knows?"

"She may."

"*May?*"

"Oriental women have a talent for surmising with astonishing precision."

Surmising, she repeated to herself, well, don't push it. That glow is coming back in his eyes. It makes me wary. Why am I wary of him, at times, but never afraid of him? *A cold brain and a menacing heart.* One day, when in the right mood, he may cut me to pieces with words or with silence, but he will not harm me. He will upset me; oh yes, regularly, square as he is. But he will not stop caring for me and protecting me. Wishful thinking? No, I am just *surmising* with astonishing precision. She smiled and said, "You think Tadashi will come to his senses?"

"Yes. He needs me, and you are irresistible." He took his first sip. "Long term."

She laughed. "Thank you." She tried to sound relaxed when she said, "Will you forget what happened tonight?"

"I am an eminent gravedigger."

"Gravedigger? Good Lord, we are talking about your memory."

He picked up his shoes, rose and stretched his torso. "Yes, we are. Let's go to bed."

She knew the pattern, by now. After a while, when he thought she was asleep, he would get up and put on his kimono and sit in his chair for hours, lost in his own world.

A few weeks of coexistence passed before Jennifer became aware of Vargas' consumption of alcohol. At first, she'd noticed only what he drank during the evenings.

She went to her office five days a week. When she came home, usually at around six o'clock, he was not always there. When he did arrive, she'd begun to smell the whisky on his breath, but she had yet to hear him slur his words or see him visibly inebriated.

High tolerance, she thought. It probably means that he's a seasoned drinker. I am going to watch this, although I haven't the faintest idea what to do about it.

One morning he came out from the bedroom took a good sip straight from the bottle and then another before he went into the bathroom. He knew she was there, and she stared in amazement as he walked by, seemingly ignoring her presence. She concluded that what she had been watching had to be an exception; he always went for a run in the morning before he spent at least one hour in the dojo. He was fanatic about his fitness, and had he not told her several times that he intended to stay that way? Something was bothering him, and he drank to anaesthetize whatever it was. Eventually he would talk, and together they would put an end to the story and he'd be back to normal.

Normal? She wished she knew what was bog-standard for a seasoned drinker.

One day they went shopping together and he did not touch a drop until late afternoon. There you are, she thought, that bottle swigging was an exception; just a coincidence, and that's all there is to it.

Saturday came without Vargas repeating the performance. Her tension eased. I was right, she thought, there is no need to worry. At noon, he suggested that they should go for an early lunch at a nearby restaurant. He had two double whiskies before the food arrived and two after the meal. He showed no signs of having as much as sniffed at a bottle.

It *is* serious, she thought and tried to fight off a shade of desperation. Nobody can drink like that without substantial experience. That is one thing, another thing is that his drinking is actually getting worse. No way did he drink like that until recently. Why? Am I doing something wrong? Has he decided that I was one monumental mistake? Dear God, I fully understand if You are reluctant to talk to a pagan like Angelo, but please help me. Please let him be honest with me so that I know where to go from here.

Honest. She suddenly remembered what he once had said: "*Whatever I tell you is the truth.*" Fine, God, but please do remind him, if nothing else.

She said, "Why do you drink so much?"

"Old habit."

"Is that true?"

"Yes and no."

"Please do not walk in circles."

"I'm sprinkling a vacuum."

She tried to control her anger. "I am sorry, but that does not convince me. You've got the most analytical mind of anyone I have ever met. You bloody well *know* why your soul is sitting erect and glistening under cascades of whisky night after night. Tell me."

He pushed his chair back. "I am leaving," he said. "Are you coming?"

They walked without talking. Perhaps he really does not know, she thought, or maybe he has a dawning suspicion of something unwelcome; a question with no answer, or a predicament unwanted.

The following day she began to monitor his drinking. She did it reluctantly; it made her feel uncomfortable, but a more vibrant voice advised her not to turn a blind eye.

His consumption was roughly a bottle a day. That did not include what he drank when away from home.

Jennifer knew that she could not confide in anybody without causing a serious dent in her relationship with Vargas and damage to her self-esteem. Gradually, she began to think that sharing the problem with a third person would also be a waste. All she could possibly achieve would be sympathetic nods, well-meant comments and worthless pieces of advice. *He needs help. Try AA. See a psychiatrist. Hide the bottles. Threaten to leave him.*

No, she thought, I am not stripping my soul and placing my relationship with him naked on the table for all to see in exchange for hackneyed platitudes and vacuous sympathy. Although her father had done his best to shield her from most of what went on in The Mission she had seen her fair share of addicts during the years, and she recalled his conclusion that nobody but the addict himself could make him stop. She knew this to be true. There was no unambiguous reason to why a person became an addict, no keys and no blueprint. Theories, yes; genes, chemical imbalance, deep-rooted psychological disturbances, a bit of each—she knew all to well that unless Vargas found a *reason* to stop, he would continue and it would get worse.

Reason. He could get cirrhosis of the liver. His brain could get perforated with more cells dead than alive. His physical demands on his body could lead to a heart attack. He could risk gangrene and amputations. *Reasons?* Those were good ones, she thought, but not good enough. He would shrug it off. She could see that even the most gruesome of pictures would not have much impact on a mind as obdurate as his. She was convinced that he was past that point aeons ago, which, in one way, made it easier for her in as much as she knew where *not* to look for a solution.

Lately, she had also sensed a certain change in his overall demeanour. He was still amusing, but his remarks and his observations were more mercenary than they used to be. He was no less gentle and considerate, but once in a while she had glimpsed evidence of his temper. He did not shout and he did not break things, but his body language was not as she remembered it from only a few months ago. His movements were more abrupt. His stare had lost some of its quality of inscrutable curiosity. A harsh edge had come into his voice. But, amidst all this, she never lost faith in his affection for her. She continued to believe that he loved her, but she also knew that, however passionate and devoted, no relationship could in the long run withstand the corrosive effect of alcohol.

Time is my enemy, she concluded. He must find a reason to quit, and he must find it soon. If only I could point at something. If only I knew where to look.

She was torn from her sleep by a voice shouting words in a language she did not understand. She switched on the light and saw him sitting upright in his bed. He breathed heavily. Perspiration poured from his head. He jolted when she touched his shoulder.

"What is it?"

He shook his head. "Some dream," he said hoarsely. He stared at her. "Did I say anything?"

"Yes, but I did not—it was not in English."

He got up. His body glistened with sweat. She put her hand on his pillow. It was stained and soaking wet. She heard water running.

Ten minutes later he came out, dressed in his robe and seemingly at ease. He said, "I'll sit up for a while."

She opened wide a window, dimmed the lights and went into the drawing room.

He sat with a glass in his hands. His breathing was normal. She thought that nobody could have guessed that this man has just woken up from what must have been a terrible nightmare. He is composed, she thought, too composed. How deep does it go?

She stood next to him. "What were you dreaming?"

"I need to collect my thoughts," he said.

She sat down. "Does that mean that you remember but you are not willing to tell me?"

He did not answer. He did not look at her.

She said, "Have you had this nightmare before?"

"Yes."

"Many times?"

"Yes."

"The very same nightmare?"

He nodded. "Not for a long time. At least six months, I think."

She crossed her ankles and leaned her head against the back of the chair. "When do you expect the next one?"

"What kind of question is that."

"It will come back, won't it?"

He looked down. "It will."

She spoke softly, "Share with me."

His eyes wandered. She saw a haunted expression on his face and she wanted to embrace him. She said, "The past cannot be undone. I once promised that I would not appoint myself jury and judge. Help me to become part of you. Please let me share your agonies and your sorrows." She lowered her head and tried to see his eyes. "I cannot understand what I do not know. Whatever problems you have, they do not go away by not talking about them. I know you are hermetic by nature and that your experiences have not made it any easier for you to open up, but you and I are not going to last unless I have your confidence. You must find the answer to what it is that holds you back."

She saw his body become rigid with tension. He put his glass on he floor. She heard a sigh from deep within when he covered his face with his hands. His fingers pressed against his skin like talons.

It was the sign she had been waiting for. She stroked his head and went back to bed.

Vargas' nightmares occurred twice during the next couple of weeks. Twice she left him alone.

On the morning of his third attack she was in no hurry to leave the breakfast table. She scanned through the newspapers, sipped her coffee and had a rare early-day cigarette. She pretended not to notice that he was watching her. She made a telephone call and announced that she was not coming in to work that day.

At ten o'clock she dressed. She knew that she looked smart in a maroon trouser suit and practical but elegant black suede shoes.

He asked, "What's up?"

"I am going shopping," she said lightly. "I need a new handbag."

"Where are you going?"

"Bond Street."

He scratched his chest and looked out the window. "I would like to come with you."

She smiled. That was a new one. In the past he'd always said *would you like me to come with you?* Progress. He wasn't in the habit of choosing his words at random.

She said, "That's sweet of you. I would love that."

Six hours earlier he had been sitting on his own, enveloped in darkness and re-living his nightmare. Behind a calm and controlled façade he was still tense, but he had volunteered to come with her.

It could be the day when she would plant her seeds and pray that they did not fall on stones.

The weather was nice, sunny and with a light breeze. The roads were quiet and the pavements were not overcrowded. It never ceased to amaze her how unpredictable the London traffic was.

They agreed to walk up Bond Street. The taxi let them off opposite the Ritz Hotel. Jennifer stopped frequently. She never tired of window-shopping. It took them fifteen minutes before they reached the corner of Asprey's. Vargas was patience personified and gave a reasonable good imitation of being interested in whatever caught her attention.

"Look at that one," she said. "Have you ever seen anything so beautiful?"

He looked. "What?"

"That bracelet in the middle, there. The gold one with the row of diamonds."

"Overdone," he said.

"No, it is not," she protested. "It's a perfect design."

He said, "Listen, I need to find a telephone and call Tadashi before noon. Why don't you go and get your handbag? I'll wait for you outside the shop."

She smiled teasingly. "You don't want to come in?"

He hesitated. "If you so wish."

"All right," she laughed. "I understand. You wait outside."

She took her time selecting her merchandise, but in the end it was she who had to wait.

"Hard luck," he said. "It took longer than I anticipated."

"Is something wrong?"

"No. Plain routine, but quite a bit of it. Anyway, here I am."

They went to a newly opened restaurant in Mayfair that she'd read about.

He only had one drink before the food arrived. When they left the table, there was still an inch left in the winebottle. He had been easygoing and communicative during the meal. Only a few times did a shadow darken his face and his concentration slipped and he was somewhere else for a brief moment.

They took their coffee in the bar. It was almost empty. They found a table out of earshot from the other two couples sitting there. He lit a cigarette and did not ask for a drink. He had turned quiet. She began to feel nervous. He is on guard, she thought; he either expects or he suspects something. He knows we are here by design and not by coincidence. I am losing my nerve, but if I chicken out today it will be all that more difficult to try again—assuming that my courage should happen to be present the second time around.

Why does he not have a drink? Why are those eyes blue and not bloodshot? Why is he sitting there like a statue chiselled in granite, waiting for the goddess of redemption to kiss life into his fossilized heart? I promised never to judge, never to condemn. Isn't that what I am doing? Yes, it is. I am scared of losing him, but that is what will happen if he does not open up and show me trust and confidence. So, then, you better listen now, listen and understand.

She stirred her coffee. She fiddled with her napkin and smiled as if a long forgotten memory all of a sudden had come to mind.

She said, "Did I ever tell you that I was once expelled from school?"

"I do not recall you did."

"I was—oh, about thirteen years of age, I think—and we had this teacher who for some reason had made me his pet hate. Thinking back, I believe he despised the female sex, actually. Age, size or shape did not come into it. Somehow, he got into his head that I was worthy of more derision than all the other girls in my class put together did. Being of Irish origin was of course a sin in itself, not to mention being Irish Catholic. Never in his entire career had he come across someone as petulant, conceited, slow, dull, insolent and hopelessly useless as the young Miss Moran. There was no limit to what a lost cause I was. One day he overstepped. He began to make snide comments about my father and The Mission, and *that* was unacceptable. I decided that time had come for revenge."

"Excellent. What did you do?"

"I borrowed a knife from a boy who I thought fancied me—at least, he said so—and I punctured all four wheels of the teacher's car. Can you believe that?"

"I can. How did you get caught?"

"How do you know I got caught?"

"There wouldn't be a moral to your story, otherwise."

She touched her nose with her little finger. "The boy told on me."

"Where can I find the dirty little rat?"

She stared at him. Then she saw the smile and relaxed. "I was told not to come back and given a letter to my parents."

"Tricky, unless you were good at copying signatures."

"Even if I had been, how could I have explained not attending school any more?"

"Education not up to standard. Anti-Irish atmosphere. Teacher pornographic—to mention a few probabilities."

She laughed. "You are not short of an answer, are you? No, seriously, my problem was that I could not lie. What an afternoon I had. Never was the walk back home so long and yet so short. But then, just before I reached the gate, I got this idea. I went in and said to my mother: "There was quite an upheaval at school today. You never guess what happened. One of the girls punctured all four tyres on a car belonging to a teacher." Mum said, "Almighty Christ, she slashed all four tyres? What a terrible thing to do." I said, "She punctured them, not slashed, but I agree, although nobody likes that teacher. The girl got a lot of sympathy from all, I must say." Then I went on to explain about the degradation that had been going on, without being too specific, and in the end Mum was entirely on the girl's side. This was the moment when I decided to own up and give her the letter. By then she was defused; my third person presentation had worked and made things so much easier for myself and—and more considerate, I'd say, as far as my mother was concerned. Wouldn't you agree?"

"Charitable. End of story?"

"Well, yes—more or less. She told me never again to lose my dignity and advised me to come and talk—" she paused for a few seconds "—instead of bottling things up."

"Good moral," he said and looked at the knuckles of his hands.

He knows, she thought. She said, "My father went off to see the headmaster, and from then on that particular teacher ignored me— distinctly the lesser of two evils. Dad paid for the tyres."

"You've got sensible parents."

"They always listened and they always tried to understand. They still do." She felt a compelling need to emphasize the purport of her story. "However understanding and positive somebody is, there are always cases when it is easier to relate a story in third person, making oneself detached, so to speak."

His eyes did not leave her face. She began to feel the silence unnerving. What was he thinking? She raised her cup and said, as casually as she could, "Don't you think so?"

He remained still. After a while, he said, "I heard you the first time."

Don't push it, she thought. She said, "I have not seen Mum for well over a week. I think I'll drop in for a couple of hours."

He rose when she got up.

She asked, "Are you leaving now?"

"I'll sit here for a few minutes."

She kissed him on the cheek. "See you later. Enjoy the afternoon."

It was seven o'clock before she got home. She switched on the lights and went into the kitchen with her shopping. On the table, neatly placed in the centre of an otherwise empty top, were a small oblong parcel and a white envelope. She listened for a moment. Then she left the kitchen and checked every single room. There was no sign of Vargas. She went back into the kitchen and opened the envelope. The motif on the card was one of Degas' ballet scenes. She unfolded the card and saw Vargas' upright and clean handwriting and read: *A good story— expertly told and its tenor beyond misinterpretation.*

No *Dear Jennifer*. No *Love, Angelo*. It was like a statement, she thought— or a message. She unwrapped the parcel and saw the name on the box. She opened it slowly. The bracelet came to life under the spotlight above. Oh God, she whispered and sank down on a chair; sweet Jesus, what has he done? She put the bracelet on and turned her wrist back and forth, unable to let go with her eyes. It is the first gift he has ever given me, she thought—no, sorry, the second; don't forget the chopsticks. Some difference. No half measures with Angelo. She placed the card upright on the table and began to store away her shopping, wearing the bracelet.

She was planning a simple Italian dish that would not take long to make. She looked at the clock.

At half past eight the dinner was ready.

At nine o'clock she was getting annoyed. They had parted almost six hours ago. Where the hell was he?

At ten o'clock she opened the lid of the bin and watched her Italian dinner disappear.

Midnight.

Why am I sick with worry? she said out loud. If anyone can look after himself, it's Angelo. No, she went on, I am not going to fool myself. My state of mind has got nothing to do with his physical well-being. I am worried because he is mercurial and because I have no idea what is going through his mind. That is the reality of my burden. Why in God's name can't he behave like a normal person, like saying in advance that he is going to be late, or leave a message, or make a telephone call? Why don't I go to bed now, wearing my bracelet, and when I wake up in the morning he is either there, next to me, or he isn't.

She buried her face in her hands. Of all the men on this overcrowded planet, why did I have to find myself someone who is difficult to distinguish from an introvert and whisky-loving grizzly bear wearing a leather jacket? Why do I love and why am I in love with a creature who believes that seclusion is the highest form of life and loneliness the purest and ultimately the most rewarding existence? The only relationship that will last, is the one he has got with himself. He has imprisoned his own mind and no one is allowed to visit. How can I share a life with a man whose soul lives in total isolation, whose concept of an acceptable existence is seclusion?

That's how it is. Anything or anybody else is an amenity, something basically superfluous and therefore of limited value. That includes myself. I am worthy of a piece of jewellery, but for heaven's sake don't stretch it to the heights of demands like a telephone call. That is *personal* involvement and, as such, beyond the pale.

No, I am not going to cry. I am going to put the bracelet back where I found it and then I am going to bed.

She got up a moment before she heard his keys in the door.

She sat down and made herself look at ease. No questions, now. No complaints and no comments. Produce a smile radiating happiness and wish the bastard welcome home.

He came in. She stared. "Is something wrong?"

He looked grim and weary. There was no warmth in his eyes when he looked at her. His mouth was small and his movements were rigid when he took off his jacket. He crossed the floor and sat down opposite her. After a while, he said, "Let us go and change into something comfortable."

They got up simultaneously. Jennifer placed the palm of her hands against his chest and asked, "What is it?"

"I have got something to tell you."

There was no smell of alcohol on his breath.

22

The land was as barren as the minds of the people living there; a land where the soil demanded much and gave scant in return. Pine trees grew on the hills and halfway up the mountains, then granite took over and vegetation became sparse and crippled and offered little or nothing even to the most hardy of animals.

Apart from growing their own potatoes, keeping chicken and small herds of sheep and cattle, most people relied on the sea. In those days the sea was full of herring and cod and mackerel. Everybody had a rowboat. Most had a small, motorized craft and some had a medium-sized smack. The wealthy ones had a trawler.

The town was an hour away by ferry. There were those who travelled to and from it every day, making a living in the building industry or at the ship yard. Some worked in shops. The superior ones worked in offices.

The people saw to their own needs by moonshining; it was widespread, illegal and overlooked. The quality could never be better than mediocre. Some industrious souls even made life better for their fellow man by running an import business; the uneven coastline and the hundreds of uninhabited islands made it a haven for smugglers. The most cherished imports were alcohol, cigarettes and tobacco. The ships came from Eastern Europe, Scotland and the odd one from Ireland. They anchored beyond the horizon and out of sight of the local lawman. He and his office were covertly part of the operation, but good manners dictated the pretence; the lawman always assumed that boats were made for fishing and nothing else. There was no logical reason why he should pay a visit to some rocky island even if the boats did.

The youngster who later called himself Martin Tauber before he became Angelo Vargas had three older sisters and a brother who was three years younger and nicknamed *Baby* because he had arrived against expectations. The family lived in their own house that had been given to them by Martin's grandfather. He broke with traditions and built himself a cottage on the property and moved out of the house when his son married.

Martin was close to his brother and to his grandfather. The three girls saw Martin as a menace and a pest. He was reluctantly accepted because God for some obscure reason had decided that they should live under the same roof. He spoke to them only when necessary, but, whatever the subject, their reply was usually in the form of a quote from the Bible, of which they had unparalleled knowledge. He thought that the girls were worthless sycophants, a view supported by the fact that their mutual parents praised the girls' love of Christ, Martin Luther and the local minister. Added to all this unadulterated devotion came the girls' adoration of their parents, a sentiment that was reciprocated, that was, to the extent that the parents were capable of loving anybody but themselves. It was a classic case of two people who never should have had children.

Baby was not nearly as saintly as were the three girls. He was a heartbreaker with his golden hair, his laughing green-grey eyes and the sweetest of dispositions. Everybody loved him, although, in the case of the two self-indulgent janitors posing as parents, it was more a question of perpetual astonishment at having produced such a bubbly and unique human being.

The grandfather loved his two grandsons. He had little time for the girls, less for his son and none for his daughter-in-law. As a young man, the grandfather had ignored all inherited, established and customary tradition. He did not become a farmer or a fisherman. For ten years he worked abroad. He went to America, and his family thought they'd never see him again since ninety-nine out of a hundred of those who went, never returned. But back he came and for the next thirty years he worked in the construction business up and down the coast. He married a local beauty. She died in childbirth and he never remarried. There was a large picture of her hanging in his living room. Martin had often caught his grandfather staring at the photograph as if he could not understand where she was.

The grandfather loved music. He had an impressive collection of 78s; Enrico Caruso, Beniamino Gigli, Paul Robeson, Marian Anderson,

Richard Tauber, Jussi Bjoerling—all the great ones. His library was second to none, and, thanks to his grandfather, at the age of four, Martin could read. They started with legends and myths and fables, and a lifelong love affair had begun. The grandfather never tired of encouraging and guiding and explaining; the realm of literature was one of immense wealth, he used to say, one of understanding, insight, experience and foresight, a world of riches that nobody could take away from you. All those writers during the centuries had been willing to share with you what they knew and what they thought and what they felt, a privilege that should not be taken lightly. You can never be lonesome if a book is within reach, he used to say.

From when Martin was three years of age, the two of them used to go for walks into the forests and up the mountains. In the beginning, the grandfather carried him on his shoulders, most of the way. For hours on end they silently enjoyed the tranquillity and the beauty and the enchantment of nature. Then they would sit down, their faces towards the blue sea, and they would talk. They had a favourite spot, a mountaintop where someone once had built a cairn. The lure of the panorama never failed; the Northeast mountain range, the hills and the woods towards the east, and, like a magnet, towards the west where in the horizon the mighty ocean disappeared in a turquoise mist.

He was six years of age when he was given the most precious of gifts by his grandfather, a hunting knife of exceptional beauty. It was a large and heavy knife; thirteen inches long and with a carved bone handle that had a rounded head made of steel. The blade itself was eight inches long, wide and curved and handmade from the finest carbon steel. The sheath was made of solid leather; there were two safety straps and a twenty-five inch long thong that went through the handle, tied with a knot. The knife was not new; the grandfather had bought it many years before, but he had never used it. "It's a tool," the grandfather said when he gave him the knife, "not a weapon. There is a difference, and I advise you to remember that. Only under extreme circumstances does a knife become a weapon." He taught him how to hone and polish the blade. One day they went to town and bought an ample supply of beeswax for the sheath. "Tools must be looked after," the grandfather said, "only then will they look after you. The way to see it," he emphasized, "is that this knife is an extension of yourself. Bear that in mind, son— an extension of yourself."

Martin never took the knife to school. His parents and sisters did not know about it. He kept it hidden in his room, and he concealed it under his clothes when he went out. Once in a while he used it; when he and his grandfather went for their walks and they came across an injured animal with no chance of surviving. Then he wielded his knife with swift efficiency, and he was not ashamed to lift his eyes and look at his grandfather afterwards because the grandfather always understood.

Martin waited two years before he showed the knife to Baby who was hugely impressed. Martin wasn't worried; Baby did not talk, he loved sharing a secret with his brother. They had begun to explore the forests and the valleys together; half the time Baby carried the knife, and he saw himself as part owner. "One day, when I get rich, I'll buy you one," Martin promised, and Baby's eyes lit up and he hoped that Martin would get loaded before next birthday.

When Martin was seven, his grandfather gave him a radio. It was an advanced piece, for its time, and he soon learned to find BBC and it became his favourite station. The grandfather had many books written in English. He also had dictionaries, and he advised him to learn the language. "Wherever you go, there will be somebody speaking English. It is the tongue of the world."

They read and listened together several times a week. Soon, he had taken a fancy to the language, but his vocabulary grew faster than his understanding of the grammar. "Take whatever time you need," the grandfather said. "Never forget to make notes when you read. A writer shares everything with you, also his grammar."

Martin agreed; he always carried a notebook and a pencil.

"It is tough going, though," he said.

"Remember Josef Korzeniowski who became Joseph Conrad," the grandfather said, "now, *that* was tough going."

There wasn't much he could say to that, so he didn't and began to buy bigger notebooks.

The year he got his radio, he and his grandfather went to town on one of the national holidays. As they sat down for a cup of coffee and a lemonade, Martin spotted a sign. "Can we go and have a look?" he said, "There is a pigeon show in the hall around the corner."

They did, and he was hooked. Four weeks later they had completed the most beautiful timber loft. They decorated the inside with white paint mixed with cresol, a good disinfectant that also carried a nice smell of tar, like an old boathouse.

The loft was more than a hundred meters behind the barn; it could be seen from the cottage but not from the house.

At the show, he had picked up some names and addresses, and he and his grandfather went back to town and returned with four pairs of homing pigeons. Martin never tired of seeing them fly across the valley and out towards the sea. That is freedom, he used to think. Occasionally, birds of prey were successful, but he took it stoically because he knew it was nature's way. Once, one of his best flyers managed to get away from a falcon, but the talons had ripped the chest open and he stitched his bird together and nursed him back to health.

Martin took to spending his evenings in the loft; he had an old oil heater and a couple of candles he had stolen from the church. He could sit there for hours with his books, reading and listening to the birds cooing their soft background music.

At times Baby showed up. They talked about life, dreams and the future until a voice cut through the air and Baby had to go back to the house.

In between the grandfather came to visit; he, too, enjoyed the birds and the soothing ambience of the loft. He did not think it was sensible to sit there and read for hours; the light was not all that good and straining the eyes could backfire later in life. Martin stole another four candles one dark night and placed all six on an apple crate only a foot away from his stool. The grandfather accepted the improvement and did not ask where the candles came from.

The loft became Martin's shrine. He did not understand it, at the time, but, later in life, thinking back, he knew that the loft had been the only place where he had felt at ease. It was a place where he had cherished the silence and the solitude, a place where he had become one with his books and where his latent urge for freedom was represented by his pigeons. It was a place that protected him from the callousness and the cruelty of the world outside, a place where he would reflect and learn by looking at his scars.

Martin and his grandfather confided in each other. For as far back as he could remember, he talked to his grandfather; there were no secrets, no excuses and no explaining away. He trusted the old man without reservation and was richly rewarded with comments, advice, suggestions, analyses, observations and explanations. The trust and the confidence were never broken, exploited or misused.

He felt that the bond between himself and his grandfather was indestructible, and that it was a bequest that could never be replaced.

Somehow it was irrelevant that the grandfather could not always come up with an answer, as was the case when Martin related about his recurring nightmare that began when he was four or five years old. From the bed in his tiny, rectangular bedroom he saw one night a grey mass, like a thick fog, emerging from the corner where the wall opposite met the ceiling. It was amorphous and noiseless and it grew and grew. It filled the room and got closer to the bed. With it came a smell of something putrid, like rotted flesh, and just before he knew that he was going to die from suffocation he woke up drenched in sweat and the grey fog shrunk rapidly and went back into the corner and disappeared.

The grandfather said that he was not an authority on the human psyche—he always spoke to him as he would speak to an adult, and the words that Martin did not understand would be explained—but the grandfather did offer an observation: "You have got a labyrinthine mind, son, but you are at a stage when you are not yet ready to interpret all of what life is trying to tell you. It will come, eventually, as you get older and wiser. Remember that experience is an unsurpassed teacher. You remember our talks about the free will, the freedom to use our minds, the freedom to feel and the freedom to allow our minds to control our emotions? If that freedom is taken away, that is, if we *allow* it to vanish, then we sentence ourselves to be suffocated by destructive and ultimately evil forces. That price is a crippled mind, son. Now, does all this have anything to do with your dream? Maybe it has. You cannot understand why you are not worthy of your parents' love. What is more significant is that you have begun to doubt if they are worthy of yours. They are incapable of loving you because they are two petty, vacuous and hugely selfish beings and you now sense strongly that they do not deserve to be loved. The grey fog in your nightmare could be your subliminal perception of your existence, for all I know. That is not at all implausible. The fog could also contain your conscience, your *struggle* with your perception."

"Why do they love Baby and the girls?"

"Your parents are possessive, obsessively so. Those four are your parents' pride, their show-offs and a façade that tells our local little world what family life and piety are all about. Never confuse vainglory with humility. That piece of confusion is so monumental that most people manage to walk through life without ever realizing the mental impact of this virulent muddle."

"Why am I different?"

"Why is a bear different from a wolf? Why are some bears and some wolves bigger and more ferocious than other bears and wolves? Now, you and I have read a bit, and we agree that it can't *all* be down to genes. It simply does not make sense that we consist of fifty percent of each of our parents, so to speak. It is as improbable that nothing is congenital as it is illogical that we are immune to environment and to environmental changes. Your father can't accept the fact that you are a bear and he is a fox. He resents that you are more intelligent than he is, something he senses like an animal senses fear, and he is not at ease with the reality that one day you'll be bigger and stronger. He has also become apprehensive about your temperament."

"Should I feel sorry for him or should I hate him?"

"Show me a bitter man, and I'll show you a man who cannot cope; a man that does not understand that he has become the victim of his own lack of integrity. No, you should not feel sorry for him. Neither is he worthy of your hate. Do not pay the price of letting bitterness cripple your mind—no human being is worth it. Be superior, Martin. It is high time he learns that a vicious kick is not an answer and that cheap disdain is not an argument."

"I have promised myself to put him in a wheelchair before I leave for good."

"Would that satisfy you?"

"Yes."

"Then look at it this way. Discard, through life, those who always have to blame someone else in any and all circumstances. Such people are life's real losers. They are the ones who cannot come to terms with their own shortcomings, their incompetence and their lack of moral courage."

"Discard?"

"Yes. You see, for those who fail to or can't look into themselves and acknowledge what's there, life is an enemy. It does not matter if this deficit is because of inability or because of lack of backbone. The result is the same. Stay clear of them. They have nothing to give."

☞

Then, in the spring of 1940, the Germans came.

The first *APPEAL!* Martin read was nailed to the telephone pole next to the school. The poster—black text on red paper—informed the nation of the background for the German presence; it was sheer necessity, and based on a desire to live in peace. Regrettably, this had been made impossible by the aggression of England and France who had declared war on Germany in September of the previous year. The warmonger Churchill, mankind's worst catastrophe, had to be stopped in his efforts to make the whole of Europe into a battleground. Hence, as of this morning, the strong forces of the German Reich had taken control of all military objects.

The appeal advised every citizen to show common sense and goodwill, and to refrain from passive or active resistance. Such acts would be pointless and crushed with whatever forces necessary.

He went home and his grandfather explained that the *Wehrmacht* had taken over the country. Martin added another dimension to the word *occupation* in his dictionary.

Little resistance were being offered; since the 1914-1918 World War successive governments had concluded that such folly could never happen again, so why waste money on defence. Within months total occupation was a reality; the royal family had fled the country and the few guns capable of firing a shot had been silenced.

In the beginning the Germans did not bother much about the islands. The camps were on the mainland and the odd visiting patrol seemed to be in a hurry. Warnings went out at first sight of arrival since the German soldiers thought it great fun to race the country roads and lanes, celebrating loudly when running over and killing dogs and cats.

Gestapo set up their headquarters in town. Passports were being issued; nobody could move from one island to another without permission, let alone visits to and from town. Ration cards followed. Meat and white bread disappeared from the market, as did all the best fish. For the next five years the diet consisted mainly of potatoes, herring and seagull.

Radios were declared illegal and confiscated. Private cars were seized without compensation. At night, no lights were allowed on unless every single window was covered with a black blind. The penetrating sound from sirens became a regular occurrence; sometimes it was a false alarm, but more often than not the threat was real enough—allied bombers kept hunting German submarines.

Martin understood that his radio had to go, but he objected when the issue of his pigeons came up.

The grandfather paused before he said, "We'll keep them. I am an old man going senile and you are a young and ignorant boy. Don't fly them too often."

Late autumn that year the grandfather began being absent for days and sometimes for more than a week.

He said to Martin, "Promise—please do not ask any questions. It is better you don't know."

Martin promised and lived with a feeling of unease ever since.

Gradually, rumours about Gestapo's activities began to circulate. Most adults stayed silent when children were around, but there were always those who didn't weigh their words. The school turned into a rich source of stories and the older boys had little difficulty finding an audience. The teachers advised caution but knew there was not much they could do. Martin picked up one careless remark after another but he remembered his promise and stayed clear. Since he wasn't known for being talkative nobody expected much anyway.

One rumour that persisted was about men in their twenties and thirties who one way or another had offended the Germans. Tales of torture flourished, and, as time went by, rumours became known facts. Before 1941 was over, Gestapo's grip had tightened; many had been tortured to death, some had been shot *trying to escape* and others had committed suicide by jumping from the top floor of the Gestapo building. They were said to be the lucky ones.

One day, in passing, he overheard the minister say to a teacher: "Our children are growing up faster than what is good for them. The trauma of what we all are going through is already etched on their minds and will stay there for as long as they live."

By then, the Germans had dropped all pretence of being the protective and friendly liberators. Posters with the heading *TO BE EXECUTED* flooded the country; a warning in plain words that anyone caught in subversive action would be summarily shot. A subjugated nation plagued by anger, fear and hatred were being kept in check by sudden arrests, arbitrary killings and deportation to prison camps in Germany.

The cold grip of terror gave the Nazi sympathizers the confidence to come out of the woodwork, and tension increased to a new level. Some of the sympathizers displayed brazen arrogance and enjoyed their unlimited freedom to excel in brutality. They were dangerous enough, but those with two faces were the lethal ones; some played the part so well that not even their families knew of their double life. Being on guard became second nature; one word in the wrong place could be one word too many.

Heinrich Himmler's introduction of *Lebensborn*—source of life—added loathing to the strain. Wehrmacht officers urged their troops to woo young women and get them pregnant—the more Aryans, the better. It was a task made less difficult by hunger; families closed their eyes when food was the reward for giving birth. A girl on a neighbouring island were given half a pig and three pairs of stockings. A week after the baby was born a German officer and a Nazi collaborator were shot in broad daylight outside the Gestapo building. The two gunmen escaped and rumours had it they'd managed to get over to Scotland.

Martin and his grandfather watched the Germans arrive on the island. From where they stood they could hear the shots and see the flames. At nightfall they knew that all males from sixteen and over had been executed. Smouldering ruins were all that was left of the buildings. The two gunmen had come from that island. The Germans issued a statement and hoped that a lesson had been learned.

Every Sunday, for eight years, he and his grandfather walked the mountains; they left at dawn and returned at dusk, regardless of weather. It's hard to think of a subject that was not touched. Not once did the grandfather shy away from whatever topic or theme Martin wanted to air. He became aware of what a unique man his grandfather was; his integrity, his sense of humour, his courage and his scrupulous honesty, his strength and his endurance.

There were times when he did not fully understand what his grandfather was saying. His knowledge and wisdom and insight were way above that of a young mind, and the old man could also be cryptic, when it suited him, a challenge that Martin enjoyed. He studiously wrote down everything he needed to mull over, and, when ready, he took it up to see if he'd got it right. It was an educational game they both relished. He often wondered why this simple and stimulating pedagogic approach was so alien to the local school where *learning to remember* was mandatory and *fearing the wrath of a merciful God* was imperative.

"Why do they think that using force and being spiteful is the best method?" he asked.

"Plain stupidity," the grandfather said. "I have never been able to fathom the value of quoting something, irrespective of whether or not it is understood. You see, only a child up to the age of five is a human being. From then on, thanks to our catatonic educational system and the mentally and emotionally destructive influence of a sanctimonious and spiritually indigent church, from then on a child is slowly regressing into a persona. The church have yet to admit that *moral* is a function of intelligence, time, place and circumstances, and—in line with most theological thinking—a verity that is undesirable is a non-concept and does therefore not exist. No preacher will ever concede that religion is basically a halo of words, and, I ask you, what in particular characterizes a halo?"

Martin made his notes. He knew that he'd need to digest this one, but at least the question itself was simple.

"The hole in the middle," he replied.

"Precisely. Why is it not difficult to imagine the universe as an image of man's mind?"

"The black holes."

"That's the picture, I'm afraid. Our inner life is dominated by too many holes, and that is why the animal called *Homo sapiens* will never resemble the gods he has created to camouflage unwittingly his own inadequacies."

"You are a true misanthrope, aren't you?"

"Just a realist, son, purely an observer of life's follies. But, that said, I agree that the sum of my experiences is that the vast majority of mankind are leeches. They suck their emotional nutrition from the life of their fellow man. Success and failure alike, blood can always be drawn. And remember this—the less they know about you, the hungrier they get. The more private you are, the more frantic becomes their desire to rip you open. Therefore, the moral is simple: never get down on your knees. Scavengers have no mercy; they do not understand how hollow their own lives are. Empathy is as alien to their psyche as is dignity."

"Choose your own path?"

"Subconsciously, you did that a long time ago. Stay on it. Never allow yourself to become a subhuman mass of prescriptions and edicts. You have begun well, but not for one day must you waver. The price you pay is solitude. Your reward is being able to walk upright."

"I shall not forget that."

"Do not. You see, most people, as they plod their way through life, lose sight of the fact that a circular room has no corners. There really is nowhere to hide, in this world. In the final analysis, you are always on your own."

"Except that I have got you."

"Yes, you have, but not forever. One day I will be gone. Use these years to establish your platform, as I did with my grandfather."

"What about your father? You never talk about him."

"He was like your father, pretty useless, the old sod. He, too, stumbled through the bleak existence he mistook for life, clinging to the one-dimensional and maudlin travesty that he called his Christian faith. "It's God's will," he used to say; calamity or boon, relying on the assumption that nobody would read his respect for the Almighty as a sign of weakness. I learned one thing from him, though—not that he was ever aware of it—and that was to differentiate between a smile and a smirk. Never trust a man who cannot be direct."

"Noted. There are not many?"

"If you meet half a dozen between now and your ninetieth year, consider yourself lucky. By the way, I have not heard you come up with a new word today."

"I have got one—*pariah*."

"Significance?"

"I feel like one."

"Wrong, son. What you are saying is that you *allow* people to make you feel like one. *Being* rejected because your standards are higher is an honour; *feeling* rejected is a declaration of failure. Are you with me?"

"I did not see it that way."

"No, but now you do. You have got a mind of your own, and you are defiant. That is the formula for everlasting unpopularity, the way the world is. Remember this, though, recalcitrance is the key to independence. Be sure to stay on that course. Petty people and their measly little imitations of an opinion are as useful as a double-barrelled rectum. Your enemy, and I have said this before, your enemy is your temper, that super-active volcano you are carrying inside you and which erupts with no predictability whatever. Now, *there's* a challenge; you either learn to channel those forces into constructive use or the volcano will destroy you."

"I still do not know how."

"Being aware of a problem is halfway there. The name of the cure is control, a self-discipline that enables you to re-direct all that energy from your fists to your head. You employ your brain the very split second you feel that the situation has become volatile. You literally stop, everything stops except that section of your grey cells that empowers you to evaluate objectively what is in your own, overall interest. I know that annihilating somebody can be tempting, but that does not necessarily make it worthwhile. Do I make sense?"

"You do. The problem is how to acquire such control."

"Look at it this way: man carries many a burden through life, and among the most corrosive of those burdens are *fear* and *fury*. Imagine that you ingest them; you absorb them into your system and convert them to power, into a latent capacity for action to be released when you so decide, that is, when your brain dictates your degree of involvement, if any. To sum up, education plus discipline equals control."

"I understand. I shall start tomorrow."

"Why not today?"

"Today is almost gone."

"Long before you reach my age, you will learn that today is life and that tomorrow belongs to nobody. Consider that an eminent piece of advice."

"I will, but I shall have to think about it. You know so much from experience; and where you understand, I am crawling through the jungle of my imagination, seeking a path leading to a glade."

"Try to see it this way: pretend for a moment that life lasts for seventy minutes instead of seventy years. At ten, you are vulnerable and confused, but never mind, there are still sixty minutes to go. At twenty, you are full of confidence, and you have all of fifty minutes to conquer life and enjoy it. But then, at sixty, you suddenly remember that time is running out. There are only ten minutes left, and you become painfully aware that each second is now as valuable as a minute was half an hour ago. That is what happens when you reach my age; you think of all that valuable time you have wasted."

"Wasted on what, Grandpa?"

"On people. Life's real time-waster is being in the company of people with whom you have nothing in common. It is so easy to get caught; it is part of our culture to endure the presence of the bigots, the hypocrites, the zealots and those just vacuous—we call it *being sociable*. Too many people get caught too early; they cannot escape—they get trapped before they are mature enough to comprehend what is happening to them. They get sucked into a certain milieu, their lives become regimented and sterile, and only when life is almost over do they ask themselves: *I did everything I had to do—why did I not do what I wanted to do?* That is the only *WHY* left in them, and they die with regrets in their hearts. It is a harsh advice, but if you want to stay sane and rational, you must shun the masses. Your acquaintances will be few and your friends fewer because only solitude can preserve an independent mind. You do not throw away those precious minutes by mixing with people when you know there's little or no reciprocity. How do you know at your age? You *sense* it, and the moment you sense it you begin to think—you ask yourself if you believe that this is where you belong. Let me give you a guideline. If somebody tries to impose on you his or her attitude to whatever it is, if they try to convince you that their imperatives must be your imperatives, and if they use every opportunity to imply their desire to convert you, then you walk away. Man's worst disease is intolerance of anybody being different, and it is contagious; only your rationale can direct you outside their sphere and only that way do you avoid contamination."

One day, when Martin was in his eleventh year, he said to his grandfather, "I have had enough. I can't stay in that house any more. The Neanderthal posing as my father does not look at me—thank heaven for small mercies—but the inane droppings in the form of sarcasms are beginning to poison Baby's life. He is losing his sparkle. He is trying to defend me, but it is not easy for Baby. The monkey is mumbling his insults before he turns his back to both of us with an air of self-righteousness, exasperation and holy innocence. The moral aphasia of the man is sensational."

The grandfather said, "I know. It is bad. Remember this, though, self-righteousness is the sea in which moral considerations drown without a whisper for help. You will meet many like him, people void of wisdom and unable to grasp that humaneness and emotional cannibalism are mutually exclusive. They are the lost cases, limited by a static inner life and a brain dominated by instinctive rejections."

"Perhaps he should stop wiping it every morning. He is an absolute asshole, Granddad, nothing but a malicious and slimy prick of a bible-reading caricature of a retarded baboon. What little he's got of a mind is irrevocably perverted and incarcerated in a minuscule world of stupidity and selfishness. Do you know what he does? I'll tell you; he stares at that saccharine-sweet pinkie-coloured painting of the Holy Virgin before he goes upstairs to fuck his parody of a wife and a mother."

The grandfather sat silent for a long while. "Martin," he finally said, "remember this: obscenities won't get you far. All you achieve by using foul language is to degrade yourself and to demonstrate poverty of mind."

The old man shielded his eyes with his right hand as the bright sunlight hit his face. With his left hand he picked up a stone. "A piece of rock can become a diamond, but only after it has been cut, shaped and polished. To produce a sparkling gem is a challenge and an achievement, son. Vying for intellectual limitation is neither."

The rising sun turned the haze over the meadows from white to lavender before it retreated into oblivion like a ghost acknowledging that the visiting hour was over. Martin put his hand on his grandfather's wrist. "Let's continue," he said and got up. "I need to let the mountain air blow through my head."

They left the cairn and walked around a precipice and further up from where they could see the vessels sailing to and from the town and the islands.

"How is your mother performing in all this?" the grandfather said.

"Slyer than ever, a venomous snake in a bucket of vomit."

"Let us look at the overall picture. You are different from your parents; your mind, your character and that distinct streak of independence in you. You question everything and accept nothing, a development for which I proudly take some credit. Such attitude does not go down well in our parochial backyard where bigotry rules. Your father is a weak man, and, true, his intelligence is not the most brilliant ever to grace our planet. His ability to cope with anything out of the ordinary is severely limited. He is the prime example if not the verification of the theory that genes have a tendency to jump a generation or two. Heavens know what made him. I do not. I also find it deplorable that each time he seeks justification for his behaviour, he buries his square head in the Bible, convinced that what he does not find in the New Testament he'll spot in the Old one. Have you ever heard him short of a quote? He was born nasty, Martin—something you have discovered long ago—and by being derogatory about all that you are and everything you stand for, he thinks that he is elevating himself onto a level above you. Such are the ways of a twisted little mind, and there is nothing that anybody can do about it."

"But—sorry to say this—isn't he after all your son?"

"That does not change the heart of the matter."

The old man pushed his cap back. He grabbed the hickory walking stick he had carved with both hands and gazed towards the ocean.

"Tell me, Granddad."

"Blood is only thicker than water if there is rapport, if there is mutual respect and affection and a genuine will to understand. Take away those conditions and blood does not matter. Never forget that."

They walked without talking for some while.

"What about my mother?"

"You summed her up well yourself. She is a spiteful cow."

Martin smiled. He said, "Accurate, but not too comprehensive."

The old man sighed. "They are made for each other. She is a replica of him and vice versa, an image in a mirror broken and darkened by age. Once, in America, I saw two snakes literally devouring each other from the tail up. That's your parents in a nutshell."

They came to the top of the mountain and looked towards the horizon. A band of thin clouds leaned on the ocean and turned crimson before disintegrating like fabrics of a veil unable to withstand the rays from the sinking sun. Martin thought of the life he was going to leave behind and he wondered if it had already come to an end. He rested his sight on an eagle sailing the winds high above, and the feeling of freedom that pumped through his veins made him gasp for air. He knew that his grandfather was watching, and they looked at each other. He saw no sadness, but he thought he could detect a flicker of stoic resignation.

They walked back to the cairn, took off their boots and socks and rested their back against the stones. Halfway down the path to the valley a giant pine tree had once been hit by lightning. The blackened branches sprawled like runes carved on a lime green slab, and Martin thought of bygone days when the tree had been strong and healthy and had looked indestructible.

Then he thought of the first summers of his childhood that he could remember, when the nights were short and the scent of the roses lingered till dawn. Later, the summers lost their sparkle and became grey and misty as purity and unawareness dwindled in the shadow of prejudice.

He had not asked before, "Why did you come back?"

The old man pulled a bar of chocolate from between the stones of the cairn and shook his head. "Is it not amazing what you can find up here, in the middle of nowhere?"

"Every time," Martin said and took his half. "Why did you come back?"

The grandfather chewed for a while. "I had this image in my mind," he said. "It was the image of a very young, beautiful and tender girl I'd met shortly before I left. For ten years I could not get that image out of my mind. I had other women, but, somehow, nobody could replace her. I began to wonder if she was just a fantasy—not that she wasn't real enough—but had I produced something in my head that never could live up to expectations? Then I realized that I would not have peace and harmony with somebody else unless I found out—so I came back. I was not wrong. It was all there."

"You still miss her."

"Every day."

An hour went. The sea prepared to swallow the sun.

Martin said, "Where do I go from here?"

The grandfather lit his meerschaum. The clouds coming in from the north had lost their creamy colour and the mountaintops became violet as the shadows grew longer. "Leave this dump and get yourself an education. There is no future here. Not for you."

"I do not know what I want to be. All kinds of thoughts are going through my head."

"Don't worry. You have got years to decide. You'll find your métier, in due time. Get yourself a diploma, some papers, and remember what we read together: *The essence of education is to learn to find what you do not know*. That is true, a piece of wisdom you can take with you everywhere and use anywhere."

"That, and a bit of luck."

The old man puffed his pipe. "Luck doesn't come into it. Do not ever rely on luck coming stumbling down the road, eager to acquaint itself with you for the price of nothing. It does not happen that way. So-called lucky people are people who know how, why and when to do what the moment they see something that may benefit them. Sometimes you act on pure instinct. At other times it is a calculated process. So-called lucky people know the difference between an opportunity and a daydream, just as they know that nothing of substance creates itself. You are not the Almighty, and neither is anybody else."

"The Almighty is an illusion, designed by and for shallow little people who cannot identify with the realities of life."

The grandfather grunted. "A nice display of arrogance, I'd say. There are times when I believe you were born an incurable pagan."

"Rather that than being an agnostic—like someone I know."

"Yes, but I wasn't in my teens when I came to my conclusion."

"Some are slow developers."

The old man laughed. He said, "Remember this—a sense of humour is a priceless gift, like a divine singing voice, but it's got to be maintained. I predict that yours will darken, in years to come. Do not forget to nurture it, but be aware of the symbiosis between the dark and the cold. They feed on each other, in your heart, and your brain could find that entertaining. Do not lose sight of who controls what."

"I shall not forget."

"Good. It will help you survive your blackest moments. Life contains it all, from the sublime to the grotesque. Bear in mind that you, and you only, are responsible for savouring each and all moments, irrespective of how they appear and what they involve and comprise."

The sun became a vast orange fireball that spit its flames through the waves and soon it was gone. The old man watched the purple sky and said, "Visit me once in a while."

Martin nearly commented that he had not left yet. Instead, he said, "I will."

Three weeks later Baby wanted to go fishing for something big; he'd got into his head that they should target a halibut or an angler or even a dogfish.

It was a fine day with only the first touch of autumn in the air. Fish were jumping off the headland, the few remaining swallows flew high and there was no raw edge to the light and pleasantly salty breeze. The sun played on the long and idle waves as though a giant had scanned the skies with a pot of liquid silver and strewn it on to the surface of the water.

Martin took the oars. He eyed a mark on the rugged coastline as the boat got closer to the bank where the big fish were lurking down under. To their surprise and delight, the first catch was a salmon, not the commonest of fish in those waters, but the second was a lumpfish that blew up when they got him on board. He wasn't good for anything, so they threw him back out again.

Then Baby yelled and clung to his line with both hands, screaming that whatever was at the other end was bigger than he was. They got so engrossed that they did not notice the heavy clouds coming in from the north and the wind that began to stroke the waters. They did not observe that the rocking of the boat was due to more than their frenzied battle with the big fish. Only when the line broke and he got away did they look up. The skies were black and the shallow waters were no longer idle and smooth. Martin grabbed the oars and rowed like possessed towards the nearest skerry. He knew that the shore was too far away. Within what felt like a few minutes the sea was rising and became an inferno of cascading froth. The clouds got blacker and more massive and the wind came howling towards them with such force that the boat careened time and again and began to take in water. The brightness of the day had turned into a ghostly twilight and the leaden sky came closer and began to lean on Martin's shoulders. The skerry was no more than a quarter of a nautical mile away; a rugged conformation of black gleaming rocks only occasionally visible.

Martin zigzagged and tried to avoid the worst impact of the huge whitecaps breaking across, threatening to swamp the boat beyond rescue. Baby clung to his seat with one hand and bailed frantically with the other. All the time he smiled and shouted *we'll make it.*

Slowly, the skerry rose from the sea. Martin cast one glance at the heavy waters where the seething surface changed from white to blue-green and again to white. He knew that he had to navigate in such a way that they were literally being washed ashore. One wrong move, and the boat would capsize and they would be sucked out and away and under for good.

He saw the big whitecap coming and shouted his instructions to Baby before letting go of the oars. As he crouched he saw Baby stand up. Martin yelled at him to lay down flat. The wave hit the boat and it flew through the air and crashed onto the rocks. Martin hit his head against the wood as he landed, but he was not unconscious and he got up.

He searched the rocks and the seaweed and scoured through driftwood and wreckage till his voice was gone and he collapsed.

The wind abated during the early hours of the evening. They managed to get a craft up to the skerry and he was brought ashore, half dead from hypothermia.

The doctor came and registered a fractured left arm and several broken ribs. He cleaned the scratches with antiseptic soap and put plasters on. The gashes on the legs and the shoulders were dabbed with iodine and stitched together.

The day after, double pneumonia set in. It was touch and go for a while. He could not attend Baby's funeral. On the day, Martin listened to the monotonous tolling of the church bells. He kept staring at the corner of his room where the grey fog was hidden.

His mother came in the few times the doctor paid a visit. The father and the sisters stayed clear. During that period, Martin finally understood what he meant to them. He also discovered what they meant to him.

The grandfather came early each morning, twice during the day and once at night-time. He fed him, washed him, monitored his progress and nursed him back to health. Little was being said. Martin had no wish to talk, and the grandfather understood. The doctor advised Martin to stay in bed for at least a month. The grandfather disagreed. Fight it, he said, get up as soon as you possibly can. Start moving. Get your strength back.

On the eighth day Martin managed to walk from the house and over to the cottage. The grandfather was sitting in the kitchen with a glass in front of him and a handrolled cigarette between his fingers. Martin sat down and shook off the dizziness. He reached for the glass and had his first taste of alcohol. He coughed violently, wiped the sweat from his forehead and said, "You are the only one who does not blame me."

"No," the grandfather said, "I am the second. You are the first."

Martin looked away. He said, "I have been thinking. A thousand times I have been thinking: what could I have done differently?"

"Nothing. You did not have an alternative. The skerry was your only option. There was no other chance of survival."

"Survival."

"Do not think that you are responsible for Baby's death. The sea took your brother. No man is stronger than the elements. You know that."

Martin said, "I can't stay here much longer. I'll leave as soon as the war is over."

"Where are you going?"

"I don't know. Somewhere. The world is a big place." He took another sip from the glass. "What is this stuff?"

"It's called Irish whisky. I was introduced to it in Dublin in—oh, well, too long ago."

"Dublin—that is in Ireland."

"Yes. An alluring city and a beautiful country. On my way to America, I stopped there. Just for the night." The grandfather tapped his nose and smiled. "I left six months later. Go and see it, one day, if you can. You will never find a more charming people. They are very Catholic, though; half the female population is called Mary, but, thankfully, not every Mary is a passionate virgin."

"I don't know too much about women."

"Wrong, son. You don't know *anything* about women. Don't worry, you'll learn. Have your fun for as long as it lasts. They shall all become yesterday's girls and you want your memories to be sweet and crowned with tender affection."

"All?"

"The time will come when you shall find one particular woman irresistible. By that I mean she'll grab your entire being and you do not want to think of life without her."

"What do I do then?"

"Get her, no matter how, but remember this: what you give must not be a reflection of what you *believe* you receive. She'll always give you more."

"How would I know if she wants me?"

The grandfather smiled. "The woman isn't born who'll drop the man she wants. She will let you know, one way or another."

The grandfather looked out the window. There was a rare expression of intensity on his face. He said, "It was in Dublin, in a pub one evening, that an old Irishman gave me a piece of advice I have carried with me forever since. Over so many drinks he told me the history of his country. He was a fabulous raconteur and he kept me fascinated for hours. Then, as we parted, he said, "Son, rely on your fellow man, but do not trust him." A contradiction, I thought, but life taught me the wisdom of his words."

"What kept you there for half a year?"

"I fell in love, twice, as it was, overnight with the country and a week later with a woman. She was a few years older and much wiser. After six months she told me that I should go to America on my own. That was it, really. What a beauty she was, and so kind. My first lesson was a good one." There was a tic under his eyes and he stared into his glass. "I wonder what happened to her."

"Why don't you come with me?"

"I am too old, now. Ten years ago, perhaps…"

"You are not that old."

The grandfather looked pensive. He got up, went over to the corner cupboard, took out the bottle and added a few drops. He put the bottle back, closed the door and slipped the key into the pocket of his vest.

"Let us think about it," he said as he sat down.

Martin nodded towards the glass, but he did not touch it. "What are we celebrating?"

"The fact that you are back on your feet."

"You were sitting here waiting for me? You knew?"

"I knew."

Nothing was said for a while. The grandfather shifted on his chair.

"What is it, Grandpa?"

"Your pigeons are gone."

"Gone? What do you mean, gone."

"Your father killed them."

Martin stared at his hands. The fury that raged through him was colder than a mid-winter's blizzard, but he did not move. He could not understand why he did not get up and why he did not explode. It

497

was as if his brain had been taken out, frozen solid and put back in again. He did not see his father's face; only a figure, the image of a rabid and demented person ravaging through the loft and the heads of the pigeons being smashed against the walls.

Martin thought of his knife; he saw the blade leave the sheath and he licked the steel on both sides and his grip tightened.

"Don't, Martin," the grandfather said and gently put his hand on his arm. "Bear this in mind: we are as entitled to remember and condemn as we are to forgive and forget."

"He does not deserve to live."

"Maybe not, but is a brief moment of pleasure worth rotting away in a prison for the rest of your life? I would not think so."

The icy white fog began to lift. He looked at his grandfather's face. The weathered skin was smooth with distinct lines but few wrinkles. Under his eyes the blue veins had become more visible, of late.

"You'll get your revenge, Martin."

"How?"

"I promise. You wait and see." He pushed the glass towards him. "One tiny drop."

Martin held up the glass as if to measure and emptied half.

"I have cleaned out the loft," the grandfather said. "Bury the memory of what you had."

"Bury."

"I did not say *forget*."

Martin bit on the callous skin of the palm of his right hand.

"By the way," the grandfather said slowly, as if his own thoughts took him by surprise, "on your last day here, whenever that may be and whatever the circumstances, go up to our cairn and remove the stone where we used to find a bar of chocolate. There will be a message for you."

Martin frowned. "Could you explain?"

"Just do it."

Three months later, Martin had regained his strength. He still attended school, but he had become even more reticent and uncommunicative. The teachers found him indifferent to most subjects and regularly sent notes to his home where his father threw them into the fire. The few boys who had been cordial in the past were no longer amiable and little whispers and snide remarks had become a daily diet. The grandfather urged him to keep his aggression under control.

It all went well until one Saturday when a school mate, mistaking Martin's reserve for passivity, became overconfident and said loudly in passing, "How is our great seafarer today?"

There was no explosion, just a display of cold, calculated and methodical demolition. Martin went back to the cottage, washed his bloodstained hands in the kitchen sink and sat down without a word.

The grandfather said, "It was bound to happen."

"My brain told me to destroy him. All I want is to be left alone."

"Fight when you believe that you have to fight," the grandfather said. "Fight for survival and fight for independence. Never fight for kudos."

"Those are nice words, but why do I sense reservation in your voice?"

"Because there is a ruthless streak in you. There is malevolence behind your temper and you must learn to control it. I have told you this before. Never allow yourself to become destructive for the sake of it. Do not become your own worst enemy. Face the fact that proclivity for violence can ultimately leave your life in ruins."

Martin stared out the window towards his empty pigeon loft.

The grandfather said, "You remember my favourite Verdi opera?"

"*The Force of Destiny*."

"That is an ingenious title, son."

"Have you not always said that we make our own destiny?"

"Make it a force, *your* force. It comes from within. Your rudder is your integrity. In ten years' time you will understand the meaning and the importance of integrity. By then you will also know how little it takes to damage probity beyond repair. Intellectual honesty and moral integrity go hand in hand. Ignore one, and there will be little left of your self-esteem." He raised his hand and stroked Martin's head.

That evening Martin could not sleep; his mind was no longer in turmoil. He could not explain this sudden state of tranquillity, but it was there and he knew that his instincts were not influenced solely by the event of the day. He recapitulated summarily his twelve years on earth and listened to the inner voice telling him to seek his own ways. The voice became stronger and more vibrant by the hour. He would move in with his grandfather, something he should have done long ago. He knew that the grandfather had been waiting for him to make this decision for himself. Come end of war he would leave. Until then, he had time to decide where to go and what to do.

He heard someone talking downstairs and thought that he recognized his grandfather's voice. He got out of bed. He opened the door and listened to the words that came towards him like arrows hissing through the night.

"He's crazy," the father said. "He almost killed another one today."

The grandfather said, "Another one?"

"You know what I am talking about."

"No. I do not know what you are talking about."

"He slew his brother," the mother said. "Do you want to know what the holy Bible says? *"For the wrongdoer will get what is coming to him for his wrongdoing; there will be no partiality."* You are the only one who thinks that he is not responsible. There will be no place in heaven for you."

"Do you not understand that you are condemning your own child?"

"He will rot in hell," the father said. "God does not forgive killers. *"And if your hand should cause you to sin, cut it off; it is better for you to enter life crippled, than to have two hands and go to Hell, into the fire that cannot be put out."* That is why God broke his arm."

The mother said, *""No one who has been born of God commits sin, for the nature of God remains within him; because he has been born of God, he cannot practice sinning. By this the children of God and the children of the devil are differentiated: anyone who does not practice righteousness, or who does not love his brother, is not from God.""*

The grandfather said, "Has it ever occurred to the two of you to try to think for yourselves?"

The silence lasted for a long while. Then Martin again heard his grandfather's voice; tired, almost dejected, "One day, soon, he will leave. Is this the way you want to end your relationship with your own son?"

""He who is from God listens to the words of God," the father said. *"Because you are not from God, you do not listen.""*

Martin heard a chair scrape against the wooden floor. An eerie quietness filled the house. Outside the wind had abated and the sighs from the waves against the shore had died down.

The grandfather said, "When you both are laid to rest in the dirt where you belong, even the worms will flee in disgust."

A door closed. Martin went back to his bed. He lay on his back and stared towards the corner where the grey fog stayed away all night.

On the morning of the third day of May 1943 the grandfather said to Martin, "I shall be away for a while."

"But you are coming back?"

The grandfather laughed. "Of course I am coming back. Stay out of trouble and walk the mountains when you get restless."

Fourteen days later, leaning against the cairn viewing the valley, Martin saw six dirt-green vehicles with black swastikas approaching his home. The cars lined up behind the house. The soldiers got out, dispersed quickly and took position behind bushes, trees and outbuildings.

He stood up. Half a kilometre from the property he spotted his grandfather coming across the neighbour's fields.

Martin began running. When he reached the foot of the mountain he saw the cars drive away.

He walked towards the house. His father stood in the doorway. When he saw Martin he turned and went back in.

Only the minister was allowed to visit the prison. He had been warned not to talk about what he saw and heard and he was not to go near Gestapo's headquarter. He spoke passable German and spent some time trying to assess the wardens. One of them was reticent but appeared sympathetic without being cordial. The minister thought that the expression on the warden's face spoke its own language when prisoners were being dragged back from interrogation.

An understanding developed. The warden turned away when exchange of pencils and bits of paper took place between the minister and the prisoners.

The minister always came to the kitchen of the house. The letters were always read out aloud. Martin stood in the porch and listened. He knew about the Inquisition and other epochs of evil through history. The Gestapo had little to learn. There were times when he could not understand that his grandfather was still alive.

At times he wondered if his parents were aware he was eavesdropping. He didn't know, and he didn't care.

One day he gave a letter to the minister who took it without a word. Three weeks later he got his grandfather's reply. The tone was optimistic. The war couldn't last much longer and they would be together again.

The minister shook his head when Martin came with his second letter. The grandfather had been sent to Germany. The minister stared past him for a fleeting moment and walked away.

The euphoria sweeping the country in May 1945 was like a warm wind carrying the intoxicating scent of eternal summer.

Then, to the sound of shackles falling to the ground, five years of repressed hatred erupted. The German soldiers kept to their barracks. Nazi sympathizers tried to hide but had nowhere to go; known torturers were not instantly turned over to the authorities. Thirst for revenge became epidemic. Right and wrong were seen in black and white with no shades of grey between. Young and old applauded when court verdicts led to executions. Books made bonfires. Women who'd had affairs with Germans were rounded up and their heads shaved. Medical experts agreed that anyone representing *The Third Reich* had to be mentally retarded and wrote off the children as subnormal and qualified only for a life in an asylum.

Those who had hidden their radios opened their doors. News from Europe came in bits and pieces. Then pictures began to arrive and Martin learned about concentration camps and what they stood for.

He wasn't aware of it, at the time, but the seed of nihilism had fallen on fertile ground.

Every morning he went up on the hill facing the bay and the road to the ferry berth waiting for his grandfather. One day he asked the minister what he knew. The minister said that the allied forces and The Red Cross did their best but there were many concentration camps and it would take time to organize the release and get everybody home.

Martin waited.

The man who came one Sunday in September was grey and bent and walked as if in pain. Martin's parents went outside. The three of them talked for a short while. Then they came through the front door and into the drawing room. Martin sat crouched behind the large sofa and could not be seen.

The man began to talk. He and the grandfather had been arrested on the same day. They had spent six months in prison before they were shipped to Germany. The grandfather was the oldest of those caught during the raid. He had been the leader of the resistance. Gestapo did their best but none had talked. Three had died. The man thought it a miracle that the grandfather had survived.

They'd all seen it as a relief when being told that they would spend the rest of the war in a German prisoners' camp. On the day of arrival they understood that the German idea of a *prison camp* was different from anybody else's.

The man spoke in a monotone voice. Occasionally, he tried to inject a light-hearted comment. In between, his voice broke.

He put all his efforts into giving a clinical picture of life in a concentration camp. At times he stopped, as if searching for words. Once in a while he paused and cleared his throat before continuing. He tried to laugh when he said he didn't know what was the worst—the inhuman working condition, the humiliation or the hunger.

Martin was aware of the cramp in his legs but he did not feel the pain. What is the man waiting for? he thought. Where is my grandfather?

The man said he was forty-two kilos when The Red Cross arrived, his weight matching his age. Then there was silence before he spoke again.

Finally, he said, "Your father died in February, two months before the Germans fled. I am so sorry."

Martin did not hear any more. After a while he dried his tears and stood up. The man stared in stunned silence.

Then he said, "Martin? Oh, he talked so much about you."

Martin walked past. His legs were wobbly but he did not stumble.

He walked across the yard and into the fields and through the woods and did not stop until he reached the foot of the mountain. He sat down on the trunk of a fallen tree and faced the icy wind that came down through the ravine. An early snowflake melted on his skin, and he inhaled the sweet scent from the fir trees. He caressed the embroidery of the tree worms and tried not to think of what the morning had brought. He continued his walk.

For some while, the fir needles were like a smooth green carpet underfoot. Then the brown earth and the grey surface of the rocks took over. He stopped at the large anthill where they always used to stop and watched the white shimmering softness of the silver birch as the first rays from the sun came through. He reached the cairn and stood in lee from the wind. He faced westward and looked at the scattered clouds coming in from the ocean like whiteclad angels dancing to the music of freedom promised.

He undid the buttons of his anorak and turned towards the valley. He saw the silver haze on the meadows below where the remains of his childhood had been buried in the greyness of dawn.

He continued walking and came back to the cairn five hours later. Only then did he allow the memories to flood his mind and he sat there till emptiness took over and the moonbeams cut through the clouds and left them frayed at the edges.

His grandfather had stood for everything that was good and dignified. His reward had been a mass grave somewhere in Germany. Yet, inside his tortured, famished and frozen body there was a spirit that could not be broken.

But men like his grandfather were exceptions in a world rotten to the core, a world that made a mockery of honesty and conscience, a world that laughed at and trampled on the purity of the virtues of the soul.

He shivered. Something in him had died. Time had come to start on a journey that he knew would always begin where the horizon ended.

Then he remembered. He removed the stone and put his hand into the cavity. He took out a parcel held together by a thin rope that smelled of tar. He untied the rope, undid the oilcloth and folded out the waxed paper. The wind played with the wad of money and he put the stone on top and pulled out the white envelope underneath. It was not sealed. He took out the paper and turned it and read in the light from the moon: *Let our stone be the altar in the shrine you one day will find.*

He put the parcel in one of his pockets and carried the stone in his hand and began his descent.

The lights were on in the kitchen of the house. He stopped when he heard voices.

"Dammit," his father said. "I'll find it even if I have to demolish the whole bloody cottage. I am sure the old scoundrel hid it just to make life difficult for me."

The mother said, "Yes, that would be typical of him. How many thousands do you think he left behind?"

"So far, God only knows. Tomorrow I shall find what is rightfully mine."

"God bless you," the mother said. " '*The Lord giveth…*' "

"We shall certainly see to that," the father interrupted.

" '*Narrow is the gate and contracted is the road that leads on to life, and few are those who discover it.*' "

"Amen."

Martin lost interest. He opened the back door, took off his boots and climbed the stairs without making a noise. He did not undress. At four o'clock in the morning he packed his few belongings and walked to the small ferry port. The first ferry left at half past five. The parcel with the money was stuck inside his belt, pressing against his stomach. He carried the stone and his hunting knife in his rucksack.

In town he walked along the waterfront until he found a café that was open. Seamen frequented it. Within an hour he had a fair idea of when and to where the few seagoing vessels were due to sail. He paid for the meal with inconspicuous notes from his meagre savings and began looking for the ship that would bring him to the first leg of his road to obscurity. She was due to leave early the next morning. He did not like the idea of having to wait for almost twenty-four hours, but there was no alternative.

The sensation of freedom and wanderlust was mixed with a feeling of being trapped; sooner or later his father would conclude that the money was gone, and, eventually, he would manage to add two and two together.

The search would commence and the town was an obvious target. Nice to be missed, Martin thought and wondered how best to keep a low profile whilst waiting.

Then he relaxed. It would take his father at least forty-eight hours to complete his rummage for the hidden treasure. During that time the whereabouts of his one and only son would be of no importance. There was, however, the risk of running into somebody who recognized him.

He found the ship tied up next to a couple of busy warehouses. He spent a good hour observing the location and took a bus to one of the suburbs where he bought a few bottles of soft drink, cheese, sausages and a loaf of bread, which he put into his rucksack. He returned to the town centre shortly after nine o'clock in the evening. He knew it would be deserted; the few cinemas operated from seven to nine and from nine to eleven. Half an hour after the last performance there would be nobody around save a handful of drunks and prostitutes. He found a café belonging to a religious sect who saw it as a moral duty to stretch the hours in case some lost soul had missed the boat either home or to salvation. They had rooms upstairs at reasonable rates. The manager was locally famous for his talents as a preacher and for his knowledge of those sections of the bible that suited the sect. The place was popular, the coffee was strong and the food gave value for money. The evangelical manager spread his gospel on the hour and was a comfort for the believer and a source of entertainment for the pagan.

Martin rented a room and paid in advance. At two o'clock in the morning he left the premises unnoticed and walked to the ship. The night was dark and windy, and it was easy to avoid the lights from the few and far between lamp posts.

He reached the warehouse from the street side and gazed around the corner. The ship was sparsely illuminated. Nobody appeared to be on duty, and the squeaky noise from the gangway was loud and reassuring. He looked around. The streets were empty. Apart from the gangway and the dull humming from a dormant town, the only other sound that could be heard was the low droning from the auxiliary diesel engine. He eyed the two lifeboats astern and walked up the gangway.

Earlier in the day he had noticed that although the ship was old, she was well maintained. He had seen that the ropes securing the canvas over the lifeboats were not as tight as they once must have been. He got away with only one cut, using his hunting knife. Well under the canvas he tied a knot and hoped that the rope would stay in place.

Martin had never owned a watch. He had no idea how long it would take him to get to Amsterdam. It had not looked all that far, recollecting the maps he had studied together with his grandfather, but he suspected that no atlas or globe would give much of an indication of the enormity of the seas and of the continents.

He peeped out when the big diesel engine could no longer be heard and there were animated voices around. The size of the Amsterdam docks amazed him. They seemed to go on for miles. Some of the ships were larger than he had thought possible. He stared at the vast number of majestic cranes and watched the incredible activity and listened to the cacophony of noises. He wondered how he could get ashore without being seen.

Within a few hours, twilight set in. It was clear that the ship was not going to return that day. The hatch-covers were still on, but he knew that at some time during the night he had to make his exit.

The hustle and bustle finally died down. He heard the crew entertaining each other with tales of expected orgies and unlimited supplies of drinks before they disappeared down the gangway. He had no idea how many were left on board; few, he reckoned, and there was no sign of them.

In the still of the night Martin abandoned his temporary home and put his feet on deck for the first time in what seemed like an eternity. His body was stiff and sore. His supply of food and liquid had been inadequate. He longed for a bath and for new clothes. He wanted to leave behind a shelter that had also served as a toilet. He wondered how long it would take to forget the smell.

Faint music came from the captain's quarters, but otherwise the ship was quiet.

He moved towards the gangway. The clicking of heels ashore was interrupting the comparative stillness. He focused and saw a guard coming out from the shadows of the cranes. It had not occurred to him that the ports would be patrolled. It was an unwelcome discovery, and he spent some time figuring out the pattern of the guards' activities. The moment came; he walked down the gangway and ran across between the cranes on his rubbersoled boots and soon he was swallowed up by the shadows from the warehouses.

There he waited till the first light of dawn. He split the money into three lots.

The next few days became an education short on amusement and rich in experience. With the exception of a small amount in Dutch guilders, he exchanged his entire capital into American dollars. He used five different banks. He bought himself a new set of clothes and found a cheap bed-and-breakfast hotel. He made a note of which ships were due for America. With his robust physique and a trace of blond stubbles he looked older than his years. On the third day he entered one of the many bars in the harbour district. The place was half-empty. Martin ordered a whisky, said *preferably Irish*, and was served without any questions being asked. He found a table and sat down. He raised his glass, sipped and whispered silently: *To you, Granddad. Thank you for all that you did for me. We shall always travel together.*

He did not notice that somebody had joined the table until the man said, "Young man, honour yourself by offering me a drink."

Martin thought, why the hell should I; then he changed his mind and said, "You English?"

"British, my boy," the man said, "British. My name is Ted, and your name is…?"

"Martin."

"A fine name, Martin. A double straight Scotch would do me a world of good, thank you very much."

Martin went over to the bar and got the drink.

"The elixir of life," Ted said. "This is very much appreciated. I really am grateful."

The man was in his fifties; of medium height and solidly built. His hair was curly and grey. Blue veins decorated his face and told their own story. His hands were strong but not steady. He cupped his glass when he drank.

"You a seaman, Ted?"

"I am indeed. First mate, as a matter of fact. There is no place I have not seen."

"Where are you going next?"

Ted's bloodshot eyes scanned the ceiling. "Right now I am having a sabbatical. I sailed during the entire war and got torpedoed a few times." His gaze drifted towards the wharf and the ships visible through the nicotine-stained windows. "Where are you heading?"

"America."

"That is a good choice. You have made a wise decision. America is the land of opportunities. It is also God's own country, according to the natives. We never should have let that colony go." Ted closed his eyes. "How are you going to get there?"

"By ship."

Ted smiled. His eyes were still closed. "Is that so? You're not a sailor, are you? If I was inclined to guess, which I am not, I would have said that you are a runaway." He opened his eyes. " Believe me, I have seen many a fine young man in your predicament, over the years. They came and they went and God knows what happened to them." He lit a small, tapered cigar. "Being a stowaway is a risky business."

"Ever been one?"

"I have been everything, or, in more Shakespearean terms, there is nothing that I have not been, broadly speaking, that is. You are looking at close to half a million hours of highly diversified experiences."

"That's a lot of hours."

"Fifty-six years."

"How do I get to America, Ted?"

"Have you got any money?"

"Very little. I have no passport."

Ted rubbed the back of his hands against his lips. "Had not my tongue been paralyzed with thirst, I probably could have told you. But, as it is…" He stared melancholy at his empty glass.

Martin went over for the second drink. Whilst he waited, he thought of his new identity. During the long hours in the lifeboat he had concluded that he had to find a name that was easy to pronounce and with a universal touch to it. Fighting boredom, he had listened to music in his head. The image of his grandfather sitting outside the cottage and Richard Tauber singing *Roses of Picardy* and *Sleepy Lagoon* had stuck. Tauber was fine. The first name came with equal ease; he took it from Jack London's *Martin Eden*. And—more important—the new Martin Tauber concluded that for the rest of his life he would keep to himself and he swore that *never again* would he get close to anybody. Never again was he going to experience the trauma that loss created.

"Awfully grateful," Ted said with a sardonic smile and drank greedily. "You really are a fine young man. The Germans occupied your country?"

Martin was taken aback and did not answer.

"I thought so," Ted continued. "The scars on your soul show on your face. I am sorry about your lost youth, but then, we all have our cross to carry. I know it's hard, but try not to let the world become your enemy. Your existence becomes harsh and lonely if you allow that to happen. I know."

Martin looked away. "How do I get on board?" he asked.

"Nothing is simpler, assuming that you have the necessary degree of audacity and the ability to look relaxed. Here," he pulled out a pencil, "give me your hand."

"Why?"

"Because I am going to write the name of one of the major ship-chandlers here."

Martin stared at the name, written in capital letters. "And then what?"

"When is she due to sail?"

"Four o'clock."

"Go and buy a crate of whisky. At around a quarter past three, when everybody is extremely busy, walk up the gangway with your crate and tell whoever wants to know that you are delivering something for the captain, compliments of the ship-chandler. Nobody will dream of stopping you. Drop the bloody crate at a convenient place and make yourself invisible till the ship is well and truly at sea."

"And then?"

"Then you surface. There is no way they are going to turn around for your sake. The rest of the scenario is even simpler; they'll take your money, put you to work and hand you over to the authorities upon arrival."

"I would like to avoid that."

"You most certainly would, but to escape without being noticed requires luck in the extreme, so don't count on it. I'd say that your best bet is to pretend that you are happy the ordeal is over, and then, with perfect timing, you make a run for it. You look fit enough. You should be able to outsprint them and get lost within a few minutes. The fat, lazy Yanks won't chase you for long." Ted fiddled with his empty glass. "Does not this invaluable piece of advice justify another drink?"

"It does."

They sat there, for a while, in silence, both lost in their own thoughts. Then Ted extended his hand and said, "There's one thing in your favour, Martin—the whole world is in chaos. Now, get going. I wish you all the best."

With his rucksack hidden under his new and roomy weatherproof jacket, he followed Ted's plan step by step. It worked to perfection. The other blessing, although in disguise at the time, was that, due to a misunderstanding with the port authorities, the country of destination was Mexico and not the United States.

☞

Vargas' narrative had stopped as abruptly as it had begun. Once in a while the flickering light from the candles had swept across his face. Jennifer had been listening to a man showing no emotions; only his lips had moved and a disembodied voice had reached her ears. She had been listening intently, her mind and her senses sharp and alert, but only when he'd said that *never again would he get close to anybody* had his voice betrayed deeper feelings. It was as if he truly had related the story of a third person with whom he was not even vaguely associated.

It is disturbing, she thought, how could anyone gain and exercise a degree of self-control that by all standards was virtually inhuman? She knew that he possessed a discipline that few would consider attainable, but the display she had witnessed filled her with a mixture of awe and desperation. How could *anybody* with such a grip on himself ever let go and allow emotions and sensitivity to enter his life and make him a partner in a relationship where empathy, rapport and reciprocity were conditions for survival?

Angelo Vargas leaned forward. He rested his elbows on his knees and looked up. Instinctively, she covered her mouth with her hand. She tried to suppress a gasp, unable to steer her eyes away from his face. The mask had gone; he looked gaunt and drawn with narrowed eyes and there were lines on his face she had not seen before. His movements were slow and jaded when he got up. There was no spring in his steps as he walked across to the cabinet. He came back with a full glass and placed it on the side table before he sat down. He fumbled with a cigarette but did not light it. She saw his body heave with an almost inaudible sigh. Then she heard his voice, a hoarse and raspy whisper, "I keep seeing Baby and those waves and my grandfather coming across the fields the day he was captured."

She wanted to move, to leap from her corner and embrace him. She wanted to press his face against her body and caress and console him and share his hurt.

She did not move. She knew that the key to the next door was within reach, and she feared that he never again so openly would allow her to accompany him down the narrow path through his past.

He still had not touched his drink. The cigarette was hidden in his fist. When she saw him lean back and stare at the ceiling she wet her lips and asked, "What happened in Mexico, Angelo?"

He kept staring. Seconds ticked away and became minutes. London was fast asleep. Only now and then a faint noise from the slumbering giant left the streets and reached the windows, tenderly fondling the dark and protective glass before falling away.

511

Would she break the spell if she got up and made a cup of tea? She dared not move. He had yet to touch his glass. His breathing was rhythmic, but then, it always was. She stretched her neck and tried to see if he had fallen asleep. She could see the contours of his head and his body. She wished that she had placed the candles with more foresight.

"Move around," he said. "Get your circulation going."

She went into the bathroom and freshened up. She wondered if she had pushed it too far. There were times when she thought Vargas' guarding of his privacy to be almost pathological, but she also knew that it would eventually prove fatal if she meekly accepted his hang-ups as sacrosanct. The barriers had to be broken down. Take it or leave it, she thought; I am not going to be your nodding shadow and neither do I believe that that's what you want. All you've got to do is *continue talking*, for God's sake. If you think of what I already know about you, what the hell is there to lose? It can't get much worse—or can it?

She walked from the bathroom to the kitchen, made a cup of coffee and went back to the sofa.

Vargas had lit his first cigarette for hours. The contents of his glass had gone down a fraction.

"Mexico," he said.

23

Martin enjoyed Veracruz, a contrast to his background more dramatic than he had ever envisaged. All he had seen of Amsterdam was in the vicinity of the ports. Here, he actually saw, for the first time, what was to him a major city.

Nobody paid any attention to him. He nodded his confirmation to those who assumed he was European, and he nodded to those who thought he was American. He found a cheap hotel and spent the days wandering about; watching, listening and becoming infatuated with the attraction of a different culture.

He was on guard and ready to vanish should he spot a face from the ship, although he assumed there had to be a number of local suspects when it came to the cook's missing fingers. But it wasn't a bad idea to be cautious, in general; he found the large number of policemen and police cars astonishing. The level of street violence was another experience. His awareness was further sharpened by the fact that he did not have a passport, and that one day his money would run out.

On the morning of his fifth day ashore, sitting at a table outside a café in Placa Constitucion, he heard a voice: "How yah all doin'?"

Martin looked in the direction of the voice and saw a man in his late twenties. He was dressed in a light blue jacket, dandelion yellow open-necked shirt, maroon trousers and snakeskin boots. "Okee-dokee," he said and came closer. Martin turned around to see whom the man was talking to. A couple of *Jarochos* sat nearby with their coffees, but they did not look up.

"Are you talking to me?" he said.

"Sure am," the man said and pulled out a chair. "Mind if Ah sit down?" He beckoned to a waiter and ordered a cup of coffee. "Mah

513

name is Henry Desormeux but everybody calls me Hank." He nodded and scratched his nose.

"Mahself, Ah'm from the proud state of Louisiana," he went on. "Sure glad to meet yah, pardner. Ever been to Nu Oh-leans?"

"No."

"Yah have *not*? Sweet Jeessuss, yah don't know what yah been missin'. Yah never listened to young Ira Lejeune or Barney Kessel or Coleman Hawkins? Yah never listened to Le Chanson de Mardi gras? Yah never had gumbo an' etouffe an' boudin? Creole cuisine is the best in the world, mon. Tell yah what. Look me up when yah get there, an' Ah'll buy yah a Big Zombie and Ah'll show yah the Old Quarter an' then some places most visitors don't never see. Okee-dokee?"

Martin missed half of what Hank was saying, but the gist of it seemed to be clear. "Sounds good, Hank."

"Lordy-Lord, never been to Nu Oh-leans!" Hank shook his head with a look of bewilderment. "What's your name?"

"Martin Tauber."

"European?"

Martin nodded. He offered no further explanation although he had yet to learn that Europe was to most Americans a place across the Atlantic where a mixture of Europeans lived, and that there wasn't much more worth saying about it.

"Ah take it that yah ain't one of them *stupid* Europeans or yah wouldn't have been here," Hank said. "Mah roots are French European on the father's side, but Ah ain't none too proud of that. Mah mother's a Cajun. That's where Ah got mah wits from."

"What is wrong with the French?"

"Ev'rything. Them dumb jerks sold Louisiana for fifteen million dollars back in 1803. *Wrong?* Fifteen million bucks for eight hunner thousand square miles. That ain't bidness, that is *stupidity*. Them French should stick to writin' adventure books an' smear paint on canvasses. That's what they're good at. Not that we complain. Yah know what Ah'm sayin'?"

"I agree."

"Yah traveller?" Hank wanted to know.

"Kind of. I want to see a bit of the world before I settle down." He thought it was a plausible explanation. The words came naturally.

"Damn good idea," Hank said without much conviction. "Myself, Ah'm a biznessman. Commodities."

Martin had no idea what Hank was talking about. "Commodities?"

"Yeah, yah know; coffee, tobacco, stuff like that. Ah run my own bidness." He paused. "See that big white car over there? Cadillac. Best vehicle in the world. It's mine. Say, Ah is goin' up to Mexico City. Care to come with me? Yah drive, Ah take it."

Martin's experience was limited to an old beat-up truck and the odd session on an antiquated tractor. "I drive," he said. "How far is it?"

"Two hunner miles, take or give. Much bigger place than Veracruz." He glanced sideways at Martin. "Actually, not a bad place to get lost, for those who so wish. Dangerous place, mind you. Life's damn cheap here in Mexico and nowhere more so than up in the City. Another thing, if yah don't mind mah sayin', beware of the po-lice. We've got a pretty corrupt lot in Nu Oh-leans, but they are boy scouts compared to them dudes up there. Good place, though. Full of opportunities assumin' yah not burdened with the mentality of a preacher. Know what Ah'm sayin'?"

"When are you leaving?"

Hank shrugged and looked world-weary. "Best time for anything is now, is mah experience. Know what Ah mean?"

Martin did not, but he nodded. "I'll come with you."

"Faan-tastic. Yah don't mind if we share the gas?"

"The gas?"

"Yeah, the gas. Not even a Cadillac runs on nothin', yah know."

"That's all right."

"Yah got some cash?"

An alarm bell rang. "Not much. I've got to be careful."

"Okee-dokee. Just askin'. Don't show it to nobody. Any selfrespectin' Mex will kill for a peso, and that's a fact. The Aztecs used cocoa beans for money, but that don't work no more."

"I listen."

"Say again?"

"I said I listen. I listen to your advice."

Hank grinned. "Yah got yah head screwed on right. Only the quick learner survives in this world. Ah guess yah have to check out from somewhere." He did not wait for a reply. "Meet me here in two hours' time, an' off we go."

"All right."

515

Hank reckoned that the drive would take them between five and seven hours. Martin enjoyed every minute. He had found Veracruz charming and interesting; its modern buildings, the old colonial style houses, the wide avenues and the narrow cobbled streets, the colourful and infectious atmosphere on Placa Constitucion, the gracious Spanish-looking women and the walnut-coloured and bowlegged little Indians, the enormous and very noisy trucks loaded with hardwood, and the rich variety of smells and foods and languages all so alien to him.

Now he saw a different Mexico; a harsh and rocky land where the *campesinos* tried to make a living from their dry and meagre plots and where the burden of existence was a far cry from the opulence of Veracruz. In his mind, he drew a parallel with his native shores, a land that demanded so much and gave so little in return. But the Mexicans' lot was different; the poverty was more abject and the quality of life was lower. Once in a while, when they stopped for a break, Martin stared into the dark eyes of the *mestizos* and saw a passivity that made him wonder if the real feeling was one of hopelessness. Each adobe seemed to be the home of numerous children, goats, chickens and dogs and made him think of health and hygiene and education and what the future could possibly hold for someone born and raised in the wilderness of nowhere.

Hank chatted incessantly and was entertaining in as much as he knew a fair bit about the country. Neither was he shy on dishing out advice on any topic that came to mind. He warned about the thin air almost eight thousand feet above sea level. He mentioned which parts of the city where no white man should set his foot. He repeatedly cautioned against the Mexicans in general and their police in particular. A more corrupt and violent city did not exist; not that New Orleans was a paradise on earth, far from it, but the Mexican capital was in a league of its own. The city was a twenty-four-hour-a-day death trap. Good for business, though; plenty of money there and lots and lots of opportunities. Armies of women, too, but better be careful, Hank admonished; a poor prostitute ain't never a clean prostitute.

"There are many cactuses here," Martin said.

"One cactus, two cacti," Hank corrected. "Them over there are magueys, by the way. That's what gives the Indians their mescal. Don't try the stuff. It's lethal for human beings. Bourbon's mah favourite."

"You don't like Indians?"

"Indians an' niggers ain't white, is all Ah'm sayin'. Yah'll learn as yah go along." Then, out of the blue, he said, "Yah ain't got no passport, have yah?"

Martin did not see much point in lying. "No," he said.

"Ah so reckoned. A piece of advice, Martin. Get yahself a pair of dark sunglasses an' buy some shoe polish and color yah hair black. Yah can get away with the way yah look for a couple a' weeks, but not in the long run. Yah better not draw attention to yahself. Be inconspicuous. Keep yah head down, is what Ah'm sayin'. Know what Ah mean?"

"I think I do."

"Okee-dokee. Only the quick learner survives in this world."

With less than an hour to go, Hank asked Martin to stop. The American smoked in silence for a while. He flicked the butt out of the window, opened the glove compartment and took out a gun. He checked it carefully. "Know anything about guns?"

"Not much."

"This is a .38 Smith & Wesson. It will stop anything coming towards you, which is what you want. I recommend that you get yourself a piece." He put the gun back. Martin wondered what had happened to Hank's accent. It was still American, but most of the drawl was gone. "Get one that is clean, no history. They cost a bit more, but it's well worth it. Don't buy a pistol."

"Why not?"

"Pistols jam. Revolvers do not."

"You expect trouble?"

"I was born and raised in New Orleans. I have seen trouble since before I could walk. Mexico is no better. I told you that. Be prepared for anything. Believe me, there are times when one bullet has got more impact than a thousand words. Even the sight of a gun can be pretty persuasive. Most people do not fancy the idea of having their brains blown out. However dumb somebody is, like a nigger or an Indian, nobody takes a liking to the notion that whatever little they have got is all of a sudden gone and it is not coming back." He laughed softly. "You read me?"

Martin nodded and wondered what future he would have in a country so close to anarchy that a decent businessman like Hank could not buy coffee beans without being armed.

Hank said, "Another thing. If some dude ask you for your passport, just say that you have got it deposited in a bank-box."

"Then what?"

"Run like hell. Mexico City is a haven for those who do not want to be found. You'll get to know it. I mean, you haven't got much of a choice, have you? You are stuck."

"I'll find a way, sooner or later."

"Sure you will. Try to make some dough. Money can buy you a passport, but a good one doesn't come cheap. I've got four."

"Why do you need four passports?"

"Only the one who can see into the future will survive. You don't know what's going to happen, do you?"

Martin resisted the temptation to argue with Hank's logic.

"I better drive, from here," Hank said.

"Is that snow, on the mountain over there?"

"That's Popocatepetl, an old volcano. Yeah, that's snow, all right. Listen, when we get to Pasco de la Reforma, I'll let you off near the Alameda Park. You will find Avenue Juarez that leads to the Zocalo. It's a big square, officially called Plaza de la Constitucion. You take it from there."

Hank waved goodbye with a grin. "Hang loose. Take care and remember everything I have told you."

Martin watched as the car slowly disappeared in the heavy traffic.

The square was teeming with people, many of them Americans. Martin felt reasonably sure that he did not look out of place. He bought a map and glanced at the piece of paper where Hank had written the names and addresses of hotels where no questions would be asked.

He followed Hank's advice. He did not take a taxi but walked the streets till he'd found the hotel he had picked, an invaluable first-day experience in a city so vast that nothing could have prepared him for the exposure.

The ordeal had taken its toll. He checked in. He locked the door, put a chair under the knob—another of Hank's hints—and laid down on the bed fully dressed with the money stuck into his trousers. He slept for twelve hours.

He woke up, hungry but rested. He had coffee and tortillas in a nearby café. He studied the map before he began to explore the city.

Five years in an occupied country had matured him beyond his age; he did not become street-smart overnight, but he learned fast. He dressed and behaved like a visitor, changed hotels at irregular intervals and never went to places where a passport might be required. The urchins, the homeless, the beggars, the junkies, the drunks, the pickpockets, the prostitutes and the streetfighters ceased to surprise him. He accepted that poverty and opulence walked side by side. He got lost in crowds listening to the mariachi bands on Plaza Garibaldi. He spent days at the packed Lagunilla flea market. He followed well-heeled Americans and the odd European to Coyacan where troubadours sang their *corridos* about Jesus Malverde and other famous bandidos. He frequented the bars of the more prestigious hotels in Polanco. He never took taxis; when he did not walk, he used the peseros buses. They were cheap and went everywhere. He discovered the library, which became his haven. Nobody asked any questions, nobody looked twice and there he could relax; read, dream and let his mind flow.

He got used to the thin air that initially had caused bouts of dizziness, and he began to get his feeling of loneliness under control.

Martin knew that apprehension about his foreseeable future was not just an academic concept. From newspapers issued in English he learned that unemployment was rife. Any chance of even a low-paid job was against all odds. With it came the danger of being discovered as an illegal immigrant. Hank had warned him about the Mexican jails; a sure way to lose your marbles, he had said, and he had supplemented with a colourful picture of the ordeal of deportation.

Martin began to wonder if he'd be better off in the United States where there appeared to be more jobs, particularly in California. How to get there without a passport remained an open question, although he had read that quite a few *pollos* got through the canyons and into San Ysidro or San Diego. But there were also stories about *la Ley de Fuga; the Law of the Flight.* It meant *run, the Americans shoot to kill.*

Martin found his way to the Alameda Park. He sat down on a bench and tried to shake off a feeling of despondency. There is always a way, his grandfather used to say, always a solution provided you keep looking.

How do you get to the top of the mountain? Not always by following a straight line. You may have to zigzag, climb to the left and climb to the right, re-rout, and—suddenly—you are there and the world is at your feet.

Martin threw breadcrumbs to the pigeons that flocked around him. He wondered what else would be at his feet in the years to come.

From the corner of his eyes he watched a man approaching the bench. He relaxed when the man sat down, put an expensive-looking oxblood briefcase on his knee and took out a bottle of tequila and a silver cup. Apart from a newspaper, there was nothing else in the briefcase.

"You look rather lost, young man," the stranger said.

Martin did not answer.

"Even worse, you are also running out of bread. May I have the privilege of offering you some lunch?"

Martin looked at the silver cup. He took it, sipped modestly and handed it back.

The man said, "Easy does it. Otherwise, it can so drastically become a habit. Or an addiction, in medical terms."

Martin changed position to get a closer look at the man who sounded like a voice from the BBC; smooth, polished, distinct and suave. He was of medium height, slender, elegantly dressed in a light grey suit, white shirt and a spinach-green tie. His shoes matched his briefcase. He had a Zapata moustache that did not fit his finely chiselled feature. His temples were grey. The look in his dark eyes was one of mild curiosity blended with faint amusement.

There was a shy smile on his face when he said in his soft baritone, "You are summing me up, I presume. That is a most commendable attitude to possess in this our rat race, which the common man calls life. I salute you." He refilled his cup. "My infallible instincts are telling me that we are spiritually related. May I offer you another drop of this nectar, which originally came into existence by distilling the Virgin Mary's urine, according to a legend I have made up myself. More touching than hilarious, come to think of it. Here, let me top it up."

"No thank you."

"You are very wise." The man looked briefly at the haze covering the sky. He placed the bottle and the cup between them on the bench and took from his pocket a gold cigarette case and a gold lighter. He lit two cigarettes and handed one to his new-found companion. "We have just drunk to spirituality. Let us now smoke to the future. A profoundly symbolic ritual, in my modest but circumspect opinion, since there is nothing so foggy as our days ahead."

Martin did not know what to make of the stranger, but at least he was company, however bizarre. The man blew a few smoke rings and watched impassively as a pigeon left a dropping on his highly polished shoe. He pulled a silk handkerchief from his breast pocket and wiped and polished his shoe before he threw the handkerchief into a wastebasket next to him.

"A lot of people would have kicked that bird," Martin said.

There was a melancholy smile on the man's face. "I have the deepest respect for all beings not human."

Strange fellow, he thought, he sounds as if he has read a bit. "Are you Mexican?" he asked.

"Forgive this terrible breach of etiquette," the man said. "I should of course have introduced myself before I sat down. Allow me to do so now." He extended his hand. "My name is Angelo Vargas."

"Martin Tauber."

"I am so pleased to meet you." Then, instead of asking the usual questions, Vargas looked at his watch. "Time for the main course," he said. He filled his cup to the rim and emptied it. "Ah! There was a bite to that one." He touched his moustache with the tip of his forefinger and nodded slowly. "Yes," he said, "I am Mexican. You have not heard of the Vargas dynasty?"

"No."

"Good for you. The family is one of the wealthiest and largest hacienda owners in the country; they are industrialists, financiers, exporters and God knows what. I am the black sheep."

"Why is that?"

Vargas let out an exaggerated sigh. "Why am I the black sheep? Because nobody loves me." He laughed. "You ought to look alarmed now, but you don't. I like that. Love is but a fleeting delusion whose existence depends entirely on our desire to believe in whichever *ignis fatuus* suitable or convenient at any one time. Let me quickly add that I am neither cynical nor misanthropic, just infinitely and incurably aware of man's fragile and incomplete emotional structure."

"You sound like a writer."

Vargas seemed taken aback for a split moment. Then he carefully adjusted his trousers, crossed his legs and said with an air of indifference, "Writing is but a stupefying escape for the esoterically minded, a flight into the realms of justification, wrath, solitude and vendetta. Add a measure of purgation amalgamated with catharsis, finely balanced, and the compulsion is complete."

Martin did not understand all of Vargas' words, but he got the thrust of it. He said, "I like the sound of that."

Vargas held up his tequila bottle. "Time for dessert." He stared at his cup. The sun caught the silver like miniature flashes against the lush greenness of the bougainvillaeas across the path. "Do you know that we have an excellent library here?" he said as if the existence of the building had occurred to him for the first time.

"Yes. I have spent some days there. It is very impressive."

"That is interesting. I deduce from this information that you are interested in literature."

"I like to read."

Vargas smiled. "The unique tourist, seeking libraries and not the magnificent monuments of our glorious past." He gave a sideways glance. "Like to read," he mused. "Who am I to question if there could possibly be a more imperious reason for seeking refuge in our temple of wisdom?"

"It is cool and quiet."

"Two irrefutable reasons. I am *so* pleased that my intuition did not let me down. It seldom does."

Martin saw which way the conversation was heading. He had no wish to delve into his past. He said, "You are a businessman?"

Vargas had a second helping of dessert. "Heaven forbid," he said with a grimace. "Can one possibly imagine a more boring, unfulfilling, morally depraved and static profession? I cannot, I am proud to say. Most businessmen are nothing but retarded jerks with a talent for figures but otherwise braindead. No, amigo, on the contrary—I am actually being paid to stay away. The venerable head of the dynasty does not desire the presence of my analytical and progressive mind, so we came to this admirable agreement where I now only exist as the recipient of a monthly cheque in return for an existence in utter oblivion. A divine solution, but then, my dear old father's omniscience is on par with that of the Pope's, and, as is the case with our revered Vatican *Bandido*, my father is convinced that among the many privileges bestowed upon him by the Almighty Lord is the indisputable right to exercise the essence of the First Commandment: *Thou shalt not have a different opinion.* That makes my father a true representative of the human race, as I see it; his sentiments are thistles thriving in the latrine he calls his mind."

The thin lines at the corners of Vargas' mouth deepened. "As a young man, I was sent to England in order to absorb whatever one is supposed to absorb at the London School of Economics. A fantastic city, London. I really enjoyed myself there. Then the Patriarch discovered that I studied practically everything except what they taught at the school, and he cruelly cut off my allowance and sent me a one-way ticket. Following a brief discussion and a lengthy monologue, he decided to send me to Harvard. I had never been to America. I thought, why not, and off I went. I was more mature, then, so I kept it going for three years as opposed to only two years in London. But, finally, as with Canossa, all roads came to an end. I returned with another non-existent diploma and a plan that worked to perfection. I had picked up sufficient left-wing jargon to make Marx look conservative. Prior to the very last family meeting I ever attended, I compiled a list of improvements that would push the Vargas dynasty into the twentieth century. My father was sitting at the end of the table and my four brothers—two older and two younger—were sitting opposite me. I began with a moving little speech about development and progress, equality, workers' participation, minimum wages and so forth. Needless to say, I was rudely interrupted several times. Within fifteen minutes my father had decided that I had no place in his empire. Neither did he harbour any wish ever to see me again, glaring at my four brothers to ensure that they shared his deep-felt sentiment. The Patriarch rounded off with a selection of profanities that my sensitivity forbids me to repeat. Mission accomplished, in other words. I was free. So, I got up, and I told him in unequivocal terms that my legal rights had been infringed, that a lengthy court case would be the regrettable outcome of his cantankerous behaviour and antiquated philosophies, and—just to make him fully comprehend the gravity of my plight—that my legal action would be funded by one or more of his many enemies. I thought he was going to have a heart attack there and then, but, sadly, no such luck. A few days later, my eldest brother found me in my favourite bar and presented me with the proposal which has been in existence ever since. May I add, to complete this picture of harmonious plethora, that my mother does not argue with the head of the dynasty, but what can you expect after six children and an equal number of miscarriages. Catholics, you know."

"Six?"

"My sister Isabella. She is the youngest and the only member of the family for whom I feel unmitigated affection. We keep in touch.

At least once a month she comes to my place and makes me the most unforgettable dinner."

"Does not your father try to stop her?"

There was a metallic clang to Vargas' laughter. "He couldn't, and he does not try. Isabella is a very strong-willed woman. She is also the only person on this earth who can make him resemble a recognizable copy of a human being. She gets her way with everything, always has. He adores her."

Martin looked at the slice of bread in his hand. He threw some more crumbs to the birds and ate the rest. "It is a bit strange, though," he said.

"You are referring to?"

"Your hatred of something you never tried."

"Business, you mean?" An expression of gloom crossed the Mexican's face. "Always look for the origin of an emotion," he said. "That is the only way to unmask your own truths. You see, from as far back as I can remember, I wanted to be an artist. I could draw, and I could write. This was anathema to my father, worthy of nothing but scorn and derogatory observations. Such being the situation, amigo, I ask you— what do you do? The answer is: you either give in, succumb, capitulate, bury your dreams and abandon your dignity, or you rebel. I saw myself conquer the art galleries and receive the Nobel price, the one-man revolution that would make Mexico proud and overshadow the cruelty of the Aztecs and the mindlessness of our civil wars. I saw myself as Rivera and Siqueiros and Azuela and Paz in one."

"What happened?"

Vargas squinted as he stared across the park. "I may show you, one day."

"Show me what?"

"The manuscript never to reach a publisher and the drawings and the paintings never to reach an exhibition hall."

"What stops you?"

Vargas' hand trembled when he once again filled his silver cup. "Kindly excuse me whilst I irrigate my mind." For a moment his face was lifeless. "One of King Alcohol's most treasured gifts to his disciples is that he never allows you to lose that most precious of all human traits, which is self-doubt." He turned and looked straight at his audience. "Does this explanation find resonance in your young and innocent soul?"

Martin sensed the naked despair in Vargas' voice and did not know what to say. He stretched his legs, put his hands on his knees and wondered how to break the silence. Vargas put the bottle and the cup back in his briefcase. Martin spotted the picture on the front page of the untouched newspaper. "What does it say?" he asked and pointed at the photo.

Vargas shrugged. "Some young American drug dealer was gunned down yesterday."

"Can I see, please?"

The photo showed a car and man lying on the ground. The two lines under the picture contained the name *Henry Desormeux*.

"Why is this article of interest to you?" Vargas asked.

"He said he was in commodities."

"He certainly was. You knew him?"

"He gave me a lift from Veracruz."

"Is that the extent of it? Nobody has seen you together?"

"He dropped me off down there, at the corner of Avenue Juarez," Martin gestured. "I have not seen him since. Not before Veracruz either, for that matter. It is five months ago."

Vargas scanned through the article. "Henry Desormeux was from one of the oldest and most respected families in Louisiana. He was an only child and had a degree in philosophy from Sorbonne. It appears that his family was unaware of this particular business activity of his. He did, however, have a reputation for being reckless and a distinct desire for being seen as a free spirit." Vargas put the newspaper back into his briefcase and closed it. "What do you know about drugs?"

"Nothing."

"Let us exercise, and I will tell you something," Vargas suggested. They walked for a few minutes. "Drugs is fast becoming a major industry in this country," he said. "Crime and corruption are practically unparalleled. Only one or two American cities are ahead of us. When it comes to the sheer number of killings per capita, this city is unchallenged. Life is not worth a peso. I do not know where you come from and what you are doing here, and neither shall I ask, but if you are looking for safety you could not have chosen a worse place. Let me add another dimension to the realities of life here in Mexico—for all you know, I am an undercover policeman. Has that occurred to you?"

Martin smiled to himself and thought about the years when one careless word or a slip of the tongue could lead to infinite misery. He had been cautious, but he shouldn't have express interest in the fate of Henry Desormeux.

"Right," Vargas continued. "You are young and you look determined, but I believe I am correct in assuming that your overall experience is limited." He nodded as if he did not expect his assumption to be confirmed. He stopped, picked up a small dead bird, walked across the lawn and placed the bird gently under a bush. He brushed a few leaves from his sleeve. "Life. We come and we go." He smiled with a tinge of sadness that Martin had come to recognize. Vargas said, "Which reminds me, I am going home. Where are you going?"

"I'll wander about for a while."

"Where do you stay?"

Martin told him.

"Never heard of it. Any good?"

"It's got a bed."

"I come here most days," Vargas said. "Who knows, we may meet again."

"Who knows."

They did. The first couple of times Martin thought nothing of it; he saw it as a coincidence since he came to the park at different hours.

After the fifth meeting he began to think that the Mexican was actually waiting for him. They talked about anything under the sun. Vargas' comprehensive cognition and acerbic observations impressed and amused him. More often than not, they sat on a bench—Vargas was not too fond of exercising—and gradually Martin sensed that the Mexican was a loner. Vargas talked about people he knew, and they were many, but, with the exception of his sister and someone called Ernesto, he never referred to anyone as a friend. Occasionally, he mentioned the rest of the family, either in humorous or satirical terms, but most of the time it was his passion for arts and history that dominated. He saw it as his duty to improve Martin's English, which was welcomed, and here the Mexican showed his gentler side and an endless patience. He refrained from asking personal questions. That both pleased and surprised Martin; it was as if his background was neither interesting nor relevant.

But, however much he enjoyed Vargas' company; it had to come to an end.

His capital was substantially reduced, and he did not fancy trying to enter the United States without a cent in his pocket.

One day he said, "Have you any idea how I can get hold of a passport?"

Vargas seemed to give the question considerable thought. "I am afraid not," he finally said. "Is it your intention to move on?"

"I have to."

"Do you have any concrete plans?"

"California. I need to find work."

Martin had spent most evenings frequenting bars. Form bits and pieces he had picked up, he knew that each year thousands of Mexicans tried to get into the United States, and that apparently a fair number succeeded. "The San Diego route," he said.

"I have heard about it," Vargas said. "It does strike me as a risky proposition."

"I know, but I haven't got much of a choice."

Vargas pondered for a long time. He sipped his tequila. He closed one eye and then the other before he at long last turned and said with a smile, "There could be an alternative."

"Which?"

Vargas drummed his fingers on his briefcase. "It is of course possible to investigate where to get hold of a passport, a legitimate one, I mean. The point, though—I am only surmising, admittedly—but the point is that we more than likely talk about costs in the region of, say, several thousand dollars."

"I see."

"Now, this means that we have to find a way to raise said amount. I am pleased to announce that such a way does indeed exist."

"How, and how long will it take?"

"You really are in a hurry, today. A few months, since you ask."

"I haven't got a few months."

"Of course you have. Move in with me, and we can commence your education tomorrow, for that matter. A glittering career is awaiting you, and its application is universal. What do you say?"

He did not know what to say. "Are you being serious?" he managed after some while.

"Not since I asked the esteemed patriarch of the Vargas dynasty to go and screw himself through the front teeth of his favourite stallion have I been more serious—and that, amigo, is a long time ago. I have got a spacious four-bedroom apartment. We won't be in each other's way. A dash of consideration, flexibility, tact and discretion, all qualities with which we are both richly accoutred, and I fail to see even the shadow of a complication."

Martin remained silent. The image of his grandfather flashed through his mind. *Rely on your fellow man, but trust nobody.*

"Another thing," Vargas went on, "I would find it deeply distressing if you left this my beloved country without giving me the opportunity to show you around. The remnants of our equivocal past are as breathtakingly beautiful as our myriads of legends are perverse, a spellbinding constellation that should appeal to an untainted mind."

Still, Martin hesitated. "I don't know," he said. "I don't know."

"Why? I am offering you the chance to learn a profession, to earn a decent living and to get a passport. What is the problem?"

Why is he doing this? he thought. He said, "I do not want to be a burden."

Vargas paused. Martin saw the doleful smile that spread across the Mexican's face. "Listen. You are young, gullible, homeless and on the run. The war didn't do you much good. Yes, I have guessed that much. I have never in my life done anything for anybody. Allow me, please, to help you to get back on your feet. Believe me, for decades I have seen young people hit the gutter never to get up again. It is not a pretty sight. One day, when I shall have my last drink, I will look back at this brief encounter and remember that I once in my life managed to conquer my selfish nature. Not the worst of epitaphs, come to think of it."

He is serious, Martin thought. "What is this career you have in mind?" he asked.

"A master criminal in a niche market."

"*Criminal?*"

"Relax, amigo. You won't get caught."

"I wasn't thinking of that."

"You were not? Moral, then; non sequitur, I am happy to emphasize. May I respectfully suggest that as of now you adopt the following maxim as part of your philosophical attitude to life: *Homo Homini Lupus.*"

"What does it mean?"

"Man is wolf to man." Vargas laughed softly and wiped his silver cup with a paper tissue. "You choose your own prey. That way you can control the limit of tragedy which is purely material and therefore of no moral consequence anyway. But even if it was—moral is a luxury, amigo, and one that you at present can ill afford." He flicked the ash from his cigarette and blew his sigh of mild resignation through his nose. "Face the facts, young man. You are poor, unprotected and forlorn. Develop and apply your moral yardstick when circumstances so allow. That most certainly is not at this stage of your life. You are facing the abyss. You either employ all means available to escape, or you let the abyss devour you for good. Embrace moral when you no longer have to run with red-hot, molten lava sizzling under your feet." He clicked his fingers and straightened up. "Why don't you go back to your plush suite, pack your bag and meet me here in two hours' time? I'll explain everything tomorrow."

Martin thought about his depleted finances, his life on the streets, his illegal existence, his accommodation and the smell of urine and sweat, and he thought about a future that had begun to look as attractive as a camp-site on Mount Everest. "Where do you live?"

"Not far. Near la Ciudadela."

It was Martin's first experience with opulence. Vargas' apartment was huge. The walls were covered with discreetly patterned textiles, and the ceilings were white. The carpets were deep and soft. The green colour reminded Martin of the pale moss through which he and his grandfather had carved their initials on the cairn. Vargas' taste in furniture was conservative, mainly rattan chairs and tables, and with an abundance of multicoloured cushions. His book collection made Martin wonder how it would feel to be rich enough to have a private library. Even the kitchen made Martin speechless; there were gadgets he did not know existed. "You cook?" he asked.

"Superbly," Vargas confirmed. "Even better than Isabella. She does not know this—or refuses to recognize it—which comes to the same, for a woman. Did you know that? Never mind. She promised to get me a car by tomorrow." He chuckled. "She is an amazing girl, Isabella. She just confiscates whatever she wants and nobody asks any questions. It is incredible what she gets away with. You'll like her. Have a seat and admire the skyline—what little you can see of it. I dread to think what pollution will do to this city in ten or twenty years' time. I'll fix us a drink."

Martin did not particularly like tequila, but he drank politely. He assumed that Vargas did not expect anybody to keep up with him. Vargas gave him a glance before he resumed studying the hardly visible skyline. "What is your preference?"

"This is fine," Martin protested.

"Alcohol is sacrosanct and should be treated with reverence and not with insouciance, amigo. I respectfully advise you never to compromise on this gift from above."

"I once tasted Irish whisky. I liked it."

"A brand not among my otherwise impressive collection, I am ashamed to say. We'll get you a case tomorrow." He looked at a cigarette burn on the carpet and rubbed it with the sole of his shoe. "My apology for descending to a level of prurient banality, but I have got a modest assortment of mistresses. They are sweet girls, but please do not pay them too much attention. I would hate any of them to think that she is unique."

"You do not want to live with a woman?"

"Good Lord in heaven! A woman is a commodity. Allow her to move in and you'll witness a metamorphosis that would make the Resurrection look plausible. A woman, *any* woman, is by nature inquisitive, domineering, pushy and possessive. Who needs it? I strongly recommend that you espouse this perspective, or you'll find before you know it that a prison is Nirvana in comparison." He took off his tie and dropped it on a cushion. "It goes without saying that you are free to use your room as you please."

Martin smiled as if a life without women was unthinkable, but he knew that his lack of experience prohibited any meaningful contribution and kept quiet.

"Enough about women," Vargas said. "There are limits to the extent one can analyze an amenity. By the way, what on earth is that piece of rock doing on top of your drawer? Are you actually travelling the world with a stone as your companion?"

"I am."

"I have no wish to lecture you on our planet's geological structure, but would you not think that rocks are available in most countries?"

"It is a special stone. It is going to be the altar of my shrine."

"That sounds mighty mysterious, amigo. As for myself, I am religiously dormant and indifferent to my fellow man's hallucinations about supernatural powers."

"It's got nothing to do with religion."

"Really? That makes it even more fascinating. However, I shall control my insatiable curiosity, as I always do. You talk if you want to."

Martin made no comment.

"Right," Vargas said. "I suggest that we honour Hosteria Santa Domingo with our presence. I could do with a decent meal. I have a feeling that as of tomorrow my peaceful existence will be but a memory, so let us celebrate the dawn of a new era."

Martin slept for ten hours. He enjoyed the largest and most powerful shower of his life, draped himself in a thick gown that Vargas had given him and went into the drawing room.

Vargas was not alone. The man sitting opposite got up and smiled warmly. He was about five-feet-five, muscular, with quick movements and piercing black eyes. His nose had been broken. A long scar ran down the left side of his neck. He was dressed in faded blue jeans, a lilac shirt and rubbersoled boots made from canvas.

"This little scumbag answers to the name of Ernesto," Vargas said. "If there ever was a man I'd call my friend, this is it. I once did him a small favour—saved him from at least ten years in jail, to be specific—and he repaid by prolonging my life one dark and memorable night when I was slightly inebriated."

"Saved," the man said and showed his perfect teeth.

"No, Ernesto. It is not in yours or mine or anybody else's power to *save* lives. That went out of fashion two thousand years ago. It was being made obsolete by the gentleman who is hanging in your bedroom. You merely *prolonged* my life, amigo." He looked at Martin and gave a shrug. "Semantic precision is not one of his virtues."

"Very pleased," the man said and extended his hand. His grip was firm. Martin could feel the calluses against his own skin.

"Ernesto's English is of mediocre quality," Vargas said. "However, his knowledge is more comprehensive than his willingness to verbalize. The reason for this psychological imbalance is his immense modesty coupled with natural shyness. It is not a problem, though. I shall translate whenever he switches over to his native tongue. That usually happens when his English vocabulary lets him down, by his own high standards, or when he gets uncontrollably emotional."

531

"Angelo a very kind man," Ernesto said. "Very deep and mucho understanding."

Vargas nodded to Martin. "That one I couldn't have composed better myself. Now, let's talk business." He paused for a moment. As he straightened his back, Martin saw a beautifully carved crystal glass next to the coffee pot. Vargas lifted the glass, swallowed half its content and put it back on the table. The expression in his eyes changed and he looked resolute yet relaxed.

He began, "Ernesto is the most skilled burglar this nation has ever produced. As a pickpocket he is unsurpassed. To call him a master is an understatement. As a streetfighter he is the pride of the city; so feared that only fools challenge him." The rest of the tequila went down. "In short, he is as talented as he is ugly. That makes him a genius, as you can see for yourself. To complete his biography, he is also a direct descendant of Cuitlahuac, brother of the more famous Montezuma, and is therefore of royal blood, all this according to himself."

The Indian laughed and caressed his drooping moustache. Martin looked at Ernesto' face; the dark complexion, the potmarks on his cheeks, the lines on his forehead and the web around his eyes. This man is probably only in his thirties, he thought—life has made him look ten years older.

Vargas seemed to read Martin's thoughts. "Whilst still an apprentice, he went in and out of jail a few times, and, believe me, our police force knows how to break a man. They failed with Ernesto, but they certainly tried their hardest. He has been wounded by the sword of reality, but there are no scars on his character."

"Ramirez," Ernesto said. His smile was gone. "His day will come."

Martin saw the flash of pure hatred in the Mexican's eyes and wondered what had happened.

Vargas said, "I sincerely hope so. Captain Ramirez does not qualify as a human being and has long lost his right to exist. Just bide your time, Ernesto."

The Indian concentrated on his coffee. The veins on his neck looked as if they wanted to leave home.

Vargas said, "Martin, show Ernesto your knife."

He went to his room, came back with the knife and gave it to Ernesto. The Indian lit up visibly. He pulled the knife from its sheath and tenderly touched the piece of art in his hand. "Beautiful," he said, "this is *real* steel. Best I have seen." The tip of his thumb slid along the length of the blade. "Very good for fighting. Not so good for throwing."

"Why not?"

"Balance. I teach you. To throw this knife will require great talent. Much skills."

Vargas said, "Right, one thing at the time. Where do we start?"

Ernesto set his eyes on Martin, shook his head and said something in Spanish.

"He does not approve of the way you look," Vargas translated. "He suggests that you get yourself a good tan and he implies that you should colour your hair. Otherwise, he says, you'll simply look too conspicuous, in the long run. Furthermore, he advocates a moustache and a pair of dark sunglasses. You get the picture, I presume."

Martin thought about Henry Desormeux' warnings. "I believe so."

Vargas clasped his hands. "Good. Why waste time? Let us get dressed and go down to Manuel Velasques' prominent establishment. He knows his stuff and is a paragon of discretion."

"Manuel is fond of life," Ernesto said.

"Yes," Vargas concurred. "That is one way of explaining Manuel's reason for prudence."

Ernesto went over to the telephone and made a quick call. He came back to his chair and said, "Only Manuel present."

"Ernesto believes in taking precautions," Vargas said. "He also believes that experience is pointless unless you make use of it. I wish I had his practical and judicious approach to life."

Manuel's premises was halfway between Guardiola and Chapel la Profesa, strategically an excellent choice with several hotels and museums in the vicinity, and the House of Representatives within walking distance. His shop was large, well lit, clean and comfortable, but save a few old Indian relics there were no signs of luxury. He employed a total of twenty people, and he paid them enough to stop them looking for employment elsewhere.

Catering for a diverse international clientele, Manuel had formulated his own version of the English language, not because he did not know any better, but because he knew that it amused his customers.

"Mr. Vargas," he beamed as they entered, "what an inexplicable solace and unadulterated encomium. This must be your confederate, I presume.

Welcome to my humble institution, sir. Are we not expecting his Royal Highness the little Aztec?"

Vargas sat down in one of the deep leather chairs next to a carved wooden table. The top was covered with newspapers and magazines. "We did not think it a good idea," he said.

"Of course not," Manuel said quickly. "Now, as you wait, Mr. Vargas, may I offer you the usual?" He disappeared behind a revolving door and came back with a bottle and two glasses on a tray.

"Not for me, thank you," Martin said. He had noticed that Manuel had locked the door once they were inside and turned the sign, and that nobody else was present. Manuel looked at the clock on the wall and said, "I directed my undergraduates to go for a coffee break. They will be back in about one hour's time. What can I do for you, sir?"

"Make him look like a Mexican," Vargas said.

Manuel rolled his eyes. "Mr. Vargas, I am neither a cosmetic surgeon nor a magician."

Vargas pulled the tray closer. "Manuel, an innovative *idea* can only come from a brain capable of more than a limited melange of instinctive reflections. Are you implying that an *idea* is to you what a glass of tequila is to the growth of a forest?"

"I can make him more sombre."

"That would not be necessary. If, on the other hand, you could darken what is visible above his neck—?"

"Ah! Colouring! *Por supesto*! That is, in retrospective, precisely what crossed my mind this very *segundo*."

"Lateral thinking," Martin said.

"Sir, you are a writer!" Manuel enthused and clasped his hands. "I have the greatest revenue for men who live by the pen."

"He means reverence," Vargas said.

Manuel ignored him. "My personal favourites are Mariano Azuela and the gringo Faulkner. Great stuff. What is your preferred theme, sir?"

"Excuse me, Manuel," Vargas said. "One can be lateral without being literal, and one can be literal without being an active member of the literati. Why don't you keep quiet and do what you are supposed to do? Darken his hair, his eyebrows and what little he's got under his nose. Advise him on how to stay that way. The same applies to his complexion."

Manuel pointed towards a chair, adjusted the blinds and began to work. Twenty minutes later Martin opened his eyes. He did not recognize himself.

"Splendid," Vargas said. "Now he is just anybody."

"Or nobody," Manuel quipped.

"I still have got blue eyes," Martin said.

"That makes you a *Gato*," Vargas said. "Rare, but not sensationally so. Gato means cat. You know, like *Manuel* means *flea*."

Manuel tossed his head and took the position of matador before the kill. "I shall refrain from retailing," he said stiffly.

"What does he mean?" Martin said.

Vargas sighed. "He means that he shall refrain from *retaliating*. Lord the Almighty is short on magnanimity compared to Manuel."

Manuel picked up two bottles from his workbench, marked one with *hair* and the other with *skin* and gave them to Martin. "You tan easily, don't you?"

He continued, "Get a tan. If you want to be as dark as Ernesto, you use this one." He gave Martin a third bottle. "I shall write down the instructions on all three. You know where to find me when you need further supplies. Just call in advance." He smiled genially. "Either way, make wearing sunglasses a consuetude."

Martin thanked him, and Vargas paid. "Magnificent, Manuel. Nobody could have done it better."

"Done what?" Manuel said and switched on a fan. "Who have I seen this morning? Four ugly little locals and one fat geriatric American. Not a good day."

Vargas smiled. Manuel let them out. "Take care, amigos," he said and closed the door.

An olive-green Willys CJ Jeep was parked outside Vargas' apartment block.

"Isabella is here," he said. "She'll be waiting upstairs. She is the only other person with a key. That's what I call *trust*."

They walked into the drawing room. The girl came towards them and embraced her brother.

"Martin," Vargas introduced. "Isabella."

They shook hands. The girl did not say anything. Martin kept quiet because he was lost for words. He had seen some eyefuls during his stay, but nothing like this goddess. Isabella was dressed in riding gear, khaki and tan. Her long black hair fell over her shoulders and framed the ivory skin of a classic beauty. She wore a richly coloured scarf tucked into her white blouse around her neck. Her slightly aslant black eyes examined him and made his throat dry and his feet itchy.

Suddenly, she smiled. He was not surprised to see that her teeth were as perfect as the rest of the girl.

She said, "You are on the run, I understand."

Vargas said, "Forgive me. I should have warned you. Isabella never saw fit to include the concept of *tact* into her education."

Isabella tilted her head. "Angelo has never before picked up a stray dog," she said, the smile now barely visible. "What have you got going for you, stranger?"

Martin began to feel annoyed. He could not see what justified the girl's rudeness, but the result was that some of his unease disappeared.

"Empathy," he said and stared back.

Her smile widened. "Great," she said and sat down. "That is exactly what Angelo needs. Are you a heavy drinker?"

"No."

"Even better." She turned to her brother. "This young man may have a good influence on you. I want to hear what he has got to say about your art."

"No!" Vargas cut in sharply. "I will show him in *due time*." He glared at his sister.

"Oh, well," she shrugged and went into the kitchen.

Vargas and Martin found a seat. "Please excuse her," Vargas said. "Isabella can't resist being outrageous. She gets a kick out of upsetting people. Are you upset, Martin?"

"Not particularly."

"She's got a heart of gold," Vargas said. He smiled. "It is not immediately apparent, but she has. I am very fond of her. You'll need a bit of time to get used to her, but, eventually, you'll find she's pure quality."

Isabella came back with a silver tray. "You are not too young to drink coffee, Martin?"

"I'll give it a shot."

"Indeed an adventurous young man." Her smile was teasing and provocative. "Where are you from?"

He was beginning to get a feeling for Isabella. "You ask too many questions," he said.

"Gosh! Why so secretive?"

"Because nothing about me is any of your business."

She laughed so contagiously that Martin smiled against his will.

She said, "Not bad, but it does make me deeply suspicious when somebody is as clam-like as you are."

"It's got nothing to do with secrecy. The term is infringement of privacy."

She studied him for a while. "What a pity that you are not ten years older, wealthy, genteel and good-looking," she said. Her tongue touched a strand of hair at the corner of her mouth. "I could have taken an interest in you."

He reddened. "My luck."

Vargas was clearly enjoying the repartee between his sister and his protégée. "When shall we have the pleasure of your company for an entire evening, Isabella?" he asked.

"Next Thursday," she said. "I presume that you eat anything, Martin?"

"Don't worry. I am not a gourmet."

Her dark eyes flashed towards him. Her skin glowed like emergency lights under water. She arrested herself and said in a silken voice, "I'll make you into one, assuming that your taste buds are not as primitive as one easily could be led to believe."

He said, "I appreciate your kindness. Angelo told me that your heart is even bigger than your behind."

Isabella spun around but calmed down when she saw the grin on her brother's face. She got up, still looking at Vargas. "Your young friend is a very fast learner," she said with a sudden tenderness in her voice. "I hope that you will both benefit from his progress." She looked at her watch. "I am off. See you next Thursday at around seven."

Martin got up. Isabella smiled with her eyes. "Goodbye, my young amigo. It has been a mixed pleasure meeting you—not *entirely* unfavourable, I hasten to add." Her voice grew softer and the expression in her eyes changed. "Look after Angelo for me."

Vargas followed her to the door and came back a few minutes later.

"How old is she?" Martin asked.

"Twenty-three. Isabella was educated in England and thereafter sent to a finishing school in Switzerland. She is quite a woman, my sister."

"So I discovered," Martin mumbled.

"She must have had about fifty proposals, so far," Vargas mused. "She does not seem to be in a hurry. It is somewhat worrying for her parents—this is Mexico—although I cannot see anyone good enough as far as my father is concerned. It is quite a dilemma for the Patriarch; he wants her to get married—actually, he has suggested one or two candidates himself—his problem is that the mere thought of losing her makes him physically ill. He can't admit it, but it is a fact. He is pathologically possessive, the old vulture." Vargas turned his gaze towards the window. He was lost in thoughts for a while. Then, abruptly, he got up. "Ernesto's present headquarters is in an old warehouse not far from the airport," he said. "Let us go and see him."

"Present—?"

"He never stays in the same place for long. You will learn a lot from him."

Ernesto willingly shared his vast knowledge and experience. For the next six months, Martin underwent a thorough course in burglary, how to become a qualified pickpocket, streetfighting and the proper use of a knife.

Ernesto had a way of finding out which houses were occupied; he never entered any premises unless they were vacated. He knew how to circumvent security and how to unlock doors without the benefit of the owner's keys. "Always wear gloves," he advised. "Never vandalize. Take money only. Getting rid of stolen objects means involving somebody else. That is an unacceptable risk. Be fatalistic. Walk away if there isn't any money lying around. Never lose your patience. Never try to open a safe. Stay one hundred percent alert every split second on the job."

Ernesto was pleased with his student's progress. Martin learned fast, and his first solo raid brought in the equivalent of forty American dollars. His own calmness surprised him, initially, but Ernesto laughed and said that youth and lack of nerves went together. "Just don't get overconfident," he warned. "That's when you start making mistakes."

Picking pockets generally paid more per hour. It was less strenuous and not much of a risk provided certain golden rules were being adhered to.

"Gringos only," Ernesto admonished, "tourists and businessmen. Leave women alone. Put the wallet under a newspaper on a restaurant's pavement table as soon as you have removed the money. Don't touch driving licences or any other papers. Tempting, but far too risky. Greed has ruined many a promising career."

Ernesto could spot an easy prey half a mile away, and after the first few attempts Martin could not believe the carelessness of most people. He brought the money back to Vargas who put it in his safe. At the end of each month, Vargas went and changed the various currencies into dollars.

Martin's laid-back attitude appealed to Ernesto, but he repeatedly warned about complacency. "One mistake, and you'll have our angels of law and order over you like a ton of horseshit. Trust me, amigo, they'll have you buried there for a very long time. It is not an experience I would recommend."

"Most certainly not," Vargas said. "He knows what he is talking about. I advise that each time you prepare for a job, you tell yourself: *I am a gringo with no passport.*"

Ernesto's attitude to streetfighting was simple; it was a waste of time, unprofitable and unhealthy. Unfortunately, it was also an inevitable part of life. He had long stopped seeking confrontations; machismo had been put in its place by common sense, and he had become good at vanishing where he in his younger days would have stood his ground. His once daily diet of fights had been reduced to four or five per month, and then only because there was no other way out.

Ernesto kept himself fit. He combined strength with speed, and his experience had taught him that ruthlessness was a matter of necessity. The jungle held no mercy; leniency was a fatal illusion, and the cemeteries were packed with the remnants of those who'd thought otherwise.

Eighteen months after being introduced to Martin, Ernesto said to Vargas, "I would not like to meet our young friend in a dark alley."

Vargas liked that. "You must have taught him well."

Ernesto nodded solemnly. "I have. He is as good as I am. That adds to the problem."

"Problem?"

"He is *loco*. I cannot explain it and I cannot define it, but there is a trait in him that is scary."

"In what way?"

"I have never killed for the sake of it, but Martin may. Unless he learns to analyze himself and get his mental house in order, he will end up his own worst enemy."

Vargas looked fondly at the little Indian. "You are a wise man. I am grateful for what you have told me. I shall do my utmost to guide him." He rubbed his neck and did not try to hide the look of bewilderment that he felt. "I wish I knew how, I must admit. Martin always seems so relaxed and easygoing."

Ernesto shook his head. "He is neither. It's a façade. The streak of violence goes deep, and he applies it with clinical detachment. There is nothing unusual about having a bit of a temper, but Martin's variety is of a nefarious nature. He does need guidance, amigo."

Vargas kept quiet for a minute. Then he said, "I shall do my best."

Ernesto raised his hand as if to emphasize. "Let us hope he will listen. I know that he has the highest regard for you."

Vargas paced the floor. His world-weary expression was gone. He looked grim and restless. "*How*, Ernesto? I do not know *how*. This situation is all new to me. I feel lost."

The Indian sipped his coffee and stared over the rim of his cup. His raven eyes shone like polished ebony in the dim afternoon light. "The primitive instincts in Martin are not far below the surface. In a way, it is as if he is seeking revenge, and he takes it out on whoever crosses his path."

"Revenge? That's interesting."

"You know?"

"No, I don't. He has never talked about his past."

"Hatred is no good. Hatred fuelled by high-octane adrenaline is worse."

"You hate Ramirez."

"Yes, I do, but I have a special reason for hating him. I don't walk around hating everybody."

"Perhaps it is part hatred and part indifference to human life."

"What does that make him?"

"That makes him a problem to himself."

"We are back to square one, amigo. As I said, you must talk to him."

Vargas picked up his glass. "I can lead him to the chamber of catharsis, but I do not know what the catalyst is." He saw the sparkle in the Indian's eyes and knew what was coming.

"Let the animal out of his cage, Angelo."

Vargas smiled. "I gathered that much—just tell me how."

"You must let him read your book. Thereafter, if he fails to understand..." Ernesto shrugged.

Vargas stared into his glass as if a universal god had left the secret of the human psyche swimming in a drop of tequila.

Ernesto went back to his headquarters and found Martin practising with his knife. Ernesto had several times recommended that Martin got a knife more suitable for all-round purposes, like Ernesto's own— a masterpiece made by William Scagel; fifteen inches long and weighing four hundred and fifty grams. It was perfectly balanced. Martin's knife was more like a Bowie, but heavier. He never explained why he wanted to stick to his imported treasure. Ernesto concluded that there had to be some sentimental value attached. The young gringo wasn't going to relinquish his possession, so better make the most of it.

Martin was doing a combination of exercises as prescribed by Ernesto when he came in; side-stepping, moving backwards, forth, ducking, jumping and circling. Ernesto stopped and leaned against a solid, vertical beam ten meters away. He watched in silence. He did not blink when the knife suddenly left his young protégéé in a perfect overhand handle throw. There was no snap of the wrist, and the follow-through movement continued to its natural end. Ernesto felt the impact on the beam. He smiled and looked at the knife six centimetres from his face.

"Good throw, amigo," he said as Martin pulled the knife out. "You are progressing well."

Martin had got hold of an Arkansas stone. He sprinkled a few drops of oil on the surface and began honing the blade. He kept it razor-sharp. Ernesto sat down on a pallet and lit a short cigar. "I need a break," he said. "I'll be off for the next two weeks."

Martin continued to hone his knife.

Ernesto said, "You have been here for almost two years, and you have yet to see the country. I know that Angelo would like to show you places. He, too, could do with a few days away from the city."

"You think so?"

"Do him a favour, and yourself, for that matter. We all need a change of climate from time to time. That applies not only to businessmen like us, but also to artists like Angelo. All batteries need to be recharged, occasionally."

Martin was satisfied with the sharpness of his knife. He looked up. He said, "Right. You need a break. Angelo needs a break." He wiped the blade with a soft cotton cloth. "And I need a break, unless I misread you."

Ernesto saw no reason to play cat and mouse with his student. "You are close to veering off in the wrong direction. I don't want that to happen. Invest a couple of weeks in analyzing yourself. Use your brain to dissect your instincts, or you will lose control and end up a *mechanic*, amigo, in the worst possible sense of the word."

"Angelo agrees with you?"

There is no way around this, Ernesto thought. "We have talked about it. He can help. He knows a few things about the human nature."

Martin put away his Arkansas stone. "Have the two of you agreed that all three of us go?"

"No. I am not coming with you."

"A pretext, in other words," Martin said and began polishing the blade with a piece of leather.

"Wrong. Maria and I are going to Oaxaca. We want to see Monte Alban."

Maria was Ernesto's wife. Martin knew that they worshipped each other. They ran several markets stands, selling fruits and vegetables. Two of their teenage children were involved, as was Ernesto's younger brother Felipe. Ernesto, who was chairman and managing director, had certain administrative duties that prevented him from being present at all times. He was also the chief buyer, which further explained irregular hours and plausible spells of absence. Ernesto was proud of his legal contribution to the Mexican economy and of his role as a pillar of society. It balanced his more rewarding activities, which he defined as a welfare-come-pension scheme, a necessity caused by the country's class-ridden, inequitable and archaic social structure. His duty was to look after his family and he had yet to discover a valid reason to abandon the maxim that the means justified the end.

Martin said, "See you when you feel sufficiently rejuvenated. Don't get lost."

He went back to the apartment and found Vargas working on one of his paintings; a colourful constellation of three figures, titled *Fallen Angel*. Vargas had long overcome his reservations about showing Martin the shrine; the door to the atelier was wide open.

Martin walked in. "Listen carefully," he said, "I need a break. It would do me good to get away for a few days. I have not seen much outside the city, and I would like to learn about your country. Is there

542

any chance that you can come with me? Perhaps Isabella can get us a car."

Vargas turned around. He had a brush stuck between his teeth. He wiped his hands on a cloth hanging on the side of the easel. He removed the brush from his mouth. "I don't know," he said and looked doubtful, "I am pretty busy, these days. Very inspired, as you may have noticed. There is nothing like a canvas if you want to exorcise your demons. Perhaps I should have said *exercise*." His laughter came like the soft smacks of pebbles hitting water.

Martin said, "We all need to recharge our batteries, from time to time. You could come back even more inspired."

Vargas put his paint tubes back in the box. He looked thoughtful and began to clean his brushes. "Let us give it a try," he said. "We can always return if we get bored."

He called Isabella about a car for the next day.

It had been Martin's impression from the start that there was not much Vargas didn't know about Mexico's history. From the floating gardens of Xochimilco to La Morena's chapel on Tepeyac Hill and to the sacred pyramids of San Juan Teotohuacan, he talked with pride about the ancient cultures of the Mayans and the Toltecs and the Aztecs. He talked with horror about the Spanish conquistadors and with passion about Montezuma and Cuauhtemoc, with sympathy about Emiliano Zapata and Pascual Orozco and Pancho Villa and their fight for *ejidos*—land reform—four hundred years later. He talked with bitterness about the wars with the United States and of the half million square miles that Mexico had been forced to concede to the Americans. His voice became hoarse with anger when he cursed the Mexican government who in 1942 had been stupid enough to agree paying compensation to the expropriated American oil companies.

In between, he added his personal observations. When they stood in front of the nearly seventy meters high pyramid, he nodded towards the ruins of the pre–Aztec city and said, "It makes me quite elated to witness history. This is what happens when our soul floats into the great nothingness from which naught shall return. All that is left is their god; the sun is still here, but the people, their civilization and their culture have vanished, never to resurface. History means nothing to anybody except historians. History is written by those in a position to do so.

History is a concept from which it is universally accepted that thou shalt not learn a damn thing. Take this pyramid, Martin; I do not dismiss the comparative convenience of reveries, but I do not believe that a state of perpetual and all-conquering fantasies does any good. What is tantamount to ignorance rewarded a few thousand years ago is still prevalent; a god—any god—is at best a consoling assumption, and, as such, of the same value and significance and succour as is wishful thinking. That was applicable to those who once ruled this soil, not to forget those being ruled. We are no different."

Martin said, "You are evidently in one of your charitable moods today. Let us see if we can find someone to sacrifice."

"I am just adding a bit of much needed perspective to history. Are you not aware that your suggestion confirms my thesis?"

"Vaguely."

"That is good. We claim that we cannot understand how the Mayans and the Toltecs and the Aztecs could allow themselves to be ruled so indiscriminately by their priests, but, in one form or another, that is exactly the case with any one generation at any one time in any one country. It is only a matter of form, presentation and ability to disguise. The substance of the message remains primarily the same: *Follow our commands. The gods have given us the power to rule. Support us, and the future is bright and promising. Defy us, and you are dead.* That is the eternal scenario. Now, what have we learned from only the last two thousand years of man's history? Have we, or have we not, noticed that every single mass murderer of alleged importance has claimed indisputable support from his god? Have we ever asked if it is a coincidence that the more religious a person professes to be the nastier is the character of that person? When did it occur to mankind that religiousness is the most magical manure for bigotry, and that zealousness is incompatible with generosity of mind? If it ever *did* strike us, when did we react? A comparative recent example—*Mein Kampf* was published in 1925, and in 1939 the vast majority of Jews were still in Germany. It is excusable that they did not attempt to read this literary masterpiece *prior* to 1934, but not thereafter. Then, the evidence began to unfold in front of their very eyes. What did they do? They did nothing. We all carry our cross through life. Mine is that I am unwilling to accept the extent of which people are prepared to claim that they just live in obeisance with the dictates from their gods. How pathetic can man get?"

Martin picked up a piece of rock and tossed it from hand to hand. "Are all members of your family as solidly anchored in the Catholic faith as you are?"

Vargas combed his moustache with all of his ten fingers before he let out a low chuckle. "Once, my father was a different man, a man of principles, a man who did what he believed was right. Back in the twenties, the state instigated a full-scale persecution of our priests. Some ten to fifteen years later only two hundred were left of what once had been over seven thousand priests. Why those two hundred were left to continue their sorcery is a question with many answers, but the true one is that this goddamn country can't do anything properly. Anyway, among those principled purifiers were my father. Then, when it dawned upon him that the church was making a comeback and that superstition is impossible to eradicate, he made a complete U-turn. At that stage of his dignified life he had also inherited the empire, and, ever since, God the Almighty and his son Expediency have ruled the emperor's life."

Martin dropped the rock. "Principles, man and his relationship with history, would that be what your manuscript is all about? Our all too non-independent nature and voluntary imprisoned existence?"

Vargas leaned against a wall and looked towards the sun. He breathed with his mouth open. "There is another dimension to it," he said. "I want you to read it."

He added, without looking at Martin, "Please."

"I would like to." He shielded his eyes and glanced at a *borracho* who staggered by, cursing as he clung to his empty bottle. "This other dimension, is that for my benefit?"

The question did not take Vargas by surprise. "It could be. Ernesto seems to think so. I have no reason to disagree."

"How would he know?"

"I read him the entire manuscript."

"Like he has seen your atelier and collection of paintings?"

"There are not many secrets between us."

Vargas' paintings impressed Martin. Each canvas was as rich in colours as it was economical in composition. With the exception of *Fallen Angel*, no title exceeded more than one word. *Experience* was used a few times, as were *Observation, Sentiment, Memory, Impression* and *Question*. They all had in common Vargas' preoccupation with Mexico's history. He acknowledged his debt to the works of Orozco, Siqueiros and Rivera, but Vargas' style was his own. He once commented, "Most artists are like politicians; commercially minded and unable to create from within. They are illustrators, not originators. Politicians paint pictures of the Promised Land—after the next election—and commercial artists paint what has already been created; wine bottles, fruit bowls and distant hills. Both professions are a playground for people whose ambitions exceed their talents, people whose walk through life is dictated by boundless vanity and infinite conceit. Their psychological make-up renders them immune to any awareness of their permanent state of dishonesty, and it precludes any conception of integrity. It would have been risible were it not for the disturbing fact that these people actually have a considerable influence on our day-to-day life."

Martin had asked, "And the writer—?"

Vargas had replied, "A writer is altogether a different animal. He cannot hide behind an oral smokescreen. He cannot excuse or explain or evade what is already done, unlike a politician or a commercial picture producer. A writer appeals to the intellect, or at least to the mind; he cannot rely on deception and he's got no second chance if facing absence of appreciation. Yes, he can always have another go, with another book, but that requires a bit more, in all respects, than producing a series of platitudes called political speeches or a canvas depicting a cucumber or a lettuce or a lane through a village."

Martin's reaction had been, "There is nothing absolute about you, is there? I like that."

Vargas had declared that he was insusceptible to irony. Martin had said, "I don't think so."

Vargas wanted to go to Morelos, where Emiliano Zapata first made his voice heard. They stood inside the cathedral at Cuerna Vaca. Vargas lifted his arms towards the ceiling. "It never fails," he said. "Each time I enter a house of worship I am being entertained by exactly the same line of thoughts, and that is—that is that this magnificent edifice was designed and constructed by the strong and the vain for the benefit and the comfort of the frail and the benighted. The kind of mindlessness we employ to convince ourselves that man is good—what travesty, what *incredible* travesty."

But by now, Martin had begun to understand Angelo Vargas. He had been drinking less during their excursions—a sign that something was heavily on his mind—and neither did Martin from the onset believe that Mexico's history and a sudden desire for fresh air were Vargas' basic reasons for their break. He had recently re-read Octavio Paz' *Luna Silvestre*. From Vargas' resume, Martin suspected that there was a link somewhere between the book and his own situation. Vargas had also seen Ernesto with unusual frequency, lately. That added to the picture.

Martin said, "I have a feeling that there is something you want to tell me."

Vargas focused on a crucifix and seemed not to hear. His right hand touched the nail through the feet of the victim. He took a step back and nodded thoughtfully.

"I have always believed that to walk through life with open eyes and an observant mind requires perseverance and moral courage," he said. "Few of us are chosen. We are the unfortunate mongrels; eternal condemnation is a guerdon in comparison. We are the spiritual nomads everyone but a kindred spirit will cross the street to avoid. Our reward, of course, the advantage and the beauty of it, is sacrosanct solitude."

"Get to the point."

Vargas folded his hands. He turned around and said, too quickly to leave an impression of indifference, "Do you know how much money you have got?"

"Twenty-two thousand three hundred dollars."

Vargas was taken aback. "How the hell did you know that?"

"I'm not too bad with figures."

"You have kept a record in your head all this time?"

"I have. I still do."

"Then you know that after deducting for a passport and a ticket to Los Angeles, you still have a decent capital left."

"I know."

Vargas began walking down the aisle. He put his hands in his pockets and looked ahead. "I am as blank about your background and why you came here as I was on the day when we first met," he said. He slowed his pace. "Please do not misunderstand—I respect the right to privacy, and I understand an inclination towards secrecy. You, amigo, are a paragon of the extreme."

"It bothers you?"

"A dilemma chained to a paradox. I have no right to know, and you have no obligation to tell me anything. What does bother me is what I interpret as lack of confidence in me."

Vargas had never before spoken so openly about personal matters. There was hurt in his voice, he stooped as he walked and he no longer looked ahead. His eyes focused on the ground.

Out in the sunshine, Martin said, "It matters to you?"

"Yes, it does matter to me." Vargas tried to smile and make his voice light-hearted. "Apart from Isabella and Ernesto, you are the only person on this earth I shall ever have the privilege to call a friend. Soon, you will be leaving, and I shall continue my pointless existence. It would have been nice…" his voice tailed off and his hand began fumbling in the pocket where he kept his silver flask.

"I have not left, yet," Martin said. That wasn't half a promise, he thought; that was a commitment. Perhaps he did owe it to Angelo Vargas; a man who had shown him nothing but kindness and without whom the gutters of Mexico City would have become a certainty.

Martin sensed that his aversion against opening up and confiding in anybody was in many ways an obstruction, an impediment that would keep most doors shut. The problem was that it worked both ways; it shielded him from intrusion, from infringement of what he firmly saw as his rights as an individual. It protected him from getting hurt and from the pit-black and ravaging despair of loss. A weak voice whispered that his clinging to intransigent solitude could in time evolve from habit to characteristic, but the voice was barely audible and contained little conviction. He had yet to meet a woman for whom he felt more than physical desire, and the notion of growing old without a companion was too distant and did not seriously enter his mind. Perhaps Angelo Vargas was right—*a paragon of the extreme.* So what? he thought, it is the way I am and it is the way I *prefer* to be. My life is my own; I am not comfortable with sharing *and nobody has a right to enter my existence.* If people need to suck blood in order to survive in their petty and shallow little world, let them suck somebody else's blood. I shall not have my memories of Baby and Granddad defiled by leeches encroaching my shrine. My good experiences and my nightmares alike can only remain treasures if I protect them from the corrosive effect of people's pathological desire to rip open and grab what they think will feed their emotional needs.

Cool it, a voice whispered. Give yourself time to think about this, as objectively as you can. He walked up to Vargas, tapped him on the shoulder and said, "How can I read your book? You know how lousy my Spanish is."

Vargas put his flask back into his pocket, shrugged and produced an expression that was meant to indicate that he had overcome his momentary attack of dejection. "It is written in English," he said.

"How come?"

"Megalomania, I suppose. My idea was to send it to some publisher in the United States and then translate it should it become a hit."

"You have actually finished it?"

"Yes, eventually I did; bridging almost five years between the first and the last word. Isabella typed it—four hundred pages."

Martin did not comment.

"Are you not going to ask what she thought about it?"

"No. I prefer to make my own judgement without the risk of being influenced."

Vargas laughed. "That would please her. She thinks you are beyond influence."

"Does she?"

"I need to find a cantina somewhere. The contents of my all too diminutive flask have gone and I could do with a sip."

They found a table in the shadow of a magnificent oak. The proprietor of the cantina was not familiar with Irish whisky, but he proudly announced that he had bourbon to offer. Martin asked for a single shot. Vargas stuck to his tequila. For a while he was lost in his own thought. Martin accepted the silence. He had no wish to pre-empt the conversation he knew would follow.

"Martin," Vargas said as if testing scolding water with his tongue, "there is something on my mind."

"You know how to surprise me."

"Yes, I know." Vargas laughed and looked relieved. "I have been thinking of—of to which extent you have managed to replant yourself. Uproot and replant, that is. When you first arrived, you must have thought that you either adapt or you perish. Am I right?"

"Something along those lines."

"I have been thinking. You always insist on paying your half of everything; food, drink, laundry, restaurants, the entire orbit. Now, you know that I am pretty well off. Paying for everything would not have made the slightest difference to me. Why do I take your money?"

"Because it is right." No better or more logical explanation occurred to him. Vargas levelled his gaze at Martin. "On the face of it, there is no reason more fundamental. As we grow up, most of us are being indoctrinated with the rights and the wrongs of this world. Then, as we grow older and realities set in, we learn to develop a selective memory which dictates what should or should not be embraced. We gain *experience*. There are one or two upheavals in our lives; we go through the odd crisis, and some of us begin to ask ourselves questions. A few of these questions are as deep-rooted as they are complicated, and one in particular did bother me for a very long time. Finally, a few years ago, I found my answer, and it is: Moral is only worthwhile as a function of conscious reflections and worthless as a product of blind, inherited acceptance."

"I would not dispute that."

"You wouldn't. Still, you offer me money because it is *right*."

Martin decided to keep quiet and listen.

Vargas smiled. "Don't feel embarrassed. I am older, wiser and I have a few more miles on the clock."

Martin had hardly touched his drink. Vargas gestured to the proprietor that it was time for a refill. He took from his pocket an etui containing his oddly shaped cigars, selected one and began tapping it on the uneven wooden tabletop. There was no sign of his lighter.

After a while, Martin said, "You are still tapping."

"Excuse me?"

"Your cigar. Why don't you light it and continue your sagacious monologue? I have a feeling that you had not finished."

Vargas looked discomfited and hid behind a cloud of smoke. He cleared his throat and said, "I was a very sociable creature, in my younger days. There was always another event to arrange, another party to be held and another restaurant to try. I was immensely popular, or so I thought." He paused and stroked his jaw as if to wipe off a sardonic smile. "You see, Angelo Vargas always paid. I had more friends than I could count, and I wallowed in their adulation. This went on for a long time, many years. One day I looked at myself in the mirror and asked one or two pointed questions. For the next few days I stayed out of circulation whilst I mulled things over. At the first night of my comeback, I suggested that we should all share the bill. From that day on, my popularity rapidly went downhill. An era was over."

"What made you pay in the first place?"

Vargas focused on the tip of his cigar. His expression of sadness was mixed with self-deprecation. He said, "Insecurity. A desire to be liked. A need to be loved." He flicked his ash onto the grass. "It cost me a vast amount of time and money to learn that affection cannot be bought, and nor can respect. The worst of it was this bottomless disappointment with myself. How could I have been so blind, so utterly and incredibly naïve? For weeks and months I felt as if my entire inner life was corroding away; my pride had all but vanished and my self-confidence had hit the rocks, swallowed by an earthquake and ground into tiny fragments never again to be a whole. What a nightmare. That year I did five paintings and began to make notes for my book. Gradually, very slowly, I managed to work myself out and away from the darkest corner of my depression." A low snarl came from Vargas' throat. "I even managed to control my drinking, and, believe me, that did not come easy. Anyway—no doubt you have by now perceived what the lesson is: *never give unconditionally.* That should bring us the *rights* and the *wrongs* as a function of the *mind.*"

"So it does."

"Never believe that the spoken reason is necessarily the real reason. Practically without exception, the real reason stems from what we instinctively deem to be of private and personal nature. It is secret, consecrated and proprietary and must therefore not be divulged to a living soul. Now, why should we not do anything *unconditionally?* Let me put it this way: Givers are easily recognized, officially appreciated and allegedly understood. I ask you; how often do we experience a taker showing gratitude *and* behaving with genuine dignity? Hardly ever. It goes against the grain. At the moment of exchange, both parties feel good because they think that's how they are supposed to feel, but that is as far as it goes. Shortly afterwards, the taker begins to sense humiliation, a feeling of being belittled and despised. His self-defence mechanism takes over. A hunger for spiteful requital develops, blended with the primitive and malignant delusion that he is really entitled to further obligements. The giver becomes resentful, and what began with an imbalance ends with a capsize."

Vargas dropped the butt of his cigar onto the grass and put his foot over it. The grinding movement was slow and methodical. "The human element. God may move in mysterious ways, but man is quite content with duplicity." He stared longingly into his empty glass. "What do you want to do now?"

"Read your manuscript."

"You want to go back?"

"Only for a couple of days."

"But there is so much I want to show you."

"A few days—or for however long it takes to read it."

Vargas gave in. He demonstrated considerable reluctance all the way to the car. Once seated, he smiled and said, "I think a break from history will benefit us. Yes, I am beginning to feel good about it. I am glad I managed to persuade you without too much fuss. It is not often you are in one of your more flexible moods."

"Careful now. I may start looking for the real reason behind this uncontrollable attack of elation."

"You are learning, amigo."

On the morning of their first day back in the city, Martin checked their supply of coffee and said, "Your manuscript, Angelo."

He watched Vargas who appeared engrossed with his morning newspaper.

"Go for a long walk," Martin said. He raised his voice, "I would like to read in peace."

Vargas looked up. "What?"

"Your book. Dig it out."

"Oh." The paper slid onto the floor. "Yes, that's right. My magnum opus. Did I promise?"

Martin waited. Vargas hoisted himself to his feet. He hid a yawn behind both hands and walked heavily towards the safe. He turned the wheel of the combination lock three times, clasped the handle, jerked it down and stopped. A sigh followed. He shook his head and opened the door. He took out a thick bundle of papers held together with a green ribbon neatly tied in a knot. "Here," he said and turned around. "Don't start reading before I've left. I shall be out for most of the day."

Half an hour later Vargas quietly closed the door behind him.

That night Isabella came and made them a meal. Vargas had returned in a state of unexpected sobriety. He did not mention the book. Martin kept quiet, assuming that Vargas did not want his sister to know.

The conversation was light and humorous, as always; only on the rarest of occasions did Isabella let her mask fall, showing a trace of surprise and indignation at Martin's apparent indifference to her charm and beauty. She knew full well that she was an exceptionally attractive woman. Why this gringo had not fallen for her, in contrast to every other male she had ever encountered, was a state of affairs she had problems coming to terms with. It did not help that Martin referred to her as *our fading beauty, our former belle* and *our well-matured spinster*, but Isabella had learned that the more she let her temperament rule, the more Martin enjoyed himself.

Her brother was less than helpful. "Quite frankly, Isabella," he had once said to her in private, "Martin must be some five or six years younger than you. He prefers girls his own age. "He is not for you, *anyway*," he had added pointedly, but Isabella missed the implication. "I am not *begging* him for an affair, for God's sake!" she'd hissed. "It's just that he—he doesn't have to be so *disrespectful!*" Vargas had shrugged and said, "He is not Mexican. You have to take into account that he comes from a different culture." This had pacified her, to some extent. As time went by, she learned to cope with the gringo's insolence and lack of breeding, a deficit she referred to whenever opportunity gave her a chance.

The mental and emotional fencing became more congenial and with a touch of unspoken fondness. What Isabella did not know, was that Vargas had warned Martin in very specific terms: "Do not get involved with my sister. Do not even think about it. I know that the two of you are attracted to each other—I am not blind—but it is an invitation to a catastrophe. The Patriarch will make his move the moment he discovers, which he will, sooner or later. Give it one hour, and every single policeman in Mexico will be looking for you. It is not what you want."

Martin heeded Vargas' advice and kept Isabella at arm's length. The conflict between the desirable and the sensible lasted for over three years.

When Vargas came home the following evening, Martin's feet were on the table. The manuscript was next to him on the sofa. "Finished," he said.

Vargas did his best to look aloof.

"Thank you for showing me your manuscript," Martin added.

Vargas looked around. He eyed a number of objects with an air of indifference. "You have."

"Yes. Quite interesting."

"*Quite? Quite interesting*? What is that supposed to mean—*quite interesting*?"

"Come down to earth. Drop your stupid mannerisms and let's talk freely. No inhibitions."

Vargas focused on his glass. The tip of his tongue played with his moustache. "I have been nervous all day," he whispered.

"Why?"

"Because your opinion matters to me."

"Thank you."

"What do you think of Chicaro?"

The Mestiz Chicaro was the main protagonist in Vargas' book. Martin said, "A remarkable transformation—the ignorant peasant becoming a great political leader." He touched the manuscript. "You described it well. You convinced *me*."

"What about Chicaro's characteristics?"

Martin thought for a moment. "Again, credible. He obviously had a strong instinct for survival, and the ferocity and the sheer vehemence of the man—I don't see anything unnatural about it. My impression is that he consciously concluded that sacrificing anything that did not benefit him was a duty, an obligation. He knew what he was doing. You got across that Chicaro's self-awareness was something he both cultivated and used extensively in his dealings with other people." Martin took a cigar from the table and lit it. "I'd say it was inevitable that the man would end up in total isolation, you describe and substantiate that most convincingly. He anticipated—no, he *knew* that the final price he had to pay for the way he conducted his life was seclusion, and he accepted it."

"A bit scary, don't you think?"

Martin pondered for a few seconds. "Not really."

Vargas laughed quietly. "I thought you'd say that."

"What is funny?"

"What is *funny*? You have just given an accurate description of yourself. There is not much difference between you and Chicaro. The more I got to know you, the more I could see the resemblance. The *scary* resemblance."

Martin kept his hand on the manuscript. "I have no particular ambitions."

"That is not the point, amigo. The traits are the same. How you employ them is irrelevant. Did you not sympathize with Chicaro? Did you not understand him? Did you not accept why and how he became what he became? Did you not commend his conclusions and his ways and his methods?"

The expression in Vargas' eyes was unfamiliar, like a thin layer of curiosity over assertiveness born by insight. He looked relaxed when he asked, "Did you, or did you not?"

"To some degree."

"To *quite* some degree, I believe. You are young enough to learn how to conduct yourself in such a way that you can escape Chicaro's worst pitfalls. Look into yourself. Confront your most destructive characteristics and take command. Do not let those instincts rule you. Can you recall that Chicaro never allowed himself to show his fury? He kept his fiery temper under control. He turned *quiet*, and the more quiet he became, the more deadly he was. Do you recognize something here?"

"Yes. You are contradicting yourself."

Vargas stroked his hair with both hands. He rested his thumbs against his eyebrows. "No, I am not," he said. "You see, there was one thing Chicaro did not take into account—he failed to acknowledge the need for safety valves. With no outlet for a variety of feelings our emotions cannot function, just as the body cannot function in a strait jacket. Our mind will turn stale and infertile if we do not allow challenges to run the entire gamut, that is, to permit ourselves an involvement that goes beyond mere clinical analyses. This is what Chicaro elided; he discarded the importance of fathoming in full the overall complexities that makes man a human being and not a robot. Ernesto agrees, by the way."

Martin looked away. "Is that so?"

"Yes. We discussed you. The three of us are friends. That means, among other things, that we should try to assist and aid when needs be."

"Do I have a right to know?"

"You have," Vargas said and related the conversation between himself and Ernesto.

Martin saw his grandfather's face and heard his voice. The chill wind came in from the north and whistled past the cairn and he shivered. So long ago.

Vargas frowned. "Is something wrong?"

"Just an echo." Martin cleared his throat and got up. "I think you should try to get your book published."

"That is out of question."

"Why did you write it?"

"It was a challenge, purely a challenge. I wanted to find out if I could give life to my observations and endure the process of doing so."

"That is it?"

"That is a hell of a lot. You see, I have been thinking ahead. Suppose I became a success and my life took on another dimension. Some are cut out for fame—I am not. I could not handle it. I cherish my life as it is; the troublefree existence, the anonymity and the placidity. You know I am a recluse by choice. Any invasion of my highly treasured privacy would probably destroy me. Faster, that is, than I manage to do by myself on my own. No, being in the position of not having to answer to anybody at any one time about anything is too precious."

"That's your reason?"

"Was I not explicit enough? As a true soulmate, you should not have any problems sympathizing with my profound assay and deliberate conclusion."

"None. I take it, then, that neither will your intriguing paintings ever be illuminated by a gallery's merciless spotlights."

Vargas caressed his chin with the nail of his thumb. "That is a different proposition. I have not made up my mind, but the idea is not entirely abhorrent to me."

"What is the difference?"

"Enormous. A bit of local fuss could turn out to be hugely amusing. I could buy a wide-brimmed hat and a long black coat and ensure that my demeanour becomes even more aloof. I could adopt an air of mystique and a façade of eccentricity. I could become the mute genius of the visual arts. That should not be difficult since nobody but the most infantile would expect a painter to have an opinion worth listening to anyway."

"Amusement and nothing else?"

"That's all. The fundamental difference is, since you ask, that you can explain away the symbolism of your paintings with an esoteric smile, but you cannot laugh away the spirit of the written word. Oil applied can never be more than a chichi commodity, at best, but if the *word* reflects your traumas then the word becomes hallowed. Even the most expressive painting remains forever static, regardless of its creator's intellect. The word knows no bound and has dimensions unattainable to the canvas."

Martin saw that a tic under Vargas' left eye had taken on a life of its own. "As long as you have convinced yourself," he said. He did not mention the Patriarch, the fear of failure and Vargas' less than cogent endeavours to make light of the dissimilarity between canvas and paper.

Vargas concentrated on a small dent in the wooden table. He touched it with his knuckles. "I have," he said. He grinned. "Subject to accepting the relativity of the concept, that is." His smile was genuine. "You know— I see myself as the perfect post-historic man; the being with no discernible inclination either to build or to destroy. An ideal epitaph, come to think of it."

"You really hate people, don't you?"

"Hate? Not at all. I just dislike them intensely. I mean, what is there to like?"

He rose, picked up his manuscript and put it back in the safe. "Any further thought about leaving?"

"No conclusion yet."

Vargas closed the safe. "There are still a lot of places you have not seen."

"Must be quite a few."

"Oh, hundreds. Perhaps one day we can fly down to Yucatan and have a look at Chichen-itza, the old Mayan city."

"We'll do that, one day."

For the next two weeks, Ignazio Chicaro played heavily on Martin's mind. He knew that he was not mature enough to anatomize fully and understand Vargas' message, but the words kept on living and so did the intention behind them.

Trying to analyze his own psyche was not new, but he accepted that many a labyrinth was still too dimly lit and that further explorations required time and patience, efforts and experience. The thought that kept nagging him was that perhaps it was all too late; the mould had been cast and only minor adjustments were achievable. Cosmetic improvements, he suspected, but no radical change. The doubts came and went. He became increasingly reticent, even in the company of

557

Vargas and Isabella who began to wonder what had happened to their young gringo friend. One day, on his own in the Alameda Park, he sat down on a bench as darkness clouded his mind and an inner voice cried to be heard. Grudgingly, he admitted that his treatment of Vargas had been short on decency and long on selfishness. Preoccupation had taken over, and this was no way to behave and certainly no way to act towards his benefactor.

He went home and waited for Vargas to show up. He was hardly inside the door before Martin got up. He stood by the large windows facing the avenue.

He was aware of the tension in his voice when he said, "You showed me your book. I'll tell you a tale."

Vargas said, "Why don't we sit down? My feet are sore."

Silence filled the room and stretched seconds into minutes and neither moved.

"Just let the words come," Vargas said at last. "It does not matter how they fall and where you begin."

Martin walked over to a chair and sat down. "I was a stowaway on a ship from Amsterdam." He rested his forearms on his thighs and pressed his palms together. "That is how I came to Veracruz. I thought that the ship was going to the United States because someone in Amsterdam said *Americas*. I misunderstood. I picked the wrong vessel. That's why I am here."

He noticed that Vargas had sat down without a glass.

"I once had a grandfather and a brother," he continued. For the next twenty minutes he gave an abbreviated, concise and unsentimental chronicle of his life till the day he departed and left his mountains behind. Much was being left unsaid, but he told enough to make him feel that he had not cheated.

During the entire narration Vargas did not move; his face was impassive and his eyes were fixed on Martin.

"And that's it," he said with an inner calm that surprised and pleased him.

"Thank you for telling me," Vargas said softly. After a while he added, "You grew up in an occupied country. Anybody who didn't cannot possibly imagine what it must have been like."

Neither spoke for a while. Vargas went over and made each his favourite drink. In between he glanced at Martin who had leaned forward, heavily supporting his upper body and clutching both knees with his hands. Drops of perspiration were visible above his eyebrows. A couple of times he inhaled sharply. He had no regrets having told Vargas, but the aftermath of re-living the past had begun to take effect. Exhaustion and giddiness set in, and he wished that he could sleep for twenty-four hours.

Vargas broke the silence. "I can see the similarities between us."

"We know how to burn bridges."

Vargas gave him a quick stare. "You do," he said. "I never touched the one between the Patriarch and my bank. The difference between being absolute and being pragmatic, I suppose, supporting my theory why we complement each other so well." An expression of embarrassment swept his face. "Do you—is it your opinion that I prostitute myself by taking money from my father?"

Martin straightened his back. The feeling of fatigue and nausea were receding. He fell back into the chair and said, "Day of judgement?"

Vargas' hollow laughter stopped as abruptly as it had begun. "Something like that."

"Your father resents paying you?"

"*Resents?*" Vargas' chuckle came from the heart. "On the day I left, I went to say goodbye. He was in his library, sitting in his big black leather chair behind his big dark mahogany desk. Before I could open my mouth, he said: "You were born a failure and you will die a failure. The only joy I shall ever get from you will be if you should muster sufficient dignity to pre-decease me, something I do not expect to savour since useless worms like you are protected by your own slime for an eternity and a half. Pardon the expression *dignity* and do not bother to look it up since its meaning is beyond your ability to comprehend. This is the last time we ever see each other. Go!" Never one to confuse the issues, my father. I saw no reason to ennoble the virulent hatred of a philistine with an appropriate comment, so I nodded politely and left."

"Paternal love," Martin said. "No wonder the Almighty Lord has been promoted to surrogate father for so many bewildered souls."

"That was roughly two decades ago," Vargas concluded. "I have not seen the Patriarch since, except for the odd glimpse in and out of a car or in and out of a building. That was the end of the legend, really, except that he once sent me a letter, informing me that my bones would never defile the family grave."

He closed his eyes and said, "Back to my question."

"No one has the right to dictate the life of another human being. It does not matter what or who they are. Your father should have given you his blessings to become an artist. Instead, he tried to squash you as an individual. When that did not work, he kicked you out. It upsets him having to pay you, and therefore you are right in taking the money. Your action is a vendetta. It is not prostitution. A whore's client does not mind paying because he gets something in return, and although the whore may despise her client, the necessity of reciprocation is based on mutuality derived from a simple understanding of rudimental symbiosis."

"Oh dear," Vargas said. "That was so eloquently worded that I am inclined to be convinced. Did you convince yourself?"

"Never thought of it before—but, yes, it does sound plausible. Anyway, what do *you* think is right? Nothing else matters, remember?"

"I remember." Vargas paused. Lines scarred his forehead. "You have fond memories of your brother and grandfather."

"Yes, I have. He was a fine man. The finest. He taught me how to understand and endure and survive injustice and unfairness. Since then, I have supplemented his teaching with the knowledge that understanding does not equal forgiveness."

"I think he also taught you that it is possible to care for another human being."

"He did. He, and my brother. I have not got it in me to be as kind and generous of mind as either of them, but I have got the guidance and I have got the memories."

Vargas' glass was empty. He crossed the floor and said, "One day you'll find a woman with whom you can share whatever you wish to share. I haven't got the guts to commit myself, but I don't think that will be your problem."

"An illusion I still keep alive."

Vargas came back. "*Still*? Amigo, you are not even twenty, yet. I am not exactly predicting a miracle."

"That may be so, but somehow I feel that the last eight years have added another ten."

"I wouldn't dispute that." Vargas strode casually towards the windows at the far end of the room. "I am glad you are not leaving yet."

But Martin knew that he lived on borrowed time. However well Ernesto had educated him, and however vigilant and careful he was, gradually the odds had shortened. Sooner or later he was bound to make a mistake, or, even if he didn't, a mere coincidence could so easily occur and land him within the reach of the law. And the law—he had long accepted the fact that justice was a concept that did not unduly bother the honourable members of the city's police force; corruption, bribes, false testimony, planting of evidence, extortion, unrestrained brutality during interrogations and even cold-blooded murder were all on the menu. No one, from top to bottom, ever grassed on a colleague unless the case was so stupidly blatant and indefensible that support would become self-destroying. Such cases were few and far between. They all looked after each other; their network was good, and there was always somebody with sufficient experience and contacts to arrange a cover-up should matters show signs of getting out of hand. As Ernesto said, "You either stay clear or you are doomed. There are a handful of decent lawyers here, but neither you nor I can afford them. Mexico is lawless except for the rich."

Martin evaluated the situation and drew his conclusions. He began to scale down. His night raids became more infrequent, and only the exceptionally careless or unforgivably naïve tourist suffered the ignominious discovery that his wallet had disappeared. As Vargas so rightly but reluctantly had pointed out, with almost twenty-five thousand dollars in his possession, he was financially secure enough to get his passport and his one-way ticket and still have a decent capital available wherever he chose to go.

But he hesitated, and he knew why. During his stay he had come to like Mexico and its people. He had become increasingly fascinated by its rich and colourful history and captivated by its amalgam of cultures. He began to make more and more excursions, most of the time on his own, but occasionally accompanied by Vargas.

Amidst all this, other bells began to chime. The world was a big place. There were so many more countries he wanted to see, and he sensed that if the day of departure was not imminent, it could or should not be too far away, either.

He knew that he was going to miss Mexico, a feeling he assumed would gradually lessen as the lure of other places and adventures took over. What he did not know was how to fill the vacuum created the day Angelo Vargas was no longer around. Even Isabella—her femininity veiled by a sharp tongue and her heart of gold inadequately camouflaged by feigned, brusque cynicism—behind the veil was an outstandingly attractive woman in qualities as well as in beauty, a paragon of all that a woman should be; yes, he knew that he would miss her, but they were never meant to be. She would become a diamond-encrusted memory with whom all women would be compared and measured, carat by carat.

Neither would it be easy to leave Ernesto behind. The stocky Indian, so generously and unreservedly willing to share his skills and experience and knowledge, enabling him to make a living and without whom his life would have been in jeopardy more than once. Martin paid Ernesto a commission, advised by Vargas, but that was purely a healthy commercial arrangement and in no way minimized Ernesto's sterling character and munificent nature. His ribald sense of humour was another asset, as was his tendency to drop little pearls of wisdom like: "*There are times when a man has to choose between his wallet and his integrity. The one who chooses the wallet is the one who never gets up on his hind legs.*" At the University of the Streets, there was no professor more qualified than Ernesto.

One rainy day Martin came home and found Vargas sitting on the edge of the sofa. His hair and moustache were soaking wet and water dripped from his coat. He stared blankly ahead and seemed not to notice that Martin had arrived.

"What is the matter?"

There was no response. Vargas sat with his hands folded, staring at nothing. His breathing was slow and the rhythm strangely staccato.

"Talk to me."

A minute or two passed. Then Vargas turned his head, as if in trance. His black eyes were void of expression. "Ramirez has taken Isabella," he said, his voice hoarse and flat.

"Taken?" But Martin knew. He knew with appalling certainty what was to follow. Still, he asked, "Please explain."

Vargas' eyes began to flicker. "He wants one hundred thousand dollars."

Detective Jesus Ramirez; murderer, torturer and extortionist, the man who had achieved such notoriety that he believed he could walk on water. The man who had such a file on his superiors that nobody dared touch him. The man who was so pathological in his mistrust and so infinitely vengeful that even the mentioning of his name was avoided for fear of repercussions. The man who had tried to break Ernesto—one of Ramirez' rare or perhaps only failure.

Now Ramirez thought he get could away with the kidnapping of a member of one of the country's most powerful and influential families—or had Ramirez finally overstretched himself and made a fatal mistake? Or had his devious mind once again developed a plan so ingenious that he would remain untouchable and be allowed to continue his glittering career?

Vargas sat still, seemingly paralyzed. Martin went over, jerked him to his feet and pushed him towards his bedroom. "Have a shower. I'll get you a drink and you let me have the details."

He could hear the water running. He placed the promised drink on the table, lit a candle and lay down on one of the rugs on the floor. He put his hands behind his neck and tried to sort out his own feelings. Fear for Isabella, yes. Worried about Vargas, yes. But there was something else, a feeling from deep inside that began to take form and shape as it drifted towards the surface and became recognizable. He knew—it was excitement, a thrill of proportions never before encountered, a challenge hitherto unknown. It took but a minute to admit the true substance and the nature of his involvement; there was more to this than despair for his friends. Thanks to Jesus Ramirez, Martin's existence had been elevated to a level where he could synchronize his brain with his instincts and attain the optimal pleasure of having every nerve-end laid open, incited by suspense and stimulated by hazard. He had little problems identifying this picture as a true image of himself. He began to relax. When Vargas reappeared, calmness had taken over.

"That drink is going to last for a while," Martin said. "I prefer rattled nerves to a muddled mind."

Vargas took the glass with both hands. A third of the tequila went down his throat.

"In chronological order," Martin said.

Vargas' hands were not steady, but his face had lost some of its haunted expression. "The telephone rang at noon, and I heard a voice say: "*Crees en al Diablo, Senor Vargas.*" Then I knew who it was."

Martin nodded. Jesus Ramirez had been given a rich variety of nicknames during the years; *el Diablo* was the one he fancied the most. "He actually presented himself?" He did not add that he saw Ramirez' audacity and self-confidence as a positive sign. "Then what?"

"He said that he and Isabella were on a picnic together, but, unfortunately, he had lost his wallet and could not pay the return fare. The ticket came to a hundred thousand American dollars. Small notes, well used. He must have thought it was funny; he couldn't stop laughing for half a minute."

"Amazing wit. What did you say?"

Vargas made a helpless gesture. "Nothing. I was in shock. Somehow, I did not believe that anything like this could happen." He added with a shrill laugh, "Could not happen! *This is Mexico.*"

"And then?"

"He said that I had twenty-four hours to raise the money, and that he would call back same time tomorrow. That was all. He hung up."

"Can you raise the money?"

"Yes. My father would pay."

"He wouldn't suspect you of being part of the scheme, or behind it, for that matter?"

Vargas looked horrified. "How can anyone think like that!"

"I can."

"You don't really believe…"

"Please. If I can, why can't somebody else? I am trying to be constructive. My whole point is, if your father gets funny, then what do we do?"

"He'll produce the money. He will have the full support of my four brothers. They will do anything for Isabella."

"How will you approach him?"

"I shall have to go out there. I hope I'll find the way," he added with a thin smile.

"It's a hell of a lot of cash, and you need it *before* noon tomorrow."

"That can be arranged."

"Who would you trust to drive you?"

Martin wrote down the name and the telephone number and dialled. Vargas spoke for only a few seconds. "This man is a friend of Ernesto's," he said to Martin. "He's in the limousine business."

Half an hour later, Vargas was on his way.

Martin paced the floor as he meticulously added detail to detail. He was satisfied with Ramirez' limitless confidence in himself, but still uneasy about the sheer simplicity of the man's methods. On the other hand, viewing the scheme from every conceivable angle; the less complicated, the better. Ramirez knew his métier. He knew what he was doing, and he understood to perfection the Mexican culture; the attitude, the mentality and the psychological complexities of a class-ridden society. He knew that the burden of proof would become onerous for the Vargas family and that the will to pursue would disintegrate as they time and again ran into a wall of silence. Nobody would rat on Ramirez; he knew too much, and he could trigger off a landslide that would bury most of his superiors. No, Ramirez was safe, protected by his own. The most likely outcome would be that he collected the money, laughed all the way to a bank abroad and returned to his duties, serving the community.

What if the Patriarch gathered his men and stormed the building? They would not dare to shoot. Ramirez would claim that he and Isabella had been secret lovers for a while, and what the hell was all the fuss about? Had they all gone absolutely *loco*? Did they not understand that an upper-class beauty like Isabella could not possibly be seen with a simple policeman? Would she not be disgraced for life? Of course she would. Have her back, please. End of romance. Word against word. No evidence. Ramirez would walk away with a smile. Within two months, somebody would throw acid in Isabella's face, or cut her up with a knife. Message delivered. Unless, that was, the Vargas family paid him to protect their precious daughter and keep quiet about the affair. No leaks to the press, guaranteed. Just a modest transfer of funds, say, once a year in advance, and harmony and balance would be restored.

Es muy sencillo, Senor Vargas. Este es un asunto serio. El amor es una emocion compleja brutalidad es un problema serio en nuestra sociedad—la moraleja del cuento es muy obvia, si?

Very obvious, indeed. Vargas senior would instantly comprehend that Jesus Ramirez was not as charitable and less of a pacifist than his more famous namesake.

Yes, he concluded, a very plausible plot, and fully within Ramirez' capabilities.

The second alternative was that Ramirez would take the money, kill Isabella and Angelo, set fire to the building and investigate the crime himself. Gradually, the episode would fade; no evidence, speculations only, and there was nothing the Vargas family could do about it—except hiring a top-class assassin and get rid of Ramirez. A small consolation—it would not bring Isabella and Angelo back.

Or maybe Ramirez planned early retirement. He was in his fifties, and this latest coup, added to his previous exploits, would ensure a comfortable future. He could disappear without a trace; Honduras, Guatemala or Brazil. Nobody would ask any questions, and soon el Diablo would be but a bad memory.

Would he take the money and allow them to be found alive a day or two later? Martin did not think so. Not even Ramirez would be that cocky. Vargas might believe so—what else could he believe—but Martin concluded that the likeliest result was two dead bodies and another emigrant.

He rang Ernesto. There was no reply. He went out and got a couple of quesadillas. He came back and dialled Ernesto's number. It rang five times before Ernesto picked up the receiver.

"I need a van for tomorrow," Martin said. "One with a trade name on it, and preferably not too shabby."

Ernesto said, "No problem. Tell me where and when. Anything else?"

"Yes," Martin said and listed a few items.

Vargas came home at half past ten in the evening. He looked grim but less dejected.

"All set," he said and took off his tie.

"Quite an ordeal?"

"You can say that again. My father aged ten years before my very eyes. I almost felt sorry for him."

"Your brothers?"

"Predictable. They went into a rage. It took me an hour to convince them that if I didn't go on my own, Isabella would be either killed or ostracized for life. They finally came to their senses."

"Any concern for your safety?"

"That was not explicitly voiced, I am sad to say." Vargas rubbed his chest and moistened his lips. "You believe that Ramirez will kill me, don't you?"

Martin did his best to look baffled. He said, "No, I don't. You know as well as I do that he is a very shrewd operator. He knows that he would not gain anything by killing you. In his book, it goes without saying that you would not discredit your own sister, and no way would the Vargas family want a scandal. All parts of his calculations. Ruthless he is, but he is also cunning and he is smart. You will be found, give it a day or two. In the meantime he'll have packed his bags and quietly slipped away."

Vargas stared at the carpet. "We shall find out."

"Consider the logic of it," Martin persisted. "Theft is one thing, murder is something entirely different. He knows the power and the influence of your family, and he does not want to spend the rest of his life looking over his shoulder any more than he already has to. It is common sense."

Yes, Martin thought, nothing but common sense, but that does not mean it is going to happen that way. During his long and eventful career, Ramirez had proved himself to be unpredictable. He had killed before. He had an intuitive feeling for expediency, and he never went out of his way to find a complex solution where simple convenience would do.

Vargas came back from the bank at eleven o'clock the next morning. He carried a briefcase. "The burden of money," he said. He breathed heavily and exercised his right hand as he let go of the luggage.

"You are badly out of form," Martin said. He opened the briefcase. "This is not what Ramirez asked for."

"I don't care what he asked for. All in well-used tens and twenties on such a short notice was just out of question. He'll take it."

He certainly will, Martin thought, but he won't be pleased.

Ramirez rang a few minutes past twelve. Vargas listened, nodded and listened again. "Yes, I know where it is," he finally said. "One and a half to two hours." Ramirez added something, and Vargas put the receiver down.

"Well?" Martin said.

"A most respectable area. Very classy."

That meant a house in one of the more affluent suburbs, Martin thought; the owners were away and a well-dressed couple was having an affair and had borrowed the place for a few nights. Ramirez would not have had any problem finding out who were away and the quality of what was available.

He asked, "Where is it?"

Vargas closed the briefcase. "Why do you want to know?"

"Because Ramirez may not bother to inform anybody about your whereabouts. All tied up, you and Isabella will be mighty thirsty by this time tomorrow. Use your brain."

Vargas stroked his moustache and exhaled through his nose. "You are not doing anything stupid...?"

Martin pretended to flare up. "What the hell *can* I do!"

"Come looking if there is no message by six o'clock this afternoon."

"Where?"

Vargas told him. He picked up the briefcase.

Martin waited for ten minutes before he pulled out his map and followed.

Vargas was familiar with the area and the address; a Spanish-style villa of the most elegant design, the pride and joy of some very wealthy people. The gate was closed but not locked. He walked through the luscious front garden and up the stairs. The massive and richly ornate door opened. Vargas stepped inside. He heard the door close behind him and the clicking of the lock.

Ramirez said, "Welcome, Mr. Vargas. Your punctuality is admirable. Please, come in."

Ramirez appeared from the shadows. He smiled and nodded towards the vast open area that was the drawing room. Vargas looked at the face that reminded him of a colourful description of Death Valley. They were of the same height, but Ramirez was prematurely grey. He had piercing black eyes and his mouth was set in a permanent snarl. His thickset body did not prevent him from moving like a cat. He had a tendency to roll his head as if trying to loosen up the muscles in his neck. He exuded a strong body odour, the kind of smell that made Vargas think of a cougar in a cage that had not been cleaned for a while. His moustache was the colour of pewter. The pockmarks on his cheeks were like miniature craters with black edges.

"Where is my sister?"

"She is enjoying herself. Can I help with the luggage?" He picked up the briefcase. "Let us go in and make ourselves comfortable. I shall fix you a drink, Mr. Vargas."

Isabella was standing along the wall. Her right hand was handcuffed to the pillar of a large, carved rosewood cabinet. Vargas could see no sign of violence.

"Would you mind releasing her?" he said.

"All in good time," Ramirez said and showed his uneven teeth. "We are not in a hurry, are we?"

Vargas sat down. He fought hard to keep his calm. "Why don't you take the money and disappear?" he said. "You know we can't talk."

Ramirez' smile radiated insincerity. "That is exactly what I have in mind. I vanish, and you can't talk." He went over to the chiffonier and came back with a glass in each hand. "This is very old Remy-Martin," he said. "Only the best for my clients." He leaned forward as he handed Vargas the drink. Ramirez' jacket was open. Only the sight of the gun was more prominent that his body smell. Vargas managed a smile. He took the glass. He avoided looking at Isabella.

"Allow me to look at the compensation," Ramirez said. He put his glass on the table, knelt down and opened the briefcase. For a moment he stared in disbelief. His face turned the colour of flesh stripped of its skin. "Bloody stupid!" he screamed. "This is not what I told you!"

"It was impossible to meet your demands on such a short notice," Vargas said and met the detective's furious stare. Ramirez rose slowly, pushed his lapels aside and placed his hands on his hips. "You are not very clever," he said. Each word dropped like an ice cube on Vargas' head. "Well, I shall survive, which is more than I can say about you and your sister. I shall now enjoy the generous Isabella's gorgeous body for a while. You will have the pleasure and the satisfaction of watching. Then, the two of you will slowly and painfully leave this world and go to heaven together."

Vargas saw the spittle in the corners of Ramirez' mouth and tensed his body. Ramirez looked at him with contempt. "Don't try anything stupid. Just consider yourself dead. It is easier that way."

"Easy does it," Martin said and took his cupped left hand from his mouth. Ramirez pivoted with incredible speed, whipped out his gun but froze for a split second as he misjudged the angle from where the voice came. Vargas saw the heavy knife going through Ramirez' throat. The tip stuck out at the back of the neck and the gun dropped with a thump onto the floor. Ramirez' hands fumbled upwards before he gurgled and collapsed. He fell heavily on his face.

Martin took the keys from Ramirez' pocket and released Isabella. He pushed Ramirez over on his back, pulled out the knife and wiped it on Ramirez' jacket. Then he went into the kitchen. They could hear water running. He came back and walked across to the door from where he had emerged. He picked up a heavy bag and stopped in front of Isabella. He looked at the dark shadows under her eyes and said, "Are you unharmed?"

"Yes," she whispered and took a step to the side as if losing her balance. He put his arm around her and guided her to a chair. "Drink some of this," he said and gave her Vargas' cognac. "Do it." He steadied her trembling hands when she drank before he turned to Vargas. "You too, Angelo."

Life was coming back into Vargas' eyes. He did not look at Ramirez. "Now what?"

"Do you think you can drive home?"

Vargas swallowed the rest of the cognac. "Yes—yes, I can drive."

Martin measured his friend. "Fine. Drive straight home. Call one of your brothers and ask him to collect Isabella. Call Ernesto's friend and get rid of the car. Thereafter you go down to Agustin's where you sit in the bar till I show up. It won't be long."

Vargas said, "I would prefer to wait at home."

Martin took a step closer to Vargas and leaned forward. He stopped when his face was an inch away. "What you prefer is irrelevant. I want you to be seen. I want *us* to be seen, in public, for a few hours."

"What are you going to do?"

"I am going to attend a funeral."

"We will wait for you," Isabella said. She had regained some of her composure.

"No, you will not. You get the hell out of here as soon as you are able to move."

Brother and sister looked at each other. "He is right," Vargas said.

They got up. Martin followed them to the door. He closed it behind them and stood by the window until the car was out of sight.

He went back into the kitchen. He searched the cupboards and found what he was looking for—a large, cast-iron pot. He filled it with water and switched on the largest of the oven's heating elements. From his bag he took a twenty-five meter long rope, thin but strong, and a five-kilo weight. He tied one end of the rope to the pot and stretched the rope in a straight line across the top of the massive writing desk in front of the windows facing the north end of the garden. He put the other end of the rope through the eye of the weight and adjusted the length so that the weight hung over the short side of the desk, some ten centimetres down. He placed a wooden chair next to the desk, under the weight. He took a thick candle and a holder from his bag and positioned the candle on the edge of the seat of the chair, slightly off-centre of the weight. He tugged gently at the rope. When he was satisfied with the degree of resistance, he pulled from the bag two five-litre cans with petrol. The wastepaper bin under the desk was empty, but he found some paper. He tore it up and filled the bin.

He grabbed Ramirez by the ankles and dragged him closer to the desk before he soaked the bin and the detective with the contents of the first can. With the second can he sprinkled the desk, the curtains alongside the doors and the floor across the room to the wall facing south. With the entrance towards the east and the secluded position of the house, the fire should get a good grip before being discovered.

He washed his hands, tested the temperature of the water in the pot with his finger, lit the candle, put on his sunglasses and picked up his bag.

Out in the garden he waited behind a bush until some children and their nanny had passed. He got into the van and took off his overall before he drove off.

He came into Puente de Alvarado and parked the van outside the San Carlos Art Gallery. He sat there until he spotted Ernesto. Martin left the key in the ignition and slid out of the van. He did not look back. He hailed a taxi, destination Agustin's.

Vargas was only into his second drink, or so he said. He did look sober. Guillermo had collected Isabella. Vargas looked at his watch. Yes, they should be well and truly home, by now.

Brother Guillermo had also insisted on taking the money with him; too late, Vargas had already put the briefcase in his safe. He had told Guillermo in plain words what to do with himself. Vargas would come out the following day and hand over the money to el Padre, together with a summary of what had happened. He had made Isabella solemnly promise ignorance as to the identity of the rescuer. That part he needed for himself. Isabella understood the significance and guessed the purpose.

"What is the purpose?" Martin asked.

"You'll know tomorrow."

"Let us have something to eat."

An expression of genuine pain filled Vargas' face. "How can you possibly...?"

"I am hungry. Keep your thoughts to yourself. We are going to spend a few hours here, and we are going to look perfectly normal. We are here to be seen. We are here to prove that we cannot have been somewhere else. Am I getting through to you?"

"I understand."

"Relax. Ramirez wasn't worth much. Mexico shall be a better place without him. My contribution, so to speak."

"May *Tezcatlipoca* be with you."

"Who?"

"The Aztec god of destiny."

They left four hours later.

Vargas came into the drawing room and found Martin sitting with his coffee and the morning papers.

"Page two," he said and turned the page for Vargas to read.

The article was brief; a property belonging to the well-known Huerta family had burned down last night. The owners were abroad. One suspected an electrical fault. It was a very valuable property, but one assumed that it was sufficiently insured. The police was looking into the matter but did not suspect foul play.

"That doesn't mean a thing," Vargas said. "Somebody could have seen the cars or Ramirez or any one of us, told the police and they are keeping quiet about it of tactical reasons. Irrespective, they may start digging, depending on who is in charge. If they do, they'll find something."

"A barbecued detective, and further investigation guaranteed."

Vargas looked absentminded. He said, "I am paying the Patriarch a visit." He opened the safe. "I should be back in four hours' time. Could you be here—please?"

"Sure," Martin said. Vargas' low-key tone of voice surprised him.

"Could you also get hold of Ernesto? Ask him to drop in tonight."

"Will do," Martin said. "I am going for a walk." He left.

When he came back, Vargas was there.

"That was quick," Martin said.

Vargas seemed to have shaken off his bout of depression. He said with a wry smile, "Yes, a rather brief get-together, I am happy to say. The Patriarch grunted like a wild boar about the money, but he conceded when Isabella gave him one of her glacial looks." He shrugged. "Apart from that, my subtlety-deficient sire made a rather pathetic attempt to thank me without losing his inestimable dignity. Not the easiest of combinations, but then he offered me the one piece of advice that renewed my belief in his otherwise questionable association with mankind. He said: "Get that damned gringo out of Mexico, *pronto*." Following this divine intermezzo, I had a brief chat with my mother and my four brothers, and a good little talk with Isabella, and that was the end of the family reunion. By the way," he added and loosened his tie and undid the top button of his shirt, "I take it that Ernesto was behind the van and your equipment."

"Who else?"

"Yes, who else. Never one to let you down."

"Why was your father upset at getting his money back?"

There was relief in Vargas' laughter. "Oh, but he didn't, you see— not all of it. Thirty-five thousand went missing. You must understand how deeply upsetting this can be for a multi-millionaire. Such people are usually very sensitive souls when it comes to what's holy on this earth."

"You took it?"

"Incorrectly phrased, amigo loco. I deducted commissions due for services rendered. Ten for Ernesto and twenty-five for you. Never do anything *unconditionally*. Remember?" He began pacing the floor. "I am afraid the Patriarch had a point," he said and tried to transform a sigh into a yawn. "Mexico has never been a safe place for you, and as of yesterday your life is hanging on an even thinner thread." He centred on the skyline and shook his head. "If they start digging, which they may well do…"

"I know. Time for a passport."

"I will make the arrangement," Vargas busied himself looking for his cigars. "With the right mixture of grease and pressure we should get you a passport within ten days." He looked at the flame from the matchstick. "I should have got you one a long time ago."

"You owe me nothing. Don't think like that."

A melancholy smile came and went. Vargas said, "Is that a fact?"

"I have to shave off my moustache and get the colour of my hair back before taking a photo," Martin said. He smiled. "I shall need to be in the sun for a few days, tanning the part under my nose."

"You tan quickly," Vargas said. "Let us go for an excursion tomorrow. I'll call Manuel whilst you remove that weasel you call a moustache."

"Aaaah!" Manuel said when they came in, "*completas el rompecabezas?*"

"No, it is not a jigsaw puzzle," Vargas said. "It's a matter of taste."

"If you say so," Manuel mumbled and beckoned Martin to the chair in the corner.

He opened his eyes when Manuel tapped him on the shoulder, signalling that the job was done. "That looks horrible," Martin said.

"Of course it does. All that colouring has done you no good. That is why I cut it short. You'll look fine in a while."

"How long is a while?"

Manuel grinned. "A few years—perhaps."

Vargas said, "Manuel is widely known as Mexico's most unsuccessful comedian. Only his punch line is worse that his timing. You'll be fine in a couple of weeks."

"Do I need to revisit my deposit of tequila?" Manuel asked.

"Too damned late," Vargas said. "We are leaving." He handed Manuel a few notes. "Here, overpaid, as always."

Manuel followed them to the door. "Martin," he said quietly, his brown eyes without the usual smile. "It was nice never to know you and never having seen you. Take care, amigo."

Martin took the Mexican's hand. "Thank you. Same to you."

On the way back they dropped in at a photographer's who Vargas knew and had Martin's pictures taken. Then Vargas insisted on a picture of the two of them together. He did it casually, but Martin knew and did not object.

"I'll have the photos and the negatives in an envelope by tomorrow afternoon," the photographer said.

They walked home. The silence was uncomfortable. Vargas was distant. Martin searched in vain for something sensible to say.

Then he began to think about his future and became preoccupied with his own thoughts.

They sat in the drawing room, staring at very little. Vargas broke the silence.

"You are going to the States, I take it?"

"Yes."

Vargas looked at the pile of books that Martin had amassed, tidily stacked on the floor. "As soon as you've got an address I can arrange for your books to be forwarded. Also, get a bank account, and I'll transfer your money." He scanned the ceiling. "You intend to stay in America?"

"I wouldn't think so. There are other places to see."

Vargas' posture did not change. "It was a most beautiful rainbow, ephemeral by nature and spellbinding for as long as it lasted," he said. "Here I am, a *borracho*, half-heartedly refusing to accept that his thinking is non-renewable and clinging to the theory that one day he will overcome his fear of failure. It is a very attractive theory, my friend, but, as is not unusual in life, ideals have a tendency to get tarnished by expediency. The human element. A new day and another stain becomes visible on the amaranthine blotting paper that our spiritual nonpareils call our soul." He made a hollow sound. "The concept of the free will is certainly alluring, but the fact remains that there is very little in life that we can control. Things happen. In most cases there is nothing we can do about it. Except to adapt, that is. Do I believe all this? Yes, I most definitely do. Subject, of course, to those rare moments of unmitigated bravery when one admits that adaptation is a bewitching euphemism for surrender." He raised his glass. "Please accept my apology. I should have let you have your passport a long time ago."

"Nobody kept me here."

Vargas drank heavily. "Oh yes, I did. I began to see you as my alter ego—the free spirit, the Byzantine mind, the man owing no allegiance to anybody, the one person who's got it in him to be anything he wants to be. That is why I could not let you go. It was as if life had come back to me, partly *with* you and partly *through* you. I even began to dream of the day when I could throw away the shackles and become my own idol; the fearless individual, the epitome of integrity, the artist who had experienced the furnace of heaven and the haven of hell and whose art conveyed it all for the whole world to see." Vargas' ironic little smile was followed by a staccato chuckle. "Just establishing my credentials."

Martin stared at the web of red veins in Vargas' eyes. "You can still do it."

"No," Vargas said wearily, "Not..." He looked away.

Martin said, "Yes, without me." He smiled. "My legacy. Don't waste it."

Vargas pressed the palms of his hands against his eyes. "The world isn't going to get any better, and neither am I. Summed up, I shall continue having one mental miscarriage after another."

"That kind of defeatism is as ludicrous as it is revolting. This is not the way I want to remember you. Publish your book whilst your father is still alive. Show your paintings whilst he is still alive. You found me one step away from the abyss. I do not want to come back and find you at the bottom of it."

Vargas turned his head. A sparkle of life brightened his eyes. "You are coming back?"

"Eventually."

There was a discreet knock on the door.

"Ernesto," Martin said and opened.

Vargas gave a detailed description of what had happened the day before. Ernesto did not interrupt and he asked no questions. Only when he was sure that Vargas had finished did the Indian look at Martin. "You must leave."

Vargas said, "We know. He'll have his passport within ten days."

"Not one day too early," Ernesto said. "The Huerta family will insist on an immediate and full investigation. That means that what's left of Ramirez will soon be found, very soon. Since it is Ramirez, somebody at top level will take over and start probing, if for no other reason than to see what may be in it for himself. Then it takes only a tiny detail, a coincidence, a fluke, and the hounds pick up the smell of the gringo. *Caramba! La libertad es un derecho humano*—but no more for Martin." He raised his hands with his palms up. "This is the end of your Mexican adventure, amigo. *El final*. Stay inside till you get your passport." Then, suddenly, he giggled. "You look funny, gringo. Even funnier than when I first saw you." He took one of Vargas' cigars and began chewing. "Thank you for killing Ramirez. My dream was to do it myself, slowly, but this is second best. After all, I trained you." He nodded thoughtfully. "It is good I can prove that I was somewhere else. My future is in Mexico. Yours is not. I shall always be grateful. Maybe one day you will come back, and we can go to the village where I was born and celebrate among my people Mexican style—yes?"

Martin said, "One day."

Vargas gave Ernesto his money in an envelope which the Indian put in his inside pocket with a brief *"Gracias"* and no further comment.

They reminisced for the rest of the evening. The drinking was only interrupted by the odd nibble from the tray of churritos, enchiladas, tacos and quesadillas that Ernesto had been sensible enough to bring along.

576

Martin licked the rim of his glass more often than he swallowed. He noticed that Ernesto used the same trick. By eleven o'clock Vargas became incoherent. Martin and Ernesto carried him to his bed. "Sweet dreams," Ernesto mumbled and took off Vargas' shoes. He put a blanket over his friend before he looked up and said, "I wish he could control it."

Martin said, "How can you control an addiction without a motive?"

Ernesto's black eyebrows shot up. "An unfortunate fact," he said. "It is sad. He is such a good man."

Martin followed Ernesto to the door.

"*Es difícil decir adiós a los amigos,*" Ernesto said. "So, I say, *for the time being, Martin.* You take care of yourself." He grabbed Martin's arms with both hands before he turned and walked quickly down the stairs.

Nine days later, Vargas handed Martin a one-way ticket to Los Angeles and his American passport. Martin opened it, grinned at the picture over his name and saw that it was stamped departure Los Angeles seven days ago.

"The real thing," Vargas said. "It remains amazing what contacts and money can do. You can now call yourself American—if you so wish."

If I so wish, Martin thought; what other alternatives have I got?

"Or you can use this," Vargas said and held up a second passport. "Except in this country, of course." His smile was strange, as if he was embarrassed, or apologetic. He did not look at Martin.

"A Mexican passport," Martin said. He tried to sound cheerful. "Well, why not have two passports?"

It was stamped departure Mexico three weeks ago. Martin turned the page. He stared at his own picture and under it the name Angelo Vargas and said, "I don't follow."

Vargas shifted in his chair. "I thought—I mean, I presume you'll not use your *original* identity ever again. It came to me that one name is as good as another." He smiled helplessly. "Tauber, Vargas—what does it matter?"

True, in that respect, Martin thought. The snag is, though, I do look distinctly un-Mexican.

Vargas read his mind. "There are fair Mexicans, you know," he said eagerly. "Not many, but they do exist. You have seen them. Their ancestors came from the north of Spain."

A valid point, he agreed silently, and I shall probably grow darker, or grey, as I get older. He said, "What is your real reason?"

The Mexican got up. He put his hands in his pockets and walked the floor nervously. After a while he said, "I do not know how to phrase it."

Martin smiled. Never before had he experienced Angelo Vargas being short on words. "Overcome your shyness and give it your best shot," he suggested.

Vargas stopped pacing. He looked weary and drawn and older than his years. "Live my life for me," he said in a subdued voice. "My dreams are getting faded. My mind can no longer recapture the purity of a new-born thought. The ideals of my youth are but feeble echoes from bygone days. The vision I once had was one of freedom and independence, owing nothing to anybody. I wanted to be the l-liberated spirit who went his own ways and t-took everything in his stride. I wanted to be someone who followed his own mind and his own rules and who did not give in to the self-serving desires of other people and who was not afraid to m-make decisions and live with the consequences. I wanted to be someone who all through his life stood on his own two feet."

He stopped and caressed an Indian statue at the end of a row of books. His shoulders were rounded. "It was just an idea, a—a concept to fill my mind and give me strength, thinking of you roaming the world free as an eagle." He stood there, immobile. Then, abruptly, he turned around. The humour in his eyes was not genuine and the smile under his drooping moustache was forced, as if he had been trapped into listening to a bad joke. "Forget it. Nobody can live the life of another. I do not want you to remember me as a m-maudlin old fool."

Martin had not taken his eyes off his friend. Never before had he heard him stammer. He said, "I'll be proud to wear your name."

He saw the tears in the Mexican's eyes and said, "When do we expect Isabella?"

Vargas blinked. "Oh, late. Ten o'clock, I believe. She does not want to stay."

"Let us go down to Agustin's," Martin said. "If we leave now, we should be back by nine-thirty."

"What if they are circling in on you?"

"They would have been here already."

Isabella came at ten o'clock. She sailed past Martin with a brief nod. They had not seen each other since the day Ramirez went missing.

"Who drove you?" Vargas asked.

"Brother Jorge. He is waiting in the car. I said I'd be down in half an hour." She sat down and rearranged the long, wide scarf that draped her shoulders. She nodded curtly as Vargas placed her drink on the table and shifted her gaze to Martin who had sat down opposite her. "I understand you are leaving tomorrow."

"I am."

Vargas put a glass of Irish whisky in Martin's hand.

The look of defiance did not leave Isabella's face. She said, "Good. Where are you going?"

"Los Angeles."

"And thereafter?"

"I don't know."

"No plans for the future, in other words. Why doesn't that surprise me?"

Martin said gravely, "But I have. I intend to make fifty million dollars within five years and then come back and marry you. By that time your maturity should match your biological age—hopefully."

Isabella's eyes darted for a second. "Very funny. Your sense of humour could have been divine had it not been overshadowed by your primitivity. I shall always remember you as an inadequately tutored primate possessing a limited variety of endearing qualities."

"Thanks to those qualities, you and I are here today," Vargas said. He smiled gently at his sister.

She got busy with her scarf.

Martin said, "It has been nice knowing you, Isabella. Who knows, the three of us may have a rendezvous one day."

Her features softened. "I hope so." Her low voice quivered. "I do hope so."

Vargas raised his glass. "To the future," he said. "May we all find what we are looking for."

They chatted amiably about very little for the next ten minutes. Then, matter-of-factly, Isabella looked at her watch and said, "Time to go, I'm afraid."

They followed her to the door. She hugged her brother and said she'd be in touch. Vargas squeezed her and kissed her hair.

Martin saw the rapid movements of her eyelids. She looked up and took a step closer. Her eyes were moist. She put both arms around his neck and kissed him. "I'll miss you," she whispered. There was a low sob in her voice. She turned and hurried down the stairs.

Martin went back to the table. He emptied his glass in one go and said, "Any more left?"

They arrived an hour before Martin's plane was due to depart. The airport was busy. They had a last drink together. They passed the cafeteria on the way to the passport control. Martin caught a glimpse of Ernesto who got busy hiding behind a newspaper.

"See you, Martin," Vargas said. He tried to sound formal. "Stay in touch." He shook his hand. "You are coming b-back one day?"

"Take care, Angelo. Focus on your future life and cut the chains that keep the eagle on the ground. You do not want to look back with regrets about a mind that promised so much and delivered so little."

He picked up his bag and walked towards the counter.

In Los Angeles he found a small and reasonable hotel not far from the airport. He opened an account in the name of Martin Tauber in a nearby bank and deposited one thousand dollars.

Within a week he had found a storage company for his books. He wrote a letter to Vargas and gave him the details. Ten days later the money arrived. There were no deductions for the passports and the ticket.

Another three weeks passed, and his books were in storage. The management assured him that temperature and humidity were automatically controlled, and, by the way, he could add as many crates as he liked, as long as he paid for them.

This, and a selection of similar experiences, convinced Martin that he had landed in a country where King Mammon was unlikely to lose his grip on his vast and adoring congregation.

Martin did not take to Los Angeles. For the next few years he travelled from border to border and from coast to coast. Sometimes he hitch-hiked with the enormous trucks roaming across the country, but mostly he rode by bus or by train, and occasionally by air. He kept a low profile. His education in Mexico came to good use as he became acquainted with the American way of life.

The big cities proved to be excellent hunting fields, as expected; owners of surplus money were aplenty. The overall level of crime was not much below that of Mexico City, but he found the American carelessness staggering. The number of voluntary displays of greenbacks were impressive and a source of instant revenue as well as amusement. Other people's cash flow situations were enough to give him a respectable standard of living. His capital from Mexico was left untouched, and he dropped burglary from his range of activities. He stayed clear of using cheques. He always dressed and behaved in a way that made him look mainstream and ordinary. At times he was Martin Tauber, and in between he was Angelo Vargas, a visitor from Madrid. The only thing that could be regarded as peculiar was that he carried a stone in his bag, but then, who would ever know.

The thought of extradition had become vague. He no longer believed that the police had discovered what had happened; either Ramirez had been too badly charred, the work involved with the large number of potential suspects had been too off-putting, or—most likely—the case had been rapidly closed out of sheer delight.

His roundtrip ended in Seattle. The beauty of the Pacific Northwest hypnotized him. On his first day he cast one long look across Puget Sound towards the Olympic Mountains, and then another towards the snow-capped Mount Rainier.

He decided to stay for a while. The city was busy enough, but there was an atmosphere of quiet charm, unlike any other place he had seen in the United States.

One day he walked into one of the many Chinese restaurants. The owner sat down and introduced himself as Tommy Chow. He had come from Hong Kong ten years earlier. Following a stint in San Francisco, which he didn't like, he had ended up in Seattle, a most agreeable place.

Chow managed to be both talkative and secretive at the same time. His tales from the Far East were alluring, and Martin's preliminary interest developed into fascination. He became a regular at Chow's. The Chinese enjoyed his one-man audience to such an extent that he one day revealed that he had been a prominent member of one of the most famous and respected Triad groups—just like Chang Kai-shek, by the way. Chow

581

sensed Martin's ignorance and went on to explain what the Triads stood for; their usefulness as part of the free market forces, the rituals, and the rivalry between the various groups. Chow further disclosed that he was a Kung Fu master, and that he also had extensive knowledge of Kempo and Hsing-I. He was, alas, too busy with his restaurant to get much practice nowadays, but he was willing to give him a couple of names and addresses should he ever contemplate visiting the great city of Hong Kong. Chow produced a map and explained what was Hong Kong and what were Kowloon and the New Territories. Over a bottle of rice wine he related the history of the place, its present situation and, for good measure, the future prospects for the next hundred years.

Martin enjoyed Chow's company. The China-man was genial, humorous, hospitable and entertaining. He could never quite decide to what extent Chow fantasized or told the truth, but, thanks to Chow's vivid descriptions, the Far East became like a magnet and he knew that he soon would be travelling across the Pacific Ocean.

Miracles do not happen but coincidences occasionally do, he thought one day when he picked up a newspaper and read an article about the great Japanese martial arts master Ryutaro Kobayashi. There was a picture of the man, a mild and placid face with an enigmatic smile.

He visited the Japanese Gardens and thought long and hard about Kobayashi and the land of the Rising Sun. He went for a three-hour stroll in Lincoln Park. He knew that there were direct routes between Seattle and the Far East. In the afternoon he went down to the ports. At dusk he knew his future, at least for some years to come.

Chow expressed deep sorrow at losing such a devotee, close friend and valuable customer. Martin promised to send a card from Hong Kong. They bade farewell with Oriental dignity followed by a round to four different bars.

Martin made his arrangements. He left the United States as Angelo Vargas, his identity ever since.

He sailed to Hong Kong where he spent fourteen months. Once, he sent a letter to Chow and expressed gratitude for kind and valuable assistance.

Martin's visa claim for Japan was based on profound interest in Japanese culture, with particular emphasis on the history of the Shoguns and a desire for knowledge of Japan's great tradition in the martial arts. He was told that the visa would not be extended, and that he would not be allowed to work during his stay. Evidence of his financial position convinced the authorities that the student should have no problems providing for himself for the permitted period of six months.

Jennifer suddenly realized that Vargas had stopped talking. The sky had turned light blue with a shimmer of red in the east. She could hear the sounds from a city preparing for another day. The light of dawn made the flame from the candles into yellow little cones, minute and unflickering. The scent that had filled the room had become almost unbearably heavy and nauseating.

She did not move. Vargas had closed his eyes, but she knew that he was not asleep. What, where and who else will emerge? she thought; will he reveal more of his soul and add further chapters to his clandestine existence, or had he called it a day?

He got up. Without a word he went into the bedroom. He lay down on his back, facing the ceiling. A minute later he was asleep.

Jennifer followed. She leaned her head against the pillow, folded her hands across her stomach and tried to relax. She turned her head and looked at him. He breathed rhythmically. There was a content, almost mellow expression on his face. His few lines were hardly visible.

An hour later, she had yet to close her eyes. Her mind was in turmoil. Finally, she wore herself out. She could not remember when she dozed off, but it was one o'clock in the afternoon when she woke up. Vargas was still asleep and appeared not to have moved.

She got out of bed, went into the kitchen and made a cup of tea. Why did this happen to me? she thought. Of all the men on this earth, why did I have to run into and fall in love and love this man? How do I explain his life before fatherhood to my children?

Her sigh echoed against the walls and came back and hit her in the throat and she swallowed and shook her head.

The bedroom was quiet. She blew away the hair that fell on her cheeks and tried to ignore the heartbeats that shook her body and filled her ears.

What do I do now, she thought; or, rather, what *can* I do? I knew from day one that *Angelo* was a misnomer if there ever was one, but...

She frowned. Give it time, a voice whispered. Get to know him better. Don't jump to conclusions. Maybe it is not as bad as it all seems at this very moment. After all, you have only seen *part* of the picture, and—think about this—are there no redeeming circumstances? Are you judging the bad you have heard against the good that you have seen? Yes, he is a rare specimen and thank God for rarity, but does that mean he is a monster and nothing else? How would I feel if I told him that, *sorry, but I can't handle you and your past, Angelo*—and he walked away for good? Do I love him any less today than I did yesterday?

She bit her knuckles. No, she whispered, the horrible truth is that I do *not* love him less.

She felt the pain and the pressure building up in her head. She rubbed her eyes. "What a mess," she mumbled. She licked the salt from the corners of her mouth and let her hands fall down on the tabletop.

A movement made her raise her eyes. Vargas stood in the doorway, watching her.

"I'll take you out to dinner tonight," he said. He looked all at ease. There was a cabalistic little smile on his face that she forever wanted to be part of her life. "I will wear my best dark suit."

"You've only got one," she said.

He nodded. "Yes. I have only got one—the best."

She read in his eyes what she wanted to read.

Over dinner, she said, "Do you think we could socialize a bit more? We hardly see anybody. I have friends and acquaintances that I do not want to lose touch with, and from time to time there are congregations at my parents' house when a contingency of Irish relatives comes over. I know you'll like that. Those parties are hilarious, very funny and entertaining."

He did not comment.

"I mean, whom do we see?" she went on. "Yasmin and Tadashi, and occasionally my parents. We should not seal ourselves off completely. You may be a hermit, but I am reasonably sociable and I think we should compromise. Isn't that fair?"

"Fair it is," he said. "The drawback is that I dislike small talk. I am inadequate as a conversationalist. You know that. Meaningless, inane little chatter bores me rigid, and when people start asking personal questions labelled as conversation I rapidly lose interest. That is—" the expression in his eyes changed "—I get irritated and inclined to walk away." His voice got a notch louder. "Why do people have this perverted tendency to probe into your life? Why do they have to delve into your entire biography? Why do they have to *know* everything about you? Why do they behave like leeches, dropping off only when there is no more blood to suck? It is ill-mannered and indecent, for that matter, and I am not going to have any part of it."

His demeanour was calm and composed, but the edge in his voice told its own story. She knew that his temper was getting closer to the surface; the theme had annoyed him, and he was bordering on intransigence.

She said soothingly, "Listen, can't we work out some formula that is acceptable to both of us?"

His eyes followed the silver carving trolley that the waiter deftly steered between tables. "You've got a point. I'll see what I can do. You like people and I do not, but with a bit of take and give it should be possible to find a compromise."

The words were convincing enough, but she did not like his expression of consummate innocence. She had accepted his unpredictability and his wicked sense of humour, but her acceptance certainly did not amount to approval. Perhaps this is what I have to live with, she thought, and—maybe—a small price to pay for possessing the whole packet. Who was without flaws?

After dinner, she asked for a liqueur. She could not understand how he could be so relaxed, so content and at ease after what he had told her the night before. It was as if it had never happened. She watched him through her eyelashes and wondered if his laid-back attitude was due to relief; he had unburdened his mind and shared with her his nightmares. Was that all it took, or was there another dimension? She could appreciate his sense of comfort—if that was what it was—but there had been nothing indicating regrets over what he had done and no compunction with the way he had developed and the course that his life had taken.

An endless series of questions went through her mind. She wanted to know more, but she sensed intuitively that any attempt to explore further would be a mistake. He had told her a lot, more than he had ever told anybody else. She was sure of that, and, patience prevailing, time was on her side. He was iconoclastic, tunnel-visioned and touchy. He responded when she was caring and attentive, and he closed up when she showed signs of being curious or inquisitive.

She put her hand over his and waited till he looked at her. "Thank you for telling me."

He turned his hand without letting go of hers.

24

After half a dozen dinner parties, at two of which her parents were present, Jennifer coldly concluded that her idea of socializing and Vargas' conception of compromise was a recipe for disaster.

"What the hell are you on about?" she said when they came home one evening from a party of twelve. "Have you gone absolutely bonkers? What is the matter with you?"

"I don't follow," Vargas said. He balanced his glass in the palm of his hand. "Could you be more explicit, please?"

"*Explicit*? At the first party we went to, you had invented the *pirko*—remember?"

Somebody had asked Vargas what he did for a living. With considerable forbearance and talent for detail he had explained that he had managed to develop a cross between a piranha and a koi, aptly named the pirko. He now had a very successful fish farm in Yorkshire where he was breeding this magnificent, colourful and only moderately aggressive specimen which he fed on barbecued hedgehogs and exported to the Far East at the practically give-away price of two thousand pounds sterling apiece.

"I remember," Vargas nodded as if he could not understand what had upset her.

"And the time thereafter you had a factory selling plastic igloos to the Scandinavians and were pleased with your share of the market in spite of increasing competition from the Koreans' inferior, cheaper and pastel-coloured designs." Jennifer was livid, so irate that she would not even contemplate sitting down. "Tonight you told Mrs. Shephard that you did absolutely nothing because young Miss Moran had plenty of money and was kind enough to look after you. Tell me honestly, are you surprised that she turned away in disgust?"

"Not at all."

"You told Anthony Pearce never to ask for a banana-split in Japan because it was a euphemism for erection and you said to Dorothy Wallis that people who socialize seven days a week do so to fill the vacuum of their personal life. Another little pearl was that each time you pass a church and hear the singing of hymns it reminds you of a herd of goats giving birth under duress, adding for good measure that priests and vicars are mental gnomes by choice. You've also likened the minds of lawyers and accountants to a fireplace without a chimney and stated that most people being friendly do so to disguise that all they're doing is to scavenge for cheap sympathy. Your favourite seems to be that the vast majority of those sporting a liberal and cosmopolitan halo are as convincing as those who pretend that supporting a charity has nothing to do with self-promotion. You remember all this?"

"Briefly."

Jennifer could feel the perspiration under her hair. She tensed her abdomen and said, "Why are you doing all this? What is your reason?"

"Reason plays only a minor part. It is a matter of temperament."

She wished that the pain in her shoulders would go away. "It is a matter of temperament to be either saturnine or mercenary. Is that what you are claiming?"

"You're close."

His poise began to feel like a burning rash. She went on, "What the hell are you aiming at? You're crazy. The only one who thinks it's funny is Dad, but then a party to him is just an excuse to have one or two drinks too many."

"Thank you. I am pleased that I haven't entirely wasted my wit."

Stay calm now, she thought. Do not explode. Keep the upper hand. Be rational. She said, "It is unfortunate that your substandard jocularity appeals to the rebel in my father." Jesus, she thought, what do I sound like?

"Or could it be that his sense of humour is more refined than that of most people, or that he has kept the divine quality of Irishness that others have lost."

"*Refinement? Irishness?* Don't give me that nonsense. Is there no way you can entertain yourself without being an embarrassment?"

Vargas focused on the drink in his hand.

"Another thing," she sibilated, the words coming fast, "you may well be one of the Almighty's more successful masterpieces of complexity, but not even you can drown your own little farrago of gods and demons, not in sorrow and not in buoyancy and least of all in whisky."

She walked into the bedroom and slammed the door behind her. A few minutes later she heard Vargas' voice, "I would like to talk to you."

No bloody way, she thought. Have another drink, Angelo.

"Please come back. There is something I would like to say."

At least he is polite, she thought and opened the door, but then he always is—until somebody upsets him. "Well?" she said.

She did not see him get up, she only noticed when he ambled lazily towards her and stopped a short yard away. His body was relaxed and he said in a low, husky voice, "Please sit down, Jennifer."

His eyes were void of expression. There was nothing menacing about his posture. She stared back. At this moment I am not his darling lovey-dovey Jennifer, she thought; I am a challenge, and one that I cannot win. He won't harm me, but I'll end up sitting down. How do I get out of this with my dignity intact? She smiled sweetly. "Of course, dear."

She took her seat. I think I have a major problem, she thought. The fact is that Angelo's zany sense of humour appeals to me. My dilemma is that most other people do not appreciate or understand his facetiousness. Is *that* the situation I can't cope with? What a prude I am. How can I possibly have it both ways? How can I be proud of my cranky man at home and ashamed of him in the company of other people? That is neither a quandary nor a paradox—it is a declaration of failure. Sorry, God, but I'm not signing it.

She watched Vargas rearrange the candles so that they could see each other better. He said, "You think that my behaviour is infantile, or, at best, cuckoo?"

She looked away.

Vargas continued, "You are wondering why I seek the company I do when I am on my own, away from home. I see people who have been where I have been. They know that there is more to life than church meetings, pension schemes, social elevation and brilliant children. They know what alcohol and heroin can do. They know what starvation is. They see violence all around. They are familiar with rejections. They do not complain, and why not? Because they have a knowledge that *your lot* only read about, if that. Man is not a rational being, Jennifer. He is not sensible. He is not pragmatic. He is not intelligent enough to analyze, understand and control his existence. He goes through life with his brain embedded in his intestines. Constantly seeping down his throat are the toxins of his religion, an invention worse than any other means of mass destruction he's ever put his mind to. Nothing will change this creature who is capable of so much and who knows so little."

"Sweet Jesus, I have lived my whole life in The Mission. I know the kind of people you are talking about."

"Kind of people. Did you not keep your distance?"

"Dad did not want me to get involved."

"I am not talking about any *kind* of people. I am talking about different situations, different perspectives and different experiences. I am talking about condemnation conceived by ignorance and raised by self-righteousness. *That* is what I do not wish to be associated with. It is one-dimensional, unrewarding, hollow and tedious."

The silence hammered her eardrums. She looked into the flame of a candle.

Vargas said, "I do not want you to feel uncomfortable with me, but I do have a problem with allowing other people to dictate my behaviour."

No, my darling, she thought; that is not a problem, it is an impossibility.

Vargas went on, "I do not think that being unconventional is necessarily synonymous with being offensive. I do not find it inspiring when people show their disdain for predicaments they have never experienced. I am not impressed when I face arrogance where attempted understanding would have been more befitting. Why is it bad form to display a reaction even if it is in an unorthodox way?"

She nodded solemnly. "So, you do not believe that if everybody had your sense of humour this world would have been even more insane than it already is."

"No, I do not. Quite the opposite. People would stop taking themselves so seriously. They would stop trying to be so ludicrously self-important and stop hiding behind a façade of affected self-esteem. They would poke and probe less and go on minding their own business and thereby accepting the entire gamut of live and let live. Wars and hostilities would be regarded as outright stupidity. The desire for conflicts would be so undernourished that the arms industry could not survive. Rather hypothetical, I agree, but so is the notion that everybody can share my sense of humour."

"Isn't that's a bit magisterial coming from a seasoned killer?" She looked down when blood rushed to her head and she realized what she had said.

Vargas showed no sign that he had heard her. He continued, "Priests could no longer make a living. A godsend, to say the least. Most politicians would be professionally dead because, as we know, deeds seldom match words. A bit of a contradiction here, by the way. With my sense of humour nobody would want to become a priest or a politician in the first place. The entire population would acknowledge that it is rather pointless to dig for gold in a salt mine. We would have business-orientated people running the country, and for spiritual solace we would seek to the hills and the forests. Nature would be revered and respected as an ally and not as a source of mindless exploitations."

"I accept that," she said, still smarting from her own comment. "I did not know that you had such thoughts."

Vargas smiled genially. "I am engaged in a detached kind of way." He rubbed his knuckles against the side of his legs and stared past her. "To conclude with my sense of humour, the moment a conversation turns sombre, dull or nonsensical I get bored out of my skin. I believe it is my human right either to divert or to clam up. This, in your opinion, classifies me as socially inept."

She said, "You expect me to accept it whenever it suits you to be outrageous, eccentric or mute?"

"No, I do not. I expect you to make a free choice. Our relationship is based on complementing and not duplicating each other. Different traits and contrasting viewpoints do not make a relationship incongruous. What makes it unbearable and eventually finishes it off is when one party constantly tries to enforce his or her entire attitude onto the other. That is a death sentence."

"Where do we go from here?"

"I shall gracefully decline each time somebody tries to serve me bullshit on a silver platter. Translated, I shall moderate myself sufficiently not to embarrass you. Just bear in mind that I am not super-human."

"Wrong prefix, and skip the *not*. You are an absolutist-human."

"We balance nicely."

She laughed. "Yes, I suppose we do. We'll succeed, won't we?" She put a hand on his shoulder.

"I never questioned that." He touched her hand.

She said, "I am sure I'll grow wiser and more tolerant as I get older."

"May the process accelerate."

She flared up. "That was a horrible thing to say!"

Vargas put his glass to his face and sniffed. "Talking about killings, those who came my way and departed to their heavenly quarters did bring it upon themselves. Whether or not they *deserved* it is in this context irrelevant." He drank. "I am referring to your appropriate allusion about my mortal activities."

Jennifer looked away. "Don't rub it in. I know that if I had been Isabella or Yasmin or Ahmed's daughter—I did not mean to make it sound as if you had appointed yourself jury, judge and executioner. I had no wish to make a moral judgement."

"That is good, because moral has got nothing to do with it. People who live by the law of the jungle have made a choice and should accept that the nature of that law is to get killed as well as kill. There are no excuses, no mitigating circumstances. My impartial conclusion is that not one of them is worth thinking twice about."

"Not one of them," she repeated. "How many?"

He shrugged. "Never mind."

Jennifer looked at him for a long time. His face was impassive.

"Are your nightmares always about your brother and your grandfather?"

"Yes."

"Your victims never haunt you?"

"They do not."

"But you do think about them, from time to time?"

"What are you getting at? My conscience?"

She was taken aback for a second. "Actually, yes—your conscience. I am trying to figure out why it does not bother you."

"That may be difficult for a Catholic."

She looked at the darkness behind the window and counted to ten. "Try me."

"What you refer to as my conscience has its limitations. Unlike religious people, I do not have an artificially developed conscience that paralyzes my mind with shoddily perceived notions about sin, guilt, remorse and fear of eternal condemnation. Conscience, as we know it, is nothing but a concept, a fabricated constellation of superstition and uncritically adopted diktats from those seeking spiritual dominance. If we do have a duty to ourselves, that duty is to use our brain as best we can. If there is a sin on this earth, that sin is to allow our brain to become a badly ventilated piece of sludge, made inactive and powerless because we permit a flimsy abstraction to deplete intellectual independence."

Very calm and oh so composed, she thought, but there is a sharp edge to his voice, an edge I hope is directed at the issue and not at me. His equanimity is the wall shielding the whirlpool inside. My Angelo is a nomad, the eternal wanderer who will never find peace. Would he *want* to be at peace with himself? I do not think so. Is he capable of defining a harmonious mind? I doubt it. And here I am, Jennifer Moran, a genuinely nice and truly Catholic girl, forever linked to a man who is a quarter-cross between an atavism, a wolf, a volcano and a Jesuit in reverse. How come? Whatever happened to decent little Jennifer who suddenly discovered that perhaps she isn't so terribly proper after all? What happened to that prim middle-class creature with her balanced mind and her clear ideas about the good and the bad and the rights and the wrongs of this world?

She pondered for a moment. What was it that Angelo had once said to her: *"Beware of the dualism in you, Jennifer. Denials do not eradicate its existence and acknowledgement is only harmful if uncontrolled."*

Yes, she had been mindful of the conflicts, of the contrasting forces in her soul since her late teens; she had been uneasy forever since and only in the company of Angelo Vargas did she feel that she could truly be herself.

What a seductive little mix-up. One day she blessed him and the next day she cursed him. If this is love, she thought—sweet Jesus, what a wicked joke. But, if it isn't love, what the hell is it?

She said solemnly, "Angelo, may God forgive me, but I'm afraid I love you."

He looked thoughtful. "The reciprocity is more amazing," he said with a gap between each word.

Wide-eyed, she opened her mouth, but no sound passed her lips. More than once had she whispered sweet little words to him; not once had he as much as attempted to intimate likewise, not in Spanish and not in Japanese and not in any other tongue known to man.

She got hold of herself. "Are you aware of what you are saying?"

"Yes."

"Stop drinking, then."

Vargas ground the butt of his cigarette with a slow, deliberate movement. He said, "I'll go for a walk."

Jennifer woke up feeling depressed. She knew that she did not have to open her eyes to establish that Vargas wasn't there. She heard no sound from the dojo; everything was eerily quiet. She got out of bed and tried to remember word by word what she'd said to him. It had been uncalled for. She had chosen a man who was a law unto himself, and her final words the night before had been unwise. He had declared his love for her and she had ruined the moment with a request that was as insensitively worded as the timing was bad. Her judgement had been too harsh and its application way out of line; she had shown herself to be callous and unforgiving in her demand.

Unforgiving. Just like Angelo, she thought with a tired smile, *unforgiving*. Then she realized she was on the wrong track; her state of mind the previous day had everything to do with conformity and nothing to do with anything else. She felt embarrassed because she had found herself unable to cope with Vargas' idea of how to entertain himself, with his stonefaced account of how he had managed to make an improbable scheme workable and then profitable. It had irritated her that he did not seem to care whether or not his audience believed him, and, perhaps not least, his indifference to the probability that some people could begin to consider him an oddball that didn't fit in.

Where do I go from here? she thought. Am I really trying to change him? That would be such a fatal mistake that I can just as well say goodbye now. One point is that Angelo will never turn into a conformist, and a second point—do I want Angelo Vargas as he is and for what he is, or do I want a hybrid, a fabricated prototype, half Vargas and half the housetrained Wilkinsons of this world, the crossbreed between a piranha and a koi? She began to giggle. It was quite funny, come to think of it. Why on earth had she not taken it in good humour and just shrugged off the episode instead of perceiving it as unacceptable social behaviour? I do have a few things to learn, she mused, and the first thing I've got to do is to get rid of my tendency to righteousness. I chose this man. I virtually handpicked him. I know more about him than does anybody else. Beyond a shadow of a doubt I know that I cannot imagine my future without him. If he walks out, my existence will become one endless, horrible ordeal, and I will forever keep looking for him every yard of the way.

And yet—as the father of my children... dear God, stop confusing me.

Nightmares. Since he had told her, Vargas had slept peacefully. That wasn't to say that it was going to last. There were still moments when she wondered if his occasional distant look masked a melancholy he would not or could not admit to. She did feel as if she had helped, in a way, and the thought was comforting, and it was attractive. The death of his brother and his grandfather, the only two people he had ever loved, and the circumstances of those losses caused his nightmares.

His nightmares had nothing to do with those he had killed.

In the short space of time since Vargas had opened up, Jennifer had come to believe that he was unaffected by the killings. He had done what he had to do, and that was all there was to it. His six or seven victims—the ones she knew about—were scumbags of no value. They had no justifiable right to exist, and no unprejudiced person could deem their demise a loss to mankind. Her Angelo had no problems with burning his bridges and never looking back.

I do not have an artificially developed conscience.

Her thoughts began to circle around her present situation; last night's unfortunate finale, Vargas gone and she sitting there without the faintest idea where he was and when he would return—assuming he did. He did spend a lot of time at home when she was at work, reading and making notes, but he also went out and she had no clear idea where he went and what he did. He didn't pay much attention to his shops, that much he had revealed. He did go on his own—always on his own—to casinos, dogtracks and racecourses, but it was not habitual. The night before he had told her that he sometimes saw people who had been where he had been. The definition of those people had been clear enough, and Jennifer believed that she understood what he meant. What she did not comprehend, or even grasped at the fringes, was what he could possibly gain from the company of addicts, gamblers, academic dropouts, ex-mercenaries, alcoholics and a diverse selection of has-beens. Why, she asked—how can these people contribute? Could the reason be that he did not have to pretend, in such surroundings; he could be his rough and unconstrained self and not be burdened with the presence of his tender and delicate partner? Perhaps, she thought, perhaps we all know each other only by the people that we shun.

She lit a cigarette and opened a window. It wasn't altogether unthinkable that he was unable to disassociate himself from the low-life of his past. Partly, she thought, but not the entire reason. There had to be something else, a factor or an element that stopped him from taking a step closer to her world. There wasn't much wrong with his brain—at least not in that respect—and throughout his life nothing had prevented him from doing what he wanted to do.

She searched in vain for a clue until a headache set in.

No, she thought; all this surmising—it isn't worth it. Today is Sunday and I am beginning to feel miserable. He's *got* to talk to me, whenever he shows up. I now know that he *can*, if he wants to.

She invited herself to lunch at her parents' and took a long, relaxing shower. With the water streaming down her face, she let her mind flow.

Jennifer gasped and stood still. "Jesus Christ in heaven," she whispered. "Why did I not think of that before? If this isn't inspiration, what is?"

She came around the corner and saw that the lights were on.

Vargas was sitting in his chair reading. "Hello," he said. "Welcome home."

She did not take off her coat and sat down opposite him. She said, "There is something I must ask you."

"Yes, dear."

"I am serious. I know your enthusiasm for questions, but I think— I believe that in fairness to both of us I have a right to know."

He closed his book, "Know what?"

"Are you bored?"

He placed the book on the side table. "Why do you ask?"

"Because I believe you are."

"Based on what?"

Oh God, she thought, not another endless mental duel. She said, "Because of the way you conduct your life. Because you are capable of more than playing cards and betting on horses and conversing with life's rejects."

He looked at her the way he had done when she first saw him, an inscrutable mask showing no emotions and his eyes expressing only impersonal curiosity. That day, she had mistaken his attitude for indifference; now, she knew that this was his way of protecting himself against an emotional booby trap, of telling the world that he could not be fazed.

"Please, Angelo."

"A bit," he said.

"Why don't you do something about it?"

A line appeared between his eyes. "I can't."

She took off her coat. "Why not? What is the problem?""

He left his chair. "Do you want a drink?"

"No, I do not want a drink. Nor am I dropping the subject."

She waited till he was seated. "I am not dropping the subject," she repeated.

He sipped twice. "My career is not over yet," he said evenly. "Until that happens, it is not easy to unwind."

The answer threw her. "Your career?"

"Yes. There is one more assignment before Tadashi and I can retire."

She did nothing to curtail her sigh of frustration. "Why don't you just get it out of the way, then?"

"We do not decide the timetable."

"You mean you have no idea?"

"I have an idea. Within two years."

"*Two years?*" She slumped back in her chair. She felt exhausted and depressed. "Is there nothing you can do about it?"

"Nothing." His eyes were no longer friendly. "No further questions."

She got up. "Just one. Can we not try to get a bit more out of our life together?" She walked across, put her hands over his eyes and kissed him. "Please try."

25

ordon Gilmore had done the ranks. Fifteen years ago, he had
established his own firm; duly appointing himself proprietor,
chairman and managing director.

Gilmore had pride in his profession. With a nose for business added
to skills, finely honed instincts, useful experience from a former life in
Scotland Yard and a sharp eye for human weaknesses, his firm had grown
from one to thirty-five employees during the years. He had a rich variety
of national and international contacts, and already as a child in the
streets of Manchester had he learned that the world was a market place
where everything was for sale; it was only a question of price, and,
sometimes, of methods.

Gilmore dressed smartly. He knew how to behave and when to speak.
He also knew when to keep quiet. A thoughtful expression, grey eyes
beaming with interest, a sympathetic nod, eyebrows indicating doubt
when appropriate; he knew the game inside out, and he played it to
perfection.

Possessing such priceless qualities, he hardly ever failed to produce
results, simply because he knew after a few minutes with a potential
client whether or not a satisfactory outcome was achievable. If he didn't
think so, he courteously recommended a competitor, usually under the
umbrella of costs, expertise and specialities.

The lady who had called had been brief. Gilmore had no idea what
she wanted. He got up when he heard a knock on the door. He adjusted
his cufflinks, buttoned his jacket and put on a concerned smile.

The moment Jennifer strode in, Gilmore thanked his Baptist God
for not having delegated one of his sidekicks to take care of the
lady's problem. She was stunningly beautiful, with a determined but

reserved look. He knew instinctively that only a star performance would do.

"Miss Moran," he said in his most silken voice. "Please take a seat."

"Thank you."

"Coffee? Tea?"

"No thank you."

He sat down. She does not look uncomfortable, he thought, just resolute in a quiet kind of way. He had seen them before, the steely ones with an abacus for a brain and with the mind of a barracuda. There was nothing and nobody he could not handle.

"What can I do for you, Miss Moran?"

Jennifer told him in clear and precise words within one minute.

"A somewhat unusual request, I dare say," he mused. "I…"

"Too complicated?" she interrupted and smiled.

A decade ago Gilmore would have blushed, but he swallowed the neatly executed insult with a slight wave of his hand and a disarming grin. He said, "I appreciate that you are not in the habit of wasting time. All I can say is that I would be more than happy to give it a try, but, due to the nature of your request, I cannot guarantee the outcome. Nobody can, as I am sure…"

"I do not recall having asked for guarantees," Jennifer cut in. "It is either obtainable, or it is not. I do realize that if it isn't, then there is nothing you or anybody else can do about it." Her discreetly made-up lips parted sideways. "Due to the nature of my request."

This one wasn't born yesterday, he thought. He said, "Very true. If I can't do it, nobody can."

"Modesty becomes you, Mr. Gilmore." She put her business card on the desk in front of him. "When can I expect to hear from you?"

"Let me see—" he paused and scribbled on a pad "—yes, eight days from today. Would that be all right?"

"Fine," Jennifer said. "How much do you want in advance?"

Gilmore made his calculations, looked up and said, "May I ask for six hundred pounds, if that is all right with you."

She wrote a cheque and extended her hand as she got up. "Thank you."

"Thank you, Miss Moran. I sincerely hope I can produce. It is obviously important to you, and I…"

"Goodbye," Jennifer said and walked out.

Christ Almighty, Gilmore thought, what an ice-maiden. I'd rather end up in a bed of stinging nettles than in a four-poster with a prude who'd make Joan of Arc appear obscene.

In the early afternoon of the eighth day, Jennifer's assistant announced that a Mr. Gilmore was on the phone. She listened for a good half minute and then she said, "I can be there by four o'clock."

She took a taxi to his office, listened politely for a few minutes to his story of how and why he had succeeded, the discretion required and so expertly executed, and, by the way and most regrettably, the costs had exceeded his original estimate. If she wanted a full breakdown, he would of course produce one. She asked for his final statement and wrote another cheque. She thanked him politely for what he had done.

By that time, Gilmore had abandoned all hope of a dinner celebrating his feat. He watched her elegant movements as she left and thought it a shame that the spiritual occupier of such a magnificent body should happen to be a frigid soul.

Jennifer continued her journey and reached her destination a couple of minutes before closing time. She accepted reluctantly that if ten days were required, so be it. She left her business card behind and went home.

The day came. Jennifer arranged the object against the back of the sofa, facing the door to the entrance hall. She lit two heavy candles and placed them on the coffee table. She rearranged and adjusted the angles till she was satisfied with the result.

She did not know when Vargas would show up, but it was getting dark and she did not think he'd be far away. She never had the advantage of being pre-warned; he did not use the lift, and she would only know when she heard his keys in the door. There were times when she could have done with the extra minute or so, something the noise from the lift would have given her, but the stairs were part of his exercise program. She knew that any objection would be ignored, apart from sounding ridiculous.

She went over to the windows facing the square and looked down. Her face was in shadow. She knew that she could not expect to see him from where she stood, but this was the spot she was going to use when he came in.

She looked briefly at the clock only to admit seconds later that she had forgotten what it had told her.

What she could see of the square was empty, but she sensed that he was close by. She could hear the pounding of her own heartbeat. Her temples were throbbing and she felt dehydrated except for the palm of her hands.

She heard the turning of the key. The door from the hallway opened. The light fell on Vargas' face. She could see no visible reaction.

For an eternity he stared at the portrait of his grandfather. Then, slowly, he walked across. He knelt down on one knee and continued to stare.

She wanted to say something, anything, but no word came to mind.

Vargas got up. He turned away from her as he did so. His walk towards the bedroom was strangely apathetic, almost sluggish.

Jennifer remained by the window. She let some minutes pass before she moved closer.

Through the door she could hear him trying to face the sudden appearance of his past.

Shortly before midnight he came out. He looked jaded but composed in a manner that told her that his self-control had taken command. He kept staring at the window through the darkness and towards a world far away.

She began to struggle with the silence. She felt physically and emotionally exhausted, drained to the point of overwhelming fatigue.

She said, "The photograph was not in a very good condition, but I had it restored and enlarged. I thought that a hand-carved wooden frame would be—would be nice."

Still, he did not speak. Please say something, she thought, please talk to me.

Vargas got up. He crouched in front of her. He placed his hands on her thighs.

"Thank you for coming into my life, Jennifer," he said quietly. "Nothing nicer has ever happened to me."

The picture stayed on the sofa for two days. On the third day, when she came home, it was hanging over the door to the dojo.

During those three days Vargas appeared not to have touched a drop of alcohol.

Jennifer began to sense a cautious optimism; could it really be that she had found the magic formula? He had re-lived his nightmares with her. He had allowed her into his past. The fact that he had opened up could only stem from confidence in her—trust blended with affection. It was not his greatest forte, showing affection, but she felt that she was beginning to know him; she believed that her ability to read him was making progress.

Weekend came, and she cursed herself for not having been more realistic. I should have known better, she thought with a tinge of bitterness as Vargas went on a two-day binge. His thirst seemed unlimited, and his consumption shocked her.

What made it worse was that he maintained his training; each morning he went for a run, followed by at least one hour in the dojo. He came out dripping with perspiration, had a shower and only then did he eat something, but less than in the past. His appetite seemed diminished, and no wonder, she thought, with his liver working overtime on alcohol.

Jennifer began to despair. Nothing had changed, except the pattern of his drinking. He had from one to five dry days, and then he plunged, all the time keeping up his rigorous physical program.

It can't last, she concluded. He is going to have a heart attack. Nobody can mis-use his body to such extent and survive.

One day she said to him, "What are you trying to do to yourself, Angelo? Why are you so hell-bent on drinking yourself to death? Is it me you hate? Tell me, what is the reason? There must be *something* that is bothering you. Just spell it out to me so that I know where I stand."

His indifference infuriated her. "Why the hell don't you answer? Talk to me! What is the matter with you?"

He lit a cigarette and filtered the smoke through his teeth. "It helps me to keep the world three feet away."

"Oh, really. And that is necessary, is it? Tell me, then, what is it you can't cope with?"

"Nothing," he shrugged. "It is the way it is. Keeps the balance, so to speak."

"Nothing," she repeated, exasperated. "*Nothing* makes you drink as if tomorrow was two weeks ago. How bloody illogical and contradictory can you get.? You are hiding, and when you are not hiding you are running away. Are your demons in such majority that you have given up fighting them? Where are your gods, Angelo? There must be *some* left. What is it that prevents you from analyzing your predicament? Where is the Angelo that came into my life with his eyes open and his spirit intact?"

His eyes followed the smoke as it slowly ascended and disintegrated.

She continued, her voice rising, "I don't care what people call it; an illness or a chemical addiction or whatever glossy little label designed to take the stigma out of an intentional dependency because *that* is all it is. How do I know? I know because some people have the character to quit. They use what is left of their brain and their guts and call it a day whilst there still is time. They make a *deliberate decision* and return from a simulated existence to a meaningful life." She inhaled sharply. "Think of what drinking does to you. Think of what it does to *us*. Also, if you have a spare moment, think of what it does to *me*."

He looked as if he was close to falling asleep.

Jennifer's face was drained of emotions. She pressed her fingers against her eyes. The vibrancy in her voice had gone. "Angelo, nothing is solved by silence. If we cannot communicate there is no point in continuing this relationship. I am not asking that we bare every corner of our souls, but I do ask for trust in each other. There will always be a moment when we need to confide and then it is good to know that the other is there. A relationship either progresses and becomes deeper and more harmonious, or it becomes tired and meaningless. Pick your choice. I know which one I want."

The ash on Vargas' cigarette was getting long.

She raised her head. "From desolation to indifference is not far. I am sorry if I make a relationship sound like a maintenance program, but in one way that's what it is."

He quenched his cigarette in his drink. "I am going for a walk," he said and left.

The emptiness was worse than the silence, and the silence was total. She began to shake. She went into the bedroom and stared at the mirror, at a face rigid with tension and eyes small and lifeless. This cannot continue, she thought, it just can't go on. He is killing us. Whatever there is between us is slowly being suffocated and soon it shall be extinct. I can't take much more of this.

She walked into the kitchen and sat down at the table. She rested her head in her hands and tried to calm down. Why did nothing add up? She loved him and he knew that she loved him. They loved each other. A man like Angelo Vargas would not live with a woman for whom he had no affection. He would not strip his soul for her. The physical attraction between them was strong and vibrant. Most of the time, their talks were captivating and spiced with his wicked observations. His humour had become blacker and the drops of vitriol fell heavier and more often than before, but not to a point where she found it unacceptably offensive.

But that was in private. What would happen if he decided to shed what little was left of his facade and he began to perform even worse in public? She had an uneasy feeling it was a question of time. The world was so obviously his enemy, and it had become equally evident that taking prisoners was a non-existing inclination.

Vargas had become a time bomb. She did not know why and she had no idea how to defuse it. He no longer had the same iron-grip on his temper; there were movements that spoke their own language and flashes in his eyes that could not be misinterpreted. Once, he had put his fist through a wardrobe door. He muttered words in a tongue she did not understand, but blessings they were not.

He was bored, he was frustrated, he had shown signs of depression and soon he could lose his rudder altogether.

But the big *WHY* still remained unanswered. I know the effect, she thought, but the cause is buried within him. I have seen the turmoil; I live with it, for God's sake, but how can I assist when he does not help me to find out where to start? Perhaps the whole thing is beyond me, even if I did know. The price for the life he has led and what he has been through is beginning to show; he is breaking down, and one day there will be nothing left to repair.

Why should it have to end like this? She loved him. Never again would she find another Angelo Vargas, and now he was drifting further and further away from her. He had become self-destructive, and the ultimate result was the ruination of their relationship.

Now what? she thought. Do I just give up? Is there no glimmer of hope somewhere on the horizon, not the tiniest little spot of blue sky somewhere high above? Are Angelo and I doomed? Were we really meant to go this way? Somehow, I cannot believe that. Only once in a lifetime do you find someone with whom you want to share everything, and then it all collapses because one is trying and the other is not.

Maybe that is the answer; we were not as perfect as I thought because somewhere along the way Angelo lost the key that would allow me to enter and face his tormented soul.

Jennifer sighed and shook her head. No, he had not lost the key. If he had, he could not have told her what he did. There was something else, another reason—or the absence of a reason. She frowned. What had he said about his Mexican friend—*how do you get rid of an addiction without a motive?* But the Mexican had not been short on motives. He had talents as a writer and a painter, and, from what she understood, he badly wanted to prove himself.

Hold on, now, she thought. Not so fast, or I'll end up mixing reason and effect and cause in the same pot. The Mexican's problem was not doubts about his talents; it was fear of failure, and that fear had been conceived and born and raised by and within himself. Deep inside he had created a dungeon, and in that dungeon the fungi grew in a darkness engendered by the shadow of the father.

Angelo's situation was more complex and less transparent. There were no loose ends she could think of. The picture of his grandfather had not had the desired effect; if anything, the problem had worsened.

Thank you for coming into my life, Jennifer. You are welcome, Angelo, don't mention it. What about *you* coming into *my* life? Why is it that what we have between us is not sufficient to drag you away from the abyss and bring into the open your qualities as a human being? Why do you keep your emotions imprisoned, shackled and starved?

She sat still for a long time. Her mind went zigzag and in circles and in straight lines as she tried to find an answer or an opening, or— if everything else failed—perhaps an omen from nowhere or from God, it did not matter; a revelation that could lead to a cue, enabling her to widen the gap between the brick-wall and the door of his cell.

I need to talk to somebody, she reflected. She sensed a patience that surprised her. I need to talk to someone with sufficient insight to shed light on aspects hitherto hidden from me.

Uncle Igor? A wise man, experienced and understanding and sympathetic, but could he possibly identify with Angelo? She did not think so. Her mother? In spite of an improved atmosphere her intuition remained the same; Kathleen still saw Angelo as a well-mannered, erudite but primitive pagan. She knew and accepted that

Jennifer loved him, but she failed to understand the devotion, if not the chemistry.

Her father? She knew the answer. His vast knowledge from decades of involvement had produced the conviction that there is no help for someone who does not want to help himself. *Motivation, Jennifer*—but she already knew that.

Tadashi? Nobody had known Angelo longer than Tadashi, but that did not necessarily mean that the Japanese would talk. Would Tadashi feel that he betrayed Angelo by becoming part of a highly personal and intimate situation? Probably.

Wearily, Jennifer rubbed her eyes and stopped abruptly as the image of Yasmin flashed by. Yasmin had never concealed her fondness of Angelo. She would stretch herself to the limit if she thought she could help.

The idea of involving someone else made her feel uncomfortable, but she knew that she was running out of options, bar walking out. As long as there was one single ray of hope she wasn't going to give up. I do love the bastard, she thought, and neither heaven nor hell is going to stop me. I can rescue the wreckage. I can build an indestructible foundation and we can live together and love each other and become inseparable forever more. All that is missing is how and where to start— a dinky little detail to which I shall soon have the answer. I *will* have the answer. Oh yes, my beloved Angelo, her thoughts went on as she got up from the table with a twisted smile; it isn't over yet, but do not ask me why, you screwed-up shit-head. At present moment you do not deserve to know what I feel for you.

Jennifer filled the bathtub and sprinkled the water with exotic herbs that Yasmin had given her. She lay with bubbles up to her nose until she began to feel sleepy. She got up, dried herself and draped a towel around her shoulders.

She walked into the dojo and stood in the centre. She faced the stone that was the altar on Angelo's shrine. Her sense of dejection was gone. She was not happy, she wouldn't go that far, but she was at ease.

The rays from the sun played with the facets of the dark granite. She went closer and eyed the stone from different angles. Remarkable, she thought, I am sure there are streaks of silver in that piece of rock. That is reassuring. It matches Angelo's head.

She walked out, closed the door and looked up at the portrait. "Give me a hand, Grandpa."

They met at the Connaught. Jennifer had briefed Yasmin over the telephone. She had no desire to circumvent the issue. Yasmin had listened without making any significant comments.

Jennifer was early. She ordered a glass of white wine and tried to concentrate on her situation in a positive and constructive manner. She was going to get straight to the point.

When Vargas had come home the night before, he had been even more distant than usual, so remote that she had asked herself if the gap between them was now so huge that any meaningful contact was no longer feasible. She had known for a while that he wasn't the embodiment of a cuddly teddy-bear; in their day-to-day life he rarely showed his affection by touch, by a pat or a gentle stroke—most of the time it simply did not seem to occur to him—but, of late, he could just as well have been physically absent. They had spoken a few words about very little. He had ended up in his chair, surrounded by candles, his mind and his eyes focused on a black hole somewhere in his private universe.

She had resorted to a rare sleeping pill and gone to bed.

"Hello," Yasmin said. The waiter pulled out her chair. "What a splendid idea. Yes," she addressed the waiter, "same for me, please." She turned to Jennifer. "You look awful. Where has all that Irish beauty gone? Drowned in the sea of love?"

"I knew you would be helpful," Jennifer said.

Yasmin smiled. The expression in her dark eyes was warm and compassionate. "That is why I am here, apart from the mere pleasure of your company." She thanked the waiter and let him out of earshot. "So, Angelo is drinking himself to death. I take it that you don't mind plain language." She lit two of her colourful cigarettes and gave one to Jennifer.

"Thank you, Yasmin. Please be direct."

"I will." Yasmin observed the smoke that seeped from her tiny nostrils. "As you evidently are aware, it is the drink that oils the locks on the door behind which a very different Angelo resides, locks that easily can spring open and allow the dragon to break free and spit his fire on anything and everybody coming his way."

Jennifer said, "I am beginning to see that." Her voice was flat. She averted Yasmin's eyes.

"Why is it that one drink for him is like feeding a shark with one sardine? How do we make him understand that he is not a shark? He is half man and half dragon. This much he does know, but we must make him *appreciate* his predicament. How? *That's* the question, Jennifer. That, and how to make him comprehend that no genie can survive forever in a bottle. Those are the bones of contention. Really, all we have to do is to get him to open his eyes."

"Is it? I never knew."

"The moment you know how to do that," Yasmin went on, ignoring Jennifer's sarcasm, "no more problems."

Jennifer could not believe her own ears. "Am I supposed to take this seriously?" she said and tried to hide her irritation.

Yasmin studied the tip of her cigarette. She said, "You should, because that is the vital question—the *only* question—and then the answer is not as complicated as you think it is."

"I am relieved."

"That is good to hear. Another truth, whilst we're at it, is that you have become mentally and emotionally short-sighted. You are allowing one single tree to obscure the entire forest, to use one of the more intelligible English aphorisms. Tell me, why do you think Angelo drinks?"

"If I knew that I would not be sitting here."

"Try again."

"Because he can't solve his conflicts."

"In what way?"

"In what way?"

"That's what I said."

"I—I don't know." Jennifer looked helplessly at Yasmin who smiled over the edge of her glass.

She said, "Look at it this way—has it ever crossed your mind that Angelo believes he is not *worthy* of you?"

"I do not think like that," she said and regretted the indignation in her voice.

"You ought to. *He* does. Let me tell you something else—surprise or no surprise—Angelo has a deeper insight into himself than has any other man I know of. He is fully aware of what he is. He is not blind to the destructive forces that lurk below the surface, and he acknowledges the dualism and the ambiguity. This knowledge has not destroyed him. It may sound strange in view of what the two of you are now experiencing, but Angelo has kept his mental and emotional equilibrium to an extent that does not equate with what he has been through. Self-imposed or not is irrelevant. He has concluded that his character and his nature do not meet with the criteria that he once himself set for being worthy of his ultimate woman. He found her, he found his shrine, but only to discover that he does not possess the qualities required being its guardian. He believes he is undeserving, and, at the same time, he is acutely aware of the irony, a paradox that gets fogged over when he immobilizes his consciousness with alcohol." Yasmin bit at the tip of her little finger and let go of her stare for a second. "The danger is that alcohol also has a tendency to strip away the constraints that keep the darker forces under control." She watched Jennifer's pale face. Her hands trembled when she fiddled with the bracelet Vargas had given her. "Those are the realities," Yasmin went on. "From these realities we shall extract a solution."

Jennifer's breathing was uneven. "I can't win—that's what you are saying, isn't it?"

"I said exactly the opposite. I said that there is a solution. Now, you think about it whilst we're having lunch. I am hungry."

She seems so carefree and happy, Jennifer thought. She has known Angelo since she was a child. She is aware of his problems and she is certainly familiar with his nature. Both she and I concede that he believes he needs his measure of Irish firewater in order to keep what he perceives as a dreadful world three feet away, and, at times, to anaesthetize his inhibitions.

Or, could it be that even someone as shrewd as Yasmin fails to distinguish between what Angelo is and what he purports to be? Do I, after all, know him better, and, if not, how come she seems so convinced that he possesses the emotional capital needed for us to survive? Only the other day, after his second drink, I said to him, "*Don't you think that life is short enough as it is? Why accelerate the process?*" He completely ignored me. He is a walking time bomb with both the battery and the detonator locked in that brain of his. He once said that the key to freedom is inside us. He is the freest spirit I have ever known; yet he cannot or will not show me that key. He lives in a twilight world of his own, and, frankly, I don't think Yasmin knows what she is talking about.

Only God understands why, but I prefer to believe that Angelo is not an iconoclast on purpose. I agree that we are all entitled to our little insecurities, but how does this observation beget any explicable vindication? Where is the answer and what is the remedy? I hope that Yasmin's solution isn't something as banal as *it is either the bottle or me.*

Jennifer struggled with her food. She put her knife and fork down and said, "Do you know that however much Angelo drinks, there is a section of his brain that stays sober and rational?"

"I know," Yasmin said without looking up. "He's a freak."

Constructive, Jennifer thought. She said, "I am going to suggest that we buy a house in the country. Correction—I am going to *insist.* I think he needs to get away from the city."

"Good thinking. He is fond of nature. Walks, other animals, the tranquillity—it can't possibly do either of you any harm. I think that's a very sensible decision."

"Don't say it," Jennifer mumbled, "I know full well that moving does not leave the problem behind."

"Of course you do, dear. What I mean is, planting him in the middle of nowhere could be conducive. After all, he does prefer pigeons and dogs to human beings."

"Conducive to what?"

Yasmin looked forlornly at her empty plate. "I could do with some pudding."

"Conducive to what?" Jennifer reiterated.

Yasmin gave a small shrug. "It was a notion that struck me when I persuaded Tadashi to settle for a life in the wilderness." She smiled and tapped her glass with her ring. "A bit more than a notion, actually. You see, it is an age-old Oriental belief that rural life enhances the growth of a man's quotient of moral fibre. Did you know that?"

"No, but I wouldn't dispute it."

"Shall we have coffee?"

"Coffee would be nice."

Yasmin gave her instructions; seemingly unaware of the waiter's undisguised infatuation. When he reluctantly left the table, she said, "Women should not be so willing to compromise, you know, so wilfully blind in their devotion. As Tadashi says, you can't make a marathon winner out of an one-legged geriatric. Quite clever, that one."

"You just lost me."

"What he means is that women should be more assertive, not

necessarily aggressive, but definitely assertive. They should make their point clearly and more often. They should stick to their guns and make a man acknowledge that a partnership does not consist of him and his shadow. If the potential and the qualifications are there, an assertive woman makes it a winner. If those factors are not there—if it's one-legged—don't waste your time. You follow?"

"That is a charming parable," Jennifer said and smiled grudgingly. "Tadashi certainly has his recipes sorted out."

Yasmin looked pleased. She said, "Yes, not bad for a Nipponese."

Jennifer said, "There is another problem. Angelo said that his career isn't over yet. I have a feeling that it bothers him."

Yasmin added a shaking of her head to her look of innocence. "Did he elaborate?"

"No. All he said was that he and Tadashi had one more assignment coming up, whatever it is, and that it could take another two years before they can retire."

"No details?"

"None. That was all he said, really. What has Tadashi told you?"

Yasmin set her lips and looked pensive. "Same thing. I am not overly worried, though. Tadashi has solemnly promised not to accept another one, irrespective of pay or perks or whatever else they'd throw at him."

"They—?"

"The clients. Tadashi has never been too specific with details, and I must admit that I'm not all that interested."

I do not believe you, Jennifer thought. Your denial is not plausible. You and Tadashi are too close for that.

Yasmin said, "Let's get back to Angelo. Another two years of frustration does not lessen the problem, does it? Time is not on your side. You have to take the initiative."

"How do I do that?" Jennifer said. She tried to dismiss from her mind that they were walking in circles. She did not avert her gaze.

The sincerity was back in Yasmin's eyes. "There is only one answer, and that is one single, simple little display of strength and courage." She picked up her gold lighter and weighed it in her hand. "Make him *want* to stop drinking. Convince him that you love him. Pledge that you complement each other, and *that* you do by rooting out the fatal misconception that he is not *worthy* of you."

A wan shadow passing for relief crossed Jennifer's face. Jesus, she thought, I don't believe this. What a waste of time.

"Is that all?" she said and heard the irony in her own voice. She knew that her lips were quivering and her smile a meaningless grimace. She wanted to get up and leave.

Yasmin reorganized the cutlery. There was a smile on her face. She placed her forearms on the table and leaned forward. "Listen to what I've got to say," she said in a hushed voice. "Let me convey something for your ears only—"

Jennifer began her search for a property. She took out a subscription on *Country Life* and contacted all the large estate agents dealing with the Home Counties. She told them in no uncertain terms what she wanted, and would they kindly avoid filling her mailbox with anything else.

From the few talks she'd had with Vargas on the subject she assumed a price bracket. Thanks to the relentless efforts of self-sacrificing agents, she began to find it difficult to divide her time between her business and her property activities. She knew that agents had a tendency to depict any property in a flattering light, but it was the first time she'd experienced the magnitude of their descriptive talents. Not everything was below standard; it was just that something or other was missing, and she relied on her instincts in those cases where she could not put her finger on what precisely was not there.

She often took Kathleen with her; her mother enjoyed it, and they usually ended up in a country pub where they discussed over lunch what they had seen.

One day, following Jennifer's negative verdict on a property, Kathleen said, "You are pretty fastidious, my girl. That's a very nice house we just saw."

Jennifer said, "Yes, but Angelo would not like the grounds. Too barren."

"But you like it."

"That is not enough. We both have to like it."

"Fair enough. What are Angelo's preferences?"

"More trees and bushes, a more uneven topography, a small stream; you know, things like that. He loves nature. After all, he comes from—" Jennifer stopped.

"You know him well, by now," Kathleen said with a laconic smile.

Oh yes, I do, Jennifer thought; he's an alcoholic loony with a handful of killings behind him, and I intend to marry him, in due time. How would you react if I told you all I know, I wonder? She said, "I know what he likes, and I know what I like. One day I shall find something that's ideal for us. Evidently, it's going to take time. These past six weeks have been quite an experience, but my property is out there, somewhere."

"If it is, you'll find it, but are you not overstretching yourself, Jennifer? Running a business and chasing houses all over the Southeast of England isn't the most perfect combination."

"I can cope."

"I know you can cope. My point is that sooner or later you'll overtax yourself."

Kathleen pretended to look at the map. "Have you and Angelo discussed selling the business? I don't mean to interfere, but you are my daughter and I do not want to see you wearing yourself out."

"But I enjoy what I am doing." She waited for the next question, knowing her mother's perseverance and reluctance to stop at half measures.

"What about the business," Kathleen continued. "You are looking for a place some fifty to eighty miles from London. Are you telling me that you are going to enjoy running the house *and* commute five days a week?" She waved her hand dismissively. "I am sure you can cope, but how are you going to get much pleasure out of either?" She waited for a few seconds. Jennifer stared at her, but said nothing.

"The business," Kathleen persisted. "What does Angelo say?"

"He does not discuss it. He says it's entirely up to me what I want to do with it."

"He is not worried about—he hasn't commented on your source of income?"

"He has no idea what I earn. He has never asked." Jennifer smiled. "He can look after me. He is not destitute."

"How do you feel about—"

"—being kept? How do you feel about Dad looking after you? What did you think after he had inherited all that money? Come on, Mum. Angelo and Dad's attitudes are exactly the same. Identical. They simply do not see it that way."

Kathleen fumbled with her handbag. "Sorry. I apologize. I have no reason to believe that Angelo won't take care of you." She put the bag on the floor.

Jennifer pulled her chair closer. "Mum, I understand you. It is a natural reaction. It would be inhuman not to be concerned." She smiled. "Inhuman you are not." She paused for a short while. "You are right. I have to make a decision about the business. I am not comfortable with the fact that I won't get much for it—I would have liked to have a bit more capital of my own. On the other hand, it *is* beginning to feel like a millstone around my neck." She smiled brightly. "Oh well, capital or freedom—I can't have it both ways." She looked at the bill and said casually, "What would you have done?"

I walked into that one, Kathleen thought. She said, "Your father gave me all the freedom I wanted, and I have praised his liberal soul ever since."

Jennifer said, "Funny. That's one of Angelo's maxims. Freedom is beyond value, he says."

Jennifer drove her mother home.

Kathleen heard Conor coming in from the back garden.

"Any luck?" he said and kicked off his wellies,

"Not yet. I am not so sure she knows what she is looking for."

"She'll know it when she sees it."

"Yes, that is probably what is going to happen. They aren't exactly looking for a half-acre plot with a dilapidated cottage on it, either. She keeps walking around saying *I could live with that but Angelo could not*—she seems to be more critical on his behalf than she is on her own."

Conor put his cap on the shelf. "It's his money."

"Strangely enough, I don't think that's a consideration. She certainly is convinced that *he* doesn't see it that way. Just like you, in that respect. I think that what she's after is a place where they can live for the rest of their lives; no regrets, no feeling of having made a mistake. That is why she is so choosy. She knows that her own happiness is important, but my impression is that Angelo's well-being is an even more significant factor."

Conor came over to the table and sat down. "Don't all women think like that?"

"Of course we do."

"Put me in the picture, please."

Kathleen filled the kettle. "My point is that Jennifer should be fifty-

fifty in her approach. Unqualified and limitless adoration backfires, sooner or later."

"Are you not being a mite judgmental now? Jennifer knows what she is doing. Angelo cannot be the easiest of men to live with. She is aware of that, and she is taking her precautions."

Kathleen's eyes opened wide. "What did you say about Angelo?"

"I may talk less than you do, but that does not mean that I *think* less and *observe* less."

"Conor, my love, how come you still surprise me, after all these years?"

"It could have been the other way round, you know. That usually happens when conclusions precedes analyses."

"I know I jump from time to time, and stop that nodding, if you don't mind. What made you say what you did about Angelo?"

"It's the nature of the man. He agrees to move, but what is happening, basically, is that Jennifer is moving him from one environment and into a different one. I don't think that city life does Angelo any good at all. What Jennifer is doing, is perfectly sensible."

"Supposing he can't adapt. He gets restless."

"That would be bad news. Jennifer knows that, and this is the reason why she is preparing the ground as best she can. I'll give it a sixty-forty chance."

"She's worried about his drinking habits. She has not said much, but I can sense it. It's got worse since that picture arrived."

"What is the story behind it? Nobody told me."

"She has not told me, either. All I know is that it's his grandfather. She hired some detective agency to find it."

Conor rested his back against the chair. "You know what that means, don't you? I am not surprised."

"What?"

"It means that she knows more about him than we have anticipated. I find that reassuring. I always thought that a clam was more communicative on personal matters than Angelo is."

"Yes, of course it is reassuring, but—"

"You still have your reservations, don't you? I thought you had mellowed a bit."

She rapped her spoon on the table. "I have, in one way. I can't fault his behaviour towards me. He is always considerate, and—" the rapping stopped. She did not look at Conor.

"Don't be timid."

The flash in her eyes went quickly. "All right. If he adores Jennifer— and there are moments when I really believe that he does—why is he clinging to the bottle?"

"You know better than to ask a question like that, and, everything else apart, I am not exactly teetotal, either."

She said tersely, "The difference is that you enjoy alcohol and he is using it."

"I agree with that." He smiled at her. "You know, there is always a chance that he will reduce his consumption when they move to an environment more favourable to a healthier life. He has got lots of interests. I know because he talks to me, and I wouldn't be surprised if that is what's on his mind. Don't forget that he wants to move."

"Does he?"

Conor took her hand. "Kathleen, not even Jennifer can persuade Angelo to do something he does not want to do. Believe me."

"Perhaps you are right, on that point." The frown was back. "You are wrong about his drinking, though."

Conor sighed. "I know. I should not have tried to console you with a feeble excuse. Angelo either finds his motive and stops, or he doesn't. There is nothing in between." He pressed the tip of his thumbs against a point under his ears. "What is the real reason for your reservations?"

She ran her fingers through her hair and looked out the window. "He is too quiet. He is too low-key, too enigmatic. I sense a darkness that I cannot explain, an immanence of enmity. It is like he's got hoarfrost on his soul. It scares me."

"We don't know what made him."

"No, but that does not make any difference. Mark my words, Conor, danger lurks inside."

That's perhaps a bit dramatic, he thought. He weighed his words, "Let us not underestimate our daughter."

"Do you know who he reminds me of?"

"Tell me."

"An Irish freedom fighter; a man who is convinced that by killing an English soldier, Ireland and the rest of the world will be a better place."

Conor glanced at the clock on the wall. "I am seeing someone at half past five," he said. "The poor soul has tried to commit suicide four times."

She watched Conor's big frame as he left the kitchen. It worried her that he had begun to stoop, of late.

I am not desperate, Jennifer thought, but I am certainly getting frustrated. It is out there, somewhere, but why is it not coming my way?

During the past ten weeks she had inspected a total of eleven properties. She had lost count of how many she had discarded by just looking at the prospectuses. One of the houses had been close to her idea of perfection; the place was beautiful, but the acreage was too small.

She knew that she had not grasped the enormity of the task when she first began, and the scarcity of top quality properties on the market still surprised her.

Then, one Friday morning, three different brochures arrived from three different top-of-the-range estate agents. Jennifer cast a quick glance over all three before she began perusing. After two hours and one telephone call she dumped one of the brochures. By noon she had made up her mind. She called the agent and asked for an appointment to be arranged.

She placed the two brochures on the coffee table. In the course of the weekend she noticed that they had been touched. Had he not wanted her to know he would have left the brochures exactly as she had placed them. Vargas did not comment, but, she thought, at least he'd had a look.

She came home late Tuesday afternoon and found Vargas at home. He was absorbed in a book about Islam and its history. He did eventually look up. He smiled briefly, but he did not ask how her day had been. He seldom did.

She went across and glanced over his shoulder. "Interesting?"

"Mmm."

She took off her jacket and hung it up. Vargas was sober. She took the brochure from her bag, placed the glossy prospectus on his lap and pulled the book from his hands.

"I think I have found our place."

"You have?"

She nodded towards the brochure. "You have seen it, have you not?"

"I looked at it. Reads well, but don't they all."

"I have just come from there."

"That's where you have been?"

"Yes. Angelo, it is *beautiful*. It is *perfect*. It's got a forest and it's got a stream, lovely gardens, outbuildings, and the house—" her happy sigh resounded like the whiff of a retreating hurricane "—the *potential*! We are going to put our own stamp on it, of course—" another sigh "—please come and have a look with me. Let us see it together."

"Now?"

She laughed. "Not now, but I am sure I can make an appointment for tomorrow."

"Fine. Let us do that."

Jennifer's lips were getting dry. She opened and closed her mouth. "I don't know how to say this—"

"What."

"The price. Have you seen the price?"

"I have."

"It's a lot of money. Can you afford it?"

"We can."

Vargas was always plural. It was time she got used to it. "I can't explain what I felt when I saw the place," she said. "It was like a dream and I was afraid to wake up. There it was, and suddenly all those wasted hours were all but forgotten." She shook her head and smiled.

"Sounds good," he said. "Let's buy it."

"But you will come with me, won't you? We should not buy it unless both of us…"

He waved a hand. "I'll come with you." He opened the brochure and looked at the pictures. "Nice place." He read for a while. "Spacious, too. Plenty of rooms."

"It is very functional."

"Yes, functional it is. You are not worried about all that space?"

Jennifer put her hands behind her back. She raised her head. "Oh, I think we can fill it, the three of us."

Vargas kept looking at the brochure. His eyelids did not move. An eternity later he lowered his shoulders and stared at her. "What did you say?"

"I am pregnant, Angelo."

He moved up and forward and did not stop until they touched. He put his hands on her hips and pressed his face against her neck.

On the Monday, Jennifer sent Yasmin a flower arrangement together with a cryptic message. Ishihara wanted to know why the flowers and why did Jennifer resort to riddles. Yasmin said it had all to do with a private little bet, and, really, it was none of Tadashi's business. One day he would find out. In the meantime, why didn't he behave like a true, dignified shogun that was quite good at keeping their flat little noses clean?

On the Tuesday, Jennifer and Vargas went to view the property.

26

The deal was agreed within ten days. Both parties were moderately happy with their ability to negotiate. They had ended halfway between Vargas's offer and the original asking price.

The next morning, over breakfast, Vargas said, "We have to make a trip to the Cayman Islands."

"Why is that?"

"That's where the money is."

"You want me to come with you?"

"You have to come with me. I spoke to Legal Lenny yesterday. He advised me to set up a trust."

Leonard Kessel was a partner in a small law-firm that Vargas used on occasions. Vargas had reasonable confidence in Kessel's competence. He knew the limits of the law, and he knew how to stretch those limits, when so required. The lawyer had originally resented Vargas's moniker, but, during the years, Kessel had discovered that the nickname had enhanced his reputation and added an air of authority in the honourable world of justice.

So much for lawyers, Vargas had said when he explained and summed up to Jennifer; show me a straight lawyer, and I'll show you a failure.

He said, "Legal Lenny has a contact in Georgetown, an accountancy firm that co-operates with a local law firm. Together, they'll set up what we want." He scrutinized her. "Perhaps you should not fly."

She laughed. "There's another five and a half months to go."

"I think you should talk to your gynaecologist."

Jennifer knew when not to argue. "I shall do that," she promised and patted his arm.

On the morning after she had told Vargas of her pregnancy, he had not gone for his customary run but straight into the dojo. After half an hour or so she had felt a vague disquiet; he was never noisy during his training, but she could always hear him. Not this time. It had been unnaturally quiet. Carefully, she'd opened the door and saw him sitting in the seiza position in front of the cabinet with the sword and the stone. She could not see his face, but she knew that his eyes were closed and she wondered what went through his mind.

Three hours later, he came out.

"Not much training today," she had said light-heartedly.

"I needed to clear my mind," was all he'd said.

Since then he had not touched a drop. Jennifer knew that miracles were in short supply. She was aware of the manifest distinction between confidence and wishful thinking, but now and then she reflected that perhaps Yasmin had shown an insight that had created the condition Jennifer herself had been close to losing faith in. But she knew it was early days. During her years at The Mission she had seen them come and go. She had seen them get up and stumble, and she had seen them never get back on their feet again. Few managed for any length of time and fewer for life. Angelo was addicted. She had no illusions about the battles he was facing, a fight that had already begun and that would go on till he either succumbed or departed. The craving never stopped; not after a week, not after a decade—she had seen, so many times, the despair on her father's face when another failure staggered into his office and confessed surrender.

She had thought of removing the bottles, get them out of sight, hide the temptation and that way make it easier for him, but she had rejected the idea almost instantly. He was too unpredictable; such an action could spark off an argument and lead to exactly the opposite of the desired effect. She sensed that she knew him sufficiently well, by now. Behind the impassive and seemingly unflappable mask a very volatile individual existed, a mercurial character whose thought and actions could not always be augured within the periphery of rationality.

She had also considered the option of counselling, but within minutes that was another idea for the dustbin. Even the vaguest and most tactful hint about a psychiatrist or the AA would have been rejected out of hand, and probably violently so. He was too private, too closed and too hell-bent on solving his own problems. She could easily imagine his arguments; *"If I can't do this on my own, build my own foundation, stand on my own two feet, then I will fail. Replacing one addiction with another, like immersing myself in AA or clinging to a psychiatrist, is no solution. I have to find my own formula. I have to find the strength and the resolution to implement it. Anything else is futile. It won't work."*

Yes, those would have been his arguments. She knew that she could not afford to dispute them, but her situation was being made easier by vibes telling her that his perspective was not entirely implausible. I do have confidence in him, she thought, I *must* have confidence in him. If anyone can do it, he can.

I shall take it all in my stride and continue to hope for the best and not only because there is no other alternative. Faith, Jennifer, faith and trust and belief and optimism, a mere one hundred percent of each.

Vargas came and sat next to her. He said, "Do you know why I have not removed the bottles?"

"Tell me."

"Wherever I go, there's alcohol. Corner shops, supermarkets, bars, hotels, other people's homes—it's everywhere. I can't close my eyes and pretend that alcohol suddenly does not exist any more. I either cling to an invisible pillar, deluding myself that the craving has vanished, or I face realities." He smiled with a trace of irony. "That's all there is to it, really. Simple."

She remembered the morning he had come out from the dojo. He had looked more serene and at ease than she'd ever before seen him. She said, "Was that what you were thinking when you meditated for half a day?"

"That was the outcome."

She battled with her mind and her heart for a minute. "Why did you quit, Angelo?"

He got up. "Because of the consequences of the effect," he said and walked into the kitchen.

She thought how difficult it still was for Angelo to put his true feelings into words. Never mind, she concluded, the result is what matters. Like with truths—its essence is more important than its presentation.

Yes, my love, I shall believe that the will is there, and I know that you do not like losing.

They flew out to The Cayman and gave themselves two days of leisure before they entered the premises of Legal Lenny's recommendation.

Alexander Greenfield, chartered accountant, senior partner and contact appointed was a man in his early forties. He was tall and skinny and with receding black hair, urbane manners and a dry wit. He greeted them warmly without being overfriendly and chatted idly about the Islands whilst they were waiting for coffee to be brought in. It was Greenfield's firm opinion that Oliver Cromwell had done the right thing when he captured Jamaica from the Spanish in 1655 and secured British control of the Islands, sealed with the Treaty of Madrid in 1670. Now, with their first constitution recently in place, the future was bright. Greenfield predicted that within a few years the Islands would become one of the world's leading tax havens, close as they were to the USA, and the British would have no incentive to abandon the pragmatism that had served them so well during the centuries.

Vargas said, "Still a haven for pirates, in other words. I seem to recall that Francis Drake made one or two guest appearances here."

"You are a friend of Mr. Kessel's?" Greenfield smiled with a shade of curiosity in his light brown eyes.

"That's stretching it," Vargas said. "We have known each other for some years. As legal crooks come, I've seen worse."

"I see." Greenfield nodded. Leonard Kessel had warned him that this particular client was neither a crude tycoon nor a walking pinstriped suit. "Mr. Kessel instructions are that you are interested in establishing a trust. Are you familiar with trusts, Mr. Vargas?"

"No."

Greenfield went into a lengthy explanation and concluded by suggesting a discretionary trust. Such an arrangement would allow Vargas to be in control for as long as he lived, and who were to be beneficiaries were his decision, and his alone. The trustees had to be respected, needless to say; there were certain rules to adhere to, but, essentially, Vargas would be in control of his funds.

"My presumption is that you have a beneficiary in mind," Greenfield said and looked at his potential client.

"Miss Moran. From what you said, I understand that upon my demise the trust will be hers, and that our expected child will be second beneficiary."

"Congratulations," Greenfield said and smiled at Jennifer. "Perhaps you would be good enough to send me the details as soon as the child is born?"

"Yes," Jennifer beamed.

Greenfield began to polish his glasses. "Now that I know what you want, I can set the wheels in motion. If you could possibly stay for another few days, we can actually have everything signed, sealed and wrapped up."

"Just as well," Vargas said. He wrote down the room number of their hotel and handed it across.

"Splendid," Greenfield said and placed his hands palms down on his desk. "That should be it, then. I will give you a call as soon as the documents are ready. The draft of your Letter of Wishes I can send over tomorrow morning, as discussed. There should not be any delays." He made a circle out of a paper clip and threw it into the wastebasket. "Is there anything else you can think of, Mr. Vargas?" His posture and the expression in his eyes made it clear that he did not believe so.

"Yes," Vargas said. He leaned back in his chair. "I need someone to phrase it for me." He paused without letting go of Greenfield's eyes. "I want this particular paragraph legally waterproof."

"But of course," Greenfield said, "and that is...?"

"In the likely event of my demise preceding that of Miss Moran, I want the trustees to guarantee an unqualified and total protection of Miss Moran's interests."

Greenfield put his glasses back on. He noticed that Vargas had moved to the left, out of reach from the bright sunshine streaming through the half-open venetian blinds. "I do not quite follow. We do have some considerable experience behind us." He tilted his head with the look of a man whose competence had been questioned.

Vargas said in a low and even voice, "I want a paragraph stating clearly and beyond interpretation that should Miss Moran become feeble of mind in her old age, then nobody—I repeat *nobody*—can possibly take advantage of her. Your experienced firm and your capable trustees will carefully examine and scrutinize *any* request for transfers of funds and *only* allow such transfers if you are convinced without a shadow of a doubt that something rotten is not going on. I shall not be there, Mr. Greenfield, and the thought of one hundred freshly baked and hitherto unknown relatives and two hundred brand new fair-weather friends crawling out from the woodwork does not appeal to me."

Jennifer viewed a picture on the wall at the other end of the office. She did her best not to smile. That's my Angelo, she thought; tactful and diplomatic he is not, but nor does he cross his lines.

Greenfield's expression had changed. He laughed softly. "I see what you mean, Mr. Vargas. Please accept my apology. I did not mean to sound arrogant. May I also compliment you on your reasoning? Not everybody thinks along those lines."

"Not everybody has got my faith in mankind," Vargas said. "Please make a similar paragraph with regard to our child or children in case something happens to both of us." He looked at Jennifer. "I have instructed Mr. Kessel concerning guardianship."

Greenfield said, "I like your realistic and unsentimental approach."

Vargas pushed his chair back further. "I presume you have no objections employing the services of my existing brokers."

"Not at all. It is an excellent firm. A number of our clients are using them. They certainly perform better than most."

He followed them downstairs.

It was not yet mid-day, but the heat from the sun hit Jennifer and she turned her face towards the breeze coming in from the sea. She took Vargas' hand and they strolled lazily down Elgar Avenue.

"Mr. Greenfield seems to think that one day there will be more banks here than there are horses in Ireland," she said.

He looked around. "Since King Midas anchored up here, the touch has stayed with them ever since. They never looked back."

They walked for a while.

"Can we take over the house at any one time now?"

"Yes—any one time as defined by the English legal system. The report from the surveyor should be there when we come back. The rest we leave to Legal Lenny and his counterpart. Give it three to four weeks, with a bit of luck."

She looked across the harbour. "Do you intend to keep the flat?"

"We do. At least for a while."

"In case of regrets?"

"Yes."

She shortened her steps. "Are you serious?"

"No. There won't be any regrets." He slowed down. "I think what happened today calls for a celebration."

The sun lost its heat. The breeze became icy and Jennifer's eyes watered. It was too good to be true, she thought. Nothing lasts forever. Anything short of forever does not add up to a fraction of a lifetime. I should have known. Well, I did. She said, "Where are we going?" She thought her voice sounded neutral.

He steered her gently to the right, down a side street. "There," he said and pointed. "The best espresso anywhere in the world."

The place was old-fashioned and charming and not too busy. Vargas studied the selection of cakes on display before he sat down. A large, black woman came over and smiled at Jennifer. "Yes, please."

"One regular coffee and two espressos, please," Vargas said without looking up.

"How'd you like your coffee, sir?"

"Your colour."

Jennifer's nose got closer to the menu. The woman leaned forward. "Jeeesus!" she shrieked, "Angelo!" She exploded with laughter. "How is you, old devil? You brought your daughter, this time!"

Vargas got up. He grinned as he embraced the woman. "Midget, my lovely nymph. How are you keeping?"

"Better than most. Can't lose any weight, but other than that, super."

Vargas kept his hands on her shoulders. His eyes measured her approvingly. "I swear, Midget, you must be down to twenty stones, now."

She giggled. "You cheek! Eighteen, I'm telling you. Maybe eighteen and a half."

"How is the family?"

"Kids is fine. My lazy, no-good slimeball of a husband is fine. The whole zoo is fine. You hanging around for a few days, Angelo, my dream?"

"A couple of days," he said. "Jennifer, this is Midget and vice versa. Midget is an old friend of mine and the best cook west of Bangkok."

Jennifer extended her hand and Midget clasped it warmly. "You look too good for him, but then, who isn't?"

"Stop flattering," Vargas said.

"You see," Midget went on, addressing Jennifer, "I know him, the old buccaneer. I is president and so far only member of his fan club."

"I'd like to apply," Jennifer smiled.

"Beware, young lady. He ain't normal." Her contagious laughter thundered across the table. She frowned and turned to Vargas. "What's the matter with you, two cups of coffee. You on the wagon or something?"

He sat down. "My gynaecologist insists."

Midget opened her mouth and rolled her eyes before she once again tried to blast the menu off the table. "Good Lord!" she screamed. "It ain't true! Another little angel shall grace this earth!" She waddled around and kissed Jennifer on top of the head. "Congratulation, my child. May the offspring be blessed with much from you and less from him. When is the peccadillo due?"

"Tonight," Vargas said. "That's why we need our coffee now."

Midget stroked Jennifer's hair. "My poor child. Did he force himself on you?"

Jennifer wondered why she did not find the conversation embarrassing. "Not entirely," she smiled.

Vargas said, "Jennifer seduced me, but the fact that I do not miss my lost innocence tells it all. We are made for each other. Isn't that nice?"

Midget sighed heavily. "Lord in heaven," she grunted, "every dog has his year. Jennifer, I wish you plenty of luck 'cause you'll need it and I hope you is as overbearing as you is beautiful."

Jennifer reddened. "Thank you, Midget."

"You take care of this diamond," Midget said sternly and glared at Vargas. "There ain't many like she around. I can tell."

"None," Vargas said.

"I'll go and get you your coffee and one of them non-calorie rum cakes. You two turtle doves must have plenty to talk about." Midget's snow-white teeth were still visible when she turned and shuffled away from the table.

"She is a character," Jennifer smiled.

He said, "That woman is unique. She has not had an easy life, but she keeps smiling. I always drop in for a chat when I'm here. Her heart is as big as the rest of her. She has even invited me home for a meal, something she really can't afford. A true, genuine lady."

Jennifer did nothing to hide her amazement. She could not recall the last time Vargas had praised anybody.

He said, "It is easy to sympathize with someone who has been where you once were yourself." He looked towards Midget who was busy behind the counter. "I do not confuse sympathy with pity, nor rapport with compassion."

No, she thought, you wouldn't.

Midget came with Jennifer's espresso and Vargas' rum cake and black coffee. "I'll get you your espresso when you is finished with that one," she said and patted him on the shoulder. "Don't slurp." She winked with dramatic exaggeration at Jennifer, laughed and walked over to the next table.

Jennifer licked the froth from her lips. "Did you ever do her a favour?" she asked casually.

"A small one. That is, I repaid one. Once, I fell asleep on the beach and was set upon by a gang of youths. Very unusual, here. Anyway, she saw it and got hold of the police before any serious damage was done. Her subsequent testimony was most helpful. Why she came forward, I still do not know."

He attacked his cake. She looked at him from an angle. "And then you repaid."

"I never owe anything to anybody."

The answer I expected, she thought. "Get even?"

He did not look up. "Always get even." He put his fork down. "I ran into her again—this place—and we began to talk. She knows one or two things about life. Good company."

She waited till he was halfway through his cake. "You've got quite a lot of money here."

He licked his fork. "We have."

She watched him work on the second half. "I am going to break my promise again," she said with a small but distinct interval between each word.

Vargas scraped up the crumbs with his teaspoon. He pulled his cup closer and readjusted the angle of his chair, crossed his legs and lit a cigarette. He said, "What promise?"

She did not like the way he said it. The old inscrutable expression was back on his face. She had an uncomfortable feeling of a sudden distance between them, a cold front that made her wish that there were no need for questions. But there was. She had to know, and there was only one way to find out. There were ways of asking, though. She said, "Tell me it isn't drug money."

"It isn't."

"You swear it is not?"

He took his time. He said quietly, "Jennifer, I have three options. I can lie to you, I can tell you the truth, and I can tell you to forget you ever asked. I do not lie to you. I have answered your question."

She closed her eyes. The relief hit her like a monsoon on a winter's day. She heard his voice: "It's tax money."

It took a moment before she realized what he had said. "Tax money?" she repeated.

"Also known as governments' money, for some bizarre reason, a complete contradiction except for politicians."

"I am not with you," she said. "Are you telling me that you work for the government?"

"Plural. Any government. It does not matter who they are or where they are. They offer us an assignment, which Tadashi and I either accept or decline. If we accept, they pay handsomely. We are only tangentially involved; we describe ourselves as glorified messengers."

"Messengers?"

"I thought you said you had one question."

Jennifer looked down. "Sorry. I got intrigued." She did not notice the smile on Vargas' face. "No more questions," she said.

There was nobody within ten yards of their table. Vargas repositioned his chair and came closer. He said, "We all know that governments can move in strange and mysterious ways. What most people are not aware of, is to what extent they all operate behind closed doors. A lot of their actions, including diplomatic activities, never reach the media. This is not only because almost any politician is passionately in love with the cloak-and-dagger image. There are times, quite a few, actually, when secrecy is justified *and* necessary. All governments get involved in covert operations, not by preference or desire perforce, but because it appears to be the only way that this world can function. Some of these agreements or deeds or actions in question can be of a sensitive nature, and, in such cases, any sensible government prefers to distance itself from the scene. Officially, they are not involved. That means that they close their diplomatic channels and resort to outsiders. That is where operators like Tadashi and I come in. It is all down to logic. If you for some reason or another can't be seen to undertake a certain assignment, get somebody else to do it."

She was wholly absorbed. "Like penetrating and destroying the Mafia or drugs cartels or things like that?"

He finished his coffee. "No. Tadashi and I would never get involved in anything of such nature. That's a complicated no-win situation. Too much is involved in too many countries, and that includes sections within law enforcement and sections of political operators."

"Is there really that much corruption?"

"It's like any other rot; it's either eliminated or it grows. Too many billions of dollars are being redistributed through too many layers of our societies; too many people are dead against squashing the rot. Their vested interest is more important than the fate of the victims and the sufferers." A smile came and went. He shrugged. "Do you see any signs that the inhabitants of our precious green planet are becoming any *less* materialistic? Moses had a point when he reacted against Aaron and his Golden Calf, but not even the mighty Yahweh was much of a match for King Mammon."

Midget placed Vargas' espresso on the table. "How about you, Miss Jennifer? Another one?"

Jennifer said, "Why not, and one of those lovely little rum-cakes as well, please."

"You don't have to feed him, you know," Midget said and nodded pointedly.

"Or her."

Midget's laughter almost shattered the windows behind them. "Now that's a sensible girl! You don't want to know, do you?"

"No, I don't."

"Was the same with me," Midget giggled. "What pops out pops out, I thought. Leave it to the Lord, I say, 'cause you'll love the little monster whatever it is. I hope it is a girl, though" she added and glanced at Vargas, "I mean—" she tried to knit her brows as she rolled her eyes "—two of *him*…"

"You are wasting your time, Midget," Vargas said. "Jennifer just told me that she does not understand more than five percent of what you're on about. She said you sound like a Scot trying to speak Chinese with a Dutch accent."

"I did not!"

She put her hands on her hips. "You just relax, my child. He's too old to improve. May the Lord Jesus have mercy with him." She put her face an inch from Vargas' and her bulging eyes locked with his. "Screwball!" she roared before she straightened up and turned her massive back on him.

"An ardent devotee," Vargas said and sprinkled brown sugar on top of his espresso. "She really does adore me. Anyway. Have I satisfied your curiosity?"

The directness of his question caught Jennifer off balance. It baffled her that he had been so open with her. In the past, each time they'd discussed a serious topic, he had been neutral. No, she thought, not neutral—impartial and detached, as if the theme could be interesting but only academically. An added quality of involvement had seemed unimaginable. He had never been short on opinions, that was not the problem, but it had always been his analytical mind speaking—his soul carefully hidden behind locked doors. Not so this time. His words had been non-partisan but his voice had not.

She said, "Well, if it isn't criminals you and Tadashi—"

"Put it this way," he interjected. "There has always been a Genghis Khan, a Napoleon, a Stalin, a Hitler or a Roosevelt on the firmament. There always will be, surrounded by equally evil-minded and power-hungry acolytes. Inevitably, their philosophies are followed by actions spelling terror, death and destruction. These paragons of Machiavellian eminence see adversaries everywhere, real and imaginary, and would address their closest advisors along these lines: *"Listen, my friends, this person is getting out of hand, and we don't like it. He no longer fits in. Now, ours is a democracy, as we all know, but we are, quite frankly, superior to this person and God is on our side. The problem is, we are not our brother's keepers and therefore we ask: does one offer a vaccine to a dog already mad with rabies? We all know the answer. What we need, is to send a message, and a pretty cut-and-dried one, at that. Does anybody have a suggestion? Oh, by the way, before you say anything—discretion is so vital that I have decided to keep the cabinet out of this."* Vargas added more sugar to his espresso. "Very cabalistic. They love it." He looked at his spoon. "That is when they need couriers like Tadashi and myself."

She dabbed her mouth. "But why?" she said. "Why can't a prime minister talk to another prime minister or president or dictator or whatever? I thought they did that."

"It isn't always feasible, or desirable, for that matter, neither direct nor through diplomatic channels. Another factor is that it isn't always the top gun that is the culprit. If newspaper editors knew all the power games and the dramas going on in the political world, they would overnight forget royalty and film stars—that kind of sapless and parasitic gossip would pale in comparison. Also, don't forget that most politicians are not famous for their brainpower. The really crafty and devious ones, those who do have an impact of global consequences, when do we catch them trying to play table tennis with a deck of cards? Only when their stealthy schemes are in the process of disintegrating, and then it is too late."

Jennifer straightened in her chair. Her back was aching. She said, "I take a dim view of that list of yours. You can't possibly compare Roosevelt with Hitler or Stalin."

"It was not meant as a list of challengers to the throne. It was merely a reference to those who leave destruction in their wake. Anyone whose intention it is to inflict total devastation on another country and, in the process, without an iota of justification, sending hundreds of thousand of children and women to their slow and meaningless death, anyone who is using a nuclear device for purely *political* purposes—all embodied in America's phoney idol—does not deserve to be remembered as any better than the rest of history's maleficent luminaries. It is no excuse that he didn't live long enough to press the button personally."

She hid behind her cup. "Oh well, he did have a reassuring smile."

"So did Dracula. What is funny? Why are you laughing?"

"Nothing. It's just the way you present things." She looked into her handbag for her mirror. "My lipstick is gone. I need to go to the ladies."

"Up to the left."

She halfway left her chair and sat down again. "Is it dangerous what you do?"

He moved his right shoulder, as if a shrug was in order. "You never know how people are going to react when facing an irreversible situation. The element of incredulity can always create an unexpected reaction. We do our homework, Tadashi and I. We eliminate as many unknown factors as we possibly can, but a hermetically sealed case does not exist. We learn whatever is humanly achievable to ascertain—or so we prefer to think—and we never let anybody know when our message is going to be delivered. If that becomes a condition, we reject the assignment. There are two major components to our advantage; the timing—which is our own—and the brevity of the deliverance. Thereafter, we are no

632

longer involved. Our mission has been accomplished and that is the end of it, as far as we are concerned. All in all, to answer your question, the degree of danger is moderate."

Jennifer felt a strange disquiet. His words made sense but the syllogistic reasoning did not. His presentation was too clinical, too smooth. Something was missing. She had no idea what; it was like staring at an ostensibly perfect picture knowing there was a flaw but unable to spot it.

"There is only one more assignment?"

"Guaranteed. I have had enough." He smiled. "My humble way of saying that my priorities have changed."

Three days later they were back in London.

Jennifer was pleased with the surveyor's report. It was thorough and extensive, clearly categorising what needed to be done without delay, what should be looked into over time, and what could be considered a matter of cosmetics.

She had known from the onset that the place was not in ideal condition—maintenance had been neglected over the last few years— and the report gave her the basis for planning ahead.

She was itching to take over. Her head was buzzing with ideas; layouts, improvements, alterations, colour schemes and furnishing. The lethargic nature of the legal process annoyed her, but she used the time as best she could, collecting samples and charts and filling one sketchpad after another. Her enthusiasm was boundless, but, as days went by, the magnitude of the job started to affect her. Neither was the baby getting any smaller, and Jennifer began to resent having to go to her office.

One night she said, "Listen, I am pretty close to hating it."

"What is *it*?"

"My business."

"Strong words. You have done an excellent job there, building it up to what it is today, and it has served you well."

"I know. That's the dilemma. I hate myself for feeling resentment towards my own creation. It should not end like that. What do you think I should do?"

He smiled. "Oh no, my girl, I am not making a decision for you."

"You are not being very helpful."

"I don't intend to be."

"Don't tell me that you have no opinion whatsoever. I refuse to believe that."

"My opinion is irrelevant. It is your business and therefore your decision. It would not do either of us any good if I voiced a preference one way or the other."

She knew he was right. "I am on my own, in other words."

"You are."

Since the day she had announced her pregnancy, Vargas had treated her as a Faberge egg balancing unsteadily on top of a fragile pedestal. He had been kindness itself twenty-four hours a day, considerate and attentive, no flashes of temper—and not one drop of alcohol.

Would it last? That remained to be seen. She had taken a chance, the biggest gamble of her life, and she would have to live with the consequences whatever happened.

She knew that her trust in him was more by instinct than by reason. He had shown her that he wanted to change his ways, but it had taken an unborn child to move him. *Bulls-eye, Yasmin.*

She put her hands on her stomach and squeezed gently. *Let us just hope, my little one,* she whispered silently, *let us pray that I do not have to produce another one every ninth months to make your father stay sober. We don't think so, do we? No, we don't. Your daddy has taken the first step towards a new and better life. Nothing in his nature tells me that he has a weakness for going back.*

"So," he said, "what about the business?"

She stared into space for a few moments. She put her cup on the table and changed into a more comfortable position. "I want to sell it. I want to spend every single minute of the day in our new home with you and our baby. I know I can cope if I have to, but I also know that I am not cut out for a dual existence."

He stayed silent.

"I won't be part of the deal," she continued. "There is no way I am staying on for even a couple of months. The buyer has to do without me, except for a limited availability on the phone. This means that I can't expect much of an offer. I can live with that." Her voice was calm and clear. "It's a small price to pay for what I really want."

He still did not comment.

"It is final. I have made my decision."

"Good."

"You approve?"

"I agree, if you don't mind a subtle but essential distinction."

His answer did not satisfy Jennifer. "Yes, but what do you *prefer*?" she persisted.

"Now that you have made your choice—" his impassive expression was gone "—I *prefer* that you stay at home with the baby."

She raised her hands in mock acquiescence. "Thank heavens I never have to drag anything out of you. Bless you, my darling, for being such a bare-faced chatterbox."

"If you had continued against your own wish to run your business, added to running a home and raising a child, you would have worn yourself out within twelve months. I fail to see the benefits. Everything and everybody would have suffered, by choice, and that is out of character. You deserve to enjoy life. You have earned it. To see you happy gives me more pleasure than anything I have ever experienced."

She had not expected a eulogy. "Good Lord," she mumbled, "when will I ever get into that head of yours?"

"Keep trying."

She set her lips. "One thing."

"What?"

"I would like our child to be raised in the Catholic faith."

"I accept that."

"You agree?"

"No, but I know what it means to you. One request, though—please omit the infallibility of the Pope."

"I will."

"In return, I shall omit that the papacy is the origin of mental tuberculosis."

"Is it necessary to be so crude?"

"Don't belittle unadorned straightforwardness."

"Do you promise to keep your profane opinions to yourself until the child is past adolescence?"

"I do. By that time, she or he will be my soulmate, anyway. Please excuse the euphemism."

"She or he. Not *he or she*," Jennifer said. She looked around. "When we were in Georgetown, you said that we shall keep this place."

"It's convenient. The market isn't too brilliant at the moment, either."

She kept her head down. "Tell me that this is not going to be your second home."

He waited till she looked up. "It is not."

Two days later, Legal Lenny called and announced that the keys could be handed over Saturday week. Jennifer wasted no time confirming the arrangement.

Come Friday night, Jennifer wanted to go to bed early. She was tired without being uncomfortable and filled with a sense of excitement that made her feel blissful and dreamy.

Vargas said that he wasn't sleepy, and, also, he had a few things on his mind.

Nothing serious.

Hours later he got up from his chair and walked across to the bottles. He stood there for a while. He looked up at his grandfather before he went over to the wall facing the square, a dark figure silhouetted against the window. He pulled the curtains and faced the sky and wondered how much was left of the night.

Angelo Vargas opened his eyes and the bright light of the morning hit him like the silvery dust from an exploding crystal ball.

27

During the short and blessedly dry months of the summer they did up most of the place. Vargas was not surprised to learn that Jennifer was a hard taskmaster. The results came with amazing speed and a minimum of aggravation. She put every ounce of her skills, experience and diplomatic talents to good use; with a couple of exceptions everybody produced to the highest standards, and those who failed were politely asked to go elsewhere.

Vargas admired her deftness and tenacity as much as he admired her taste and her ability to grasp details and entire concepts.

In spite of her condition, Jennifer displayed a drive and a seemingly indefatigable zest that astonished him. More than once did he plead with her to slow down. In her eighth month she began to listen, but by then most of the work on the house had been completed. He seldom interfered. The exceptions were all decisions on security, the interior design of the cottage he had chosen for himself and his books, and the usage of the barn.

Yasmin, at long last, had found her house. She had shared Jennifer's experience with endless viewing of not-quite places.

A couple of times, during re-decoration, they had visited each other. The properties were fifteen minutes apart. A picturesque country lane with trees and bushes connected. The proximity pleased them.

Yasmin had yet to become pregnant. It worried her, and she clung to the hope that an idyllic and quiet life would be conducive to their efforts.

Parkhurst had bowed to the inevitable when Yasmin and Tadashi announced their move and that they would no longer need the West

Wing. Parkhurst's consolation was that they were all within easy distance from each other.

A week before the baby was due, Jennifer and Vargas moved up to London. They left the care of the property to a full-time gardener employed and installed in one of the cottages.

Kathleen and Conor visited daily, flush with excitement and loaded with presents. Vargas tried not to behave like a caged animal. The only one unperturbed was Jennifer. She radiated a serene happiness. Conor kept searching for words he could not find and masked his confusion by constantly nodding. Both he and Kathleen wanted to know if the baby's name had been decided, but Jennifer laughed and said she wasn't in a hurry. What she *had* decided was that the child was *not* going to be named after anybody; he or she should have his or her own identity.

Anu was born one bright and sunny late autumn's morning. Vargas stared at his little bundle as if he was facing a miracle beyond comprehension. He touched her hand and her black hair with the tip of his finger and said, "She's got blue eyes."

"All babies have got blue eyes," Jennifer said, tired but elated, sitting up with her daughter in her arms.

"You mean they could change?"

She smiled. "They possibly will."

Vargas said, "I opt for green, like these—" he pulled an etui from his pocket and placed it next to Anu's chubby little fist, resting on Jennifer's bosom.

"Oh Lord," she said, "what have you done now?" She took out the necklace. The emeralds sparkled in perfect setting. Her smile widened. "You are crazy, Angelo. It is absolutely beautiful."

"Good match," He locked the necklace under her hair and kissed the top of her head. His hand cupped Anu's little fist and his thumb stroked her soft and wrinkled skin.

Jennifer closed her eyes. From her teens she had known that she had wanted her first child to be a girl, and for almost as long she had known that her name would be Anu. Once, visiting Ireland with her parents, they had been driving through County Kerry and her father had pointed at the mountains, the Paps of Anu, and he had explained how they came to get the name. "The mother goddess," he'd said, "also known as Ana or Buanann which means *the lasting one*. Same deity as Dana. Personally, I prefer *Anu*."

That was it; no other name ever entered her mind. She had told Vargas the story, and he had rolled the name over his tongue once and said, "Anu it is."

She opened her eyes and saw his smile. He stared at Anu, fast asleep.

Jennifer recovered quicker than anybody except she had dared anticipate, but they decided to stay in London for another three days. Kathleen and Conor were delighted about the name Jennifer had chosen. Conor had forgotten the circumstances, but he was not slow to claim credit when Jennifer reminded him. Kathleen could not think of a name prettier and more apt. They offered to baby-sit if Jennifer and Vargas should wish to go out, even for a few minutes.

One day they took up the offer and went to a French restaurant; a place where they knew the owner and were guaranteed what Vargas always referred to as value for money.

After the meal they walked for a few minutes. They passed a car show room, and Jennifer stopped. "Look at that one," she said and pointed at a racing green Jaguar XK-150. "Isn't that something else? Look at the lines. They don't make cars like that any more, do they? What an absolute beauty."

"Not bad."

"Is it fast?"

"Reasonably."

"I wonder why it is so expensive. That is a lot of money for a second-hand car."

"There are not too many of those around. My guess is that it is in pretty good condition—you know, one owner's pride and joy—but the time has come to cash in, for some reason or another."

They walked till Jennifer got tired and took a taxi back.

Kathleen and Conor were slow to leave, but finally they said goodnight.

Jennifer said after they'd left, "I shouldn't really say this, but in a way I am glad they don't live too close. Mum is absolutely nutty about Anu, and Dad isn't much better."

Vargas said, "It's the novelty. They'll come down to earth, eventually."

Jennifer did not look convinced. She said, "I am glad we are going back tomorrow. I am homesick. Not that this isn't our home, too," she added quickly. "You know what I mean."

Vargas smiled. "I think I do. By the way, would you mind if we go back on Saturday instead of tomorrow? I've got a few things to arrange in the morning." He looked apologetic. "It saves me coming up again next week."

"All right," she said, disappointed, "but can we leave early on Saturday, then?"

"Whenever you are ready."

They came down the drive and Jennifer saw the highly polished Jaguar in the sunshine, in front of the garages.

"Oh Jesus, Angelo," she gasped. She clasped her mouth and tried not to wake Anu. "I can't say a word without—"

"Enjoy it," Vargas said.

"Is it really mine?"

"Yours alone."

Vargas stopped and took Anu in his arms. Jennifer stepped out. She went over to the Jaguar and walked around it a few times. "What a beauty," she sighed. "Maybe I can drive over to Yasmin's this afternoon. That should be a good little test." She laughed. "You are very good at baby-sitting, aren't you?"

"None better."

They went inside. Anu's bedroom was next to theirs. Vargas had installed a number of gadgets in order to supervise her well-being at any one time.

Anu suddenly voiced her displeasure. Jennifer sat down. "The poor little darling is hungry. Did you know that babies who are being breast-fed grow up to be healthier and stronger and more balanced than those who are not?" She giggled. "I am sure *you* were breast-fed."

Vargas placed Anu in Jennifer's arms. He did not look at her. I should not have said that, she thought.

He said, "Where are the diapers?"

They bathed Anu together and dressed her. Vargas saw Jennifer's esoteric smile and did not know that his tenderness was part of her joy.

The chiming of church-bells echoed through the valley when Jennifer decided to go for a spin in her Jaguar. She came back two hours later with Yasmin and Tadashi following in their brand new black Bentley.

Ishihara suggested that he and Vargas should go for a walk.

It had rained the night before. The grass was a darker green where the light from the morning sun had yet to reach the westward slopes of the meadows. They jumped the stream chuckling lazily and crystal clear past the paddocks, climbed the rails and walked in the shade of the chestnut and beech trees.

They reached a glen where there once had been a small cottage. Ishihara sat down on the remnants of a wall and pulled out a cigar. "Care for one?" he offered.

Vargas said, "You know I never smoke when I go for my walks." He leaned against a huge sycamore tree and watched a buzzard circling high above.

Ishihara said, "Our man is running."

Vargas continued to watch the buzzard. "He sounds like a cat," he said.

Ishihara looked up. "What?"

"The bird. He sounds like a cat."

"Yes, he does. Did you hear what I said?"

"Our man is running."

Ishihara chewed on his cigar. He avoided eye contact. "We cannot afford to miss out on this one."

Vargas sat down at the foot of the tree. His forearms rested on his knees. His hands were loose and relaxed. "Speak for yourself."

Ishihara swore silently behind the smoke and cursed the day when Jennifer Moran cast her net over his friend and ally Angelo Vargas. The timing could not have been worse. Yes, he corrected, it could and it was. The arrival of that child was even more unfortunate—the timing of the entire scenario of Vargas' love life was incredibly inconvenient. Ishihara glared at the dark green moss complementing the colour of his brown suede boots and wondered how to placate, soothe and convince Vargas—in that order.

"I do speak for myself," he said. "I need the money."

Vargas focused on an ant promenading across his left hand. "How come?"

Time to play it straight, Ishihara thought. Vargas was clearly reluctant. One false move, and he would walk away never to come back. "Do you not need the money?"

"No."

A single drop of sweat ran down Ishihara's spine. He picked up a small twig and began poking holes in the ground. "You mean, even now, with Jennifer and the baby and the property—" he tried to slacken the muscles in his neck "—I say you are facing some pretty costly times ahead."

"I had no idea."

Just a shade of irony, Ishihara thought; he doesn't even bother to be sarcastic. How bloody stupid can I get? This is going nowhere, fast. Vargas had never shown any interest in high finance and the glamour of business, but he was as prudent and shrewd as they came. He must at least have trebled his money, Ishihara thought. No wonder he is not worried. Neither would I have been, had I been sitting on his capital. He said, "Sorry. I had no intention of lecturing you."

"You gave a passable imitation."

"I apologize." Ishihara snapped the twig in two and threw the pieces away. "I need the money. I am not destitute, far from it, but I am not as well off as I should have been. This is a chance of a lifetime, more rewarding than anything we have ever done before, but you know the core—" he straightened his back "—without you I am stuck. I can't do it on my own. You know that."

Vargas got interested in a pair of rabbits showing increasing boldness. "What happened to your money, Tadashi?"

At long last, Ishihara thought. He swallowed a sigh. There is only one sensible route to take now, and that is to look into his blue eyes and tell it exactly as it is. His own priorities are with Jennifer and the baby. He will drop me on even a hint of suspicion of something duplicitous. Tread where ordinary angels don't dare, young Tadashi. Appeal to his few noble instincts and create a carrot of sympathy.

He picked up a long slender straw, split it in half and dangled each like a pair of antennae in the air. "Not all my investments have been successful," he said matter-of-fact. "Hard luck, a couple of times. I also made the odd misjudgement. Added to that, the re-launching of Igor Parkhurst's career cost me a few pennies, and so did our entrance into the higher strata of social life. All in all, our standard of living is high. What worries me is that I do not have the extra reserve which takes the tension out of future planning. I am not saying that we can't survive on what we've got, even survive well, for that matter, but the absence of that ancillary buffer zone makes me a tad nervous." Ishihara paused. He half expected to be confronted with the purchase of his new Bentley.

Vargas looked at a couple of deer grazing a few hundred meters away. He said, "You haven't finished."

This is either going very well, Ishihara thought, or it is going top gear to hell. Even after all these years I can't read my friend the gaijin. He said, "The property is in Yasmin's name." He opened his fingers and let go of the straw. "That adds to her protection, but it does not seal it. Supposing somebody knocks me off. That is not completely improbable, and if it so happens, she will find herself in the middle of an almighty mess. People are very good at making claims—fabricated, construed, wholly unsustainable and un-provable makes no difference— she will have to employ legal advice and costs start snowballing. The funds will dry up. She will be left with a property she can't afford to keep and a child or two suffering from the lack of protection that money gives. I am not saying it *will* happen, I am saying it *can* happen. We have both made a variety of enemies during the years, and anyone still alive can hit back." He smiled wryly. "My trust in the common man's decency and integrity dried up decades ago. I refer to what Yasmin can run into if she ends up in the hands of the wrong lawyers."

Vargas seemed preoccupied listening to a skylark.

One last shot, Ishihara thought; if this one doesn't make an impact, nothing will. He tried to eliminate any trace of passion in his voice when he said, "I intend to set up a trust for Yasmin, a trust that literally nobody else can touch. She is everything to me, and a safety net like that would give her—and me—peace of mind." Did Angelo hear that? he wondered.

He looked at Vargas who appeared fascinated by two squirrels chasing each other. Vargas said, "What are your plans for the future?"

You bastard, Ishihara reflected, you heard me. Well, the fight isn't over yet.

"The future?" He broke the stem of a mushroom and sniffed at it. "The future will be food. I intend to write cookery books. I want to introduce Japanese cuisine on a wider scale to this country, including a television series, an idea which has found response with a producer I know. I also plan to take over Itoh's restaurant."

He let out a low whistle and went on, "Itoh-San wants to retire and he asked me if I would be interested in buying the place, which I am. A chain of top-class establishments would suit me fine." He held the mushroom close to his nose. "Fungi make delicate food," he said. "I wonder what this is."

"It's a red-spotted agaric."

"Most attractive. Is it poisonous?"

"Yes. Have one."

Ishihara laughed and dropped it. "The future is food," he said.

"Restaurants are hands-on business," Vargas said.

"I know, and I want to get involved. Not on a daily basis; no way is the business going to run me, but I have plans for a control system that will make it difficult for anyone to cheat me."

"Difficult and dangerous?"

Ishihara grinned. "Part of the package. Fear is a good motivator." He brushed away a bumblebee bewildered by the mild season and mistaking after-shave for the real thing. "What about you?"

"I am going to open an art gallery in London."

Ishihara remembered Vargas' sketches and drawings from their days in Japan. "I know you are good," he nodded. "That's an excellent idea."

Vargas laughed. "Not my work," he said. "That is strictly a personal and private safety valve. No, other people's efforts. There's a lot of talent out there, artists with little money and fewer contacts and no realistic chance of ever making it. I am thinking of those who have something to say and the talent to express it, artists who are not afraid of speaking their mind. Artists who can convey their thoughts and impressions and their experiences onto the canvass and who are still idealistic enough to stick to their guns. Artists who do not seek instant stardom manifested by vulgarity and an ability to shock." Vargas turned his head. "With the help of your marketing skills and numerous contacts I should be able to break even after a couple of years. From then on it is up and forward only."

Ishihara said, "I would be delighted to help. What a marvellous idea. Jennifer must be pleased."

"She doesn't know about it."

Ishihara looked puzzled. "Why not?"

"Because I am going to call it *Jennifer Vargas* and give it to her. She will have no idea until the day of the opening when she sees the name and walks through the doors."

Ishihara smiled. "I'd never thought you'd end up an old romantic."

Vargas moved a few feet away from the big sycamore tree. The light from the sun sliced through the branches and painted little figures on the grass. "Yasmin came to see me," he said.

"Oh."

"Drop your pretence, Tadashi."

"She said she would, but she did not tell me…"

"She didn't have to."

Ishihara pressed his knees together. He did not feel comfortable. His eyes followed the busy schedule of a nuthatch. "No, she didn't," he said.

"This is the last one," Vargas said quietly. "Never again."

Ishihara looked into his eyes and nodded. He had seen that stare before. "Never again," he said. "I, too, look forward to a different life." For a while he listened to the breeze fondling the leaves and the orchestra of the birds and the humming of the insects whilst he thought of what would be his final and most accomplished masterpiece.

Vargas had sat down. He rested his back against the sycamore.

"I predict a landslide," Ishihara said.

"Early days."

Ishihara shook his head vigorously. "No," he emphasized, "there is nobody around to beat Caldwell. The incumbent is tired and fed up. Achieving Alaska and Hawaii as the forty-ninth and fiftieth state and saying hello to Khrushchev and goodbye to Batista seems to have knocked out what little was left of his spirit. He's been regretting from day one that he took on a second term, and, as we have seen on so many occasions, he couldn't care less about a vice-president so hell-bent on proving what a jerk he is. Who else is there? The Republicans are in disarray. There is no way they can get their act together and produce a plausible candidate within next autumn, unless they're witless enough to go for the vice-president. The only other possible contender who could add some colour to the show is that chap from Massachusetts—Milland. So far, he's been sitting on the fence."

"You are reasonably sure that not even the Americans will see Caldwell as the inexperienced lightweight of a dilettante that he is?"

"Did they see through Roosevelt? Did they see through Truman? Both were vacuous criminals, but elected they were. One is a dead icon and the other is still being consulted. No, I am not worried, Angelo. The Americans never learn. Caldwell has got big white teeth, an enormous grin and those peculiar mannerisms that the majority of voters find so reassuring, mistaking façade for substance." Ishihara switched over to a broad American accent. *"Hi folks, Ah'm Cliff Caldwell, the chosen one, the one yya'll have been waitin' for, the one blessed by the good Lord above to be ev'rythin' at any one time to all of the American people. Together we'll make our great country even greater. God bless America and god bless me and God bless yya'll. Vote for me, folks, 'cause there ain't nothin' Ah cain't promise and there ain't no promise Ah'll do my darnest to do somethin' about. God bless yya'll."*

Vargas smiled. "I take it you give him a bit more credit than that. True, he is a pretty face with no record to speak about, but he has got this non-descript charisma that so easily infatuates the Americans."

"Yes, but what I said will be the essence of his message. No, do not misunderstand me. Our friend from Kentucky is a master orator by American standards, and, who knows, he may turn out to be shrewder and more guileful than any of them since the great creator of the New Deal. Like Roosevelt, Caldwell is a hypocrite par excellence, but he could play the game so well that not even two terms in office will make the Americans understand his talent for deceit. You and I know what Caldwell is at. He has never let trivia like conscience, honesty and consideration stand in his way. He has shown an ability to manipulate. He is revealing signs of this magical knack of keeping people fascinated even when they know he is lying. He knows how to convert mistakes into virtues and errors into future challenges. His aptitude for turning with the wind and still make people subscribe to his sincerity is no less than remarkable. His timing is above average. All in all, his faculties are perfect for the nation he wants to lead. He is a god of our time in the shape of a chameleon. People believe in him because they must have someone to believe in, and other gods are in decline. He'll be a great president, just what God's own country needs."

"Is he beginning to believe in his own hype?"

Ishihara unwrapped another cigar. "There are some welcoming signals," he said, "and nothing suits the General better. What surprises me is that Caldwell can be so totally blind to the danger that Forster represents."

"He does not know that it exists. That is the genius of the General, keeping such a low profile that he is virtually invisible. Added to this is his gift for conning people into believing that he has no political ambitions. Caldwell may have a few things going for him, but he is a lethargic amateur compared to Abraham Forster." Vargas looked up through the branches and squinted. "He is in for a rude awakening, our young senator."

"He certainly is," Ishihara said. His eyes sparkled. "What a divine situation, two opportunists ending up grossly underestimating each other." He listened to the whistle from a train and gazed across the meadows. In the distance he could see the tiny figures of Yasmin and Jennifer walking the garden.

Vargas said, "Let us hope that we do not overrate Caldwell."

"What options has he got?"

"Two, but that does not mean he's got the guts to carry out number one."

"You think he'd rather be kicked out of office and live the rest of his life as a disgraced failure? No way. Also, don't forget his darling wife, little Sheryl. A diamond is softer than wax in comparison, and she is as familiar with *scruples* as you are with conformity."

"Esther," Vargas said.

"Excuse me?"

"A lady from the Old Testament. You should read about her, and you may well conclude that Sheryl is Esther reincarnated."

"Is it important?"

Vargas laughed. "Ask one of your Shinto gods."

"I will. I shall also ask the appropriate deity to cast a spell over you so that you do not confuse me any more. It is not very nice."

"Who says I am nice?"

"Nobody, except Yasmin and Jennifer, but they are females and, as such, magnanimous beyond the extreme."

The breeze played with the grass. A field mouse sprinted from behind a bush into the safety of the blackened stones.

Ishihara said, "It's not too far away now, and then it is all over."

They walked back, saying little.

28

Abraham Forster made his stars in Korea. He as adored by his men and respected by his superiors. Pentagon saw him as a true professional. The White House was pleased because the General was a-political and never gave interviews. On the quiet he praised President Truman for originally giving General Douglas MacArthur command of the sixteen UN forces, and on the quiet he praised President Truman for sacking MacArthur on the 11th of April 1951 and appointing General Matthew B. Ridgway. Generals shouldn't mess with politics, was Forster's motto.

He received his orders without questioning wisdom or motives. Any instruction was carried out with the precision and the foresight of a born chess-player. With the exceptions of a few well planned and masterly performed occasions, the American people did not hear Abraham Forster's name. The most significant of those occasions was the announcement of the General retiring from active service, widely reported by the media. The extent of the media coverage surprised those who bothered to think about it; why was this unknown soldier suddenly so hot with all major news corporations? The answer to the question was swept away by a tidal wave of patriotism and never broke the surface.

The General lived through a few weeks of glory and appreciation before he allowed Pentagon, the White House and the American people to believe that he had gracefully accepted being dispatched to an anonymous existence under the discarded helmet of an unpopular but necessary war.

As the name *Korea* became increasingly hard for the American people to swallow and digest, there were those who wondered why Abraham Forster had become such an icon. The generally accepted assumption was that he had represented everything that was humanly and militarily good, decent and honourable in the American people under duress.

Forster had been involved in the Inchon and Yalu River massacres. The moment he sensed that the carnage could cause large, long and indignant headlines, he engineered the records and disassociated himself with the actual operational event. When justice, honour and decency cast their shadows over the court martial of the unfortunate perpetrators, Forster had already orchestrated both the build-up and the aftermath. He himself had become a non-participating and morally shocked superior with no prior knowledge. With customary skills he simultaneously attacked and condoned the ill-fated soldiers involved. In a conversation with his wife he predicted that the inexperienced, opportunistic, self-righteous and politically browbeaten cowards in Pentagon would prefer to forgive and forget, as would the worthless caricature of a gold-digging commercial failure in the White House. Soon, Forster augured, the intoxicating blend of chauvinism, arrogance and megalomania mistaken for patriotism would sweep from the streets and into the corridors of power, and Washington and the rest of America would be back to normal.

Forster's own rewards were continued credibility, reverence and another star.

Everybody knew that he was a soldier of distinction, the pride of the American people and a true son of a great nation. Most Koreans and their Chinese comrades did not share this opinion, but they were only a bunch of unwashed bandits and ethnically too inferior to count anyway. The only exception Forster ever made, was Mao Tse-Tung, whom Forster respected as a tactician almost as brilliant as himself.

Forster's retirement speech was a masterpiece of native pride, blended with personal modesty and resignation mingled with deep-felt gratitude. The American people mourned the loss of a great warrior's invaluable services, and he disappeared from the firmament and into a precisely measured degree of inconspicuousness.

Forster, like Caldwell, was born and raised in Kentucky. Caldwell was pure and undiluted white. Forster had a few drops of black in him. It was not instantly evident from his complexion, but Negroid features were faintly present on his broad and strong face. Also, his hair gave him away; although it had turned iron grey already when in his thirties, the texture was unmistakable.

Forster's parents split up and vanished shortly after his birth, and his maternal grandmother brought him up. The lady was deeply religious; she had joined the church of a local preacher whose most burning desire was to make life as miserable as possible for his fellow man. Armed with carefully selected sections of the Old and the New Testament, the preacher was convinced that his mission could not fail. Grandma had become one of his most ardent disciples.

At the age of three Abraham Forster had become aware of his mixed origins. The seed of a deep hatred had been planted, and ever since his first day at school he refused to speak to his grandmother who had been brainless enough to screw a full-fledged nigger. Luckily, the grandmother died just before Forster's tenth birthday, the date he had chosen as the moment of retribution. Her departure deprived him of his chance to knock her off and conveniently avoided a local scandal, and he acknowledged later in life that the disposal of Grandma Nigger-Fucker would have done his career no good.

The feeling of belonging neither here nor there made young Abraham Forster exceptionally combative, intensely shrewd and immensely ambitious. Early in his teens, he weighed with clinical precision the options available to him. A future in the armed forces came out the clear winner. It wasn't the place to accumulate wealth, under normal circumstances, but everything had its price and he was convinced that his rewards would be promotion and power, followed regularly by further promotions and more power.

His studies had taught him that man once discovered that war was the solution to peace; peace followed war, and thereafter war followed peace. Man's passion for bloodletting followed man's need for a break, plus time to re-arm and rebuild what had been destroyed. The conclusion was simple; there would always be armed forces.

His second observation was that, in view of the way his country had conducted itself in the past, it would more than likely continue to follow the pattern in the future. The risk of redundancy was negligible.

Young Abraham knew that to become a cadet at West Point and leave as an officer was a long shot but not an impossibility. The fifth black man ever to enter the academy—Henry Ossian Flipper, born a slave —had done just that; he left West Point commissioned as a Second Lieutenant in the U.S Army as far back as 1876.

All Forster needed was someone to open the door. A local businessman of considerable status experienced inconvenience from his talkative mistress, and Forster solved the problem with deadly precision. The businessman contacted friends in high places and repaid his young trouble-shooter.

Forster cut a lonely figure at his hard-earned place at West Point. His natural aggression and sensitivity to anything resembling racism made him unpopular, but he finished West Point with top marks.

Soon after leaving behind the theoretical phase of his martial education, he decided to re-invent himself. He utilised all his considerable talents and his massive will power and emerged as a new and different Abraham Forster. The new Forster was sociable, tolerant, moderately humorous, likeable without resorting to being overfriendly, and incisive without being pushy. He never forgot a favour or a kind gesture. He was generous within his means, but he also ensured that his amiable and modest attitude was never mistaken for timidity.

Forster was still at an educational stage when America's inveterate respect for liberty and democracy made Roosevelt persuade his people to defend Europe's right to reject the intentions of The Third Reich, conveniently assisted by Japan's golden handshake at Pearl Harbour. Forster missed out on a divine opportunity, and for some years he was worried that the theories of his education would not be put into noble practice whilst he was still young and trigger-happy.

Then came Truman and his unselfish decision to assist liberty and democracy in Korea. Forster became forever grateful to what he in a rare, unguarded moment described as the worst political folly of the failed shopkeeper's many stupidities. This slip of the tongue came about long after the war; Truman had joined the rank of has-beens, and the United States was temporarily too busy with internal problems to defend freedom and liberty and more freedom and a bit of democracy anywhere else.

By that time, Forster had nothing but contempt for politicians, a specie he saw as phoney by nature and deceitful by profession. The vast percentage of Republicans was insular, selfish, hubristic and intolerant. They were geographically, historically and culturally ignorant, and everything they stood for in life was steered by the balance of their bank accounts.

The Democrats were no better, in most respects; what happened to make them more despicable, in particular, was their ludicrous misconception that being leftist gave them intellectual respectability.

One late evening, assisted by a bottle of Jack Daniels, Forster told his wife what he thought about the Congress, the Senate, Pentagon, the White House historically and in general, and, not least, the revered Roosevelt, historically and in particular. The reason for his outburst was that Mrs. Forster for the n'th time had accused her husband of infidelity. This pastime had become so blatantly evident that he had long stopped denying and trying to cover up. The difference, that evening, was that Sophie Forster's tried and tested patience had come to an end; she demanded a divorce. Moreover, she had a very clear and most disagreeable idea of how to split his whacking fortune. Another recently developed concept but one she kept to herself for tactical reasons, was that she could see several major advantages in a second marriage because by then one had learned to say *go-screw-yourself-you-bastard* with a smile that radiated sincere belief in mutual rapport and empathy.

Forster dissented. A divorce was completely unnecessary. Why not, instead, show a united front when needed and otherwise lead their separate lives? For the sake of marital harmony forever after, and with an eye on his assets, he promised that he would definitely be more discreet in the future. A divorce always had a cloud of scandal hanging over it; he did not need that, and he would not think that she did, either. He then went on to paint an attractive picture of their future in Washington; he had worked out a plan on how to cultivate political influence. His ultimate target was to gain access to the White House. He was not drunk enough to go into details, but Sophie Forster had known Abraham since their schooldays together in Kentucky. She knew from long experience that her husband was sufficiently equipped and adequately qualified to make realities out of his dreams. She nodded thoughtfully as he promised to cut down on his carnal activities, a problem he would overcome, however complicated; Washington was full of female predators with a voracious appetite for rich, famous and powerful men. The mere scent of this blend of aphrodisiacs was more than enough to remove the safety pin in any two-legged hand-grenade that thought she had something to offer.

Another factor, however unwelcome in itself, was that he was getting older now, though much wiser, thank God. He had, of late, concluded that it was no longer an absolute imperative to fall foul of anything without a dick, in contrast to, say, that bigot Roosevelt and other prominent sleazebags dominating Washington's tarnished history ever since Jefferson rode into the sunset in 1809.

Sophie Forster nodded again. Yes, she did understand him—understanding not being synonymous with approbation, if he didn't mind—but, in view of the pothole ride of their matrimonial experience, she would need some time to contemplate all aspects of his sketchily outlined project. Furthermore, considering the hurt, the suffering and the humiliations he had caused her during the decades, a two-million-dollar bank account in her own name would enable her to think clearer, and possibly also faster.

It was a shot in the dark; her problem was that she did not know the extent of her husband's wealth. Forster's problem was that he did not know whether Sophie knew about the methods employed to create his fortune. He had always been obsessively cautious and secretive, but he did not delude himself into believing it was possible to fool everybody all of the time, and especially not the one who lived under the same roof.

Sophie Forster noticed his hesitation and sensed that for once she could be sitting with all four aces. She asked him if by the White House he actually meant the Presidency; an idea she found utterly implausible since not only was he void of political experience, but, more significantly, he wasn't white enough.

His answer put her mind at ease and convinced her that he was still the same crafty jackal he'd always been. Him *president?* That was as probable as the Pope getting into his head to canonize Stalin or an orthodox rabbi becoming the next king of Saudi Arabia. He, Abraham Forster, had his ambitions, true enough, but when had he been short on a belly-full of realism? No, his plan was quite a simple one; so streamlined and uncomplicated that nobody would have the faintest suspicion and everybody would be stunned into temporary silence when he one day suddenly emerged as the new Chief of Staff. Now, this would take a few years. He would have to find the right person to become president; actually, he had somebody in mind, but the kid wasn't ready yet. In the meantime, Forster would cultivate and nurture whatever contacts necessary enabling him to establish a solid political foundation. To conclude, the spadework required among dumb, corrupt, vain and egotistical senators and congressmen was such that the presence and the assistance of a loyal wife would be distinctly helpful—so, what about it? It wasn't absolutely *essential*, he hoped that she did not misunderstand. If she *insisted* on a divorce, well…

Forster had been around long enough to acknowledge that the eternal constellation of *Male* and *Female* wasn't merely a question of gender; far from it, the real issue was one of *Culture* dominated by way of reasoning and, not least, tackling emotions.

Sophie Forster upped the ante from two to five million. Abraham Forster unlocked the door to the department in his brain that contained *Culture* and conceded. For a moment his lack of resistance surprised her. Then she figured that the loss of five million bucks was less detrimental to his plan than what the effect of a public divorce would have been.

Sophie Forster decided to cooperate. She asked who the vehicle was. She did not disagree with his choice of Cliff Caldwell, the up-and-coming senator from their native Kentucky. She had met Caldwell several times, and she had been impressed with his boyish charm, easy manners and seemingly considerable political acumen. He was from a once wealthy family of stud farm owners, but during the years their fortune had steadily declined due to fluctuating markets, hard luck and the element known as poor management. To make things worse, Caldwell had married a belle from Virginia without first checking her family's financial status. Their story ran parallel to that of his own clan, but Sophie Forster agreed with her husband there were times when character should overrule common sense, particularly if it should turn out to be an omen in disguise for somebody else. She knew that Forster had become Caldwell's benefactor and sponsor. Only years later did she learn that this apparent act of charity had its long-term purpose and implications, something she had suspected but could not prove. All summed up, his plan did not take her by surprise, and she began to wonder what it would feel like to become part of Washington's highest echelons.

Sophie Forster was white; when Forster had proposed all those years ago she knew that being a genuine blonde had been a contributing factor to her attractiveness, but she did not discount that his feelings for her were mostly genuine.

In time to come, she had let her once blonde hair turn grey without resorting to the magic of bottles, and she carried herself with dignity and natural grace. She was still a beautiful woman, well respected wherever she went and admired for the way she tackled her husband's concupiscence and indiscretions. Their three children, two sons and a daughter, adored their mother and tolerated their father. The grandchildren, eleven in all, worshipped their grandmother and endured their grandfather. Sophie Forster did nothing to upset the balance of what she saw as a just equipoise of graded sentiments; it was fair compensation, and the shaky equilibrium supported her long-term strategy vis-à-vis her husband.

Her father was a third generation Sicilian who had married a second generation Swede. He had been a law-abiding and honourable man who all his life had nursed a fascination with Sicily's culture and history, in particular the darker sides of the island's traditions. The concept of *omerta* became part of Sophie's upbringing. From when she could talk, Sophie knew there were moments in life when silence could be advantageous, as well as necessary.

She harboured her suspicions about her husband's entrepreneurial activities and tactics with supreme discretion, and although Forster trusted nobody, herself included, he was human, after all, and little signs could go a long way with somebody close enough to observe and shrewd enough to analyse, weigh up and conclude.

The more Sophie Forster thought about her husband's plan, the more she liked it. She knew of his contempt for Washington's megalomaniac bureaucracy, and she secretly began to admire his ambition to create a meritocracy and weed out all that made America wobbly, inefficient, hypocritical and ridiculous. Strength appealed to her—one of her reasons for saying yes all those years ago—and she found his vision so infatuating that before the night was over she had decided to stay by him; subject to irretrievable confirmation of the transfer of five million bucks.

Abraham Forster duly obliged, and Sophie began to take renewed interest in the house they had bought off California Street on Kalorama Heights. He asked her to begin to work on the wives of certain senators and congressmen, and whilst he still regularly commuted to the heart of his business empire in Kentucky, she now rarely joined him.

Sophie Forster decided to end her first and only affair, a brief fling with the Japanese ambassador. He took it with stoical dignity, partly because he was soon to be transferred to London, and partly because her idea of eroticism did not match his own fantasies. During their last night together she mistook his quietness for hurt feelings and, consumed by sympathy, a still vivid flame of passion and an uncomfortable blend of guilt, remorse and cognac, she cast aside her Sicilian inheritance and told him about the General's plan to revive America's pride and glory. The Japanese listened respectfully. He nodded politely when appropriate, and during the entire narration he concealed to perfection his disdain for a bunch of hairy barbarians whose behaviour had become increasingly asinine since Pearl Harbour. The conquest of the wife of someone who had surfaced as a national hero after rescuing a country by destroying it appealed to the ambassador's sense of humour. She was a white feather among other white feathers in his cap, and now the poor cow sought redemption by taking him to the private garden of her husband's clumsily planted and niggardly fertilized little beans. It was hilarious, no less.

Caldwell! The ambassador shook his head without moving a muscle whenever he heard the name and repeated silently his prediction that within a short century America would have gone the way of the Roman Empire.

Whilst Sophie Forster caressed his muscular arms—the ambassador had been a kendo master in his youth—he decided to repay her confidence in a way that further tickled his subtle brand of drollery. He asked her if she knew how the revered General had laid the foundation of his now formidable fortune, how a salaried soldier could turn into a Croesus overnight, so to speak.

She sensed something unpleasant and said, yes, of course she did, whereupon the ambassador stared at the ceiling for a while before he closed his eyes and said it was time for him to go to sleep and for her to go home.

Curiosity, together with the notion of useful information for future exploitation, won the day. She admitted that she wasn't quite so much in the picture as she ought to have been; there was indeed a secretive side to the General, or paranoid, to be perfectly candid.

It didn't take much prodding to make the ambassador postpone his beauty sleep. He asked her if she could remember a story that broke the news some years ago; a Korean general granted asylum after the war and who, together with his shrimp trawler, had been blown out of the water by an explosion forever unaccounted for. She had a brief recollection, but the story, too, died quickly, and she never had a reason to give it a second thought.

The ambassador picked his words with care and precision. He told her that the Korean had become steadily more desperate; he had left behind a tidy pile of a few million dollars when hurriedly departing from Seoul due to rumours of having been a mite too intimate with the North Koreans. For some dim reason he seemed to think that the American government owed it to him to extract the money from the new regime—a fantasy too ludicrous for words—or, alternatively, pay him out of Uncle Sam's pocket, which was equally ludicrous. His lost fortune became an obsession; nobody in Washington took him seriously—a fact he simply did not comprehend—and he became increasingly irrational in his behaviour. What had begun as a bad joke turned into a serious nuisance and from there into a veritable plague.

Having exhausted all sources of American origin, the Korean turned to the Russians who for a while kept him mentally afloat with hollow promises. Why the Russians bothered, the ambassador could not explain, but then the Russians did a lot of things that nobody could explain, themselves included.

One day, during a cocktail party, the Korean spotted the Japanese ambassador and approached him. It flashed through the Korean's mind like a divine revelation—or so he said—that who but a fellow Oriental could open the doors and make the Americans listen and pay heed to justice and fair play?

He pulled the ambassador aside and confided in him the same old sorry story that even the chauffeurs now knew by heart, but added that he sat on some explosive information that could blow Capitol Hill half-way across the Atlantic. He had been reluctant to use it, but… the threat hung ominously in the air. The ambassador wasn't too impressed; the Korean was a proven nutcase, but, on the other hand, a lot of funny things had been going on in Korea, so why not listen for a few minutes?

Well aware of the American passion for eavesdropping, the ambassador suggested that they should meet the following day, after dark, and go for a walk. This they did.

The Korean's story was indeed interesting. It told how General Abraham Forster had founded his financial empire by jamming immeasurable quantities of heroin into the bodies of American soldiers being sent home for burial; a not too complicated task, since there had been some 27,000 to choose from. The stuff had been shipped from Tangshan in China to Inchon in Korea, and this activity went on for two years. The General only called it a day a few months before Washington decided to withdraw their victorious forces from Korea's

657

bloodstained soil. The General's timing was perfect. Four of his closest partners in his ingenious enterprise, those who knew and could prove that they knew, were sent on a fact-finding mission, seemingly routine, but, unluckily, with fatal outcome. The General, caring as ever, did not rest until their bodies had been found, and that was the closing chapter in the General's handbook on how to get rich in the Orient. Those on American soil receiving the stuffed corpses—four co-operative and less than upright citizens, in the Korean's estimate—all met with tragic accidents. So did the veteran who had acted as go-between and the middleman who had carried out the General's instructions and deposited the money. Both encountered an unknown and obviously professional assassin since they disappeared without a trace and so did the assassin.

From then on, not one single live American knew the source of the supply. The distributors suddenly discovered that their contacts had vanished, and that the merchandise was no longer available.

Most interesting, the ambassador had said when the Korean had finished his tale. Tactfully handled, this was decidedly a constructive, persuasive and justifiable argument—properly presented—the Japanese could not see that Washington had the stomach for a scandal of such magnitude. He promised to get in touch with the right people and revert within two weeks. The Korean thanked him profusely, and they parted.

The ambassador went home, smiling to himself. He had no sympathy with the Korean and his ill-gotten lost fortune. Admittedly, it could have been fun to rattle the Americans to the bone, but the reality was that such an act would do Japan Incorporated no good at all. These were sensitive times, Nippon's financial, technical and economical conquest was well on its way; chunks of America were already in Japanese hands, and this was not the hour to rock the boat and make the Americans even more Oriental-hostile than they already were. Peace and quiet had to prevail; any hiccup could prove diversionary and therefore unwelcome, and no way should a schizophrenic little Korean be allowed to put a spanner in the wheel. Action had to be taken sooner rather than later. If the Korean discovered that even the mighty and supposedly friendly Japanese had turned against him, he would eventually figure out that he had no choice but to run to a reporter with access to the national media. This was potentially suicidal, a concept the Korean must have had arrived at and the reason why he had not done so long ago, but then, the ambassador thought, a cornered rat could do funny things if being kept cornered with no means of escape.

No way, the ambassador concluded. The day after he sent a message to General Abraham Forster and proposed a meeting.

Eight days later the Coast Guard spotted the wreckage of a shrimp trawler and picked up sufficient debris to establish ownership, but not even the never-resting Washington gossip machine could be bothered to get enthused over the demise of a deranged former ally.

Sophie Forster wanted to know if anybody else knew about this. The ambassador convinced her that such was not the case. Discretion was his trademark and, apart from that, what good would it do? To whisper such a sordid little story into the ears of any other American would be utterly meaningless, a sentiment with which she instantly agreed.

The ambassador did not see much mileage in telling her that his own private and personal offshore pension fund had improved considerably, all of a sudden. Neither did he feel obliged to inform her that her highly regarded husband had wisely concurred when the ambassador had pointed out that getting rid of a Korean fruitcake was a mite simpler than eliminating a Japanese ambassador—the killings had to stop somewhere—and, by the way, certain precautions had been taken. They drank to the mutually acceptable fact that silence had its price, and thereafter they drank to the amazing coincidence that there were seven letters in silence, million and dollars.

The ambassador also kept to himself that Americans were not the only human creatures equipped with ears, and that, during a trip to London, he had confided in his old friend Tadashi Ishihara. They had known each other for a very long time; Ishihara loved to be entertained with amusing anecdotes from the seedy side of politics—and which side wasn't, the ambassador had long stopped asking—also, his friend Ishihara was an ardent collector of snips and pieces of intelligence. The ambassador never asked why; minding one's own business was a prerequisite for continued friendship, and not for a moment did he believe that Ishihara would dream of sharing this amusing yarn with anybody else.

For some reason, Ishihara had found it particularly intriguing that Forster aimed for the White House, using Cliff Caldwell as a vehicle, but Ishihara's only question had been if the ambassador thought that Caldwell had sufficient appeal to be taken seriously as a candidate for presidency. Yes, the ambassador believed so; Caldwell was a silver-tongued worm who at least half the population would consider a delicatessen. He definitely had a talent for the kind of phraseology making diarrhoea-thin bullshit sound like divine revelations under a halo of dignity. In other words, being all frontage with nothing behind, he would be swallowed and digested as ideal for the job.

Sophie Forster said goodnight to the man who that night ceased to be her lover and went home, intoxicated with the power her new-found knowledge had bestowed upon her. What an ace, what a gem of an information, what a superb and magnificent tool suddenly in her hands—just a pity she didn't know all this prior to her request for the five million greenbacks. She could easily have made it ten, and he would have obliged. She began to wonder how much money her darling spouse actually had. Before she went to bed, sitting in solitude with a glass of sherry, she made a vow. She would force him to reveal the extent of his finances, and, gradually, she would begin to bleed him. Nothing life threatening, but enough to secure herself, her children and her grandchildren a carefree and opulent life.

A bittersweet smile played around the corners of Sophie Forster's mouth. A fine blue web of veins showed on her eyelids. A tinge of scarlet flushed her cheeks, and her breathing became heavy as figure upon figure danced like dervishes through her mind.

Ignoring the wishes of the South Korean President Syngman Rhee and the aspirations of General Abraham Forster, the United States, carrying the banner of the United Nations, had signed a humiliating armistice on the 27th of July 1953. Reluctantly accepting that the Korean conflict was over, Forster salted his money away in various offshore accounts and gave himself time to ponder. Dealing in drugs was out; an opportunity had come, he had exploited it, and now it was gone. He was not aware of any suspicions against him; the evidence had been erased and it was time to think like a law-abiding citizen. He was firmly convinced that the United States would not enter into another war for a long time—ergo, no more golden opportunities—and he decided to retire whilst he was still young enough to embark on another career and make positive use of his millions.

It did not take long for Forster to determine what he wanted to do. For the next couple of years he invested his time in nurturing his image. He visited veterans' hospitals, he became active in a carefully selected assortment of charities, he gave lectures at universities, and he began making trips to Washington where his unassuming nature and generous and understanding attitude soon made him popular with an increasing number of politicians, none of whom saw him as a threat, a-political as he was. Practically all of the embassies enjoyed the company of this liberal, steadfast, knowledgeable and objective American, indeed a rare animal. He participated in television debates about his great and cherished country's past, present and future; his learning on American history was impressive even to historians. Each fee he received he modestly gave to charity—but, alas, somehow this was seldom kept confidential, as promised. There were always unprincipled people who wallowed in the cheap sensationalism of leaks and breach of trust; lurid vultures, as he was forced to call them.

Forster built up his dossier with the same systematic approach he had employed during his previous occupation. With his property in Kentucky supplementing his reputation he went to his local bank in Lexington and asked for a two-million-dollar loan. The world was a madhouse, sadly—who would know better than a professional soldier— and the fact remained that a lot of countries were in the market for arms. Did it not make sense that the United States met this requirement and not, say, France or Germany or the United Kingdom or—God forbid—the Soviet Union? The United States was sitting on this colossal surplus from Korea; would it not be more sensible to dispose of it against payment instead of letting it corrode away? As long as those lunatics from South America or overseas or wherever were so hell-bent on acquiring armaments, why not oblige? Nothing was going to stop those guys; America was not the world's policeman any more, and, in the General's considered opinion, imbalance of power between nations, large or small, was simply not conducive to peace and stability on earth.

He proudly showed them his newly acquired licence. With a minimum of formalities the loan was granted on generous and flexible terms.

Abraham Forster showed his gratitude and amply rewarded each member of the Board of Directors.

Most African leaders knew that General Abraham Forster shared their view on American imperialism. They shared his contempt for politicians who explained and analysed with supreme authority hardship never experienced and to whom human suffering caused by wars were mere academic concepts. They knew that he disagreed with Washington's tendency to interfere with other countries' internal affairs. They knew that he despised the American attitude of lofty moralism. They knew that he sympathised with the 24th Infantry Regiment—the only black unit in the entire armed forces except for the officers—and that he deplored the court-martial of the 32 blacks condemned and found guilty of panicking and otherwise doing a lousy job in Korea; half of them sentenced to death or life imprisonment and the rest receiving 10 to 15 years. The new chapter in American race relations being opened by President Truman's decision to desegregate in 1948 had certainly benefited himself, as it happened, but the treatment of the 24th Regiment had been nothing but a racial matter and a gross insult to all black men.

What they did not know, was that Forster never repeated such sentiments in the presence of a white audience. His black brethren were convinced that in Forster they had found an American whose guts and integrity could not be disputed, and they loved his countenance as much as they worshipped his demeanour. One by one they became his friends—Forster's private definition of friendship being more a matter of convenience than of substance and time—and an empire was born. The warlord, who as a young man had dreamed of power and glory attainable by ordering young men to kill other young men, had found his true vocation. It was distinctly more sensible and immensely more rewarding to sell a gun than to tell somebody to use it.

Forster soon discovered that although the loan from the bank was helpful, it was far from adequate; his business grew rapidly, and he found himself seriously under-capitalized. With the assistance of some carefully selected and handsomely paid straw-men, one local and five out of state lawyers, he laundered ten million dollars through the casinos of Reno, Las Vegas and Monaco over a period of twelve months.

For a while he did not sell anything a man could not carry, and he struggled; some were slow payers and some did not pay at all, but little by little, gaining more experience by the day, he established a foot-hold. Within four years from his first sale, he was the world's largest individual arms dealer.

Forster followed a policy of openness; he co-operated wholly with all governmental bodies involved. This paid off. Forster was seen as a patriot, a formidable source of revenue, and a highly reliable channel of clandestine military and political intelligence. In return, he never encountered the petty bureaucratic problems befallen lesser operators.

But Forster's greatest achievement was not his incredible commercial success, nor the respect of successive administrations; the masterpiece was *anonymity*—hardly anybody knew his line of business.

When Forster severed all contacts with the media and cut out public appearances, it did not take long to become the forgotten hero of a war that few wanted to remember and fewer wanted to talk about.

Once again, Forster had re-invented himself. He had turned into his own image of Cardinal Richelieu, the Grey Eminence whose energy thrived in darkness and who preferred the shadows when performing his activities. His personal contacts were top brass only, a handful of senators and congressmen, and, abroad, never below ministerial level.

There were no inconvenient ethical principles in the way. Forster could not care less whether his client was democratically elected, whether he was a sergeant promoting himself to Field Marshal one day and President the next, whether he was a well-meaning fantasist of a school teacher who had decided to become his country's saviour—they all needed arms to defend and protect the freedom of their people, and they all had an ego in need of massage.

The day-to-day running of Forster's business had been taken over by Michael Sheldon, a Korean veteran who Forster had known since their days together at West Point. Seldon had returned from the war a bitter and disillusioned man. After a brief spell attempting to return to society and a normal life, he failed to adapt to the contempt dished out by the American people on the survivors of a war the veterans had never asked for. Seldon quit his job as technical director of a security firm and went to Mississippi where he joined an ultra-right militant group, loosely associated with the Ku Klux Klan.

One day, dressed in his camouflage gear, Sheldon visited a bar in Vicksburg and began drinking. There were three men present; a sluggish and obese barman, a black man in his late fifties, and Sheldon. The Negro dropped a few snide remarks about the stupidity of extremism, and, guessing that he was dealing with a veteran, the black man began to question the bravery required to slaughter children and women. Seldon went into a rage. He pulled his gun and shot the Negro between the eyes. The barman called the local Sheriff who arrived within minutes, handcuffed Sheldon and dumped him in the nearest available cell.

During the evening Seldon sobered up and began to contemplate his predicament. He asked if he could make a telephone call. This was granted, and he called his ex-commanding officer. Forster listened and said that he could be there around noon the next day.

Forster duly showed up. He carried a briefcase that contained a concealed camera. He asked the Sheriff for a few minutes of privacy with client Sheldon. The Sheriff had no objection. He genuinely believed that Forster was the prisoner's lawyer. After a short while Forster asked to be let out of the cell. He eyed the Sheriff with a profoundly sorrowful expression. Then Forster nodded towards a bar across the street and said that he badly needed a drink. Would the Sheriff be kind enough to join? Never one to turn down a break, the Sheriff consented after ten seconds of professional deliberation. Aware of his own importance, he gave a lengthy instruction to his baffled deputy, and off they went.

Twenty minutes later the deputy saw his boss and the lawyer drive off in the Sheriff's car. Within the hour they were back in the office.

It was time for the deputy to have his lunch. He sauntered over to the local diner where the waitress told him that the lawyer had offered to pick up the tab later.

The Sheriff unlocked the door to Sheldon's cell and went back to his desk. Forster opened his briefcase and took out two brown envelopes. He handed them to Sheldon together with a concise message.

Sheldon could not agree more. Self-defence was not a crime and never would be, hopefully.

The barman, a white and God-fearing Christian, praise the Lord, was more than willing to testify to this effect.

Forster stepped out of the cell and the Sheriff stepped in. He made a funny comment about paying for one's crime but stopped laughing when he saw that the other two clearly did not understand the joke. The brown envelope got lost inside his shirt and behind the belt decorating his impressive belly. Then he picked up the telephone. All three looked out the window and listened to the humdrum of the ceiling fan until the barman arrived. The Sheriff got busy with his paperwork. The barman went into the cell. Forster stood outside, as he did when the Sheriff went in, holding the briefcase in front, and with the appropriate facial expression to match.

Forster thanked the Sheriff for his time and complimented his diligence, his high moral standards and his legal faculties. The barman offered a drink on the house which Forster accepted before he caught the bus that would take him to the locals' primitive idea of an airport.

It did not worry Forster that he had left the sunny state of Mississippi thirty thousand dollars poorer. His briefcase contained what he saw as a future investment, including photos and suitable objects with fingerprints of a Sheriff and a barman.

The Sheriff, on his part, praised Sheldon for his choice of lawyer; white niggers were indeed few and far between.

Forster got Sheldon an up-and-coming defence lawyer; ambitious, cunning, rapacious and black. The trial was brief. Sheldon had minded his own business, quietly enjoying a single shot of whisky, when the black man became aggressive and insulting. Getting no reaction from Sheldon, probably the psychological reason behind the Negro's offensive behaviour, he became menacing and had pulled a knife. Sheldon had retreated, trying to avoid the knife which was cutting big holes in the air, but, finally, with his back against the wall and with nowhere to go, yes, Sheldon had pulled his gun, but only after several warnings had he fired. The Sheriff confirmed that the black man was a trouble-maker with violent tendencies, something nobody else had ever known about, and the ugly knife found on the floor did have the dead man's finger prints on it. His family could not recall ever having seen the knife before, but evidence was proof and dissensions were not.

Duly acquitted, Sheldon accepted Forster's invitation—or was it an order—to come to Kentucky. Forster explained the essence of his commercial activities, its growth and potential, and he concluded by making it clear to Sheldon that the business required a hands-on director in charge of daily operation. Thanks to his background Sheldon knew the commodities; everything else was a matter of tuition, and Forster was willing to invest whatever time needed to make Sheldon a valuable colleague. One thing, though, Forster stressed; back in the old days Sheldon had been an extrovert, humorous, sympathetic and courteous young man. Nobody could help him to become that person once again— that he had to do himself. Sheldon believed that this was possible; with the kind of money Forster had offered him, anything was possible. Another little detail was that Sheldon had no choice, and he knew it. Forster had put a pair of golden handcuffs on the table. Behind them, somewhere in Forster's possession, was access to the real ones. Forster had shown him the photos of freedom bought, and Sheldon had no illusions about his benefactor's ruthless character.

Sheldon joined, learned and flourished. He became a born-again Christian, married a girl from one of the best families around, and earned his reputation as one of society's pillars. Most people were moved by his unswerving loyalty to Forster, another pillar, and over time Seldon managed to bury the image of a cell on death row in the middle drawer of his consciousness. He and his family enjoyed the trappings of wealth and status, and both he and Forster carefully avoided the one subject that could bring discord to their relationship.

It did not bother Sheldon that whilst he was heavily involved in most all technical aspects of the business, he was never part of Forster's financial manipulations. Forster operated a number of offshore companies, and his on-shore enterprises were a complex and intricate conglomerate where in particular the sales of chemicals and major equipment were dealt with by Forster himself. Sheldon never learned the true turnover or the actual profits made, and neither did he discover where the money ended up. He was too wise to try to investigate and sensible enough not to ask. He knew that it certainly was not for tax reasons; Forster paid more than he actually had too, an opinion often voiced by the firm of accountants they used. Sheldon resigned himself to the conclusion that Forster knew what he was doing, and that he, Michael Sheldon, was better off being kept in the dark.

As time went by, Forster again became interested in the overall welfare of the nation. He bought a house in Washington and renewed his contact with a few selected charities and welfare organizations. His deeds were pure benevolence; politically, he had no profile and no apparent inclinations. He did befriend the young and promising Democrat senator Caldwell, the state's favourite son, but, clear to everybody, it never went beyond social association.

Having repaid his loan to the bank and using the bank's services forever after, up to a point, Forster had been invited to join the Board of Directors. He gracefully accepted. One weekend, at a shooting party, Caldwell mentioned in passing that he intended to apply for a loan. His family was growing, as were his commitments, and he needed a larger house. Forster shook his head, took the young man aside and warned him against such a financial liability until the senator had established himself more firmly in Washington, and, as things went, till he had picked up a few bones. The bank had its principles and guidelines. It would almost certainly reject Caldwell's application; the necessary security simply wasn't there.

Another unfortunate fact was that all banks leaked, like it or not, and did Caldwell need such a humiliation? Forster could not imagine so. On the other hand, Forster could very well understand the situation. He had once been young and destitute. It would be a privilege for him to offer personally the assistance that Caldwell needed. A private loan—nothing wrong with that—and on more flexible terms than any bank could offer. All in writing, of course, and, needless to say, within the limits of the law. Something to think about?

Caldwell went home to his wife. The next day he called Forster and accepted the offer.

Forster prepared the document. It was remarkably short but why complicate things between friends? Caldwell scanned through it and silently praised the Good Lord above for the existence of Abraham Forster. The ceremony took place in the impressive library in Forster's luxurious home.

Just before Caldwell was going to sign, his attention was diverted by Forster who deftly swapped one document with another from an assortment of paperwork on his desk.

The first document read *interest free loan to be re-paid at convenience* and the second read *in return for specific political favours.* Forster steadied the paper with both hands, covering the text, and Caldwell signed. Forster handed Caldwell a transfer slip but no copy of the document.

As advised by Forster, the elated senator went to Frankfort and introduced himself to a bank he had not used before. The money was deposited into a joint account in the name of Cliff and Sheryl Caldwell.

Forster and Caldwell began to see more of each other. Caldwell enjoyed the company of the kind, wise and experienced businessman with such a glorious past. Forster treated the young political lion with respect and consideration.

More and more of Forster's time was being spent in Washington. With increasing but not conspicuous frequency he invited Caldwell to luncheons and dinners with important senior politicians. Caldwell could not believe his luck. His star continued to rise. One or two desirable committees came his way, and all the time he had Forster in the background whenever advice was needed.

Taking a break from time to time was a healthy principle, Forster one day told Caldwell on the plane back from Washington. Unwind, forget it all and just relax for a few days. Forster himself preferred a spot in the sun, like Panama or Puerto Rico or Florida. Why not join forces one long weekend, recharge the batteries and come back rejuvenated and eager to re-enter the treadmill of life?

Forster mentioned the date for his forthcoming mini-holiday to Panama. Caldwell consulted his wife, received her permission and accompanied Forster.

It was the first of several vacations together. Caldwell learned to enjoy himself in a way he had never before savoured. Forster knew all the best beaches, the best hotels and the best company. He was relaxed, easy-going, entertaining and generous. His dearest hobby was to take photographs with his marvellous Nikon. He also knew such an incredible number of interesting people, and there was nothing he loved more, almost childishly so, than to show off his best shots of Caldwell surrounded by charming and engaging characters.

When Caldwell first hinted at presidential aspirations, Forster donated five million dollars to an offshore account, but omitted to mention that the company was registered in Caldwell's name. *Funds for the future*, as Forster described it, adding with a fatherly smile that one day the United States of America would cry out for a president in the mould of Lincoln.

Caldwell hesitated, at first. A vague instinct told him to be on guard, but the hurt expression on Forster's face was enough to drop further objections. Forster was his benefactor and his mentor and as clean as they came, utterly trustworthy and more discreet than most. He obviously could afford and knew how to channel money where and when needs be, and to run for president was indeed an expensive affair. Without Forster's help there was no way Caldwell could even afford to dream of becoming president, that much he knew and acknowledged.

Caldwell thanked Forster for his act of unselfish largesse; how could this incredible kindness and support ever be repaid —?

Repaid? Forster shook his head in disbelief. He was a soldier and a patriot, and to see a young American of Caldwell's stature as president was a more than ample reward.

Caldwell did not tell his wife about the offshore account. It took a backseat in one of the smaller cubicles of his memory bank.

Sophie Forster never forgot her vow. She had the General by the balls, and she knew how to squeeze. Her wealth, together with that of her children and grandchildren, steadily grew. She had acquired her own properties in Washington and Kentucky, and she began to see more of her family than she once had dared hope. If she could not visit them, they visited her. She seldom bothered to inform Forster about her various arrangements. On the face of it, he did not seem to care. That suited her almost as much as it suited her children. She knew that he still had his affairs, but at least he had become sensible and considerate and appeared to perform his somatic acrobatics neither in Washington nor in the state of Kentucky. This she appreciated, acknowledging that Washington was by far the country's largest multi-building whorehouse and that Kentucky was brimful of hot little fillies who recognised a high-priced stallion when they saw one.

Everything went so well for Sophie Forster in her effortless accumulation of riches that she one day decided to ascend from the marshland of exorbitant demands to the Himalayas of uninhibited greed.

Her once dear husband listened in silence, nodded in between and said that he would make the necessary transactions.

Three weeks later, crossing the Massachusetts Avenue, Sophie Forster was hit by a car. She died in the ambulance on its toilsome way to the hospital. The driver of the accident car was a black youth stoned out of his mind. He was an old acquaintance of the police and had an impressive record of never being short of a few thousand dollars without ever having had a job. He collapsed and expired from an overdose two days later. The police were at a loss to explain how such a tragedy could possibly happen to someone in the protective custody of the boys in blue.

Sheldon called Forster who was in Africa on business and conveyed the sad news. Forster came back and went straight into mourning for three full months, interrupted only by the odd nightly interstate helicopter flight required to discharge his juices and maintain his testosterone equilibrium so vital to his sanity.

His sorrow was there for all to see, and, although he was unapproachable, everybody felt for him and hoped for the day to come when he would recover from his trauma.

He did, eventually, after ninety days. The community admired his dignity and they all welcomed him back from his private hell of sorrow and despair. Caldwell, in particular, was tremendously supportive, being a close friend. He and his wife did whatever they could, as tactfully as humanly possible, to assist Forster on his long road back to a meaningful existence and a life worth living. Their Christian attitude evoked considerable veneration, and more and more agreed with Forster in his assessment of the young senator; he had all the qualities called for to be an outstanding president, compassion being one of them.

Quietly, like a mild breeze across the Sea of Galilee, the gospel spread. It came to Washington, and the number of followers multiplied and Caldwell walked on water. The people flocked around him and nowhere were there room for a Pontius Pilate in their midst, let alone a Judas Iscariot.

Abraham Forster was satisfied. Soon, nothing could stop Caldwell becoming America's next president. Forster would be appointed the president's Chief of Staff. After three years the vice-president would resign, due to ill health. Forster would fill his position. Caldwell would get re-elected, but within a short year of the second term he'd be struck down by a mysterious illness. The presidency, inevitably, would be left in the capable hands of Vice-president Abraham Forster.

It was all predetermined, prearranged and with every detail in place. Caldwell could not fail to become president, and, under the guidance of Forster, re-election would be a formality.

Forster smiled to himself each time he thought about it, sitting in solitude in his library and planning the long-term strategy of an omnipotent United States of America. The harsh reality, he knew, was that the nation was still too young, too immature and too confused to come to grips with its racial complexity. The American people were not yet ready to opt for a coloured president, however qualified. He stood no chance of being elected, not this century and probably not the next, either.

Abraham Forster laughed softly and thanked his distant God for a democracy so flexible and a constitution so liberal that occasionally elections were not required.

A new dawn was coming. Soon the sun would shine on each and all, and the length of a man's shadow would no longer be dictated by the colour of his skin.

29

Jennifer and Yasmin did not pay much attention to the American primaries. They watched the odd program on television and saw the entire event as a colourful, overhyped and somewhat ridiculous circus.

As one candidate after another fell by the wayside, the media became increasingly starved on gossip. The eventual winners, the Democrat Cliff Caldwell and the Republican George Milland, were both men with a past void of full-grown skeletons in the cupboard; one or two slips and mishaps here and there, yes, but nothing lurid or revolting, nothing that could create abominable and eye-catching headlines. Some rumours whispered in the wind, tales were being fabricated and assumptions drawn, but before long the media and the American people began to think that the two candidates were a cut above the majority of their predecessors.

Both won their candidacy by a wide margin, but on either side of the Atlantic two worried men resided—Forster in the United States and Ishihara in England. The reason for their apprehension was George Milland. The Republicans had pulled the same masterstroke as the Democrats; a potential icon from nowhere, a young, able and rational politician who inspired confidence and whose political agenda was sane and thoroughly plausible.

There were few basic differences between their programs. Both parties had deftly pinched from each other, and they adapted their style whenever and to whatever they found useful. Experienced pundits agreed that the battle for the presidency would be won on the television screen. The polls that at one stage had predicted a walkover for Caldwell were down to fifty-fifty, and most observers agreed that this time they would get a race for their money.

Milland came across as the more sombre of the two. He did nothing to conceal the grey of his temples. He moved with the ease of a fit man. His gaze did not wander. His small but even teeth showed less readily than those of Caldwell's and his laughs were shorter.

The Democrats knew that they had a problem on their hands; Milland was composed, he was cool and his sincerity was alarmingly convincing. He had the footwork of Sugar Ray Robinson and the relentless stamina and punching power of Rocky Marciano. Without exception, Milland answered a question with an answer and not with an evasion or with a counter-question. Forster soon became aware of Milland's forte, and he acknowledged that Caldwell could have problems going the distance with Milland. Loss on points, technical knockout or blasted out of the ring all came to the same.

Forster intensified the training and the preparations, and Caldwell did not disappoint. He became incisive, bold and assertive without losing his natural charm. He reduced the frequency and shortened the width of his smile. He became more euphonic, gave himself more time before he answered questions, treated hecklers with mild ridicule and stared unflinchingly and longer at anyone addressing him.

The final television duel between the two candidates became a memorable event. Seasoned commentators, experienced observers and shrewd punters had Milland ahead up to and including the penultimate round. Then, during the last three minutes, Caldwell showed what he was made of, or, as Forster saw it, what *he* had done with the raw material and produced as the final product. With electrifying charisma and with an aura of utterly convincing probity, Caldwell surprised everybody except Forster by promising significant individual and corporate tax cuts within eighteen months. This was a complete U-turn from the Democrat manifesto, and it caught Milland flat-footed. The bell went before he could get his act together and go for a desperately needed ten-and-out; he reeled against the ropes unable to regain the initiative, defeat masking his face.

Forster had long been aware of the age-old experience that voters everywhere were prepared to sideline their brains should it come to the crunch; it was the harmonious and well-tuned voices from the heart, the stomach and the wallet that decided what went into the ballot box.

Caldwell won by less than two hundred thousand votes, a result that stunned and infuriated the Republicans almost as much as it pleased the Democrats. Caldwell was accused of cheating, but he explained with blue-eyed credibility and syllogistic reasoning that only lately had the American economy taken a turn for the better—it was there for all to see, by the way—and that it would have been wrong to incorporate such a promise *only* if what he saw as a *reality* had not been backed by facts. The statement made Wall Street raise an eyebrow, but Caldwell was not deterred. He was going to stand by his vow. Together, he and the American people would see to that.

Ishihara and Vargas sat up all night and watched Caldwell's rise to eternal prominence. In the early hours of the morning Ishihara called Vargas and suggested a few hours' sleep before they met in Vargas's dojo.

They went through a sparring session before Ishihara sat down. He shook his head. He said, "That news conference was amazing. Caldwell impressed me with his effortless casuistry. He's quite a talent, our new president."

"He is a politician."

"He surely is, but don't you find it interesting how their opportunism and their truths and their lies can balance on the thin edge of expediency, and how the final selection between the three depends entirely on a cynical evaluation of degrees of probability?"

Vargas loosened the belt on his gi. He said, "Go back through history and tell me when political integrity was not an oxymoron."

"I know, but I still find it captivating that people everywhere and at any one time are prepared to swallow these verbal excrements. I mean, even Hitler came to power with almost fourteen million votes behind him."

"The human element."

Ishihara rubbed the soles of his feet. "It won't be long, now. Forster has got to show his colours before Caldwell enters the White House. Then, instantly, Caldwell has to explain why Forster is to become the Chief of Staff. The more he delays it, the more of an upheaval he risks. Poor Caldwell, he doesn't know what he's in for." Ishihara grinned. "I've got to admit that Forster really is a most incredible man. He has played his hand to absolute perfection. Caldwell can't even turn and say that if *he* goes down, Forster will follow—he won't. Forster is sitting on a rock, and Caldwell is one step away from the quagmire. Forster can prove everything and Caldwell can prove nothing. He's quite a master tactician, our General. Caldwell hasn't got a choice—it's either him or Forster."

"That's the choice—assuming Caldwell is ruthless enough."

"True. Every plan has its components of unknowns, as we have seen so many times in the past, but what else can Caldwell do?"

"Hope and pray."

"What happens if Caldwell does *not* eliminate Forster? How can Caldwell possibly live with a situation like that? He can't." Ishihara cracked his finger joints and began to kneed his calves. "Do you believe he can?"

"Yes."

For a split second Ishihara looked flabbergasted. "Impossible," he said. "He'd be a nervous wreck within six months." He chewed on his tongue. His eyes got smaller. "Are you saying that it is *not* going to happen?"

"No."

"For heaven's sake, Angelo—"

"Esther."

"What?"

"Sheryl Caldwell. She'll make it happen." Vargas smiled thinly and looked at the palms of his hands. "You must learn to read characters. Caldwell will hesitate, dither and struggle with his fears. No such compunctions with little Sheryl. We could not have asked for a more reliable ally—ergo, happen it will."

"How do you know all this?"

"I listened to everything you told me. Then I did my sums. You should try it, one day—listen and sum up."

Ishihara laughed and looked out the wide-open barn doors. "Soon," he said. "Very soon. The day is close when Igor Parkhurst will be invited to lunch by his old friend Pritchard-White." He curled his toes and smiled. "The final contribution to our pension fund is only months away, Angelo, and we can become renowned gallery owner and master chef. Apropos, have you mentioned to Jennifer about Yasmin and Hiroshi whilst I am away?"

Yasmin's patience had at long last been rewarded; Hiroshi Ishihara, the first samurai of the Tokugawa lineage to be born outside of Japan, was six weeks old. During the first month of his birth, his proud sire had been mentally and emotionally out of reach, but a composed Yasmin had gently managed to haul him in from the Milky Way and the sensation had been reduced from miracle to marvel.

Hiroshi had arrived three weeks prematurely, and only eight days after Ishihara had come back from his first reconnaissance to the United States. The close experience with unpredictability had sharpened his protective instincts, and he had made it clear that he would not allow Yasmin to be alone with the child.

"Not a problem," Vargas said. "I shall take it up with Jennifer in due course."

Ishihara stretched his arms above his head with a satisfied look on his face. "I think we can expect a call from Uncle Igor any day, now."

"Any day?"

"Mark my words. I give it two weeks, maximum."

"End of February or early March," Vargas said.

Ishihara lowered his arms. "What makes you say that?"

"Logic."

"What logic?"

"It is unlikely that Caldwell will jump to conclusions the moment Forster tells him what is going to happen. Caldwell will need time to think things over. He will have to tell Sheryl. He will need to find an accomplice; that is, Sheryl will have to make her husband summon up the guts needed to call in Tony Bianconi, confide in him and ask him to arrange a brighter future. Now, would you have done that as President-elect or as President inaugurated and installed in the White House?"

Ishihara sat silent for a time. "I see. That means a delay of several months." He punched the floor with both fists. "This is not very professional, but because of Hiroshi I hate even thinking of delays."

"There is nothing we can do about it. It would be folly to make a further investment before we have heard from Pritchard-White."

Ishihara knew that Vargas was right. To use another considerable amount of money and time in the United States for a final and up-to-date scrutiny without having been commissioned was lunacy. The intelligence had to be as fresh as humanly possible. Ishihara cursed silently; he should not had let himself be influenced by the birth of his child. Sentiments could lead to the kind of circumstances where mistakes were being made; his mind elsewhere, and all it took was one or two tiny but vital pieces of information to slip through the net and Vargas got killed, or, worse, never saw the outside of a prison wall again.

Even the most insignificant coincidence could lead to catastrophic results. During the years, Ishihara had prided himself with always having everything at his fingertips, backed up by a series of contingency plans stretching from the very plausible to the nearly unthinkable. Maybe he was beginning to lose his edge; it had been a long time since their last assignment, and complacency was the illegitimate child of affluent idleness.

Ishihara got up and went over to the doors. The ground was covered with dead leaves whisking across the grass flattened by an early morning downpour. He looked at the tall and dark green pine trees standing proud and indifferent to the wind.

Let me assume that Angelo does not come back, he thought. We always ask for fifty percent up front. That means five million in the box, irrespective. I cannot lose. Jennifer does not know about the nature of the assignment and ditto about any financial arrangement. Does she *have* to? No. Angelo can direct every penny of it into an account in her name. He can leave instructions with his lawyers or his trustees in case he does not come back. Angelo is the one who will negotiate with Bianconi, as always, and there is nothing I can say or do about it. Will Jennifer give me half if Angelo does not return? Only if he has left instructions for her to do so. I can *not* lose? Ishihara heard his own staccato chuckle and closed his mouth. Let me take this one step further, he continued his reflections. Let me assume I make an intelligence slip, but Angelo survives and comes back. Will he give me my share or will he say I have not earned it? Supposing he does say that. What can I do about it? I can accept it gracefully, never talk to him again and try to live my life with *minus five million dollars* written across my heart. Or I could kill him and terrorise Jennifer to hand over my half. Then his Middle-East contacts will come looking for me. It won't take them long, and I have Yasmin and Hiroshi to think of.

Ishihara closed his eyes and did a series of *ibukis*. All of this has gone through Angelo's mind, he thought. There is no escape. I shall do my best. The rest I leave in the hands of my gods.

He finished his breathing exercises and turned to Vargas. "I need to sharpen up, physically and mentally. We never could afford mistakes, and this time least of all." He bowed. "Let us start with a few *katas*."

Two hours later Ishihara drove off. Vargas went back to the house. He found Jennifer sitting at the kitchen table with a pencil between her teeth and a pad in front of her. Anu was on the floor, practizing backward crawling with breath-taking speed.

Vargas said, "Hello, my beauties. Busy times?"

Jennifer dropped the pencil. "My parents are coming for the weekend. I told you." She squinted and pressed her tongue against her front teeth. "I think my fridge is too small."

"Get another one."

"Where do I put it?"

Vargas sat down. "Yes, it is a bit cramped, this place. You've only got five hundred square metres to play with. Build an extension." He rubbed his thighs. "I'll go and get you another fridge this afternoon."

She smiled warmly. "You can be such a darling, Angelo."

He looked at Anu. "Come to Daddy, little princess."

Anu gave a grunt but did not bother to look up. "Her vocabulary is still limited," he said and frowned.

Jennifer rolled her eyes. "Yes, I find that rather alarming, myself. Practically all babies her age are already familiar with the classics, I've heard. What on earth can we do?" She looked at him. "Perhaps your genes didn't click in properly."

He touched the tip of her nose and went for a glass of milk.

She chewed on her pencil and pretended to concentrate on her immediate acquisitions whilst thinking how Vargas had mellowed, a process that had begun when he stopped drinking and that had improved further when Anu came into his life. He was friendlier with people and he smiled more often; admittedly, that didn't take much, but he also chose his words with greater care and consideration. She would not go so far as to call him sociable, but he did try, and he did show progress. He had conquered the art of saying *excuse me* without making it sound like a confrontation, and those who asked about background and family suddenly found themselves talking about their own lives. Vargas had become adept at changing subjects and his strategy never failed. There were those who wanted to know why he did not drink alcohol, and had he never…? to which he casually remarked that he had never taken to the stuff, as simple as that, accompanied by a shrug intimating indifference. He had also begun to describe himself as a *country squire* when people became inquisitive about how he was making a living; a *retired* country squire, and the explanation was always the same—he had sold his rubber plantation in Malaysia. All the other fanciful versions—

rude and capricious taunts, as Jennifer once had thrown at him—had been dropped, and, although never a conversationalist, he had become less reticent.

Overall, she concluded, he treated people with shade more respect—or less disdain, whichever—than before, but she had a feeling that he had reached his peak, and there he would stay. Regardless, it was a distinct improvement, and thank heavens for that.

Vargas said, "Tadashi is going away for some weeks. He asked if Yasmin and Hiroshi could stay here. We are probably talking about end of January."

She looked up, puzzled. "That's a fair bit away."

"I guess he wanted to be reassured. I said I did not think you would object."

"Of course I would not object. Yasmin can't be on her own in that big house, not with a baby. Why is Tadashi travelling again?"

"He is winding up a few loose ends."

Jennifer put her hands on the table. She played with the pencil. Her eyes were clear and her stare direct. "Has this to do with your last assignment?"

"Yes." He raised his glass whilst still looking at her. "Just a few more months, and it will all be over."

She forced a smile. "Thank God." She rolled the pencil towards him. "Have you got any plans for the future?"

He smiled and took her hands. "I have, but it is going to be a surprise. Something we can do together, long-term. You will love it. I know you will."

"Oh please tell me!"

He shook his head. "No. I have planned it as a surprise, and that's the way it is going to be. I want to see your face when—well, when it happens."

"When?"

"Not later than end of March." He smiled at her. "Don't try to pump me."

"You have made me very curious."

"It will be worth waiting for." He picked up Anu and placed her on his knee. "Hello, my beauty queen. What have you been doing today?" Anu shook her dark curls, giggled and reached for the milk glass.

Jennifer said, "Careful. I don't want milk all over my new table cloth."

Vargas took Anu tenderly by the wrist and steered her hand away. "No spill, princess. Mummy will be upset. We don't want that, do we?"

Anu tried again. Vargas kissed her hand. "Daddy said no."

She looked at him with her big green eyes, wriggled ecstatically and shot forward. This time she succeeded. Vargas picked up the glass. Jennifer leaned across the table, took Anu's hand and gave it a light pat. "Naughty girl!"

Vargas' grip on Jennifer's forearm was so painful that she gasped. "Don't you *ever* hit her again," he said, his voice so husky and strained that the words came like a snarl.

She tried to compose herself. "You are hurting me," she said quietly. He lifted his head and let go of her arm.

Jennifer rose from the table and walked across to the window facing the yard. Anu prattled busily. Vargas stroked her hair.

It took several minutes before Jennifer spoke. Her voice was low and controlled when she said, "I do not want our daughter to become a spoiled brat who can get away with whatever pleases her. I do not want her to grow up not knowing what is right and what is wrong. I want her to learn manners, to learn how to behave and to learn how to conduct herself. We cannot give her a harmonious and healthy and proper upbringing without guiding her. If we do this in a sensible way she will one day become a young lady who is sure of herself. She will know who she is, what she is and where she stands. She will be equipped to meet life as a balanced person and not as a rich man's irresponsible and ill-mannered daughter. That is our obligation to her, and it is my intention to fulfil my duties. I hope that you will help me. Your reaction was irrational and I ask you not to insult me by apologizing."

Carefully, Vargas put Anu back on the floor. He looked at Jennifer. Why do I remain unable to decipher that expression, she thought, that look of mild but detached curiosity? What is behind it? It is *not* indifference—that is what I used to think—but what is it? Is he still summing me up?

Vargas turned without a word and walked out. He came back two hours later and found Jennifer and Anu in the garden.

He said, "Your fridge will be here tomorrow."

He knelt down and put a finger under Anu's chin. "Been a good girl whilst Daddy was away? We don't want you to grow up a spoilt brat of a rich man's ill-mannered daughter, you know. We want you to become a real lady, like the one who seduced your father."

Jennifer turned away to hide her smile.

You devil, she thought with a tenderness that made her close her eyes. You are two different persons, Angelo Vargas, and I love you both, God help and forgive me.

30

Forster slipped out of Washington in the early hours of the grey autumn morning following Election Day. He went as quietly as he had arrived. Caldwell stayed on for a few days. He was still trying to come to grips with the fact that he was going to be next president of the United States.

Forster had vanished without a word, not even a goodbye. For a while Caldwell did not take much notice until suddenly he was being confronted with questions about the composition of his government. Most of the prominent positions had been debated and analysed beforehand; the party's elders, the power-brokers and whoever else who had a say, or thought they did, had voiced their opinions about desirable posts for the president to consider. There were many brilliant people around, and, evidently, there were not so few favours to be re-paid. There were influential persons one should not offend, and then there was the future to consider, politically and financially. Caldwell began to sense the enormity of the ruthless politicking that was going on, combined with an increasingly uncomfortable feeling of being out of his depth. The brutal realities of his position and of his future hit him like a sudden tornado and he struggled to keep his smile in place. The constant whispering in his ear became nerve-racking. He knew that he needed to sit down with someone he could trust, someone who could help him navigate through the rocky waters whilst he was still close to land and the Plutonian realities of the big ocean had yet to be encountered.

Forster had been around for weeks. Where the hell was he now in this hour of need?

Caldwell made a dignified exit, and he and his wife returned to the comparative peace of Lexington. He was greeted as a hero; mostly, he thought, because people did not know how to spell *celebrity*. His few, old and trusted friends joined forces with an untold number of brand new friends. They all revelled in his triumph.

Forster stayed out of the fray; not on one single occasion did he show up. Neither did he call. This baffled Caldwell, but then, on reflection, the General was such an unassuming man. He probably waited for things to calm down—or, it suddenly occurred to Caldwell, for him to call Forster, which he eventually did.

"Hello, Abraham," he said. "How are you doing?"

"Very well indeed, thank you. How are you holding up?"

"Not bad—not bad. I have been here for four days."

"Yes, I know. Television has not concentrated on much else. It has been a joy to watch you, my son. I congratulate the American people with their choice of president."

My son. That was a new one. Caldwell said, "Listen, Abraham, I need to talk to you."

Forster did not answer.

He continued, "I need your help. I can see one or two problems ahead. You know, the odd complications with people—I don't think I fully understood what a rat race it is up there, until now."

"Anything in particular?" Forster asked mildly.

"Well, let me put it this way—I have to clear my mind."

"Any time, Cliff. Why don't you come over for a drink, at your convenience?"

"Today?"

"I am here."

A maid opened the door. She advised that the General was in his library. Caldwell went in. Forster was standing by his desk. He had a sheet of paper in one hand and a glass in the other.

Forster smiled. "Cliff! Good to see you again." He put the paper and his glass on the desk and extended his hand. "Once again, my congratulations. How does it feel, Mr. President? You must be absolutely thrilled. A drink?"

"I could do with an Old Crow. Neat, please."

Forster poured the drink and topped up his own. "Let us sit down over there," he suggested and beckoned towards a pair of heavy, black leather chairs. "They are, as you know, very comfortable."

They sat down.

"Cheers," Forster said.

Caldwell said, "You disappeared rather quickly." He was not sure if he'd managed to keep a slice of accusation out of his voice.

"Oh well," Forster said and clinked the ice in his glass. "The day belonged to you." He raised his gaze. "My old role had come to an end—as simple as that."

Caldwell took a sip, and then another, before he scanned the walls and said, "I know it wouldn't have been possible without you, Abraham." He paused, still looking around. His voice trembled when he continued, "I do not know how to thank you. How can I ever repay everything you have done for me?"

Caldwell was unable to interpret the smile on Forster's face. Abashment? Modesty? "You always give and you never take. I—I simply..." he shrugged with an expression of mild despair on his face. "It is embarrassing. I just do not have any idea what I can do for you in return." He shrugged again and looked into his glass.

"I do," Forster said.

Caldwell's eyebrows moved. "Oh?" he said and showed his teeth. Expectations radiated from his eyes. "What's on your mind?"

"Chief of Staff."

"Say again?"

"Chief of Staff."

Caldwell laughed. "I always enjoyed your baroque sense of humour, Abraham, the arabesque way in which your mind moves. You like throwing jokes like little napalm bombs, don't you, even if they are not meant to go off."

"This one is, except that it is not a joke," Forster said.

Caldwell lowered his glass. "Sorry, I am a bit lost here. I mean, it *is* a jest..." he tried to smile but drank instead.

Forster crossed his legs. He kept his glass cupped in his hands. He said softly, "Why can't I be serious?"

Caldwell searched for words. Here I am, he thought, with a hell of a lot of problems which I need to talk to him about, and all he can do is have me on. He coughed into his handkerchief. "Abraham, I came here to thank you and because I can really do with your help. Can we stop playing games and get down to brass? I have to go back to Washington, and, believe me, there are a few complications ahead."

"I believe you."

"Fine," Caldwell responded quickly and clasped his hands. "Shall we begin with…"

"Chief of Staff."

Caldwell leaned back. He rested his head against the solid ridge of the chair and tried to control his irritation. "This is not funny any more," he said in a flat voice.

"It was never intended to be funny. You are the new Mr. President. I am the new Chief of Staff." Forster put his glass on the table and got up. "That is how it is. No joke, and certainly not funny in any other way I can think of."

He walked across the large bay windows and looked towards the sky. "Accept it gracefully and with dignity, Cliff, and thank your God for Abraham Forster." He turned and stood erect like an officer on duty. "I made you president. I will ensure that you become a good president. I will ensure that you get re-elected. Without me you are nothing, not even mediocre. That has not occurred to you, has it?"

Caldwell said, "No, it has not." He injected a touch of weary indifference into his voice, "I don't know what the hell you are talking about." He tried to catch Forster's eyes, but the General stared past him. There was an unfamiliar shine in his gaze.

Forster spoke slowly, "Without me you will not survive. Washington is a more savage jungle than you have yet to discover. I can guide you through the minefields, past the booby traps and the ambushes and out of sight from the snipers. You are but a recruit, a greenhorn, a rookie and an inexperienced kid who on your own will be eaten alive within six months. You know as little about infighting as you know about anything else. Please don't delude yourself. You do need me."

Caldwell said lightly, "I'll learn." He was pleased with the way he controlled his anger.

"You won't get the chance to learn. You will be in a political wheelchair without knowing who placed you there. You will become a caricature and a scapegoat, more inept than Herbert Hoover and more ridiculous than Woodrow Wilson." Forster's eyes became little slits. "You are not exactly on thick ice, my boy, with a massive fortune behind you and a venerated and blue-blooded family to consult. You have got *nobody*—except Abraham Forster."

"Amen," Caldwell said. "I think I am going home. Dean Goodman is to become my Chief of Staff. He is an excellent choice, I have been told." Christ, he thought, Abraham is either more drunk than he looks, or he is slowly but surely going mad. I'll talk to him tomorrow. Hopefully he's got his marbles back, by then. "Thanks for the drink, General," he said.

"Dean Goodman is a dodo. A scan of his brain would come out blank. Your vice-president Matthew Rackow is as useless as he is insignificant. When the mid-wife pulled him out she left his identity behind. What you have got with those two is a couple of colourless sycophants. They'll prove as effective and reliable as a pair of crutches made of glued-together champagne glasses."

Forster was pleased with the word *colourless*. It had the sweet smell of molasses mixed with gunpowder. Like *success*, which was equally sweet and far from monochrome. At present Cliff Caldwell was *colourless*, and when he returned to his natural whiteness he would still look anaemic. In a few years time America would have a president who would turn upside-down the entire nation's concept about *colour*. Abraham Forster's lips parted. His eyes had the gloss of a man unfamiliar with incertitude.

Forster said, "Have another drink."

Caldwell's stare was blank. There were beads of perspiration on his forehead. He said, "No thank you. I wish you a good night's sleep."

"It will be better than yours," Forster said. He took a few steps nearer when Caldwell left his chair.

"I beg your pardon?"

Forster said, "I do not think you will sleep at all, unless you come to your senses."

"*I* come to my senses?"

"Correct."

Caldwell sat down again. "Listen, Abraham," he said patiently and did his utmost to sound reasonable, "I couldn't make you Chief of Staff even if I wanted to. You know how these things work. The Senate will never approve. I may be president, but I am certainly not the Almighty."

"I know how these things work," Forster said and sat down opposite Caldwell. "That is why I know you won't have any problems. You *insist* on me. You *compromise* on something else—that's how things work. I know those guys. I knew them before you left school. My rating among them is pretty high, as you are well aware of. I know how they play, Republicans and Democrats alike. I know their weaknesses. I know what they are made of. I know the chinks in everybody's armour. I know that our new president will face a very hostile Congress with a solid Republican majority—something you appear not to have picked up. You still think that you do not need me?"

Caldwell said, "Abraham, you are not a politician. You have never been one. I do not want to hurt you, but you are asking for the impossible. Nobody will take you seriously. Let me think about some arrangement; you know, like advisory capacity—something like that."

Forster smiled. "Cliffie boy, you have just committed the eighth deadly sin, which is to believe that we know what is going on in somebody else's mind."

He walked over to his desk. "Talking about being taken seriously," he drawled and picked up a sheet of paper, "what do you think about this one?" He sauntered back and dropped the paper casually on the table in front of his guest.

Caldwell picked it up. He read quickly. "That's a grotesque joke!" he spluttered. "I never signed anything like this!"

"Is it not your signature?"

Caldwell's eyes were fixed on the document. He did not answer.

"I swapped the papers," Forster said. "That is the one you signed. Payment for favours. Not a loan."

"You won't get away with this," Caldwell whispered hoarsely. "*Political favours*—how absurd can you get?"

Forster put his hand in the pocket of his burgundy smoking jacket and pulled out a handful of photographs, which he spread in front of Caldwell. "Look at these."

Caldwell frowned. He shook his head, robot-like.

"This one," Forster suggested and pointed with his index finger. "That is you in the company of Wilfredo Gomez. Best of pals, it looks like. Mr. Gomez is a very prolific drug-dealer. Still at large, I should add. He is also a killer. That one, that is you and Joachim Steiner, the arms smuggler. Shall I name all the other ones and what they do for a living? It was a pity I couldn't join you around the table, but somebody had to take the pictures."

Caldwell was ashen. His hands shook visibly. Forster went over to his desk. He came back with another piece of paper.

"Your offshore account. Some of the money came from Mr. Gomez, some from Mr. Steiner and some from other nice people you have cultivated. I presume I don't have to emphasize that I have all the necessary evidence, in case you want details."

Caldwell closed his eyes. His breathing came like gasps from a man suffering severe chest pain.

Forster eyed him with contempt. "You are a sparrow among eagles, my boy," he said and took away his pieces of persuasion. "I am your Chief of Staff, Cliff, and the sooner you announce it, the better. I sincerely hope that we now fully understand each other."

Caldwell opened his eyes and put his hands between his knees. He pressed hard.

"If I go down I'll drag you with me."

Forster smiled benignly. "How?"

Caldwell did not know. His mind was spinning and he wanted to throw up.

"You don't," Forster said. "There is no link. The pictures will reach the media from nowhere. The offshore money did not come from me— to which the bank can testify—and the money for your house came from a source which does not lead back to me." The smile widened. "How can you drag me down with you? Your argument is as effective as a regurgitated aphrodisiac."

Caldwell twiddled with his handkerchief. He pressed it against his mouth. He wiped his eyebrows. He looked up towards the ceiling with lifeless eyes. The raspy noise from his breathing filled the room.

Forster watched.

Ten minutes later Caldwell had regained sufficient self-control to speak. He said, "I understand, Abraham. You are my Chief of Staff. I shall find something else for Dean Goodman—and a plausible explanation."

"No president worth his salt has ever been accused of being short on plausible explanations," Forster said amiably. He raised his glass. "To harmony, tolerance, wisdom and experience. God bless America, the President and his Chief of Staff. Apocalypse postponed."

Facing and surrendering to the inevitable had helped Caldwell to recover. "I really did underestimate you," he said. "I was naïve enough to *believe* that you did it for me. That is what's called blind trust, isn't it?"

"It wasn't a question of under- or overestimating me," Forster said. "The simple fact is that you did not read me at all. That is not blind trust, young man. That is self-generated insanity." Forster placed his right hand over his heart. His smile became patronizing. "It is a shocking state of affairs when your best advice to anybody is: *trust nobody*. The long history of man taught us that—correction, taught the few of us who bother to read history. Most politicians don't, and those who do fail to take heed."

Caldwell sat slumped in his chair. He was too drained to listen. Forster stroked the grey crop on his head tenderly with the palm of his hand. Then he suddenly made a fist and slammed it onto the top of the table. Caldwell jolted. He stared wild-eyed at Forster's open mouth and flaring nostrils.

"The elite!" Forster shouted. He threw his head back as if to avoid a left jab from an imaginary opponent. "It is only the *elite* who learn from history. I know. The elite has long understood that we will never reach the stage when it is more attractive to protect innocence than it is to misuse it. Do not forget that, and you might begin to grow up." He wagged a finger. The condescending grin lingered on. "The *elite*, Cliff. There are not many of us."

"Can I go now?" Caldwell said.

"Do that. Tomorrow we shall get down to hard work. We shall start from scratch and move from there. Up and up, that is. Pleasant dreams, Mr. President."

Caldwell found his way out.

Forster kicked off his shoes and put his feet on the table. He folded his hands behind his neck and stared through the ceiling and out towards the great universe beyond where dreams floated freely and barriers did not exist.

Caldwell would not do anything silly; the poor jerk so badly wanted to be president. The thought of pending scandals petrified him, but not enough to make him commit suicide. Bar taking his own life, what other options did he have? No, Caldwell would concur, adjust and survive. He was a human sponge—*a born politician*—credit, in all fairness, where credit's due.

There would be no need to use the evidence. Just as well, Forster mused with the shadow of a smile, since the publication of any of it would effectively torpedo his own ambitions—no Caldwell, no Chief of Staff. It was a deterrent, and, as such, it would work precisely because of Caldwell's disposition. Forster was ninety-nine percent sure that he had read him correctly. No great military man would ever say *one hundred percent*; there was always this *one*-percent left, hanging in the air, somewhere, the one-percent that represented the unforeseen, the out-of-character element, the unpredictable and the patently idiotic.

Forster rested the cool rim of the glass against his lower lip. Say Caldwell could no longer withstand the pressure of knowing that he could be wiped out overnight. Say he confided in somebody who in turn confided in somebody else, or the kid became so self-absorbed that he had a nervous break-down—which was all right as long as it did not happen within the first three years—yes, the perils of the unexpected were always present. No plan involving other people could be hermetically virus-proof. That was a fact of life, and, as such, a calculated risk that had to be taken.

Forster sipped. His plan was odds-on to succeed. If Caldwell went to hell, at least he would go on his own.

Forster gathered his material and put it back in the safe. A complete set of copies was in a sealed envelope in Glen Morrit's office. Morrit was Forster's local legal advisor, a man of stature and a lawyer of note. His file on Morrit was extensive, a neat bundle of intelligence so explosively discriminating that Glen Morrit did not take a coffee break without Forster's permission.

He had contemplated a third set, this to be deposited with one of his offshore companies, but he had decided against it. Bankers were notoriously unreliable, untrustworthy and deeply dishonest. He knew that quite a few bankers entertained themselves by peeping into their clients' safety boxes. The more he thought about it, the more he became convinced that any decent and upright person should have as little as possible to do with this scum of the earth, displaying such a disgraceful and unethical behaviour.

Forster spread his legs, straightened his back and took the stance of Napoleon.

Caldwell would either play ball, or he would shoot himself. Stripping the entire matter down to its bare essence, there was nothing in between. Based on an objective scrutiny of the kid's mental makeup, he would go for the ball and shun the gun.

Forster grinned. He added a few drops of bourbon into his glass. All his vast experience with men under pressure told him that Caldwell would turn into a good soldier, happy to take orders from one whose destiny it was to command.

☞

Sheryl Caldwell came across as fragrant, quiet, shy, winsome and demure, a part she'd played to perfection since she was three years of age. Cliff Caldwell was convinced that no psychiatrist was sufficiently qualified to spot her true character; she would have run rings around an entire herd of them.

Many a long year had come and gone since Cliff Caldwell learned that his darling wife was anything but the irresolute and puzzled little doll he'd once thought he had married. There was steel in the lady, and that steel was acid-proof. It had been produced by a forger with access to heavenly counsel, and it withstood any corrosive attack. It could not break, and it could not bend.

Cliff Caldwell went home. He got into the kitchen unseen. He went over to the sink and turned on the tap. He cupped his hands and the water pushed the phlegm back in place. He sneaked into the toilet and stared at himself in the mirror. He looked as if he had been for a walk in a blizzard. His eyes were watering and his lips were blue. The skin on his face looked like sickly-pink sandpaper.

Cliff Caldwell took off his tie and dropped it on a chair. He undid the top button of his shirt and saw that the sweat on his upper lip had dripped onto his chin. He wiped his face with a paper tissue and walked into the drawing room.

Sheryl Caldwell listened with unblinking and expressionless eyes whilst her husband related his tête-à-tête with Abraham Forster. Only when she was sure there was no more to come did she speak.

She began, "You fucked-up, braindead caricature of a dickhead, how moronic can you get? I told you all along that your badly diluted nigger is a slimy creep, but were you *compos mentis* enough to listen? Evidently not."

Caldwell bowed his head in shame. *Mea culpa*, he thought, but he refrained from saying it loud. It would not have made an impact.

Sheryl continued, "Furthermore, why didn't your limited assembly of brain cells make you ask the simplest of all questions, namely: is it even remotely possible that an authorized killer turned licensed apocalypse merchant took you under his wings because his golden heart is the size of the state of Kentucky? That is how any *sane* person would have reasoned." She continued to circle him. The heels of her tiny shoes tapped against the wooden floor. "And now," she purred, "are we now supposed to believe that the General wants to become Chief of Staff just because he is in need of exercising his adrenaline?" She sat down on a high chair with a straight back, her knees pressed together and her delicate little hands folded in her lap.

Caldwell was not able to read the expression in her cobalt-blue eyes. He clicked his teeth and frowned. "What do you mean?"

Her perfectly shaped lips parted. Her voice came across like a diamond-cutter on glass, "Yes—what can I possibly mean?" Her head was bobbing. "This is really intricate, isn't it, darling? Let us go back to the beginning, my precious Cliff. You led me to believe that we had a loan from the bank, but there was no loan. The money was given to you by the General. That means, technically, that the General owns most of this house. You never repaid a cent. That alone can kill you overnight as a politician. You have been photographed in the company of notorious criminals—drug barons, killers and arms smugglers. You accepted an offshore account—" Sheryl rolled her eyes "—an *offshore account* to the tune of five million dollars in your *own* name. The General can prove that the money came from among others your drinking buddy Wilfredo Gomez, probably the worst sample of mankind that Puerto Rico has ever produced." She lit a cigarette. The smoke seeped from the left corner of her mouth. "None of this did I know anything about. Isn't it both nice and reassuring to be so close to your wife, Cliff?"

He avoided her stare. His mouth felt as if a deceased racoon had replaced his tongue. His pulse had reached third gear.

Sheryl Caldwell's smile would have made Lucretia Borgia feel like a saintly and virgin nun. "Did you ever query why Forster raised all those millions for your campaign fund? Did you ever wonder *how* he did it? Did it not *ever* strike you that Forster could be as harmless as a landmine under a pile of fifty-dollar notes?

Oh no, not you, Cliff. You are as surprised as Hoover was when once caught telling the truth. You *trusted* the piece of shit. Well, you certainly showed consistency. Your friendship with the sonofabitch made you as proud as an uninitiated prick, and your kudos made you as blind as it made you mindless. Sacred Christ, how in hell could you be such an imbecile? Even Washington deserves better than to be contaminated by your deportment."

His neck shrunk. The bile in his mouth grew. He wanted to vomit and locked his jaws. From afar he heard his wife's voice, "All in all, Mr. President, the General has got you hanging by your nuts. That is square one, Cliff."

Caldwell rubbed his tongue against his front teeth. His mind was numb, and, which was worse, it was also empty.

Sheryl said, "Next step. What do you think is the General's target in life?"

"He wants to be Chief of Staff," Caldwell rasped. "I told you."

She smiled. Her face had the heart-warming appeal of a cut and crumbling wedding cake. "Dearest Cliff, you did. However, I wasn't asking what your great mentor wants to be come *January*. I asked for your intelligent opinion about Forster's *target* in life. Please, try not to confuse the two."

Caldwell wished that he could stop perspiring. "I don't follow," he said.

"You don't? I accept that. Let us try to apply a touch of elementary logic, then. Try to imagine *who* Abraham Forster is, and then *what* he is. Ask yourself a few questions about his colour, his careers—plural—his wealth, his tactics, his strategies, his Washington contacts—Cliff Caldwell included—does not the answer give itself?"

Caldwell was lost. "What?" he said.

"Abraham Forster wants to succeed you as president of the United States."

Caldwell gasped. "He'll never be elected!"

Her laughter could have given a nightingale an inferiority complex. She said, "No, he wouldn't. But he doesn't *have* to be elected, you see. He'll fill the vacancy created when Cliff Caldwell resigns."

"You're out of your mind, Sheryl!"

Her expression was an even blend of pity and contempt. "Forster's plan is so simple in its ingenuity that it cannot fail," she said, carefully lifting a tress from her forehead. "Forster will stay Chief of Staff until your vice-president suddenly resigns due to medical reasons, say, within roughly two years of your first term. Abraham Forster becomes the new vice-president—do remember that you haven't got a say—and within the end of the first term he is the most experienced creature in the White House. You perform well, and Forster tells you to go for re-election, which you do or else. He stays on as vice-president. Then, within half a year or thereabouts of your second term, you have to retire. Forster will come up with a perfectly sane and credible reason. Who is then the president of the United States?" She winked at him, but there was malice in her eyes. "You are perfectly right; the bloody cur knows that niggers don't get elected presidents. All he needed was a canny and innovative plan requiring *one* secret vote and that vote he bought from you. Not bad, my darling. You must be proud of yourself."

Caldwell gulped. He felt as if he'd swallowed a pound of hash. "I need some water. Please get me some water."

She got up. "Don't faint on me, darling. We haven't finished yet."

She came back with a glass of ice and water in one hand and a tumbler quarter-full of bourbon in the other. "Here," she said. "Calm down. Don't drink too fast."

Sheryl walked across to the windows overlooking the paddocks. She thought of her father Joshua Beaufort and of her childhood in Virginia. During her adolescence he had warned her repeatedly to be wary of any man who combined success with a low profile. How right the old fox had been. She was in no doubt about the advice he would have given her had he lived to hear of Abraham Forster and his scheme.

She turned and noticed that half of Caldwell's bourbon had been absorbed. "Feeling better now?" she asked.

He nodded. The giddiness was gone and his body wasn't on fire any more. He looked into his glass with an empty stare and said, "What do we do now? Forster is going to wreck our life—" the sigh came like the dying gasp from a wounded sheep "—it is a nightmare."

Sheryl's family could be traced back to the early part of the seventeenth century. She had loved listening to her father's tales from the good old days before slavery was abolished. Beaufort's hatred against the blacks did not stem so much from the fact that they were of a different pigmentation as from the catastrophic reality that they were too dumb to understand that they were inferior. A logical consequence of this deficiency was that niggers were incapable of conducting themselves in a fashion acceptable to the superior white race. It did not help that blacks were repulsively ugly, although this added jest by Mother Nature was possible to live with. Neither did it contribute to co-existence on the same planet that they reeked like a heap of rotting corpses. Beaufort had known all his life that God had made a serious mistake when He created the talking ape. Beaufort was equally clear in his opinion of that white trash Abraham Lincoln, a goddamn no-good, primitive and sly peasant; a traitor of such enormity that Judas was a saintly and well-meaning choir boy in comparison.

Another of Joshua Beaufort's insightful opinions was that there was only one thing worse than being black, and that was being a mongrel. This Beaufort had preached whenever he was in the mood, which was daily, and Sheryl had not forgotten. Being a mongrel spelled that at some stage a *white* person had been involved. Any other transgression, individual or in total, faded into oblivion when equated with the unspeakable act of one white, male or female, screwing or being screwed by a nigger.

Now, Beaufort had sermonized, waving a fist, praise the Lord and all His angels that there were remedies for such a crime against God and mankind—evidently, God could not control everything—and the simplest of those remedies was a bullet in the neck. The glorious invention of firearms had been inspired by the Almighty Himself—who else—partly because He had finally realized His mistake, and partly because it was a quick, dignified and inexpensive way of culling the breed and exterminate the mongrels. Sheryl smiled when she recalled what her father had claimed as scientifically proven: "*A mongrel is lethal because he has enough brain cells to plan and implement afflictions and calamities of unsuspected proportions on innocent whites.*"

Sheryl Caldwell pirouetted and faced her husband. He sat slumped in his chair, clinging to his tumbler with both hands. He looked hopelessly lost and dejected. His face had taken the colour of mother-of-pearl, and his nostrils moved as if he half expected a free sniff of cocaine. A typical politician, she thought; his intellect does not match his conceit, and when cornered he gets paralyzed.

She said, "Well, Mr. President, what is your solution?"

He did not move.

"You want to give up, don't you?" she said. "You are sitting there contemplating how to tell the world that, sorry, but I've just discovered I've got a heart condition, or something, and farewell White House and goodbye future."

She walked over to him, sat down on the edge of the chair and let her fingers slide through his khaki-coloured hair. "We shall eliminate the problem," she said softly. "We will do so shortly after the inauguration."

It took a while, but finally he looked up. "How?" he said tonelessly.

She knew there was nobody else in the house; the maid had gone shopping and the children were at school, but she still looked around before she leaned closer and whispered into his ear, "The General will be in his grave before Easter. There is no other solution. I know that, and you know that."

He wanted to move his head, but she held it firmly between her hands. She came closer. He could feel her teeth nibbling on his earlobe. "Hush-hush, baby. Either, you and your family are being destroyed, or that fate befalls the General. It is him or us." She let go of him and went back to her chair. Her eyes made Caldwell think of a pair of translucent moonstones in an oval setting.

She said, "We shall work out a plan, my apple-pie; a simple, economical and above all workable plan. You cannot do it on your own. At present moment you are as powerless as an egg in an incubator. We need the assistance of other people. That is unavoidable. It is also unfortunate, since it increases the element of risk. No plan is waterproof, but let me emphasize—however unnecessarily, I hope—that even a high degree of risk is worth taking when we consider the alternative. Having said that, you only need to confide in one other person, and if he is what I have reason to think that he is, any link between you and the timely death of Abraham Forster simply will not exist."

Caldwell managed to shake his head. "People just don't walk around assassinating each other," he muttered. He looked ten years older than he did on Election Day.

Sheryl Caldwell tilted her head. "Welcome to Year One, my little bubble."

The silence was heavier than an executioner's axe. He said, "But…"

"They do," she interrupted. "They do it all the time. Your problem is that you have never experienced realities. All you can refer to is a brief and closeted little job in your younger days. Tell me, what have you actually encountered when it comes to real life? You are the *classic* politician. You have never been exposed to the cruel and shabby truths out there. You moved from a small cocoon and into a bigger cocoon. You feed on thin air and your tenets have their roots in expediency and narcissism. Your brittle, little theories are masqueraded as altruism and they are as changeable as the winds. The only true target you've ever had in your life has been to win an election. The quintessence of your existence is the smell of power and the illusion of being important. Without exception, you politicians are a bunch of perverted and pathetic little crooks. You spend most of your time inventing laws to protect yourselves and legislating regulations to hog-tie the rest of the population."

She tapped her forefinger on the nearby side table. "Look at me, Cliff. There are more crimes instigated in Washington than in the rest of the United States put together. Most of those crimes we do not hear about, and do you know why? Because only the unsuccessful politician gets caught, the one too inept to commit the perfect crime. Perfect crimes are either never discovered or never exposed, Cliff, or they wouldn't be perfect."

He coughed. "There are not many perfect crimes."

"Oh yes, there are. The reason we don't hear about them is called *corruption*, a useful piece of depravity as widespread as any other sleaze dominating your world. Together with cronyism you have an umbrella the exact size of Washington."

Caldwell throat was burning. He coughed again.

Sheryl said, "Have a sip. You sound like a mechanical frog. Haven't you got any intelligent comment to make about the centre of the universe you're soon going to rule?"

Caldwell didn't feel like adding anything to his wife's analysis. He feebly raised his left arm and said, "Who can help us?" He watched her slender little body getting up and coming closer. She took a sip of his bourbon and walked the floor in silence for a while. She stopped four feet away and said, "Toni Bianconi."

He was lost. "Say again?"

"No, my darling," she said patiently. "I refuse to believe that you do not know who I am talking about."

He clasped his head with both hands. "Of course," he mumbled. He looked up. "How did *you* know?"

"Oh dear," Sheryl Caldwell said. Her eyes embraced the large, curved sofa covered with colourful textiles. "How does one come to know *anything*?" She took off her shoes, placed herself in the corner of the sofa and stretched her legs. "You may recall that I have spent some time in Washington," she said. "What in holy hell did you think I was doing up there?"

Caldwell waited for an explanation. He had no idea.

She said, "I familiarized myself with the place. *Familiarized*, Cliff. Do you understand? I got to know people. I learned who is who behind the scene. I detected who are time-wasters, who are time-servers and who have *real* juice. I discovered who are those *not* on The Hill assigned for *what* when it comes to friendly persuasion. I found out who are being consulted when more surreptitious methods are required. I call it my *Little Black Book of Amenities*, and only an idiot would fail to acquire one." Sheryl stopped for breath. Her contempt filled the room like smoke from burning tyres. "Some call it *doing your homework*. We are going to spend eight years in that can of worms, and I'm afraid your good looks alone aren't sufficient to make you a great and proficient president." She pressed her knees together, snatched a banana from the fruit bowl and began to peel.

Caldwell saw the shadow of his head move on the wall. His brain felt as active and useful as the tusk of a mastodon. Sheryl threw the peel back into the bowl. She continued, "Before I tell you what you so plainly don't know, let me draw you a picture which should put your mind at ease and make you see the perspectives of what we intend to do. Imagine yourself as a district attorney. After a while you get political ambitions and decide to run for office. Halfway through the race you are being presented with a murder case. Somebody gets arrested, but in your heart of hearts you know that the poor shit is innocent. However, you need to be seen as someone who can perform, someone who lives up to his promises on law and order, for instance. So, you get the hapless dimwit convicted and condemned to fry. Do you at any one point turn around and say: "Sorry, but the suspect is innocent." Of course you don't. Your entire career would disappear down the gutter overnight unless the *real* killer shows up, but let us assume for the moral of the story that he doesn't. The one in the cell is all you've got. Here comes the funny part—you admit to yourself that you haven't *really* got that much of a problem. There isn't much left of your conscience; during the years it has slowly but surely eroded because you came to understand that *conscience* is an extravagance that no true politician can afford. Justice? Justice is what prevails at any one time for the one who is sitting with the best hand." Sheryl licked her fingertips. "As of January, my precious one, *you* are the foremost exponent of American justice. Do you follow?"

Caldwell nodded. His mouth twitched when his brain reminded him of what a smile looked like. He thought of her analogy and scratched the inside of his thighs. Sheryl was right. Things went on all the time.

She said, "Except that you and I are talking about the General, and the word *innocent* is as applicable as it was for Billy the Kid and Al Capone."

"Yes," he said. "That makes it much easier. I mean, it's rational."

"Isn't it? Now, let me tell you what else I did in Washington, and, I must say, it was amazingly easy the moment I got the knack of it." Her blue eyes rested on the chandelier over the staircase. She moistened her ruby red lips.

"What?" he said eagerly.

"Washington confirmed what I suspected. Most politicians are not alarmingly brainy. Take them outside their kindergarten where the vocabulary is non-political, and they are as confident as monkeys on an iceberg. This, added to their overall behaviour, their demeanour and their mannerisms makes it comparatively easy to sort the boys from the men. You quickly learn to distinguish what a man is and what he wants you to believe that he is. You learn that most of them are bumblebees; unimportant little non-entities who borrow their light from the real luminaries, bumblebees who languidly try to pretend that they've got a personality and whose idea of portraying significance and substance boils down to gossiping and name-dropping. Add bragging, and you have the turd summed up and presented inside a coconut shell. If he is also inclined to gloat, which is usually the case, you have got the ideal medium for whatever message you wish to broadcast. Now, isn't this interesting? Yes, it is, because it means that you and I have an entire army of bumblebees at our disposal. Believe me, that will prove more useful than you at present can imagine."

"For what?" Caldwell said.

"For dropping hints about the General's poor health. Just remember to underline that this is *highly* confidential, and it'll be all over Washington faster than the bullet that got rid of Lincoln."

"Forster's demise will not come as a surprise?"

"Bravo."

He looked at her. "I have met Tony Bianconi. I remember him."

She clapped her hands. Her cold and uncompromising stare went through him and left ice water on his spine.

She said, "Tony Bianconi is going to be your one and only ally."

"But I have only said hello to him a couple of times. I do not know the man."

"Nobody knows Tony Bianconi."

Caldwell frowned. "But—" he looked increasingly confused "—hasn't one of his sons got a prominent position in the FBI?"

Sheryl studied her fingernails. "Strangely enough, I am aware of that." Her voice oscillated like the tuning of a racing car. "Could anything suit us better?"

"I don't get it."

"On the day when Abraham Forster goes to his final rotting place, someone has to move in and get rid of the evidence against you. Mr. Bianconi will arrange for his son to perform this task. Junior will bring the evidence to Daddy, who in turn will destroy it. Daddy will give Junior a plausible explanation for the action, and Junior will not probe. He knows his dad. Father and Son Incorporated have worked well before, and I cannot see why this should be an exception. It is a perfect combination, Mr. President. One does not catch elephants with mouse traps."

"How much to I tell him?"

"Do not dream of playing hard-ball with Tony Bianconi. You tell him everything."

"When do I tell him?"

She put her hands on her bosom and used her eyelashes as a pair of safety nets.

"You tell him a couple of weeks after we're installed in the White House. It is important that it is *the President* who asks his advice—not the president-elect. Don't worry, sweetheart. Time will fly like the last day on death row."

Caldwell's fingers moved deep inside his pockets. He said, "I was just thinking—why should Mr. Bianconi help us with—with this?"

"For two reasons. He loves it." She did not continue, and she did not smile, either.

"What am I missing?"

"Tony Bianconi is a past master at collecting favours. He finds his profession very useful, in this respect."

"And—?"

"You don't know that his second eldest son is running for New York?"

"Mayor?"

"Yes, dear. Mayor. That is the second reason."

"So, with myself and the whole party machinery…"

"Precisely, my love, in that order. That'll be Tony's modest price."

Caldwell opened the double doors to the veranda. He went outside and walked down the stairs to the lawn.

Sheryl Caldwell could see herself in the large mirror over the fireplace. The afternoon sun gave her skin the soft hue of a peeled mango. She smiled. She was going to be one hell of an unusual first lady. She pulled the fruit bowl closer and turned her glass upside down. She watched the ice cubes as they melted. The water made the fruits look cold and glossy and strangely alive. Soon there was nothing left but a few drops that clung to the skin and then silently slid off and vanished.

Just like the General, she thought. In a few months' time he would be reduced to a wet stain that would dry up and fade into nothingness.

She turned her eyes towards the ceiling. Her father was watching. She could see the proud smile on his face.

She lit a cigarette and placed it between the forefinger and the index finger of her left hand. Her right hand massaged her flat little belly.

31

Antonio Bianconi neither agreed nor differed whenever it was being claimed that J. Edgar Hoover ruled, manipulated and destroyed by using knowledge as his weapon. It was, after all, commonly accepted that everybody had a past. Did anybody walk through life without something he or she wished to hide? Bianconi didn't think so. Maybe anybody of significance—significance as defined by Hoover— was worth keeping a file on or maybe not. The prerogative was Hoover's, and he was entitled to his opinions. True, during the years of his reign from 1924 onwards, the FBI's archives became what he intended it to become—an arsenal and a goldmine. On the other hand, USA was a democracy and it was up to each individual president to curb Hoover's power, if the president so wished.

Bianconi, like most of those who walked the corridors of power in the capital, knew that few people respected Hoover. Fewer still did not fear him. His grip on Washington in particular and the nation in general was as legendary as the tales and myths of his bravery, exploits and achievements were fallacious.

No president risked making a move within the spheres of the FBI's influence—spheres as defined by Hoover—without consulting the Director. Any politician with a desire to survive did his utmost to stay clear; experience taught them all that this was impossible, and second best became not consciously doing anything that could offend Hoover's delicate sensitivity.

Bianconi was all too aware that neither did Washington's army of advisors escape the FBI's attention. Such people had influence. The Director saw no reason to make an exception for anyone with the potential to re-arrange whichever cards were on the table at any one time. The damage he did to the American democracy did not bother him. The feat of single-handedly transforming Washington to a permanent farce evaded him. Everybody had a past, and it was the Director's right and duty to register any impropriety in the interest of the nation— interest as defined by Hoover. Successive governments had kept him in his post, and the unsubstantiated presumption that they did not dare to sack him underlined his value to the nation.

Antonio Bianconi had been an advisor to Herbert Hoover for a couple of years when Franklin D. Roosevelt became president, and the relationship with the White House continued. Hoover had taken an intense dislike to the young lawyer; he was smart and intelligent, which was bad, and he had the confidence of the president, which was worse. The real tragedy, however, was that Tony Bianconi was clean. The entire FBI followed instructions from above and overstretched itself in trying to find something, but not even a parking ticket appeared. Tony Bianconi remained as elusive as a butterfly in a rain forest, and Hoover's loathing grew. He tried everything from bugging and innuendoes to rumours and falsifications. Nothing stuck.

A year after the inauguration, Roosevelt gave a party at the White House. Both Hoover and Bianconi were present. Towards the end of the evening Hoover suddenly voiced his appreciation of the government's fight against organized crime. The observation was followed by a comment about the Italian Mafia, the part it had played in America's history, and how its power had come to an end.

He rounded off by alluding to the dubious character and cunning nature of anyone of Italian origin. Whilst doing so, he stared for a few seconds at Bianconi.

Nobody in the room mistook Hoover's remark for a tasteless joke. Roosevelt was visibly uncomfortable, and the guests turned quiet. The only one who appeared unaffected was Bianconi. He smiled benignly, walked up to Hoover and whispered something in his ear. Hoover went white. For a moment he seemed paralyzed, and he did not attempt a reply. Shortly after he left the party.

The episode became Washington's hot topic until it died from malnutrition. To nobody's surprise, Hoover refused to divulge; he became violently hostile the few times somebody dared to mention it. Bianconi followed his simple principles and kept his knowledge to himself. The assumption formed was that Bianconi's little gem had nothing to do with Hoover's homosexuality or any other trivia concerning his private life; at some stage the Director had committed a constitutional crime, and Bianconi could prove it.

Bianconi continued as advisor to Roosevelt, followed by Truman and Eisenhower. They all wanted to know the hold he had on Hoover—some even demanded it—but each time Bianconi produced his shy little smile and whispered, "*Dammit—I wish I could remember!*"

The relationship between Hoover and Bianconi reached its nadir with the Harry Dexter White affair. Roosevelt had appointed White to Assistant Secretary of the Treasury, and Truman followed up in 1946 by making White the United States executive director of the International Monetary Fund. Truman knew through Bianconi that White was a spy. However, Bianconi advised Truman not to dismiss White; *keep him in office and that's how we keep an eye on him.*

When Hoover learned what the FBI should have discovered, he went livid and composed the feeble excuse that the agency never made recommendations or drew conclusions. The sneer on everybody's face did not get any less visible when the FBI never managed to compile sufficient evidence to persuade a grand jury to indict White.

From then on, Hoover hated Bianconi with a passion hitherto not registered for anybody and waited patiently for the day to come when revenge could be executed. Promoting Bianconi's son was one of the moves Hoover saw as worthy of a grand master.

This made Tony Bianconi smile. His signet was discretion blended with dexterity, and its application was unconditional. He never deviated from what he himself called his simple philosophy in life and others described as an immensely potent conjuration. Long experience had also taught him that irrationality was seldom an asset.

His sons were devoted students.

Tony Bianconi had his income as a senior partner in a Washington law firm, and there was not a single cent attached to his name that the IRS did not know about. He was sometimes referred to as *The Incorruptible*, a quality lesser mortals deemed impossible. His more commonly used nickname was *Second Opinion*.

First opinion was Clark Clifford who had been picked from obscurity in 1946 when Harry Truman had his serious problems with the mineworkers. Following this triumph, Clifford participated in founding the National Intelligence Agency, which was superseded by the CIA.

Before the year was over, Clifford had assisted in structuring the Marshall Plan.

As America's political *eminence grise* Clifford had few rivals. His reputation as a fixer grew steadily, and he became as famous as Bianconi stayed anonymous. Clifford worked solely for the Democrats. Bianconi could not care less who was in charge, and his non-political stance earned him the ear of every president from Herbert Hoover onwards.

Nobody underestimated Clark Clifford's capacity as advisor, but Washington was reasonably convinced that there at times could be problems that required a second opinion, skipping the first, and that the solution of whatever was on the agenda needed a brain that was as astute and experienced as it was ruthless.

Nobody ever learned what Bianconi and any one president talked about. Bianconi knew that without his integrity intact he was finished, and the various presidents had their own reasons for keeping quiet.

Late in Bianconi's career, his eldest son received another promotion within the FBI. There were those who saw the irony in this and took it with a smile, and there were those who tried to raise an issue. For a while aspersions flowered and multiplied, but Bianconi Junior's credentials were as impeccable as his father's reputation was rock solid. The Director's backing supported the confidence, President Eisenhower stayed neutral and opposition withered away without scratching the surface.

Shortly afterwards, two things happened. Bianconi's second son declared his interest in becoming New York's next mayor, and Tony Bianconi announced his retirement at the end of the year. He was getting on a bit, and he would like to enjoy the evening of his life with his wife Maria. They had not seen as much of each other during the years as they would have wished, and it was time to pull in the oars and enjoy the uninterrupted presence of the best friend he'd ever had.

He was thankful that he and his family had been allowed to serve this great country, and he knew that he would think back on his career with pride and gratitude.

Tony Bianconi knew that if he was being called to the White House within six months of a new presidency, then the President had a serious problem. It was equally certain that the problem had existed before inauguration; it had followed the new incumbent into the Oval Office. Six short weeks was a new record, though, so uniquely ahead of anybody else that young Cliff Caldwell had to be a desperate man.

Tony Bianconi drove slowly. The rain hit the surface of the road like jets from a pressure cleaner. He tried to avoid the mist sprayed from the car in front. He hummed an old Johnny Cash tune. There was no point in wasting time and energy guessing; he had dropped that habit decades ago. Cliff Caldwell would stutter and fumble and part-explain and walk in circles for a while, but, eventually, he would get to the point. Whatever his problem was, Bianconi did not think that the President would present something unheard of; a conflict or a dilemma that Bianconi had not been confronted with once or more before. If he should venture any hypothesis at all, it would be that somewhere in the wings a menacing shadow lurked, a shadow that neither Caldwell the person nor Caldwell the President had been able to shake off.

Bianconi smiled. It was beyond him why anybody wanted to be president. Poor fool, he thought; Caldwell had no idea what was in store for him. For the next four years, possibly eight, he would be surrounded by hangers-on, sycophants, wannabes, philistines, could-have-beens, fantasists, leeches and simians, each of whom would fight his own corner. Eventually, the President would learn the game—hopefully—as he would learn that the ambience of the White House was not conducive to ideals like trust and loyalty.

Bianconi swung up in front of the gates. He showed his pass and was whisked through. He thought of John Adams, the first president to move into what was then an unfinished White House, and who, on his second night, wrote to his Abigail: "*I pray Heaven to bestow the best of blessings on this House and on all that shall hereafter inhabit it. May none but honest and wise men ever rule under this roof.*"

The words were carved in the mantelpiece of the State Dining Room. Bianconi had more than once wondered if the presidents he had known had ever taken on board and digested those words.

An aide guided him to the Oval Office. Bianconi resisted a comment that he had been familiar with the place for a few decades.

Cliff Caldwell stood by the window, the American flag suitably to his right. He turned when Bianconi entered, walked past the desk and extended his hand. "Thank you for coming, Mr. Bianconi."

Bianconi saw the dry skin on Caldwell's forehead; a few white specks were stuck to the eyebrows and he kept touching his hairline with the edge of his left hand.

"The honour is mine," Bianconi said and stared at Caldwell for longer than it took to pronounce the words. He saw neither appreciation of the slight satire, nor any glimpse of humour in Caldwell's blue eyes. Bianconi went on, "May I take this opportunity to congratulate you with your victory, Mr. President."

Caldwell smiled, a fleeting grimace that did nothing to lighten up his visage. "Thank you," he said, swung around and went back to the window.

Bianconi noticed that Caldwell twice pressed the cap of his right shoe into the pile of the carpet, and that he walked like a man unsure of which direction to take.

"It does not rain any more," Caldwell said.

Bianconi knew what was coming. The moment he had entered the office, he had spotted Caldwell's coat hanging over the back of a chair. Bianconi shifted his own coat from left to right arm and waited.

Caldwell said, "Would you mind if we go for a walk?"

The ghost of Hoover, Bianconi thought; suspicions of microphones everywhere. Surely the President's problems couldn't be something as trite as advice on how to de-bug the entire White House discreetly. No, that would be too trivial, even from a greenhorn like Caldwell. The President was a seriously worried man, but there was also a hint of determination in his body language, an expression indicating that whatever it was that bothered him, he wanted to get rid of it, fast.

"Not at all, Mr. President."

They put on their coats and went outside. Caldwell looked around a few times as if to ensure that the two-legged guard dogs kept their distance. Bianconi nodded approvingly. Caldwell's coat had been at hand. His shoes were made of thick leather with solid rubber soles. So far, the President had conducted himself with an air of calm and authority. Perhaps there was more to this kid than most pundits expected.

"It is my understanding that you are one of life's greatest chess-players, Mr. Bianconi," Caldwell said and put his hands behind his back.

"Kind words, Mr. President."

Again, Caldwell looked around. He tried hard to remember the exact words he so carefully had rehearsed for hours on end.

"You do know why you are here," he began. "I have a problem which needs to be solved without delay." He cleared some grit from his throat. The words came fast and hard like pebbles dropping into a milk bottle. "There is nobody else I can talk to. I am familiar with your reputation and your abilities, Mr. Bianconi, and I hope you can do for me what I understand you have done for several of my predecessors."

Not bad, Bianconi thought and put on his gloves. He had heard worse introductions. A bit early, however, to comment.

"I emphasize that apart from my wife and the person involved no living soul knows about this," Caldwell said.

"Is that person aware of my presence here today?"

"The gentleman in question is having lunch with Senator Myers who is still vigorously opposed to the promotion."

"I see," Bianconi said. "Abraham Forster."

"You don't miss much, do you?" Caldwell said with a trace of humour.

"Not much, Mr. President." He knew that Caldwell's insistence on Forster as Chief of Staff had raised objections, but only Myers had come forward with arguments heavy enough potentially to prevent the promotion. Myers had been dead against. He had claimed that Forster was nothing but an arms-dealing pirate with far too many shadowy contacts, and that he eventually would prove to be a stain and a burden that any government could do without. Most insiders saw Myer's opposition as personal; it was well known that he disliked the person Forster, but there were also the odd rumours that Myers was deeply upset because Forster once had reneged on a promise of financial reward in connection with sales of arms to China. Myers had been around for a long time. He was as influential as he was cantankerous and stubborn, and Bianconi could see Caldwell and Forster's need for a truce with the old grizzly bear. It did not make it easier that Myers had a passion for exercising that least popular of all human rights—speaking his mind in unequivocal terms loudly and whenever it pleased him. Bianconi did not think that one single free lunch would be sufficient to pacify Myers. Leastwise, Caldwell's problem was not Myers, it was the General.

Caldwell looked to the right, to the left and over his shoulder. "I am going to inform Mr. Forster of your visit," he said. "I do not want him to hear it from somebody else, which he will if I don't. My explanation will be that I want to know how best to tackle the Speaker who, as you know, made some remarks two days ago about the need for tighter reins. It was a clear personal insult, the way he phrased it, and I reckon that Mr. Forster will swallow my reasoning. He does not think that I am particularly cunning, nor that I have much guts. He does know that you and the Speaker are old friends."

Bianconi kept his silence.

"The case is that Forster has got me by the balls," Caldwell said with less fluency.

Bianconi listened to his experience and continued his silence.

Caldwell said, "Let me tell you the entire story."

Bianconi listened. He did not nod. He did not shake his head, nor did he interrupt. He stared ahead and he knew, before Caldwell was halfway through, where it all would lead.

"I understand, Mr. President," he said when he was sure that Caldwell had finished.

Caldwell stopped and faced Bianconi with a stony stare. "It is a nightmare scenario, Mr. Bianconi. Having Abraham Forster as president in four years' time is a fate that should not befall the United States of America. I honestly believe that the man's megalomania will turn into insanity. America run by a madman will be the end of us."

A touching little speech, Bianconi thought. What could be more important than the welfare of our great nation? Who does this amateur think I am?

A terse smile appeared on Caldwell's face. "America does not need Abraham Forster, and neither do I."

That's better, Bianconi reflected; now we are getting closer to the real issue.

"I prefer to be as direct as I possibly can," Caldwell went on in a monotonous tone. "Please accept that it is not my intention to insult your intelligence. If I hesitate or—or correct myself it is because I am not very familiar with a situation like this."

"I appreciate that, Mr. President."

They continued walking. Bianconi smiled ruefully. They never came to him with simple little stupidities. They came when their imbroglio was by definition primarily personal and tangentially political. Not all of them knew the difference, but it was there; it was *always* there.

Bianconi's biggest problem was to make them comprehend and admit the true nature of their request—and its consequences.

Like when there was someone they wanted to get rid off. Well, he thought, Forster fits the category of unwanted species; Bianconi knew enough about the General and his background to acknowledge that Caldwell's reason coincided with what benefited the nation.

Right or wrong, he continued his line of thought, it does not matter. I am getting too old for this, but I shall do this one. I shall do it for my son. To become mayor of New York without the back up of the party machinery could prove difficult.

Caldwell would oblige. It was time for action, once again, and for words that could not be misinterpreted.

"You want Abraham Forster out of the way, Mr. President."

"Yes, I do. I want him eliminated."

Caldwell's directness surprised Bianconi. He had expected the young president to be vague and cagey and manipulative and to cause Bianconi to phrase, repeat and underline the solution.

"I understand, Mr.President. May I also respectfully add that it is going to be extremely difficult? A man like Abraham Forster has more than likely taken his precautions."

"I know he has. One set of evidence is in his home in Kentucky, in his safe, and the other is with his legal advisor Glen Morrit, I believe. Forster has complete control over Morrit."

"Excuse me for saying so, Mr.President, but that is the easy part. What we must avoid at all costs is a political atmosphere created by a demise open to suspicion. That is the tricky part. May I further include that Mr. Forster, who is exceptionally suspicious by nature, does walk around with his eyes open."

"I understand that much," Caldwell said. "That is why you are here. In other words, all I need is your assurance that you can take care of my problem."

They walked for a while, neither too keen to continue the dialogue. Bianconi wondered if Caldwell understood the risk he was running as intimately as he sensed that allowing Forster to live represented a hazard of monstrous proportions. Caldwell was not strong enough to live in a vacuum where his only companion was *doubt*—the *what-if* syndrome would finally wear him down and he would crack up, one way or another. To his credit, Caldwell seemed to have reached the same conclusion. A cornered rat contemplated neither negotiations nor contingency plans for some ambiguous armistice; Caldwell's was a classic case of desperation impersonating strength and decisiveness.

Caldwell kicked at a twig and stared towards the leaden sky, heavy with snow.

"Forster is a weed," he said. "God only knows how that weed will spread and what damage it will do if allowed to flourish."

"I agree," Bianconi said. He had never been impressed with Eisenhower, and it irked and saddened Bianconi to see his country slide towards mediocrity and ultimately disintegration. It was anybody's guess if Caldwell had what it took to stem the tide, but one thing was certain— with Forster around, the young President would be too paralyzed even to try.

Bianconi had more than once wondered how Forster had managed to finance his capital-demanding arms empire. Something didn't add up, and the passing of the General's money-grabbing wife was too much of a coincidence to be an accident.

Forster was as ruthless as they came. He had undoubtedly killed, both in and out of uniform. All in all, he was as needed as a paedophile in a girls' scout camp.

Bianconi said, "The problem may be solved—" he avoided saying *your* problem "—that is, if the man we need is still around—" taking care saying *we* and not *you.*

"Who is he?" Caldwell said.

Bianconi suppressed a smile. "I am sure you would prefer not to know, Mr. President."

"Of course," Caldwell said hastily. "I mean, just the profile—"

Young Caldwell has got a hell of a lot to learn, Bianconi thought— well, that's natural. He said, "The man we need must not be an American citizen. Neither must he reside in this country. He must be able to enter and leave without a trace, and—this is the crunch—he must be able to procure the General's death supposedly from natural causes, say, a heart attack. A pretty tall order, I'd say."

"Does such a person exist?"

"He does exist, but rumours have it that he is retired." He cast a quick sideways glance at Caldwell, noticing the frown and that his jaw fell.

"You know this person?" Caldwell asked.

"I know of him," Bianconi said. "I have never met him." There are lies and lies, he thought; this is a white one. The President should have known better than to ask.

"Has he worked for us before?"

"Indirectly—in a manner of speaking."

Caldwell got the message, but he still had to reassure himself: "And he is as good as you—as they say he is?"

Bianconi wished that he were back in his comfortable chair in his warm and cosy study. Cold weather did not do his rheumatism much good. His left ankle, fractured many years ago, had begun to send signals to his brain. He said, "Does the word *Safehaven* mean anything to you, Mr. President?"

"No," Caldwell said.

Bianconi liked the answer. Most of the young man's predecessors would have said: *Refresh my memory* or *It rings a bell—fill me in.*

Bianconi eyed the naked trees. He listened for a moment to the wind playing fiddle on wet and rigid branches.

He began, "The year after Hitler came to power, he made a deal with the Swiss government, ensuring the secrecy laws necessary for the Nazis to deposit without any question being asked where the money and the gold came from. We all know the answer to that question, of course, but what amazes a lot of people is how the Swiss have managed to get away with it for so long. However, under the Roosevelt administration, an attempt was made to disclose the true story of the Swiss and their untold billions of other people's money. That is how *Safehaven* came about, conceived by our own Treasury and State Department. They made a decent effort for as long as it lasted, but due to resistance from the British government—chauvinistic and anti-Semitic as always—all efforts came to a halt. That was the real reason, neatly camouflaged by our State Department and the British Foreign Office, emphasizing other priorities caused by the Cold War emerging." Bianconi put his hands in his pockets and shuddered. "But not everybody forgot *Safehaven*. Some years ago, a group of German Jewish families sent a couple of representatives to Switzerland. They argued that the Swiss were sitting on fifty million dollars of the families' money, and could the families have the money back, please? During the meeting the Germans used the word *Safehaven*—of which the Swiss had indeed a clear recollection—but the original *Safehaven* was so long ago, and

711

the Swiss failed to put it into its proper context. To nobody's surprise, the Swiss flatly denied any knowledge of such money, and, on the face of it, the meeting came to nothing. A few months later one of the top directors of Credit Suisse was found dead in his office. In his *office*, Mr. President, from heart failure. Some while thereafter the Germans returned, asked for their money and got the same arrogant negative response. Just before leaving, the Germans once again dropped the word *Safehaven*, and again it failed to click. Within ten days, a second director was found dead in his luxurious home outside Geneva, a home that was considered as impenetrable as Fort Knox.

The funny thing was that the Swiss authorities were pretty sure that the director had been poisoned, yet no trace of toxins could be detected. The Germans paid a third visit, asked for their money, whispered *Safehaven* and left without waiting for a reaction. A brilliant tactic, I'd say. Anyway, the Swiss police did everything in their power to trace the killer of their two esteemed citizens, but to no avail. The Swiss government decided not to confront the German government, and a quiet transfer of fifty million dollars took place." Bianconi nodded and tried to ignore the cold that penetrated his bones.

"That was our man?" Caldwell said.

"Yes, it was. There's a limited handful of highly professional hitmen around, but none have his pre-eminence. He is the only one who can do it exactly the way we want it to be done."

"What would it take to get him out of retirement?"

"A lot of money, Mr. President. We talk megabucks, relatively speaking." Bianconi smiled wryly and added, "I know for a fact that our man has a high opinion of his own worth."

Caldwell grinned. "I have not been President for long, but I understand that presidents have funds available for emergencies."

"The money can be found. I can point you in the right direction. Very few need to be involved. Nobody will ever know the *true* purpose, and the receiver will take care of whatever it takes when it comes to his own identity. The stratagem is simple. Two payments for unspecified services getting lost in a black hole under an appropriate heading. It is not unheard of, Mr. President."

"*Two* payments?"

"Half up front and half on completion. Standard terms."

Caldwell whistled. "Can we forget the second half?"

So much for presidential integrity, Bianconi thought. They are all the same; creepy little cheats behind a glittering façade. Once, it used to surprise me. Then experience taught me that avarice, dishonesty and subreption fill a chamber in their brains where perceptive and intelligent people have cells activated in a constructive and judicious manner. That is why such people find their success outside of politics.

He said cuttingly, "No, Mr. President, we can *not* forget the second payment, if for no other reason—" he stopped short of being dramatic "—they would get to us, sooner or later. It could be you, it could be me, or it could be a member or two of our families. You do not want to live with that, Mr. President, and neither do I."

"Of course not, Mr. Bianconi," Caldwell said quickly. " It was just a bad joke. *They*—?"

"It's a team. One does the intelligence, and the other the actual job. I have also been told that they have a few associates," he said pointedly, "back-up, if so required."

Caldwell said, "I understand." He wanted to drop the subject. "How soon can you act?"

"I can leave the day after tomorrow and be back on the seventh day."

Caldwell turned around. "Let us go back," he suggested. "I'm getting cold."

A hundred yards from the house he stopped and gazed towards the great universe where guardian angels resided. "What about the evidence?" he said.

"My son will take care of it. Very few will participate in that operation. There will be a convincing explanation. Nobody will see the evidence apart from my son who has to make sure he's got the right envelopes. Whatever is in them will be destroyed without delay."

"And Mr. Morrit, the lawyer?"

"Same procedure. We shall have enough ammunition to secure Mr. Morrit's wholehearted co-operation and everlasting silence."

"Will we know the date?"

Bianconi sighed silently and wanted to shake his head. "No, Mr. President. It can take weeks, and it can take months. We—or I, rather—will know within one hour after completion. That is how they operate. I appreciate their strategy."

No wonder everybody puts on their velvet gloves when they deal with this guy, Caldwell thought. I am beginning to understand how he got his reputation. He said, "I hear that your son Guiseppe has a wish to run New York."

"The boy has got great plans for the city," Bianconi smiled.

"With a bit of support he shouldn't fail to get there."

"That would be appreciated, Mr. President."

Caldwell unbuttoned the top of his coat and commenced walking. "Shall we have coffee in the library?" he said. "I like that room."

Bianconi nodded. His mind was elsewhere.

32

Bianconi had booked a suite at Claridge's, his regular abode each time he visited London. In his younger days he had tried a variety of the city's prestigious hotels, but he had found that none had the same unique blend of dignified, high-class and low-profile atmosphere as Claridge's.

Being recognized as a long-standing patron and treated accordingly was another bonus. Bianconi did not deny that it tickled his vanity. He had often said to Maria that he was looking forward to times ahead when the two of them could book in for a whole month and use the days to explore the treasures of a great city; the tome of duties a thing of the past and forever closed.

Bianconi left no markers; he paid for everything himself. The first president he had worked for, Herbert Hoover, had unashamedly and with patronizing arrogance behind an amiable façade taken it for granted that cash was the key to any door. An alarm bell rang, and Bianconi went home and discussed the matter with his wife. They quickly agreed on a more subtle principle; whatever Bianconi did for the high and mighty should be done as a *favour*—and he would collect one in return. Those without honour—an apt euphemism for acumen—would never ask him again, but neither would they have anything on him. All in all, this modus operandi had worked well; the inevitable deficit here and there and now and then, as was to be expected, but, seen as a long-term strategy, Bianconi was satisfied with what he had achieved for his family and for himself.

It was early morning when he arrived at the hotel. As soon as he had unpacked he stripped to his underwear and lay down on the bed, sipping a glass of complimentary champagne. He closed his eyes, unleashed his imagination and decided to entertain himself by thinking the unthinkable, which was to write his memoirs. It was an exercise he found hugely amusing. He could see the headlines and hear the news bulletins and witness the panic-stricken faces of past and present politicians and high-ranking bureaucrats; what a sensation it would be, what a mass crucifixion of men who had been democratically elected and trusted with office. If only people knew what was going on of deals and pacts and arrangements and assassinations. To open the eyes of the public to whatever took place in the name of politics would be the gift of several millenniums.

Bianconi let out a low chuckle. Officially, men like himself and Angelo Vargas did not exist. Even the vilest, most contemptible and corrupt regime could not bring themselves to admit that they employed methods like quietly getting rid of some undesirable subject. Genocide and mass murder, yes; nobody had yet discovered a method of sweeping a few thousand corpses under a carpet, but the odd and carefully selected elimination of a troublesome opponent was an entirely different matter. *We do not do that sort of thing!*

Bianconi could not think of any other profession so ludicrous and hypocritical as politics; yet, he was part of this catatonic rat race, and it did not bother him. It was a living, and a challenging one, at that; it kept him mentally active, and, all summed up, the world was a pit overloaded with nonentities that came and existed and disappeared. Morals and ethics and faiths were concepts invented by a creature too vain to acknowledge that life was but an ephemeral affair without any other value than the physical significance of temporary existence. Everything else was a bi-product, and the most precious was one's own family where significance began and consequences ended. Everything else was nugatory; Tony Bianconi did not believe that man was sufficiently equipped ever to be able to distinguish between development and progress, between a turbid and materialistic society and a society where man was eager to unfold sources of care and consideration. What remained constant was man's ability to destroy, his talent for intolerance and his faculty for blaming the world for most if not all of his own shortcomings and mistakes.

Bianconi afforded himself another glass of complimentary champagne. He thought of his childhood and of his youth in New York, the city that had played such an important part in his upbringing. His whole family had been devout Catholics, but the streets had got the better of young Antonio. At the age of twelve there wasn't much left of the once wide-eyed, innocent and uncritical choirboy. He remembered the twenty-two stone Father Bernard whose equally obese soul had wobbled with sanctimonious indignation each time he had been forced to admit that the spirit of the church had lost to the imperative of the concrete jungle. Father Bernard had followed up his acerbic predictions with the caveat that there were limits to what an all-forgiving God could accept of blatant and nihilistic insouciance. According to Father Bernard, the anarchy of the streets was utterly reprehensible, and—God forgive—it was patently *dishonourable*. Honour, in Father Bernard's book of revelations, was the antithesis of sin and therefore the key to salvation. Poor Father Bernard. Everybody thought him a slow learner and practically dyslectic when it came to the lyrics of the municipal wilderness.

Later in life, Bianconi came to agree with Father Bernard, although without sharing the same criteria. Honour, in the form of integrity and united with a manipulative intelligence, could be used as a shield when so needed and a sword when so desired, a combination that secured an intriguing and fascinating career in a world where machination was the only order of the day.

Tony's father, Salvatore Bianconi, had been a mild-mannered and unassuming man who had wanted to become a lawyer, but circumstances interfered. Instead, he became a bus driver who took shifts to provide for his family. Bianconi still remembered his father's smile when being asked if law was an *honourable* profession, and the answer: "No, my son. The existence of the entire legal profession proves that crime pays. A legal education—please pardon the irony—teaches you what you can do and what you can't do. You learn about the pitfalls and you learn about the loopholes and, if you are smart enough, you also acquire the experience of how to exploit both. From this you'd extract the conclusion that there isn't much dissimilarity between a mobster and a lawyer. The advantage of the latter category is that the Internal Revenue are inclined to consider you less of a crook."

Antonio Bianconi became a lawyer. He joined a medium-sized law firm in New York and was a partner within five years. The turning point came when he successfully defended a famous and corrupt politician. A smaller but vastly more profitable firm in Washington came with an offer that Bianconi could not refuse. The firm's clients were mainly politicians and their rich variety of associates. The sniff of sordid artifice had been too irresistible, and Bianconi never looked back. A brief encounter with a friend of Herbert Hoover prior to the 1929 election provided Bianconi with the break-through that created the foundation of his future.

Bianconi sighed. A rueful smile deepened the lines on his patrician face. He thought of his meeting with Caldwell and of Abraham Forster who soon would be reduced to a few ounces of ash and who would no longer pose a threat to the new and honourable leader of the Western World.

What a funny and simple little world, he thought, What primitive games men played with each other. *Checkmate. Next game…*

Bianconi carefully stretched his legs and cursed his rheumatism. It had become worse, the last couple of years. Time had come to pack it in. He would buy a place in the sun where he and Maria could spend the winters away from a cold and soulless Washington and walk on the beach and relish the privilege of being a distant spectator whatever happened—to whomever it happened.

Bianconi mobilized his willpower and got one leg at a time onto the floor. He went into the bathroom and filled the tub. He found the jar with miraculous herbs he always carried with him and sprinkled the water generously. He did not know why the herbs worked, but the soluble multi-coloured little grains definitely had a pain-relieving effect on his aching joints and limbs. The water was hot, but Bianconi was not to be deterred. After a few minutes he began to relax. There was nothing on the agenda apart from a quick telephone call to arrange next day's meeting with Gregory Pritchard-White; Bianconi suffered badly from jet lag and he always took the first day off. He would walk the streets of London for a while, have lunch at a nice Italian restaurant, a not too late dinner at the hotel, and then, hopefully, a good night's sleep.

It was Tony Bianconi's experience that tomorrows, if they came, had a tendency to sort themselves out.

☞

They met in the lounge. Gregory Pritchard-White had arrived when Bianconi came downstairs. The twelve years they had known each other had made little impact on their relationship; it was cordial, but no more. Both acknowledged silently mutual dislike, but neither was unprofessional enough to allow such sentiments to influence their dealings. A few words of courtesy were quickly done with whilst they waited for their gin and tonic. Bianconi lowered his heavy eyelids and watched the Englishman who had adopted an expression of weary nonchalance.

"Cheers," Pritchard-White said and raised his glass. "May you live to see the sun go down." His smile was designed to tell the world that radiating warmth and empathy wasn't in his best interest.

Bianconi nodded solemnly. "Likewise, although that is not much of an accomplishment on this crowded little island permanently under a cloud."

"Touché," Pritchard-White offered generously, "but at least we are not torn apart by tornadoes and hurricanes bestowed so richly on God's own country."

The American said, "Granted. Here, not even the cobwebs are being blown away, as one does register time and again."

So much for the weather, Pritchard-White thought, let's get down to basics. "What is your particular predicament this time, Tony?"

Bianconi poured more tonic into his glass. "Merely a local little hiccup," he said. "Nothing that requires co-operation between our respective boy scout clubs."

The comment annoyed Pritchard-White. He knew that Bianconi had scant regard for practically any country's secret service, Mossad possibly excepted. In Bianconi's opinion, the CIA, the MI6 and everybody else's equivalent had a tendency to botch up more than they repaired. "A local little hiccup," he repeated, "yes, that makes sense. That's why you are here, and that is why we have this meeting."

"Precisely," Bianconi said. He ignored the Englishman's sarcastic tone. "All I need is a favour."

"Now, isn't that unusual? Anyway, I shall be happy to oblige. As always."

"Is Vargas still around?"

Ah, Pritchard-White thought, a local little hiccup, and he needs Vargas. He lowered his voice and said with an amiable smile, "Is your new president in a mess already, Tony? Skeletons tumbling in and out of his cupboard?"

"Nothing of the sort," Bianconi said as if he found the subject tiresome.

"We need to untangle a couple of crossed lines, that's all. Purely internal; nothing for our satellites to worry about."

Pritchard-White almost winced, but he managed to produce a condescending grin. Bianconi was the only American he'd ever met who had a sharp, ironic and—a miracle—a genuine satirical sense of humour. It wasn't so much the reference itself that irked Pritchard-White, it was the fact that the laid-back American still managed to take him by surprise. "And this unimportant, simple and run-of-the-mill little wire-crossing requires the expertise of the world's most accomplished electrician, Tony? Yes, that *really* makes sense. One can't be too careful when it comes to the need for top quality work, can one?"

Bianconi said, "Exactly my philosophy. We see eye to eye, Gregory—as always."

"Don't we just. Yes—to answer your question—our friend is still here. He's got a very nice country house where he lives with a most attractive woman of Irish extraction and a darling of a one-year old daughter." He shook his head in mock sympathy and thoroughly enjoyed himself. "It is difficult to see him coming out of retirement."

Bianconi leaned forward. "And Ishihara?"

"Same thing, I am afraid. Country estate, wife and child. Well, the wife you knew about, of course, but the child is brand new. He and Vargas actually live only fifteen minutes apart." The spite in Pritchard-White's voice was unmistakable, and Bianconi detested it almost as much as he disliked the information itself. He decided to defuse the Englishman's obvious malice and said with a hint of resignation, "Fancy that—Angelo has a family. A bit of a surprise, I must admit. Quite an about-turn, but then, I guess he deserves a different life." He looked up. His eyes showed nothing but mild compassion. "Not that I ever got to know him, I mean, who did, but I can't say I disliked him. A closed book, if there ever was one," he added and took one careful sip from his glass. "Understandable, considering his profession, but also for personal reasons, I reckon. He never lets you down, Vargas. You could always trust him, and that's more than we can say about most of his colleagues."

Pritchard-White sensed that the air was leaving the balloon. "He is just a hitman," he said with an air of disdain.

Bianconi put his glass down. "And you and I are just manipulating organizers," he said mildly. "Does that mean that we are not human beings?"

Pritchard-White looked at his watch. He said, still eyeing his timepiece, "I have the deepest respect and admiration for Italian philosophers, but I am afraid I haven't got the time to participate in the analyses of human nature at present moment. Shall we revert to the subject over dinner one night? I would be only too delighted to absorb the drips of wisdom from an eloquent, articulate and most renowned sage."

The web of wrinkles around Bianconi's eyes spread like cracks in dry soil. "Let us do that," he said. "I have always marvelled at your ambition to mature and grow as a person."

Pritchard-White fiddled with his cufflinks. "You are being exceedingly generous." He made a pyramid with his hands. "What is it you want me to do?"

"Convey a message to Vargas. I want to see him. I'll be outside Hamleys in Regent Street at twelve noon tomorrow."

Pritchard-White thought quickly. "My advice would be the day after tomorrow."

"So be it."

"That's it?"

The goddamn Brit is aching to know what it is all about, Bianconi mused, but he knows for certain that he never will. He is doing a decent job, though, hiding his disappointment. He does realize that there is no question of involving his clumsy and overdramatic outfit, and that's annoying the daylight out of him. It has a most attractive corrosive effect, but his inflated self-importance does not let him question any further. I shall forever relish this nice, final memory of my esteemed collaborator. He said, "Please give me the honour of inviting you out to dinner before I go back. I am retiring, after this."

"Seriously?"

"I am seventy-one years of age, my friend. Time for the paddock of no return." He stroked his chin and looked pensive. "This implies that I shall never again cast my tired old eyes on any client, associate or contact if I can possibly avoid it. It's final. I want to enjoy my sunset years in harmony."

Pritchard-White felt a touch of disappointment. He had never taken to the American's laid-back mannerisms, but nobody could deny that Bianconi's skills and professionalism were unsurpassed. He was one of a kind, a man whose word was his bond, and, as such, an increasingly rare phenomenon in the shady world of top-level wheeling and dealing.

Britain would miss his expertise and his reliability. Pritchard-White shook his head and said, "Who is going to replace you?"

Bianconi shrugged. "It is not a position, as you know."

Correct, Pritchard-White thought as he slowly emptied his glass. Tony Bianconi just happened to be the most convenient coincidence ever to emerge from the United States. With his retirement, nothing could be the same again. No longer would there be a shock absorber between British intelligence and the unrefined morons from the Americans' secret service. It would be less complicated to replace the Pentagon's whole bunch of top brass than to find another Tony Bianconi. Well, everything had to come to its inevitable end, but still, it was such a bloody shame that 10 Downing Street and the White House no longer would benefit from the invaluable services of this genuine master of clandestine engineering. Pritchard-White had met many a clever man in his world of intrigues and deceptions, but Tony Bianconi was the only one that could truly be classified as a *mechanic*. He was unique.

"Let us make it Thursday," Bianconi said.

"I beg your pardon?"

"Dinner. Thursday night."

"Yes—yes, of course. Can't wait."

Pritchard-White got up, nodded briefly and left.

A vague smile spread across Bianconi's face. He sank deeper into his chair. He held up his hands. They were not as steady as they used to be, and the liver spots looked like an assembly of squashed ants. He asked for another gin and tonic and rested his eyes at the ceiling. It is nice to be missed, he thought, but nicer still not to miss it at all.

33

Igor Parkhurst felt physically ill. He stood at the foot of the staircase leading to the kitchen and stared at the dark and menacing sky. The clouds ripped each other apart and the wind from the north tore at his shirt and rumpled his grey and curly hair. He did not feel the cold; in fact, he thought, he sensed nothing but fear, nausea and dejection. The old terror was back. His life, that had improved so dramatically, had once again been smashed to pieces, and this time he did not believe that he would recover.

Nemesis never left, really. He just hid behind a rock for a while and then, suddenly, he was back with a vengeance and life disintegrated like a dilapidated riverbank and all life was being swept away by the water and did not return.

It was the end, Parkhurst thought; he could not take any more. He was too old, too incompetent and too flaccid to fight the machinery of Her Majesty's Government. *Fate* had given him a brief comeback, and it had been nice, but now *Fate* had tapped him on the shoulder and whispered that the party was over.

It did not matter what Fletcher had said, that it was all a silly little game with no consequences, probably, and that Parkhurst was just an errand boy for petty people infatuated by the exercise of power.

It wasn't as simple as that. There was something sinister behind it all. Parkhurst did not know what, but his instincts told him that Fletcher's *game* had undertones yet to come into play. Fletcher had been neither consistent nor convincing in his logic. He had contradicted himself. His reasoning had been flawed. One day the missing pieces in the jigsaw puzzle would slot into place and then—then the picture had been designed in such a way that it would explode upon completion. The ordeal would be over, but included in its finality was the sorry exit of Igor Parkhurst.

He went over to his car and touched the bonnet with his fingers. The metal was still warm. He listened to the cracking noises from the engine cooling down.

Pritchard-White had been pleasant enough during their lunch together. He had been suspiciously civilized throughout. He had complimented Parkhurst on his latest play, performing in the West End, and he had praised Parkhurst's *excellent* television series of John Steinbeck's works. The atmosphere had been urbane and innocuous; sheer culture from first to second last minute. Parkhurst had sat there, bemused, wondering about the purpose of the get-together, but only when they'd left the table had Pritchard-White come to the point in the most casual of manners. "Oh, Mr. Parkhurst," he had said as if it was a detail of no real importance, "could you please ask Mr. Vargas to be outside Hamleys in Regent Street tomorrow, twelve noon?" Then he had thanked Parkhurst for a most enjoyable lunch, wished him luck with future creations and vanished in a taxi.

Parkhurst drove home. His head was buzzing. Twice, he nearly collided with other cars. Immediately inside he poured a stiff cognac, which he swallowed without sitting down. He threw his coat and jacket over a kitchen chair and ventured outside. *Ask Mr. Vargas to show up.* How simple could it get? Why couldn't Pritchard-White call Vargas and convey the message himself? True, Vargas was ex-directory, but Pritchard-White could get hold of the number if he so had wished.

Parkhurst leaned against the car. He scratched his head. What the hell was going on? Why use *him* as a go-between? There had to be a purpose somewhere. Parkhurst shivered and put his hands in his pockets. He went inside for another cognac. He knew that he had to drive over and see Vargas, but the chance of being stopped for drink driving on a country lane was minimal. Besides, the risk was less than negligible compared with his needs.

After a few more immodest sips, the alcohol began to take effect. His mind focused on his friends and benefactors Tadashi Ishihara and Angelo Vargas. Nice, respectable businessmen, on the face of it. One made his living on the stock market and the other from fruits and vegetables. One was university educated, the other self-taught. One was good with people, the other less so.

He tried to organize his thoughts. Behind the charm and the humour, Ishihara was contemptuous of anybody not Japanese, and of most of those too, for that matter. Vargas was indifferent to mankind in general. Ishihara's attitude was steered by a sharp intellect that provided him with acutely accurate observations. Vargas' perspectives were a function of a life having had its share of maleficent and disconcerting experiences. Ishihara was entertaining, but his mind could also produce a torrent of abuse, invectives, dissections and scorn. He was lethal because he could be merciless; he was knowledgeable, and he possessed a remarkably precise intuition. Vargas kept his ominous silence, a quiet stream without any visible swirls, floating along lazily from somewhere and into a sea of darkness.

Parkhurst shuddered. He rested his elbows on the table. He clinched his glass with both hands and forced himself to smile and to think that his heart still had a few beats in reserve. The lull had gone the moment he'd zeroed in on his two friends.

After a while he calmed down. Those two, they scared him. They made him feel unsettled and ill at ease. And yet—what a paradox—they had helped him in his hour of need, for which he was genuinely thankful—*and* he enjoyed their company. They had Jennifer and Yasmin, two of the most magnificent women ever created; kind, warm, affectionate, sensible, loyal—he wouldn't know where to stop.

Didn't that tell something about Ishihara and Vargas? It had to. Parkhurst knew that he was losing track of his objective. He pushed his glass aside and straightened up.

The *big minus* was that he knew nothing about the *true* profession of Ishihara and Vargas. Pritchard-White's request could not possibly stem from a newborn fascination for bonds and Polish sausages. Had not Ishihara indicated that they worked as some kind of couriers? It was a fact that they had travelled together extensively during the years. It was a fact that neither regarded human life as sacrosanct. Both behaved as if solipsism was the only philosophy worthy of consideration. Neither had ever shown any recognizable concern over news of terrorism, wars and other calamities that made ordinary, decent people shake their heads and wonder what the world was coming to.

They had gone out of their way to befriend him. They had assisted with money, efforts and moral support. Thanks to them he had come back into the limelight, famous anew and with an income to match.

It was no coincidence. Parkhurst glanced at the clock over the hand-painted cabinet he'd inherited from his parents. He put on his jacket and his coat and grabbed the car keys.

Jennifer opened the door. "Uncle Igor," she smiled, "what a pleasant surprise." She kissed him on both cheeks and stepped aside. "Come in. I'll make some coffee."

"That is kind of you, Jennifer, but—is Angelo here?"

Jennifer studied him closely. "Are you all right?"

He knew that his smile was too broad to be convincing. "Yes, thank you, I am fine. I am—I had to drive up to London and back again today. A fair distance, I'd say, at my age. I am a bit tired, that's all." His eyes drifted.

Jennifer pointed towards the long, low building behind the sycamore trees and said, "Angelo is in the cottage. *His* cottage, as he says."

"Do you think I can disturb him?"

"He said he was going to reorganize his books—again. Nothing vitally important, in other words. Of course you can. Would it take long?"

"No, just a few minutes."

"Fine. Bring him back with you, and I'll have the coffee ready."

She watched him trudge towards the cottage, an ageing, grey figure with no spring in his steps. Something has upset him, she thought. I hope Angelo can sort it out.

Parkhurst knocked twice. It took a few seconds before Vargas opened the door. He showed no surprise. "Come in," he said.

They went through the small entrance hall and into the lounge. The carpet was covered with meticulously arranged hardbacks and colourful rows of paperbacks.

Vargas said, "Have a seat. Don't kick my books."

Parkhurst stepped carefully towards a large easy-chair and sat down.

Vargas stood a few yards away and stared at him.

"Somebody wants to meet you outside Hamleys in Regent Street tomorrow, twelve noon," Parkhurst said. He was feeling out of breath.

Vargas did not move. There was no change of expression on his face.

"That's all, really," Parkhurst added.

"No, it isn't."

"Excuse me?"

"Do you know who it is?"

"No, I do not."

"Who told you?"

"Oh, sorry—it was Mr. Pritchard-White. He was kind enough to invite me to lunch today. I had the honour of paying. We talked about literature, theatre, politics and God knows what, and then, when we were leaving, he asked me to convey this message." He tried a grin. "Very mysterious, I'd say."

"Demons move in baffling ways, Igor."

Parkhurst had run out of words. The chair was comfortable. He wished he could take a nap.

Vargas said, "Let's go and have some coffee."

Parkhurst made a move, but the remnants of his stomach muscles would not cooperate.

"How are you going to get out of that chair?" Vargas said with a look of genuine concern.

Parkhurst struggled and silently cursed a body that no longer would do what it was being told to do.

"Here," Vargas said and reached out. Parkhurst felt a grip around his right wrist, firmer than strictly necessary, he thought, and was yanked to his feet.

"Thanks," he mumbled. "It is very comfortable, that chair."

"Ideal for profane meditation," Vargas said.

They walked over to the house where Jennifer was waiting; three cups on the table, sugar, milk and biscuits. She cast them a quick glance as they came in. Parkhurst was red in the face and looked exhausted. Vargas was as relaxed as she had ever seen him. She helped Parkhurst with his coat, patted his shoulder and said, "Would you like a tiny cognac?" She turned to Vargas. "Uncle Igor has had a hectic day. He's been all the way up to London"

"Has he really?"

Parkhurst said, "I wouldn't mind a wee one, thank you."

"So, what's new?" Jennifer asked.

He blew away the steam from his coffee. "Oh, not much, really. I am working on a new play. I must confess that I am struggling, at the moment, but that always happens, in between."

Vargas said, "How is your carnal predicament?"

"Angelo!" Jennifer rebuked sharply. The twinkle in her eyes contradicted her tone of voice.

Parkhurst laughed, feeling relieved. "Not bad, I am happy to say. Valerie is different—" he huffed and tasted his coffee "—either that, or I never learn."

"She is very sweet," Jennifer said. "I am sure it will all work out." She leaned closer to Parkhurst. "You certainly deserve it."

Vargas said, "Has she moved in?"

"Not yet, but we are talking about it. Soon, I hope." He looked from Vargas to Jennifer. "She enjoyed so much our Christmas here. We both appreciated it very much. It was the nicest Christmas I've had for a long time." He smiled fondly at Jennifer. "You've got a heart of gold, my girl."

She looked at her godfather for a while before she answered. "You've had a Christmas or two on your own, haven't you."

Parkhurst looked down. "A few," he said. He moved forward on his chair. "Well, I'd better get back. It has been a long day. Thank you for your hospitality."

Jennifer followed him to the door.

She came back and found Vargas sitting in the same position. He did not seem to be in a hurry to get back to his cottage.

She cleared the table. "What was that all about?"

Vargas took a fruit juice from the fridge. He stood by the window and stared at the milky-blue January sky. "He conveyed a message."

"Has this to do with your assignment?"

"Yes."

She found a chair. "I do not understand. Why is Uncle Igor involved?"

"The people employing our services prefer not to have direct contact. They use messengers. It is a precaution. In this particular instance, Igor knows the person in charge, socially, and was asked to convey a message."

"You are saying that it was a coincidence, that it could have been just anybody?"

He turned and faced her. "Yes. It could have been anybody."

He went into the boot room and put on a heavy weatherproof jacket. "I am going over to see Tadashi."

The knot in Jennifer's stomach swelled and began to move. She folded her hands and tried hard to sound casual, "When are you leaving for your assignment?"

Vargas came back into the kitchen. "As soon as Tadashi is back, in about three weeks time."

She swallowed. The burning sensation in her throat did not go away. "How long will it take? When are you coming back?"

"It is difficult to predict. What I *do* know is that I *am* coming back, and that this is my last assignment. No more. From then on, my life is you and Anu."

He is hearing my heartbeats, she thought. She smiled. "A dream come true," she said and hoped that her words sounded light-hearted and not melodramatic.

He came closer. His lips touched her ears. "So it is." She thought she heard a vibration in his voice.

She got up when she heard the engine start. She went over to the window and waved, a habit from the first days of moving in. It had become a ritual. She looked at the antique clock placed between an old-fashioned coffee grinder and a small copper urn. It was still half an hour before she could wake up Anu from her daily nap.

Igor Parkhurst had drunk only some of the cognac she had served him. She emptied the glass in the sink and thought about the first Christmas she had arranged in her own house.

Her parents had been there. They had stayed for four days. Uncle Igor and his friend Valerie and Yasmin and Tadashi and little Hiroshi had come over. She had prepared Christmas Day dinner assisted by her mother, Yasmin and Valerie.

Before they all had gathered in the drawing room, she had found Angelo standing there on his own, staring into the flames. She'd had to call his name twice before he reacted.

Later in the evening, when the children had gone to bed, Angelo had disappeared and was nowhere to be seen in the house. On instinct she had opened the main door. She had found him sitting in his shirtsleeves, staring at the sky.

"What is it, Angelo?"

"As a child I used to wonder which star the magi had followed," he said. "Most of the Christmas cards were simple little coloured drawings of Mary and Joseph and the child in the manger. They all had halos. One Christmas I stood in front of the fire. Baby came and stood next to me. I had my hands in my pockets. He did the same. I took my hands out and hooked my thumbs into my belt. He did the same. It was a nice moment."

She put her arm around him. "You never went back, did you?"

"No. There was nothing to go back to."

"You never went back to Mexico either, did you?"

He shook his head. "I thought about it, now and then, but I just went on with my life and it never happened."

She leaned her head against his shoulder and thought about the cairn somewhere in those faraway mountains and the stone he had placed on the mantelpiece where it would stay forever. She thought of all those years of wandering and of his restless soul and whispered, "You have found your haven."

He did not move. His body was rigid. She could feel the coldness of his skin through his thin shirt.

She said, "You want a drink, don't you?"

It took a while before he answered, "Not any more."

"Let's go inside," she said. "You must be freezing."

He kissed the top of her head. His lips rested against her hair. "Did I ever thank you for luring me into your life?"

Jennifer smiled. She pressed her head against his neck. "You did, but I don't mind hearing it again."

"Before you came out I sat here thinking about how I was heading towards nowhere before I met you. That is not a very nice place to be." He squeezed her gently. "I also thought how I used to feel that I was not worthy of you."

She laughed. "What tipped the balance?"

"Anu."

Jennifer's eyes clouded over. She pressed her body close to his. "Let us go inside."

One day, she thought, one day I will understand you, Angelo Vargas, but sure as heaven above it will take some time.

Jennifer looked at the clock. She went upstairs to wake up Anu.

Parkhurst drove slowly, aware of being over the limit. He was tired, and the black dog of depression was still wagging its tail.

He cheered himself up by thinking about Valerie Hopkins who had come into his life the previous summer, an intelligent, well-preserved and humorous woman who had means of her own and a mind of her own.

Since his resurrection, Parkhurst had happily drifted along on the shallow and choppy waters of London's social ocean; cocktail parties, gallery openings, book sessions and whatever events he thought would suit his affable nature and promote his image. They had met on one such occasion; there had been an instant rapport. She had seen all his plays and she could quote from his books passages he could not remember having written. At first, he had been cautious; no, he had been *suspicious*, but, as their relationship developed and he learned more about her, he began to believe that there was little to fear. Valerie Hopkins was not a gold-digger. As time went by, he saw more and more evidence of a genuine and harmonious character. She was in her early fifties and had been married once before. She had two grown-up and well-educated children, both married. She was on speaking terms with her ex-husband; they had dinner twice a year where they spoke mainly about the children and the grandchildren and about bits and pieces of what took place in their own and separate lives.

Parkhurst liked that. No animosity, just a whiff of a sophisticated and urbane atmosphere, two people listening to the faint but tolerable echoes of what once had been.

He also saw more of his own children, now. His re-emergence to prominence had not escaped them. They came regularly once a month and stayed for up to one full hour before they departed with a cheque each.

Parkhurst had finally accepted the situation; he was pleasant when they arrived and stoical after they had gone. He had lodged their character and behaviour under the category *Life's Dustbin for Moral Embryos,* and there wasn't much else he could do about it. At least they didn't criticize him as much as they used to, small mercies being better than none, and he had stopped blaming himself for having assisted in producing them in the first place. It was a touch of pure *amour-propre* and, presumably, better than none.

Two of his three ex-wives had tried to improve their financial circumstances, but Britain's well-oiled and impartial legal system had put an end to the matter and declared that enough was enough. The original agreement stood, and that's where the story should and did end. Each had promptly married their latest boyfriend. Parkhurst sent flowers to each of the blushing brides and wished them all the luck they deserved. He preferred to think that the ambiguity wasn't lost on them.

Parkhurst smiled and promised himself a nightcap. He stretched his arms and yawned with satisfaction. A good night's sleep, now…

The grin left his face. Where did Ishihara and Vargas fit in with Pritchard-White? The three of them clearly knew each other. Logic said that they were on the same side. Logic answered the question whether men like Ishihara and Vargas really needed a wretch like Igor Parkhurst to get whatever they were after.

He slumped in his chair and closed his weary eyes. It *was* a game. Unscrupulous people without mercy were playing it; he was a pawn in that game and he had no idea why or what it was all about.

It would probably all be revealed, in time, but there was no worse soul-eroding emotion than uncertainty.

34

Tony Bianconi pulled his tweed hat further down towards his ears and wished that he were in the Bahamas. He had always hated the wintry winds whipping through the streets of the big cities. Another unpredictable shower had washed away what little sympathy he'd had for the season when he woke up to the greetings from a bewildered ray of sunshine peeping through his window earlier in the morning. He had also been frivolous enough to walk from Claridge's to Regent Street, however short the distance. The sidewalks were crowded, and although he found the average Englishman more civilized than the average American, he nevertheless cursed himself for not having suggested an in-door rendezvous with Vargas.

Bianconi looked from one toy to another and wondered how many manufacturers would go bust if parents began to teach their children that there wasn't much glory in the destruction of man and property.

I am losing my grip, he thought; when was a Christmas or a birthday supposed to be an event when common sense and tolerance ruled the mind of those assumed to know and to guide?

"Hello, Tony."

Bianconi adjusted his eyes to the window and nodded to Vargas' reflection on the glass. "Hello, Angelo." He turned around. "Good to see you. You don't get any older, do you?"

"I found the spring of eternal youth."

"Tell me, please. Lead the way."

"Sorry, Tony. She's private."

Bianconi laughed and dried his eyes with the back of his gloves. "I heard. She must be some woman."

"She is."

"Like my Maria. Well, we deserve a good partner, my friend. God knows we need one." He shook his shoulders and turned his back to the wind. "We are not staying here, are we? I'm freezing my butt off."

"All arranged."

Vargas hailed a taxi. The cab stopped in a side street off Marylebone Road. The small restaurant in front displayed a *Closed* sign. Bianconi looked around.

Vargas said, "That's the place."

Bianconi nodded. Vargas had stopped surprising him. They went in. No lights were on, but a candle was burning on a circular table in the corner furthest away from the door.

Bianconi smiled. "I have always thought that your heart was merely an organ, Angelo. It seems that I now have to attach some romantic odour to it."

A figure emerged from the small corridor leading to the kitchen.

"Greetings, Alberto," Vargas said.

"Top of the morning," Alberto said with a heavy Italian accent. His black eyes sparkled. "May I take your coats, gentlemen?"

They sat down. Alberto reappeared with a bottle of red wine and a tall glass containing a non-descript liquid. He waited stoically till Bianconi had tasted the wine.

"Perfect," he said and looked at the label. "My compliments, Alberto. Nobody can compete with Veneto."

Alberto nodded as if Bianconi has said something superfluous and went back to his kitchen.

Bianconi said, "You are not joining me?"

"I quit."

Bianconi took a mouthful and let the wine caress his tongue for a while. "Some woman," he mumbled.

"Some women," Vargas said.

Bianconi put his glass down. "I stand corrected. I heard you have a daughter. Congratulations, my friend. You must be very proud."

"That's premature, but I am certainly pleased."

"And Tadashi has a son?"

"A true replica of his father, poor little gnome. Ugly thing. Let us hope there is room for improvement."

Bianconi hid his amusement behind a worried mask and said gravely, "He must have inherited *something* from his mother."

"Early days. One can only hope," Vargas said and lit a cigarette. "What else have you heard? Your British idol was evidently in a talkative mood when you met."

Bianconi poured olive oil spiced with garlic and chilli on his side plate and reached for the bread. He broke off a piece, dipped and chewed slowly.

"Take your time," Vargas said.

Bianconi swallowed. "He said you've retired, that's all."

"Peculiar. Why on earth did he utter such a libellous rumour?"

Bianconi began to feel less comfortable within himself. "So, it's true," he said.

"Nobody goes on forever. You don't, I don't."

I hope to God he is bargaining, Bianconi thought. He said, "Have I ever played anything but straight with you?"

"Don't get sentimental. Get to the point."

Bianconi did not hesitate. "I have got a serious problem, and I mean *serious*."

"The General."

"How the hell—" Bianconi broke off and stared at Vargas.

"Credit Tadashi," Vargas said. "He concluded that much years ago. It has clearly gone the way he predicted."

"Amazing," Bianconi muttered, "absolutely amazing. That guy is clairvoyant."

"Just exceptionally perspicacious, apart from his talent for using his psychological abacus. Amazing? No, Tony. In retrospect, knowing the history of your problem, it is not even mildly surprising."

Alberto arrived with the starters; sundried tomatoes over fried cod. Bianconi sniffed with delight. "This looks absolutely superb," he smiled.

"Marvellous stuff," Alberto said.

Bianconi stretched his neck. "You should have stayed in Italy," he said, peering at Alberto. "They've got a sense of humour down there, matching their modesty."

"We all make mistakes," Alberto said and waddled back to his kitchen.

Bianconi tasted the food. "He's right, you know." A smile spread across his face. "Marvellous stuff. How did you find this place?"

"Remember Otto Meltzer?"

"Oh dear, Mr. Mercenary himself. Who can forget him? A pity they didn't get him in the Congo. He's still around?"

735

"Not as a mercenary. He packed it in years ago. He finally discovered that his frayed reputation had superseded his technical skills. Today he is a respectable trader; weapons, explosives, drugs, women—you name it. I see him from time to time. He has mellowed, over the years. His favourite pastime now is to sit in front of an audience and extract dramatic tales and awesome stories from his ever-growing memory bank. This place is his headquarter. He and Alberto go back a long time, and Alberto does not talk."

"Neither can Alberto be making much money," Bianconi commented. "Serving two people can't be too profitable."

Vargas smiled. "Quite the opposite. Alberto is well looked after. Whoever uses this place pays the full amount for a packed restaurant, wine and service included."

"Discretion rewarded—I should have guessed. After all, he *is* Italian." Without taking his eyes from his plate, Bianconi leaned closer to Vargas and said, "Do you know how the General made his money—originally, that is?"

"By stuffing young American corpses with heroin before they were shipped from Korea and home to a dignified and well deserved funeral."

"Oh God," Bianconi said and put down his knife and fork, "oh God. Who else knows about this?"

"Ishihara, myself and one more person. The rest are dead, among them the General's wife, as you know."

Bianconi was silent for a long time. He shoved his plate away and sipped his wine several times before he said, "I am beginning to understand Cliff Caldwell."

Vargas did not answer. Alberto came to collect the plates.

"Marvellous stuff," Bianconi said and tried to sound chirpy—Forster's business methods were still on his mind.

His eyes expressed melancholy but his voice was firm when he said, "I am retiring, Angelo. This is my last job."

"Sensible. You have earned it."

"That makes two of us. Give me one of your cigarettes. The first of the year," he added. He touched the flame of the candle. "I know you are reluctant, but you wouldn't be here if it was dead in the water."

"Wouldn't I?"

Bianconi looked away. "Sorry, I should not have said that." He rotated the cigarette between his fingers and watched the smoke. "Do this one for me."

"For you?"

"For me. I have got two very good reasons for asking. One is that my country and the rest of the world are better off without a rotten, menacing sonofabitch like Forster around. The second—or the first, rather—is that my son Guiseppe is aiming for the mayorship of New York. Without the president and the party behind Guiseppe, he doesn't stand much of a chance. Forget the person Caldwell. Apart from being the catalyst, he is irrelevant."

"The long line from George Washington to date implies to me that the American people and whoever is their president at any one time do deserve each other."

Bianconi shrugged off a smile. "That may be so, but Caldwell is a lesser evil than Forster."

Vargas said, "Ten."

"That is steep."

"Life isn't cheap."

"You are making it difficult for me."

"Give my condolences to your president for having torpedoed the American economy."

Bianconi laughed quietly. "You've got to admit that ten million is on the other side of munificence."

"I am prepared to do you a favour, Tony, but not without adequate compensation. I trust that you appreciate my implicit definition of reciprocity."

"Caldwell is very inexperienced. He will never understand that figure."

"Play on his lack of experience and tell him it's the going rate for black-mailing generals. He'll find the money—with your help."

"He's nervous enough as it is. Ten million is to Caldwell a lot of money to pinch from the Treasury. He'll learn, but it will take time. That's what we haven't got—time."

"How much did you and the Brits pay to get rid of Count Folke Bernadotte back in 1948—five, wasn't it? That is a long time ago. You mustn't ignore the horrible effects of inflation, Tony."

"Correct, but I have no intention of telling that to this guy."

"I have a suggestion if you want to economize," Vargas said. "Have a chat with Otto Meltzer. He'll do it for a crate of wine."

Bianconi hummed. "All right. I shall see to it. Have you got your instructions?"

Vargas pulled an envelope from his inner pocket. He shook it, and another smaller envelope fell on the table. "All there," he said and put the larger envelope back in his pocket.

"Cautious as ever," Bianconi mumbled.

Vargas said, "By the way, did Caldwell hit on the brilliant notion of getting away with paying only fifty percent?"

"He did, but I think I convinced him that it wasn't a very good idea."

"I want the full amount up front. The moment that has been confirmed, Tadashi will be on his way."

"I understand."

"You haven't got much regard for Caldwell—that is, even less than for the average politician?"

"He is shallow, greedy and venal. So be it—they all are, by degree. Caldwell has only himself to thank for his predicament. He is cornered, and he is frightened. Desperation can make a man confused, and the bridge from bewilderment to irrationality can be a short one."

"I never knew."

The deep lines between Bianconi's eyes did not go away. "You'll have to be at your sharpest, Angelo."

Alberto came with the pasta, meat sauce, bread and a different bottle of olive oil. "This one is spicy," he said and put the bottle down hard on the table. "Apart from its heavenly taste is also delays senility. Enjoy it, gentlemen." He brushed his hands against his apron and left with a worried look.

"There will be no link if I disappear," Vargas said. "Whoever eliminates me will have no idea why, and Caldwell feels safe."

"I don't know if that's the way he thinks, but I do not put it past him. He did not hesitate much when it came to Forster, and once you start..."

"The vicious circle. Yes, I have read about it."

Bianconi smiled. "Sorry. I haven't got much to teach you when it comes to understanding and taking risks." He shrugged. "It is still beyond me why God created man. Not much to be proud of, is there? What a cock-up."

"The human element and its unpredictability is a source of amusement, if nothing else. Try to look at it that way. When are you leaving?"

"Saturday."

"Give me a call Thursday next at three o'clock in the afternoon, your time," Vargas said and quoted his cottage number. He went on, "I presume your scrambler is in good working condition."

"No home is complete without one." He looked at Vargas. "What is the word?"

"Icarus. I'll call you one hour after mission accomplished."

"Icarus," Bianconi repeated with a low chortle. "Apt."

"Let us enjoy the meal. I recommend Alberto's coconut ice cream. Tell me your plans for the future."

Over coffee, Vargas said, "Do me a small favour, Tony. Call Pritchard-White and tell him to be outside Selfridges in Oxford Street at ten o'clock tomorrow morning."

"That sounds ominous. He's got no idea what this is all about, you know."

"He will when he reads about it."

"Yes, I guess the arrogant ass-wipe will draw his conclusions."

"Unavoidable."

"I see your point. I'll call him."

Alberto came in. Bianconi thanked him with genuine appreciation.

"Bravissimo," Alberto said. "Born and bred in America, but Italian enough to display decorum and gratitude. Going back to your hotdogs and your hamburgers soon?"

"You don't approve?"

"Culinary insults, Signor, but what can one expect from two hundred and twenty million plebeians. Had another one in here, the other day. His table manners would have made an untrained chimpanzee look refined."

Vargas put an envelope under Alberto's chin and said, "Bow your head and remember to blow out the candle when we're gone."

Alberto clutched the envelope against the top of his chest, grabbed the plates and walked off with an expression of mild scorn.

"Excuse me, Alberto," Bianconi said. "How did you know I am of Italian origin? I know that Mr. Vargas has not said anything, so how come?"

Alberto half turned. "Your friend Mr. Vargas couldn't compete with a new-born mynah bird. That aside, I don't need anybody to tell me the obvious. You have got Sulla's profile and Cicero's tongue, Signor. What else does one need to spot a patrician bloodline?"

"Thank you," Bianconi said. He was touched.

"Yeah. Such a pity with your goddamn accent, though," Alberto said with a look of sincere regret.

Vargas said, "Alberto's kindness is only overshadowed by his ability to make spaghetti." He looked at the chef. "Can't you see that our patrician guest is close to tears? You are overdoing your compliments again."

The silence lasted for several minutes. Bianconi said, "That should be it, then. It has been nice knowing you, Angelo."

Bianconi got up. He found his coat and put it on. He stood there, for a while, both hands holding the brim of his hat. "Take care, my friend."

Vargas replied with a smile.

He telephoned Jennifer from the flat and said that he was going to stay overnight. He had a meeting the following morning. Jennifer said that she understood. She would be fine.

Dusk had yet to arrive, but Vargas lit three candles, tossed a small pillow onto the floor, found his cigarettes, his lighter and an ashtray and lay down on his back.

Take care, Tony had said. Interesting. Did he assume or did he know that Caldwell's intention was to waste the one who eliminated Forster?

Tony Bianconi had almost completed his part of the operation; all that was left was to get the money transferred and for him and his son to get rid of the evidence. Then Tony would retire, and, presuming that Vargas succeeded, whatever happened thereafter was none of Tony's concern.

They had been on good terms, during the years, and they had never failed, but this was a game where the concept of trust did not exist. Caldwell would assume that the one who disposed of Forster knew too much. Taking out that person made sense. Finding someone competent and ignorant of the set-up was a question of money. The CIA had their contacts. There were a few good and experienced old-timers around. There were also some young, ambitious and hungry newcomers who would be eager to make their mark; unknowns, and therefore more dangerous.

Vargas lit a cigarette. He watched the thin spiral of smoke ascending towards the ceiling. For the first time in his life he wished that he could back out. So much had happened since Ishihara had told him about the American general and outlined Forster's ambitions, his strategies and his ultimate target. Surmising, yes, but had not Tadashi been incredibly accurate? Vargas had not remonstrated. On the contrary; this was going to be their final triumph, the crown on a long and illustrious career coming to an end when they were still in their prime.

That was then. That was long before Jennifer. Long before he had realized that another life could become a reality; the vague dream of peace and harmony and someone to share with, a dream carefully kept under lid and never allowed to influence his existence. Then she came along, out of the blue, and the dream came closer and wasn't so vague any more. Against his instincts, sharpened by decades of experience, he had begun to think that life had more to offer than he hitherto had been prepared to anticipate. It had thrown him off balance. For a long time he had not fully understood that Jennifer accepted him, that she wanted to be with him. He had not dared believe that she wished to share her life with him, knowing his past and knowing his disposition and the characteristics that made him a loner, a social misfit and a man whose attitude towards mankind was dominated by taciturn contempt.

Fully understood?

Angelo Vargas smiled. No, he had not understood it at all. He had thought, all along, that one day Jennifer would walk out, that it would come to a point where she would have had enough of his entire being and everything he stood for. His dream would collapse and he would walk away from the crash, taking with him nothing but a few memories. Alcohol had helped him to suppress the dream, to prevent it from taking over his life and dominate his existence, to lessen the impact of the blow when Jennifer walked out. Alcohol had been the safety valve that had let off the pressure when needed and made him cope with a world alien to him; Jennifer's world, inhabited by people whose conduct and standards and behaviour he had found strange and artificial. Alcohol had immunized against loneliness, against this terrible feeling of isolation, of floating around in a capsule and watching a world he was incapable of joining. Yes, he could communicate, to some extent, but there was never any feeling of rapport or a sense of belonging anywhere, and he had long lost the urge to wonder why he felt so secure in his own company and so ill at ease with anybody else.

He had misjudged Jennifer. From the moment he first saw her, he knew that she was an exceptional woman, and that he wanted to get to know her. She had responded, and it had not taken him long to decide the next step. He had chosen Lebanon, Japan and Hong Kong as fragments of the portrait depicting the person. He had let her accept or reject at will. He had *expected* her to flee in horror and disgust, but she had stayed. Surprise had collided with hope.

Her acceptance had not been enough for him. His innate lack of trust in anybody continued to rule, and alcohol assisted. His fear of reliving the trauma when he lost his brother and his grandfather continued to dominate. He had kept on testing her, but it was she who had put the final test to him.

Her pregnancy had made him accept that his dream had become a reality. She had convinced him that her affection was not a temporary infatuation, that she really cared for him. That was when he knew he had to mend his ways should he wish to link his future with a woman who could give meaning to his life and whose equal did not happen twice.

Perhaps he had not misjudged her, after all. In her, he had seen what he *wanted* to see—and it had been there, all of it, all of the time.

During the years, he had questioned his ability to love since his brother and grandfather. Slowly, the question gave an answer. Until Jennifer, he had presumed that he had lost the emotional depths for genuine affection. It had become a thing of the past, so long ago; the treadmill of life had withered away emotions that once had led to attachment. He had found consolation in his conviction that he could never again get hurt.

Jennifer had made him admit that a tiny doubt must have had been present all along. He had scrutinized his callousness and he had begun to wonder if his attitude had been born and dictated by a need for protection—or, could it be a measure of each? Did non-existing sympathy and absence of empathy with practically anybody define and emphasize unadulterated misanthropy, or did it mean that what he had to give could not be stretched beyond one particular and very special woman and the child or children that were his own? Or both?

Lately, he had wondered if this trait, which seemed so plausible, had run parallel with his indifference towards his victims. There had been no remorse after he had mutilated the Belgian cook in Veracruz. There had been no remorse ever since. It was as if he'd stood outside of himself and watched with no more than clinical interest when other men died. Their demise had meant nothing to him. His participation in their departure had been the execution; to perform a well-paid job; it did not upset him, but neither did it give him any sense of pleasure. His prey was men like himself, men who had chosen a perilous path leading a merciless game of decadence and depravity where some survived and others did not. Moral judgement did not enter the equation. It was never a question of who deserved to live or die in the world of power struggle with all its nuances. Questions of rights and wrongs and of morals and ethics were effectively erased by the nature of the game and by the persuasion of its participants.

Ishihara's original idea, way back in Japan, had been clear-cut and uncomplicated. Political assignments only; all requests from individuals operating outside this perimeter to be rejected, and no involvement with internal family feuds.

It had been an interesting life, but it had run its course. Since meeting Jennifer he had felt like a prizefighter facing the choice between retirement whilst still on top, or take one more pay-day with its inherent and inevitable risk of defeat. The opponent Abraham Forster represented such a risk, not because of the time in the ring, but because of the shadows in his corner. Tony Bianconi could not be relied upon; he had never served anybody but himself, and rightly so, and he was an expert at closing his eyes when so deemed desirable. Tony would not instigate any attempt to get rid of Forster's liquidator; such an act he would see as unnecessary and possibly counter-productive, but neither would he lift a finger to prevent it happening. A mild protest, perhaps, a discreet warning or a low-key advice to keep the operation as simple as possible, but there it would end.

The danger was that Caldwell thought he knew better; a young and inexperienced man trying to be clever and apply his own rules to a game he knew nothing about, believing in his ignorance that by eliminating Forster' assassin there could be no come-backs.

Such reasoning excluded the fact that Tony's choice was non-domicile and non-resident. It excluded the fact that whomever Caldwell involved would live on the doorstep of his mind. It excluded the threat he could have avoided by heeding Tony's simple conception.

Elimination of links was an art. It required experience, common sense and the ability to evaluate. Nothing that Caldwell had done so far gave reason to believe that he was any more familiar with those golden rules than he was with reading people like Abraham Forster.

All summed up, Vargas thought, he could have done without this one. Complications looming in the background were part of the package and did not worry him unduly, but then there were Jennifer and Anu and the less than compelling phenomenon that the only valid basis for the assignment was Ishihara's financial predicament. Not much of a justification, strictly speaking—nobody but Tadashi was responsible for his own life and for his own actions—but Vargas knew that he could not back out.

Could not?

The only valid basis?

Angelo Vargas smiled and closed his eyes. *Could not.* His commitment to Ishihara and Bianconi was of no value. No card in the deck had the word *honour* printed on it, and neither of those two would raise an eyebrow if he changed his mind. Resentment, yes—surprise, no.

His decision to go ahead had nothing to do with Ishihara and Bianconi. It had to do with himself, with an underlying desire never to have to question whether he was still capable of facing a challenge as monumental as Abraham Forster. Who else could do him, undetected, and then vanish without a trace? One or two. Who else could do so in such a way that any coroner would accept death by natural causes? Nobody else. They had come to him because of his superior record. They had come because the only alternative was a lunatic, and that kind of substitute was the last person Caldwell and Bianconi needed.

Vargas knew that the more he'd thought about it, the more irresistible the assignment had become. The long period of inactivity had done him no good. Boredom had set in. He had missed the action; the planning, the preparations and the electrifying sensation of balancing on the sharp edge of the sword. The dark forces were still there. The challenge of the *last assignment* had become close to an obsession. His adrenaline was still flowing. The smell of danger was still sweeter than the scent of wallflowers on a warm summer's day.

Until Jennifer, the concept of any *last assignment* had not crossed his mind. Now, he had promised—and he was happy with his pledge. No more. After Abraham Forster, the demons would be satisfied and calm down. They would become settlers and never again leave the hidden valley and climb the mountains and demand yet another confrontation.

Looking back, the only regrettable factor was that it had not happened earlier, before he had met Jennifer, but such was life and the dice had been thrown.

Did she know? He thought so. There was something in the air that he could not define, like a tiny echo or a faint whisper. Since their trip to the Cayman Islands there had been one or two indications that she had begun to suspect the true nature of his profession. He had heard the almost inaudible shade of despair in her voice when they talked about his retirement. He had seen the expression in her eyes when he made his promise, a look that made him feel that her intuition had encircled the reality of his chosen path. Still, not a word had been said; she believed his promise and they both knew that he was not going to break it.

After Abraham Forster, there was nothing more to prove.

Angelo Vargas listened to the cooing of the pigeons and wished that his grandfather and brother could have met Jennifer.

Pritchard-White was as cold and miserable as the weather when he waited for Vargas to show up outside of Selfridges. Already five minutes late. Another couple of minutes and that would be it. Bloody foreigners, who the hell did they think they were? Pritchard-White shuddered and stamped his feet. It was a bit early for lunch, but maybe Vargas had a lot on his mind and their parley would be concluded over a nice meal in a first-class restaurant.

Tony Bianconi had given no clue about his real reason for visiting London, but Pritchard-White was as patient as he was curious. He had been quietly pleased when he'd learned that Vargas wanted to see him. The hitman wasn't noted for being talkative, nor for wasting time, and with Bianconi in the background it had to be not just important but *very* important. Tony was an old man, now, and both he and Vargas were on the brink of retirement; clearly something significant, something *big* was going to happen. But *who, why and where*—those were the questions.

Pritchard-White adjusted his scarf. Once again he cursed the climate and thought of his soccer coupons and his eight hundred premium bonds and the condo he wanted to buy in the West Indies. What a way to wrap it up; the children out of the way and nothing but the sun and the beaches and the income from a few hundred thousand added to his pension; a well-deserved life of leisure, with absolutely nothing to do except what pleased him. He hadn't had much luck, so far, with his soccer coupons; those illiterate and empty-headed ball-kicking slobs who called themselves footballers weren't what they used to be, but almost every Saturday some asshole won big money and...

"Good morning," Vargas said.

Pritchard-White swore silently and turned around. He wondered how Vargas had managed to creep up on him. Then he noticed that Vargas' coat was dry. He must have come through the shop. Pritchard-White looked at his watch a bit longer than it took him to register the time. He thought that would make his point, but he did not expect an apology.

"Good morning," he said stiffly and gave a slight nod. "I hope our conference will take place somewhere else."

"You are not in the mood for a walk?"

"Most certainly not. Only when being indoors do I find this climate agreeable."

"As you wish. Let's go somewhere else. I know of a warm and cosy place."

Vargas gave an address and added, "I advise that we go in separate cars. Follow not earlier than five minutes after I've left."

Pritchard-White repeated the address. He had never heard of the place. He said, "Right. One can't be too careful, can one?"

"One can't. Ask for Mr. White when you arrive. You are Mr. Black."

"Now, isn't that appropriate."

"I thought so. See you there." Vargas hailed a taxi and was gone.

Pritchard-White followed precisely five minutes later. It's probably one of these nice little family-run restaurants, he thought—discreet, private and with excellent food and wine. He sank back in the seat, rubbed his hands and decided not to waste any mental energy on the purpose of the meeting. It would soon enough surface. A confident demeanour, physical passivity, an air of confidence and a stiff upper lip had always served him well. He doubted that Vargas could spring a surprise causing as much as a blink of an eye.

"Here we are," the cabby said. "Enjoy yourself and don't overdo it."

Pritchard-White leaned forward and looked up. It was a health club. He stared in disbelief at the sign and said, "Are you sure this is the right address?"

"What do you mean *am I sure*. Of course I am bloody sure. That's the address you gave me." The cabby turned around. "Listen matey, I've been driving for forty years, and—"

"All right. Could I have a receipt, please?"

He went inside. How frightfully funny, he thought. Mr. Vargas does indeed have a refined sense of humour. Well, what could one expect from a reptile of a foreigner?

The reception area was brightly lit, with comfortable furnitures and four white-clad and attractive girls behind the counter.

One of them said, "Can I help you, sir?"

"Yes, please. My name is Mr. Black. I believe that Mr. White is expecting me."

A manicured finger stopped somewhere down the page of the book in front of her. She turned it and said, "Sir, if you would be good enough to sign here, please."

Pritchard-White filled in his fictitious details and took off his coat. "Would you care to show me where I can find Mr. White, please?"

The girl laughed. "Show you? I don't think so, sir. Mr. White is in the sauna."

"Of course," Pritchard-White said and kept his composure. "Of course. Sorry, I have never been here before."

"Through the glass doors," the girl pointed. "Turn right and you will see the sign for the cloakrooms. The sauna is at the very end of the corridor. Your key, sir."

Stay calm, Pritchard-White reminded himself as he undressed. Be your usual self. You are not to be fazed. You are going to stay on top of the situation, as always. No way shall this degenerated alien get the better of you.

He took a towel, wrapped it around his waist and walked stiffly towards the sauna.

"Welcome," Vargas said and splashed more water on the stones.

Neither the gesture nor the hissing sound amused Pritchard-White. He tried not to blink when the steam hit his eyes. He sat down on the uncomfortably hot wooden bench and said, "You have got a suspicious mind, Mr. Vargas. I wasn't wired, and nobody is following us." He looked around at the all too close pinewood walls. "An ideal place, I'd say."

"Warm and cosy."

"Indeed, and a true reflection of your sense of humour."

"Don't get lost in the spicy pickle of hermetic psychology. I never mix business with humour."

Pritchard-White waited for Vargas to continue, but he merely wiped his forehead and seemed to enjoy himself.

Pritchard-White looked at his host's tanned and finely tuned body. Suddenly, he became aware of his own thin arms and long and spindly legs and the hair like a squashed black widow on his white and sunken chest. The heat was getting close to unbearable. He said, "What can I do for you, Mr. Vargas?"

"Nothing."

"I beg your pardon?"

"Nothing," Vargas repeated.

Pritchard-White forced a smile and wished he'd brought a second towel. "I am afraid I don't follow. Why are we here?"

"Why do you think Tony Bianconi came to town?"

"I haven't got the faintest idea."

"Right, but you do consider it probable that you'll eventually find out."

Pritchard-White shrugged. "I am under the impression that whatever is on Tony Bianconi's mind does not concern my country. I have therefore no interest in the matter."

Vargas stared at the ceiling ten inches above his head. "Is that right?"

"Of course it is right. You know the game as well as I do."

"That is why I do not believe you."

"Suit yourself."

"Thank you. Has it not occurred to you that you are already involved?"

"Excuse me?"

"You arranged the meeting between Mr. Bianconi and myself through Igor Parkhurst."

"All I did was to convey a message via Mr. Parkhurst. That hardly amounts to involvement."

"You made Mr. Parkhurst a go-between."

"So what?"

Vargas threw more water on the stones. When the steam cleared, he said, "Go-betweens usually meet with an accident."

Pritchard-White moved uneasily on the bench. "Mr. Parkhurst is of no importance whatsoever. We simply can't be bothered. He is small-time, too insignificant. He is not worth the effort."

Vargas said, "A link is a link. Degrees of significance have not hitherto dictated your actions. On the contrary, I would say. Not only do you deem it necessary, you also find it irresistible to combine the roles of jury, judge and executioner. Who knows, it may even appeal to your sublime sense of humour."

Pritchard-White moved a few inches away from the heater and tightened his towel. It irked him that he had to look up since Vargas sat on the top bench, but suffering in silence was better than collapsing. "It is pure business," he said and wiped the sweat from his nose.

Vargas said, "That's the word—business."

Pritchard-White said wearily, "Excuse me, Mr. Vargas, but what is it exactly you want from me, apart from nothing?"

Vargas said, "Mr. Ishihara has a family. So do I. If anything happens to anyone, regardless of circumstances and however accidental it may look, please remember that you, too, have a family."

"Good Lord! We would never…"

"Cut it out. I know how you operate. You are a bunch of odious little chaps who consider yourselves untouchable." He paused and waited for Pritchard-White to look up. It did not happen. Vargas shrugged. "I presume you know that Parkhurst is Jennifer Moran's godfather. You do not touch him, and you sever all contact with him as of today."

Pritchard-White kept his rage under control. "Or you will see me dead, is that it?"

Vargas said, "No, but I guarantee you that you'd wish you were dead." He picked up the ladle and began to scatter water with rhythmic movements.

The heat was becoming insufferable; Pritchard-White closed his eyes and tried to make himself smaller. He said, "I do not take lightly to threats, Mr. Vargas." He blinked and glared at Vargas with narrowed eyes.

Vargas smiled. "Strange," he said.

"What is strange?"

"You have been around for decades," Vargas said. "Don't you think it's time you learn to differentiate between a threat and a statement?"

"Are we finished, Mr. Vargas?"

"I believe we are."

Pritchard-White got up, fastened his towel and reached for the door handle.

"Remember the key," Vargas said.

"I have got it in my hand, thank you."

"The key *word*—nothing."

"Goodbye, Mr. Vargas."

"Don't forget to shower."

Outside, in the corridor, Pritchard-White took a few of his deepest breaths as the cool air embraced his burning body. He walked slowly towards the cloakroom, took a luke-warm shower, put on a gown that was too short and sat down on the nearest comfortable chair. There was nobody else around. He sighed and rubbed his eyes with the tip of his fingers and tried to suppress a rising sense of indignation and vengefulness. Vargas had treated him like some unimportant little shit from a minor department. He had been forced to swallow one insult after another. Who the hell did this barbarous sub-human maniac of a primitive hitman think he was? Vargas knew very well that involving families was indeed a rare occurrence.

Pritchard-White breathed heavily through his nose and scanned the ceiling. His head pivoted from side to side. Parkhurst was different. Let him off the hook, and the silly old fool could be dumb enough to write a play or a story or even an entire novel about his life in the shadow of Her Majesty's government. Nor was it inconceivable that Parkhurst could surmise or discover by accident the identity of whomever it was that Bianconi and Vargas had in mind. One could not be too careful, and Parkhurst, like everybody else, would soon be forgotten. A neatly arranged accident, a colourful funeral, a flowery obituary, and that would be it.

Pritchard-White crossed his legs and folded his hands over his stomach. *Statement—not threat.* Vargas had no scruples, none at all. The only one who could compete with his callousness and utter lack of consideration was his Japanese partner. What a pair, and what incredibly hard luck that Parkhurst should happen to be the godfather of the Moran woman, and that she, in turn, had decided to share wigwam with the incarnation of bestial nastiness.

Pritchard-White began to feel more at ease. The worst seething had abated, and the erupting geyser of fury and hatred was spitting less severely. His head was still perspiring. He dried his hair and massaged his scalp with a hand towel and wondered against professional insight if Igor Parkhurst really was worth bothering about. After all, there were alternatives. Parkhurst did not *necessarily* have to stop a locomotive with his front teeth in order to be silenced. Perhaps something as simple as a signature could do the job. *We have decided to release you from your duties, Mr. Parkhurst. You do realize, of course, that total silence is required for the rest of your life. Code of Secrecy, Mr. Parkhurst. You are aware that such does exist, are you not? Good. Sign here, please. Any breach, ANY breach, however minor …need we say more? Thank you, Mr. Parkhurst, and farewell.*

That would most likely do it. The old fart was easily scared. On top of that, he was overweight and in his seventies and would probably pack it in soon, anyway. Statistically, he should be dead already.

Pritchard-White looked at himself in the large mirror on the wall opposite, showed his teeth and got up from his chair. Vargas could turn up any minute, now. Pritchard-White had no desire to continue the dialogue.

He dressed methodically and was out and away as quickly as his dignity allowed.

☞

Ishihara was cutting wood in one of the stables when he heard the car. He went outside, waved at Vargas and began walking towards him. "A most rewarding morning, I take it?"

"Informative," Vargas said.

"Do I detect a slight reservation?"

"Those people have their own code of conduct."

So do we, my friend, Ishihara thought. He said, "Should I draw the conclusion that you are not satisfied?"

Vargas locked his car. "I have my doubts about Pritchard-White. He is not entirely rational."

Ishihara said, "Excuse me, but who do you think is going to nick your car in front of my mansion, three hundred yards away from a quiet country lane?"

"Old habits," Vargas said and put the keys in his pocket. "The avenue of complacency is littered with the bones of those who mistook silence for safety. Where is the vigilant Tadashi I once knew? Life isn't over yet, amigo. Don't let yourself go."

Ishihara took off his gloves. "So, you don't have much confidence in Her Majesty's diligent servant."

"I don't."

"What makes you think he didn't get the message?"

"He got the message, all right. The stumbling block could be his monumental arrogance."

"Exactly the way I summed him up. He is a true representative of the medium-to-upper echelon of the British society." Ishihara shook his head. "It's rather strange, really. Who the hell do they think they are? Why is even *attempted* self-assessment such an unknown concept to them?"

"They can't help it. There's a gene missing."

"That is sad, don't you think?"

"Where is Yasmin?"

Ishihara unbuttoned his jacket. "Jennifer called this morning. They went shopping, and from there back to your place for a gossipy lunch. I reckon we have got a couple of hours. Let's go inside."

Vargas took off his coat and found an ashtray before he sat down. Ishihara made Japanese tea.

"Are you hungry?" he asked.

"No, and neither are you. You need to lose a stone."

"I haven't got fat on my brain."

"You will, unless you pull yourself together."

"Here," Ishihara said and put the tray on the table. "Help yourself." He turned a chair and rested his arms on the top of the back. He said, "I gather that Pritchard-White must be left in no doubt." He paused for a few seconds. "You do not believe that he will come to his limited senses as a result of your no doubt urbane conversation?"

"I can't risk it."

"Tell me what happened."

Vargas did, and Ishihara laughed. "Perfect," he said. "The ideal setting for a hot topic." He took one of Vargas' cigarettes. "I agree with you. It is indeed a grave possibility that Pritchard-White now is so seriously offended that he could be tempted to demonstrate his superiority. I take it you have a plan."

Vargas nodded. His fingers caressed the Japanese teapot. "Do you remember the day you introduced yourself to Igor Parkhurst?" he said.

"I certainly do. Nice little pub."

"There was an interruption."

"The Black-and-White Minstrel Show," Ishihara said. "Unforgettable." He pulled a tissue from his pocket and blew his nose. "Not the most prominent members of our adopted country, I'd say. My recollection is one of limited competence."

"Sufficient for what I've got in mind."

Ishihara smiled. "I am all ears."

Vargas outlined his plan. Only when he had finished did Ishihara speak.

"Sounds good," he said. "That should make it clear to Pritchard-White Esquire that even a nature as charitable as yours should not be pushed too far."

35

Otto Meltzer had seen sunnier days. His finances were not what they used to be. His social life had taken a dip, as had practically everything else. Few knew better than Meltzer that life could be compared with an unknown route through the wilderness of blackest Africa.

Once, Otto Meltzer had been proud of his physique; five-foot-eleven, athletic and fast. Rich food, sweet wine and years of inactivity had added three stones. Meltzer no longer strutted; he walked with his feet well apart, like a man trying to avoid getting blisters on the inside of his thighs. Only his mien remained the same; Meltzer conducted himself with the air of the conqueror that owned the world but without a clear idea of what to do with it.

Meltzer did not think that anybody else knew what to do with it, either. Petty little minds reigned everywhere. Shabby deals were being reached behind closed doors. Nations united behind mountains of documents containing rules and regulations impossible to implement, which, as Meltzer saw it, was precisely the intention. Permanent confusion had made stealth and corruption respectable parts of the structure; the world had become a gravy train accelerating with such speed that a catastrophe was inevitable. There were no visions any more, no one with the ideals and the qualities of a true *Fuhrer*, only a bunch of mediocre politicians whose ego, greed and vanity were in inverse proportion to their wits.

Otto Meltzer reflected and reminisced to the tunes of *Gotterdammerung*. Wagner was his favourite. The beauty of his music was only surpassed by the composer's political philosophies. Meltzer had read *Das Judentum in der Musik*. What a dual talent. Meltzer's eyes shrouded over. He brushed a tear from his cheek as his mind suddenly touched the sad fact that his old contacts had all but vanished. Younger men had taken over. During the last decade, Meltzer had suffered. His discreet feelers had become a waste of time. For some obscure reason nobody seemed to appreciate the value of experience any more. It was like everybody was brushing him aside just because he was no longer a *young* mercenary. It was an utterly stupid and short-sighted attitude, Meltzer thought; what kind of record did they have, these kids? What had they been through and what did they know when the going got tough? Yes, he was into his sixties now and had not participated in respectable wholesale slaughter for longer than he cared to remember, but there had to be something seriously wrong with a world completely ignoring the immeasurable benefits of knowledge and practise. To top it all—Meltzer quaked as the memories flooded his mind—*to top it all*; some years ago a black bugger of an African politician had actually told him face to face that *he, the redoubtable Otto Meltzer,* was well past his best. They could not use a man whose brain was centred under the nail of his trigger finger. Meltzer was proud of his reputation for being trigger-happy. He had made it clear to the politician that dead men neither shot back nor talked, and wasn't that something to bear in mind? No, the politician had said, it wasn't always something to bear in mind, since even in Africa it was difficult to successfully interrogate dead people.

Meltzer had then lowered his fee, but the politician, that stinking *untermenschen* of a corrupt *mutterfocker,* had just laughed and said with visible *schadenfreude* that Meltzer's market value was on a par with the droppings from a baby baboon.

It had taken Meltzer a full week and twelve bottles of whisky to get over the insult. Then, as his hangover receded, Meltzer began to take stock. He did not accept that his days of distinction were over; sooner or later someone would acknowledge the need for competence and experience, but, whilst waiting, Meltzer had to make a living.

He owned outright his small flat in Maida Vale, but there was precious little left of his savings. Meltzer was good enough with figures to realize that his cash flow situation would become painfully acute in the not too distant future unless he found contributory sources.

London was a wide open market for a vast number of seedy activities; it was a world that Meltzer knew inside out, and he decided to become a supplier of commodities. He started with firearms, an area where few could match him. He expanded quickly into the easy money of prostitution, covering both sexes and offering any variety of corporal pleasures known to man. Within a year he had progressed into drugs, which completed his portfolio. He stayed clear of the big boys and took care never to cross the paths of ethnic groups; he made a living, and he knew in his heart of hearts that the chance of making mega-bucks would probably never again materialize. If he could not travel to countries in disarray, it followed that he could not legally steal, plunder and rob—the source of his once respectable fortune—which again meant that the days were gone when he was the darling of several bank managers, local and otherwise; wet little turds who invited him to lunch when he did not need them.

Added to his commercial activities, Meltzer began to develop his latent talent as a raconteur. He knew that he could be repetitive, so, like his social idol Oscar Wilde, Meltzer spent hours every day creating punch lines, observations and witticisms. He was realistic enough to admit that his sense of humour was not in the same league as his memory; accordingly, there was only one solution, and that was to plod on and gradually increase his arsenal of one-liners without forgetting any of the old ones along the way.

Meltzer held court in select, offbeat restaurants. As his reputation as an unconventional entertainer grew, gone were the days when he had to pick up the tab.

One evening, standing on the pavement looking for a taxi, he heard a voice behind him: "Good evening, Mr. Meltzer."

Meltzer turned and saw a man who looked like a younger version of Ibn-Saud. The man moved one step forward and there were less than three feet between them. Meltzer took his hands up from the pockets of his Burberry coat and shifted the weight onto his right leg. The man in front of him was barely half of Meltzer's size, but Meltzer was far too experienced to be fooled by appearance.

"My name is Mohammad," the man said. "We would like to employ your services. Is there a place where we can talk in private?"

Meltzer had emptied two bottles of Blue Nun in the course of the evening, but he was not drunk. "You want my services," he repeated as he studied the deadpan face of the Middle-Eastern.

"We do," the man nodded. He looked quietly confident.

Meltzer knew better than to ask who *we* were. "My place," he said and hailed a taxi.

Neither spoke during the ride. The flat was in darkness. Meltzer switched on the lights and locked the door behind him.

"Please sit down," he said.

Only then did the man move. He did not take off his long leather jacket.

"Something to drink?" Meltzer asked. His smile revealed a third of his teeth missing. His tongue kept appearing between the gaps like an eel looking for a way out.

Mohammad said, "No thanks. I am fine."

Meltzer liked that. It was very professional. He sat down. "Go ahead," he said.

Mohammad spoke with a heavy accent, but his pronunciation was distinct and he did not search for words. When he finished, he crossed his legs and leaned back in the chair. His smile was benign enough, but Meltzer thought that somehow it did not fit the expression in the dark eyes under black and straight brows.

"I see," Meltzer nodded. "Ten grand."

"Interesting," Mohammad said. His smile was in place. "That is exactly the figure we had in mind."

Meltzer cursed silently. He still had no idea who *we* were. This was obviously on a need-to-know basis, and just as well. "I meant ten for the equipment and ten for the job," he said and waved his right arm as if to indicate that this should have been clear to Mohammad from the onset.

"So did we," Mohammad said. "My apology for not expressing myself in an unambiguous fashion."

Meltzer rose to get himself a schnapps. "You are not Jewish?" he said and corked the bottle.

"What if I am?"

Meltzer sat down heavily and took a solid sip before he planted the glass hard on the table. Yes, he had been reduced to a wheeler-dealer and a merchant of cheap commodities, but he still had a few principles left. No true Aryan should ever forget what the Jews had done to Germany. Their crimes and misdemeanours had directly caused the Second World War, among other atrocities, and ultimately the fall of The Third Reich and the eclipse of der Fuhrer. It was the bloody

Jews who had ruined his once mighty *Vaterland*, and it pained him deeply each time he remembered that Deutschland was no longer *uber alles*.

"Forty," he said resolutely.

"Do I look Jewish?" Mohammed said.

Yes, Meltzer thought, you fockin' well do. You all look the same, down there. You are equally repugnant, and your godamn religion is all there is between you. *Gott im Heaffen*—did not Herr Wagner know what he was talking about?

"Certainly not," Meltzer said.

"Correct. I am not Jewish. For the record, Mohammad is not the most common of Jewish names."

"Good point. I couldn't care less where you come from. I am a professional."

"When can you deliver?"

Meltzer's mind accelerated. He stared at the ceiling for a minute. His eyelids moved with military precision. "The last day of the month," he said.

"That is ten days from today," Mohammad stated.

"Precisely," Meltzer agreed. "You see, I have to be extremely careful and selective and…"

"I did not ask for an explanation. We accept the last day of the month. Another member of our group will contact you on the day. His name is also Mohammad."

I am sure it is, Meltzer thought. He took off his glasses and polished the lenses with a handkerchief that had not been washed for a while.

"Half now and half on delivery," Mohammad said. His right hand moved slowly and disappeared behind the lapel of his jacket. One by one, five brown envelopes were placed side by side on the table. "Twenties only, all used."

Meltzer did not react.

Mohammad slid forward and got to his feet. "It has been a pleasure, Mr. Meltzer."

Meltzer grinned. "How did you hear about me?"

"You have an outstanding reputation," Mohammad said. He walked towards the door. "In fact, you are probably more notorious than you know about."

Meltzer nodded thoughtfully. "I probably am." He unlocked the door. "Maybe we can do business again."

"Who knows?" Mohammad said. He walked down the stairs.

Meltzer had another schnapps. Only when he sat down did he open the envelopes. He removed the rubber bands from each bundle and spread the five hundred twenty-pound notes across the table. He laughed. "Easy," he said. "Easy, and no risk to speak about. Do this one well, which shouldn't be difficult, and you are on the comeback trail." He glanced at his watch and poured the rest of the schnapps back into the bottle.

Otto Meltzer searched through his collection of records, found *Der Ring Des Nibelungen* and lay down on the sofa. With a bit of luck, the intended target was a Jew.

☞

Janos Szecheny considered himself as British as any, and he had a passport to prove it. He had kept his original name out of reverence for the proud Magyars from whom he descended. It did not bother him that few could pronounce his name correctly and fewer could spell it, but it did upset him that hardly any of his adopted compatriots knew so little about the illustrious history of his land of birth; a tragic situation which was nigh impossible to digest and therefore sufficient reason in itself never to change his name.

His parents had sided with Imre Nagy in 1956. Like so many others, they had fled when the Russian tanks entered the scene. Together with their one and only son, Karoly and Eva Szecheny spent ten months as unwelcome guests in Austria before they finally made it to London where they settled for good.

They ended up in a council flat in Hackney. Young Janos quickly adapted. His English became close to fluent within a year. His father, an engineer by education, tried hard to get work befitting his qualifications, but his inability to master the language was against him. Eventually, he accepted a job as a handyman.

Karoly and Eva Szecheny did not enjoy living in exile. They missed their families, their friends and the unique atmosphere of Budapest, the city they thought more beautiful and charming than any city anywhere else. Slowly, but surely, they faded. On the day of the first anniversary of their arrival, Karoly Szecheny quietly passed away; a broken, bitter man with many a deep line of resignation etched on his once handsome face. Eva Szecheny did not have the strength or the will to continue an existence without her tragic and dearly loved husband. Within four months she was gone.

Janos stayed in the flat until he had scraped together enough money to move. He found a tiny place in Notting Hill where he replanted his clipped and tender roots.

Since he had no education to speak of, Janos decided to try his luck as a professional boxer, but he lacked the killer instinct and the ferocity that caught the headlines. Technically, he was good, but after six fights on the under-cards, Janos acknowledged that he was no Laszlo Papp and that he could not afford to continue.

For a while he kept his day-job with a scrap dealer. It paid the bills, just about, but the company was family-owned. With two sons in the business, Janos knew that any chance of a future was as remote as becoming middleweight champion of the world.

Janos had matured fast since his parents died, and he knew his way around London. He got involved with illegal gambling, discovered a latent talent as a card mechanic, and for a while he enjoyed his easy-going and profitable life-style. Then, one day, some no-good loser squeaked. Janos found himself behind bars in the local police station where he ignored for hours rude questions and coarse accusations.

It did not take long before Janos grasped that the police were not overly interested; he was let off with a warning and re-entered the sunshine with fortified impudence. Through grateful contacts he managed to get an excellent cover-job as a dustman. He continued his gambling with more caution and finesse, and he dreamed of the day when he could go back to the city of his early childhood. Many a late night did he see himself approaching the Szabadsag Bridge where the all-conquering Teruel looked down at him. He stopped halfway across and stared into the Danube where the water was clear and blue and not brown and muddy. He sunned in the Varosliget City Park. He sauntered down Andrassy Utca and had coffee at Muvesz and later a drink at Ruszwurm. He wrapped cakes in his napkin and went to Vorosmarty Square where he fed the pigeons. At night he went back to his suite at the Gellert Hotel. One day he would find the property he'd been looking for. Who could say, maybe a life was waiting for him there and he could put down his fragile roots for whatever was left of his less than alembicated life.

The only drawback was that his ability to save money was critically close to non-existent. Once or twice a year he cursed his own extravagance, but Janos knew that he was hopelessly trapped. He was still young and there was so much to enjoy; restaurants, pubs, women, dog tracks, race meetings, a new car—the money went out as fast as it came in and sometimes faster. Each New Year's Eve he vowed to put aside ten percent of his earnings, earmarked for his visit to Hungary. Three hundred and sixty five days later he lifted his champagne glass and swore that from now on he would take his pledge seriously.

It never happened. His life-style became more and more expensive to maintain, and Janos' overdraft grew. He drifted into petty crimes and became a trustworthy middleman; a handler of this and a loader of that; he could always be relied upon to receive and to deliver. He was sensible enough never to cheat on those with more juice. The unsentimental and down-to-earth perspective of his modus operandi, combined with shrewd judgement and the necessary attention to the needs of a select variety of police officers kept him out of prison, and his unfailing sense of discretion was as recognized as it was widely admired.

Janos supplemented these qualities with a high sartorial standard but without being ostentatious. He maintained assiduously his aptitude for sociability; he fitted in everywhere with apparent ease and took care always to keep a low profile.

One day, at the end of some very long and strenuous hours, somebody offered him a shot of heroin. Janos accepted. The stress and the tension of a life in shadowland had begun to wear him down; the heroin elevated him to a heaven of euphoric relaxation. The darker side of his soul faded out of sight. Nirvana embraced him and his tears flooded his chest until realities returned and sent him crashing down to earth.

Within a few months, Janos was addicted. He managed to keep it hidden from his business world, of that he was certain. He was equally sure that his ability to perform remained undiminished.

His only problem was one of financial nature; his newfound passion did not come cheap. Either something had to go, or he had to make more money.

One frosty March afternoon Janos went down to his local for a pint of beer. He was preoccupied with an annual budget he had revised several times without ending up in the black. He was at least twelve grand short; he had no clear idea where to collect the kind of money that would eradicate his deficit, nor, for that matter, did the notion of further economizing amuse him.

He stared miserably into the froth of his beer, so lost on permutations and short on ideas that he did not bother to look at the man who sat down opposite.

The man cleared his throat and spat on the floor.

Screw it, Janos thought, my concentration is gone. He lifted his eyes and focused when he recognized Kemal, a drug dealer of no insignificant standing in the local community.

Kemal had been a wild man in his younger days. He had the face of a fighter who'd never associated the art of pugilism with the advantage of defence. As he matured, he revised his life-style and began to hire more physically adept associates to take care of the persuasive bits of his business strategy.

Kemal was also known as The Emissary. He possessed an uncanny knack for picking the right people for whatever other right people wanted done. Janos and Kemal only knew each other by appearance and reputation. Janos was too street-wise to get his stuff locally; he had a supplier in Brixton. The Turks and the blacks had little or nothing to do with each other except on the odd occasion when the question of boundaries cropped up. Janos was reasonably sure that there were no common market research and no exchange of other vital business information between them.

Kemal found a matchstick and placed it between his teeth. "Cumberland Hotel ten o'clock sharp tomorrow morning," he said. "Go straight up."

Janos watched the tiny red head of the matchstick moving back and forth under Kemal's black and impressive moustache.

"To where?"

Kemal took a small piece of paper from the breast pocket of his suede jacket. Janos read the three digits.

"The suite number," Kemal said. He grabbed Janos' lighter and put the flame to the paper. Janos wondered why the Turks always dramatized things.

He said, "I'll be there."

Kemal leaned across the table. "We haven't done business before," he said. "My cut is twenty percent."

"Extortionate," Janos said.

Kemal removed the matchstick. He licked the corners of his mouth. "Non-negotiable," he said. For a second his black eyes were aglow.

Janos drank from his beer. He looked long enough at the fingernails on his left hand to demonstrate to both Kemal and himself that he was not fazed. It was improbable that Kemal knew the nature of whatever somebody wanted, but it wasn't unlikely that he knew or would learn about the amount in question. Janos reckoned he had enough problems as it were without adding a bloodthirsty Turk to the collection.

"All right," he said.

Lines appeared on Kemal's forehead as he got up. "Stay healthy," he grinned and walked out.

Janos lit a cigarette. So, Kemal knew. That meant that also other people knew. Oh well, he thought with a shrug; it was inevitable, come to think of it.

Janos knew that he wanted to quit his addiction to heroin, but he doubted his own willpower. He had thought about getting help, and he had wondered if some deterrent existed. This job tomorrow—supposing it paid well—perhaps he should make a trip to Singapore for a couple of weeks since it was better to go cold turkey than to hang.

Janos smiled ruefully. No, he would go to Budapest and take it from there.

The next morning Janos showed up at The Cumberland ten minutes ahead of time. He was wearing a dark suit, white shirt, red-and-green striped tie, navy blue overcoat and classy black shoes. He carried a slender and elegant black briefcase. The lobby was busy. He looked neither left nor right as he headed for the lifts.

He knocked twice and waited for a good minute before the door opened.

"Good morning," the man said and extended his hand. "My name is Mohammad. Come in, please. Do take off your coat."

Janos hung up his coat and placed his briefcase on the floor.

"What is in the briefcase?" Mohammed said."

"It is empty."

Mohammad laughed. "Very good." He walked into the lounge. Janos followed. This must cost a bomb, he mused as he looked around. This chap's got money.

There was a coffee tray on the table.

"May I?" Mohammed said.

"Thank you. Black with one sugar, please."

Mohammad said, "Please sit down. Make yourself comfortable."

Janos picked a chair and studied his host. Mohammad was in his fifties, about five-foot-ten, sturdily built and with powerful hands. He sported a moustache like most Arabs that Janos knew about. The large diamond ring on his left little finger and the heavy gold watch did not look out of place. Mohammad moved with the grace of a man sure of himself. His velvety voice matched his amiable comportment.

"We need a van driver," Mohammad said as he sat down. He balanced the cup and saucer in his left hand.

Christ in heaven—a *van driver.* Now, isn't *that* amusing, Janos thought. He knew that he looked impassive.

"We need a driver who can take a van from A to B and otherwise follow our instructions with mathematical precision," Mohammad continued.

Janos waited patiently. He wasn't unfamiliar with obscure preludes to compositions of complex nature.

"The driver needs to become acquainted with two gentlemen in North London, one black and one white." Mohammad smiled as if the colour scheme tickled him. " It is my understanding that you have no hang-ups about blacks."

Janos said, "Business is business."

Mohammad nodded. "I appreciate your down-to-earth attitude. Furthermore, it rests upon the driver to ensure that the aforementioned gentlemen receive a parcel on a certain day and that they follow the driver's commands to the letter."

They sipped coffee simultaneously.

Mohammad said, "That's it. Would you be interested?"

Janos put his cup back on the saucer with elaborate care. "I have three questions, if I may," he said.

"That is to be expected. Please go ahead."

"What stops the two gentlemen from picking up the van from A, drive it to B and deliver in one go?"

Mohammed's lower lip protruded. "That is a logical question. The reason is that neither of them is in possession of the required mental infrastructure. It will be too complicated for them—something is bound to go wrong, and we cannot afford any mess-up. They are, however, capable of removing a parcel from the van, carry the parcel to a place pointed out to them, and then disappear. That is their limit, I'm afraid. Also," he went on and smiled genially, "by now it has probably occurred to you that *you* do not wish to be seen."

Janos understood. "The element of risk on my part is limited, then," he said.

"It is non-existent if you do exactly what you are being asked to do. Third question?"

"How much?"

"Twelve grand in all, of which you promise one each to your assistants."

Janos turned the ring he wore on his right-hand little finger. The stone was an amethyst. He had heard that it prevented addictions.

"*Promise?*" he echoed.

Mohammed's moustache hid his nostrils when he showed his large and white teeth.

He said, "They leave the van with the parcel. You pretend to look for a parking space up the road."

"I drive off?"

"Slowly."

"I understand."

"Good. With regard to the Turk, if I may be so free as to offer a piece of advice? Don't get him excited. Give him his ten percent."

"Thank you. It is my intention."

And no risk involved, Janos thought, well-well-well. This is obviously big, but if I try to negotiate I'm out.

Mohammad took a photograph from his inner pocket and placed it on the table. He pointed with a massive finger, "That is Sammy the Skunk, and that is Mescaline Mike."

Janos did not touch the photo. "A handsome pair," he said.

Mohammad smiled politely. "Get your briefcase."

Janos did as he was told. When he returned he saw that Mohammad held an envelope in his hand..

"Here," he said. "Five today and seven when you return the van. Everything will be arranged. You will receive further instructions the day before your services are required. That is nine days from today."

Janos put the envelope in his briefcase.

"Thank you for coming," Mohammad said and followed Janos to the door.

Janos put on his coat and said, "Thank you for asking me."

"You are welcome," Mohammad said and smiled jovially. "We know you are the right man for the job. Have a good day."

Janos went home and changed into designer jeans, a tailor-made blue cotton shirt, maroon Italian boots and his most expensive Italian leather jacket. He took the underground up to North Finchley.

He decided to call himself Jimmy Forbes.

It did not take Sammy and Mike long to warm to Jimmy. He was easy-going, friendly and generous, not least generous. For five full days they enjoyed free drinks, two meals a day and a loan of a hundred pounds each to be repaid as soon as they'd got their overdrafts sorted out.

Jimmy was sympathetic to the philosophy that equal opportunity looked good on paper but was a load of nonsense in real life. He listened to their woes and misfortunes with an expression of deep concern. He concurred wholeheartedly with the observation that the world was indeed a rotten place. Nor was mankind much better, and the police— all three of them shook their heads in unison the few times that the dreaded scum of the earth slipped into the conversation and allowed half a minute of silence to speak for itself.

One early afternoon, when the three of them enjoyed a pint in The Virile Slug, Sammy suddenly said, "I tried to call you last night, but I couldn't find you in the book."

"I am ex-directory. Why did you try to call me?"

Sammy chewed on the nail of his right-hand thumb. "I was just wondering, you know, if we could make that loan two hundred," he said without letting go of his thumb. "My bank manager is on holiday. He won't be back until next week."

Janos said, "Sure. I can arrange that."

"Why are you ex-directory?" Mike said.

"Precautions."

"What for?"

"Oh, you know—" Janos frowned and looked away "—people in my business must keep their head down."

Mike said, "So what's your business then?"

766

"Don't pry," Sammy said. "It is none of our business what his business is." He was worried that the extra hundred quid could be in jeopardy if Mike offended Jimmy.

Janos said, "You wonder why I come all the way from Chelsea every day, don't you? I can understand that."

Sammy had a cold. He sniffed, but the drop under his nose got bigger. "We don't wonder," he said. "We reckoned you're on holiday." He tapped the tip of his nose. The drop fell on the table. He wiped it away with the sleeve of his jacket.

"*I* didn't," Mike said angrily.

"You wouldn't want to know," Janos said and lowered his voice. "It is not quite—you know what I mean?"

The glance between Sammy and Mike dragged out for so long that a mole would have picked it up.

Janos went on, "You see, I have a delivery coming up soon in this area, but I can't talk about it." He looked towards the ceiling and then into his glass. "You guys have been really helpful, though, showing me around."

Sammy wasn't aware that they had, but he accepted that advanced criminals worked in sophisticated ways. He said, "You're most welcome. We're just glad to help."

"With what?" Mike said. He scratched his scrotum. His eyes darted from Sammy to Jimmy.

"Shut up," Sammy said. "Let the man talk."

"He just said he couldn't," Mike said. He was beginning to feel irate.

"He can't if you keep interrupting all the time."

Mike let out a burp. "I could do with another pint."

Janos said, "Make it three."

Sammy pushed his long, yellow-grey hair away from his face and smiled apologetically. "He's got a good heart," he whispered, "He means it well. He's a bit daft, but not all that dumb, really."

Mike came back with the beers. He licked the froth from his fingers. "Deliver what?" he said.

Janos gave a short and enigmatic smile. "You wouldn't want to know. I mean, you've become mates of mine and it is better that way." He showed the palm of his hands as if he, too, regretted that their intimate friendship prohibited further disclosure.

But Sammy smelled money and was not prepared to let go without an honest attempt. "You're sure there's nothing we can do?" he asked and sucked his teeth to disguise any impression of keenness.

Janos pondered for a while. The other two barely breathed whilst they waited for the outcome of their mate's exercise in contemplative perceptiveness.

"All right," Janos said at long last. "I need two reliable chaps. You know faces around here. Who can you recommend?"

Sammy kicked Mike on the shin and said, "That's a very good question, that one, Jimmy. You see, most people around here are useless." He picked his ear and dropped what he found on the floor. "Worse than useless, actually," he continued and looked at Mike. "Who can we trust around here?"

"Nobody," Mike said with genuine affection.

"There we are," Sammy said and waved his hand in utter dismissal.

"Oh well," Janos said. He looked dejected. "I'll find a solution, somehow."

"Except us, of course," Sammy said. The glow of his cigarette got closer to his nose. For a while he looked cross-eyed. "We are extremely trustworthy. Wouldn't you say so, Mike?"

"Absolutely."

Janos gave himself plenty of time to let the revelation sink in. "You do realize that this operation is not entirely without..." he paused and closed his eyes for a few seconds. "You know what I mean?"

"No better way to make a living," Sammy said.

"None," Mike confirmed.

Janos finished his beer. "Originally, I was going to try to do this on my own if I couldn't find anybody I could trust," he said gravely. "Point is, you guys have given me some food for thought."

"When is this operation taking place?" Sammy said.

"Tomorrow."

"That isn't much notice."

"That's the way we work."

"Sure," Mike said and rearranged the position of his balls. "How much?"

"I get two grand for the job and I'll give you a monkey each. Can't be fairer than that."

"Impossible to be fairer than that," Sammy agreed. "We're in."

"Both of us," Mike ratified.

Janos collected his cigarettes and his lighter. "Deal," he said solemnly and shook their hands in turn. "One thing," he added and adopted a stern look, "you must stay absolutely sober for the rest of the day. It is vital that you are alert and on your toes tomorrow. Also, I would appreciate if you'd look as—if you could appear at your most presentable."

Sammy rubbed the stubs on his cheeks. "Expect to see two oil paintings, matey."

"Piece of cake," Mike said and put his nose under his armpit.

"Good. At eleven sharp tomorrow morning you will see a white van saying *W. A. Smith Books*. When I stop outside here, you enter through the back door. Don't jump. Do it naturally. Further instructions will be given as we drive to the designated address. I'll have the money with me and you'll get paid the moment you have delivered and are back in the van. Questions?"

"It's *W. H. Smith*," Sammy said.

Janos smiled. "Few are as hawk-eyed as you." He tapped his chin with the fingers of his right hand. "My employers do not want to infringe intellectual rights."

Sammy dug out a single gum from his trouser pocket and began chewing. It had a sedative effect on him. "That's clever," he said.

Janos got up from the table and nodded in a military fashion. "See you tomorrow." He walked out.

"Blimey," Sammy grunted. "A monkey for delivering a parcel. I think Jimmy boy is in with the right people, you know. Let's keep him sweet."

"Why?"

Sammy licked his fingernails. "Because he's got contacts," he said patiently. "We help him and we treat him nicely. In return, he'll provide us with a more interesting future than we've had so far. You follow?"

"No."

"What?"

"First he says he needs two chaps to help him. Then he says he's gonna do it all by himself. Then he says he'll give us a monkey each to help him. He don't make sense."

"Mike," Sammy said as if talking to a child, "it's called psychology. Ducking and diving. Smoke-screening. That's what makes a great criminal. You should read more books."

"How do we look presentable?" Mike said.

"You've got a shower in your place, haven't you?"

"I think so."

"Let's go and find out how it works."

They were outside The Virile Slug at half past ten, freshly scrubbed and dressed in their best outfits. Sammy had hidden most of his locks under an over-sized baseball cap. He had cut and cleaned his nails and used up a canister of body spray on himself and another on Mike who at one point had groaned about the risk of becoming unrecognizable.

Janos was on time. Sammy and Mike walked towards the van, opened the back door and climbed inside.

Janos said, "Good morning. You see that parcel there?" It stood in the middle of the floor. It measured forty-five by forty-five by sixty inches. It was cellotaped and heavily roped.

Sammy said, "We do."

"Lift it. One hand each."

They did. Mike had no problem, but Sammy's face turned scarlet. "Hell," he groaned, "what's in it?"

"You now understand why I need some help," Janos said. "It's too heavy for one man, really."

Mike nodded. Top class criminals didn't necessarily have strong hands. It all added up. "Sure, mon," he said. He spat into his palm and rubbed it against Sammy's back.

Janos said, "See the two overalls there? Put them on."

The overalls were white and had *BOOKS* written in red on the back. "Keep your cap on," Janos told Sammy who had made a move to take it off. "You want to look the part, don't you? Now," he went on and beckoned at the bench behind them, "sit down and listen carefully to my instructions."

Mike touched the parcel with the tip of his shoe. "What's in it?"

"Gold bars."

Mike and Sammy looked at each other. Mike's lips stuck out. Sammy put in an effort to look indifferent but forgot to control his nostrils.

Janos turned in his seat. He said amicably, "Listen, chaps, don't get any ideas. *We* did not steal them. *We* do not melt them down and *we* do not try to sell them. *We* are just delivering, remember? Pay is related to risk, and I swear to you—" he gave each a hard and uncompromising stare "—I swear to you that you don't want to irritate my employers. They can be very, very nasty if things don't go their way."

The silence didn't last long. Sammy said, "Sure. It was just a question. Don't get upset."

Janos shook off his tough-guy expression. He said, "No problems. We read each other. Now, this is what we do. The place is about ten minutes drive from here. I stop in front of the gate, and you take the parcel between you up to the front door. It is important that the label is facing the door so that the man can read it instantly. Have a look. It is very, very important. The moment the man steps aside, you carry the parcel just inside the door, put it down and leave immediately. Got it?"

Sammy had another look at the label. "It's a code, isn't it?" he said.

"Of course it is a code. These chaps are not amateurs—" Janos showed a fist "—and neither are we. Let us prove to them that we are worthy of their confidence."

Mike stuck two fingers in his mouth and removed some leftovers from his breakfast. "You forgot something," he said and completed his meal.

"What?"

"You forgot to tell us to ask for a receipt."

"Christ," Janos mumbled and watched the busy street for a few seconds. "A receipt won't be necessary," he said calmly. "Please do exactly what I have told you to do. *Nothing else.* Do not screw up things now. No personal initiative is required. Just follow orders." He put on his hard-man stare. "*Nothing else,*" he repeated with a merciless clang to his voice.

Mike said, "Easy, mon. We never screw up. Don't worry. I just thought..."

"Don't," Janos interrupted and started the engine.

His own instructions had been clear enough: drive off quietly the moment Sammy and Mike reach the front door of the house. No explanation given, and no questions asked.

The traffic was light. They came to the road and Janos slowed down to a crawl.

"There," he said and nodded, "to the left. The one with the black door and the two urns on top of the stairs."

Sammy stretched his neck. He said, "I can see it. It is nice and quiet around here."

Janos stopped the van. Sammy and Mike got out.

Janos said, "I can't park here. I'll find a spot a bit further up the road."

Sammy and Mike took the parcel between them and began walking. They had ensured that the label faced forward. Janos put the car in first gear and pretended to look for an empty space. He saw his two mates reach the stairs and increased the speed. He rounded the corner and was out of sight.

Otto Meltzer smiled when he saw the van disappear. His stolen Ford was parked alongside the opposite pavement. He had unrestricted view of the black door eighty meters away.

Sammy and Mike walked with short steps as they carried Otto Meltzer's hitherto most sophisticated little device, neatly placed amidst a stack of engineering bricks. Meltzer's smile widened when he saw them put the parcel down and Sammy rang the doorbell.

Meltzer reached for his remote control. He waited till Sammy rang for the second time and they both took a step forward as if listening for a sign of life inside. The parcel stood one foot behind them.

Otto Meltzer pressed the button and hummed with satisfaction when his bomb behaved precisely as it was supposed to do. The door, the framework and some of the walls on each side blew in and not out, decorated with odds and ends of Sammy and Mike. The bang was not alarmingly loud, and the smoke was hardly noticeable.

Meltzer put the remote control in his inner pocket, reversed the car into a driveway and drove off. He kept well within the speed limit.

During the afternoon he watched the news on television and rewarded himself with a few extra schnapps when he learned about the attempted assassination of a high-ranking civil servant. BBC showed tact and consideration, but a commercial channel mentioned Pritchard-White by name. Meltzer nodded sagely when the IRA was being named as the most likely perpetrator. He shook his head when the reporter informed that the civil servant had been in his office miles away. Neither had his wife been at home. She did charities on Wednesdays. The four children had all been at school. A spokesman for Scotland Yard could reveal that they had indeed found some clues. He expected rapid development toward solving this abominable crime.

Later in the evening, Meltzer celebrated at Alberto's, drinking more than was his habit but not enough to become careless. He staggered only slightly when he walked to the taxi half past midnight, and he sang *Lili Marlene* in German all the way home. The cabbie was compensated with an extra tenner for having had to listen to the performance.

Otto Meltzer was found with a broken neck at the bottom of the stairs early in the morning. The police concluded that he must have lost his balance, being well over the limit, and tumbled all the way down.

A week later, an elderly and nosy neighbour of Janos Szecheny informed the police that the young man had not been seen for days. Nor had there been any annoying Gypsy music for the same length of time, and that was even more unusual.

The police broke down the door and found Janos laying face down on the floor. A syringe lay one foot away from his right hand. The officer in charge took one long look at the grey scar tissue on Jano's left arm and made his notes.

The police concluded that there were no suspicious circumstances. The coroner settled for death by overdose. He had no reason to believe otherwise; heroin was a killer, full stop.

Not many came to the funeral. A soon forgotten grave became the final home of Janos Szecheny, and there his body ravaged with heroin and with traces of potassium chloride slowly decomposed and his soul rested peacefully forever more.

Gregory Pritchard-White had no illusions about who had been behind the explosion that gave him a chance to redecorate his residence with taxpayers' money, but he kept his secret to himself. He analyzed the situation and resolved to bear in mind the difference between a threat and a statement. The image of himself permanently placed in a wheelchair was not an attractive one. He had a wife and four children to consider, as well.

A quick investigation showed that Vargas together with Jennifer Moran had enjoyed a lengthy breakfast at Claridge's before they attended an auction at Sotheby's where they successfully bid for a Frank O'Meara. Thereafter they went to The Ritz for afternoon tea before they travelled home by car.

Yasmin Ishihara had been looking after the children that day; she stayed at Vargas' property whilst her husband was abroad. Each time one or both women were on their own, some chaps of foreign-looking origin could be spotted in the vicinity.

Igor Parkhurst heard the tyres against the gravel and went outside.

"Hello, Angelo," he said. "What an unusual and pleasant surprise. Please come in."

"No, thank you," Vargas said. He left the car door open and walked up to Parkhurst. "The chapter is closed. Pritchard-White will never again bother you."

Parkhurst had seen the news on television. He began to feel unwell. "I—I do not understand," he said. The trees behind the garage swayed from side to side. He gripped the railing.

Vargas said, "You do understand, Igor." He moved closer. "You are free of your nightmare. It was never more than a grotesque joke, but you took it seriously and now it is gone."

Parkhurst stared, unable to speak. He saw a smile on his guest's face.

Vargas said, "I am not here. You and I never had this talk."

Parkhurst gulped. He wet his lips and said, "No."

"Good," Vargas said and went back to his car.

36

Ishihara came back from the United States on a Sunday. During the afternoon he telephoned Vargas.

Ishihara was not too happy about the prospects of spending the entire Monday in Vargas' barn, but he mellowed when he saw that the fireplace had been completed and that it worked to satisfaction. The beech wood burned with a quiet flame. The odd log from an old apple tree added to the scent. The fragrance reminded Ishihara of springtime in Japan and made him momentarily nostalgic.

I do miss the place from time to time, he thought; it's quite natural, I suppose, but what is there to go back to? He shook his head and sat down on the floor.

"An interesting trip," he said and sipped the tea that Vargas had prepared. "We are indeed facing a cagey customer. Our friend the General is unpredictable, to say the least."

Vargas waited.

Ishihara continued, "He isn't too popular with the White House staff. His reputation is one of being bullish, arrogant and extremely possessive of the President. Evil tongues have it that the mixed-blood chip on Forster's shoulder has grown considerably since he moved in; he seems to have a penchant for absorbing imaginary as well as real insults. He cannot stand being opposed. There has already been a noticeable turnover of personnel. He is obviously determined to keep an iron grip on everything that is going on. He demands respect bordering on servility, and he rules by terror. The overall perception of Caldwell is that of a weak and diffident man, a concept that is beginning to find response also on The Hill. Now—and this is interesting—both sides of The House have a high regard for Forster; practically every Democrat speaks well of him, and the Republicans are still prepared to give him the benefit of the doubt. He plays his cards well, no question about it."

Vargas stared into the flames.

Ishihara went on, "So does Caldwell. I do not believe that Forster suspects him of anything sinister. Forster does show Caldwell respect and courtesy when seen together, but little signs tell me that Forster deems Caldwell incapable of representing even a mild threat in any one direction. Caldwell's greatest asset is his wife. She is clearly an immensely shrewd woman. So far, she has stayed out of the limelight, most of the time. She is well liked. There is little doubt that she is the brain behind whatever move is necessary for their survival. Our petite Sheryl looks like a porcelain doll and behaves like one, so to speak. Washington has yet to discover what she is made of. She is at least as ruthless as her husband's omnipresent Chief of Staff."

"You do not believe he has seen through her?"

"No, I do not, and I have got two reasons: one is that she plays her part to absolute perfection—sweet, anonymous, pretty and vacuous—and, two, Forster is not very good at reading women. I would not say that he treats them with open contempt or sees them as only partly useful commodities that can be discarded at will, but his acumen in this respect is limited. His libido is not of old, either. He does not screw around the way he used to. He is actually down to one woman—broadly speaking, I should add—and she hasn't even moved in with him."

"If Forster has seen through Sheryl Caldwell, he has taken his precautions," Vargas said.

Ishihara was quiet for a moment. "Let us include that possibility," he said.

Vargas kept staring at the fireplace. "I do. You mentioned that Forster is unpredictable."

"Yes, he is. There is no fixed pattern to what he does. For instance, sometimes he drives himself and at other times he has got a driver who is also a trained bodyguard. Forster can leave the White House early, and he can stay there all night. One day he goes to a highly renowned restaurant, and the next time you can find him in some sleazy little ethnic outfit."

Ishihara pulled a map from his briefcase, unfolded it and pointed with his index finger. "His abode is here," he said. "It has got a very sophisticated alarm system, supplemented by two rottweilers."

He described the house in detail. Vargas listened with his eyes closed.

"Forster's girlfriend stays overnight four or five times a month, but most of the time he's got the place to himself," Ishihara said. "How conscientious he is with his alarm system I do not know. That's anybody's guess."

"How come?"

"Forster radiates confidence. He walks and talks and behaves like a man who has got nothing to fear, an attitude I find strange in view of his past."

"Add Washington's criminal record."

"Forster always drives to wherever he is going. If it is off the beaten track, the bodyguard is there."

"Forster is armed?"

".38 Smith & Wesson. We must assume he knows how to use it. Shoulder holster."

"The bodyguard?"

"A Colt .45. Shoulder holster. A stub-nosed Magnum strapped to his leg."

"Not fond of taking prisoners."

"His name is Dan Mandoki, and he is a nasty piece of work. Forster picked him from obscurity somewhere in Idaho. A search showed that Mr. Mandoki is a multiple killer who owes his life and his freedom to Forster—surprise, surprise."

"A bit careless of the General."

"It can look that way," Ishihara agreed, "but bear in mind that Washington isn't a haven for purists, saints and boy scouts. The prevailing selfishness and moral standards are such that the devil himself would not feel comfortable there."

"Does Forster ever go back to Kentucky?"

"Once a month, on average, and always on his own. No bodyguard and no girl friend. It is as if he seeks a fleeting moment of freedom. There is no doubt that Forster is a more relaxed man in Lexington than he is in Washington."

"Over-confidence is a dangerous enemy," Vargas said.

"It most certainly is, but look at what he's got away with, during the years. My impression is that his incredible success has dulled his senses, and, if so, he is not aware of it. If I am right, this can only be to our benefit."

Ishihara pulled out another map. "This is Lexington. Here is where Forster resides. As I said, Forster is a different person when on native soil; jovial, easygoing and seemingly without a worry in the world. There is a middle-aged couple living permanently in the house. The alarm is on when they are both out, which doesn't happen all too often. There are no dogs."

Ishihara took out a thick envelope and placed a series of photographs on the floor. "Forster's Washington residence," he said and began explaining.

Two hours later they had been through the pictures and the blueprints of both properties.

Vargas said, "Good job, Tadashi. I am beginning to get an idea."

For the next three hours they examined their master plan, followed by several contingency plans. Then they revised, changed and adapted before they started all over again.

It was a drill they had been through so many times before. They only stopped when they knew that saturation point had been reached and there was nothing more to add.

"I can't think of anything else," Ishihara said and handed Vargas the notes containing the detailed information about transport and accommodation. Vargas read each page carefully; airlines operating to and from the two cities, bus companies, arrival and departure times, car dealers, an assortment of hotels, restaurants frequented by Forster and their opening hours and facilities, regularity and patrol activities of the police and security firms, guard dogs in the vicinity of Forster's properties, and make and model of the alarm systems.

"The rest is up to improvisation, as usual," Vargas said. He placed the sheets on the floor. "There will be an unknown factor or two, here and there—little surprises which nobody can foresee. Makes it exciting."

"It's the last one, Angelo."

Vargas put his hands behind his back and stretched his torso. He did not answer.

Ishihara closed his briefcase and said, "When?"

"I don't know."

Ishihara stirred his tea. He took a sugar cube from the bowl and began to chew. The breeze cuddled the vines on the barn walls. He could hear the engine of a small aircraft. The iron claw clutching his chest tightened its grip. Vargas looked distant.

Ishihara said, "What do you mean?"

"Anu is not well."

The grip loosened. "What is wrong with her?"

"It could be an infection. It could also be asthma."

Ishihara put his spoon back on the saucer. "There are antibiotics for infections. Asthma she will grow out of."

"Not this week."

"I know, but—it's not all that unusual. All children have minor hiccups. I mean, only the other day Yasmin told me that Hiroshi…"

"I am not leaving until she is better," Vargas said.

Ishihara levelled his gaze and hoped that the wind coming through the doors had blown away the sigh that had forced its route past his throat. At least it wasn't a question of second thoughts. He said, "I understand."

"I want to know what it is," Vargas said. "Infection, asthma or whatever."

Ishihara could not see the fountain, but he listened to the soothing splashing of the water. He thought of the necessity of a third trip to the United States. Inevitable, apparently, but, after all, no more than an unwelcome nuisance, considering what was at stake.

"We probably talk about a few weeks, then," he said. "You let me know, and I'll go back for a final check."

"No need. As long as Forster keeps his two properties, the situation remains the same. That we can find out from here. I take it that Keizo Morita is still with the Washington embassy?"

"Yes, he is. That part of it is not a problem."

"What is?"

Ishihara felt as if his mind was swimming upstream. "I don't like it. We have always been up-to-date, down to the last minute, so to speak. A lot of things can happen between now and—and whenever you arrive."

"Things always happen. That is why we have contingency plans. That is why I have never been on an assignment where I did not have to improvise."

Ishihara thought for a while. Vargas was right; not much could change. Forster was a static target; it was either Washington, or Lexington. Any sudden or unexpected predicament had to be dealt with on the spot. As usual.

He got up and looked at his watch. "I'd better rush home," he said. "Give Jennifer and Anu a hug from me. Call me tomorrow, will you?"

He waved as he left.

Vargas sat there, for a while. His eyes were fixed on the fireplace and the flames dying out.

Two weeks later Anu was free of her infection. Vargas stayed put for another fortnight. Only when he was convinced that she was back to her bubbly self did he begin to make his preparations.

Kathleen and Conor had been staying for a few days. Conor was getting serious about his retirement. He had taken his first deliberate step—the acquisition of a brand new Land Rover that instantly became his pride and joy—*very countryish*, Kathleen had complimented. He was still in agony about closing down The Mission, but one night, after dinner, he admitted that his heart was no longer there. Both his mind and his body were telling him to call it a day. Kathleen and Jennifer tried to ease his worried soul by suggesting they should start to look for a property. Conor consented. He showed his determination by asking if Kathleen and he could stay for a few more days.

Accompanied by Jennifer and Anu and with a map of the county, they began their exploration. "*Not too close,*" Vargas had suggested to Jennifer. She agreed, but had added, "Not *too far away, either.*"

One grey and misty morning but with promise of sunshine they again waved farewell for the day.

Vargas went over to his cottage. He dialled the combination of his safe and took out a thick wad of dollars. He went through his collection of passports and driving licences. Each document looked reasonably seasoned, but had never been used. Each would be destroyed having served its purpose. Vargas made his choice, wrote down a few coded telephone numbers on a piece of paper and put everything in a medium-sized canvas bag. He took out a box made from semi-hard rubber. It contained what looked like an artist's tools; brushes, crayons, knives and pencils. He dismantled the brushes and checked the wires inside. An A-5 and an A-4 sketchpad completed the melange.

He walked back to the house and found a three-quarter long sports coat he'd had made. The coat was equipped with a dozen inner pockets, all with zippers. He distributed the contents of the bag into the pockets. The box and the pads he put at the bottom of his valise. It was small enough to be accepted on board as hand luggage. He chose a limited selection of clothes, zipped up the bag and hung it inside his wardrobe.

Late afternoon he heard Conor's car. He met them outside. He lifted up Anu and kissed her on both cheeks. He exchanged a few words with Kathleen and Conor before they went over to the guest cottage.

Jennifer put her carrier bags on the table and said, "When, Angelo?"

"Tomorrow morning."

She came across. She put her arms around his neck.

He held her. "Nothing will stop me coming back to you and Anu."

Jennifer did not have a restful night.

The worst of the traffic was over when they came into Cromwell Road. It was a dull morning, mild with no wind and a few spots of rain in the air.

Vargas said, "Stop outside the Hyde Park Hotel."

The Bentley came to a halt. Vargas got out. He took his valise from the back seat and nodded. "See you."

Ishihara' hands rested on the steering wheel. He looked to his left. "See you," he said.

He watched in the mirror as Vargas hailed a taxi and disappeared. A doorman approached the Bentley. Ishihara waved him off. It's funny, he thought; all these years, and not once has Angelo asked me how I manage to accumulate such a mountain of intelligence. Neither, for that matter, have I asked him where, when and how. What we share is only the simple little *why*. We do indeed have a perfect partnership. I regret having to see our successful operation being dissolved, but such is life. What lasts forever?

Ishihara re-joined the traffic.

37

Vargas took the train to Liverpool and the ferry over to Ireland. He paid cash on both occasions. He spent two nights in Dublin, each night in different hotels, before he flew to Paris, using a German passport. Two days later he flew to Frankfurt on a Dutch passport. He waited for twenty-four hours before he purchased a tourist class ticket with Lufthansa to New York. He used a British passport.

He booked in for one night at a small hotel on the edge of Bryant Park at West 40th Street and Sixth Avenue.

The next morning he checked out from the hotel. He went to New Jersey and bought a one-year old Buick.

He stayed one night in Atlantic City and drove from there to Philadelphia where he found a large multi-store car park in one of the rougher outskirts of the city. He left the keys on the roof of the car and walked out.

He stayed one night in Philadelphia. He bought a two year old Chrysler and drove to Baltimore. He followed the same procedure as in Philadelphia, except that this time he left the keys in the ignition.

He arrived in Washington by bus, chose one of Ishihara's recommended hotels near Union Station and booked in for one night. He spent the evening going over in his mind the layout of Forster's house, the garden, the neighbourhood and the streets. Late evening he found a restaurant half a mile from the hotel. He had a quick meal and walked back to his room.

He checked out the next morning, settled his bill in cash, and began walking towards Pennsylvania Avenue. At some point he caught a Metro bus which took him to the Saint Matthew's Cathedral. He found the hotel he was looking for and booked a room for one night. The place was more up-market than the previous hotel; it had a safe placed on the floor in the cupboard.

Vargas did not bother with the safe. He distributed his driving licences, passports and money evenly in the inside pockets of his jacket. He left the hotel and began his exploration.

On the eleventh day he went to the Arlington National Cemetery, across the Potomac River. He thought of those who had given their lives for freedom, democracy and presidents. He wondered how many of the young dead ones had carried back their contribution to Abraham Forster' fortune. He saw the tears on the faces of those around him and mused silently if the United States would ever build a memorial for the families of those who had survived but whose lives had been ruined. He did not think that America would find such an idea tasteful. More probable, in this city of pride and memorials, would be an Americanized Arc de Triomph praising the investment that Korea had been, allowing a great nation to develop more advanced technology of destruction to be employed should freedom, democracy and access to resources come under threat sometime in the future, somewhere.

Vargas looked towards the grey and heavy skies and adjusted his cap. A penetrating wind came across from the Potomac River. There were flurries of snow in the air.

He went back and walked the Constitution Avenue for a while, towards the Ellipse. He found a place that looked reasonably empty. He chose a table in the corner furthest from the door. He took off his cap and asked for a cup of coffee.

During his days in Washington he had not joined the congregation of admirers outside the White House. He had shunned the FBI Building and avoided Capitol Hill. He had spent only one night in any one hotel, each time under a different name. He had worn different disguises, nothing outré, just sufficient not to be instantly associated with the person from the day before.

He had bought a reversible coat large enough to wear over his jacket. He had an assortment of caps, different in shapes and colours.

He knew that it was not impossible to follow his trail, but it would take a highly skilled and experienced professional to do so.

Tony Bianconi had said it would be illogical to interfere; Caldwell would not be that mindless. Vargas smiled. Logic wasn't one of man's most prominent characteristics. Fear and irrationality were.

Vargas drank his coffee and asked for another. He skipped *please* and other civilities not favoured by Americans. So far, he had avoided anything resembling a dialogue. He was good at accents, but he had no wish to get involved in the natives' passion for exchanging personal information. His attitude was that of a grumpy visitor from out of state. He took care to come across as absentminded. He always carried a book to hide behind when he sensed the presence of a chatterbox.

He tried not to think of Jennifer and Anu. He had been away for close to three weeks, but contacting Jennifer was out of question.

Again, Angelo Vargas smiled. Always, in the past, he'd had nobody to think about and nobody to come back to. How much longer? A week, perhaps, maybe two. He could not tell.

He blew away the steam from his coffee. Something did not hang together. Abraham Forster did not drive himself. There was always a limousine available for him. The driver was his bodyguard Mandoki.

A couple of times Forster had invited guests to his house. So far, he had not frequented any restaurant—not once in six days.

Forster's alarm system was advanced, but, like any technicality, it was not insuperable. The two rottweilers were a time-consuming nuisance, but no more. A small treat each and they would nod off for an hour and nobody would be any wiser.

The problem was the woman whose permanent presence he had not known about. Ishihara had said that Forster's girlfriend stayed overnight four or five times a month. That was no longer so; at one point, since Ishihara's departure, she had moved in. One night, at a Japanese restaurant, Vargas had exchanged a few words with Keizo Morita from the embassy. Morita had said the rumour in town was that Forster had secretly married the woman.

There was no pattern to her behaviour. When she went out, Mandoki came with the limousine. She was fond of big fur hats, scarves, tinted glasses and knee-high boots.

Not many would believe that Forster and his girlfriend both had died from a heart attack within five minutes of each other. That was an open invitation to a murder hunt. Nor was she part of the deal. Vargas knew that he could not kill her just because she represented an obstacle. He was a contract killer, not a murderer. He had made this condition clear to Ishihara from the very beginning, and Ishihara had said that he understood.

Vargas did not think so. Ishihara was not the one who had to live with the direct impacts of their deeds. That made the difference between *professing* to know and *knowing*, between *observing* and *experiencing*.

Ishihara was a good ally and as trustworthy as could be expected, but Vargas had known for a long time that in the final analysis he was on his own. Nothing could ever change that.

Some of his colleagues called it *pride* and others called it *principles*, refusing to kill innocent bystanders. Vargas called it common sense. They all operated in the same sty; the survivors were those who managed to keep their heads above the surface.

Vargas placed a cube of sugar on his teaspoon. He dipped the spoon in his coffee and thought about his options. Forster liked restaurants, but he had not been to one for a week. The natural conclusion was that his girlfriend did not share this passion, and Forster had not pushed it. For how long he would play the part of the devoted companion was anybody's guess.

Forster's Washington home was out. The choice was between a restaurant and his place in Kentucky, but he had yet to move in either direction. A restaurant would have been ideal; Forster had prostate problems and went for a leak several times during an evening. It could all be over within a couple of minutes. From there, Vargas would seek the nearest crowded bar, de-camouflage, make a brief telephone call to Tony Bianconi and go for a stroll.

Vargas drew invisible figures on the table with his teaspoon. He pretended to read a few pages of his book. He thought about the game that required so much persistence, restraint and patience. How many more days before Forster dropped his pretence and went to a restaurant? How many more days before he went back to his Kentucky hideaway?

On the Thursday he bought a second-hand Pontiac and said he would pick up the car the next day.

Friday morning he checked out from his hotel. He took a bus to the airport. The department hall was teeming. He sat for an hour here and an hour there, pretending to read newspapers. From time to time he drifted around for a while. In between, he had a cup of coffee. He kept an eye on the entrance doors and the desks for flights to Lexington. The late flight was direct, and the most likely choice.

Forster appeared at three o'clock in the afternoon. He was on his own. Vargas picked up his valise. He passed close enough to hear fragments of the conversation between Forster and the airline attendant.

He left the building and took a bus that stopped close to the car dealer. An hour later he was on his way to Pittsburgh. He never exceeded the speed limits. In Penn Hills he left the car with the key in the ignition. He flew to Cincinnati where he purchased an almost new Oldsmobile. Near Newport he booked in at a motel where he slept for six hours.

He timed the distance and left Newport so that he would arrive in Lexington mid-afternoon.

He found a vast parking area adjacent to a busy shopping mall, made a note of where he had left the car and took a bus to the city centre. He had a light meal and sauntered around window-shopping for a while. At quarter to four in the afternoon he saw Forster leave his favourite restaurant, followed by five male companions.

Forster's weekends in Lexington were perfectly regimented, according to Ishihara. So far, he'd got it right. Come evening, Forster would either entertain at home or be the guest of one of the local bigshots. He would round off the day with a nightcap on his own in his library. Sunday morning he went to church. In the afternoon he could be found either on his preferred golf course or in a private club with his admirers. His womanizing days seemed to be over. Vargas wondered if the woman in Washington knew something that made Forster follow the narrow path.

The day was mild with a hazy sunshine. There was no wind. Vargas wandered about, had a few breaks and waited for darkness to come.

Shortly before dusk he returned to the shopping mall. He bought a pint of milk and some fruit. He took half a dozen extra paper bags. From a hardware shop he purchased a pair of scissors and twenty meters of half-inch thick rope. He found his car and moved it to a deserted area. He changed into a black tracksuit and a pair of black rubber-soled lightweight shoes he'd bought in Washington. He took out his enlarged money belt from his valise and transferred from the pockets of his jacket all documents and his tools into the belt before he put it around his waist under the jacket of the tracksuit. He tied the rope above the belt and hid the pair of scissors under the driver's seat.

Vargas fed on grapes and apples whilst going over in his mind the details of Forster's house and its vicinity. The time was eight o'clock. The night was dark and cloudy. The weather forecast had predicted no rain.

Forster' place was twenty minutes away, careful driving. Vargas started the engine. He found the address he was looking for, a quiet side road one mile from Forster's property. He parked the car between two streetlights. He heard distant music. There was no sign of life on the road.

Vargas darkened the skin under his eyes, put on a small dark beard, a moustache, a pair of glasses and a knitted black cap before he locked the car and jumped the fence of the nearest property.

He did not hurry. He used hedges, trees and bushes as he moved from one property into the next, avoiding those where he knew there were dogs. It took him an hour and fifteen minutes to reach the perimeter of Forster' ten acre estate.

He could see the house from where he stood. It was quiet. Lights came only from the windows facing north. The quarter of a mile driveway stretching towards the opposite side of the building was well lit, but the miniature garden lamps scattered around were too far apart to represent any hazard.

Ishihara had warned about the generous number of spotlights that switched on the instant anything moved within reach of the sensitivity cells. Vargas did not underestimate the obstacle, but he knew that in most people's experience the culprit was an animal. The majority of those installing such devices usually became complacent and seldom bothered to instigate a thorough search unless they heard noises they could not identify.

He kept his distance from the house until he could see the garage complex. Both the double doors were up. He saw a large four-wheel drive and a small saloon car. Forster's Cadillac was missing.

Vargas went back to the spot where he had entered the property. Shielded by cedar trees, he moved closer. He stopped when he reached a gazebo sited at the edge of the largest of the lawns. The night was darker than he'd wished, but from the map in his head he knew the layout from where he was and the distance to the dogwood shrubs under the balcony fronting Forster's library.

He used a hedge as his cover and inched forward. He stopped when he knew he was within ten yards of activating the spotlights mounted on the north-west gables of the building. Between himself and the bush under the balcony was a small lawn, a flowerbed with a path of solid slabs, and the patio.

Vargas checked his shoe laces and did a set of ten breathing exercises before he sprinted across the lawn. From behind the dogwood bush he eyed a good acre of the property lit up by the spotlights. He heard a door he could not see being opened. A male voice expressed annoyance. Then the lights went out, and the door slammed shut.

The patio was not entirely in the dark; the lampposts in the driveway reflected their yellow light onto the windows on the ground floor sufficiently for Vargas to see. He sat still for several minutes before he took off his shoes and pulled a small brush from his pocket. He removed all traces of soil and grass from the footwear.

He pressed his back against the wall and undid the rope around his waist. He threw the rope over the rail of the balcony and hoisted himself up. He got a good grip on the metal bars and swung over. He took out his tools and began working on the locks. Within a minute he was inside. He locked the doors and checked the lined, heavy curtains reaching the floor before he looked around.

Only one lamp was burning, a Chinese vase with a dark shade standing on a small hand-carved table inside the door leading to the hallway. Vargas reckoned there had to be six to eight hundred books on the shelves. He wondered if Forster had read them all. The air was stale from leather and polish and cigars. Vargas moved around on the thick maroon carpet. He admired Forster's taste in antiques and Indian art. An ornate clock on the mantelpiece chimed ten times.

Vargas prepared himself for a two to three hours wait in tranquil solitude. The room was not cold, but he wished someone would come and attend to the fireplace; the glow from the embers would not last through the night and he would have to keep still until it suited Forster to show up.

Vargas sat down in one of the massive leather chairs closest to the balcony. The chair was in darkness, facing the hallway. He would be behind the curtains before anybody could enter the room and switch on more lights.

Music came from the kitchen area. He did not think that he would be disturbed. If the butler or his wife had been instructed to keep an eye on the fireplace, they would have done so by now. Nevertheless, there were no guarantees. He made himself comfortable and discarded from his mind any desire for a cigarette.

Two hours and forty-five minutes later he heard a car arrive.

Forster locked himself in. He followed his traditional pattern and good-humouredly chided the butler and his wife for waiting up. The ritual lasted for a few minutes before he bade them goodnight and walked upstairs for a cigar, a nightcap and some pleasing thoughts about his future.

After the fateful night when he had told his ill-starred wife more than she'd ought to hear, Forster had never again allowed himself to get inebriated; he drank to feel comfortably relaxed but no more, and only when in Lexington. Here, Washington was a universe away; he felt at ease from the moment he arrived and he returned to the rat race feeling recharged, rejuvenated and ready for another Machiavellian intermezzo. Another ten months, Forster figured, and Dean Goodman would begin to wish he'd never entered politics. More dead wood would follow in the wake, replaced by Forster's Kentuckian inner circle; four of whom he had dined with that very evening and whose loyalty, devotion and indebtedness could not be questioned. A few years from now and that spineless jerk Caldwell would be one of history's minor footnotes, replaced by a man whose destiny it was to reign. Men like Alexander the Great, Caesar and Napoleon had all failed, ultimately, because they had lacked the ability to take into account the probable future consequences of their actions. They had been like farmers who could sow but not harvest; they did not properly foresee what even tomorrow would bring, they did not understand the implications and the value of contingencies and precautions, and they had relied on the wisdom and support of gods that did not exist.

Forster went to his bedroom and changed into a pair of white cotton pyjamas, a dark blue silk gown and a pair of monogrammed slippers before he strolled leisurely down the hall to his cherished library. He switched on the concealed lights over the bookshelves and walked across to the cabinet where his exclusive selection of bottles stood like soldiers on parade. He chose a Monte Christo from his humidor and cut and lit it whilst he briefly pondered if Caldwell could be idiotic enough to suggest making Castro a permanent enemy.

Forster reached for his favourite green label Jack Daniels. A superb Cuban, two fingers of the most superlative nostrum ever invented, half an hour or so in his thinking chair, and he would sleep like an angel for seven peaceful hours.

He held his cigar in his left hand. He put the bottle back, raised his glass and said, "To Abraham Forster."

The forearm pressing against his larynx and the hand firmly placed on the left hand side of the back of his head belonged to someone who knew what he was doing. Forster did not move. He tried to control his breathing. His knowledge of unarmed combat told him that he was a split second away from a broken neck. His only option was not to resist. He knew that the feeling of surprise and alarm could at any moment give way to shock, but he also expected the perpetrator to talk.

It did not happen.

Seconds ticked by. Forster fought hard not to swallow. "Fine," he at last whispered hoarsely, "you've got me, whoever you are. What do you want? Name it. I can get you anything."

The pressure from the hand against the back of his head eased. Forster closed his eyes. Money, he thought and wanted to smile. *Money*—the essence of man's universe and the key to survival if not salvation.

The forearm crushing against his larynx remained in place, but the hand slid down under his left arm. Forster felt the palm of the hand resting against his rib cage. "A million?" he whispered. "No questions asked. I can arrange..."

Forster had never before experienced the pain that shot through his abdomen and across his chest. A red fog blurred his sight. He gasped when the scream from deep inside could not reach his lips. He fell to the floor. His hands tried to rip away the agony.

Vargas turned the broken cigar in Forster's hand, preventing the glow from touching the carpet. He left the glass where it had landed and sat down in Forster's favourite chair. He waited till no more smoke came from the cigar before he took off one of his gloves and placed a finger behind Forster's ear. He cast a final glance on Forster' lifeless body. He put the glove back on and left the house through the main entrance door.

The butler's self-contained apartment was in darkness and the curtains drawn. Vargas walked across the green paving towards the garages. He continued till he was out of reach of the spotlights before he turned north and left the property from where he had come in.

He got to his car fifty minutes later, changed quickly and drove twenty miles to a public telephone box outside a 7-Eleven. He dialled Tony

Bianconi's number and heard him answer in a tired and guttural voice, "Yes?"

"Icarus," Vargas said and hung up.

The rest was up to Tony and his son. The news would be that Abraham Forster had died from a heart attack. There would be a moving speech by President Caldwell, the statutory glowing obituary and an impressive military funeral. End of dream for the General. End of career for the hitman. Those who lived by the sword—Vargas smiled wryly and steered his car towards Interstate 64. Death was indiscriminate and paid no due to time, place, cause or method.

Vargas thought about his own last day on earth. He saw himself as an old man sitting under a regal oak tree. That would be perfect; difficult to plan, though, but one could always hope.

In New Albany he had breakfast in a small café before he found a motel. He emptied the car and took everything into his room. He cut up the gloves, the tracksuit, the shoes, the caps, the beard, the moustache, the glasses and the rope. He put the pieces in the six bags. He cleaned the pair of scissors, broke it in two and put the two halves in separate bags. He tied a knot on each bag.

He badly needed some sleep but he stuck to his plan and went out and bought a jacket in one shop and a pair of trousers in another. On both occasions he obtained a large, non-transparent carrier bag. He put three of the paper bags in each carrier, placed them under his king-size bed and lay down. He slept for two hours.

He spent the afternoon walking about. He had an early dinner and slept for five hours during the night.

He checked out at half past eight the next morning and drove around for some hours, getting rid of the bags and the carriers at eight different refuse sites and skips reasonably far apart. He disposed of the car in his usual manner, leaving no fingerprints. He took a bus to Louisville Airport where he sat in the same spot for two hours with his back to the wall of a cafeteria. During his entire stay he had not detected any signs of being followed. Nobody showed up at the airport.

Vargas arrived at Idlewild Airport with sufficient time in hand to shop around. Air France to Paris was full and Lufthansa had a technical problem, but there were tourist seats available on SAS to Copenhagen. He bought a return ticket, used an American passport and walked to

791

the gate. In Copenhagen he modified his appearance to fit a British passport.

Only when he walked the corridors of the Heathrow terminal did Angelo Vargas think of Jennifer and Anu.

He glanced at his watch when he left the building. In two hours' time he would be home.

38

When William Westcott left the port of Dover he did not look forward to the long journey ahead of him. Once, driving had been fun. Those days were long gone. He had been a truck driver for over twenty years and the loneliness of each new trip filled him with dread and a hint of despair.

Westcott put his vehicle into third gear and adjusted his position. He was a big man, six-foot-one and over fifteen stones, but what had once been a strong and muscular body was now an aching reminder of nature's cruel game with age and decay.

He opened the window and let fresh air circulate. He liked the smell of the countryside. Another ten miles and he would be home.

He glanced at the fuel gauge out of habit and remembered that he had filled up twenty minutes ago. He stretched his left leg and cursed his aching body and fumbled in his pocket for another handful of painkillers. Again, his tired eyes routinely swept the instrument panel.

Westcott frowned, angry with himself for doing sixty miles per hour when he should have stayed at forty, or less. *What the hell are you doing*, he growled and dropped his bottle. *Concentrate, for God's sake!* He grabbed his gear stick. His feet moved. The S-bend came towards him at what seemed like uncontrollable speed. He tried to manoeuvre closer to the edge of the narrow road but suddenly he was only yards from the bend and his thirty-eight tonner would not stop.

William Westcott felt the impact tear through his body. He heard the screeching of metal being ripped and he screamed in horror when the green sports car disappeared under his massive engine.

☞

Igor Parkhurst had discreetly suggested that they should all come to his place after the funeral. Kathleen and Conor had accepted.

The local church had been packed. Almost everybody from the village had attended. There were also thirty or forty men that Parkhurst did not recognize. Half of them were Orientals; all sombre men in dark suits who did not introduce themselves. They quietly offered their condolences to Kathleen and Conor and left immediately after the service.

Conor had called Ireland and expressed his wish that nobody came over. The only ones present were Igor Parkhurst and his friend Valerie Hopkins, and Yasmin and Tadashi Ishihara. Parkhurst and Valerie had arranged food, coffee and wine. Parkhurst put cognac and Irish whisky on the table, leaving each to their choice.

Parkhurst struggled to keep his emotions under control. He tried to keep the conversation flowing and wished that Conor would opt for a whisky. It did not happen. Valerie was calm and serene. She looked at her friend and quietly handed him a cognac. "Here," she said. "Maybe you should sit down, Igor."

Parkhurst clung to his glass with both hands.

"Would anyone mind if I opened a window?" Valerie asked.

Nobody answered, but Conor shook his head. The light breeze came with a scent of spring. Ishihara moved closer to the window and stared towards the forest across the fields. It had not been easy to convince Kathleen and Conor Moran that he did not know Vargas' whereabouts and therefore could not get hold of him. It had been even harder to admit that no date could be given for Vargas' return.

Ishihara inhaled and moistened his lips. Igor Parkhurst had believed him; he had said to Kathleen and Conor that there was no way Ishihara would tell anything but the truth. Thereafter Conor had telephoned and apologized and said that the funeral would take place without delay. Ishihara had said that he understood and pledged that he would be there for Vargas when he came home. Conor again apologized before he asked if Yasmin and Tadashi would be kind enough to come after the service.

Ishihara lowered his head. For once in his life he truly despaired. He knew that the blow would be devastating, but he did not know how his friend would react.

Ishihara felt a hand on his shoulder. He turned his head and put his arm around Yasmin.

794

She whispered, "I know what you are going through, Tadashi."

He nodded. The ache in his stomach would not go away. He saw that Kathleen had sat down. She was looking at him. The old fire had gone from her eyes. Her hair had lost its shine. The expression on her face was one of resignation and hopelessness.

Conor stood behind her. His hands clutched the back of the chair. His posture was hunched and his face an ashen mask of sorrow and bewilderment.

Parkhurst had emptied his glass. He had managed to keep the conversation going; kind of, he thought. He signalled with his eyes to Valerie who poured him some more before she smiled softly at Conor and gave him a glass of Irish whisky.

Ishihara rested his eyes at the grey-blue smoke from a distant bonfire spiralling towards oblivion and wondered when he could leave without appearing ill-mannered. Yasmin nudged him gently and he followed her and they sat down on the sofa, close together.

Parkhurst began talking about his latest conversation with a local farmer. Kathleen interrupted and said, "You will be there, Tadashi?"

Ishihara folded his hands and looked back. He had lost count of how many times he had heard the question. "I will be there," he said benignly. "Please do not worry."

She bowed her head. "I feel so sorry for him."

Truly a remarkable woman, Ishihara thought. He did not know what to say.

Yasmin said, "We shall be there for him. We will do all we can."

"He will walk into an empty house," Conor said. He frowned and put his glass on the table.

Ishihara said, "No, Conor. I have arranged for some friends to keep watch. They will contact me the instant they see Angelo coming. I will be there."

Kathleen and Conor had followed Parkhurst's advice to stay overnight. "Maybe tomorrow," Kathleen said.

Not likely, Ishihara thought, not even next week. "Whenever," he said softly.

He reached for Yasmin's elbow when he got up. Silently, he extended his hand to Kathleen and then to Conor. When Yasmin embraced them he looked away.

They drove home. Yasmin rested her head on Ishihara's shoulder.

39

The night had surrendered to a morning heavy with rain when Ishihara received the call. Graphite grey clouds moved like worn-out phantoms. The smell of ozone ripped his nostrils. Lazy patches of fog left water dripping from the trees.

Yasmin saw the look in his eyes and took his hands in hers. She wanted to say something but they both knew the futility of advice.

Tadashi Ishihara did not know how to break the news; all he could do, he thought, was to show up and hope that he would find the words at the least awkward moment.

Yasmin followed him to the car. She was red-eyed and her body trembled as from sudden exposure to freezing cold. Her voice was thin and unrecognizable when she said, "Bring him back with you, Tadashi."

"If I possibly can."

When he reached the gate he looked in the mirror and saw that she was standing in the same spot with her arms across her chest.

One mile down the lane he ended up behind a tractor large enough to fill the space between the hedges. Ishihara knew that there was no place to pass for another mile. The farmer was not in a hurry.

Ishihara cursed. He had given himself an extra ten minutes for possible delays. At this sped, Vargas would be the first to arrive. His taxi had been spotted when it passed a petrol station seven miles away.

Ishihara was tempted to honk his horn but decided against. He knew from experience that any sign of aggravation would only upset the farmer and he would slow down to near standstill just for the fun of it. Ishihara looked at the clock on the dashboard. He wiped his forehead with a cloth he kept for dusting and cleaning.

Then, all of a sudden, the farmer spotted the entrance to a cottage on the right-hand side. He got his colossal machine partly out of the way and waved cheerfully. Ishihara shot by, only vaguely aware of the hard twigs of the hedge scratching the paintwork of his car.

With half a mile to go he saw the taxi drive away, increasing the speed as the lane widened. Soon the car was out of sight.

The main entrance door of the house was open when he arrived. He sat motionless for a few minutes.

He got out and slammed the door behind him.

Vargas came out. He was still wearing his jacket.

Ishihara took a few steps closer. "They are not here, Angelo."

"So I discovered," Vargas said. His voice was strained.

He has read me, Ishihara thought. He knows. Now what? He wanted to avert his eyes but moved forward till there were only a few yards between them. He kept his stare and said, "They are no longer here."

He heard his own words as if coming from somebody else. "There was an accident, a car crash. They did not survive." He looked down, unable to watch. When he raised his head, Vargas was gone.

Ishihara pressed the back of his hands against his eyes and followed. He found Vargas in the drawing room. He was still wearing his jacket. He sat in his chair and his forearms rested on the sides. He stared ahead towards the far-away hills.

Ishihara sat down on a high-chair. There was a coffee table between them. He watched Vargas' profile.

"I am so sorry, Angelo."

There was no reaction. Ishihara waited for a while. He listened to the silence. Then he said, "It happened on the day you left." Again he held back, hoping for a response.

Vargas did not move. Ishihara said, "The funeral took place on the following Friday. We—we didn't know when you would be back and—" no, he thought, do not say that Kathleen and Conor would not wait, *could* not wait. Say nothing more, except—he went over to the French doors and watched a flock of jackdaws battling against the wind coming from the forest. He did not turn around when he said, "Let us go back to my place. Stay with us for a few days." He moved his head, enough to see Vargas frozen in the same position.

No, Ishihara thought, I knew. Not yet. He said, "I'll be back later."

He closed the entrance door but he did not lock it.

Half an hour later he related to Yasmin each and every word he had said and Vargas' lack of reaction. Her hands shook when she lifted the teapot and filled their cups.

"I could do with something stronger," Ishihara said. He saw the expression in her eyes and added, "Later."

She said, "What do we do?"

"I don't know." He pressed his thumbs against his temples and closed his eyes. "I cannot recall the last time I felt so utterly helpless."

Her frown did not go away. She kept clasping her hands. "What do we do, Tadashi? What is Angelo going to do?"

Ishihara stirred his tea. He watched the dance of the leaves. "I wish I knew." He looked at her. "You know, on the way back home it struck me that—that even after all this time I do not really know Angelo. I do not understand him. I never have. During all these years we were closer than most in so many ways, and yet there was this distance between us. He never opened up. He only allowed me to see what he wanted me to see." Ishihara felt the muscles in his back becoming rigid. He tried to smile. "That wasn't much, really. The only one allowed access to his world was Jennifer."

They heard noises from the playroom. Yasmin got up. She said, "We both go over in the afternoon."

"He may listen to you," Ishihara said. He wished that he had sounded more convincing.

They went over four hours later. Hiroshi was belted up in his baby chair strapped to the back seat. They left him in the car. Ishihara was two steps ahead of Yasmin. She looked as if she had not slept for a while. Twice she stopped and made little noises.

Ishihara said, "Locked. He has locked the door."

They stared at each other. It was still daylight, but the clouds were dark and low.

"I can check the garage," he said.

She shook her head. "Wait here," she said and went around the corner.

She saw Vargas sitting in his chair. He had his jacket on. His forearms rested on the sides of the chair.

There is only one reason why he has locked the door, she thought and continued towards the far end of the building. She stopped in front of the window facing Vargas and pressed her nose against the glass. He could not avoid seeing her, but still she made a small circular movement with her hands. She could not see his eyes. He must be aware of my presence, she thought, yet there is not a flicker of reaction. She stood with her face against the glass for several minutes. Then she walked back to the car.

"He is just sitting there," she said and hid her face in her hands. "He does not want to know."

He put his arms around her. "Maybe tomorrow," he said. "We will come back tomorrow. Let us give him twenty-four hours to himself. That is what he wants, I think."

They returned late afternoon the following day and noticed that at some time Vargas had used his car; it was parked outside. The garage door was closed.

"Good sign," Ishihara nodded. His hand moved towards the bell.

Yasmin said, "No, not the bell. Open the door and knock a few times. He will hear us if he wants to."

And the door is locked if he wants to be on his own, Ishihara thought and pushed down the heavy brass handle. "Locked," he said.

"We have got a key," Yasmin said. "Give me the key."

"That is not a good idea. The door would not have been locked if he wanted to see either or both of us."

"But—"

"Please believe me. We do *not* use the key."

Her eyes searched his face. "What do we do?"

"We go home and try again tomorrow."

"What if Angelo still has not unlocked the door?"

Ishihara put his hands in his pockets. He felt the cold metal of the keys. The clouds split and the rays from the sun swept across the yard. "I will think of something," he said. He took her hand.

Ishihara could not sleep. He sat up most of the night. By daybreak he was no nearer knowing what to do. When Yasmin came down, he looked weary and dejected. He sat at the kitchen table with his hands cupped around his coffee long gone cold.

Yasmin made him a fresh cup. She lit one of his small cigars and gave it to him. He looked into her eyes and said, "No answer."

She ran her fingers through her hair and sat down. She said, "He is bound to move, sooner or later." She tried to inject some cheerful pragmatism into her voice. "Don't you think?"

"He has already."

"But not to see us. Do you think he went over to Igor's?"

"No. He would have come here had he wanted to see anybody." He placed his palms on the tabletop and pushed. "I am beginning to move in circles," he said and got up. "I shall try to get some sleep."

He came down four hours later. He was dressed in jeans and a thick sweater. The look of fatigue was still there. Yasmin had been out for a walk with Hiroshi. The fresh air had done her good.

"You look better," he said.

"You don't. Not much of a rest, I gather."

Ishihara lifted up his son and kissed him on the forehead. "Let us do something—go shopping, have lunch somewhere, whatever."

"No conclusion, Tadashi?"

He said, "Perhaps. I am going to give Angelo three days. If he still does not open the door, I am going to use the key."

"I'll come with you."

Hiroshi giggled. Ishihara rubbed noses. "I don't think so," he said in a flat voice. "Angelo is unpredictable. He may no longer control his own mind. I am not saying that something is going to happen, but if it does, I do not want you to watch. That is not the way you are going to remember him."

Yasmin's eyes turned black. "*Remember*—?"

Ishihara stroked Hiroshi's head and gently tugged his earlobe. "Angelo is not going to stay around for much longer. Come. Let us go shopping."

Yasmin did not move. "Before we go, Tadashi—the money must have crossed your mind."

He stopped in his track. "It has. That is the second reason why I want to see him." He shrugged. "Or the first—pick your choice."

Yasmin pulled at the collar of her blouse.

Ishihara took out his notebook and compared his sketch with the position of the wheels on Vargas' car. It had not been used. An eerie stillness hung over the house; it was as if life had been banned and all creatures sensed a doom they did not wish to challenge.

Ishihara walked across the yard. He passed the kitchen and stopped when he came onto the patio facing south. He shielded his eyes with both hands, leaned closer and looked in.

Vargas had taken off his jacket. He sat in the same chair. His position was unchanged. On the floor to his left was a crate. On the side table to his right were a glass and a bottle of whisky.

Ishihara counted six empty bottles under the table.

Vargas' face was vandalized by grief and alcohol. The smoothness of his skin was gone. Deep lines were etched on his forehead. There were dark and heavy bags under the hollow stare of his eyes. His mouth was open. His hands gripped the sides of the chair like the rigid clutching of a dead man.

Ishihara blinked and wiped his cheeks. *No*, he thought, *this is not the way to go, Angelo.*

He went back to the main entrance door and put his key in the Yale lock. The key turned, and turned again. He has blocked it, he thought. I can't get in. What I need now is an axe and a jemmy. He sensed a rising fury. One way or another I am going to get you out, he thought. I'll be back, Angelo.

"No," Yasmin said when he told her. She touched his arm with her fingers. "That is not the way to do it."

"There is no other way."

She increased her pressure and said, "Yes, there is. In two days' time he has run out of whisky."

"Then what?"

"Remove the battery from the car. Show him a couple of bottles through the window and see what happens. He'll come out."

Ishihara smiled wearily. "Not bad. It could work." He paused. "What if it doesn't?"

"I—" her voice trailed off. She looked past him.

"You do not want me to go in, do you?"

She did not answer.

He rolled his head till he heard the cracks from his neck. "I can always get out faster than I got in," he said with a smile that was meant to be reassuring. "I'll do the car tomorrow."

She said, "You look drained. I'll go over to Igor and borrow some sleeping pills."

"Don't bother," he said. He stretched and got up. "I will be all right. Tomorrow is not far away."

☞

Ishihara looked through the darkness at the green hands of the alarm clock. He quietly slid out of his bed. He listened for a moment to Yasmin's breathing before he closed the door. He took a gown from the bathroom and went downstairs.

Only the outside lights were on. He left it that way. He went into the study and pulled the curtains from the windows. He stood motionless for a long time. He stared towards Vargas' haven.

Ishihara lit a candle. He found a bottle of cognac and filled his glass before he sat down.

He drank and watched the spectacular brightness over the horizon where a scarlet veil spread across a velvet sky.

Later in the day, Ishihara received a message from London. Vargas' car had been found in a long-term car park at Heathrow Airport.

Ishihara made a call to the chief of the local fire brigade.

Two days later Ishihara put on his overall and heavy boots. Yasmin said she wanted to come. Ishihara objected and went on his own.

There was nothing left of the house. The ruins were smouldering in places.

Ishihara covered his hands with a pair of thick gloves and began his search. Four hours later he straightened his back and went to his car.

The stone was nowhere to be found.

40

After three hours of walking up the mountainside they came to a plateau and the Ninja stopped. They let go of the ropes around the large canvas-wrapped parcels they carried in each hand, took off their backpacks and sat down.

The early morning sun painted the valleys violet and the pine forests turned dark green when the first long shadows cast their spell on the ravine below.

Yoshiri Sakaigawa enjoyed his regular excursion to Shirakawa-go, more so now than in his younger days. Once, he used to live there. Little had changed; a couple of hundred Gassho-zukuri farm houses, a few Minshuku inns, the small rice paddies surrounded by flower beds, the beauty of the Shokawa river, the serenity of the Shinto shrine and the magnificence of the pine-covered mountains. Shirakawa-go still represented the Japan he loved; the history, the culture and the traditions, so different from the big cities desecrated by foreign influence.

Sakaigawa did not contradict that he was a relic. His heart belonged to the Edo period when the Tokugawa dynasty ruled and the shoguns took care of those who harboured unhealthy alien ideas. Those days were gone, regrettably, but, praise the gods, nobody could deny a man his right to live in the past if he so wished.

They had come to the village together. For the first time in twelve months, Vargas had volunteered to join him. Sakaigawa was secretly pleased. He was fond of his village and proud of its halcyon beauty and the vestige of a bygone era.

After months of silence he chatted happily with people and translated in between to Vargas who was silent but not unfriendly.

They walked around for a couple of hours whilst the locals took care of the provisions generously offered free of charge since everybody knew that the Ninja had no money. He was an icon, a remnant from days of pride and glory, the history of the immortal samurais personified. Anchored in facts and not according to myths and legends, he was the last of the great Ninjas. He was revered in the village and far beyond, and, as he dryly observed to Vargas, when were gods and semi-gods alike ever burdened with something as prosaic as cash?

"What do you do in return?" Vargas had asked.

"Ah, simple," Sakaigawa had replied. "I nurture their dreams."

Towards the end of the visit, Sakaigawa wanted to go to the Jinja and pay his respect to the gods. Vargas knew what it meant to Sakaigawa and said he would like to come. He had been there before, an eternity ago when he and Tadashi Ishihara first visited Shirakawa-go in their search for the elusive Ninja.

They came to the Torii. Vargas stopped and placed his hands on one of the solid pillars as if caressing the wood of the gate. Sakaigawa watched silently. He waited till Vargas was ready to continue.

"I am going to have a word with Amaterasu," Sakaigawa said. "The spring is late this year and I am not happy about it."

Vargas agreed. There was too much snow in parts of the mountains. Hopefully the Sun Goddess would listen and exercise her influence.

They came to the water trough where Sakaigawa rinsed his mouth and washed his hands. Vargas kept in the background. Sakaigawa clapped his hands three times to make the gods aware of his presence before he bowed his head and began to pray.

None of the worshippers seemed to find anything strange about Vargas' being there. They acknowledged him with customary politeness and then ignored him. He watched Sakaigawa who appeared to have a lot on his mind. His prayers went on and on. Evidently there was more than one god whose attention he required.

They went back to the village and picked up their provisions. Soon they were lost amid the pine trees at the foot of the mountain.

They sat on the plateau and viewed the valley. Sakaigawa said, "I have noticed that you still do not pray, Angelo-San."

Vargas selected a leaf from a small bush. He chewed for a while. "Your culture has many gods. You worship your ancestors, your heroes and your kami. You are open-minded. You embrace Confucius and Buddha and you cultivate the importance of family and loyalty. You have no scriptures and no ordained code of moral and ethics." Vargas removed the leaf and looked towards the sky. "The religion I faced when growing up had nothing *but.* You rely on wisdom on earth. I was taught to fear the wrath of mythical beings ruling life and death and life thereafter. It found no response in me, Sensei. The seeds of occultism fell on soil insufficiently fertile. I have no gods to pray to and no sense of loss for it being so."

"Then there is no emptiness," Sakaigawa said.

"There is, but not for religious reasons."

Sakaigawa folded his hands behind his neck. He scanned the pale blue sky that arched the eastern mountains. He was pleased. During the first ten months Vargas had barely said a word. He had arrived without offering any explanation.

From the very first day he had been roaming the mountains on his own. He had stayed away for a week or more, at times. It was only during the last two months they had been training together and Vargas had begun to talk.

One night, sitting by the campfire, Vargas had suddenly told in a monotonous voice about Jennifer and Anu and what had happened. Sakaigawa listened. He offered neither consolation nor advice. He thought of his own past and he knew that nobody but Vargas himself could find the path through the jungle of his mind. He had finally opened up, and that, to Sakaigawa, was the first sign of wounds beginning to heal.

Sakaigawa knew that there was little he could say. Vargas' hurt went too deep. His encounter with happiness had been all too brief and his loss would forever embrace his entire being. But he had talked, and now Vargas had come to the village and that was another shade of progress, however tiny. Sakaigawa did not think that Vargas would ever again find peace of mind. He would drift from place to place, forever restless, knowing that what he once had found would never come back.

"Time to go," Sakaigawa said and looked at the sinking sun. He got up. "Night is not far away."

He took the lead. Both used short steps and leaned forward as they walked. It was dark before they reached Sakaigawa's abode. They unpacked and had the campfire blazing within twenty minutes.

Sakaigawa prepared the meal, Sansai-soba and Oyakodon. In between he glanced at Vargas who stared into the flames.

"Here," Sakaigawa said and held out one of his hand-made wooden trays. "My most delicious and healthy vegetable and noodles mix and my energy-enhancing and succulent chicken and egg on rice."

They ate in silence. He is still too scraggy, Sakaigawa thought, but at least he is no longer picking at the food.

Sakaigawa cleared the utensils away and came back with his one and only indulgence, the locally produced milky-white, thick and potent sake he allowed himself now and then. He sat down in the lotus position and stretched his back. He did not take his eyes off Vargas who was sipping his sake seemingly transfixed by the lure of the red and yellow flames caressing the night.

For a while Sakaigawa listened to the music from the nearby waterfalls. He watched the stars as they appeared like calligraphy from a brush dipped in gold and applied on soft blue satin. He thought of the day a year ago when Vargas had arrived from nowhere and asked if he could stay. He had given no explanation. Sakaigawa sensed a tragedy. He asked no questions. He offered Vargas to stay for as long as he wished and left it at that.

During those first ten months they had not seen much of each other. Vargas preferred to be on his own and he had little or no desire to communicate.

Then, one evening, Vargas came back and looked more tense and haggard than usual. Sakaigawa warmed up some sake and tacitly handed Vargas a thimble. After a while, when Sakaigawa knew that some of the tension had gone, he began reciting from the works of Basho, his favourite poet. Finally, Vargas fell asleep. Sakaigawa covered him with a blanket and kept the fire alive all through the night.

From then on Vargas stayed away less and for shorter periods of time. He listened to Sakaigawa's tales of the past and nodded when he stopped and on occasions he asked the odd question. Sakaigawa's well of myths, legends and history was bottomless; he talked as fluently and eloquently about famous ninjas like Fujibayashi, Momochi and Hattori who had added their colours to sixteenth century Japan as he talked about the Nara, the Heian and the Kamakura periods. His favourite, though, was the Edo period. Sakaigawa could lose himself for hours with stories about the great Tokugawa who, among countless achievements, had managed to keep Japan pure and free from Christians and other barbarians. But, alas, Tokuwaga was not entirely faultless. He had got into his head to ban the ninjas and he had almost succeeded, but, apart from this inexplicable attack of temporary dementia, Tokugawa represented and incarnated the spirit that made Japan face and conquer the challenges arising over the next four hundred years.

Sakaigawa's most revered hero was Musashi Miyamoto, the swordsman without equal of the Edo period and author of *Gorin-no-sho* from which Sakaigawa often quoted with repeated emphasis on Miyamoto's advice that in order to master the sword one must first master one's spirit. Sakaigawa had countless stories about Miyamoto, a warrior who was as wise as he was fearless and thus an example to all, irrespective of their chosen passage through life.

That evening, Vargas said, "Forgive my curiosity, Sensei, but where did you learn English?"

Progress, Sakaigawa thought. He said, "In Tokyo, just after the war. Now and again my services were required there, and I decided that it would be to my advantage to understand the language of the gaijins flooding the city. It was not a happy time. The Americans had their orders to behave in a cordial manner, or so it was alleged, but they treated us all as if we were Burakumins, worthless outcasts, primitive and inferior. What the Americans forgot was that we were at the foot of the mountain, from where there is only one way, and they were at the top of the mountain, from where there is also only one way." Sakaigawa looked at the pale and late winter moon scarcely visible behind billowy clouds. "Or maybe they just did not understand. Yes, that is more probable; they never did and they never will. However, a Japanese who had lived in America for many years and returned in time to escape their concentration camps, gave me what I think is called a crash course. Then a client, a man who had recognized the dawn of a new and very different era, gave me some English books including *Chambers Dictionary*, which you have seen. That is how I acquired my knowledge. I know most of my books by heart, so, once in a while, I need to supplement my library. I have contacts in Matsumoto, Takayama and Tokyo. They are always helpful."

"But how do you maintain it? Nobody around here speaks English."

"Not difficult, Angelo-San. I always read out loud, and all my discussions with the English poets and writers are in their own language.

A most efficient method." He smiled as if enjoyed an insight that was his alone. "Shakespeare is an adequate bard, but I do find Byron lacking in depth and Keats short on weighty perceptions. Neither are as close to the earth where we all belong as most Japanese and Chinese poets." He turned his weatherworn face towards Vargas. "Where were you when the accident happened?"

"On my way to America for my last assignment," Vargas said. He looked at the silhouette of the mountains where a single flash of lightning cut across the sky. He tilted his head as if he was listening to the distant thunder.

Sakaigawa said softly, "Angelo-San, I am eighty-two years of age and, I suspect, autumn is trickling into my life. Let me tell you what I have learned. Once, when I was at the height of my power, I consciously concluded that my code of conduct and ethics could have no room for the soothing luxuries of doubt and remorse. I eliminated by reasoning any moralistic objection to taking a human life. I rendered superfluous the need to justify my actions. My attitude became like an abstract isolated in an existence of its own, floating in a private universe where the black holes were but inexplicable facts that needed no scientific or any other explanation. Did I feel emptiness? Yes, I did, for a while. Did I feel loneliness? No, I did not. Loneliness came to me when my wife died, but this terrible trauma somehow transformed itself over the years into a treasure, a shrine where I could forever worship her memory. Did I then not carry any burden since her departure? Yes, I did, and it is flowing like snowflakes through my veins." Carefully, he put a log on the fire and returned to his motionless position.

Vargas said, "Which burden?"

"The futility of human encounter. It is a fate chosen for me by the gods and therefore beyond contention."

"You accept that?"

"There is no choice. I do not question what the gods have decided."

Vargas stared at the golden sparks from the embers of the dying campfire. "How to achieve peace of mind."

Sakaigawa smiled. "Or how to live with oneself."

"You are telling me to re-enter my journey from nowhere to nowhere?"

"I am telling you nothing, except that I found and learned to move with the rhythm of life. It is a confession, not a recommendation." Sakaigawa

808

paused. "Unless, that is, you are overwhelmed by a desire to enter the kingdom of the gods of your forefathers. I experienced that predicament myself a couple of times in my younger days, but then I concluded it was more compelling to face the rising sun of another day."

Vargas kept silent. He had closed his eyes. The empty ceramic cup rested in his hand. Sakaigawa saw no movement when he poured another few drops of sake. He said, "Ignorance would claim that men like you and I, with our proclivity to violence, are cursed by life and blessed by death. That is but a universal misconception. What makes a man is his character, and not his methods. The uneducated and one-dimensional will say that the method reflects a man's character. The truth is that the shallow and the weak are ruled by his instincts and the reflective and the strong rules his instincts. A man can cheat and lie, betray and deceive, pretend and corrupt, seduce and pervert—all very common, but is such behaviour morally any better than to dispose of a worthless human being?" Sakaigawa chuckled. "I do not believe it is. The difference between you and I and all the righteous ones is that we have no need to cling to mawkish delusions. I have no regrets."

The moon was gone and the mountains stood dark and gloomy in the silence of the night.

Sakaigawa said, "What happened in America?"

Vargas told his story. Sakaigawa nodded. "I taught you well."

"You did, Sensei."

Sakaigawa poked into the embers. He did not take his eyes off the tiny yellow flames. "Tadashi-San must be worried about his money."

"He will get his share."

Sakaigawa put his stick down and said, "I shall rest my tired limbs." He went into the cottage, rolled out his futon and lay down on his left side. He could see Vargas change position but he did not get up.

From then on they spent every day together. Vargas seemed to be more at ease; gradually, he came out of his shell and their talks became less one-sided. Sakaigawa asked about the stone that Vargas had placed next to Sakaigawa's gods. Vargas told about his brother and grandfather and the cairn on another mountain in another world.

Sakaigawa said, "I am honoured to have your stone in my shrine, but I must ask you again—how come you do not pray?"

"I have no need to pray. The stone is a symbol, a memento from the part of my life when I first understood the exquisiteness of unconditional affection. You may think that the stone and my memory of those I loved are my gods, and in your world this is so. I am unable to see myself as anything other than a biological unit that has arrived, exists and who will one day vanish. Religion, any religion, is to me but an academic concept. As such it is of some interest, like culture and history and anthropogeny, but it is not within my reach to be moved by ecclesiastical performances or to accept that divinity is not a pathetic fantasy with its origin in man's frail and insecure mind."

They walked uphill. The fog lifted like shreds of silk gently swept away by the mild spring breeze. Far below they could see the pine trees laced in the early morning mist. The rays from the rising sun played with the emerald dew on the ground. The air carried a fragrant promise of an early summer. They watched the purple cliffs shadowing the distant valleys of Shirakawa-go.

They continued for an hour before Sakaigawa stopped and pointed. "Let us sit down over there. I have got something to tell you."

Vargas rested his eyes on a crown eagle circling high above. He listened to the sonorous humming of the waterfalls.

"*Hinkaku*," Sakaigawa said. "Dignity."

"I know the word, Sensei."

Sakaigawa bowed his head. He seemed to shrink as he gracefully touched the ground with his fingers. "Angelo-San," he said slowly, his weathered and wrinkled face turned towards the sun, "you must use your mind as the waterfalls use the mountains to cascade free and pure and strong. You must use your mind as the river is using the hills and the fields to flow with ease yet powerfully and unable to be stopped. You must use the ocean when the day comes for the river of your mind to cease its flow and become one with the universe. For me, the ocean is near. You must still watch it from afar. Always remember that time and distance are nature's own measures. Stay true to your belief— it must not escape your mind that nature is divine and man is not." He clenched his hands and pressed his knuckles against the thin layer of soil covering the rock. "Your world is more than the obscurity of these mountains."

Vargas did not reply.

Sakaigawa said, "When you talked about your past, the wisdom of Confucius came to me. "*Those who leave their native lands are like a river— never stopping, always rushing, day and night.*"" He smiled and his voice became soft. "Can you imagine a river standing still? One of life's many fallacies is that peace of mind is a benediction. It is not. Our only blessing is our ability to live with the disarray inside." He raised his hands and pressed them together upwards as he turned. "Cherish your memories, Angelo-San. Treat them as precious pearls and not as drops of acid. What you lost will become your treasure."

They sat in silence for a long time. Finally, Vargas said, "You know I am going away."

"Soon," Sakaigawa said. "I know."

They walked the entire day. The wind came from the north and made the trees chant melancholy. The snow-covered peaks of the mountains turned silver in the soft light of the evening sun.

The next morning Sakaigawa quietly watched when Vargas packed his bag. He went outside and left the bag on the ground. His eyes swept the mountains before he turned to Sakaigawa and bowed.

"Thank you, Sensei."

Sakaigawa showed no emotions, but his voice was low when he bowed and said, "The mountains will always be here."

"They will," Vargas said. "So will you, Sensei."

He picked up his bag, adjusted the shoulder strap and began walking. He did not look back.

☞

He stayed awake for most of the journey from Japan to Grand Cayman.

After two days of resting and walking the beach he began to feel better. On the third day he arranged for the transfer of Tadashi's share and went to see Midget. She listened in silence and understood when he declined her invitation to an evening meal.

☞

There was little activity at Owen Roberts Airport. He walked into the cool and almost empty terminal. Bored airline personnel chatted idly trying to pass time. The bar was open. Only two other people were sitting there, an elderly couple slowly munching hamburgers and sipping beer. They did not talk to each other.

Vargas chose a corner table and placed his hold-all on a chair. The waitress came over.

He said, "Can you get me an ashtray, please?"

Her smile was tired. "Certainly, sir."

Vargas sat down. "Thank you," he said.

She pulled a pad and a pencil from her pocket. "What else can I get you, sir?"

"Irish whisky, please."

"Oh," she said and turned towards the counter, "I'm not sure…"

"Jack Daniels will do. Large, please. No ice."

Her smile became genuine. "You got it. On the tab, sir?

"Please."

"Right," she said and scratched her head with the pencil. "I am Enid." She pointed at her nametag. "It's so quiet here…" she shrugged and expected him to understand.

"Nice to meet you, Enid."

She came back with the drink and put a coaster under the glass.

"Thank you," Vargas said.

She badly wanted to have a chat, but he did not look the type. He was reserved, kind of, like he was preoccupied with his own thoughts and would rather be left alone. She said, "You're welcome." She tried to catch his eyes. He did not look up. "Oh," she said, "I forgot."

She came back with the ashtray. She saw the stranger making an effort, like coming out of a dream. He thanked her.

The birds were quiet in Conor's loft. He had found the bottle and poured with a mischievous little smile. It was as if they had known each other for a long time. They had both been forthright. They had talked about travelling and Conor had expressed his regrets that he had seen so little of the world.

"I like airports. They kind of remind me of our existence; an analogy, so to speak, of our life here on earth."

"How come?"

"You arrive, you sit there, in the terminal, or you maunder about; people passing by, you see your destination up on the board and then—the final call. Sort of sums it up, doesn't it?"

"And then we vanish."

"We are only lost if we do not know where to go."

"A bewitching parable, Conor, but exclusively for the redeemed."

A bird had flapped his wings and Conor had taken him in his hands.

"Let me put it this way, then. We sit here, the prey of our demons and our gods who guide us towards the final destination, and who, in the meantime,

play their little games with us; all those seemingly inconspicuous and at times inexplicable one-acts that we interpret as coincidences or fate."

Vargas looked up when the woman brushed by and placed her belongings on the chair at the next table. She gave him a casual glance, dropped *The Washington Post* on the tabletop, asked for a martini and headed for the restrooms. Her movements were measured. She walked with confidence. She had the looks of a darker blonde Grace Kelly.

The newspaper was facing him. There was a large photograph of her on the front page. The picture did her justice; she had reasons to be proud of it. The caption read *Shock Retirement*.

Vargas scanned the three brief columns. The woman had been one of USA's brightest television stars, now calling it a day. There was a lengthy article on page four for those who wanted to know more.

Vargas leaned back. The woman returned. She put her shoulder bag on her lap, took out her pack of cigarettes and shook her head.

"May I have a light, please?" she asked.

Vargas obliged.

"Where are you going?" she asked.

"London."

"First class?"

He nodded.

"So you are the other one," she said. "We are the only two. It's going to be a long and dreary flight."

She inhaled and looked out the window. A few clouds crossed a sky as blue as cornflowers and made her think of elusive demons chasing ethereal virgins from genesis to infinity.

She smiled and blew a smoke ring. "May I suggest that we keep each other company?"

Vargas emptied his glass. "Perhaps we should," he said.

A chat with Abraham Forster's widow could be entertaining.